P. D. JAMES OMNIBUS

P. D. JAMES OMNIBUS

UNNATURAL CAUSES

SHROUD FOR A NIGHTINGALE

AN UNSUITABLE JOB
FOR A WOMAN

faber and faber

P. D. James Omnibus
first published in 1982
by Faber and Faber Limited
3 Queen Square London WC1N 3AU
Printed in Great Britain by
Fakenham Press Limited, Fakenham, Norfolk
All rights reserved

Unnatural Causes
first published in 1967
Shroud for a Nightingale
first published in 1971
An Unsuitable Job for a Woman
first published in 1972

British Library Cataloguing in Publication Data

James. P. D.
P. D. James omnibus.
I. Title
823'.914[F]   PR6060.A467
ISBN 0-571-11851-8

Contents

UNNATURAL
CAUSES

Book One

I

The corpse without hands lay in the bottom of a small sailing dinghy drifting just within sight of the Suffolk coast. It was the body of a middle-aged man, a dapper little cadaver, its shroud a dark pin-striped suit which fitted the narrow body as elegantly in death as it had in life. The hand-made shoes still gleamed except for some scruffing of the toe caps, the silk tie was knotted under the prominent Adam's apple. He had dressed with careful orthodoxy for the town, this hapless voyager; not for this lonely sea; nor for this death.

It was early afternoon in mid October and the glazed eyes were turned upwards to a sky of surprising blue across which the light south-west wind was dragging a few torn rags of cloud. The wooden shell, without mast or rowlocks, bounced gently on the surge of the North Sea so that the head shifted and rolled as if in restless sleep. It had been an unremarkable face even in life and death had given it nothing but a pitiful vacuity. The fair hair grew sparsely from a high bumpy forehead, the nose was so narrow that the white ridge of bone looked as if it were about to pierce the flesh; the mouth, small and thin-lipped, had dropped open to reveal two prominent front teeth which gave the whole face the super-cilious look of a dead hare.

The legs, still clamped in rigor, were wedged one each side of the centre-board case and the forearms had been placed resting on the thwart. Both hands had been taken off at the wrists. There had been little bleeding. On each forearm a trickle of blood had spun a black web between the stiff fair hairs and the thwart was stained as if it had been used as a chopping block. But that was all; the rest of the body and the boards of the dinghy were free of blood.

The right hand had been taken cleanly off and the curved end of the radius glistened white; but the left had been bungled and the jagged splinters of bone, needle sharp, stuck out from the receding flesh. Both jacket sleeves and shirt cuffs had been pulled up for the butchery and a pair of gold initialled cuff links dangled free, glinting as they slowly turned and were caught by the autumn sun.

The dinghy, its paintwork faded and peeling, drifted like a discarded toy on an almost empty sea. On the horizon the divided silhouette of a coaster was making her way down the Yarmouth Lanes; nothing else was in sight. About two o'clock a black dot swooped across the sky towards the land trailing its feathered tail and the air was torn by the scream of engines. Then the roar faded and there was again no sound but the sucking of the water against the boat and the occasional cry of a gull.

Suddenly the dinghy rocked violently, then steadied itself and swung slowly round. As if sensing the strong tug of the on-shore current, it began to move more purposefully. A black-headed gull, which had dropped lightly on to the prow and had perched there, rigid as a figure-head, rose with wild cries to circle above the body. Slowly, inexorably, the water dancing at the prow, the little boat bore its dreadful cargo towards the shore.

2

Just before two o'clock on the afternoon of the same day
Superintendent Adam Dalgliesh drove his Cooper Bristol
gently on to the grass verge outside Blythburgh Church and,
a minute later, passed through the north chantry-chapel door
into the cold silvery whiteness of one of the loveliest church
interiors in Suffolk. He was on his way to Monksmere Head
just south of Dunwich to spend a ten-day autumn holiday
with a spinster aunt, his only living relative, and this was his
last stop on the way. He had started off from his City flat
before London was stirring, and instead of taking the direct
route to Monksmere through Ipswich, had struck north at
Chelmsford to enter Suffolk at Sudbury. He had breakfasted
at Long Melford and had then turned west through Laven-
ham to drive slowly and at will through the green and gold of
this most unspoilt and unprettified of counties. His mood
would have wholly matched the day if it weren't for one
persistent nagging worry. He had been deliberately putting
off a personal decision until this holiday. Before he went back
to London he must finally decide whether to ask Deborah
Riscoe to marry him.

Irrationally, the decision would have been easier if he
hadn't known so certainly what her answer would be. This
threw upon him the whole responsibility for deciding whether
to change the present satisfactory status quo (well, satisfactory
for him anyway, and it could be argued surely that Deborah
was happier now than she had been a year ago?) for a commitment which both of them, he suspected, would regard as
irrevocable no matter what the outcome. There are few
couples as unhappy as those who are too proud to admit
their unhappiness. Some of the hazards he knew. He knew

that she disliked and resented his job. This wasn't surprising nor, in itself, important. The job was his choice and he had never required anyone's approval or encouragement. But it was a daunting prospect that every late duty, every emergency, might have to be preceded by an apologetic telephone call. As he walked to and fro under the marvellous cambered tie-beam roof and smelt the Anglican odour of wax polish, flowers and damp old hymn books, it came to him that he had got what he wanted at almost the precise moment of suspecting that he no longer wanted it. This experience is too common to cause an intelligent man lasting disappointment but it still has power to disconcert. It wasn't the loss of freedom that deterred him; the men who squealed most about that were usually the least free. Much more difficult to face was the loss of privacy. Even the loss of physical privacy was hard to accept. Running his fingers over the carved fifteenth century lectern he tried to picture life in the Queen-hithe flat with Deborah always there, no longer the eagerly awaited visitor but part of his life, the legal, certificated next of kin.

It had been a bad time at the Yard to be faced with personal problems. There had recently been a major reorganization which had resulted in the inevitable disruption of loyalties and of routine, the expected crop of rumours and discontent. And there had been no relief from the pressure of work. Most of the senior officers were already working a fourteen-hour day. His last case, although successful, had been particularly tedious. A child had been murdered and the investigation had turned into a man hunt of the kind he most disliked and was temperamentally least suited for—a matter of dogged, persistent checking of facts carried on in a blaze of publicity and hindered by the fear and hysteria of the neighbourhood. The child's parents had fastened on him like drowning swimmers gulping for reassurance and hope and he could still feel the almost physical load of their sorrow and guilt. He had been required to be at once a comforter and father-confessor, avenger and judge. There was nothing new to him in this. He had felt no personal involvement in their

grief, and this detachment had, as always, been his strength, as the anger and intense, outraged commitment of some of his colleagues, faced with the same crime, would have been theirs. But the strain of the case was still with him and it would take more than the winds of a Suffolk autumn to clean his mind of some images. No reasonable woman could have expected him to propose marriage in the middle of this investigation and Deborah had not done so. That he had found time and energy to finish his second book of verse a few days before the arrest was something which neither of them had mentioned. He had been appalled to recognize that even the exercise of a minor talent could be made the excuse for selfishness and inertia. He hadn't liked himself much recently, and it was perhaps sanguine to hope that this holiday could alter that.

Half an hour later he closed the church door quietly behind him and set off on the last few miles of the journey to Monksmere. He had written to his aunt to say that he would probably arrive at half-past two and, with luck, he would be there almost precisely on time. If, as was usual, his aunt came out of the cottage at two-thirty she should see the Cooper Bristol just breasting the headland. He thought of her tall, angular, waiting figure with affection. There was little unusual about her story and most of it he had guessed, picked up as a boy from snatches of his mother's unguarded talk or had simply known as one of the facts of his childhood. Her fiancé had been killed in 1918 just six months before the Armistice when she was a young girl. Her mother was a delicate, spoilt beauty, the worst possible wife for a scholarly country clergyman as she herself frequently admitted, apparently thinking that this candour both justified and excused in advance the next outbreak of selfishness or extravagance. She disliked the sight of other people's grief since it rendered them temporarily more interesting than herself and she decided to take young Captain Maskell's death very hard. Whatever her sensitive, uncommunicative and rather difficult daughter suffered it must be apparent that her mother suffered more; and three weeks after the telegram was received she

died of influenza. It is doubtful whether she intended to go to such lengths but she would have been gratified by the result. Her distraught husband forgot in one night all the irritations and anxieties of his marriage and remembered only his wife's gaiety and beauty. It was, of course, unthinkable that he should marry again, and he never did. Jane Dalgliesh whose own bereavement hardly anyone now had the time to remember, took her mother's place as hostess at the vicarage and remained with her father until his retirement in 1945 and his death ten years later. She was a highly intelligent woman and if she found unsatisfying the annual routine of housekeeping and parochial activities, predictable and inescapable as the liturgical year, she never said so. Her father was so assured of the ultimate importance of his calling that it never occurred to him that anyone's gifts could be wasted in its service. Jane Dalgliesh, respected by the parishioners but never loved, did what had to be done and solaced herself with her study of birds. After her father's death the papers she published, records of meticulous observation, brought her some notice; and in time what the parish had patronizingly described as "Miss Dalgliesh's little hobby" made her one of the most respected of amateur ornithologists. Just over five years ago she had sold her house in Lincolnshire and bought Pentlands, a stone cottage on the edge of Monksmere Head. Here Dalgliesh visited her at least twice a year.

They were no mere duty visits, although he would have felt a responsibility for her if she were not so obviously self-sufficient that, at times, even to feel affection seemed a kind of insult. But the affection was there and both of them knew it. Already he was looking forward to the satisfaction of seeing her, to the assured pleasures of a holiday at Monksmere.

There would be a driftwood fire in the wide hearth scenting the whole cottage, and before it the high-backed armchair once part of his father's study in the vicarage where he was born, the leather smelling of childhood. There would be a sparsely furnished bedroom with a view of sea and sky, a comfortable if narrow bed with sheets smelling faintly of wood-smoke and lavender, plenty of hot water and a bath long enough for

a six-foot-two man to stretch himself in comfort. His aunt was herself six foot tall and had a masculine appreciation of essential comforts. More immediately, there would be tea before the fire and hot buttered toast with home made potted meat. Best of all, there would be no corpses and no talk of them. He suspected that Jane Dalgliesh thought it odd that an intelligent man should choose to earn his living catching murderers and she was not a woman to feign polite interest where she felt none. She made no demands on him, not even the demands of affection, and because of this she was the only woman in the world with whom he was completely at peace. He knew exactly what the holiday offered. They would walk together, often in silence, on the damp strip of firm sand between the sea's foam and he pebbled rises of the beach. He would carry her sketching paraphanalia, she would stride a little ahead, hands dug in her jacket pockets, eyes searching out where wheatears, scarcely distinguishable from pebbles, had lighted on the shingle, or following the flight of tern or plover. It would be peaceful, restful, utterly undemanding; but at the end of ten days he would go back to London with a sense of relief.

He was driving now through Dunwich Forest where the Forestry Commission's plantations of dark firs flanked the road. He fancied that he could smell the sea now; the salt tang borne to him on the wind was sharper than the bitter smell of the trees. His heart lifted. He felt like a child coming home. And now the forest ended, the sombre dark green of the firs ruled off by a wire fence from the water-coloured fields and hedges. And now they too passed and he was driving through the gorse and heather of the heathlands on his way to Dunwich. As he reached the village and turned right up the hill which skirted the walled enclosure of the ruined Franciscan friory there was the blare of a car's horn and a Jaguar, driven very fast, shot past. He glimpsed a dark head, and a hand raised in salute before, with a valedictory hoot, the car was out of sight. So Oliver Latham, the dramatic critic, was at his cottage for the weekend. That was hardly likely to inconvenience Dalgliesh for Latham did not come to Suffolk

for company. Like his near neighbour, Justin Bryce, he used his cottage as a retreat from London, and perhaps from people, although he was at Monksmere less frequently than Bryce. Dalgliesh had met him once or twice and had recognized in him a restlessness and tension which found an echo in his own character. He was known to like fast cars and fast driving, and Dalgliesh suspected that it was in the drive to and from Monksmere that he found his release. It was difficult to imagine why else he kept on his cottage. He came to it seldom, never brought his women there, took no interest in furnishing it, and used it chiefly as a base for wild drives around the district which were so violent and irrational that they seemed a kind of abreaction.

As Rosemary Cottage came into sight on the bend of the road Dalgliesh accelerated. He had little hope of driving past unobserved but at least he could drive at a speed which made it unreasonable to stop. As he shot past he just had time to see out of the corner of his eye a face at an upstairs window. Well it was to be expected. Celia Calthrop regarded herself as the doyen of the small community at Monksmere and had assigned herself certain duties and privileges. If her neighbours were so ill-advised as not to keep her informed of the comings and going of themselves and their visitors she was prepared to take some trouble to find out for herself. She had a quick ear for an approaching car and the situation of her cottage, just where the rough track across the headland joined the road from Dunwich, gave her every opportunity of keeping an eye on things.

Miss Calthrop had bought Brodie's Barn, re-named Rosemary Cottage, twelve years previously. She had got it cheap and by gentle but persistent bullying of local labour, had converted it equally cheaply from a pleasing if shabby stone house to the romanticised ideal of her readers. It frequently featured in womens' magazines as "Celia Calthrop's delightful Suffolk residence where, amid the peace of the countryside, she creates those delightful romances which so thrill our readers." Inside, Rosemary Cottage was very comfortable in its pretentious and tasteless way; outside, it

had everything its owner considered appropriate to a country cottage, a thatched roof (deplorably expensive to insure and maintain), a herb garden (a sinister looking patch this; Miss Calthrop was not successful with herbs), a small artificial pond (malodorous in summer) and a dovecote (but doves obstinately refused to roost in it). There was also a sleek lawn on which the writers' community—Celia's phrase—was invited in summer to drink tea. At first Jane Dalgliesh had been excluded from the invitations, not because she didn't claim to be a writer but because she was a solitary, elderly spinster and therefore, in Miss Calthrop's scale of values, a social and sexual failure rating only a patronising kindness. Then Miss Calthrop discovered that her neighbour was regarded as a distinguished woman by people well qualified to judge and that the men who, in defiance of propriety, were entertained at Pentlands and who were to be met trudging along the shore in happy companionship with their hostess were frequently themselves distinguished. A further discovery was more surprising. Jane Dalgliesh dined with R. B. Sinclair at Priory House. Not all those who praised Sinclair's three great novels, the last written over thirty years ago, realized that he was still alive. Fewer still were invited to dine with him. Miss Calthrop was not a woman obstinately to persist in error and Miss Dalgliesh became "dear Jane" overnight. For her part she continued to call her neighbour "Miss Calthrop" and was as unaware of the rapprochement as she had been of the original disdain. Dalgliesh was never sure what she really thought of Celia. She seldom spoke about her neighbours and the women were too rarely in each other's company for him to judge.

The rough track which led across Monksmere Head to Pentlands was less than fifty yards from Rosemary Cottage. It was usually barred by a heavy farm gate but today this stood open, biting deep into the tall hedge of brambles and elders. The car bumped slowly over the potholes and between the stubble of hay which soon gave way to grass and then to bracken. It passed the twin stone cottages belonging to Latham and Justin Bryce but Dalgliesh saw no sign of either

man although Latham's Jaguar was parked at his door and there was a thin curl of smoke from Bryce's chimney. Now the track wound uphill and suddenly the whole of the headland lay open before him, stretching purple and golden to the cliffs and shining sea. At the crest of the track Dalgliesh stopped the car to watch and to listen. Autumn had never been his favourite season, but in the moment which followed the stopping of the engine he wouldn't have changed this mellow peace for all the keener sensitivities of spring. The heather was beginning to fade now but the second flowering of the gorse was as thick and golden as the first richness of May. Beyond it lay the sea, streaked with purple, azure and brown, and to the south the mist-hung marshes of the bird reserve added their gentler greens and blues. The air smelt of heather and woodsmoke, the inevitable and evocative smells of autumn. It was hard to believe, thought Dalgliesh, that one was looking at a battlefield where for nearly nine centuries the land had waged its losing fight against the sea; hard to realize that under that deceptive calm of veined water lay the nine drowned churches of old Dunwich. There were few buildings standing on the headland now but not all were old. To the north Dalgliesh could just glimpse the low walls of Seton House, little more than an excrescence on the edge of the cliff, which Maurice Seton, the detective novelist, had built to suit his odd and solitary life. Half a mile to the south the great square walls of Priory House stood like a last bastion against the sea and, on the very edge of the bird reserve, Pentlands Cottage seemed to hang on the brink of nothingness. As his eyes scanned the headland a horse and buggy came into sight on the far north track and bowled merrily over the gorse towards Priory House. Dalgliesh could see a stout little body hunchbacked in the driving seat and the whip, delicate as a wand, erect by her side. It must be R. B. Sinclair's housekeeper bringing home the provisions. There was a charming domestic touch about the gay little equipage and Dalgliesh watched it with pleasure until it disappeared behind the shield of trees which half hid Priory House. At that moment his aunt appeared

at the side of her cottage and gazed up the headland. Dalgliesh glanced at his wrist. It was thirty three minutes past two. He let in the clutch and the Cooper Bristol bumped slowly down the track towards her.

3

Stepping back instinctively into the shadows of his upstairs room, Oliver Latham watched the car as it bounced gently up the headland and laughed aloud. Then he checked himself, silenced by the explosive sound of his laughter in the stillness of the cottage. But this was too much! Scotland Yard's wonder boy, still reeking from his latest blood sport, had come most promptly upon his cue. The car was stopping now on the crown of the headland. It would be pleasant if that damned Cooper Bristol had broken down at last. But no, it looked as if Dalgliesh was pausing simply to admire the view. The poor fool was probably relishing in advance the sweets of a fortnight's cossetting at Pentlands. Well, he was in for a surprise. The question was, would it be prudent for him, Latham, to stay around and watch the fun? Why not? He wasn't due back in town until the first night at the Court Theatre on Thursday week and it would look odd if he dashed back now so soon after his arrival. Besides, he was curious. He had driven to Monksmere on Wednesday expecting to be bored. But now, with luck, it was promising to be quite an exciting holiday.

4

Alice Kerrison drove the buggy behind the fringe of trees
which shielded Priory House from the northern part of the
headland, bounced down from her seat and led the mare
through the wide crumbling archway to a row of sixteenth
century stables. As she busied herself with the unharnessing,
grunting a little with the effort, her practical mind complacently reviewed the morning's work and looked forward
to the small domestic pleasures to come. First they would
drink tea together, strong and over-sweet as Mr. Sinclair
liked it, sitting one each side of the great fire in the hall.
Even on a warm autumn day Mr. Sinclair liked his fire. And
then before the light began to fade and the mists rose,
they would take their daily walk together across the headland.
And it wouldn't be a walk without a purpose. There was
some burying to be done. Well, it was always satisfactory to
have an object and for all Mr. Sinclair's clever talk, human
remains however incomplete were still human remains and
were entitled to respect. Besides, it was high time they were
out of the house.

5

It was nearly half-past eight and Dalgliesh and his aunt, their dinner over, sat in companionable silence one each side of the living room fire. The room, which occupied almost the whole of the ground floor of Pentlands, was stone walled with a low roof buttressed by immense oak beams and a floor of red quarry tiles. In front of the open fireplace, where a wood fire crackled and spurted, a neat stack of driftwood was drying. The smell of wood smoke drifted through the cottage like incense; and the air vibrated endlessly with the thudding of the sea. Dalgliesh found it hard to keep awake in this rhythmic, somnambulant peace. He had always enjoyed contrast in art or nature and at Pentlands, once night had fallen, the pleasures of contrast were easily self-induced. Inside the cottage there was light and warmth, all the colours and comfort of civilized domesticity; outside under the low clouds there was darkness, solitude, mystery. He pictured the shore, one hundred feet below, where the sea was spreading its fringe of lace over the cold, firm beach; and the Monksmere bird reserve to the south, quiet under the night sky, its reeds hardly stirring in the still water.

Stretching his legs to the fire and wedging his head still more comfortably into the high back of the chair, he looked across at his aunt. She was sitting, as always, bolt upright and yet she looked perfectly comfortable. She was knitting a pair of woollen socks in bright red which Dalgliesh could only hope were not intended for him. He thought it unlikely. His aunt was not given to such domestic tokens of affection. The firelight threw gules on her long face, brown and carved as an Aztec's, the eyes hooded, the nose long and straight above a wide mobile mouth. Her hair was iron grey now, coiled into

a huge bun in the nape of her neck. It was a face that he remembered from childhood. He had never seen any difference in her. Upstairs in her room, stuck casually into the edge of a looking glass, was the faded photograph of herself and her dead fiancé taken in 1916. Dalgliesh thought of it now; the boy, in the squashed peak cap and breeches which had once looked slightly ridiculous to him but now epitomised the romance and heartbreak of an age long dead; the girl half an inch taller, swaying towards him with the angular grace of adolescence, her hair dressed wide and ribbon bound, her feet in their pointed shoes just showing beneath the slim flowing skirt. Jane Dalgliesh had never talked to him of her youth and he had never asked. She was the most self-sufficient, the least sentimental woman that he knew. Dalgliesh wondered how Deborah would get on with her, what the two women would make of each other. It was difficult to picture Deborah in any setting other than London. Since her mother's death she hardly ever went home and, for reasons which they both understood only too well, he had never gone back to Martingale with her. He could only see her now against the background of his own City flat, of restaurants, theatre foyers and their favourite pubs. He was used to living his life on different levels. Deborah was not part of his job and as yet she had no place at Pentlands. But if he married her, she would necessarily have some share in both. Somehow, on this brief holiday he knew he had to decide if that was what he really wanted.

Jane Dalgliesh said:

"Would you like some music? I have the new Mahler recording."

Dalgliesh wasn't musical, but he knew that music meant a great deal to his aunt and listening to her records had become part of a Pentlands holiday. Her knowledge and pleasure were infectious; he was beginning to make discoveries. And, in his present mood, he was even ready to try Mahler.

It was then they heard the car.

"Oh, Lord," he said. "Who's this? Not Celia Calthrop, I hope." Miss Calthrop, if not firmly discouraged, was an

inveterate dropper in, trying always to impose on the solitariness of Monksmere the cosy conventions of suburban social life. She was particularly apt to call when Dalgliesh was at the cottage. To her a personable and unattached male was natural prey. If she didn't want him herself there was always somebody who did; she disliked seeing anything go to waste. On one of his visits she had actually given a cocktail party in his honour. At the time he had enjoyed it, intrigued by the essential incongruity of the occasion. The little group of Monksmere residents, meeting as if for the first time, had munched canapes and sipped cheap sherry in Celia's pink and white drawing room and made inconsequent polite conversation while, outside, a gale screamed across the headland and the sou'westers and storm lanterns were stacked in the hall. Here had been contrast indeed. But it was not a habit to encourage.

Jane Dalgliesh said:

"It sounds like Miss Calthrop's Morris. She may be bringing her niece. Elizabeth is home from Cambridge convalescing from glandular fever. I think she arrived yesterday."

"Then she ought to be in bed. It sounds as if there are more than two of them. Isn't that Justin Bryce's bleat?"

It was. When Miss Dalgliesh opened the door they could see through the porch windows the twin lights of the car and a confusion of dark forms which gradually resolved themselves into familiar figures. It looked as if the whole of Monksmere was calling on his aunt. Even Sylvia Kedge, Maurice Seton's crippled secretary, was with them, creeping on her crutches towards the stream of light from the open door. Miss Calthrop walked slowly beside her as if in support. Behind them was Justin Bryce, still bleating inconsequently into the night. The tall figure of Oliver Latham loomed up beside him. Last of all, sulky and reluctant came Elizabeth Marley, shoulders hunched, hands dug into her jacket pockets. She was loitering on the path and peering from side to side into the darkness as if dissociating herself from the party. Bryce called:

"Good evening Miss Dalgliesh. Good evening Adam.

Don't blame me for this invasion. It's all Celia's idea. We've come for professional advice my dears. All except Oliver. We met him on the way and he's only come to borrow some coffee. Or so he says."

Latham said calmly:

"I forgot to buy coffee when I was driving from town yesterday. So I decided to call on my one neighbour who could be trusted to provide a decent blend without an accompanying lecture on my inefficient housekeeping. If I'd known you were having a party I might have waited until tomorrow."

But he showed no inclination to go.

They came in, blinking in the light and bringing with them a gust of cold air which billowed the white wood smoke across the room. Celia Calthrop went straight to Dalgliesh's chair and arranged herself as if to receive an evening's homage. Her elegant legs and feet, carefully displayed to advantage, were in marked contrast to her heavy, stoutly-corseted body with its high bosom, and her flabby mottled arms. Dalgliesh supposed that she must be in her late forties but she looked older. As always she was heavily but skilfully made up. The little vulpine mouth was carmine, the deep-set and downward sloping eyes which gave her face a look of spurious spirituality much emphasized in her publicity photographs were blue shadowed, the lashes weighted with mascara. She took off her chiffon headscarf to reveal her hairdresser's latest effort, the hair fine as a baby's through which the glimpses of pink, smooth scalp looked almost indecent.

Dalgliesh had only met her niece twice before and now, shaking hands, he thought that Cambridge had not changed her. She was still the sulky, heavy-featured girl that he remembered. It was not an unintelligent face and might even have been attractive if only it had held a spark of animation.

The room had lost its peace. Dalgliesh reflected that it was extraordinary how much noise seven people could make. There was the usual business of settling Sylvia Kedge into her chair which Miss Calthrop supervised imperiously, although she did nothing active to help. The girl would have

31

been called unusual, perhaps even beautiful, if only one could have forgotten those twisted ugly legs, braced into calipers, the heavy shoulders, the masculine hands distorted by her crutches. Her face was long, brown as a gypsy's and framed by shoulder length black hair brushed straight from a centre parting. It was a face which could have held strength and character but she had imposed on it a look of piteous humility, an air of suffering, meekly and uncomplainingly borne, which sat incongruously on that high brow. The great black eyes were skilled in inviting compassion. She was now adding to the general fluster by asserting that she was perfectly comfortable when she obviously wasn't, suggesting with a deprecating gentleness which had all the force of a command that her crutches should be placed within reach even though this meant propping them insecurely against her knees, and by generally making all present uncomfortably aware of their own undeserved good health. Dalgliesh had watched this play-acting before, but tonight he sensed that her heart wasn't in it, that the routine was almost mechanical. For once the girl looked genuinely ill and in pain. Her eyes were as dull as stones and there were lines running deeply between her nostrils and the corners of her mouth. She looked as if she needed sleep, and when he gave her a glass of sherry he saw that her hand was trembling. Seized by a spasm of genuine compassion, he wrapped his fingers around hers and steadied the glass until she could drink. Smiling at her he asked gently:

"Well, what's the trouble? What can I do to help?"

But Celia Calthrop had appointed herself spokesman.

"It's too bad of us all to come worrying you and Jane on your first evening together. I do realize that. But we're very worried. At least, Sylvia and I are. Deeply concerned."

"While I," said Justin Bryce, "am not so much worried as intrigued, not to say hopeful. Maurice Seton's disappeared. I'm afraid it may only be a publicity stunt for his next thriller and that we shall see him among us again all too soon. But let us not look on the gloomy side."

He did, indeed, look very far from gloomy, squatting on a

stool before the fire like a malevolent turtle, twisting his long neck towards the blaze. His had been, in youth, a striking head with its high cheekbones, wide mobile lips and huge, luminous grey eyes under the heavy lids. But he was fifty now and becoming a caricature. Though they seemed even larger, his eyes were less bright, and watered perpetually as if he were always fighting against a high wind. The receding hair had faded and coarsened to dull straw. The bones jutted through his skin giving him the appearance of a death's head. Only his hands were unchanged. He held them out now to the fire, soft-skinned, white and delicate as those of a girl. He smiled at Dalgliesh:

"Lost, believed safe. One middle-aged detective writer. Nervous disposition. Slight build. Narrow nose. Buck teeth. Sparse hair. Prominent Adam's apple. Finder, please keep. . . . So we come to you for advice, dear boy. Fresh, as I understand it, from your latest triumph. Do we wait for Maurice to make his reappearance and then pretend we didn't notice that he got lost? Or do we play it his way and ask the police to help us find him? After all, if it is a publicity stunt, it would only be kind to co-operate. Poor Maurice needs all the help in that direction he can get."

"It's not a joking matter, Justin." Miss Calthrop was severe. "And I don't for one moment think that it's a publicity stunt. If I did, I wouldn't come worrying Adam at a time when he particularly needs a peaceful, quiet holiday to recover from the strain of that case. So clever of you, Adam, to catch him before he did it again. The whole case made me feel sick, physically sick! And now what will happen to him? Kept in prison for a few years at the State's expense, then let out to murder some other child? Are we all mad in this country? I can't think why we don't hang him mercifully and be done with it."

Dalgliesh was glad that his face was in shadow. He recalled again the moment of arrest. Pooley had been such a small man, small, ugly and stinking with fear. His wife had left him a year before and the inexpert patch which puckered the elbow of his cheap suit had obviously been his own work.

33

Dalgliesh had found his eyes held by that patch as if it had the power to assert that Pooley was still a human being. Well, the beast was caged now and the public and press were free to be loud in their praise of the police work in general and of Superintendent Dalgliesh in particular. A psychiatrist could explain, no doubt, why he felt himself contaminated with guilt. The feeling was not new to him and he would deal with it in his own way. After all, he reflected wryly, it had seldom inconvenienced him for long and never once had it made him want to change his job. But he was damned if he was going to discuss Pooley with Celia Calthrop.

Across the room his aunt's eyes met his. She said quietly:

"What exactly do you want my nephew to do, Miss Calthrop? If Mr. Seton has disappeared, isn't that a matter for the local police?"

"But is it? That's our problem!" Miss Calthrop drained her glass as if the Amontilado had been cooking sherry, and automatically held it out to be refilled.

"Maurice may have disappeared for some purpose of his own, perhaps to collect material for his next book. He's been hinting that this is to be something different—a departure from his usual classical detective novel. He's a most conscientious craftsman and doesn't like to deal with anything outside his personal experience. We all know that. Remember how he spent three months with a travelling circus before he wrote *Murder on the High Wire*. Of course, it does imply he's a little deficient in creative imagination. My novels are never restricted to my own experience."

Justine Bryce said:

"In view of what your last heroine went through, Celia darling, I'm relieved to hear it."

Dalgliesh asked when Seton had last been seen. Before Miss Calthrop could answer, Sylvia Kedge spoke. The sherry and the warmth of the fire had put some colour into her cheeks and she had herself well under control. She spoke directly to Dalgliesh and without interruption.

"Mr. Seton went to London last Monday morning to stay at his Club, that's the Cadaver Club in Tavistock Square. He

34

always spends a week or two there in October. He prefers London in the autumn and he likes to do research for his books in the Club Library. He took a small suitcase with him and his portable typewriter. He went by the train from Halesworth. He told me that he was going to make a start on a new book, something different from his usual style, and I got the impression he was rather excited about it although he never discussed it with me. He said that everyone would be surprised by it. He arranged for me to work at the house for mornings only while he was away and said he would telephone me about 10 o'clock if he had any messages. That's the usual arrangement when he's working at the Club. He types the manuscript in double spacing and posts it to me in instalments and I make a fair copy. Then he revises the whole book and I type it ready for the publishers. Of course, the instalments don't always connect. When he's in London he likes to work on town scenes—I never know what's going to arrive next. Well, he telephoned on Tuesday morning to say that he hoped to post some manuscript by Wednesday evening and to ask me to do one or two small mending jobs. He sounded perfectly all right, perfectly normal then."

Miss Calthrop could contain herself no longer.

"It was really very naughty of Maurice to use you for jobs like darning his socks and polishing the silver. You're a qualified shorthand typist and it's a dreadful waste of skill. Goodness knows, I've enough stuff on tape waiting for you to type. However, that's another matter. Everyone knows my views."

Everyone did. There would have been more sympathy with them if people hadn't suspected that dear Celia's indignation was chiefly on her own account. If there was any exploiting to be done she expected priority.

The girl took no notice of the interruption. Her dark eyes were still fixed on Dalgliesh. He asked gently:

"When did you next hear from Mr. Seton?"

"I didn't, Mr. Dalgliesh. There was no call on Wednesday when I was working at Seton House but, of course, that didn't worry me. He might not telephone for days. I was there

again early this morning to finish some ironing when Mr. Plant rang. He's the caretaker at the Cadaver Club and his wife does the cooking. He said they were very worried because Mr. Seton had gone out before dinner on Tuesday and hadn't yet returned to the Club. His bed hadn't been slept in and his clothes and typewriter were still there. Mr. Plant didn't like to make too much fuss at first. He thought that Mr. Seton might have stayed out for some purpose connected with his work—but he got worried when a second night went by and still no message. So he thought he'd better telephone the house. I didn't know what to do. I couldn't contact Mr. Seton's half-brother because he's recently moved to a new flat and we don't know the address. There aren't any other relations. You see, I wasn't sure whether Mr. Seton would want me to take any action. I suggested to Mr. Plant that we should wait a little longer and we agreed to phone each other the minute there was any news, and then just before lunch time, the post arrived and I got the manuscript."

"We have it here," proclaimed Miss Calthrop. "And the envelope." She produced them from her capacious handbag with a flourish and handed them to Dalgliesh. The envelope was the ordinary commercial, buff-coloured, four by nine inch size and was addressed, in typing, to Maurice Seton, Esq., Seton House, Monksmere, Suffolk. Inside were three quarto sheets of inexpert typescript, double spaced. Miss Kedge said dully:

"He always addressed the manuscript to himself. But that isn't his work, Mr. Dalgliesh. He didn't write it and he didn't type it."

"How can you be sure?"

It was hardly a necessary question. There are few things more difficult to disguise than typing and the girl had surely copied enough Maurice Seton manuscripts to recognize his style. But before she had a chance to reply, Miss Calthrop said:

"I think it would be best if I just read part of it."

They waited while she took from her handbag a pair of immense jewelled spectacles, settled them on her nose, and

36

arranged herself more comfortably in the chair. Maurice Seton, thought Dalgliesh, was about to have his first public reading. He would have been gratified by the listeners' rapt attention and possibly, too, by Miss Calthrop's histrionics. Celia, faced with the work of a fellow craftsman and sure of the audience, was prepared to give of her best. She read:

"Carruthers pushed aside the bead curtain and entered the night club. For a moment he stood motionless in the doorway, his tall figure elegant as always in the well-cut dinner jacket, his cool ironic eyes surveying with a kind of disdain the close packed tables, the squalid pseudo-Spanish decor, the shabby clientèle. So this was the headquarters of perhaps the most dangerous gang in Europe! Behind this sordid but commonplace night club, outwardly no different from a hundred others in Soho, was a master mind which could control some of the most powerful criminal gangs in the West. It seemed unlikely. But then, this whole fantastic adventure was unlikely. He sat down at the table nearest the door to watch and wait. When the waiter came he ordered fried scampi, green salad and a bottle of chianti. The man, a grubby little Cypriot, took his order without a word. Did they know he was here? Carruthers wondered. And, if they did, how long would it be before they showed themselves.

"There was a small stage at the end of the Club furnished only with a cane screen and a single red chair. Suddenly the lights were dimmed and the pianist began to play a slow sensuous tune. From behind the screen came a girl. She was blonde and beautiful, not young but mature and full bosomed, with a grace and arrogance which Carruthers thought might indicate White Russian blood. She moved forward sensuously to the single chair and with great deliberation began to unzip her evening dress. It fell about her knees to the ground. Underneath she wore nothing but a black brassiere and G string. Sitting now with her back to the audience she twisted her hands to unhook the brassiere. Immediately from the crowded tables there came a hoarse murmuring. 'Rosie! Rosie! Come on Rosie! Give! Give!'"

Miss Calthrop stopped reading. There was complete

silence. Most of her listeners seemed stunned. Then Bryce called out:

"Well, go on Celia! Don't stop now it's getting really exciting. Does Rosie fall on the Hon. Martin Carruthers and rape him? He's had it coming to him for years. Or is that too much to hope?"

Miss Calthrop said:

"There's no need to go on. The proof we need is there."

Sylvia Kedge turned again to Dalgliesh.

"Mr. Seton would never call a character Rosie, Mr. Dalgliesh. That was his mother's name. He told me once that he would never use it in any of his books. And he never did."

"Particularly not for a Soho prostitute," broke in Miss Calthrop. "He talked to me about his mother quite often. He adored her. Absolutely adored her. It nearly broke his heart when she died and his father married again."

Miss Calthrop's voice throbbed with all the yearning of frustrated motherhood. Suddenly Oliver Latham said:

"Let me see that."

Celia handed the manuscript to him and they all watched with anxious expectancy while he scanned it. Then he handed it back without a word.

"Well?" asked Miss Calthrop.

"Nothing. I just wanted to have a look at it. I know Seton's handwriting but not his typing. But you say that he didn't type this."

"I'm sure he didn't," said Miss Kedge. "Although I can't exactly say why. It just doesn't look like his work. But it was typed on his machine."

"What about the style?" asked Dalgliesh. The little group considered. At last Bryce said:

"One couldn't really call that typical Seton. After all, the man could write when he chose. It's almost artificial, isn't it? One gets the impression he was trying to write badly."

Elizabeth Marley had been silent until now, sitting alone in the corner like a discontented child who has been dragged unwillingly into the company of boring adults. Suddenly she said impatiently:

38

"If this is a fake it's obvious we were meant to discover it. Justin's right. The style's completely bogus. And it's too much of a coincidence that the person responsible should have hit on the one name which would arouse suspicion. Why choose Rosie? If you ask me, this is just Maurice Seton trying to be clever and you've all fallen for it. You'll read all about it in time when his new book comes out. You know how he loves experimenting."

"It's certainly the sort of childish scheme that Seton might think up," said Latham. "I'm not sure I want to be an involuntary participant in any of his damn silly experiments. I suggest we forget the whole thing. He'll turn up in his own time."

"Maurice was always very odd and secretive, of course," agreed Miss Calthrop. "Especially about his work. And there's another thing. I've been able to give him one or two useful little hints in the past. He's definitely used them. But never a word to me subsequently. Naturally I didn't expect a formal acknowledgement. If I can help a fellow writer I'm only too happy. But it's a little disconcerting when a book is published to find one or two of one's own ideas in the plot and never a thank you from Maurice."

"He's probably forgotten by then that he didn't think them out for himself," suggested Latham with a kind of tolerant contempt.

"He never forgot anything, Oliver. Maurice had a very clear mind. He worked methodically too. If I dropped a suggestion he'd pretend to be only half interested and mutter something about trying to work it in sometime or other. But I could see from the look in his eyes that he'd seized on it and was only waiting to get home to file it away on one of those little index cards. Not that I resented it really. It's just that I think he might have acknowledged the help occasionally. I gave him an idea a month or so ago and I bet you anything it will appear in the next book."

No one accepted the offer. Bryce said:

"You're absolutely right about him, Celia. One contributed one's own mite from time to time. God knows why except

that one does get the occasional idea for a new method of murder and it seemed a shame to waste it when poor Seton was so obviously near the end of his resources. But, apart from that predatory gleam in his eye—not a sign of appreciation, my dears! Of course, for reasons you all appreciate, he gets no help from me now. Not after what he did to Arabella."

Miss Calthrop said:

"Oh, my idea wasn't for a new method of murder exactly. It was just a situation. I thought it might make rather an effective opening chapter. I kept telling Maurice that you must capture your readers from the very start. I pictured a body drifting out to sea in a dinghy with its hands chopped off at the wrists."

There was a silence, so complete, so sudden that the striking of the carriage clock drew all their eyes towards it as if it were chiming the hour of execution. Dalgliesh was looking at Latham. He had stiffened in his chair and was grasping the stem of his glass with such force that Dalgliesh half expected it to snap. It was impossible to guess what lay behind that pale, rigid, mask. Suddenly Bryce gave his high, nervous laugh and the tension broke. One could almost hear the little gasps of relief.

"What an extraordinarily morbid imagination you have Celia! One would never suspect. You must control these impulses, my dear, or the League of Romantic Novelists will hurl you out of the Club."

Latham spoke, his voice controlled, colourless. He said:

"All this doesn't help with the present problem. Do I take it that we're agreed to take no action about Seton's disappearance? Eliza is probably right and it's just some nonsense Maurice has thought up. If so the sooner we leave Mr. Dalgliesh to enjoy his holiday in peace the better."

He was rising to go as if suddenly wearied of the whole subject when there was a loud, authoritative knock on the cottage door. Jane Dalgliesh lifted an interrogative eyebrow at her nephew then got up quietly and went through the porch to open it. The party fell silent, listening unashamedly. A caller after dusk was rare in their isolated community.

Once night fell they were used to seeing only each other and knew by the instinct of long experience whose footstep was approaching their door. But this loud summons had been the knock of a stranger. There was the soft, broken mutter of voices from the porch. Then Miss Dalgliesh reappeared in the doorway, two raincoated men in the shadows behind her. She said:

"This is Detective Inspector Reckless and Sergeant Courtney from the County C.I.D. They are looking for Digby Seton. His sailing dinghy has come ashore at Cod Head."

Justin Bryce said:

"That's odd. It was beached as usual at the bottom of Tanner's Lane at five o'clock yesterday afternoon."

Everyone seemed to realize simultaneously how strange it was that a Detective Inspector and a Sergeant should be calling after dark about a missing dinghy but Latham spoke before the others had formed their questions:

"What's wrong Inspector?"

Jane Dalgiesh replied for him.

"Something very shocking, I'm afraid. Maurice Seton's body was in the boat."

"Maurice's body! Maurice? But that's ridiculous!" Miss Calthrop's sharp didactic voice cut across the room in futile protest.

"It can't be Maurice. He never takes the boat out. Maurice doesn't like sailing."

The Inspector moved forward into the light and spoke for the first time.

"He hadn't been sailing, Madam. Mr. Seton was lying dead in the bottom of the boat. Dead, and with both hands taken off at the wrists."

6

Celia Calthrop, as if relishing her own obstinacy, said for the tenth time.

"I keep telling you! I didn't say a word about the plot to anyone except Maurice. Why should I? And it's no good harping on about the date. It was about six months ago—perhaps longer. I can't remember just when. But we were walking along the beach to Walberswick and I suddenly thought that it would make a good start to a detective story if one described a handless corpse drifting out to sea in a boat. So I suggested it to Maurice. I certainly never mentioned it to anyone else until tonight. Maurice may have done so, of course."

Elizabeth Marley burst out irritably:

"Obviously he told someone! We can hardly suppose that he cut his own hands off in the cause of versimilitude. And it's stretching coincidence too far to suggest that you and the murderer happened to think of the same idea. But I don't see how you can be so certain that you didn't talk about it to anyone else. I believe you mentioned it to me once when we were discussing how slow Maurice was to get his plots under way."

No one looked as if they believed her. Justin Bryce said softly, but not so softly that the others couldn't hear:

"Dear Eliza! So loyal always." Oliver Latham laughed and there was a short, embarrassed silence broken by Sylvia Kedge's hoarse belligerent voice.

"He never mentioned it to me."

"No dear," replied Miss Calthrop sweetly. "But then, there were a great many things which Mr. Seton didn't discuss with you. One doesn't tell everything to one's maid. And that, my dear, was how he thought of you. You should

have had more pride than to let him use you as a household drudge. Men prefer a little spirit, you know."

It was gratuitously spiteful and Dalgliesh could sense the general embarrassed surprise. But no one spoke. He was almost ashamed to look at the girl but she had bent her head as if meekly accepting a merited rebuke, and the two black swathes of hair had swung forward to curtain her face. In the sudden silence he could hear the rasping of her breath, and he wished he could feel sorry for her. Certainly Celia Calthrop was intolerable; but there was something about Sylvia Kedge which provoked unkindness. He wondered what lay behind that particular impulse to savagery.

It was nearly an hour since Inspector Reckless and his Sergeant had arrived, an hour in which the Inspector had said little and the rest of the company, except Dalgliesh and his aunt, had said a great deal. Not all of it had been wise. Reckless had settled himself on arrival in a high chair against the wall and sat there still, solid as a bailiff, his sombre eyes watchful in the light of the fire. Despite the warmth of the room he was wearing his raincoat, a grubby gaberdine which looked too fragile to sustain the weight of its armour of metal buttons, buckles and studs. On his lap he nursed with careful hands a pair of immense gauntlet gloves and a trilby hat as if fearful that someone was going to snatch them from him. He looked like an interloper; the minor official there on sufferance, the little man who dares not risk a drink on duty. And that, thought Dalgliesh, was exactly the effect he aimed to produce. Like all successful detectives, he was able to subdue his personality at will so that even his physical presence became as innocuous and commonplace as a piece of furniture. The man was helped by his appearance, of course. He was small—surely only just the regulation height for a policeman—and the sallow, anxious face was as neutral and unremarkable as any of a million faces seen crowding into a football ground on a Saturday afternoon. His voice, too, was flat, classless, giving no clue to the man. His eyes, wide spaced and deep set under jutting brows, had a trick of moving expressionlessly from face to face as people spoke

which the present company might have found disconcerting if they had bothered to notice. By his side, Sergeant Courtney sat with the air of one who has been told to sit upright, keep his eyes and ears open and say nothing, and who is doing just that.

Dalgliesh glanced across the room to where his aunt sat in her usual chair, she had taken up her knitting and seemed serenely detached from the business in hand. She had been taught to knit by a German governess and held the needles upright in the Continental manner; Celia Calthrop seemed mesmerised by their flashing tips and sat glaring across at them as if both fascinated and affronted by her hostess's unusual expertise. She was less at ease, crossing and un-crossing her feet and jerking back her head from the fire as if she found its heat intolerable. It was certainly getting hot in the sitting room. All the other visitors, except Reckless, seemed to feel it too. Oliver Latham was pacing up and down, his brow wet with sweat, his restless energy seeming to raise the temperature still higher. Suddenly he swung round at Reckless:

"When did he die?" he demanded. "Come on, let's have some facts for a change! When did Seton die?"

"We shan't know that precisely until we get the P.M. report, Sir."

"In other words, you're not telling. Let me phrase it an-other way then. For what hours are we expected to provide alibis?"

Celia Calthrop gave a little squeak of protest but turned to Reckless as anxiously as the rest for his reply.

"I shall want a statement from all of you covering the time Mr. Seton was last seen, which was I understand, seven-thirty on Tuesday evening, until midnight on Wednesday."

Latham said:

"That's putting it a bit late surely? He must have been shoved out to sea long before midnight. Sunset and evening star and one clear call for me. . . . I'll begin, shall I? I was at the New Theatre Guild first night on Tuesday and after-wards went on to a party given by our dear theatrical knight.

44

I got back to my flat shortly after one and spent what remained of the night with a friend. I can't say who at present but I expect I'll be able to give you the name tomorrow. We got up late, lunched at the Ivy, and parted when I got out my car to drive down here. I arrived at my cottage shortly after seven-thirty yesterday evening and didn't go out again except to take a short walk along the beach before bed. Today I've spent driving around the country and getting in supplies. After dinner I discovered I hadn't bought any coffee and came to the one neighbour who could be relied upon to provide a drinkable blend without a coy accompanying lecture on men and their inefficient housekeeping. To make it easy for you, I would emphasis that I have, apparently, an alibi for the time of death—presuming him to have died on Tuesday—but not for the time he was sent off on his last journey, presuming that to have been yesterday night."

During the first part of this recital Miss Calthrop had assumed a quick variety of expressions—curiosity, disapproval, lubricity and a gentle sadness—as if trying to decide which suited her best. She settled for the gentle sadness, a good woman grieving once more over the frailty of men.

Inspector Reckless said quietly:

"I shall have to ask you for the lady's name Sir."

"Then you'll ask in vain, at least until I've had a chance to talk to her. Charming of you to assume that it was a woman, though. Look Inspector, be reasonable! If I had anything to do with Seton's death I should have fixed my alibi by now. And if I set out to concoct a false one it would hardly involve a woman. Apart from considerations of misplaced chivalry we could hardly fox you for long. No one remembers all the details. You would only have to ask what we talked about, who drew the curtains, on what side of the bed I slept, how many blankets, what we ate for breakfast. It amazes me that anyone tries to concoct an alibi. One would need a better head for detail than I lay claim to."

"Well, you seem to be in the clear, Oliver," proclaimed Celia severely. "It is a matter of murder after all. No reasonable woman could make difficulties."

Latham laughed.

"But she's not reasonable, my dear Celia. She's an actress. Not that I'm expecting trouble. My father gave me one piece of useful advice. Never go to bed with a woman if either of you would be embarrassed to admit the fact next morning. It's a little restricting to one's sex life but now you can see the practical advantages."

Dalgliesh doubted whether Latham found it in fact so very restricting. In his sophisticated circle few people minded a liaison becoming public provided it enhanced their standing, and Oliver Latham, wealthy, handsome, urbane and reputedly hard to get, stood high in the market. Bryce said peevishly:

"Well, you've nothing to worry about then if, as seems likely, Seton died on Tuesday night. Unless, of course, the Inspector is unkind enough to suggest that your sleeping partner would provide you with an alibi in any case."

"Oh, she would provide almost anything if asked nicely," said Latham lightly. "But it would be dangerous surely. It's a question of histrionics. As long as she was playing the gallant little liar, risking her reputation to save her lover from jail, I should be all right. But suppose she decided to change her role? It's probably as well that I shall be requiring her merely to tell the truth."

Celia Calthrop, obviously tired of the general interest in Latham's sex life, broke in impatiently:

"I hardly think I need to describe my movements. I was a very dear friend of poor Maurice, perhaps the only real friend he ever had. However, I haven't any objection to telling you, and I suppose it may help to clear some one else. Every piece of information is important, isn't it? I was at home for most of the time. On Tuesday afternoon however, I drove Sylvia to Norwich and we both had our hair washed and set. *Estelle's* near the Maddermarket. It makes a pleasant little treat for Sylvia and I do think it's important not to let oneself go just because one lives in the country. We had a late tea in Norwich and I took Sylvia home at about eight-thirty; then I drove back to my cottage. I spent yesterday morning working—I

46

dictate on tape—and I drove to Ipswich yesterday afternoon to do some shopping and call on a friend, Lady Briggs of Well Walk. It was just a chance call. Actually she wasn't in, but the maid will remember me. I'm afraid I got a little lost coming home and wasn't back until nearly ten. By then my niece had arrived from Cambridge and she, of course, can vouch for me for the rest of the night. Just before lunch this morning Sylvia telephoned to tell me about the manuscript and Maurice being missing. I wasn't at all sure what to do for the best but when I saw Superintendent Dalgliesh driving past this evening I rang Mr. Bryce and suggested that we all come to consult him. By then I had a premonition that something was dreadfully wrong; and how right I am proved!"

Justin Bryce spoke next. Dalgliesh was intrigued by the readiness with which the suspects were volunteering information for which no one had yet officially asked. They were reciting their alibis with the glib assurance of converts at a revivalist meeting. Tomorrow, no doubt, they would pay for this indulgence with the usual emotional hangover. But it was hardly his job to warn them. He began to feel a considerably increased respect for Reckless; at least the man knew when to sit still and listen.

Bryce said:

"I was at my Bloomsbury flat in town until yesterday too but if Seton died late on Tuesday night I'm definitely out of the running my dears. I had to telephone the doctor twice that night. I was really dreadfully ill. One of my asthma attacks; you know how I suffer Celia. My doctor, Lionel Forbes-Denby can confirm it. I phoned him first just before midnight and begged him to visit at once. He wouldn't come, of course. Just told me to take two of my blue capsules and ring again if they hadn't acted in an hour. It was really naughty of him. I told him I thought I was dying. That's why my type of asthma is so dangerous. You can die with it if you think you're going to."

"But not if Forbes-Denby forbids it, surely?" said Latham.

"That's all very well, Oliver, but he can be wrong."

"He was Maurice's doctor, too, wasn't he?" asked Miss

47

Calthrop. "Maurice always swore by him. He had to be terribly careful of his heart and he always said that Forbes-Denby kept him alive."

"Well he should have visited me Tuesday night," said Bryce, aggrieved. "I rang again at three-thirty and he came at six but I was over the worst by then. Still, it's an alibi."

"Not really, Justin," said Latham. "We've no proof that you rang from your flat."

"Of course, I phoned from the flat! I told you. I was practically at death's door. Besides, if I sent a false message and was rushing around London murdering Seton what would I do when Forbes-Denby turned up at the flat? He'd never treat me again!" Latham laughed:

"My dear Justin! If Forbes-Denby says he isn't coming he isn't coming. And well you know it."

Bryce assented sadly; he seemed to take the destruction of his alibi remarkably philosophically. Dalgliesh had heard of Forbes-Denby. He was a fashionable West End practitioner who was also a good doctor. He and his patients shared a common belief in the medical infallability of Forbes-Denby and it was rumoured that few of them would eat, drink, marry, give birth, leave the country or die without his permission; they gloried in his eccentricities, recounted with gusto his latest rudeness and dined out on the recent Forbes-Denby outrage whether it were hurling their favourite patent medicine through the window or sacking the cook. Dalgliesh was glad that it would be Reckless or his minions who would have the task of asking this unamiable eccentric to provide medical information about the victim and an alibi for one of the suspects.

Suddenly Justin burst out with a violence that caused them all to turn and stare at him:

"I didn't kill him, but don't ask me to be sorry about it! Not after what he did to Arabella!"

Celia Calthrop gave Reckless the resigned, slightly apologetic look of a mother whose child is about to make a nuisance of himself but not altogether without excuse. She muttered confidentially:

"Arabella. His Siamese cat. Mr. Bryce thought that Maurice had killed the animal."

"One didn't think, Celia. One knew." He turned to Reckless.

"I ran over his dog about three months ago. It was the purest accident. I like animals. I like them, I tell you! Even Towser who, admit it Celia, was the most disagreeable, ill-bred and unattractive mongrel. It was the most horrible experience! He ran straight under my wheels. Seton was utterly devoted to him. He practically accused me of deliberately running the dog down. And then, four days later, he murdered Arabella. That's the kind of man he was! Do you wonder someone has put a stop to him?"

Miss Calthrop, Miss Dalgliesh and Latham all spoke at once thus effectively defeating their good intentions.

"Justin dear, there really wasn't a particle of proof. . . ."

"Mr. Bryce, no one is going to suppose that Arabella has anything to do with it."

"For God's sake Justin, why drag up. . . ."

Reckless broke in quietly:

"And when did you arrive at Monksmere, Sir?"

"Wednesday afternoon. Just before four. And I didn't have Seton's body in the car with me either. Luckily for me, I had trouble with the gear box all the way from Ipswich and had to leave it in Baines garage just outside Saxmundham. I came on by taxi. Young Baines brought me. So if you want to check the car for blood and fingerprints you'll find it with Baines. And good luck to you."

Latham said:

"Why the hell are we bothering, anyway? What about the next-of-kin? Dear Maurice's half-brother. Shouldn't the police be trying to trace him? After all, he's the heir. He's the one with the explaining to do."

Eliza Marley said quietly:

"Digby was at Seton House last night. I drove him there."

It was only the second time she had spoken since the Inspector's arrival and Dalgliesh sensed that she wasn't anxious to speak now. But no one hoping for a sensation could

have wished for a more gratifying response. There was an astounded silence broken by Miss Calthrop's sharp, inquisitorial voice:

"What do you mean, drove him there?"

It was, thought Dalgliesh, a predictable question.

The girl shrugged:

"What I said. I drove Digby Seton home last night. He telephoned from Ipswich station before catching the connection and asked me to meet him off the eight-thirty train at Saxmundham. He knew Maurice wouldn't be at home and I suppose he wanted to save the cost of a taxi. Anyway, I went. I took the Mini."

"You never told me about this when I got home," said Miss Calthrop accusingly. The rest of the party shifted uneasily, apprehensive that they might be in for a family row. Only the dark figure sitting against the wall seemed utterly unconcerned:

"I didn't think you would be particularly interested. Anyway, you were pretty late back, weren't you?"

"But what about tonight? You didn't say anything earlier."

"Why should I? If Digby wanted to beetle off again somewhere it's no business of mine. Anyway, that was before we knew that Maurice Seton was dead."

"So you met Digby at his request off the eight-thirty?" asked Latham, as if anxious to get the record straight.

"That's right. And what's more, Oliver, he was on the train when it pulled in. He wasn't lurking in the waiting room or hanging about outside the station. I bought a platform ticket, saw him get off the train and was with him when he gave up his ticket. A London ticket, incidentally; he was complaining about the cost. The ticket collector will remember him, anyway. There were only about half-a-dozen other passengers."

"And presumably he hadn't a body with him?" asked Latham.

"Not unless he was carrying it in a hold-all measuring about three feet by two."

"And you drove him straight home?"

50

"Of course. That was the idea. Sax is hardly a haunt of gaiety after eight o'clock and Digby isn't my favourite drinking companion. I was just saving him the cost of a taxi. I told you."

"Well, go on, Eliza," encouraged Bryce. "You drove Digby to Seton House. And then?"

"Nothing. I left him at the front door. The house was quiet and there were no lights. Well, naturally. Everyone knows that Maurice stays in London during mid October. Digby asked me in for a drink but I said that I was tired and wanted to get home and that Aunt Celia would probably be home and waiting up for me. We said goodnight and Digby let himself in with his own key."

"He had a key, then?" interposed Reckless. "He and his brother were on those terms?"

"I don't know what terms they were on. I only know that Digby has a key."

Reckless turned to Sylvia Kedge.

"You knew about this? That Mr. Digby Seton had open access to the house?"

Sylvia Kedge replied:

"Mr. Maurice Seton gave his brother a key about two years ago. From time to time he did mention asking for it back but Mr. Digby used it so seldom when his brother wasn't at home that I suppose he thought it didn't matter letting him keep it."

"Why, as a matter of interest, did he want it back?" enquired Bryce. Miss Calthrop obviously considered this the kind of question that Sylvia should not be expected to answer. With an expression and voice clearly indicating "not in front of the servants", she replied:

"Maurice did mention the key to me on one occasion and said that he might ask for it to be returned. There was no question of not trusting Digby. He was merely a little worried in case it got lost or stolen at one of those night clubs Digby is so fond of."

"Well, apparently he didn't get it back," said Latham. "Digby used it to get into the house at about nine o'clock

last night. And no one has seen him since. Are you sure the house was empty, Eliza?"

"How could I be? I didn't go in. But I heard no one and there were no lights."

"I was there at half past nine this morning," said Sylvia Kedge. "The front door was locked as usual and the house was empty. None of the beds had been slept in. Mr. Digby hadn't even poured himself a drink."

There was an unspoken comment that something sudden and drastic must indeed have occurred. There were surely few crises which Digby Seton would not suitably fortify himself to meet.

But Celia was speaking.

"That's nothing to go by. Digby always carries a hip flask. It was one of those little idiocyncracies of his that used to irritate Maurice so. But where on earth can he have gone?"

"He didn't say anything to you about going out again?" Latham turned to Eliza Marley. "How did he seem?"

"No, he didn't say anything; I'm not particularly perceptive of Digby's moods but he seemed much as usual."

"It's ridiculous!" proclaimed Miss Calthrop. "Digby surely wouldn't go out again when he'd only just arrived. And where is there for anyone to go? Are you sure he didn't mention his plans?"

Elizabeth Marley said:

"He may have been called out."

Her aunt's voice was sharp.

"Called out! Nobody knew he was there! Called out by whom?"

"I don't know. I only mention it as a possibility. As I was walking back to the car I heard the telephone ring."

"Are you sure?" asked Latham.

"Why do you keep on asking me if I'm sure? You know what it's like up there on the headland; the quietness; the loneliness and mystery of the place; the way sound travels at night. I tell you, I heard the phone ring!"

They fell silent. She was right, of course. They knew what it was like on the headland at night. And the same silence, the

52

same loneliness and mystery waited for them outside. Despite the heat of the room Celia Calthrop shivered. But the heat was really getting intolerable.

Bryce had been crouching on a low stool in front of the fire feeding it compulsively from the wood basket like some demonic stoker. The great tongues of flame leapt and hissed around the drift wood; the stone walls of the sitting room looked as if they were sweating blood. Dalgliesh went over to one of the windows and wrestled with the shutters. As he pushed open the pane the waves of sweet cold air passed over him, lifting the rugs on the floor and bringing in like a clap of thunder the surge of the sea. As he turned again he heard Reckless' flat, unemphatic voice:

"I suggest someone takes Miss Kedge home. She looks ill. I shan't want to talk to her tonight."

The girl looked as if she were about to remonstrate but Elizabeth Marley said with brief finality:

"I'll take her. I want to get home myself. I'm supposed to be convalescent and this hasn't exactly been a restful evening, has it? Where's her coat?"

There was a little spurt of activity. Everyone seemed to feel relief in action and there was much fuss over Sylvia Kedge's coat, her crutches and her general comfort. Miss Calthrop handed over her car keys and said graciously that she would walk home escorted, of course, by Oliver and Justin. Sylvia Kedge, surrounded by a bodyguard of helpers, began to hobble her way to the door.

It was then that the telephone rang. Immediately the little party froze into a tableau of apprehension. The raucous sound, at once so ordinary and so ominous, petrified them into silence. Miss Dalgliesh had moved to the telephone and lifted the receiver when Reckless rose swiftly and without apology took it from her hand.

They could make little of the conversation, which on Reckless' part was conducted briefly and in monosyllables. He seemed to be speaking to a Police Station. For most of the time he listened in silence interspersed with grunts. He ended:

"Right. Thank you. I shall be seeing him at Seton House

first thing in the morning. Goodnight." He replaced the receiver and turned to face the waiting company who were making no effort to hide their anxiety. Dalgliesh half-expected him to disappoint them but instead he said:

"We've found Mr. Digby Seton. He has telephoned Lowestoft Police Station to say that he was admitted to hospital last night after driving his car into a ditch on the Lowestoft Road. They are discharging him first thing tomorrow morning."

Miss Calthrop's mouth had opened for the inevitable question when he added:

"His story is that someone telephoned him just after nine o'clock last night to ask him to go at once to Lowestoft Police Station to identify his brother's body. The caller told him that Mr. Maurice Seton's corpse had come ashore in a dinghy with both hands chopped off at the wrists."

Latham said incredulously:

"But that's impossible! I thought you said the body wasn't found until early this evening?"

"Nor was it, Sir. No one telephoned from the Lowestoft Police yesterday night. No one knew what had happened to Mr. Maurice Seton until his body came ashore this evening. Except one person, of course."

He looked round at them, the melancholy eyes moving speculatively from face to face. No one spoke or moved. It was as if they were all fixed in a moment of time waiting helplessly for some unavoidable cataclysm. It was a moment for which no words seemed adequate; it cried out for action, for drama. And Sylvia Kedge, as if obligingly doing her best, slid with a moan from Eliza's supporting arms and crumpled to the floor.

7

Reckless said:

"He died at midnight on Tuesday, give or take an hour. That's my guess based on the stage of rigor and the general look of him. I shall be surprised if the P.M. doesn't confirm it. The hands were taken off some time after death. There wasn't much bleeding but it looked as if the seat of the dinghy had been used as a chopping block. Assuming that Mr. Bryce was telling the truth and the dinghy was still beached here at five o'clock Wednesday afternoon, he was almost certainly pushed out to sea after the tide turned an hour later. The butchery must have been done after dusk. But he had been dead then for the best part of eighteen hours, maybe longer. I don't know where he died or how he died. But I shall find out."

The three policemen were together in the sitting room. Jane Dalgliesh had made an excuse to leave them alone by offering them coffee; from the kitchen Dalgliesh could hear the faint tinkling sounds of its preparation. It was over ten minutes since the rest of the company had left. It had required little time or effort to revive Sylvia Kedge and once she and Liz Marley were on their way, there had been a general tacit agreement that the excitements of the evening might now be drawn to a close. The visitors looked suddenly bedraggled with weariness. When Reckless, as if gaining energy and animation from their exhaustion, began to question them about a possible weapon, he was met by weary incomprehension. No one seemed able to remember whether he or she owned a chopper, a cleaver or an axe, where these implements were kept or when they had last been used. No one except Jane Dalgliesh. And even Miss Dalgliesh's calm admission

that she had lost a chopper from her wood shed some months previously provoked no more than mild interest. The company had had enough of murder for one night. Like overexcited children at the end of the party, they wanted to go home.

It was not until Miss Dalgliesh had also left them that Reckless spoke of the case. This was to be expected but Dalgliesh was irritated to discover how much he resented the obvious implication. Reckless was presumably neither stupid nor crassly insensitive. He would utter no warnings. He wouldn't antagonize Dalgliesh by inviting a discretion and co-operation which both of them knew he had the right to take for granted. But this was his case. He was in charge. It was for him to decide at leisure which pieces of the puzzle he would lay out for Dalgliesh's inspection; how much he would confide and to whom. The situation was a novel one for Dalgliesh and he wasn't sure he was going to like it.

The room was still very close. The fire was dying now into a pyramid of white ash but the heat trapped between the stone walls beat on their faces as if from an oven and the air smelt heavy. The Inspector seemed unaffected by it. He said:

"These people who were here this evening, Mr. Dalgliesh. Tell me about them. Do they all call themselves writers?"

Dalgliesh replied:

"I imagine that Oliver Latham would call himself a dramatic critic. Miss Calthrop likes to be known as a romantic novelist, whatever that may mean. I don't know what Justin Bryce would call himself. He edits a monthly literary and political review which was founded by his grandfather."

Reckless said surprisingly:

"I know. *The Monthly Critical Review*. My father used to take it. That was in the days when sixpence meant something to a working man. And for sixpence the *Monthly Crit.* gave you the message, warm and strong. Nowadays it's about as pink as the *Financial Times;* advice on your investments, reviews of books which nobody wants to read; cosy competitions for the intelligentsia. He can't make a living out of that."

56

Dalgliesh replied that, so far from making a living, Bryce was known to subsidize the review from his private income. Reckless said:

"He's apparently one of those men who don't mind people thinking he's a queer. Is he, Mr. Dalgliesh?"

It was not an irrelevant question. Nothing about a suspect's character is irrelevant in a murder investigation, and the case was being treated as one of murder. But, irrationally, Dalgliesh was irritated. He replied:

"I don't know. He may be a little ambivalent."

"Is he married?"

"Not as far as I know. But we surely haven't yet reached the point when every bachelor over forty is automatically suspect?"

Reckless did not reply. Miss Dalgliesh had returned with the tray of coffee and he accepted a cup with grave thanks but with no appearance of really wanting it. When she had again left them he began noisily sipping; his sombre eyes above the rim of the cup fixed on a water colour of avocets in flight by Jane Dalgliesh which hung on the opposite wall. He said:

"They're a spiteful lot, queers. Not violent on the whole. But spiteful. And there was a spiteful crime. That secretary girl, the cripple. Where does she come from, Mr. Dalgliesh?"

Dalgliesh, feeling like a candidate at a viva voce examination, said calmly:

"Sylvia Kedge is an orphan who lives alone in a cottage in Tanner's Lane. She is said to be a highly competent shorthand typist. She worked chiefly for Maurice Seton but she does quite a bit for Miss Calthrop and Bryce. I know very little about her, about any of them."

"You know enough for my needs at present, Mr. Dalgliesh. And Miss Marley?"

"Also an orphan. Her aunt brought her up. At present she's at Cambridge."

"And all these people are friends of your aunt?"

Dalgliesh hesitated. Friendship was not a word his aunt used easily and he thought it doubtful whether she would in fact speak of more than one person at Monksmere as a

57

friend. But one does not willingly deny one's acquaintances when they are about to be suspected of murder. Resisting the temptation to reply that they knew each other intimately but not well, he said cautiously: "You had better ask my aunt. But they all know each other. After all, it's a small and isolated community. They manage to get on together."

Reckless said:

"When they're not killing each other's animals."

Dalgliesh didn't reply. Reckless added:

"They weren't particularly upset were they? Not a word of regret the whole evening. Being writers you'd think one of them might have managed a stylish little epitaph."

"Miss Kedge took it badly," suggested Dalgliesh.

"That wasn't grief. That was shock. Clinical shock. If she isn't better tomorrow someone should get a doctor to her."

He was right, of course, thought Dalgliesh. It had been shock. And that in itself was interesting. Certainly the evening's news had been shocking enough, but would it have been quite so shocking to someone to whom it wasn't news? There had been nothing faked about that final faint and it hardly suggested guilty knowledge.

Suddenly Reckless got up from his chair, looked at his empty cup as if uncertain how it came to be in his hand and replaced it with slow deliberation on the coffee tray. Sergeant Courtney, after a moment's hesitation, did the same with his. It looked as if they were at last preparing to go. But first there was something which Reckless had to be told. Since it was a perfectly straightforward piece of information which might or might not prove to be important, Dalgliesh was irritated at his reluctance to get it out. He told himself that the next few days were going to be difficult enough without letting Reckless inveigle him into a mood of morbid self-analysis. Firmly he said:

"There's something you ought to know about that fake manuscript. I may be wrong—there's not a lot to go on—but I think I recognize the description of the night club. It sounds like the Cortez Club in Soho, L. J. Luker's place. You probably remember the case. It was in 1959. Luker shot his

partner, was sentenced to death, but was released when the verdict was quashed by the Court of Criminal Appeal."

Reckless said slowly:

"I remember Luker. Mr. Justice Brothwick's case wasn't it? The Cortez Club would be a useful place to know if you were hoping to pin a murder on someone. And Luker would be as good a man to pin it on as any."

He walked to the door, his Sergeant following him like a shadow. Then he turned for a last word.

"I can see that it's going to be a great advantage having you here, Mr. Dalgliesh."

He made it sound like an insult.

8

The contrast between the brightness of the sitting room and the cool darkness of the autumn night was absolute. It was like stepping into a pit. As the door of Pentlands closed behind them Celia Calthrop experienced a moment of blind panic. The night pressed around her. She breathed darkness like a physical weight. It was as if the air had thickened with night, had become a heaviness through which she had to fight her way. There was no longer direction nor distance. In this black and numinous void the sullen, melancholy thudding of the sea sounded on all sides, so that she felt menaced and rooted like a lost traveller on some desolate shore. When Latham shone his torch on the path the ground looked unreal and very far away like the surface of the moon. It was impossible that human feet could make contact with this remote and insubstantial soil. She stumbled and would have lost her balance if Latham hadn't gripped her arm with sudden and surprising force.

They started together on the inland path. Celia, who had not expected to walk home, was wearing light, high-heeled shoes which alternately skidded on the smooth sea pebbles which littered the path or sank into soft patches of sand so that she lurched forward in Latham's grip like a graceless and recalcitrant child. But her panic was over. Her eyes were getting accustomed to the night and with every stumble forward the roar of the sea grew fainter and less insistent. But it was a relief when Justin Bryce spoke, his voice unaltered, ordinary:

"Asthma is a peculiar complaint! This has been a traumatic evening—one's first contact with murder—and yet one feels quite well. Yet last Tuesday one had the most appalling

attack with no apparent cause. One may get a reaction later of course."

"One certainly may," agreed Latham caustically. "Especially if Forbes-Denby doesn't confirm one's alibi for Tuesday night."

"Oh, but he will, Oliver! And one can't help thinking that his testimony will carry rather more weight than anything your sleeping partner may say."

Celia Calthrop, gaining confidence from their nearness, their normality, said quickly:

"It's such a comfort that Adam Dalgliesh happens to be here. After all, he does know us. Socially I mean. And being a writer himself I feel that he belongs at Monksmere."

Latham gave a shout of laughter.

"If you find Adam Dalgliesh a comfort I envy your capacity for self-deception. Do tell us how you see him, Celia! The gentleman sleuth, dabbling in detection for the fun of it, treating his suspects with studied courtesy? A kind of professional Carruthers, straight out of one of Seton's dreary sagas? My dear Celia, Dalgliesh would sell us all to Reckless if he thought it would enhance his reputation one iota. He's the most dangerous man I know."

He laughed again and she felt his grip tighten on her arm. Now he was really hurting her, hurrying her forward as if she were in custody. Yet she could not bring herself to shake free. Although the lane was wider here, the ground was still uneven. Stumbling and slipping, her feet bruised and her ankles aching, she had no chance of keeping up with them except in Latham's remorseless grip. And she could not bear to be left alone. Bryce's voice fluted in her ear.

"Oliver's right you know, Celia. Dalgliesh is a professional detective and probably one of the most intelligent in the country. I don't see that his two volumes of verse, much as I personally admire them, can alter that."

"Reckless is no fool though." Latham still seemed amused. "Did you notice how he said hardly a word but just encouraged us to babble on in our childish, egotistical way? He probably learned more from us in five minutes than other

suspects would tell him in hours of orthodox questioning. When will we learn to keep our mouths shut?"

"As we've nothing to hide I don't see that it matters," said Celia Calthrop. Really Oliver was extraordinarily irritating tonight! One might almost imagine that he was a little drunk. Justin Bryce said:

"Oh, Celia! Everyone has something to hide from the police. That's why one is so ambivalent about them. Wait until Dalgliesh asks why you kept referring to Seton in the past tense, even before we heard that his body had been found. You did, you know. Even I noticed it so it must have struck Dalgliesh. I wonder whether he'll feel it his duty to mention the matter to Reckless."

But Celia was too tough to be intimidated by Bryce. She said irritably. "Don't be stupid Justin! I don't believe you. And, even if I did, it was probably because I was speaking of Maurice as a writer. And one does somehow feel that, as a writer, poor Maurice has been finished for quite a time."

"God yes!" said Latham. "Dead and done for. Finished. Written out. Maurice Seton only wrote one effective passage of prose in his life but that was straight from the heart all right. And from the brain. It produced exactly the effect he intended. Every word selected to wound and the whole— lethal."

"Do you mean his play?" asked Celia. "I thought you despised it. Maurice always said that it was your notice that killed it."

"Celia darling, if my notice could kill a play, half the little pieces now running in London would have folded after the first night." He jerked her forward with fresh impetus and for a minute Justin Bryce lagged behind them. Hurrying to catch them up he called breathlessly:

"Maurice must have been killed on Tuesday night. And his body was pushed out to sea late on Wednesday evening. So how did the murderer get it to Monksmere? You drove from London on Wednesday Oliver. It wasn't in the boot of your Jaguar, was it?"

"No dear," said Latham easily. "I'm very particular what I carry in the boot of my Jaguar."

Celia said complacently:

"Well, I'm in the clear. Sylvia can give me an alibi until late on Tuesday and that's obviously the crucial time. I admit that I was out alone on Wednesday night but Reckless will hardly suspect me of mutilating the body. And that reminds me. There's one person who doesn't even claim an alibi for Tuesday or Wednesday, Jane Dalgliesh. And what's more—it was her chopper!"

Latham said:

"Why in God's name should Miss Dalgliesh wish to kill Seton?"

"Why should any of us want to?" retorted Celia. "And I'm not saying she did. I'm merely pointing out that it was apparently her chopper."

Bryce said happily:

"I wanted to at one time. Murder Seton, I mean. After I found Arabella I could willingly have killed him. But I didn't. All the same, I can't feel sorry about it. I wonder if I ought to ask to view the body after the inquest. It might shock me out of this insensitivity which I can't feel is at all healthy."

But Latham was still meditating on the missing chopper. He said fiercely:

"Anyone could have taken it! Anyone! We all walk in and out of each other's houses at will. No one here locks up anything. There's never been the need. And we don't even know yet that it was the weapon."

"My dears," said Bryce. "Consider this and calm yourselves. Until we know the cause of death we can't even be sure that Maurice was murdered."

9

They left her at the door of Rosemary Cottage and she watched them disappear into the night. Justin's high voice and Latham's laugh came back to her long after their figures had merged with the darker shadows of hedgerow and tree. There were no lights in the cottage and the sitting room was empty. So Elizabeth was in bed. She must have driven home fast from Tanner's Cottage. Her aunt was uncertain whether to be glad or sorry. She had a sudden need of company but she couldn't face questions or arguments. There would be much to discuss, but not tonight. She was too tired. She switched on the table lamp and, kneeling on the hearthrug, poked ineffectually at the slates and ashes of the dead fire. Then she got unsteadily to her feet, grunting with the effort like an old woman, and let herself down into an armchair. Opposite her an identical chair loomed squat and solid, plump with cushions, empty and poignant. Here Maurice had sat on that October afternoon six years ago. It was the day of the Inquest; a day of cold and sudden squalls. There had been a good fire that evening. She had been expecting him and had taken care that both she and the room were ready. The firelight and the one discreet lamp had shed a nicely-calculated glow over the polished mahogany and cast soft shadows on the soft pinks and blues of cushions and carpet. The tray of drinks had been set ready to hand. Nothing had been left to chance. And she had waited for him as eagerly as a young girl before her first date. She had worn a dress of soft blue-grey wool. It had really made her look quite slim, quite young. It still hung in her wardrobe. She had never cared to wear it again. And he had sat opposite her, stiff and black in his formal mourning, an absurd little mannikin with his black tie and armband, his

64

face rigid with grief. But she hadn't understood then that
it was grief. How could she? It was impossible that he could
be grieving for that shallow, egotistical, monstrous nym-
phomaniac. Of course, there had been the shock of hearing
that Dorothy was dead, had killed herself, the horror of
identifying the drowned body, the ordeal of the inquest, of
facing the rows of white, accusing faces. He knew what they
were saying all right, that he had driven his wife to suicide. No
wonder he had looked shocked and ill. But grief? It had never
occurred to her that he might grieve. Somehow she had taken
it for granted that there must, in his heart, have been a spring
of relief. Relief that the long years of torment and self-control
were over at last, that he could begin to live again. And she
would be there to help him, just as she had helped with her
sympathy and advice when Dorothy was alive. He was a
writer, an artist. He needed affection and understanding.
From tonight he need never be alone ever again.

Had she loved him, she wondered. It was difficult to
remember. Perhaps not. Perhaps it had never been love as she
imagined love to be. But it had been as close as she would ever
get to that longed-for, elusive, oft-imagined cataclysm. She
had dealt with its counterfeit in nearly forty novels; but the
coin itself had never come within her grasp.

Sitting in front of the dead fire she recalled the second when
she had known the truth, and her cheeks burned at the
memory. Suddenly he had begun to cry, awkwardly as a child.
In that moment all artifice had been forgotten. Only pity
remained. She had knelt beside him, cradling his head in her
arms, murmuring her comfort and love. And then, it had
happened. His whole body stiffened and withdrew. He looked
at her, catching his breath, and she saw his face. It was all
there. Pity, embarrassment, a trace of fear—and hardest of all
to accept—physical repulsion. In one bitter moment of
complete clarity she had seen herself with his eyes. He had
been grieving for that slim, gay, beautiful creature; and an
ugly middle-aged woman had chosen that moment to throw
herself into his arms. He had recovered himself, of course.
Nothing had been said. Even the dreadful sobbing had been

cut off in mid-gasp like that of a child suddenly offered a sweet. She reflected bitterly that there was nothing like personal danger to take the edge off grief. Somehow, gracelessly, she had stumbled back to her own chair, her face burning. He had stayed for as long as politeness dictated and she had handed him his drinks, listened to his sentimental reminiscences about his wife—dear God, had the poor fool forgotten so soon?—and feigned interest in his plans for a long holiday abroad, "to try to forget". It was six months before he had thought it prudent to revisit Rosemary Cottage alone and even longer before he began tentatively to establish the understanding that she would be available whenever he wanted to escort a woman in public. Just before he left for his holiday he had written to tell her that she was named in his Will "in appreciation of your sympathy and understanding on the death of my dear wife". She had understood all right. It was the kind of crude, insensitive gesture which he would consider an adequate, appropriate apology. But her first reaction hadn't been anger or humiliation; she had merely wondered how much it would be. Since then she had wondered increasingly; and now the question had a fascinating immediacy. It might, of course, be a mere hundred or so. It might be thousands. It might even be a fortune. After all, Dorothy was reputed to have been a wealthy woman and Maurice hadn't anyone else to leave it to. He had never had much use for his half-brother and lately they had grown even further apart. Besides, didn't he owe it to her?

A slant of light from the hall fell across the carpet. Silently, Elizabeth Marley came into the room, her feet bare, her red dressing gown glowing in the half light. She stretched herself out stiffly in the chair opposite her aunt, her feet towards the dying fire, her face deep in the shadows. She said:

"I thought I heard you come in. Can I get you anything? Hot milk? Ovaltine?"

The tone was ungracious, embarrassed, but the offer was unexpected and Miss Calthrop was touched.

"No thank you dear. You go back to bed. You'll catch cold. I'll make the drink and bring yours up."

The girl did not move. Miss Calthrop made a fresh attack on the fire. This time a tongue of flame hissed round the coals and she felt the first welcome warmth on hands and face. She asked:

"You got Sylvia home all right? How did she seem?"

"Not too good. But then, she never does."

Her aunt said:

"I wondered afterwards whether we ought to have insisted that she stay here. She really looked very ill, not safe to be alone."

Elizabeth shrugged. "I did tell her that we had a spare bed until the new *au pair* girl comes and that she was welcome to it. She wouldn't consider it. When I pressed her she became overwrought, so I left it. After all, she's thirty, isn't she? She's not a child. I couldn't force her to stay."

"No, of course not." Celia Calthrop thought that her niece would hardly have welcomed Sylvia in the house. She had noticed that most women were less sympathetic to the girl than were men, and Elizabeth made no secret of her dislike. The voice from the armchair asked:

"What happened after we left?"

"Nothing very much. Jane Dalgliesh seems to think that he may have been killed with her chopper. Apparently she missed it about four weeks ago."

"Did Inspector Reckless tell you that he was killed that way?"

"No. But surely. . . ."

"Then we still don't know how he died. He could have been killed in a dozen different ways and his hands chopped off after death. I imagine that they were. It wouldn't be an easy thing to do if your victim were alive and conscious. Inspector Reckless must know if it happened that way. There wouldn't be very much bleeding for one thing. And I expect he knows the time of death to an hour or so even without the P.M. report."

Her aunt said:

"Surely he died on Tuesday night? Something must have happened to him on Tuesday. Maurice would never walk out

of his Club like that and spend the night away without a word to anyone. He died on Tuesday night when Sylvia and I were at the pictures."

She spoke with stubborn confidence. She wished it to be so, therefore, it must be so. Maurice had died on Tuesday night and her alibi was assured. She added:

"It's unfortunate for Justin and Oliver that they happened to be in town that evening. They've got alibis of a sort, of course. But it's a pity all the same."

The girl said quietly:

"I was in London on Tuesday night too." Before her aunt could speak she went on quickly:

"All right, I know what you're going to say. I was supposed to be on a bed of sickness in Cambridge. Well, they let me up earlier than I told you. I took the first fast train to Liverpool Street on Tuesday morning. I was meeting someone there for lunch. No one you know. Someone from Cambridge. He's gone down now. Anyway he didn't turn up. There was a message of course, very polite, very regretful. It's a pity, though, that we arranged to meet where we were known. I didn't much enjoy seeing the head waiter look sorry for me. Not that I was surprised really. It isn't important. But I wasn't going to have Oliver and Justin gossiping over my affairs. I don't see why I should tell Reckless, either. Let him find out for himself."

Celia thought:

"But you told me!" She felt a surge of happiness so acute that she was glad that they sat in the shadows. This was the first real confidence she had ever received from the girl. And happiness made her wise. Resisting the first impulse to comfort or question she said:

"I'm not sure, dear, that it was sensible of you to spend the whole day in town. You're not really strong yet. Still, it doesn't seem to have done you any harm. What did you do after lunch?"

"Oh, worked for the afternoon in the London Library. Then I went to a news theatre. It was getting latish then so I thought I'd better stay the night. After all, you weren't

expecting me at any particular time. I had a meal at the Coventry Street Lyons and then managed to get a room at the Walter Scott Hotel in Bloomsbury. Most of the evening I spent just walking in London. I suppose I collected my key and went to my room just before eleven."

Miss Calthrop broke in eagerly:

"Then the porter will be able to vouch for you. And perhaps someone will remember you at Lyons. But I think you were right to say nothing about it for the present. It's entirely your own concern. What we'll do is to wait until we know the time of death. We can reconsider the whole matter then."

It was difficult for her to keep the ring of happiness from her voice. This was what she had always wanted. They were talking together, planning together. She was being asked, however obliquely and unwillingly, for reassurance and advice. How odd that it should take Maurice's death to bring them together. She babbled on:

"I'm glad you're not upset about the luncheon date. Young men today have no manners. If he couldn't telephone you by the day before at the latest, he should have made it his business to turn up. But at least you know where you stand."

The girl got up from the chair and walked without speaking to the door. Her aunt called after her:

"I'll get the drinks and we'll have them together in your room. I won't be a moment. You go up and get into bed."

"I don't want anything, thank you."

"But you said you'd like a hot drink. You ought to have something. Let me make you some Ovaltine. Or just hot milk perhaps."

"I said I didn't want anything. And I'm going to bed. I want to be left in peace."

"But Eliza. . . ."

The door closed. She could hear nothing more, not even a soft footfall on the stairs. There was nothing but the hissing of the fire and, outside, the silence, the loneliness of the night.

10

Dalgliesh was woken next morning by the ring of the telephone. His aunt must have answered it quickly for the ringing stopped almost immediately and he dozed again into that happy trance between waking and sleeping which follows a good night. It must have been half an hour before the telephone rang again, and this time it seemed louder and more insistent. He opened his eyes wide and saw, framed by the window, a translucent oblong of blue light with only the faintest hairline separating the sea and the sky. It promised to be another wonderful autumn day. It was already another wonderful autumn day. He saw with surprise that his watch showed ten-fifteen. Putting on his dressng gown and slippers, he pattered downstairs in time to hear his aunt answering the telephone.

"I'll tell him, Inspector, as soon as he wakes. Is it urgent? No, except that this is supposed to be his holiday . . . I'm sure that he'll be glad to come as soon as he's finished breakfast. Goodbye."

Dalgliesh bent over and placed his cheek momentarily against hers. It felt, as always, as soft and tough as a chamois glove.

"Is that Reckless?"

"Yes. He says he is at Seton's house and would be glad if you would join him there this morning."

"He didn't say in what capacity I suppose? Am I supposed to work or merely to admire him working? Or am I, possibly, a suspect?"

"It is I who am the suspect, Adam. It was almost certainly my chopper."

"Oh, that's been taken notice of. Even so, you rate lower

than most of your neighbours, I imagine. And certainly lower than Digby Seton. We police are simple souls at heart. We like to see a motive before we actually make an arrest. And no motive so gladdens our heart as the prospect of gain. I take it that Digby is his half-brother's heir?"

"It's generally supposed so. Two eggs or one, Adam?"

"Two, please. But I'll see to them. You stay and talk. Didn't I hear two calls? Who telephoned earlier?"

His aunt explained that R. B. Sinclair had rung to invite them both to dinner on Sunday night. She had promised to ring back. Dalgliesh, paying loving attention to his frying eggs, was intrigued. But he said little beyond expressing his willingness to go. This was something new. His aunt, he guessed, was a fairly frequent visitor to Priory House but never when he was at Pentlands. It was after all well understood that R. B. Sinclair neither visited nor received visitors. His aunt was uniquely privileged. But it wasn't hard to guess the reason for this innovation. Sinclair wanted to talk about the murder with the one man who could be expected to give a professional opinion. It was reassuring, if a little disillusioning, to discover that the great man wasn't immune to common curiosity. Violent death held its macabre fascination even for this dedicated non-participant in the human charade. But, of course, Dalgliesh would go to dinner. The temptation was too great to resist. He had lived long enough to know that few experiences can be so disenchanting as meeting the famous. But, with R. B. Sinclair, any writer would be willing to take the risk.

Dalgliesh made an unhurried business of washing-up after his breakfast, put on a tweed jacket over his sweater, and hesitated at the cottage door where a jumbled collection of walking sticks, left by past guests as hostages against a happy return, tempted him to add a final touch to the part of an energetic holiday-maker. He selected a sturdy ash, balanced it in his hand, then replaced it. There was no point in over-doing the act. Calling "Goodbye" to his aunt he set off across the headland. The quickest way would have been by car, turning right at the road junction, driving about half a mile

on the Southwold Road, then taking the narrow but reasonably smooth track which led across the headland to the house. Perversely, Dalgliesh decided to walk. He was, after all, supposed to be on holiday and the Inspector's summons had made no mention of any urgency. He was sorry for Reckless. Nothing is more irritating and frustrating to a detective than any uncertainty about the extent of his responsibility. In fact, there was none. Reckless was in sole charge of the investigation and both of them knew it. Even if the Chief Constable decided to ask for the help of the Yard it was highly improbable that Dalgliesh would be given the case. He was too personally involved. But Reckless would hardly relish conducting his investigation under the eyes of a C.I.D. Superintendent, particularly one with Dalgliesh's reputation. Well, it was hard luck on Reckless; but harder luck, thought Dalgliesh, on himself. This was the end of his hope of a solitary, uncomplicated holiday, that blessed week of undemanding peace which almost without effort on his part was to soothe his nerves and solve his personal problems. From the first this plan was probably an unsubstantial fabrication built on tiredness and his need to escape. But it was disconcerting to see it fall so early into ruin. He was as little inclined to interfere in the case as Reckless was to seek his help. There would have been tactful telephone calls to and from the Yard, of course. It would be understood by all concerned that Dalgliesh's familiarity with Monksmere and his knowledge of the people concerned would be at the Inspector's service. That was no more than any citizen owed the police. But if Reckless thought that Dalgliesh craved any more positive participation he must be speedily disillusioned.

It was impossible not to rejoice in the beauty of the day and as he walked much of Dalgliesh's irritation fell away. The whole headland was bathed in the yellow warmth of the autumn sun. The breeze was fresh but without chill. The sandy track was firm under his feet, sometimes passing straight between the gorse and heather, sometimes twisting among the thick brambles and stunted hawthorn trees which formed a succession of little caverns where the light was lost and the

path dwindled to a thread of sand. For most of the walk Dalgliesh had a view of the sea except when he passed behind the grey walls of Priory House. It stood four square to the sea within a hundred yards of the cliff edge and was bounded on the south by a tall stone wall and on the north by a fringe of fir trees. At night there was something eerie and unwelcoming about the house which reinforced its natural privacy. Dalgliesh thought that Sinclair if he craved seclusion could hardly have found a more perfect site. He wondered how long it would be before Inspector Reckless violated that privacy with his questions. It would hardly take him long to learn that Sinclair had a private flight of steps leading to the beach from his land. Assuming that the body had been taken to the boat and not the boat rowed some considerable distance along the coast to the body, it must have been carried down to the beach by one of three paths. There was no other access. One way, and perhaps the most obvious, was Tanner's Lane which led past Sylvia Kedge's cottage. As the dinghy had been beached at the bottom of Tanner's Lane this would have been the most direct route. The second was the steep and sandy slope which led from Pentlands to the shore. It was difficult enough in daylight. At night it would be hazardous even to the experienced and unburdened. He could not see the murderer risking that route. Even if his aunt did not hear the distant car she would know that someone was passing the cottage. People who lived alone and in so remote a place were quick to sense the unfamiliar noises of the night. His aunt was the most detached, and incurious of women to whom the habits of birds had always appeared of greater interest than those of humans. But even she would hardly watch unconcerned while a dead body was carried past her door. There would, too, be the problem of carrying the corpse the half mile along the shore to where Sheldrake was beached. Unless, of course, the killer left it half buried in the sand while he collected the dinghy and rowed it to the corpse. But that would surely add unnecessarily to the risks and it would be impossible to remove all traces of sand from the body. More to the point, it would require oars and

73

rowlocks. He wondered whether Reck[...] had checked on these.

The third way of access to the be[ach] was by Sinclair's steps. These were only some fifty yar[ds...] [fr]om the bottom of Tanner's Lane and they led to a smal[l] [sec]luded cove where the cliffs, taller here than at any other [...]t, had been crumbled and eroded by the sea into a gent[le] [c]urve. This was the only part of the beach where the killer[—if] killer there were— could have worked on the corpse [...] [witho]ut fear of being watched either from the north or sout[h...] [o]nly in the unlikely event of one of the local inhabitants [...] [choos]ing to take a late walk along the shore would there be d[...] of discovery; and in this place, once dusk had fallen, t[he] [co]untryman did not choose to walk alone on the shore.

Priory House was behind Dalglies[h...] and he had come to the thin beech wood which fringe[d...] [Ta]nner's Lane. Here the earth was brittle with fallen leave[s...] [t]hrough the lattice of the bare boughs there was a haze [which] could have been sky or sea. The wood ended [sudden]ly and Dalgliesh clambered over a stile and dropped i[nto the] lane. Immediately before him was the squat, red-brick [cot]tage where Sylvia Kedge had lived alone since the death [of her] mother. It was an ugly building, as uncompromisingly [p]athetic as a doll's house with its four small windows, each he[avily cu]rtained. The gate and the front door had been widene[d...] [presu]mably to take the girl's wheel chair, but the change [...] [do]ne nothing to improve the proportions of the hous[e...] attempt had been made to prettify it. The diminutiv[e...] [as diffi]cult garden was a dark patch cut in two by a gravel path[...] [pa]int on doors and windows was a thick, institutional [...] Dalgliesh thought that there must have been a Tanner [at those] [...]e here for generations, each built a little higher up th[e...] [un]til it too crumbled or was swept away in the great stor[...] [No]w this square, red, twentieth-century box stood firm t[o...] chance against the sea. Obeying an impulse, Dalgliesh [...] [...]l open the garden gate and walked up the path. S[...] his ears caught a sound. Someone else was explorin[g...] the corner of the house came the figure of Elizabet[h...] Unembarrassed,

74

she gave him a cool glance and said: "Oh, it's you! I thought I heard someone snooping around. What do you want?"

"Nothing. I snoop by nature. Whereas you, presumably, were looking for Miss Kedge?"

"Sylvia's not here. I thought she might be in her little dark room at the back but she isn't. I've come with a message from my aunt. Ostensibly she wants to make sure that Sylvia's all right after the shock of last night. Really, she wants her to come and take dictation before Oliver Latham or Justin nab her. There's going to be great competition for La Kedge, and I've no doubt she'll make the most of it. They all like the idea of having a private secretary on call for two bob a thousand words, carbons supplied."

"Is that all Seton paid her? Why didn't she leave?"

"She was devoted to him, or pretended to be. She had her own reasons for staying, I suppose. After all, it wouldn't be easy for her to find a flat in town. It'll be interesting to know what she's been left in the Will. Anyway, she enjoyed posing as the loyal, overworked little help-meet who would be so happy to transfer to auntie if only it didn't mean letting poor Mr. Seton down. My aunt never saw through it, of course. But then, she's not particularly intelligent."

"Whereas you have us all neatly catalogued. But you're not suggesting that someone killed Maurice Seton to get his shorthand typist?"

She turned on him furiously, her heavy face blotched with anger.

"I don't care a damn who killed him or why! I only know that it wasn't Digby Seton. I met him off that train Wednesday night. And if you're wondering where he was on Tuesday night, I can tell you. He told me on the drive home. He was locked up in West Central Police Station from eleven o'clock onwards. They picked him up drunk and he came before the Magistrate on Wednesday morning. So, luckily for him, he was in police custody from eleven o'clock on Tuesday night until nearly midday on Wednesday. Break that alibi if you can Superintendent."

Dalgliesh pointed out mildly that the breaking of alibis was

75

Reckless's business, not his. The girl shrugged, dug her fists into her jacket pockets, and kicked shut the gate of Tanner's Cottage. She and Dalgliesh walked up the lane together in silence. Suddenly she said:

"I suppose the body was brought down this lane to the sea. It's the easiest way to where Sheldrake was beached. The killer would have to carry it for the last hundred yards, though. The lane's much too narrow for a car or even a motor cycle. He could have got it by car as far as Coles's meadow and parked the car on the grass verge. There were a couple of plain clothes men there when I came past, looking for tyre marks. They won't get much joy. Someone left the gate open last night and Coles's sheep were all over the lane this morning."

This, as Dalgliesh knew, was not unusual. Ben Coles, who farmed a couple of hundred unproductive acres on the east of the Dunwich Road did not keep his gates in the best of repair and his sheep, with the blind perversity of their kind, were as often in Tanner's Lane as in their own meadow. At tripper time the lane became a shambles when the bleating flock in full cry mingled with the herd of horn-happy motorists frantically trying to edge each other out of the only parking space in the lane. But that open gate might have been highly convenient for someone; Coles's sheep in their happy scamperings might have been following an old local tradition. It was well known that, in the smuggling days, the flocks were driven nightly along the sheep paths which crossed the Westleton marshes so that all traces of horses' hoofs were obliterated before the Excise Officers made their morning search.

They walked on together until they came to the stile which gave access to the northern half of Monksmere Head. Dalgliesh was pausing to say goodbye when the girl suddenly blurted:

"I suppose you think I'm an ungrateful bitch. She makes me an allowance, of course. £400 a year in addition to my grant. But I expect you know that. Most people here seem to."

There was no need to ask whom she meant. Dalgliesh could

ve replied that Celia Calthrop was not the woman to let her
nerosities go unremarked. But he was surprised by the
ount. Miss Calthrop made no secret of the fact that she
no private income—"Poor little me. I'm a working girl. I
every penny I get"—but it was not therefore assumed
she lacked money. Her sales were large and she worked
, incredibly hard by the standards of Latham or Bryce
were apt to assume that dear Celia had only to lean back
comfortable armchair with her tape recorder on and her
hensible fiction would gush forth in an effortless and
rewarding stream. It was easy to be unkind about her
But if one were buying affection, and the price of even
tant toleration was a Cambridge education and £400 a
much might be necessary. A novel every six months; a
stint in *Home and Hearth*; appearances whenever her
uld get them on those interminably boring television
short stories written under one name or another for
en's weeklies; the gracious appearances at Church
where the publicity was free even if the tea had to be
He felt a spasm of pity for Celia. The vanities and
ns which were such a source of amused contempt to
nd Bryce suddenly appeared no more than the
appings of a life both lonely and insecure. He won-
ther she had really cared for Maurice Seton. And
ed, too, whether she was mentioned in Seton's

Marley seemed in no hurry to leave him and it
t to turn away from that resolutely persistent
as used to being a confidante. That, after all, was
b. But he wasn't on duty now and he knew well
ho confided most were apt to regret it soonest.
ad no real wish to discuss Celia Calthrop with
hoped the girl didn't intend to walk all the way
se with him. Looking at her he could see where
f that £400 allowance went. Her fur lined jacket
r. The pleated skirt of thin tweed looked as if
lored for her. Her shoes were sturdy but they
nt. He remembered something he had once

77

heard Oliver Latham say; he couldn't remember when
why. "Elizabeth Marley has a passion for money. One fin
it rather engaging in this age when we're all so busy preten
ing to have minds above mere cash."

She was leaning back against the stile now, effectiv
blocking his way.

"She got me to Cambridge, of course. You can't do
without either money or influence if you're only modera
intelligent like me. It's all right for the alpha people. Ev
one's glad to get them. For the rest of us it's a matter
right school, the right crammers, and the right nam
your application form. Aunt could manage even that. Sl
a real talent for making use of people. She's never afr
being a vulgar nuisance which makes it easier of cour

"Why do you dislike her so much?" enquired Dalgl

"Oh, it's nothing personal. Although we haven't n
common, have we? It's her work. The novels are bad
Thank God we haven't the same name. People ar
tolerant at Cambridge. If, like the waterman's w
was a receiver of stolen property under guise of k
brothel no one would care a damn. And nor would I
column she writes. It's utterly humiliating! Worse
the books. You know the kind of muck." Her voic
sickly falsetto. "Don't give in to him, dear. Men are
one thing."

In Dalgliesh's view men, including himself,
were but he thought it prudent not to say so. Sudd
middle-aged, bored and irritated. He had neither
expected company and if his solitude had to be
could have named more agreeable companion
peevish and dissatisfied adolescent. He hardly h
of her complaint. She had dropped her voice a
were blown from him on the freshening breeze.
the final mutterings. "It's so completely amor
sense of the term. Virginity as a carefully pres
eligible males. In this day and age!"

"I haven't much sympathy with that point o
Dalgliesh said. "But then, as a man, your

78

doubt consider me prejudiced. But at least it's realistic. And you can hardly blame Miss Calthrop for dishing out the same advice week after week when she gets so many letters from the readers wishing they'd taken it in the first place."

The girl shrugged: "Naturally she has to adopt the orthodox line. The hag rag wouldn't employ her if she dared to be honest. Not that I think she knows how. And she needs that column. She hasn't any money except what she earns and the novels can't go on selling for ever." Dalgliesh caught the note of anxiety in her voice. He said brutally.

"I shouldn't worry. Her sales won't fall. She writes about sex. You may not like the packaging but the basic commodity will always be in demand. I should think your £400 is safe for the next three years."

For a moment he thought she was going to smack his face. Then surprisingly, she gave a shout of laughter and moved away from the stile.

"I deserved that! I've been taking myself too seriously. Sorry for boring you. You're on your way to Seton House, I suppose?" Dalgliesh said that he was and asked if he should give any message to Sylvia Kedge if she were there.

"Not to Sylvia. Why should you pimp for auntie? No, it's to Digby. Just to say that there will be meals for him at the cottage until he gets fixed up if he cares to come. It's only cold meat and salad today so he won't be missing much if he can't make it. But I don't suppose he'll want to depend on Sylvia. They hate each other. And don't get any wrong ideas, Superintendent. I may be willing to drive Digby home and feed with him for a day or two. But that's as far as it goes. I'm not interested in pansies."

"No," said Dalgliesh. "I wouldn't suppose that you were."

For some reason she blushed. She was turning away when, prompted by no more than mild curiosity, Dalgliesh said:

"One thing intrigues me. When Digby Seton telephoned to ask you to meet him at Saxmundham, how did he know you weren't at Cambridge?" She turned back and met his gaze without embarrassment or fear. She didn't even

appear to resent the question. Instead, to his surprise, she laughed.

"I wondered how long it would be before someone asked that. I might have known it would be you. The answer's simple. I met Digby in London, quite by chance, on Tuesday morning. At Piccadilly Underground to be precise. I stayed in London that night and on my own. So I probably haven't an alibi. . . . Are you going to tell Inspector Reckless? But of course you are."

"No," replied Dalgliesh. "You are."

11

Maurice Seton had been fortunate in his architect and his house had that characteristic of all good domestic building: it seemed indigenous to its site. The grey stone walls curved from the heather to buttress the highest point of Monksmere Head, with a view north over Sole Bay and south over the marshes and the bird reserve as far as Sizewell Gap. It was an unpretentious and agreeable building, single-storied and L-shaped, and built only fifty yards from the cliff edge. Presumably, these elegant walls, like those of Sinclair's sturdy bastion, would one day crumble into the North Sea, but there seemed no immediate danger of it. The cliffs here had a strength and height which gave some hope of permanence. The long arm of the L faced south-east and was composed almost entirely of double-glazed windows which opened on to a terrace of paved stones. Here Seton had taken a hand in the planning. Dalgliesh thought it unlikely that the architect had chosen to set up the two ornate urns which marked the ends of the terrace and in which a couple of bushes, their boughs contorted by the cold winds of the Suffolk coast, were failing to thrive, nor the pretentious sign swinging between two low posts on which the words, "Seton House" were carved in Gothic lettering.

It didn't need the car parked at the terrace edge to tell Dalgliesh that Reckless was there. He could see no one, but he knew that his approach was being watched. The tall windows seemed full of eyes. One of them was ajar. Dalgliesh drew it open and stepped into the living room.

It was like walking on to a stage set. Every corner of the long narrow room was warm with light as if bathed in the glare of arc lamps. It was a modern set. From centre back an

open staircase curved to the upper storey. Even the furniture contemporary, functional and expensive-looking added to the air of impermanence and unreality. Almost the whole of the window space was taken up with Seton's desk, an ingeniously designed fitment with a complex of drawers, cubboards and bookcases spreading each side of the central working surface. It had probably been made to the owner's specification, a functional status symbol in light polished oak. On the pale grey walls there were two popular Monet prints unimaginatively framed.

The four people who turned to watch unsmiling as Dalgliesh stepped over the window sill were as immobile and carefully disposed about the room as actors who have taken up their pose ready for the curtains to rise. Digby Seton was lying on a couch placed diagonally across the centre of the room. He was wearing a mauve dressing gown of artificial silk over red pyjamas and might have looked more the part of romantic lead had it not been for the cap of grey stockinette which fitted close to his head and came down level to his eyebrows. The modern method of bandaging is effective but scarcely becoming. Dalgliesh wondered whether Seton had a temperature. He would hardly have been discharged from hospital unfit and Reckless, who was neither inexperienced nor a fool, would have telephoned the doctor to make sure that the man was fit to be questioned. But his eyes were unnaturally bright and a red moon burnt high on each cheekbone so that he looked like a gaudy circus clown, a bizarre focus of interest against the grey couch. Inspector Reckless sat at the desk with Sergeant Courtney by his side. In this morning light Dalgliesh saw the boy clearly for the first time and was struck by his pleasant good looks. He had the type of honest, open face which looks out of advertisements extolling the advantages of a career in banking for the intelligent and ambitious young man. Well, Sergeant Courtney had chosen the police. In his present mood Dalgliesh thought it rather a pity.

The fourth player was hardly on stage. Through the open door which led to the drawing room Dalgliesh caught a

glimpse of Sylvia Kedge. She was sitting at the table in her wheelchair. There was a tray of silver in front of her and she was engaged in polishing a fork with as little enthusiasm as a bit player who knows that the attention of the audience is elsewhere. She lifted her eyes momentarily to Dalgliesh and he was shocked by the misery in her drawn face. She looked very ill. Then she bent again to her task.

Digby Seton heaved his legs from the couch, walked deliberately to the dining room door and prodded it gently shut with his stockinged foot. None of the policemen spoke.

Seton said:

"Sorry and all that. Don't want to be rude, but she gives me the willies. Damn it all, I've said I'll pay her the £300 Maurice left her! Thank God you've come, Superintendent! Are you taking over the case?"

It could hardly have been a worse beginning. Dalgliesh said:

"No. It's nothing to do with the Yard. Surely Inspector Reckless has explained to you by now that he's the officer in charge?"

He felt that Reckless deserved that snide innuendo.

Seton protested:

"But I thought they always called in the Yard to tricky cases of murder?"

"What makes you think this is a case of murder?" asked Reckless. He was slowly sorting out papers from the desk and did not turn to Seton as he spoke. His voice was quiet, unemphatic, almost uninterested.

"Well, isn't it? You tell me. You're the experts. But I don't see how Maurice could have cut off his own hands. One perhaps, but hardly two. If that's not murder, then what is it? And damn it all, you've got a Scotland Yard chap on the spot."

"On holiday, remember," said Dalgliesh. "I'm in exactly the same position as you."

"Like hell you are!" Seton twisted himself into a sitting position and groped under the couch for his shoes.

"Brother Maurice hasn't left you £200,000. God, it's crazy!

83

It's unbelievable! Some sod pays off an old score and I get a fortune! Where the hell did Maurice get that kind of money, anyway?"

"Apparently partly from his mother and partly from the estate of his late wife," replied Reckless. He had finished with the papers and was now going through a small drawer of index cards with the methodical intentness of a scholar looking for a reference.

Seton gave a snort of laughter.

"Is that what Pettigrew told you? Pettigrew! I ask you, Dalgliesh! Trust Maurice to have a solicitor called Pettigrew. What else could the poor devil be with a name like that? Pettigrew! Doomed from birth to be a respectable provincial solicitor. Can't you picture him? Dry, precise, sixtyish, resplendent watch chain and pin stripes. God, I hope he knows how to draw up a valid Will."

"I don't think you need worry on that score," said Dalgliesh. Actually, he knew Charles Pettigrew who was his aunt's solicitor. It was an old firm but the present owner, who had inherited from his grandfather, was a capable and lively thirty year-old, reconciled to the tedium of a country practice by the nearness of the sea and a passion for sailing. He said:

"I gather you've found a copy of the Will?"

"It's here." Reckless passed over the single sheet of stiff paper, and Dalgliesh scanned it. The Will was short and soon read. Maurice Seton, after instructing that his body be used for medical research and afterwards cremated, left £2,000 to Celia Calthrop, "in appreciation of her sympathy and understanding on the death of my dear wife", and £300 to Sylvia Kedge, "provided she has been ten years in my service at the time of my death". The remainder of the estate was left to Digby Kenneth Seton, on trust until he married, and then to revert to him absolutely. If he died before his half-brother or died unmarried the estate went absolutely to Celia Calthrop. Seton said:

"Poor old Kedge! She's lost her £300 by two months. No wonder she looks sick! Honestly, I'd no idea about the Will. At least, I knew that I would very likely be Maurice's heir.

He more or less said so once. Anyway, he hadn't anyone else to leave it to. We've never been particularly close but we did have the same father and Maurice had a great respect for the old man. But £200,000! Dorothy must have left him a packet. Funny that, when you consider that their marriage was pretty well on the rocks when she died."

"Mrs. Maurice Seton had no other relatives then?" asked Reckless.

"Not that I know of. Lucky for me, isn't it? When she killed herself there was some talk of a sister who ought to be contacted. Or was it a brother? Honestly, I can't remember. Anyway, no one turned up and no one but Maurice was mentioned in the Will. Her father was a property speculator and Dorothy was left pretty well off. And it all came to Maurice. But £200,000!"

"Perhaps your half-brother did well with his books," suggested Reckless. He had finished with the card index but was still seated at the desk, making entries in a note book and seemingly only half-interested in Seton's reactions. But Dalgliesh, himself a professional, knew that the interview was going very much according to plan.

"Oh, I shouldn't think so! Maurice always said that writing wouldn't keep him in socks. He was rather bitter about it. He said that this was the age of 'Soap-powder fiction'. If a writer hadn't a gimmick no one was interested. Bestsellers were created by the advertisers, good writing was a positive disadvantage and the public libraries killed sales. I daresay he was right. If he had £200,000 I don't know why he bothered. Except, of course, that he liked being a writer. It did something for his ego, I suppose. I never understood why he took it so seriously, but then, he never understood why I wanted my own Club. And I'll be able to have it now. A whole chain of them if things go my way. You're both invited to the opening night. Bring the whole of West Central with you if you like. No sneaking in on expenses to check on the drinking and see that the floor show isn't too naughty. No women sergeants tarted up to look like provincial tourists on the spree. The best tables. Everything on the house. D'you know, Dalgliesh, I

85

could have made a go of the Golden Pheasant if only I'd had the capital behind me. Well, I've got it now."

"Not unless you also get a wife," Dalgliesh reminded him unkindly. He had noted the names of the trustees in Seton's Will and couldn't see either of those cautious and conservative gentlemen parting with trust funds to finance a second Golden Pheasant. He asked why Maurice Seton had been so anxious for Digby to marry.

"Maurice was always hinting that I ought to settle down. He was a great one for the family name. He hadn't any children himself—none that I know of anyway—and I don't suppose he was keen to marry again after the Dorothy fiasco. Besides, he had a dicky heart. He was afraid, too, that I might set up house with a queer. He didn't want his money shared with a pansy boy friend. Poor old Maurice! I don't think he'd recognize a queen if he met one. He just had the idea that London, and West End Clubs in particular, are full of them."

"Extraordinary!" said Dalgliesh dryly. Seton seemed unaware of the irony. He said anxiously:

"Look, you do believe me about that phone call, don't you? The murderer phoned me as I arrived here Wednesday night and sent me off on a fool's errand to Lowestoft. The idea was to get me away from the house and make sure I hadn't an alibi for the time of death. At least, I suppose that was the idea. It doesn't make sense otherwise. It puts me in a spot all right. I wish to God that Liz had come in with me. I don't see how I can prove that Maurice wasn't in the house when I got here or that I didn't take a late night walk on the beach with him, conveniently armed with the kitchen knife. Have you found the weapon, by the way?"

The Inspector replied briefly that they hadn't. He said:

"It would help me, Mr. Seton, if you could remember more about this phone call."

"Well, I can't." Seton sounded suddenly peevish. He added sullenly: "You keep asking me about it and I keep telling you! I don't remember. Damn it, I've had a bloody great bang on the head since then! If you told me I'd imagined the whole

86

thing I wouldn't be surprised except that it must have happened or I wouldn't have taken out the car. I was dog tired and I wouldn't have set off to Lowestoft just for the fun of it. Someone phoned. I'm sure of that. But I can't remember what the voice sounded like. I'm not even sure if it was a man or a woman."

"And the message?"

"I've told you, Inspector! The voice said it was speaking from Lowestoft Police Station, that Maurice's body had come ashore in my dinghy with the hands chopped off—"

"Chopped or cut?"

"Oh, I don't know! Chopped I think. Anyway, I was to go to Lowestoft at once and identify the body. So I set off. I knew where Maurice keeps the car keys and luckily the Vauxhall had plenty of juice in her. Or unluckily. I damn near killed myself. Oh, I know you're going to say it was my fault. I admit I had a pull or two from my hip flask on the way. Well, do you wonder! And I was bloody tired before I started. I had a lousy night on Tuesday—the West Central's hardly a hotel. And then that long train journey."

"And yet you set off for Lowestoft straight away without bothering to check?" asked Reckless.

"I did check! When I got to the road it occurred to me to see if Sheldrake had really gone. So I drove down Tanner's Lane as far as I could and walked to the beach. The boat wasn't there. That was good enough for me. I suppose you think that I ought to have rung back the police station but it never occurred to me that the message might be a hoax until I was on my way and then the easiest thing was to check on the boat. I say. . . ."

"Yes?" enquired Reckless calmly.

"Whoever phoned must have known that I was here. And it couldn't have been Liz Marley because she'd only just left when the phone rang. Now, how could anyone else have known?"

"You could have been seen arriving," suggested Reckless. "And I suppose you put the lights on when you got in. They could be seen for miles."

"I put them on all right. The whole bloody lot. This place gives me the creeps in the dark. Still, it's odd."

It was odd, thought Dalgliesh. But the Inspector's explanation was probably correct. The whole of Monksmere Head could have seen those blazing lights. And when they went out, someone would know that Digby Seton was on his way. But why send him? Was there something still to be done at Seton House? Something to be searched for? Some evidence to be destroyed? Was the body hidden in Seton House? But how was that possible if Digby was telling the truth about the missing boat?

Suddenly Digby said:

"What am I supposed to do about handing the body over for medical research? Maurice never said anything to me about being keen on medical research. Still, if that's what he wanted. . . ."

He looked from Dalgliesh to Reckless enquiringly. The Inspector said:

"I shouldn't worry about that now, Sir. Your brother left the necessary instructions and official forms among his papers. But it will have to wait."

Seton said: "Yes. I suppose so. But I wouldn't like . . . I mean, if that's what he wanted. . . ."

He broke off uncertainly. Much of the excitement had left him and he was looking suddenly very tired. Dalgliesh and Reckless glanced at each other, sharing the thought that there would be little more to be learnt from Maurice's body once Walter Sydenham had finished with it, the eminent and thorough Dr. Sydenham whose textbook on forensic pathology made it plain that he favoured an initial incision from the throat to the groin. Seton's limbs might be useful for raw medical students to practise on, which was probably not what he had had in mind. But his cadaver had already made its contribution to medical science.

Reckless was preparing to leave. He explained to Seton that he would be required at the inquest in five days' time, an invitation which was received without enthusiasm, and began putting his papers together with the satisfied efficiency of an

insurance agent at the end of a good morning's work. Digby watched him with the puzzled and slightly apprehensive air of a small boy who has found the company of adults a strain but isn't sure that he actually wants them to leave. Strapping up his brief case, Reckless asked his last question with no appearance of really wanting to know the answer:

"Don't you find it rather strange, Mr. Seton, that your half-brother should have made you his heir? It isn't as if you were particularly friendly."

"But I told you!" Seton wailed his protest. "There wasn't anyone else. Besides, we were friendly enough. I mean, I made it my business to keep in with him. He wasn't difficult to get on with if you flattered him about his bloody awful books and took a bit of trouble with him. I like to get on with people if I can. I don't enjoy quarrelling and unpleasantness. I don't think I could have stood his company for long but then I wasn't here very often. I told you I haven't seen him since August Bank Holiday. Besides, he was lonely. I was the only family he had left and he liked to think that there was someone who belonged."

Reckless said:

"So you kept in with him because of his money. And he kept in with you because he was afraid of being completely alone?"

"Well, that's how things are." Seton was unabashed. "That's life. We all want something from each other. Is there anyone who loves you, Inspector, for yourself alone?"

Reckless got up and went out through the open window. Dalgliesh followed him and they stood together on the terrace in silence. The wind was freshening but the sun still shone, warm and golden. On the green-blue sea a couple of white sails moved fitfully like twists of paper blown in the wind. Reckless sat down on the steps which led from the terrace to the narrow strip of turf and the cliff edge. Dalgliesh, feeling unreasonably that he could hardly remain standing since it put Reckless at a disadvantage, dropped down beside him. The stones were unexpectedly cold to his hands and thighs, a reminder that the warmth of the autumn sun had little power. The Inspector said:

"There's no way down to the beach here. You'd have thought Seton would want his own way down. It's a fair walk to Tanner's Lane."

"The cliffs are pretty high here and there's little solid rock. It could be tricky to build a stairway," suggested Dalgliesh.

"Maybe. He must have been a strange sort of chap. Fussy. Methodical. That card index, for instance. He picked up ideas for his stories from newspapers, magazines, and from people. Or just thought of them for himself. But they're all neatly catalogued there, waiting to come in useful."

"And Miss Calthrop's contribution?"

"Not there. That doesn't mean very much though. Sylvia Kedge told me that the house was usually left unlocked when Seton was living here. They all seem to leave their houses unlocked. Anyone could have got in and taken the card. Anyone could have read it for that matter. They just seem to wander in and out of each other's places at will. It's the loneliness I suppose. That's assuming that Seton wrote out a card."

"Or that Miss Calthrop ever gave him the idea," said Dalgliesh. Reckless looked at him.

"That struck you too, did it? What did you think of Digby Seton?"

"The same as I've always thought. It requires an effort of will to understand a man whose passionate ambition is to run his own Club. But then, he probably finds it equally difficult to understand why we should want to be policemen. I don't think our Digby has either the nerve or the brains to plan this particular killing. Basically he's unintelligent."

"He was in the nick most of Tuesday night. I gave West Central a ring and it's true all right. What's more he was drunk. There was nothing feigned about it."

"Very convenient for him."

"It's always convenient to have an alibi, Mr. Dalgliesh. But there are some alibis I don't intend to waste time trying to break. And that's the kind he's got. What's more, unless he was acting just now, he doesn't know that the weapon wasn't

a knife. And he thinks that Seton died on Wednesday night. Maurice couldn't have been in this house alive when Digby and Miss Marley arrived on Wednesday. That's not to say that his body wasn't here. But I can't see Digby acting the butcher and I can't see why he should. Even if he found the body here and panicked he's the sort to hit the bottle then belt off back to town, not to plan an elaborate charade. And he was on the Lowestoft not the London Road when he crashed. Besides, I don't see how he could have known about Miss Calthrop's pleasant little opening for a detective story."

"Unless Eliza Marley told him on the way here."

"Why should she tell Digby Seton? It's not a likely topic for conversation on the drive home. But all right. We'll assume that she did know and that she told Digby or that, somehow or other, he knew. He arrives here and finds his brother's body. So he immediately decides to provide a real life mystery by chopping off Maurice's hands and pushing the body out to sea. Why? And what did he use for weapon? I saw the body, remember, and I'd swear those hands were chopped off, not cut, nor sawed, chopped. So much for the kitchen knife! Seton's chopper is still in the pantry. And your aunt's —if that was the weapon—was stolen three months ago."

"So Digby Seton is out. What about the others?"

"We've only had time for a preliminary check. I'm taking their statements this afternoon. But it looks as if they've all got alibis of a sort for the time of death. All except Miss Dalgliesh. Living alone as she does, that's not surprising."

The flat monotonous voice did not change. The sombre eyes still looked out to sea. But Dalgliesh was not deceived. So this was the reason for the summons to Seton House, for the Inspector's unexpected burst of confidence. He knew how it must look to Reckless. Here was an elderly unmarried woman living a lonely and isolated life. She had no alibi for the time of death nor for Wednesday night when the body was launched out to sea. She had an almost private access to the beach. She knew where Sheldrake lay. She was nearly six foot tall, a strong, agile country woman, addicted to strenuous walking and accustomed to the night.

Admittedly she had no apparent motive. But what did that matter? Despite what he had said to his aunt that morning Dalgliesh knew perfectly well that motive was not the first concern. The detective who concentrated logically on the "where", "when", and "how", would inevitably have the "why", revealed to him in all its pitiful inadequacy. Dalgliesh's old chief used to say that the four L's—love, lust, loathing and lucre—comprised all motives for murder. Superficially that was true enough. But motive was as varied and complex as human personality. He had no doubt that the Inspector's horribly experienced mind was already busy recalling past cases where the weeds of suspicion, loneliness or irrational dislike had flowered into unexpected violence and death.

Suddenly Dalgliesh was seized with an anger so intense that for a few seconds it paralysed speech and even thought. It swept through his body like a wave of physical nausea leaving him white and shaken with self disgust. Choked with this anger he was luckily saved from the worst follies of speech, from sarcasm, indignation or the futile protest that his aunt would, of course, make no statement except in the presence of her solicitor. She needed no solicitor. She had him. But, God, what a holiday this was proving to be!

There was a creak of wheels and Sylvia Kedge spun her wheelchair through the french windows and manœuvred it up beside them. She didn't speak but gazed intently down the track towards the road. Their eyes followed hers. A post office van, brightly compact as a toy, was careering over the headland towards the house.

"It's the post," she said.

Dalgliesh saw that her hands were clamped to the chair sides, the knuckles white. As the van drew up before the terrace he watched her body half rise and stiffen as if seized with a sudden rigor. In the silence which followed the stopping of the engine, he could hear her heavy breathing.

The postman slammed the van door and came towards them, calling a cheerful greeting. There was no response from the girl and he glanced puzzled from her rigid face to the still

figures of the two men. Then he handed Reckless the post. It was a single, foolscap envelope, buff coloured and with a typewritten address.

"It's the same kind as before, Sir," he said. "Like the one I gave her yesterday." He nodded towards Miss Kedge, then, still getting no response, backed awkwardly towards his van muttering "goodmorning."

Reckless spoke to Dalgliesh:

"Addressed to Maurice Seton, Esq. Posted either late on Wednesday or early on Thursday from Ipswich. Postmarked midday yesterday."

He held the envelope delicately by one corner as if anxious not to impose more finger prints. With his right thumb he edged it open. Inside there was a single sheet of foolscap paper covered with double spaced typescript. Reckless began to read aloud:

"The corpse without hands lay in the bottom of a small sailing dinghy drifting just within sight of the Suffolk coast. It was the body of a middle-aged man, a dapper little cadaver, its shroud a dark pin-striped suit which fitted the narrow body as elegantly in death as it had been tailored to in life. . ."

Suddenly Sylvia Kedge held out her hand.

"Let me see."

Reckless hesitated, then held the sheet before her eyes.

"He wrote it," she said hoarsely. "He wrote it. And that's his typewriting."

"Maybe," said Reckless. "But he couldn't have posted it. Even if this went into the box late on Wednesday night he couldn't have put it there. He was dead by then."

She cried out:

"He typed it! I know his work, I tell you. He typed it! And he hadn't any hands!"

She burst into peal upon peal of hysterical laughter. It rang over the headland like a wild echo, so startling a flock of gulls that shrieking their alarm they whirled from the cliff edge in a single white cloud.

Reckless looked at the rigid body, the screaming mouth,

with speculative unconcern, making no move to comfort or control her. Suddenly Digby Seton appeared in the french windows, his face white under the ridiculous bandage.

"What the hell. . . ?"

Reckless looked at him, expressionless, and said in his flat voice:

"We've just heard from your brother, Mr. Seton. Now isn't that nice?"

12

It took some little time to pacify Miss Kedge. Dalgliesh had no doubt that her hysteria was genuine; this was no play-acting. He was only surprised that she should be so upset. Of all the little community at Monksmere Sylvia Kedge alone seemed to be genuinely shocked and distressed at Seton's death. And, certainly, the shock was real enough. She had looked and behaved like a woman maintaining a precarious self-control which had snapped at last. But she made visible efforts to pull herself together and was at last well enough to be escorted back to Tanner's Cottage by Courtney who had succumbed entirely to the pathos of her drawn face and plead-ing eyes and who pushed her wheelchair down the lane like a new mother displaying her fragile newborn to the glares of a potentially hostile world. Dalgliesh was relieved to see her go. He had discovered that he did not like her and was the more ashamed of the emotion because he knew that its roots were unreasonable and ignoble. He found her physically repellant. Most of her neighbours used Sylvia Kedge to gratify, at small expense, an easy impulse to pity while ensuring that they got their money's worth. Like so many of the disabled she was at once patronized and exploited. Dalgliesh wondered what she thought of them all. He wished he could feel more sorry for her but it was difficult not to watch, with a kind of contempt, the way in which she made use of her disability. But then what other weapons had she? Despising the young constable for his easy capitulation and himself for lack of feeling, Dalgliesh set off back to Pentlands for lunch. He walked back by the road. It took longer and was less interesting but he had always disliked retracing his footsteps. The route took him

past Bryce's cottage. As he reached it an upstairs window was opened and the owner shot his long neck out and called:

"Come in Adam, dear boy. I've been watching out for you. I know you've been spying for that dreary little friend of yours but I don't hold it against you. Just leave your rhino whip outside and help yourself to whatever drink you prefer. I'll be down in a jiffy." Dalgliesh hesitated then pushed open the cottage door. The little sitting room was as untidy as always, a repository of bric-à-brac which could not appropriately be housed in his London flat. Deciding to wait for his drink, Dalgliesh called up the stairs:

"He's not my dreary little friend. He's a highly competent police officer."

"Oh no doubt!" Bryce's voice was muffled. Apparently he was pulling clothes over his head. "Competent enough to nab me if I'm not cunning. I was stopped for speeding on the A 13 about six weeks ago and the officer concerned—a beefy brute with one of those metamorphic glares, was most uncivil. I wrote to the Chief Constable about it. It was a fatal thing to do, of course. I see that now. They've got it in for me all right. My name's on a little list somewhere, you may be sure."

He had padded into the room by now and Dalgliesh saw with surprise that he did indeed look concerned. Murmuring reassurance he accepted sherry—Bryce's drinks were always excellent—and settled himself in the latest acquisition, a charming Victorian high-backed chair.

"Well, Adam. Give, as they say. What has Reckless discovered? Such an inappropriate name!"

"I'm not altogether in his confidence. But another instalment of manuscript has arrived. It's rather better written this time. A description of a handless body in a boat and typed apparently by Seton himself."

Dalgliesh saw no reason why Bryce should be denied this bit of information. Sylvia Kedge was hardly likely to keep it to herself.

"Post when?"

"Before lunch yesterday. From Ipswich."

Bryce wailed his dismay.

"Oh no! Not Ipswich! One was in Ipswich on Thursday. One often is. Shopping you know. One hasn't an alibi."

"You're probably not the only one," Dalgliesh pointed out consolingly. "Miss Calthrop was out in her car. So was Latham. So was I, come to that. Even that woman from Priory House was out in the buggy. I saw her as I drove over the headland."

"That would be Alice Kerrison, Sinclair's housekeeper. I don't suppose she went any further than Southwold. Probably fetching the groceries."

"On Thursday afternoon. Isn't it early closing?"

"Oh Adam dear, what does it matter? I expect she was just out for a drive. She'd hardly drive the buggy as far as Ipswich just to post an incriminating document. She hated Seton, though. She was housekeeper at Seton House before his wife died. Sinclair took her on after Dorothy killed herself and she's been there ever since. It was a most extraordinary thing! Alice stayed with Seton until after the inquest, then, without a word to him, she packed her bags and walked up to Priory House to ask if Sinclair had a job for her. Apparently Sinclair had reached the point when the urge for self sufficiency didn't extend to the washing-up and he took her on. As far as I know neither has regretted it."

"Tell me about Dorothy Seton," invited Dalgliesh.

"Oh, she was lovely, Adam! I've got a photograph of her somewhere which I must show you. She was madly neurotic, of course, but really beautiful. Manic depressive is the correct jargon, I believe. Exhaustingly gay one minute and so down the next that one felt positively contaminated with gloom. It was very bad for me, of course. I have enough trouble living with my own neurosis without coping with other people's. She led Seton a terrible life, I believe. One could almost pity him if it weren't for poor Arabella."

"How did she die?" enquired Dalgiesh.

"It was the most appalling thing! Seton strung her up from that meat hook in the beam in my kitchen. I shall never forget the sight of that darling furry body hanging there

elongated like a dead rabbit. She was still warm when we cut her down. Look, I'll show you."

Dalgliesh had been half dragged into the kitchen before he grasped that Bryce was talking about his cat. He successfully fought down the first impulse to nervous laughter and followed Bryce. The man was shaking with anger, grasping Dalgliesh's forearm in a surprisingly powerful grip and gesticulating at the hook in impotent fury as if it shared Seton's guilt. There seemed no immediate chance of getting any information about Dorothy Seton's death now that Arabella's end was so vividly recalled. Dalgliesh sympathized with Bryce. His own love of cats was as great if less vocal. If Seton had indeed wantonly destroyed a beautiful animal out of malice and revenge it was difficult to regret him. More to the point, such a man must have made his share of enemies.

Dalgliesh enquired who had found Arabella.

"Sylvia Kedge. She had come up to take some dictation for me and I was delayed arriving from London. I got here about five minutes later. She had phoned Celia to come and cut Arabella down. She couldn't reach the body herself. Naturally both of them were terribly upset. Sylvia was physically sick. We had to push the wheelchair to the kitchen sink and she threw up all over my washing up. I won't dwell on my own sufferings. But I thought you knew all the details. I asked Miss Dalgliesh to write. I hoped you might have come down to prove Seton did it. The local police were quite hopeless. Now, if it had been a human being, think of the fuss and nonsense! Just like Seton. It's so ridiculous. I'm not one of those sentimentalists who think that human beings are more important than any other form of life. There are too many of us anyway and most of us neither know how to be happy ourselves nor make any one else happy. And we're ugly. Ugly! You knew Arabella, Adam. Wasn't she the most beautiful creature? Didn't you feel it was a privilege to watch her? She was life-enhancing."

Dalgliesh, wincing at Bryce's choice of words, said the appropriate complimentary things about Arabella who had indeed been a beautiful cat with every appearance of knowing

it. His aunt had told him of the incident in one of her fortnightly letters but not surprisingly had made no mention of Bryce's request that he should come down and take over the investigation. Dalgliesh forebore to point out that no actual evidence had been produced against Seton. There had been a great deal of anger, ill-feeling and suspicion but remarkably little rational thought applied to the problem. But he had no stomach for solving it now. He induced Bryce to return to the sitting room and asked again how Dorothy Seton had died.

"Dorothy? She had gone to Le Touquet for an autumn holiday with Alice Kerrison. Things were pretty bad between her and Seton by then. She had become terribly dependent on Alice and I suppose Seton thought it would be a good idea if there were someone to keep an eye on her. When they had been away a week Seton realized that he couldn't face living with her again and wrote to say he wanted a separation. No one knows what exactly was in the letter but Alice Kerrison was with Dorothy when she opened it and said at the inquest that it upset Mrs. Seton terribly and that she said they must go home at once. Seton had written from the Cadaver Club and the house here was empty when they got back. Alice said that Dorothy seemed all right, perfectly calm and really much more cheerful than usual. She began preparing supper for the two of them and Dorothy wrote at her desk for a short time. Then she said she would go for a walk along the beach to see the moon on the sea. She walked to the bottom of Tanner's Lane, stripped herself naked, put her clothes in a neat pile with a stone on top and walked out to sea. They recovered the body a week later. It was suicide all right. She left a little note under the stone to say that she realized now that she was no use to herself or to anyone else and had decided to kill herself. It was a very direct note, perfectly clear, perfectly lucid. I remember at the time thinking that most suicides talk about ending it all. Dorothy just wrote that she had decided to kill herself."

"What happened to the letter that Seton wrote her?"

"It was never found. It wasn't with Dorothy's belongings and Alice didn't see her destroy it. But Seton was quite open

about it. He was sorry but he had acted for the best. It had become impossible to go on. I didn't realize exactly what living with Dorothy had done to him until I saw his play two years later. It was about marriage to a neurotic but in the play it's the husband who kills himself. Well, naturally. Seton wanted to cast himself in the major role. Not literally, of course. Still, he might just as well have played the part. He couldn't have been much worse than poor Barry. Not that one can blame the actors. Such a very bad play, Adam! And yet written with a kind of terrible honesty and pain."

"Were you there?" enquired Dalgliesh.

"Bang in the middle of the third row of the stalls my dear, and curling with embarrassment. Seton was in a box. He'd got Celia with him and one must say she did him proud. Hardly a stitch above the waist and tinkling away with imitation jewellery like a Christmas tree. Do you think Seton wanted people to think she was his mistress? I've a feeling our Maurice liked to be taken for a naughty boy. My dear, they looked like a couple of minor emigré royalties. Seton even wore a decoration. A Home Guard medal or something of the kind. I was with Paul Markham, such a sensitive boy. He was in tears by the end of the first act. So, admittedly, were a good third of the audience but in their case I suspect it was tears of laughter. We left in the first interval and spent the rest of the evening drinking at Moloneys. I can bear quite an amount of suffering provided it's not my own but I do draw the line at public executions. Celia, gallant girl, stuck it out to the last. They even had a party at the Ivy afterwards. When I think of that evening, oh Arabella, how thou art revenged!"

"Latham's notice was Latham at his most vicious wasn't it? Did you get the impression that he had a personal interest in killing the play?"

"Oh, I shouldn't think so." The large eyes bent on Dalgliesh were as innocent as a child's but Adam had a considerable respect for the intelligence behind them.

"Oliver can't tolerate bad writing nor bad acting and when they come together it tends to make him savage. Now if Oliver had been found dead with his hands hacked off one

could have understood it. Half those illiterate little secondary-mods who swan around London calling themselves actresses could have done it happily given the wit."

"But Latham knew Dorothy Seton didn't he?"

"Oh Adam! How you do go on about a thing! Not very subtle, my dear. Yes, he knew her. We all did. She was a great dropper-in. Sometimes drunk and sometimes sober and equally tedious either way."

"Were she and Latham lovers?" enquired Dalgliesh bluntly. As he expected Bryce was neither disconcerted nor surprised by the question. Like all inveterate gossips he was fundamentally interested in people. This was one of the first questions he would ask himself about any man or woman in his circle who seemed to find each other's company agreeable.

"Celia always said so, but then she would. I mean the dear girl can't conceive of any other relationship between a heterosexual man and a pretty woman. And where Latham's concerned she's probably right. One could hardly blame Dorothy, stuck in that glass-house with Seton, so dull. She was entitled to find consolation anywhere so long as it wasn't with me."

"But you don't think Latham was particularly fond of her?"

"I don't know. I shouldn't have thought so. Poor Oliver suffers from self-disgust. He pursues a woman, then, when she falls in love with him, he despises her for lack of discrimination. The poor dears simply can't win. It must be so exhausting to dislike oneself so much. Now I'm lucky. I find myself fascinating."

The fascination was beginning to pall on Dalgliesh. He glanced at his watch, said firmly that it was 12.45 and his lunch would be ready and made to go.

"Oh, but you must see that snap of Dorothy. I've got it somewhere. It will give you some idea how lovely she was."

He opened the sliding lid of his writing desk and rummaged among the piles of paper. Dalgliesh thought that it looked a hopeless task. But there must have been some order in

the chaos for, in less than a minute, Bryce had found what he wanted. He brought the photograph over to Dalgliesh.

"Sylvia Kedge took it when we were picnicking on the beach one July. She does quite a bit of amateur photography."

There was certainly nothing professional about the photograph. It showed the picnic party grouped around Sheldrake. They were all there, Maurice and Digby Seton; Celia Calthrop with a sulky looking child recognizable as Liz Marley; Oliver Latham and Bryce himself. Dorothy Seton, wearing a bathing costume, was leaning against the hull of the dinghy and laughing at the camera. The snap was clear enough but it told Dalgliesh nothing except that she had an agreeable figure and knew how best to show it off. The face was that of a pretty woman but no more. Bryce looked at the snap over his shoulder. As if struck by this fresh evidence of the perfidy of time and memory he said sadly. "Funny . . . It doesn't really give one any idea of her. . . I thought it was better than this. . ."

Bryce came to the cottage gate with him. As Dalgliesh was leaving an estate car came lurching up the lane and stopped with a bump at the gate. From it bounded a sturdy, black-haired women with legs like jambs above her white ankle socks and schoolgirl sandals, who was greeted by Bryce with squeaks of pleasure.

"Mrs. Bain-Porter! You haven't brought them! You have! How perfectly sweet of you."

Mrs. Bain-Porter had the deep, rich, upper-class female voice which is trained to intimidate the helots of empire or to carry across any hockey field in the teeth of a high gale. Her words boomed clearly in Dalgliesh's ears.

"When I got your letter yesterday I thought I'd take a chance. I've brought the three best from the litter. It's so much nicer to choose them in your own home I think. Nicer for them too."

The back of the car was opened now and Mrs. Bain-Porter, helped by Bryce, was carefully lifting out three cat baskets from which there rose at once an agitated

squealing, treble descant to Mrs. Bain-Porter's bass and Bryce's joyful chirpings. The concert party disappeared through the cottage door. Dalgliesh trudged home to his lunch in contemplative mood. It was one of those little things which can mean everything or nothing. But if Mrs. Bain-Porter got a letter from Julian Bryce on Thursday it was posted on Wednesday at the latest. Which meant that on Wednesday Bryce had either decided to take a chance on Seton's cat-killing propensities, or had known that there was no longer anything to fear.

13

On Friday afternoon the suspects walked, drove or were driven to the small inn just outside Dunwich which Reckless had taken as his headquarters and there made their statements. They had always thought of the Green Man as their local pub—indeed they took it for granted that George Prike ran the place principally for their benefit—and the Inspector's choice was criticised as showing crass insensitivity and a general disregard for the comfort of others. Celia Calthrop was particularly bitter although she used the Green Man less than most and was scathing in her denunciation of George's folly in allowing himself to be inveigled into such an invidious position. She was not at all sure she would be happy to continue to buy her sherry from George if she were going to be reminded of Inspector Reckless every time she had a drink and a visit to the Saloon Bar would become intolerably traumatic. Latham and Bryce shared her view of the Inspector. Their first impression of him hadn't been favourable and thinking it over later they decided that they disliked him. Perhaps, as Bryce suggested, a too-close acquaintance with Seton's Inspector Briggs had spoilt them for the real thing. Briggs, who was occasionally called Briggsy by the Honourable Martin in an excess of spurious camaraderie, had a humility which they hadn't detected in Inspector Reckless. Despite his eminence at the Yard Briggsy was always happy to play second fiddle to Carruthers, and so far from resenting the Honourable Martin's interference with his cases, made a practice of calling him in when his special expertise was required. Since Carruthers was an expert on wine, women, heraldry, the landed gentry, esoteric poisons and the finer points of the minor Elizabethan poets, his opinion was

frequently invaluable. As Bryce pointed out, Inspector Briggs did not turn people out of their favourite pub nor gaze at them fixedly from dark, morose eyes as if hearing only half they were saying and disbelieving that. Nor did he give the impression of regarding writers as no different from lesser men except in their capacity to invent more ingenious alibis. Inspector Briggs' suspects, if required to make statements—which was seldom—made them in the comfort of their own homes attended by obsequious policemen and with Carruthers present to ensure, in the nicest possible way, that Inspector Briggs kept his place.

They were careful not to arrive at the inn together; the artless confidences of Thursday night had been followed by a certain wariness. By Friday afternoon there had been time to think and Seton's death was seen less as a bizarre excursion of fiction into life than as a highly embarrassing fact. Certain unpalatable truths were recognized. Seton, admittedly, had last been seen alive in London, but his mutilated body had been floated out to sea from Monksmere Beach. It hardly needed any complicated calculations with charts, wind force or tide drift and race, to convince anyone of that. He might well have run into trouble in London in his naive search for copy, but the forged manuscript, the severed hands, the telephone call to Seton House, had a more local flavour. Celia Calthrop was the most voracious supporter of the London-gang-of-crooks theory, but even she could advance no convincing explanation of how the criminals knew where Sheldrake was beached or why they had chosen to bring the corpse back to Suffolk. "To throw suspicion on us, of course", was generally thought to beg more questions than it answered.

After the statements were made there was a certain amount of telephoning. Cautiously, as if half-believing that the lines were being tapped, the little community exchanged those scraps of information, rumour or guesswork which pieced together probably told as much as there was to know. They were reluctant at present to meet each other, afraid of what they might be told, or worse, inadvertently tell. But they were avid for information.

Telephone calls to Pentlands were invariably answered by Jane Dalgliesh, courteous, uncooperative and uncommunicative. No one liked to betray himself by asking to speak to Adam except Celia Calthrop and she met with such little success that she found it more convenient to believe that he had nothing to tell. But they spoke to each other, gradually abandoning caution in their need to confide and their hunger for news. The snippets of information, most of which changed subtly in the telling and some of which were founded on hope rather than fact, built up an incomplete and amphigoric picture. No one had changed his or her story and the various alibis for Tuesday night which had been put forward with such eager confidence had stood up to such investigation as there had been time for. It was understood that Latham's house guest had made no trouble in supporting his story, but as Reckless was completely uncommunicative and Latham was maintaining a gentlemanly reticence, the general curiosity about her name seemed likely to remain unsatisfied. The news that Eliza Marley had admitted to spending Tuesday night in London created a certain amount of pleasurable speculation, stimulated by Celia's frequent and unconvincing explanations of her niece's need to visit the London Library. As Bryce said to Latham, one could understand it if the poor girl had been at Redbrick but there had been quite a number of books in Cambridge when he was up. Both Bryce's and Latham's cars had been examined by the police but the owners had made so little protest over the proceedings that it was commonly agreed that they had nothing to fear. It was reported that Dr. Forbes-Denby had been gratifyingly offensive to Inspector Reckless on the telephone while Bryce was at the Green Man and had insisted on regarding Bryce's telephone call as a matter of sacred confidence between himself and his patient. Eventually, however, on Bryce's almost hysterical insistence he had agreed that it had been made. Celia's story that she had given Seton the idea for a floating corpse was supported by an old Walberswick fisherman who called at the Green Man to say that he remembered Mr. Seton enquiring some months previously where a body

in a dinghy would come ashore if it were pushed out from Monksmere Beach. As no one had doubted Celia's statement this wasn't regarded as more than mildly interesting. In face of their united wish to find support for the London-gang-of-crooks theory it was depressing that no one except Bryce had seen any strangers at Monksmere on the Wednesday night. He had been outside bringing in wood from his shed shortly after seven when a motor cyclist had come roaring down the lane from the road and had reversed just outside his cottage. Justin abominated motor cycles and the noise had been quite unendurable. He had shouted his protest and the lad had retaliated by roaring up and down in front of the cottage for several minutes, making what Bryce described as obscene gestures. Eventually with a parting blast of his horn he had roared away. It wasn't known what Reckless made of this although he did ask Bryce for a full description of the cyclist, and would probably have noted it down if Bryce had been able to provide it. But the man had worn a black leather suit with helmet and goggles and Bryce could say no more than that he was obviously young and his manners were abominable. But Celia was sure he was a member of the gang. What else would he be doing at Monksmere?

By midday on Saturday the rumours had grown and multiplied. Digby had been left one hundred thousand, two hundred thousand, half a million; the post-mortem was held up because Dr. Sydenham couldn't discover the cause of death; the cause of death was drowning, strangulation, poison, suffocation, haemorrhage; Forbes-Denby had told Reckless that Seton was good for another twenty years; Seton's heart was liable to give out at any moment; Adam Dalgliesh and the Inspector were hardly on speaking terms; Reckless would have arrested Jane Dalgliesh if only he could have discovered a motive; Sylvia Kedge was being very difficult and wouldn't accept the legacy of £300 which Digby had offered to pay her; Reckless had called at Priory House late on Friday night and he and his men had been seen with torches on the cliff path; the inquest was to be held on Wednesday at two-thirty. Only on the last was there unanimity. The inquest was certainly

arranged for the following Wednesday. Digby Seton and Sylvia Kedge had been summoned to attend. Those who had a choice in the matter were uncertain whether their presence would arouse curiosity, help allay suspicion or be prudent as showing a proper respect for the dead.

On Saturday morning it was made known that Inspector Reckless had left Monksmere for London by car late on Friday and wasn't expected back until Sunday morning. Presumably he had gone to check on the London alibis and investigate the Cadaver Club. There was no surprise that he was expected back so shortly. It was plain that he knew only too well where his business lay. But even this temporary absence was a relief. It was as if a cloud lifted from Monksmere Head. That gloomy, silently accusing presence had taken his preoccupations elsewhere and the air felt freer for his going. He left behind a restlessness which found relief in action. Everyone seemed anxious to get away from Monksmere. Even Jane Dalgliesh and her nephew who were the least affected by Reckless, were seen to set off early along the beach in the direction of Sizewell laden with painting paraphernalia, binoculars and knapsacks. It was obvious that they wouldn't be back until after dark. Latham drove off soon afterwards; the Jaguar was doing sixty-five when it passed Rosemary Cottage and Celia observed tartly that Oliver was off again on one of his attempts to break his neck. She and Eliza were to take Sylvia Kedge on a picnic to Aldeburgh but Eliza changed her mind just before they were due to start and set off on a solitary walk to Walberswick. No one knew what Digby Seton had planned, but a telephone call to Seton House by Miss Calthrop who hoped to persuade him to join the picnic, met with no reply. Bryce told everyone that he was driving to a country house sale just outside Saxmundham where he hoped to bid for some seventeenth-century porcelain. By half-past nine he too was far away and Monksmere was left to the half dozen autumn trippers who came in ones and twos throughout the day to park their cars in Tanner's Lane and to the occasional couple of walkers from Dunwich or Walberswick trudging along the sand dunes to the bird sanctuary.

Reckless must have driven back to Monksmere late on Saturday. When dawn broke his car was already outside the Green Man, and soon after nine o'clock Sergeant Courtney had rung most of the suspects to request their presence at the inn. The invitation was perfectly polite but no one was under the illusion that there was any choice in the matter. They took their time about arriving and, once again, there was a tacit understanding that they wouldn't arrive together. Sylvia Kedge was collected as usual in a police car by Sergeant Courtney. There was a feeling that Sylvia was, on the whole, quite enjoying herself.

Maurice Seton's portable typewriter was ready for them at the Inn, placed squat and shining on the edge of a small oak table in the saloon bar. The attentions of the finger print men and the typewriter experts seemed to have given it an added lustre. It looked at once ordinary and menacing, innocent and dangerous. It was, perhaps, the most intimate object that Seton had owned. Looking at the gleaming keyboard it was impossible not to think with repugnance of those bleeding stumps, to wonder what had happened to the severed hands. They knew at once why it was there. They were required to type two passages of prose; the description of Carruther's visit to the nightclub and of the handless corpse, drifting out to sea.

Sergeant Courtney, who was in charge of the exercise, was beginning to fancy himself as a student of human nature and the different reactions of his suspects provided gratifying material. Sylvia Kedge took some time to settle herself but once started the strong fingers, bony as a man's, danced above the keys to produce, in an incredibly short time, two accurate copies elegantly set out and perfectly typed. It is always satisfying to see a job performed perfectly and Sergeant Courtney received Miss Kedge's effort in respectful silence. Miss Dalgliesh, who arrived at the Inn twenty minutes later, was unexpectedly competent. She had been used to typing her father's sermons and the Church magazine and had taught herself with the aid of a manual. She used all five fingers correctly although her speed was only moderate and, unlike

Miss Kedge, she kept her eyes firmly on the keys. Miss Calthrop, staring at the machine as if she hadn't seen one before, protested shortly that she couldn't type—all her work was dictated on tape—and didn't see why she should waste her time trying. Eventually she was persuaded to make a start and after thirty minutes' effort, produced an appallingly typed two pages which she flourished at the Sergeant with the air of a vindicated martyr. Observing the length of Miss Calthrop's nails, Courtney was only surprised that she had managed to depress the keys. Bryce, when he could bring himself to touch the typewriter, was surprisingly quick and accurate although he found it necessary to keep up a scathing commentary on the style of the prose. Latham was almost as expert as Miss Kedge and rattled away in sullen silence. Miss Marley said briefly that she couldn't type but had no objection to trying. She refused Courtney's help, spent about five minutes examining the keyboard and the carriage and settled down to the laborious task of copying the passage, word by word. The result was quite creditable and Sergeant Courtney privately marked Miss Marley as an intelligent worker, in contrast to her aunt's assessment of "Could do better if she tried". Digby Seton was hopeless, but even Courtney couldn't believe that the man was faking. In the end, to everyone's relief he was allowed to give up. Predictably, none of the copies, including Digby's abortive effort, bore any resemblance to the originals. Sergeant Courtney, who believed that the second, and probably the first also, had been typed by Maurice Seton, would have been surprised if they had. But the final verdict would not be his. The copies would now be sent to an expert and examined for more subtle similarities. He didn't tell his suspects this; but then, he didn't need to. They hadn't read their Maurice Seton for nothing.

Before they left the inn their finger prints were taken. When her turn came, Miss Calthrop was outraged. She began for the first time to regret the desire to economize which had made her earlier decide not to seek the help of her solicitor. But she mentioned his name freely, together with that of her

Member of Parliament, and the Chief Constable. Sergeant Courtney, however, was so reassuring, so understanding of her feelings, so anxious for her help, so different in every way from that uncouth Inspector, that she was at last persuaded to cooperate. "Silly old bitch," thought the Sergeant as he directed the pudgy fingers. "If the rest of them make half this fuss I'll be lucky to be through before the old man gets back."

But the rest of them made no fuss at all. Digby Seton was tediously facetious about the whole proceedings, attempting to hide his nervousness by an exaggerated interest in the technique. Eliza Marley was sulkily aquiescent, and Jane Dalgliesh's thoughts appeared to be elsewhere. Bryce disliked it most. There was something portentous and irrevocable about parting with a symbol so uniquely peculiar to himself. He understood why primitive tribes were so careful that no scraps of their hair should fall into an enemy's hand. As he pressed his fingers on the pad with a moue of distaste he felt that virtue had gone out of him.

Oliver Latham jabbed his fingers into the pad as if it were Reckless's eye. When he looked up, he saw that the Inspector had come quietly in and was watching him. Sergeant Courtney got to his feet. Reckless said:

"Good evening, Sir. That's just a formality."

"Oh, I know all about that, thank you. The Sergeant has trotted out all the routine reassurance. I was wondering where you'd got to after your trip to town. I hope you enjoyed yourself questioning—as you would no doubt term her—'my lady friend'. And the porter at the flat? Duncombe was cooperative, I hope?"

"Everyone was very helpful, thank you, Sir."

"Oh, I'm sure they were! I've no doubt they enjoyed themselves immensely. Things are a bit quiet in town at present. I must be providing the best bit of gossip in weeks. And as we're all being so cooperative, what about a little cooperation from your end? I suppose there's no objection to my knowing how Seton died?"

"None at all, Sir—in due course. But we haven't got the P.M. report yet."

"Your chap's being a bit slow, isn't he?"

"On the contrary, Sir. Dr. Sydenham is very quick. But there are still a number of tests to be done. This isn't a straightforward case."

"I should rank that remark, Inspector, as the understatement of the year."

Taking his handkerchief from his pocket Latham carefully wiped his already clean fingers. Watching him the Inspector said quietly:

"If you're so impatient, Mr. Latham, why not ask some of your friends? You know as well as I do that someone at Monksmere could tell you precisely how Maurice Seton died."

14

Since his half-brother's death Digby Seton had taken to
dropping in at Rosemary Cottage for meals, and his neighbours didn't fail to remark with wry amusement on just how
often the Vauxhall was to be seen parked on the grass verge
outside the cottage. They conceded that Celia was unlikely to
discourage the company of a very rich young man but
Digby's motives were less obvious. No one assumed that the
charms of Eliza attracted him or that he saw in her sullen
gracelessness a means of getting his hands on Maurice's
capital. On the whole, people thought that he probably
preferred Celia's food, uninteresting though it was, to the
tedium of driving twice a day into Southwold or the effort of
cooking for himself and that he was glad to get out of the way
of Sylvia Kedge. Since the murder the girl had haunted
Seton House with the persistence of a funeral mute waiting
for her pay. The obsessional care which she had given to
Maurice's work now seemed to be devoted to his house and
she tidied, polished, cleaned, counted linen and dragged herself about on her crutches, duster in hand as if she expected the
late owner to reappear any minute and run his finger over the
window ledges. As Digby told Eliza Marley, it made him
nervous. He had never liked Seton House which, despite its
bright modernity, he found curiously sinister and depressing.
Now, when those smouldering black eyes were liable to turn on
him from every corner and cupboard, he felt he was living in
one of the gloomier Greek dramas with the Eumenides lurking
outside ready to make their entrance.

The remark had interested Eliza since it suggested that
Digby might be more perceptive and sensitive than was
commonly assumed. Without being in the least attracted to

him physically she was beginning to find him interesting, even a little intriguing. It was surprising what the possession of £200,000 could do for a man. Already she could detect the subtle patina of success, the assurance and complacency which the possession of power or money invariably gives. The glandular fever had left her depressed and fatigued. In this mood, without the energy to work and fretted by boredom, almost any company was better than none. Despising the easy capitulation to self interest which had changed her aunt's opinion of him overnight from Maurice's problem brother to a perfectly charming young man, she nevertheless was beginning to admit that there might be more in Digby Seton than met the eye. But not much more.

He hadn't accepted Miss Calthrop's invitation to dinner on Sunday night but he turned up at Rosemary Cottage shortly after nine and having arrived was apparently in no hurry to leave. It was now nearly eleven but he was still there, swivelling himself to and fro on the piano stool and spasmodically playing snatches of his own or other people's tunes. Eliza, curled into her fireside chair, watched and listened and was in no hurry for him to go. He didn't play badly. There was no real talent there, of course, but when he was taking trouble, which was seldom, he was agreeably competent. She remembered that there had once been talk by Maurice of making a pianist out of Digby. Poor Maurice! That was when he was still desperately trying to persuade himself that his only living relative had some qualities to justify the relationship. Even when Digby was still at school his modest successes, the time he had won the boxing championship, for example, had been trumpeted by Maurice as major achievements. It was unthinkable that Maurice Seton's half-brother should be entirely without some talent. And nor was he. He had, single-handed, designed and built Sheldrake and had sailed her with competence even if his enthusiasm had only lasted a couple of seasons. But this hearty gamesmanship, in some way so untypical of Digby, was hardly likely to impress an intellectual snob like Maurice. In the end, of course, he had given up pretending just as Celia had given up hope that her niece was

pretty, that she was going to have an orthodox success as a woman. Eliza glanced across at the large coloured photograph of herself that bore witness to Celia's humiliating and ludicrous ambitions. It had been taken when she was eleven, three years after the death of her parents. The thick dark hair was preposterously curled and ribboned, the white organdie dress with its pink sash looked vulgarly inappropriate to such a heavy featured and graceless child. No, it hadn't taken her aunt long to shed that particular delusion. But then, of course, it had been succeeded by another; dear Eliza, if she couldn't be pretty, had to be clever. Now the theme was: "My niece has a brilliant brain. She's at Cambridge, you know." Poor Aunt Celia! It was petty to grudge her this vicarious intellectual pleasure. After all she was paying hard cash for it. But Eliza felt some sympathy with Digby Seton. To an extent both of them had suffered from the pressure of another's personality, both had been accepted for qualities which they had no hope of ever possessing, both had been marked down as a bad buy.

On impulse she suddenly asked him:

"Which of us do you think killed your brother?"

He was syncopating a number from one of the recent London shows, inaccurately and rather too loudly for comfort. He had almost to shout above the noise of his own row:

"You tell me. You're the one who's supposed to be clever."

"Not as clever as Aunt makes out. But clever enough to wonder why it was I you phoned to meet you at Saxmundham. We've never been particularly friendly."

"Perhaps I thought it was time we were. Anyway, assuming I wanted a free lift to Monksmere, who else could I phone?"

"There is that. And, assuming you wanted an alibi for the time of the train journey."

"I had an alibi. The ticket collector recognized me; and I had an interesting chat with an old gentleman in the carriage about the naughtiness of the modern generation. I expect he would remember me. I can prove I was on that train, darling, without your help."

"But can you prove where you got on?"

"Liverpool Street. It was pretty crowded so I don't suppose anyone noticed me; but let Reckless try to prove that I didn't. Why are you so suspicious all of a sudden?"

"I'm not really. I don't see how you could have done it."

"Thank you for nothing. Nor do the police at West Central Station."

The girl shivered and said with sudden force: "Those hands —it was a horrible thing to do. Horrible! Don't you feel that? Particularly to a writer. Horrible and significant. I don't think you hated him that much."

He dropped his hands from the keys and swung round to face her.

"I didn't hate him at all. Damn it, Eliza! Do I look like a murderer?"

"How should I know? You're the one with the motive. £200,000 worth."

"Not until I get a wife. What about applying for the job?"

"No thank you. I like men to have an I.Q. at least approximate to mine. We wouldn't suit. What you want for the Club, surely, is a glamorous blonde with a forty-inch bust, a heart of low carat gold, and a mind like a calculating machine."

"Oh no!" he said seriously. "I know what I want for the Club. And now I've got the money I can pay for it. I want class."

The door into the study opened and Miss Calthrop poked her head through and gave them a vaguely puzzled look. She spoke to Eliza:

"I seem to have lost one of my new tapes. You haven't seen it, I suppose?"

Her niece's only response was a disinterested shrug but Digby sprang to his feet and peered hopefully around the room as if expecting the reel to materialize on top of the piano or pop out from under the cushions. Watching his ineffectual antics Eliza thought:

"Quite the little gentleman, aren't we? He's never bothered with Auntie before. What the hell is he playing at, anyway?"

The search was, of course, unsuccessful and Digby turned his charming deprecatory smile on Miss Calthrop.

"So sorry. It doesn't seem to be here."

Celia, who had been waiting with ill-concealed impatience, thanked him and went back to her work. As soon as the door closed behind her Digby said:

"She's taking it rather well, isn't she?"

"Taking what?"

"Maurice's Will. After all, if it weren't for me she'd be a very wealthy woman."

Did the fool really imagine that they didn't know it, that the arithmetic had somehow escaped them? She glanced across at him and caught his look of secret satisfaction, complacent, amused. It came to her suddenly that he must know something about Maurice's death, that the secret smile meant more than a momentary satisfaction at their disappointment and his own good luck. It was on the tip of her tongue to utter a warning. If he really had discovered something he would be in danger. He was typical of the fool who stumbles on part of the truth and hasn't the sense to keep his mouth shut. But she checked herself, irritated by that glimpse of secret satisfaction. Probably she was only being fanciful. Probably he had guessed nothing. And if he had? Well, Digby Seton would have to look after himself, would have to take his chance like the rest of them.

15

In the dining room at Priory House, dinner was nearly over. Dalgliesh had enjoyed his meal. He wasn't sure exactly what he had expected. It could have been a six course dinner served on Sévres china or a nut cutlet eaten off wooden plates and followed by communal washing-up. Neither would have surprised him. They had, in fact, been given an agreeable chicken casserole cooked with herbs and followed by a salad and cheeses. The Bordeaux rouge had been cheap and a little rough but there had been plenty of it and Dalgliesh, no wine snob, had never subscribed to the view that the only proper alternative to good wine is no wine at all. He sat now, content, almost happy, in a gentle daze of well-being and let his eyes wander over the immense room, where the four of them sat, dwarfed as puppets, round the simple oak table.

It was easy to see that the house had once been part of a monastery. This room must have been the refectory. It was a huge version of the sitting room at Pentlands but here the oak hammer beams smoked with age, arched against the roof like great trees and merged into a black void nearly twenty feet above the faint sphere of the six tall candles which lit the dining table. The fireplace was the stone hearth of Pentlands but magnified into a small cavern in which the great logs burned steady as coal. The six vaulted windows to seawards were shuttered now but Dalgliesh could still hear the murmur of the sea and, from time to time, a soft moan which suggested the wind was rising.

Alice Kerrison sat opposite Sinclair, a plump, quiet, self-possessed woman, sure of her place and chiefly concerned, as far as Dalgliesh could see, to ensure that Sinclair over-ate. When they were first introduced he had the immediate

sensation that he had met her before, that he had even known her well. Then almost instantly he realized why. Here, personified, was the Mrs. Noah of his childhood's Noah's ark. Here was the same straight hair, black and smooth as paint, drawn back from a centre parting into a tight little bun at the nape of the neck. Here was the same dumpy and compact figure with its tiny waist and the well recalled face, round, ruddy cheeked and beaded with two bright eyes. Even her clothes were familiar. She wore a plain black dress, long sleeved and bordered at neck and cuffs with narrow bands of lace. The whole was as evocative of the doldrums of childhood Sundays at his father's vicarage as the sound of Church bells or the morning smell of clean woollen underwear.

He glanced across at her as she poured the coffee and wondered what her relationship with Sinclair was. It was hard to guess. She didn't treat him as if he were a genius; he didn't treat her as a servant. Obviously she enjoyed looking after him but there was something matter-of-fact, almost irreverent in her calm acceptance of him. At times, bringing the food to the table together as was their obvious habit, conferring a little anxiously over the wine, they seemed as close and secret as conspirators. He wondered what had prompted her to pack her bags that morning, six years ago, and leave Maurice Seton for Sinclair. It struck him that Alice Kerrison probably knew more about Seton and his relationship with his wife than anyone else in the world. He wondered what else she knew.

He let his eyes slew round to where Sinclair sat with his back to the fire. The writer looked smaller than his photographs suggested but the broad shoulders, the long, almost simian arms, still gave an impression of great strength. His face was thickening with age so that the features were smudged and amorphous as an underexposed print. The heavy folds of skin hung about his face. The tired eyes were sunk so deep under the springing brows that they were almost invisible, but there was no mistaking the proud carriage of his head nor that great dome of white hair which shone now like a burning bush in the light of the fire, reinforcing the impression of some archaic Jehovah. How old was he, Dal-

gliesh wondered. The last of his three great novels had been published over thirty years ago and he had been middle-aged then. Three books were a slight foundation for such a solid reputation. Celia Calthrop, peeved by her failure to persuade Sinclair to participate in a Monksmere Literary Festival, accept the dedication of one of her novels, or even invite her to tea, was fond of saying that he was overrated, that it was quantity as well as quality that constituted greatness. Sometimes Dalgliesh thought that she had a point. But, always, one returned to the novels with a sense of wonder. They stood like great rocks on the foreshore where so many literary reputations had crumbled like sandcastles in the changing tide of fashion. Priory House would one day disappear beneath the sea but Sinclair's reputation would stand.

Dalgliesh was not so naive as to suppose that a great writer is necessarily a good talker nor presumptious enough to expect Sinclair to entertain him. But his host had not been silent during the meal. He had spoken knowledgeably and appreciatively of Dalgliesh's two volumes of verse but not, his guest felt, out of any desire to please. He had the directness and self absorption of a child. As soon as a topic ceased to interest him he changed the subject. Most of the talk was of books although he had no further interest it seemed in his own, and his favourite light reading was, it appeared, detective fiction. He was completely unconcerned with world affairs. "Men will either have to learn to love each other, my dear Dalgliesh, in the entirely practical and unsentimental use of the word or they will destroy themselves. I have no further influence either way." And yet, Dalgliesh felt that Sinclair was neither disillusioned nor cynical. He had detached himself from the world but neither out of disgust nor despair; it was merely that, in extreme old age, he had simply ceased to care.

He was talking now to Jane Dalgliesh, discussing apparently whether the avocet was likely to nest that year. Both of them were giving the subject the serious attention which other topics had failed to excite. Dalgliesh looked across the table at his aunt. She was wearing a cherry red blouse in fine wool, high necked and with the sleeves buttoned almost as

high as the elbows. It was an appropriate dress for dining out on the cold eastern seaboard and she had worn it with little variation as long as he remembered. But now, inexplicably, it was in fashion and to her individual, dégagé elegance was added the hint of a contemporary smartness which Dalgliesh found alien to her. Her left hand was resting against her cheek. The long brown fingers were heavy with the family rings which she wore only in the evenings. In the candle light the rubies and diamonds struck fire. They were talking now of a skull which Sinclair had recently picked up on his stretch of the beach. It was usual for the drowned graveyards to yield up their bones and, after a storm, walkers on the shore could expect to find an occasional femur or scapular bleached by the sea and friable with age. But it was less usual to find a whole skull. Sinclair was discussing its probable age and with some expertise. But so far there had been no mention of that other, more recent body. Perhaps, thought Dalgliesh, he had been wrong about the motive for this dinner party. Perhaps Sinclair wasn't interested in Seton's murder after all. But it was difficult to believe that he had merely had a whim to meet Jane Dalgliesh's nephew. Suddenly his host turned to him and said in his slow, rumbling voice:

"I suppose a great many people ask you why you choose to be a detective?"

Dalgliesh answered evenly:

"Not many whom I care to answer . . . I like the job; it's one I can do reasonably well; it allows me to indulge a curiosity about people and, for most of the time, anyway, I'm not bored by it."

"Ah yes! Boredom. The intolerable state for any writer. But isn't there something else? Doesn't being a policeman protect your privacy? You have a professional excuse for remaining uninvolved. Policemen are separate from other men. We treat them, as we do parsons, with superficial fellowship but essential distrust. We are uneasy in their company. I think you are a man who values his privacy."

"Then we are alike," suggested Dalgliesh. "I have my job. you have Priory House." Sinclair said:

"It didn't protect me this afternoon. We had a visit from your colleague, Inspector Stanley Gerald Reckless. Tell Mr. Dalgliesh about it, Alice."

Dalgliesh was wearying of disclaiming any responsibility for Reckless but was curious to know how Sinclair had discovered the Inspector's full names. Probably by the simple expedient of asking.

Alice Kerrison said:

"Reckless. It isn't a Suffolk name. He looked ill to me. An ulcer most likely. Worry and overwork maybe. . . ."

She could be right about the ulcer, thought Dalgliesh, remembering the pallor, the pain-filled eyes, the deep clefts between nose and mouth. He heard the calm voice continue:

"He came to ask if we had killed Mr. Seton."

"But with more tact, surely?" suggested Dalgliesh.

Sinclair said:

"He was as tactful as he knew how to be. But that's what he came for, nevertheless. I explained to him that I didn't even know Seton although I had tried to read one of his books. But he never came here. Just because I can no longer write myself I'm under no obligation to spend my time with those who never could. Fortunately Alice and I can give each other an alibi for Tuesday and Wednesday nights which we understand are the significant times. I told the Inspector that neither of us had left the house. I am not sure that he altogether believed me. Incidentally, Jane, he asked whether we had borrowed your chopper. I deduced from that question that you had unwittingly supplied the weapon. We showed the Inspector our two choppers, both in excellent order I am glad to say, and he could see for himself that no one had used them to chop off poor Maurice Seton's hands."

Alice Kerrison said suddenly.

"He was a wicked man and he's better dead. But there's no excuse for murder."

"In what way was he wicked?" asked Dalgliesh.

The question was a formality. He was going to be told whether he wanted it or not. He could feel Sinclair's amused

and interested eyes searching his face. So this was one reason for the dinner party. It wasn't just that Sinclair hoped to gain information. He had some to give. Alice Kerrison was sitting bolt upright, her face blotched with emotion, her hands clasped under the table. She gave Dalgliesh the truculent, half-pleading look of an embarrassed child and muttered:

"That letter he wrote to her. It was a wicked letter, Mr. Dalgliesh. He drove her to death as surely as if he'd forced her into the sea and held her head under the water."

"So you read the letter?"

"Not all of it. She handed it to me almost unthinking and then took it back again when she'd pulled herself together. It wasn't a letter any woman would want another woman to read. There were things in it I couldn't ever tell a soul. Things I'd rather forget. He meant her to die. That was murder."

Dalgliesh asked:

"Can you be sure he wrote it?"

"It was in his handwriting, Mr. Dalgliesh. All five pages of it. He only typed her name at the top, nothing more. I couldn't mistake Mr. Seton's hand." Of course not, thought Dalgliesh. And Seton's wife would have been even less likely to mistake it. So Seton had deliberately driven his wife to suicide. If this were true it was an act of wanton cruelty greater in degree but of the same nature as the killing of Bryce's cat. But somehow this picture of a calculating sadist was subtly out of focus. Dalgliesh had only met Seton twice but the man had never struck him as a monster. Was it really possible that this pedantic, nervous and self-opinionated little man with his pathetically over-valued talent could have nourished so much hatred? Or was this scepticism merely the arrogance of a detective who was beginning to fancy himself as a diagnostician of evil? After all even if one gave little Crippen the benefit of the doubt, there were still plenty of nervous, ineffectual men on record who had proved far from ineffectual when it came to getting rid of their wives. How could he, after two brief meetings, know the essential Seton as well as Alice Kerrison must have known him? And there was

the evidence of the letter, a letter which Seton, whose carefully filed correspondence at Seton House was all typewritten, had taken the trouble to write with his own hand.

He was about to ask what Dorothy Seton had done with it when the telephone rang. It was an incongruously strident noise in the silence of that immense, candle-lit room. Dalgliesh, startled, realized that he had unreasonably taken it for granted that there was no electricity at Priory House. He peered around for the instrument. The bell seemed to be ringing from a bookcase in the dark recess at the far end of the room. Neither Sinclair nor Alice Kerrison made any move to answer it. Sinclair said:

"That will be a wrong number. No one ever rings us. We only have the telephone in case of emergency but the number isn't in the book." He glanced across at the instrument complacently as if gratified to know that it was actually in working order. Dalgliesh got up: "Excuse me," he said. "But it may be for me." He groped for the instrument and laid hold of its smooth coldness among the impedimenta which littered the top of the bookcase. The irritating noise ceased. In the quiet he could almost believe that everyone present could hear Inspector Reckless speaking.

"Mr. Dalgliesh? I'm speaking from Pentlands. Something has happened which I think you should know about. Would it be convenient for you to come now?"

Then, as Dalgliesh hesitated, he added:

"I've got the P.M. report. I think it will interest you."

He made it sound like a bribe, thought Dalgliesh. But he would, of course, have to go. The formal, unemphatic tone of the request didn't deceive either of them. If they had been working on a case together Superintendent Dalgliesh would have summoned Inspector Reckless, not the other way round. But they weren't working on a case together. And if Reckless wanted to interview a suspect—or even the nephew of a suspect —he could choose his own time and place. All the same, it would be interesting to know what he was doing at Pentlands. Miss Dalgliesh hadn't locked the cottage when they left for Priory House. Few people at Monksmere bothered to lock

up and the possible murder of a neighbour hadn't induced his aunt to change her habits. But it was unlike Reckless to make himself so at home.

He made his excuses to his host who accepted them with little sign of regret. Dalgliesh suspected that Sinclair, unused to company other than his aunt, was glad enough to see their party reduced to the familiar three. For some reason of his own he had wanted Dalgliesh to hear Alice Kerrison's story. Now it had been told and he could speed his guest with satisfaction and some relief. He merely reminded Dagliesh to pick up his torch on the way out and instructed him not to return for his aunt as he and Alice would escort her home. Jane Dalgliesh seemed happy enough with this arrangement. Dalgliesh suspected that she was being tactful. Reckless had only asked to see him and his aunt had no wish to be an unwelcome third even in her own house.

He saw himself out, stepping into darkness so impermeable that at first his eyes could distinguish nothing but the white blur of the path at his feet. Then the clouds moved from the face of the moon and the night became visible, a thing of forms and shadows heavy with mystery and pungent with the sea. Dalgliesh thought how in London one could rarely experience the night, riven as it was by the glare of lights and the restlessness of men. Here it was an almost palpable presence so that there moved along his veins the stirring of an atavistic fear of darkness and the unknown. Even the Suffolk countryman, no alien to the night, could hardly walk these cliff paths without a sense of mystery. It was easy to understand how the local legends had grown that sometimes, on an autumn night, one could hear the muffled beat of horses' hoofs as smugglers brought their kegs and bales from Sizewell Gap to hide them in the marshes or carry them inland across the desolate Westleton heathlands. Easy, too, on such a night to hear from the sea the faint bells of long drowned churches, St. Leonard's, St. John's, St. Peter's and All Saints clanging their dirges for the souls of dead men. And now there might be new legends to keep the countryman indoors on the autumn nights. The October legends. One of a naked woman, pale

under the moon, walking through the waves to her death: one of a dead and handless man drifting out on the tide.

Dalgliesh perversely decided to walk home along the edge of the cliff. It would add fifteen minutes to his journey but it wouldn't hurt Reckless, comfortably ensconced at Pentlands, to wait another quarter of an hour. He found the path with his torch and followed the little pool of light which moved before him like a wraith. He looked back at the house. It was formless now, a black mass against the night sky with no sign of habitation except the thin shafts of light between the dining room shutters and one high round window which blazed out like a cyclops eye. While he watched, the light went out. Someone, probably Alice Kerrison, had gone upstairs.

He was nearing the edge of the cliff now. The waves thudded more clearly in his ears and somewhere, piercingly shrill, a sea bird called. He thought that the wind might be rising although it was still little more than a strong breeze. But here, on this exposed headland, it was as if sea, land and sky shared a perpetual and gentle turbulence. The path was becoming more overgrown. For the next twenty yards it was little more than a tortuous clearing through the brambles and gorse whose thorned branches caught at his legs. He was beginning to think that it would have been wiser to take the inland path. The gratification of making Reckless wait struck him now as irrational and childish and certainly not worth the ruining of a pair of perfectly good trousers. If Seton's body had been carried from Priory House through this prickly jungle there should be some evidence of its passing. Reckless would certainly have gone over the ground with care; he wondered what, if anything, he had found. And it wasn't only the path. There would be the forty or so rackety wooden steps down to the beach to be negotiated. Sinclair was a strong man despite his age and Alice Kerrison was a healthy countrywoman; but Seton small as he was, would have been literally a dead weight. It would have been an exhausting, almost impossible journey.

Suddenly he saw a white shape to the left of the path. It was one of the few remaining tombstones on this part of the cliff.

Most of them had long since crumbled with age or been swept under the sea to yield in time their quota of bones to the human debris washed up by the tides. But this one stood and, on impulse, Dalgliesh went over to examine it. It was taller than he had expected and the lettering was cut clear and deep. Crouching low, he shone his torch on the inscription:

In Memory of
Henry Willm. Scrivener
Shot from his horse by a party of
smugglers while travelling in these
parts, 24th Sept. 1786.
The cruel balls have pierced me to the heart
No time have I to pray ere I depart.
Traveller pause, thou knowest not the Day
When thou must meet thy Maker on the Way

Poor Henry Scrivener! What ill chance, Dalgliesh wondered, had brought him travelling on the lonely road to Dunwich. He must have been a man of some substance. It was a fine stone. He wondered how many years it would be before Scrivener, his stone and its pious exhortation were in turn swept away and forgotten. He was scrambling to his feet when the torch jerked in his hand and shone full on the grave itself. He saw with surprise that someone had opened it. The turf had been replaced, the brambles twisted together again to form a dense and prickly panoply, but the grave had undoubtedly been disturbed. He knelt again and gently shifted the soil with his gloved hands. It was light and friable. Hands other other than his had been there before. Within a few seconds he unearthed a femur, then a broken scapular and, finally, a skull. Henry Scrivener had been given companions in death. Dalgliesh guessed at once what had happened. This was Sinclair or Alice Kerrison's way of disposing of the bones they found on the beach. All of them were very old, all bleached by the sea. Someone, and he thought it was probably Alice, had wanted to give them a reburial in consecrated ground.

He was musing over this fresh insight into the ways of that

odd couple at Priory House and turning the skull over in his hands when he caught the soft thud of approaching footsteps. There was a rustle of parted branches and suddenly a dark figure was standing over him, blotting out the night sky. He heard Oliver Latham's light, ironic voice:

"Still detecting, Superintendent? You look, if I may say so, like an under-rehearsed First Grave Digger. What a glutton for work you are! But surely you can let poor Henry Scrivener rest in peace? It's a little late, I should have thought, to start investigating that particular murder. Besides, aren't you trespassing?"

"Rather less than you are at the moment," said Dalgliesh evenly.

Latham laughed:

"So you've been dining with R. B. Sinclair. I hope you appreciated the honour. And what did our great apostle of universal love have to say about Seton's peculiarly unpleasant end?"

"Not much."

Dalgliesh scooped a hole in the soft earth and began covering up the skull. He smoothed soil over the pale forehead and trickled it into the eye sockets and the gaps between the teeth. Without looking up he said:

"I didn't know you were fond of nocturnal walks."

"It's a habit I've only recently taken up. It's most rewarding. One sees such interesting sights."

He watched Dalgliesh as the reburial was completed and the turfs replaced. Then, without speaking, he turned to go. Dalgliesh called quietly after him:

"Did Dorothy Seton send you a letter shortly before she died?"

The dark figure stood stock still, then slowly turned. Latham asked softly:

"Is that any concern of yours?" And, as Dalgliesh hesitated he added.

"Then why ask?"

Without another word he turned again and disappeared into the darkness.

16

The light was on over the cottage porch but the sitting room was almost in darkness. Inspector Reckless was sitting alone in front of the dying fire rather like a guest who, unsure of his welcome, is making a propitiatory gesture of economizing on the lights. He rose as Dalgliesh entered and switched on a small table lamp. The two men faced each other in its soft but inadequate glow.

"Alone Mr. Dalgliesh? You had some trouble perhaps in getting away?"

The Inspector's voice was expressionless. It was impossible to detect either criticism or enquiry in the flat statement.

"I got away all right. I decided to walk back along the cliff. How did you know where to find me?"

"When I found the cottage empty I supposed you and Miss Dalgliesh would be dining somewhere in the district. I tried the most likely house first. There are developments which I wanted to discuss with you tonight and I didn't want to talk on the phone."

"Well, talk away. But what about something to drink?"

Dalgliesh found it almost impossible to keep the note of cheerful encouragement from his voice. He felt uncomfortably like a housemaster jollying along a promising but nervous examination candidate. And yet Reckless was entirely at ease. The sombre eyes gazed at him with no trace of embarrassment or servility. "For God's sake, what's wrong with me?" thought Dalgliesh. "Why can't I feel at ease with the man?"

"I won't have anything now, thank you Mr. Dalgliesh. I thought you'd be interested in the pathologist's report, I got it early this evening. Dr. Sydenham must have been up all

last night with him. Would you like to take a guess at the cause of death?"

"No," thought Dalgliesh, "I wouldn't. This is your case and I wish to God you'd get on with solving it. I'm not in the mood for guessing games." He said:

"Asphyxia?"

"It was natural causes, Mr. Dalgliesh. He died of a heart attack."

"What?"

"There's no doubt of it. He had a mild angina complicated by a defect of the left antrim. That adds up to a pretty poor heart and it gave out on him. No asphyxia, no poisoning, no marks of violence apart from the severed hands. He didn't bleed to death, and he didn't drown. He died three hours after his last meal. And he died of a heart attack."

"And the meal was? As if I need to ask!"

"Fried scampi with sauce tartare. Green salad with French dressing. Brown bread and butter, danish blue cheese and biscuits, washed down with Chianti."

"I shall be surprised if he ate that at Monksmere," said Dalgliesh. "It's a typical London restaurant meal. What about the hands, by the way?"

"Chopped off some hours after death. Dr. Sydenham thinks they may have been taken off on Wednesday night, and that would be logical enough, Mr. Dalgliesh. The seat of the dinghy was used as a chopping block. There wouldn't be much bleeding but if the man did get blood on him there was plenty of sea to wash it away. It's a nasty business, a spiteful business, and I shall find the man who did it, but that's not to say it was murder. He died naturally."

"A really bad shock would have killed him, I suppose?"

"But how bad? You know how it is with these heart cases. One of my boys has seen this Dr. Forbes-Denby and he says that Seton could have gone on for years with care. Well, he was careful. No undue strain, no air travel, a moderate diet, plenty of comfort. People with worse hearts than his go on to make old bones. I had an aunt with that trouble. She survived two bombing-outs. You could never count on killing

a man by shocking him to death. Heart cases survive the most extraordinary shocks."

"And succumb to a mild attack of indigestion. I know. That last meal was hardly the most appropriate eating for a heart case, but we can't seriously suppose that someone took him out to dinner with the intention of provoking a fatal attack of indigestion."

"Nobody took him out to dinner, Mr. Dalgliesh. He dined where you thought he might have done. At the Cortez Club in Soho, Luker's place. He went there straight from the Cadaver Club and arrived alone."

"And left alone?"

"No. There's a hostess there, a blonde called Lily Coombs. A kind of right-hand woman to Luker. Keeps an eye on the girls and the booze and jollies along the nervous customers. You know her, I daresay, if she was with Luker in fifty-nine when he shot Martin. Her story is that Seton called her to his table and said that a friend had given him her name. He was looking for information about the drug racket and had been told that she could help." Dalgliesh said:

"Lil isn't exactly a Sunday school teacher but, as far as I know, she's never been mixed up in the dope business. Nor has Luker—yet. Seton didn't tell her the name of his friend, I suppose?"

"She says that she asked but he wouldn't tell. Anyway, she saw the chance of making a few quid and they left the Club together at nine-thirty. Seton told her that they couldn't go back to his Club to talk because women weren't admitted. That's true; they aren't. So they drove around Hyde Park and the West End in a taxi for about forty minutes, he paid her five quid for her information—I don't know what sort of a yarn she pitched him—and he got out at Paddington Underground Station leaving her to take the cab back to the Cortez. She arrived back at ten-thirty and remained there in view of about thirty customers until one in the morning."

"But why leave in the first place? Couldn't she have spun him the yarn at his table?"

"She said he seemed anxious to get out of the place. The

131

waiter confirmed that he looked nervy and on edge. And Luker doesn't like her to spend too much time with one customer."

"If I know Luker he'd take an even poorer view of her leaving the Club for forty minutes to take a trip round Hyde Park. But it all sounds very respectable. Lil must have changed since the old days. Did you think it a likely story?"

Reckless said:

"I'm a provincial police officer, Mr. Dalgliesh. I don't take the view that every Soho tart is necessarily a liar. I thought she was telling the truth, although not necessarily the whole truth. And then you see, we've traced the cab driver. He confirmed that he picked them up outside the Club at nine-thirty and dropped Seton outside the District Line entrance at Paddington about forty minutes later. He said they seemed to be talking together very seriously for the whole of the journey and that the gentleman made notes in a pocket book from time to time. If he did I should like to know what happened to it. There was no pocket book on him when I saw the body."

Dalgliesh said:

"You've worked quickly. So the time he was last seen alive is pushed forward to about ten-ten. And he died less than two hours later."

"Of natural causes, Mr. Dalgliesh."

"I think he was intended to die."

"Maybe. But I'm not arguing with facts. Seton died at midnight last Tuesday and he died because he had a weak heart and it stopped beating. That's what Dr. Sydenham tells me and I'm not going to waste public money trying to prove that he's wrong. Now you're telling me that someone induced that heart attack. I'm not saying it's impossible. I am saying that there's no evidence yet to support it. I'm keeping an open mind on this case. There's a lot we don't know yet."

That remark struck Dalgliesh as a considerable under-statement. Most of the facts Reckless didn't yet know were surely almost as crucial as the cause of death. He could have catalogued the unanswered questions. Why had Seton asked

to be dropped at Paddington? Who, if anyone, was he on the way to meet? Where had he died? Where was his body from midnight on Tuesday onwards? Who moved it to Monksmere and why? If the death had indeed been premeditated how did the murderer contrive so successfully to make it look like natural death? And this led on to a question which Dalgliesh found the most intriguing of all. Having done so, why didn't he leave the body in London, dumped perhaps at the side of the road to be later identified as that of a middle-aged, unimportant detective novelist, who had been walking in London on his own mysterious business and had been overcome by a heart attack. Why bring the body back to Monksmere and stage an elaborate charade which couldn't fail to arouse suspicion of foul play and which would inevitably bring the whole Suffolk C.I.D. buzzing around his ears?

As if he could read Dalgliesh's thoughts Reckless said:

"We've no evidence that Seton's death and the mutilation of his body are directly related. He died of natural causes. Sooner or later we shall find out where. Then we shall get a lead on the person responsible for all the subsequent nonsense; the mutilation; the false telephone call to Digby Seton —if it were made; the two manuscripts sent to Miss Kedge— if they were sent. There's a joker in this pack and I don't like his sense of humour; but I don't think he's a killer."

"So you think that it's all an elaborate hoax? With what purpose?"

"Malice, Mr. Dalgliesh. Malice against the dead, or the living. The hope of throwing suspicion on other people. The need to make trouble. For Miss Calthrop, maybe. She doesn't deny that the handless corpse in a dinghy was her idea. For Digby Seton. He stands to gain most by his half-brother's death. For Miss Dalgliesh, even. After all, it was her chopper."

Dalgliesh said:

"That's pure conjecture. The chopper's missing, that's all we know. There's no evidence whatsoever that it was the weapon."

"There's evidence now. You see, it's been returned. Switch on the lights, Mr. Dalgliesh, and you'll see."

The chopper had, indeed, been returned. At the far end of the room stood a small eighteenth-century sofa table, a delicate and charming thing which Dalgliesh remembered from his childhood as part of the furniture of his grandmother's sitting room. The chopper had been driven into the centre, the blade splitting the polished wood almost in two, the shaft curving upward. In the bright centre light which now flooded the room Dalgliesh could see clearly the brown stains of blood on the blade. It would be sent for analysis, of course. Nothing would be left to chance. But he had no doubt that it was Maurice Seton's blood.

Reckless said:

"I came to let you know the P.M. report. I thought you might be interested. The door was half open when I arrived so I came in, calling for you. I saw the chopper almost at once. In the circumstances I thought I'd take the liberty of staying around until you arrived."

If he were gratified by the success of his little charade, he made no sign. Dalgliesh hadn't credited him with a dramatic instinct. It had been quite cleverly stage managed; the soft conversation in the gloaming, the sudden blaze of light, the shock of seeing something beautiful and irreplaceable wantonly and maliciously destroyed. He would have liked to have asked whether Reckless would have broken his news with such spectacular éclat if Miss Dalgliesh had been present. Well, why not? Reckless knew perfectly well that Jane Dalgliesh could have driven that chopper into the table before she and Dalgliesh left for Priory House. A woman who could cleave off a dead man's hands to provide herself with a little private entertainment was hardly likely to jib at the sacrifice of a sofa table in the same cause. There had been method in the Inspector's excursion into drama. He had been hoping to watch his suspect's eyes for the absence of that first unmistakable flicker of surprise and shock. Well, he hadn't got much out of Dalgliesh's reaction. Suddenly, cold with anger, he made up his mind. As soon as he could control his voice he said:

"I shall be going to London tomorrow. I would be grateful

if you would keep an eye on this place. I don't expect to be any longer than one night."

Reckless said:

"I shall be keeping an eye on everyone at Monksmere, Mr. Dalgliesh. I shall have some questions for them. What time did you and your aunt leave the cottage?"

"At about six-forty-five."

"And you left together?"

"Yes. If you're asking whether my aunt popped back on her own to fetch a clean hankie the answer is no. And, just to get the record straight, the chopper was not where it is now when we left."

Unprovoked, Reckless said calmly:

"And I arrived here just before nine. He had nearly two hours. Did you tell anyone about the dinner engagement, Mr. Dalgliesh?"

"No. I didn't, and I'm sure my aunt wouldn't have talked about it. But that's not really significant. We can always tell at Monksmere whether people are at home by the absence of lights."

"And you always leave your doors conveniently unlocked. It's all made very easy. And if things run true to form on this case, either all of them will be able to produce alibis, or none of them will." He walked over to the sofa table, and pulling an immense white handkerchief from his pocket he wrapped it round the shaft of the chopper and jerked the blade out of the table. He carried it to the door, then turned to face Dalgliesh:

"He died at midnight, Mr. Dalgliesh. Midnight. When Digby Seton had been in police custody for over an hour; when Oliver Latham was enjoying himself at the theatrical party in full view of two Knights, three Dames of the British Empire and half the culture hangers-on in London; when Miss Marley was safely tucked up in her hotel bed as far as I or anyone else knows; and when Justin Bryce was battling with his first attack of asthma. At least two of them have foolproof alibis and the other two don't seem particularly worried. . . . I forgot to tell you, by the way. There was a telephone call

for you while I was waiting. A Mr. Max Gurney. He wants you to ring back as soon as possible. He said that you knew the number."

Dalgliesh was surprised. Max Gurney was the last of his friends to ring him when he was on holiday. More to the point, Gurney was a senior partner in the firm which published Maurice Seton. He wondered whether Reckless knew this. Apparently not, since he made no comment. The Inspector had been working at tremendous pace and there were few people connected with Seton who hadn't been interviewed. But either he hadn't yet got round to seeing Seton's publisher, or he had decided that there was nothing to be gained.

Reckless finally turned to go:

"Goodnight, Mr. Dalgliesh. . . . Please tell your aunt that I'm sorry about the table. . . . If you're right about this being murder we know one thing about our killer, don't we? He reads too many detective stories."

He was gone. As soon as the departing roar of his car had died away, Dalgliesh telephoned Max Gurney. Max must have been waiting for he answered immediately.

"Adam? Good of you to telephone so promptly. The Yard were very naughty about letting me know where you were but I guessed it might be Suffolk. When are you coming back to town? Could I see you as soon as you do?"

Dalgliesh said that he would be in London next day. He could hear Max's voice lighten with relief.

"Then could we lunch together? Oh, lovely. At one o'clock say? Have you any preference about the place?"

"Max, weren't you once a member of the Cadaver Club?"

"I still am; would you like to lunch there? The Plants really do one very well. Shall we say one o'clock then at the Cadaver? Are you sure that's all right?"

Dalgliesh said that nothing would suit him better.

17

In the ground floor sitting room of the dolls' house in
Tanner's Lane Sylvia Kedge heard the first sighs of the rising
wind and was afraid. She had always hated a stormy night,
hated the contrast between the violence around her and the
deep calm of the cottage wedged damply into the shelter of the
cliff. Even in a high wind the surrounding air was heavy
and still as if the place bred a miasma of its own which no external force could disturb. Few storms shook the windows or
set the doors and timbers of Tanner's Cottage creaking. Even
in a high wind the branches of the elder bushes which clustered against the back windows only moved sluggishly as if
they lacked strength to tap against the panes. Her mother,
squatting in animal comfort in the fireside chair, used to say:
"I don't care what anyone says. We're very snug in here. I
shouldn't like to be at Pentlands or Seton House on a night
like this." It was her mother's favourite phrase. "I don't care
what anyone says." Spoken always with the truculence of the
widow with a grievance, permanently at odds with the world.
Her mother had had an obsessional need of snugness, of smallness, of security. To her all nature was a subtle insult and in the
peace of Tanner's Cottage she could shut from her thoughts
more than the violence of the wind. But Sylvia would have
welcomed the onslaught of cold, sea-heavy gusts against her
door and windows. It would at least have reassured her that
the external world existed and that she was part of it. It
would have been infinitely less harrowing than this unnatural
calm, this sense of isolation so complete that even nature
seemed to pass her by as unworthy of notice.

But tonight her fear was sharper, more elemental than the
unease of loneliness and isolation. She was afraid of being

murdered. It had begun as a flirtation with fear, a nicely judged indulgence of that half pleasurable frisson which a sense of danger can bring. But suddenly and terrifyingly, her imagination was out of control. Imagined fear had become fear itself. She was alone in the cottage, and helpless. And she was horribly afraid. She pictured the lane outside, the path soft and moist with sand, the hedges rising black and high on either side. If the killer came for her tonight she would have no chance of hearing his approach. Inspector Reckless had asked her often enough and her answer had always been the same. It would be possible for a man treading warily to pass by Tanner's Cottage at night unseen and unheard. But a man burdened with a corpse? That had been more difficult to judge but she still thought it possible. When she slept she slept soundly with windows closed and curtains drawn. But tonight he wouldn't be carrying a body. He would be coming for her, and alone. Coming perhaps with a hatchet, or a knife, or twisting a length of rope in his hands. She tried to picture his face. It would be a face she knew; it had not needed the Inspector's insistent questions to convince her that someone living at Monksmere had killed Maurice Seton. But tonight the familiar features would be changed into a mask white and rigid with intent, the face of the predator stalking light footed towards his prey. Perhaps he was even now at the gate, pausing with his hand on the wood, wondering whether to risk the soft creak as it swung open. Because he would know that the gate creaked. Everyone at Monksmere must know. But why should he worry? If she screamed there would be no one near to hear. And he would know that she couldn't run away.

Desperately she looked round the sitting room at the dark and heavy furniture which her mother had brought with her when she married. Either the great ornate bookcase or the corner cupboard would have made an effective barrier to the door if only she could have moved them. But she was helpless. Heaving herself from the narrow bed she grasped her crutches and swung herself into the kitchen. In the glass of the kitchen cabinet she saw her face reflected, a pale moon with eyes like black pools, the hair heavy and dank like the hair of a drowned

woman. A witch's face. She thought. "Three hundred years ago they would have burned me alive. Now they aren't even afraid of me." And she wondered whether it was worse to be feared or pitied. Jerking open the cabinet drawer she seized a fistful of spoons and forks. These she balanced in a row on the edge of the narrow window ledge. In the silence she could hear her own breath rasping against the pane. After a moment's thought she added a couple of glasses. If he tried to climb in through the kitchen window at least she would have some warning in the tinkle of falling silver and the smashing of glass. Now she looked round the kitchen for a weapon. The carving knife? Too cumbersome and not really sharp enough. The kitchen scissors perhaps? She opened the blades and tried to pull them apart but the rivet was too strong even for her tough hands. Then she remembered the broken knife which she used to peel vegetables. The tapering blade was only six inches long but it was keen and rigid, the handle short and easy to grasp. She whetted the blade against the stone edge of the kitchen sink and tested it with her finger. It was better than nothing. Armed with this weapon she felt better. She checked again that the bolts on the front door were secure and placed a row of small glass ornaments from the corner cupboard on the window ledge of the sitting room. Then, without taking the braces from her legs she propped herself upright on the bed, a heavy glass paper weight on the pillow beside her, the knife in her hand. And there she sat, waiting for fear to pass, her body shaken with her heart beats, her ears straining to hear through the far away sighing of the wind, the creak of the garden gate, the tinkle of falling glass.

Book Two

I

Dalgliesh set out next morning after an early and solitary breakfast, pausing only to telephone Reckless to ask for Digby Seton's London address and the name of the hotel at which Elizabeth Marley had stayed. He didn't explain why he wanted them and Reckless didn't ask but gave the information without comment except to wish Mr. Dalgliesh a pleasant and successful trip. Dalgliesh replied that he doubted whether it would be either but that he was grateful for the Inspector's cooperation. Neither troubled to disguise the irony in his voice. Their mutual dislike seemed to be crackling along the wire.

It was a little unkind to call on Justin Bryce so early but Dalgliesh wanted to borrow the photograph of the beach party. It was several years old but was a good enough likeness of the Setons, Oliver Latham and Bryce himself to help an identification.

Bryce came padding down in response to his knock. The earliness of the hour seemed to have bereft him of sense as well as speech and it was some time before he grasped what Dalgliesh wanted and produced the snap. Only then, apparently, was he struck with doubt about the wisdom of handing it over. As Dalgliesh was leaving he came scurrying down the path after him, bleating anxiously: "You won't tell Oliver that I let you have it, will you Adam? He'll be absolutely furious if he learns that one is collaborating with the police. Oliver is the teeniest bit distrustful of you, I'm afraid. One must implore secrecy."

Dalgliesh made reassuring noises and encouraged him back to bed, but he was too familiar with Justin's vagaries to take him at his face value. Once Bryce had breakfasted and

143

gained strength for the day's mischief he would almost certainly be telephoning Celia Calthrop for a little cosy mutual speculation about what Adam Dalgliesh could be up to now. By noon all Monksmere including Oliver Latham would know that he had driven to London, taking the photograph with him.

It was a comparatively easy journey. He took the quickest route and, by half past eleven, he was approaching the city. He hadn't expected to be driving into London again so soon. It was like a premature ending to a holiday already spoilt. In a half propitiatory hope that this might not really be so, he resisted the temptation to call at his flat high above the Thames near Queenhithe and drove straight on to the West End. Just before noon he had garaged the Cooper Bristol in Lexington Street and was walking towards Bloomsbury and the Cadaver Club.

The Cadaver Club is a typically English establishment in that its function, though difficult to define with any precision, is perfectly understood by all concerned. It was founded by a barrister in 1892 as a meeting place for men with an interest in murder and, on his death, he bequeathed to the Club his pleasant house in Tavistock Square. The Club is exclusively masculine; women are neither admitted as members nor entertained. Among the members there is a solid core of detective novelists, elected on the prestige of their publishers rather than the size of their sales, one or two retired police officers, a dozen practising barristers, three retired judges, most of the better known amateur criminologists and crime reporters and a residue of members whose qualifiction consists in the ability to pay their dues on time and discuss intelligently the probable guilt of William Wallace or the finer points of the defence of Madeline Smith. The exclusion of women means that some of the best crime writers are unrepresented but this worries no one; the Committee take the view that their presence would hardly compensate for the expense of putting in a second set of lavatories. The plumbing at the Cadaver has, in fact, remained virtually unaltered since the Club moved to Tavistock Square in 1900 but it is a

canard that the baths were originally purchased by George Joseph Smith. The Club is old-fashioned in more than its plumbing; even its exclusiveness is justified by the assumption that murder is hardly a fit subject for discussion in front of women. And murder at the Cadaver seems itself a civilized archaism, insulated from reality by time or the panoply of the law, having nothing in common with the sordid and pathetic crimes which took up most of Dalgliesh's working life. Murder here evokes the image of a Victorian maidservant, correct in cap and streamers, watching through a bedroom door as Adelaide Bartlett prepares her husband's medicine; of a slim hand stretched through a Glasgow basement railing proffering a cup of cocoa and, perhaps, arsenic; of Dr. Lamson handing round Dundee cake at his wealthy brother-in-law's last tea party; or of Lizzie Borden, creeping, axe in hand, through the quiet house in Fall River in the heat of a Massachusetts summer.

Every club has its peculiar asset. The Cadaver Club has the Plants. The members are apt to say "What shall we do if we lose the Plants?" much as they might ask "What shall we do if they drop the Bomb?" Both questions have their relevance but only the morbid dwell on them. Mr. Plant has sired—one would almost believe for the benefit of the Club—five buxom and competent daughters. The three eldest, Rose, Marigold and Violet, are married and come in to lend a hand. The two youngest, Heather and Primrose, are employed in the dining room as waitresses. Plant himself is steward and general factotum and his wife is generally acknowledged one of the best cooks in London. It is the Plants who give the Club its atmosphere of a private town house where the family's comfort is in the hands of loyal, competent and discreet family servants. Those members who once enjoyed these benefits have the comfortable illusion that they are back in their youth, and the others begin to realize what they have missed. Even the eccentricities of the Plants are odd enough to make them interesting without detracting from their efficiency and there are few Club servants of whom this can be said.

Dalgliesh, although he was not a member of the Club, had

occasionally dined there and was known to Plant. Luckily, too, by that curious alchemy which operates in these matters, he was approved of. Plant made no difficulties about showing him round or answering his questions; nor was it necessary for Dalgliesh to emphasise his present amateur status. Very little was said but both men understood each other perfectly. Plant led the way to the small front bedroom on the first floor which Seton had always used and waited just inside the door while Dalgliesh examined the room. Dalgliesh was used to working under scrutiny or he might have been disconcerted by the man's stolid watchfulness. Plant was an arresting figure. He was six feet three inches tall, and broad shouldered, his face pale and pliable as putty with a thin scar sliced diagonally across his left cheekbone. This mark, the result of an un-dignified tumble from a bicycle on to iron railings in his youth looked so remarkably like a duelling scar that Plant had been unable to resist adding to its effect by wearing a pince-nez and cropping his hair en brosse, like a sinister Commander in an anti-Nazi film. His working uniform was appropriate, a dark blue serge with a miniature skull on each lapel; this vulgar conceit, introduced in 1896 by the Club's founder, had now, like Plant himself, been sanctified by time and custom. Indeed, members were always a little puzzled when their visitors commented on Plant's unusual appearance.

There was little to be seen in the bedroom. Thin terylene curtains were drawn against the grey light of the October afternoon. The drawers and wardrobe were empty. The small desk of light oak in front of the window held nothing but a clean blotter and a supply of club writing paper. The single bed, freshly made up, awaited its next occupant. Plant said:

"The officers from the Suffolk C.I.D. took away his type-writer and clothes, Sir. They looked for papers, too, but he hadn't any to speak of. There was a packet of buff envelopes and about fifty sheets of foolscap and a sheet or two of un-used carbon paper but that's all. He was a very tidy gentle-man, Sir."

"He stayed here regularly every October didn't he?"

"The last two weeks in the month, Sir. Every year. And he

always had this room. We've only got the one bedroom on this floor and he couldn't climb stairs because of his bad heart. Of course, he could have used the lift but he said he hadn't any confidence in lifts. So it had to be this room."

"Did he work in here?"

"Yes Sir. Most mornings from ten until half past twelve. That's when he lunched. And again from two-thirty until half past four. That's if he was typing. If it was a matter of reading or making notes he worked in the library. But there's no typing allowed in the library on account of disturbing other members."

"Did you hear him typing in here on Tuesday?"

"The wife and I heard someone typing, Sir, and naturally we thought it was Mr. Seton. There was a notice on the door saying not to disturb but we wouldn't have come in anyway. Not when a member's working. The Inspector seemed to think it might have been someone else in here."

"Did he now? What do you think?"

"Well, it could have been. The wife heard the typewriter going at about eleven o'clock in the morning and I heard it at about four. But we wouldn't either of us know whether it was Mr. Seton. It sounded pretty quick and expert like but what's that to go on? That Inspector asked whether anyone else could have got in. We didn't see any strangers about but we were both busy at lunch time and downstairs most of the afternoon. People walk in and out very freely, Sir, as you know. Mind you, a lady would have been noticed. One of the members would have mentioned it if there'd been a lady about the Club. But otherwise—well I couldn't pretend to the Inspector that the place is what he'd call well-supervised. He didn't seem to think much of our security arrangements. But, as I told him Sir, this is a Club not a police station."

"You waited two nights before you reported his disappearance?"

"More's the pity, Sir. And even then, I didn't call the police. I phoned his home and gave a message to his secretary, Miss Kedge. She said to do nothing for the moment and she would try to find Mr. Seton's half-brother. I've never met the

gentleman myself but I think Mr. Maurice Seton did mention him to me once. But he's never been to the Club that I remember. That Inspector asked me particularly."

"I expect he asked about Mr. Oliver Latham and Mr. Justin Bryce too."

"He did, Sir. They're both members and so I told him. But I haven't seen either gentleman recently and I don't think they'd come and go without a word to me or the wife. You'll want to see this first floor bathroom and lavatory. Here we are. Mr. Seton used this little suite. That Inspector looked in the cistern."

"Did he indeed? I hope he found what he was looking for."

"He found the ballcock, Sir and I hope to God he hasn't put it out of action. Very temperamental this lavatory is. You'll want to see the library, I expect. That's where Mr. Seton used to sit when he wasn't typing. It's on the next floor as I think you know."

A visit to the library was obviously scheduled. Inspector Reckless had been thorough and Plant was not the man to let his protégé get away with less. As they crushed together into the tiny claustrophobic lift, Dalgliesh asked his last few questions. Plant replied that neither he nor any member of his staff had posted anything for Mr. Seton. No one had tidied his room or destroyed any papers. As far as Plant knew there had been none to destroy. Except for the typewriter and Seton's clothes, the room was still as he had left it on the evening he disappeared.

The library, which faced south over the square, was probably the most attractive room in the house. It had originally been the drawing room and, except for the provision of shelves along the whole of the west wall, looked much as it was when the Club took over the house. The curtains were copies of the originals, the wallpaper was a faded pre-Raphaelite design, the desks set between the four high windows were Victorian. The books made up a small but reasonably comprehensive library of crime. There were the notable British Trials and Famous Trials series, text books on medical jurisprudence, toxicology and forensic pathology, memoirs of

judges, advocates, pathologists and police officers, a variety of books by amateur criminologists dealing with some of the more notable or controversial murders, text books on criminal law and police procedure, and even a few treatises on the sociological and psychological aspects of violent crime which showed few signs of having been opened. On the fiction shelves a small section held the Club's few first editions of Poe, Le Fanu and Conan Doyle; for the rest, most British and American crime writers were represented and it was apparent that those who were members presented copies of their books. Dalgliesh was interested to see that Maurice Seton had had his specially bound and embellished with his monogram in gold. He also noted that, although the Club excluded women from membership, the ban did not extend to their books, so that the library was fairly representative of crime writing during the last one hundred and fifty years.

At the opposite end of the room stood a couple of show cases containing what was, in effect, a small museum of murder. As the exhibits had been given or bequeathed by members over the years and accepted in the same spirit of uncritical benevolence they varied as greatly in interest as, Dalgliesh suspected, in authenticity. There had been no attempt at chronological classification and little at accurate labelling and the objects had been placed in the show cases with more apparent care for the general artistic effect than for logical arrangement. There was a flintlock duelling pistol, silver mounted and with gold-lined flashpans which was labelled as the weapon used by the Rev. James Hackman, executed at Tyburn in 1779 for the murder of Margaret Reay, mistress of the Earl of Sandwich. Dalgliesh thought it unlikely. He judged that the pistol was made some fifteen years later. But he could believe that the glittering and beautiful thing had an evil history. There was no need to doubt the authenticity of the next exhibit, a letter, brown and brittle with age from Mary Blandy to her lover thanking him for the gift of "powder to clean the Scotch pebbles"—the arsenic which was to kill her father and bring her to the scaffold. In the same case was a Bible with the signature "Constance Kent" on

the flyleaf, a tattered rag of pyjama jacket said to have formed part of the wrapping around Mrs. Crippen's body, a small cotton glove labelled as belonging to Madeline Smith and a phial of white powder, "arsenic found in the possession of Major Herbert Armstrong." If the stuff were genuine there was enough there to cause havoc in the dining room and the show cases were unlocked. But when Dalgliesh voiced his concern Plant smiled:

"That's not arsenic, Sir. Sir Charles Winkworth said just the same as yourself about nine months ago. 'Plant', he said 'if that stuff's arsenic we must get rid of it or lock it up.' So we took a sample and sent it off to be analyzed on the quiet. It's bicarbonate of soda, Sir, that's what it is. I'm not saying it didn't come from Major Armstrong and I'm not denying it wasn't bicarb that killed his wife. But that stuff's harmless. We left it there and said nothing. After all, it's been arsenic for the last thirty years and it might as well go on being arsenic. As Sir Charles said, start looking at the exhibits too closely and we'll have no museum left. And now, Sir, if you'll excuse me I think I ought to be in the dining room. That is, unless there's anything else I can show you."

Dalgliesh thanked him and let him go. But he lingered himself for a few more minutes in the library. He had a tantalizing and irrational feeling that somewhere, and very recently, he had seen a clue to Seton's death, a fugitive hint which his sub-conscious mind had registered but which obstinately refused to come forward and be recognized. This experience was not new to him. Like every good detective, he had known it before. Occasionally it had led him to one of those seemingly intuitive successes on which his reputation partly rested. More often the transitory impression, remembered and analyzed, had been found irrelevant. But the sub-conscious could not be forced. The clue, if clue it were, for the moment eluded him. And now the clock above the fireplace was striking one. His host would be waiting for him.

There was a thin fire in the dining room, its flame hardly visible in the shaft of autumn sunlight which fell obliquely across tables and carpet. It was a plain, comfortable room,

reserved for the serious purpose of eating, the solid tables well spaced, flowerless, the linen glistening white. There was a series of original "Phiz" drawings for the illustrations to Martin Chuzzlewit on the walls for no good reason except that a prominent member had recently given them. They were, Dalgliesh thought, an agreeable substitute for the series of scenes from old Tyburn which had previously adorned the room but which he suspected the Committee, tenacious of the past, had taken down with some regret.

Only one main dish is served at luncheon or dinner at the Cadaver Club, Mrs. Plant holding the view that, with a limited staff, perfection is incompatible with variety. There is always a salad and cold meats as alternative and those who fancy neither this nor the main dish are welcome to try if they can do better elsewhere. Today, as the menu on the library notice board had proclaimed, they were to have melon, steak and kidney pudding, and lemon soufflé. Already the first puddings, napkin swathed, were being borne in.

Max Gurney was waiting for him at a corner table, conferring with Plant about the wine. He raised a plump hand in episcopal salute which gave the impression both of greeting his guest and of bestowing a blessing on the lunches generally. Dalgliesh felt immediately glad to see him. This was the emotion which Max Gurney invariably provoked. He was a man whose company was seldom unwelcome. Urbane, civilized and generous he had an enjoyment of life and of people which was infectious and sustaining. He was a big man who yet gave an impression of lightness, bouncing along on small, high-arched feet, hands fluttering, eyes black and bright behind the immense horn-rimmed spectacles. He beamed at Dalgliesh.

"Adam! This is delightful. Plant and I have agreed that the Johannisberger Auslese 1959 would be very pleasant, unless you have a fancy for something lighter. Good. I do dislike discussing wine longer than I need. It makes me feel I'm behaving too like the Hon. Martin Carruthers."

This was a new light on Seton's detective. Dalgliesh said that he hadn't realized that Seton understood wine.

"Nor did he, poor Maurice. He didn't even care for it greatly. He had an idea that it was bad for his heart. No, he got all the details from books. Which meant, of course, that Carruther's taste was deplorably orthodox. You are looking very well, Adam. I was afraid that I might find you slightly derange under the strain of having to watch someone else's investigation."

Dalgliesh replied gravely that he had suffered more in pride than in health but that the strain was considerable. Luncheon with Max would, as always, be a solace.

Nothing more was said about Seton's death for twenty minutes. Both were engaged with the business of eating. But when the pudding had been served and the wine poured Max said:

"Now, Adam, this business of Maurice Seton. I may say I heard of his death with a sense of shock and" —he selected a succulent piece of beef, and speared it to a button mushroom and half a kidney— "outrage. And so, of course, have the rest of the firm. We do not expect to lose our authors in such a spectacular way."

"Good for sales, though?" suggested Dalgliesh mischievously.

"Oh no! Not really dear boy. That is a common misconception. Even if Seton's death were a publicity stunt, which, admit it, would suggest somewhat excessive zeal on poor Maurice's part, I doubt whether it would sell a single extra copy. A few dozen old ladies will add his last book to their library lists but that isn't quite the same thing. Have you read his latest, by the way? *One for the Pot,* an arsenic killing set in a pottery works. He spent three weeks last April learning to throw pots before he wrote it, so conscientious always. But no, I suppose you wouldn't read detective fiction."

"I'm not being superior," said Dalgliesh. "You can put it down to envy. I resent the way in which fictional detectives can arrest their man and get a full confession gratis on evidence which wouldn't justify me in applying for a warrant. I wish real life murderers panicked that easily. There's also

the little matter that no fictional detective seems to have heard of Judges' Rules."

"Oh, the Honorable Martin is a perfect gentleman. You could learn a lot from him, I'm sure. Always ready with the apt quotation and a devil with the women. All perfectly respectable of course but you can see that the female suspects are panting to leap into bed with the Hon. if only Seton would let them. Poor Maurice! There was a certain amount of wish fulfilment there I think."

"What about his style?" asked Dalgliesh who was beginning to think that his reading had been unnecessarily restricted.

"Turgid but grammatical. And, in these days, when every illiterate debutante thinks she is a novelist, who am I to quarrel with that? Written I imagine with Fowler on his left hand and Roget on his right. Stale, flat and, alas, rapidly becoming unprofitable. I didn't want to take him on when he left Maxwell Dawson five years ago but I was outvoted. He was almost written out then. But we've always had one or two crime novelists on the list and we bought him. Both parties regretted it, I think, but we hadn't yet come to the parting of the ways."

"What was he like as a person?" asked Dalgliesh.

"Oh, difficult. Very difficult, poor fellow! I thought you knew him? A precise, self-opinionated, nervous little man perpetually fretting about his sales, his publicity or his book jackets. He overvalued his own talent and undervalued everyone else's, which didn't exactly make for popularity."

"A typical writer, in fact?" suggested Dalgliesh mischievously.

"Now Adam, that's naughty. Coming from a writer, it's treason. You know perfectly well that our people are as hard-working, agreeable and talented a bunch as you'll find outside any mental hospital. No, he wasn't typical. He was more unhappy and insecure than most. I felt sorry for him occasionally but that charitable impulse seldom survived ten minutes in his company."

Dalgliesh asked whether Seton had mentioned that he was changing his genre.

"Yes, he did. When I last saw him about ten weeks ago. I had to listen to the usual diatribe about the decline of standards and the exploitation of sex and sadism but then he told me that he was planning to write a thriller himself. In theory, of course, I should have welcomed the change, but, in fact, I couldn't quite see him pulling it off. He hadn't the jargon or the expertize. It's a highly professional game and Seton was lost when he went outside his own experience."

"Surely that was a grave handicap for a detective writer?"

"Oh, he didn't actually do murder as far as I know. At least, not in the service of his writing. But he kept to familiar characters and settings. You know the kind of thing. Cosy English village or small town scene. Local characters moving on the chess board strictly according to rank and station. The comforting illusion that violence is exceptional, that all policemen are honest, that the English class system hasn't changed in the last twenty years and that murderers aren't gentlemen. He was absolutely meticulous about detail though. He never described a murder by shooting, for example, because he couldn't understand firearms. But he was very sound on toxicology and his forensic medical knowledge was considerable. He took a great deal of trouble with rigor mortis and details like that. It peeved him when the reviewers didn't notice it and the readers didn't care."

Dalgliesh said:

"So you saw him about ten weeks ago. How was that?"

"He wrote and asked to see me. He came to London purposely and we met in my office just after 6.15 when most of the staff had left. Afterwards we came on here to dine. That's what I wanted to talk to you about Adam. He was going to alter his Will. This letter explains why." He took a folded sheet of writing paper from his wallet and handed it to Dalgliesh. The paper was headed "Seton House, Monksmere Head, Suffolk." The letter, dated 30th July, was typed and the typing, although accurate, was inexpert, with something about the spacing and the word division at the end of lines which marked it as the work of an amateur. Dalgliesh realized

immediately that he had recently seen one other typescript by the same hand. He read:

Dear Gurney,

I have been thinking over our conversation of last Friday— and here I must digress to thank you again for a most enjoyable dinner—and I have come to the conclusion that my first instinct was right. There is absolutely no sense in doing things by half. If the Maurice Seton literary prize is to fulfil the great purpose which I plan for it the capital outlay must be adequate, not only to ensure that the monetary value of the award is commensurate with its importance, but also to finance the prize in perpetuity. I have no dependents with a legitimate claim on my estate. There are those people who may think they have a claim but that is a very different matter. My only living relative will be left a sum which hard work and prudence will enable him to augment should he choose to exercise these virtues. I am no longer prepared to do more. When this and other small bequests have been made there should be a capital sum of approximately £120,000 available to endow the prize. I tell you this so that you may have some idea of what I intend. As you know my health is not good and although there is no reason why I should not live for many years yet, I am anxious to get this affair under way. You know my views. The prize is to be awarded biennially for a major work of fiction. I am not interested particularly in encouraging the young. We have suffered enough in recent years from the self-pitying emotionalism of the adolescent writer. Nor do I favour social realism. A novel should be a work of imaginative craftsmanship not the dreary shibboleths of a social-worker's case book. Nor do I restrict the prize to detective fiction; what I understand by detective fiction is no longer being written.

Perhaps you will think over these few ideas and let me know what you suggest. We shall need trustees of course and I shall consult lawyers in regard to the terms of my new Will. At present, however, I am saying nothing about this plan to anyone and I rely on you to be equally discreet. There will

inevitably be publicity when the details are known but I should much deplore any premature disclosures. I shall, as usual, be staying at the Cadaver Club for the last two weeks in October and I suggest that you get in touch with me there.

Yours sincerely,

MAURICE SETON.

Dalgliesh was conscious of Gurney's little black eyes on him as he read. When he had finished he handed back the letter, saying:

"He was expecting rather a lot of you, wasn't he? What was the firm getting out of it?"

"Oh, nothing, my dear Adam. Just a lot of hard work and worry and all of course for the greater glory of Maurice Seton. He didn't even restrict the prize to our list. Not that it would have been reasonable, I admit. He wanted to attract all the really big names. One of his chief worries was whether they would bother to apply. I told him to make the prize large enough and they'd apply all right. But £120,000! I never realized he was worth that."

"His wife had money. . . . Did he talk to anyone else about his plan do you know, Max?"

"Well, he said not. He was rather like a schoolboy about it. Tremendous swearings to secrecy and I had to promise I wouldn't even telephone him about it. But you see my problem. Do I, or do I not, hand this over to the police?"

"Of course. To Inspector Reckless of the Suffolk C.I.D., to be precise. I'll give you his address. And you'd better phone him to say it's on the way."

"I thought you'd say that. It's obvious, I suppose. But one has these irrational inhibitions. I know nothing of his present heir. But I imagine that this letter gives someone a whacking great motive."

"The best. But we've no evidence that his heir knew. And, if it's any comfort to you, the man with the strongest financial motive also has the strongest alibi. He was in police custody when Maurice Seton died."

"That was clever of him . . . I suppose I couldn't just hand this letter over to you, Adam?"

"I'm sorry, Max. I'd rather not."

Gurney sighed, replaced the letter in his wallet, and gave his attention to the meal. They did not talk again of Seton until lunch was over and Max was enveloping himself in the immense black cloak which he invariably wore between October and May, and which gave him the appearance of an amateur conjuror who has seen better days.

"I shall be late for our Board meeting if I don't hurry. We have become very formal, Adam, very efficient. Nothing is decided except by resolution of the whole Board. It's the effect of our new buildings. In the old days we sat closeted in our dusty cells and made our own decisions. It led to a certain ambiguity about the firm's policy but I'm not sure that was such a bad thing . . . Can I drop you anywhere? Who are you off to investigate next?"

"I'll walk, thank you Max. I'm going to Soho to have a chat with a murderer." Max paused, surprised.

"Not Seton's murderer? I thought you and the Suffolk C.I.D. were baffled. D'you mean I've been wrestling with my conscience for nothing?"

"No, this murderer didn't kill Seton although I don't suppose he would have had any moral objections. Certainly someone is hoping to persuade the police that he's implicated. It's L. J. Luker. Remember him?"

"Didn't he shoot his business partner in the middle of Piccadilly and get away with it? It was in 1959, wasn't it?"

"That's the man. The Court of Criminal Appeal quashed the verdict on grounds of misdirection. Mr. Justice Brothwick, through some extraordinary aberration, suggested to the jury that a man who made no reply when charged probably had something to hide. He must have realized the consequences as soon as the words were out of his mouth. But they were said. And Luker went free, just as he'd said he would."

"And how does he tie up with Maurice Seton? I can't imagine two men with less in common."

"That," said Dalgliesh, "is what I'm hoping to find out."

2

Dalgliesh walked through Soho to the Cortez Club. With his
mind still freshened by the clean emptiness of Suffolk he
found these canyoned streets, even in their afternoon doldrums, more than usually depressing. It was difficult to
believe that he had once enjoyed walking through this shoddy
gulch. Now even a month's absence made the return less
tolerable. It was largely a matter of mood, no doubt, for the
district is all things to all men, catering comprehensively for
those needs which money can buy. You see it as you wish.
An agreeable place to dine; a cosmopolitan village tucked away
behind Piccadilly with its own mysterious village life, one of
the best shopping centres for food in London, the nastiest and
most sordid nursery of crime in Europe. Even the travel
journalists, obsessed by its ambiguities, can't make up their
minds. Passing the strip clubs, the grubby basement stairs,
the silhouettes of bored girls against the upstairs window
blinds, Dalgliesh thought that a daily walk through these
ugly streets could drive any man into a monastery, less from
sexual disgust than from an intolerable ennui with the same-
ness, the joylessness of lust.

The Cortez Club was no better and no worse than its
neighbours. There were the usual photographs outside and
the inevitable group of middle-aged, depressed-looking men
eyeing them with a furtive lack of interest. The place wasn't
yet open but the door yielded to his push. There was no one
in the small reception kiosk. He went down the narrow stairs
with their scruffy red carpet and drew aside the curtain of
beads which divided the restaurant from the passage.

It was much as he remembered it. The Cortez Club, like
its owner, had an inate capacity for survival. It looked a little

smarter although the afternoon light showed up the tawdriness of the pseudo-Spanish decorations and the grubbiness of the walls. The floor was cluttered with tables, many only large enough for one and all too closely packed for comfort. But then, the customers did not come to the Cortez Club for family dinner parties, nor were they primarily interested in the food.

At the far end of the restaurant there was a small stage furnished only with a single chair and a large cane screen. To the left of the stage was an upright piano, its top littered with manuscript paper. A thin young man in slacks and sweater was curved against the instrument picking out a tune with his left hand and jotting it down with his right. Despite the sprawled attitude, the air of casual boredom, he was completely absorbed. He glanced up briefly as Dalgliesh came in but returned immediately to his monotonous stabbing at the keys.

The only other person present was a West African who was pushing a broom in leisurely fashion around the floor. He said in a low, soft voice:

"We're not open yet, Sir. Service doesn't begin until six-thirty."

"I don't want to be served, thank you. Is Mr. Luker in?"

"I'll have to enquire Sir."

"Please do so. And I'd like to see Miss Coombs too."

"I'll have to enquire, Sir. I'm not sure that she's here."

"Oh, I think you'll find that she's here. Tell her please that Adam Dalgliesh would like to speak to her."

The man disappeared. The pianist continued his improvisation without looking up, and Dalgliesh settled himself at the table just inside the door to pass the ten minutes which he judged Luker would feel it appropriate to keep him waiting. He spent the time thinking of the man upstairs.

Luker had said that he would kill his partner and he had killed. He had said that he wouldn't hang for it and he didn't hang. Since he could hardly have counted on Mr. Justice Brothwick's cooperation, the prediction had shown either uncommon prescience or remarkable confidence in his own luck. Some of the stories which had grown around him since

his trial were no doubt apocryphal but he was not the man to repudiate them. He was known and accepted by the professional criminal classes without being one of them. They gave him the reverent half-superstitious respect of men who know exactly how much it is reasonable to risk, for one who in one irretrievable stride has stepped outside all the limits. There was an ambience of awe about any man who had come so close to that last dreadful walk. Dalgliesh was sometimes irritated to find that even the police weren't immune to it. They found it hard to believe that Luker, who had killed so casually to satisfy a private grudge, could content himself with running a string of second-class night clubs. Some more spectacular wickedness was expected of him than the manipulation of Licensing Laws or Income Tax returns and the selling of mildly erotic entertainment to his dreary expense account customers. But if he had other enterprises, nothing as yet was known of them. Perhaps there was nothing to know. Perhaps all he craved was this prosperous, semi-respectability, the spurious reputation, the freedom of this no-mans-land between two worlds.

It was exactly ten minutes before the coloured man returned to say that Luker would see him. Dalgliesh made his own way up the two flights to the large front room from which Luker chose to direct not only the Cortez but all his Clubs. It was warm and airless, over-furnished and under-ventilated. There was a desk in the middle of the room, a couple of filing cabinets against one wall, an immense safe to the left of the gas fire and a sofa and three easy chairs grouped around a television set. In the corner was a small washstand basin. The room was obviously designed to serve both as an office and a sitting room and succeeded in being neither. There were three people present; Luker himself, Sid Martelli, his general factotum at the Cortez, and Lily Coombs. Sid, in his shirt sleeves, was heating himself a small saucepan of milk on a gas ring at the side of the fire. He was wearing his usual expression of resigned misery. Miss Coombs, already in her evening black, was squatting on a pouffe in front of the gas fire varnishing her nails. She raised a hand in salute and gave Dalgliesh a wide,

unworried smile. Dalgliesh thought that the manuscript description of her, whoever had written it, fitted her well enough. He couldn't personally detect the Russian aristocratic blood but this hardly surprised him since he knew perfectly well that Lil had been bred no further east than the Whitechapel Road. She was a large, healthy-looking blonde with strong teeth and the thick, rather pale skin which stands up well to ageing. She might be in her early forties. It was difficult to tell. She looked exactly as she had when Dalgliesh had first seen her five years earlier. Probably she would look much the same for another five years.

Luker had put on weight since their last meeting. The expensive suit was strained across his shoulders, his neck bulged over the immaculate collar. He had a strong, unpleasant face, the skin so clear and shining that it might have been polished. His eyes were extraordinary. The irises were set exactly in the centre of the whites like small grey pebbles, and were so lifeless that they gave the whole face a look of deformity. His hair, strong and black, came down low to a widow's peak imposing an incongruous touch of femininity to his face. It was cut short all over and shone like dog's hair, glossy and coarse. He looked what he was. But when he spoke his voice betrayed his origins. It was all there; the small town vicarage, the carefully fostered gentility, the minor public school. He had been able to change much. But he had not been able to alter his voice.

"Ah, Superintendent Dalgliesh. This is very pleasant. I'm afraid we're booked out this evening but Michael may be able to find you a table. You're interested in the floor show no doubt."

"Neither dinner nor the show, thank you. Your food seemed to disagree with the last of my acquaintances who dined here. And I like women to look like women, not nursing hippopotami. The photographs outside were enough. Where on earth do you pick them up?"

"We don't. The dear girls recognize that they have, shall we say, natural advantages, and come to us. And you mustn't be censorious, Superintendent. We all have our private sexual

fantasies. Just because yours aren't catered for here it doesn't mean that you don't enjoy them. Isn't there a little saying about motes and beams? Remember, I'm a parson's son as well as you. It seems to have taken us rather differently, though." He paused as if for a moment interested in their separate reactions, then went on lightly:

"The Superintendent and I have a common misfortune, Sid. We both had a parson for dad. It's an unhappy start for a boy. If they're sincere you despise them as a fool: if they're not you write them off as a hypocrite. Either way, they can't win."

Sid, who had been sired by a Cypriot bartender on a mentally subnormal skivvy, nodded in passionate agreement.

Dalgliesh said:

"I wanted a word with you and Miss Coombs about Maurice Seton. It isn't my case so you don't have to talk if you don't want to. But you know that, of course."

"That's right. I don't have to say a damn word. But then I might be in a helpful accommodating mood. You can never tell. Try me."

"You know Digby Seton, don't you?"

Dalgliesh could have sworn that the question was unexpected. Luker's dead eyes flickered. He said:

"Digby worked here for a few months last year when I lost my pianist. That was after his Club failed. I lent him a bit to try and see him over but it was no go. Digby hasn't quite got what it takes. But he's not a bad pianist."

"When was he last here?"

Luker spread his hands and turned to his companions:

"He did a week for us in May, didn't he, when Ricki Carlis took his overdose? We haven't seen him since."

Lil said:

"He's been in once or twice L.J. Not when you were here though." Luker's staff always called him by his initials. Dalgliesh wasn't sure whether the idea was to emphasise the general cosiness of their relationship with him or to make Luker feel like an American tycoon. Lil went on helpfully, "Wasn't he in with a party in the summer, Sid?"

Sid assumed an expression of lugubrious thought:

"Not summer, Lil. More like late spring. Didn't he come in with Mavis Manning and her crowd after her show folded up in May?"

"That was Ricki, Sid. You're thinking of Ricki. Digby Seton was never with Mavis."

They were as well-drilled, thought Dalgliesh, as a song and dance act. Luker said smoothly:

"Why pick on Digby? This isn't murder and, if it was, Digby's safe enough. Look at the facts. Digby had a rich brother. Nice for both of them. The brother had a dicky heart which might give out on him any minute. Hard luck on him but, again nice for Digby. And one day it does give out. That's natural causes, Superintendent, if the expression means anything at all. Admittedly someone drove the body down to Suffolk and pushed it out to sea. And did some rather messy and unpleasant things to it first, I hear. It looks to me as if poor Mr. Seton was rather unpopular with some of his literary neighbours. I'm surprised, Superintendent, that your aunt cares to live among these people, let alone leaving her chopper handy for the dead."

"You seem well informed," said Dalgliesh. He was remarkably quickly informed too. Dalgliesh wondered who had been keeping him so clearly in the picture.

Luker shrugged.

"There's nothing illegal in that. My friends tell me things. They know I'm interested in them."

"Particularly when they inherit £200,000 ?"

"Listen, Superintendent. If I want money I can make it, and make it legally. Any fool can make a fortune outside the law. It takes a clever man, these days, to make it legally. Digby Seton can pay me back the fifteen hundred I lent him when he was trying to save the Golden Pheasant if he likes. I'm not pressing him."

Sid turned his lemur-like eyes on his boss. The devotion in them was almost indecent.

Dalgliesh said:

"Maurice Seton dined here the night he died. Digby Seton

is connected with this place. And Digby stands to inherit £200,000. You can't blame people if they come asking questions, particularly as Miss Coombs was the last person to see Maurice alive."

Luker turned to Lil:

"You'd better keep your mouth shut, Lil. Or, better still, get yourself a lawyer. I'll phone Bernie."

"What the hell do I want Bernie for? I've told it all to him once when that C.I.D. chap was here. I'm telling the truth. Michael and the boys saw him call me over to his table and we sat there until nine-thirty when we left together. I was back here by ten-thirty. You saw me Sid, and so did the whole bloody Club."

"That's right. Superintendent. Lil was back by half past ten."

"Lil should never have left the Club," said Luker smoothly. "But that's my concern, not yours."

Miss Coombs appeared magnificently unconcerned at the thought of Luker's displeasure. Like all his employees she knew exactly how far she could go. The rules were few and simple and were well understood. Leaving the Club for an hour on a slack evening was venial. Murder, under certain well-understood circumstances, was probably venial too. But if someone at Monksmere hoped to pin this killing on Luker he was in for a disappointment. Luker was not the man to do murder for someone else's benefit nor did he trouble to cover up his tracks. When Luker killed he had no objection to leaving his prints on the crime.

Dalgliesh asked Lil what had happened. There was no more mention of lawyers and no difficulty in getting her story. Dalgliesh did not miss Lil's quick glance at her boss before she began her story. For some reason best known to himself Luker was willing to let her talk.

"Well, he came in at about eight o'clock and took the table nearest the door. I noticed him at once. He was a funny little man, small, very neat, nervous-looking. I thought he was probably a Civil Servant out for a spree. We get all types here. The regulars usually come with a party but we get the odd

solitary chap. Mostly they're looking for a girl. Well, we don't cater for that kind of thing and it's my business to tell them so." Miss Coombs assumed an expression of pious severity which deceived no one and wasn't intended to. Dalgliesh enquired what had happened next.

"Michael took his order. He asked for fried scampi, green salad, bread and butter and a bottle of Ruffino. He seemed to know exactly what he wanted. No mucking about. When Michael served him he asked if he could speak to me. Well I went across and he asked me what I would drink. I had a gin and lime and drank it while he started picking at the scampi. Either he hadn't an appetite or he just wanted something to push around the plate while we were talking. He got quite a bit of the meal down eventually but he didn't look as if he was enjoying it. He drank the wine, though. Fairly put it away. Nearly the whole bottle."

Dalgliesh enquired what they had talked about.

"Dope," said Miss Coombs frankly. "That's what he was interested in. Dope. Not for himself, mind you. Well, it was plain enough he wasn't a junkie and he wouldn't have come to me if he was. Those boys know well enough where they can get the stuff. We don't see them in the Cortez. This chap told me that he was a writer, a very well known one, quite famous, and that he was writing a book about dope peddling. He didn't tell me his name and I never asked. Anyway, someone had told him that I might give him some useful information if he made it worth my while. Apparently this friend had said that if you want to know anything about Soho go to the Cortez and ask for Lil. Very nice, I must say. I've never seen myself as an authority on the dope racket. Still, it looked as if someone was trying to do me a good turn. There was money in it and the chap wasn't the sort to know whether he was getting genuine information. All he wanted was a bit of local colour for his book and I reckoned I could provide that. You can buy anything you want in London if you've got the cash and know where to go. You know that ducky, as well as I do. I daresay I could have given him the name of a pub or two where they say the stuff is passed. But what good would that

be to him? He wanted a bit of glamour and excitement and there's no glamour about the dope racket, nor the junkies neither, poor devils. So I said that I might be able to give him a bit of information and what was it worth? He said ten quid and I said O.K. And don't you go talking about false pretences. He was getting value."

Dalgliesh said that he was sure Miss Coombs always gave value and Miss Coombs, after a brief struggle, decided prudently to let the remark pass. Dalgliesh asked:

"Did you believe this story of being a writer?"

"No dear. Not at first, anyway. I'd heard it too often before. You'd be surprised the number of chaps who want to meet a girl 'just to get authentic background for my new novel.' If it's not that then they're doing sociological research. I'll bet they are! He looked that type. You know, insignificant, nervous and eager at the same time. But when he suggested we should take a taxi and I could dictate the stuff to him and he type it straight away, I began to wonder. I said I couldn't leave the Club for more than an hour at most and I'd rather we went to my place. When you don't know who you're playing keep to the home ground, I always say. So I suggested we took a taxi to my flat. He said all right and we left just before nine-thirty. That right, Sid?"

"That's right Lil. Nine-thirty it was." Sid lifted sad eyes from his glass of milk. He had been contemplating, without enthusiasm, the puckered skin which had slowly formed on its surface. The smell of hot milk, sickly and fecund, seemed to permeate the claustrophobic office. Luker said:

"For God's sake drink the stuff or chuck it away, Sid. You make me nervous."

"Drink it up, darling," encouraged Miss Coombs. "Think of your ulcer. You don't want to go the way of poor Solly Goldstein."

"Solly died of a coronary and milk never helped that. The opposite I should think. Anyway, the stuff's practically radioactive. Full of strontium 90. It's dangerous, Sid."

Sid trotted to the washbasin and poured the milk away. Resisting the urge to throw open the window Dalgliesh asked:

"How did Mr. Seton appear while you were sitting together?"

"Nervy, dear. Excited but on edge at the same time. Michael wanted to move him to another table, it's a bit draughty near the door, but he wouldn't budge. He kept looking at the door while we were talking."

"As if he was expecting someone?"

"No dear. More as if he wanted to make sure it was still there. I half expected him to do a bunk. He was an odd fish and no mistake."

Dalgliesh asked what had happened when they left the Club.

"The same as I told that C.I.D. chap from Suffolk. We got a taxi at the corner of Greek Street and I was going to give the cabbie my address when Mr. Seton suddenly said that he'd rather just drive around for a bit and would I mind. If you ask me he'd suddenly got cold feet. Scared of what might happen to him, poor little twerp. Anyway, that suited me and we cruised around the West End a bit and then went into Hyde Park. I strung him a bit of a yarn about the dope racket and he made notes in a little book. If you ask me he was a bit drunk. Suddenly he got hold of me and tried to kiss me. Well, I was a bit fed up with him by then and didn't fancy being pawed about by that little twit. I got the impression that he only made a pass because he thought he ought to. So I said I ought to be back at the Club. He asked to be put down outside Paddington Underground and said he'd take a tube. No hard feelings. He gave me two fivers and an extra pound for the taxi fare."

"Did he say where he was going?"

"No. We came up Sussex Gardens—it's one way only down Praed Street now, as you know—and put him down outside the District Line. But he could have crossed the road to the Bakerloo I suppose. I didn't watch to see. I said goodbye to him at about quarter past ten outside Paddington Underground and that's the last I saw of him. And that's the truth."

Even if it weren't, thought Dalgliesh, it was difficult to see

how the story could be disproved. There was too much corroborative evidence and Lil was the last woman in London to be panicked into changing a good story. It had been a waste of time coming to the Cortez. Luker had been unnaturally, almost suspiciously cooperative but Dalgliesh had learnt nothing which Reckless couldn't have told him in half the time.

Suddenly he felt again some of the uncertainties and the inadequacies which had tormented the young Detective Constable Dalgliesh nearly twenty years ago. When he took out Bryce's photograph of the beach party and handed it round it was with no hope of success. He felt like a doorstep salesman proferring his unwanted rubbish. They looked at it politely enough. Perhaps, like kindly householders, they were rather sorry for him. Doggedly persevering, he asked whether any of the people shown had been seen at the Cortez Club. Lil screwed up her eyes in an agony of effort while holding the snap at arm's length, thus effectively blurring her vision. Lil, Dalgliesh remembered, was like most women. She lied most effectively when she could convince herself that, essentially, she was telling the truth.

"No, dear, I can't say I recognize them. Except Maurice Seton and Digby, of course. That's not to say they haven't been here. Better ask them."

Luker and Sid, less inhibited, merely glanced at the photograph and averred that they hadn't seen the subjects in their lives.

Dalgliesh looked at the three of them. Sid had the pained, rather anxious look of an underfed little boy, hopelessly at sea in the world of wicked adults. Dalgliesh thought that Luker might be secretly laughing if the man had ever been known to laugh. Lil was looking at him with the encouraging, motherly, almost pitying look which, he thought bitterly, was usually reserved for her customers. There was nothing more to be learned from them. He thanked them for their help—he suspected that the note of cool irony wasn't lost on Luker—and let himself out.

3

When Dalgliesh had left Luker jerked his head at Sid. The little man left without a word or a backward glance. Luker waited until his footsteps had been heard going downstairs. Lil, alone with the boss, showed no particular anxiety but settled herself more comfortably in the shabby armchair on the left of the gas fire and watched him with eyes as bland and incurious as the eyes of a cat. Luker went to a wall safe. She watched his broad back as he stood there, motionless, turning the combination lock. When he turned round she saw that he held a small parcel, the size of a shoe box, covered with brown paper and loosely tied with thin white string. He laid it on his desk.

"Have you seen this before?" he asked.

Lil disdained to show curiousity.

"It came for you by this morning's post, didn't it? Sid took it in. What's wrong with it?"

"Nothing's wrong with it. On the contrary it is an admirable parcel. I've undone it once, as you can see, but it was a very neat little job when it arrived. You see the address? L.J. Luker, Esq., The Cortez Club, W.1. Neat capital letters, characterless, printed in Biro. Not very easy to identify that hand. I like the esquire. My family is not armigerous as it happens, so the writer is being a little pretentious but as he shares that failing with my Income Tax inspector and half the tradesmen in Soho, we can hardly consider it a clue. Then there's the paper. Perfectly ordinary brown paper; you can buy it in sheets from any stationer. And the string. Do you see anything remarkable about the string, Lil?"

Lil, watchful, admitted that there was nothing remarkable about the string. Luker went on:

"What is rather strange, though, is the amount of postage he—or she—paid. At least a shilling on the generous side by my estimate. So we take it that the parcel was stamped outside a post office and then pushed over the counter at a busy time. No waiting for it to be weighed. There would be less chance of the customer being noticed that way."

"Where was it posted?"

"In Ipswich on Saturday. Does that mean anything to you?"

"Only that it was posted a hell of a long way from here. Isn't Ipswich near that place where they found Maurice Seton?"

"The nearest large town to Monksmere. The nearest place where one could be certain of being unrecognized. You could hardly post this in Walberswick or Southwold and expect that no one would remember."

"For God's sake, L.J.! What's in it?"

"Open it and see for yourself."

Lil advanced cautiously but with an assumption of unconcern. There were more layers of the brown wrapping paper than she had expected. The box itself was revealed as an ordinary white shoe box but with the labels torn away. It looked very old, the kind of box that could be found tucked away in a drawer or cupboard in almost any house. Lil's hands hovered over the lid.

"If there's some bloody animal in here that jumps out at me I'll kill you L.J., God help me if I don't. I hate damn silly jokes. What's the stink, anyway?"

"Formaline. Go on, open it."

He was watching her closely, the cold grey eyes interested, almost amused. He had her worried now. For a second her eyes met his. Then she stepped back from the desk and, reaching forward, flipped off the lid with one jerk of her wrist.

The sweetly acrid smell rose like an anaesthetic. The severed hands were lying on their bed of damp cotton wool curved as if in a parody of prayer, palms touching briefly, finger tips pressed together. The puffy skin, what was left of it, was chalk white, and so crumpled that it looked as if the phalanges were loosely clothed with a pair of old gloves which

would peel off at a touch. Already the flesh was shrinking from the butchered wrists and the nail of the right index finger had shifted from its bed.

The woman stared at the hands, fascinated and repelled. Then she seized the lid of the box and rammed it home. The cardboard buckled under her force.

"It wasn't murder, L.J. I swear it! Digby hadn't anything to do with it. He hasn't the nerve."

"That's what I would have said. You've told me the truth Lil?"

"Of course. Every word L.J. Look, he couldn't have done it. He was in the nick all Tuesday night."

"I know all about that. But if he didn't send these, who did? He stood to make £200,000 remember."

Lil said suddenly:

"He said that his brother would die. He told me that once." She gazed at the box, fascinated and horrified.

Luker said:

"Of course he was going to die. Some time. He had a dicky heart, didn't he? That's not to say Digby put him away. It was natural causes."

Lil may have detected some tinge of uncertainty in his voice. She glanced at him and said quickly:

"He's always been keen to come in with you L.J. You know that. And he's got £200,000."

"Not yet. And he may never get his hands on it. I don't want a fool in with me, capital or no capital."

"If he put Maurice away and made it look like natural death, he's not all that of a fool, L.J."

"Maybe not. Let's wait and see if he gets away with it."

"And what about . . . those?" asked Lil jerking her head towards the innocuous looking box.

"Back in the safe. Tomorrow I'll get Sid to parcel them up and send them off to Digby. That should tell us something. It would be rather a nice touch to enclose my visiting card. It's time Digby Seton and I had a little talk."

4

Dalgliesh closed the door of the Cortez Club behind him and gulped in the Soho air as if it were as sweet as the sea wind on Monksmere Head. Luker had always had this effect of seeming to contaminate the atmosphere. He was glad to be out of that stuffy little office and free from the stare of those dead eyes. It must have rained briefly while he was in the Club for the cars were hissing over a wet road and the pavement was tacky under his feet. Soho was wakening now and the narrow street was swirling its gaudy flotsam from kerb to kerb. A stiff breeze was blowing, drying the road as he watched. He wondered if it were blowing on Monksmere Head. Perhaps even now his aunt would be closing the shutters against the night.

Walking slowly towards Shaftesbury Avenue he pondered his next move. So far this dash to London, prompted by angry impulse, had told him little that he couldn't have learnt in greater comfort by staying in Suffolk. Even Max Gurney could have told his news over the telephone although Max was, of course, notoriously cautious. Dalgliesh didn't altogether regret his journey; but it had been a long day and he wasn't disposed to make it longer. It was the more irritating, therefore, to find himself harrassed by the conviction that there was still something to be done.

It was difficult to decide what. None of the possibilities was attractive. He could visit the fashionable and expensive flats where Latham lived and attempt to get something out of the hall porter but, in his present unofficial capacity, he was unlikely to succeed. Besides, Reckless or his men would have been there before him and if Latham's alibi could be broken they would have broken it. He could try his luck at the eminently respectable Bloomsbury Hotel where Eliza Marley

claimed to have spent last Tuesday night. There too his reception would hardly be cordial and, there too, Reckless would have been before him. He was getting a little tired of following in the Inspector's footsteps like a tame dog.

He could take a look at Justin Bryce's flat in the City; but there seemed little point in it. Since Bryce was still in Suffolk there could be no chance of seeing inside and he didn't imagine that there was much to be learned from an examination of the building itself. He already knew it well since it was one of the pleasanter architectural conceits in the City. Bryce lived over the offices of the *Monthly Critical Review* in a small eighteenth century courtyard off Fleet Street, so carefully preserved that it looked wholly artificial. Its only outlet to the street was through Pie Crust Passage, almost too narrow for a single man. Dalgliesh didn't know where Bryce garaged his car but it certainly wasn't in Pie Crust Court. He had a sudden fantastic vision of the little man staggering down Pie Crust Passage with Seton's body slung over his shoulder and stowing it in the back of his car under the interested gaze of the local traffic wardens and half the City police. He wished he could believe it.

There was, of course, another way to spend the evening. He could telephone Deborah Riscoe at her office—she would be almost due to leave—and ask her to join him at his flat. She would come, of course. Those days, sweet to the memory despite their occasional torments, when he could never be sure that she would come, were over now. Whatever else she might have planned for the evening, she would come. Then all the boredom, the irritation and the uncertainties would find at least a physical relief. And, tomorrow, the problem would still remain, casting its shadow between him and the first light.

Suddenly he made up his mind. He turned briskly towards Greek Street, hailed the first taxi that he saw, and asked to be put down outside Paddington Underground Station.

He decided to walk from Paddington Underground to Digby Seton's address. If Maurice Seton had come this way he might have taken a bus or even another taxi (had Reckless

checked on that, Dalgliesh wondered) but the chances were that he had walked. Dalgliesh timed himself. It took exactly sixteen minutes of fast walking before he arrived at the archway of brickwork and crumbling stucco which led into Carrington Mews. Maurice Seton might have taken longer.

The cobbled entrance was uninviting, ill-lit and smelt strongly of urine. Dalgliesh, unobserved, since the place was obviously deserted, passed under the archway into a wide yard lit only by a solitary and unshaded bulb over one of a double row of garages. The premises had apparently once been the headquarters of a driving school and a few tattered notices still clung to the garage doors. But they were dedicated now to a nobler purpose, the improvement of London's chronic housing shortage. More accurately, they were being converted into dark, under-sized and over-priced cottages soon, no doubt, to be advertized as "bijou town residences" to tenants or owners prepared to tolerate any expense or inconvenience for the status of a London address and the taste for contemporary chi-chi. The existing double garages were being halved to provide a downstairs room while retaining space for one small car, and the lofts enlarged to form a couple of cells for bedroom and bath.

Digby Seton's cottage was the only one completed and the decor was depressingly orthodox. It had an orange door with a brass knocker in the shape of a mermaid, window boxes at the two minute square windows, and a lamp in a wrought iron holder above the lintel. The lamp wasn't alight but this was hardly surprising since, as far as Dalgliesh could see, it wasn't connected to the power. It struck him as being coy without being attractive and vulgar without being functional; in this it was symbolic of the whole house. The orange window boxes were sagging with their weight of caked earth. They had been planted with chrysanthemums and, when fresh, their gaiety had no doubt justified another two guineas on the rent. But the flowers, once golden, were now faded and brittle, the dead leaves stank of decay.

He prowled around the cobbled yard shining his pocket torch into the dark eyes of the windows. The two adjoining

garages with the rooms above were now being modernized. The interiors had been completely stripped and the double garage doors taken off so that he could step inside the shell and note with interest that there was to be a connecting door between the sitting room and the garage. Everywhere there was a smell of new timber, paint and brickdust. The district had a long way to go, of course, before it became socially acceptable let alone fashionable, but it was on the way up. Digby had merely been the first to sniff the returning tide.

And that, of course, led to the intriguing question of why exactly he had come here. It wasn't an unlikely house for him to choose. In many ways this squalid little status symbol was entirely appropriate to Digby. But wasn't it altogether too much of a coincidence that he had chosen a house so convenient for murder? It was within twenty minutes walk of where Maurice Seton had been put down; it was in a dark inconspicuous yard which, once the workmen had left, would be uninhabited except for Digby; it had a garage with a direct door into the house itself. And there was another fact, perhaps the most significant of all. Digby Seton had only recently moved and he hadn't given his new address to anyone at Monksmere. When she had wanted to contact him after Maurice's death Sylvia Kedge hadn't known where to find him. And this meant that Maurice, if indeed he had been sent to Carrington Mews by Lily Coombs, wouldn't have known that it was Digby who was waiting for him. Certainly, Maurice had gone from the Cortez Club to his death. And Digby was the only suspect who was connected with the Club.

But all this was no more than suspicion. Nowhere was there any proof. There was no evidence that Lil had directed Maurice here; even if she had, Lil was capable of an obstinate adherence to a good story that would have been commendable in a better cause. It would need stronger measures than any English police force would tolerate to persuade Lil to talk. There was no proof that Maurice had been in the Mews. Dalgliesh couldn't get into the locked cottage but Reckless or his men would have been over it; if there had been anything

to find they would have found it. There wasn't even any proof that Maurice had been murdered. Reckless didn't believe it, the Chief Constable didn't believe it and probably no one else did except Adam Dalgliesh, stupidly persistent, blindly following his hunch in the teeth of the evidence. And, if Maurice had been murdered, the biggest problem remained. He had died at midnight when Digby Seton and indeed most of the other suspects, had an unbreakable alibi. Until one could discover the "how" it was pointless to concentrate on the "who".

Dalgliesh shone his torch for the last time round the deserted yard, over the stacked timber under its tarpaulin cover, the piles of new bricks, the garage doors with their peeling notices. Then he passed under the arch as silently as he had entered and made his way to Lexington Street and his car.

It was just outside Ipswich that the tiredness hit him and he knew that it wouldn't be safe to drive much further. He needed food. It had been a long time since his substantial lunch with Max and he had eaten nothing since. He was perfectly happy to spend the night in a lay-by but not to wake in the early hours with a gnawing hunger and no chance of an early breakfast. But the problem was that it was too late for a pub and he had no intention of stopping at a country club or small hotel to do battle with the proprietor's fixed determination to serve meals only at regulated hours and at a price and quality to deter all but the starving. After a mile or two, however, he found an all night transport cafe, advertised by the black phalanx of lorries parked around its doors and the blaze of light from its low windows. The place was full, the air thick with smoke and jangling with talk and the cacophony of the juke box, but he sat undisturbed at a corner table, bare-topped but clean, and was served with a plate of eggs, sausage and crisply fried chips and a pint mug of hot, sweet tea.

Afterwards he went in search of the telephone, inconveniently placed in a narrow passage between the kitchen and the parking yard, and put through a call to Pentlands. There was no need to telephone. His aunt wasn't expecting him back at any particular time. But he was suddenly uneasy about

her and determined if there were no reply to drive on. He told himself that it was an irrational anxiety. She might well be dining at Priory House or even be taking a solitary walk along the beach. He had discovered nothing to suggest that she was in any danger; but still there was this sense that all was not well. It was probably only the result of weariness and frustration, but he had to know.

It seemed an unusually long time before she answered and he heard the quiet, familiar voice. If she was surprised at his call she didn't say so. They spoke briefly against the clatter of washing-up and the roar of departing lorries. When he replaced the receiver he felt happier but still uneasy. She had promised him to bolt the cottage door tonight—thank God she wasn't the woman to argue, question or laugh over a simple request—and he could do no more. He was half irritated by this worry which he knew to be unreasonable; otherwise, whatever his tiredness, he must have driven on.

Before leaving the telephone booth a thought struck him and he searched in his pocket for a further supply of coins. It took longer to get through this time and the line wasn't clear. But eventually he heard Plant's voice and asked his question. Yes, Mr. Dalgliesh was quite right. Plant had telephoned Seton House on Wednesday night. He was sorry that he hadn't thought to mention it. Actually he had been phoning about every three hours that evening in the hope of getting Mr. Seton. About what time? Well, as far as he could remember at about six, nine and twelve o'clock. Not at all. Plant was only too glad to have been of help.

Was it any help? Dalgliesh wondered. It proved nothing except that Plant's unanswered call could have been the ringing telephone heard by Elizabeth Marley when she left Digby at Seton House. The time was about right and Reckless hadn't been able to trace the other call. But that didn't mean that no one had made it. He would need stronger evidence than this to prove Digby Seton a liar.

Ten minutes later Dalgliesh parked under the shelter of the hedge at the next lay-by and settled himself in the car as comfortably as was possible for a man of his height. Despite

the pint of tea and the indigestible supper sleep came almost immediately and for a few hours it was deep and dreamless. He was awoken by a spatter of gravel against the car windows and the high keening of the wind. His watch showed three-fifteen. A gale was blowing and, even in the shelter of the hedge, the car was rocking gently. The clouds were scudding across the moon like black furies and the high branches of the hedge, dark against the sky, were groaning and curtseying like a chorus row of demented witches. He eased himself out of the car and took a short walk down the deserted road. Leaning against a gate he gazed out over the dark flat fields, taking the force of the wind full in his face so that it was difficult to breathe. He felt as he had as a boy on one of his solitary cycling trips when he would leave his small tent to walk in the night. It had been one of his greatest pleasures, this sense of complete loneliness, of being not only without a companion but with the knowledge that no one in the world knew exactly where he was. It was a solitude of the spirit as well as of the body. Shutting his eyes and smelling the rich dampness of grass and earth, he could imagine himself back in childhood, the smells were the same, the night was familiar, the pleasure was as keen.

Half an hour later he settled himself to sleep again. But before he dropped into the first layer of unconsciousness, something happened. He had been thinking drowsily and without effort of Seton's murder. It had been no more than the mind's slow recapitulation of the past day. And suddenly, inexplicably, he knew how it could have been done.

Book Three

I

It was just after nine o'clock when Dalgliesh got back to Pentlands. The cottage was empty, and for a moment, he felt again the foreboding of the night. Then he saw the note on the kitchen table. His aunt had breakfasted early and was walking along the shore towards Sizewell. There was a jug of coffee ready to be reheated and the breakfast table was laid for one. Dalgliesh smiled. This was typical of his aunt. It was her habit to take a morning walk along the beach and it would never occur to her to vary the routine merely because her nephew was flying backwards and forwards between London and Monksmere in chase of a murderer and might wish her to be immediately available to hear his news. Nor would she imagine that a healthy male was incapable of getting his own breakfast. But, as always at Pentlands, the essential comforts were there, the kitchen was warm and welcoming, the coffee strong, and there was a blue bowl of new laid eggs and a batch of home-baked rolls still warm from the oven. His aunt had obviously been up early. Dalgliesh breakfasted quickly, then decided to stretch his car cramped legs by walking along the shore to meet her.

He jumped his way down the uneven path of sand and rock which led from Pentlands to the beach. The leaping sea was white capped to the horizon, a brown-grey waste of heaving water, empty of sails and with only the sturdy silhouette of a coaster against the skyline. The tide was coming in fast. Lurching over the stones of the upper beach, he found the ridge of fine shingle which ran half-way between the sea's edge and the plateau of marram grass which fringed the marshes. Here walking was easier although, from time to time, he was forced

to turn his back to the wind and fight for breath. Buffetted and foam-flecked, he squelched onward over the shingle finding the occasional and welcome stretch of firm serrated sand, and pausing from time to time to watch the smooth green underbelly of the waves as they rose in their last curve before crashing at his feet, in a tumult of flying shingle and stinging spray. It was a lonely shore, empty and desolate, like the last fringes of the world. It evoked no memories, cosily nostalgic, of the enchantments of childhood holidays by the sea. Here were no rockpools to explore, no exotic shells, no breakwaters festooned with sea weed, no long stretches of yellow sand sliced by innumerable spades. Here was nothing but sea, sky and marshland, an empty beach with little to mark the miles of outspate shingle but the occasional tangle of tar splotched drift wood and the rusting spikes of old fortifications. Dalgliesh loved this emptiness, this fusion of sea and sky. But today the place held no peace for him. He saw it suddenly with new eyes, a shore alien, eerie, utterly desolate. The unease of the night before took hold of him and he was glad to see, rising from the sand dunes, the familiar figure of his aunt braced like a flag staff against the wind, the edges of her red scarf flying.

She saw him almost immediately and came towards him. As they met and stood together, fighting for breath against a sudden gust of wind, there was a harsh "kraaank" and two heron flew low overhead, pounding the air with heavy, laborious wings. Dalgliesh watched their flight. Their long necks were drawn in, their delicate brown legs stretched straight behind them like a slipstream.

"Heron," he said with mock triumph.

Jane Dalgliesh laughed and handed him her field glasses.

"But what do you make of these?"

A small flock of grey-brown waders was twittering on the edge of the shingle. Before Dalgliesh had time to note more than their white rumps and blackish, down-turned beaks, the birds rose in one swift direct flight and faded into the wind like a wisp of thin white smoke.

"Dunlin?" he hazarded.

"I thought you might say dunlin. They're very similar. No, those were curlew-sandpipers."

"But the last time you showed me a curlew-sandpiper it had pink plumage," protested Dalgliesh.

"That was last summer. In the autumn they take on the buffish plumage of the young birds. That's why they look so like the dunlin. . . . Did you have a successful time in London?"

Dalgliesh said:

"Most of the day I spent following rather ineffectually in Reckless's footsteps. But during the course of a too-large lunch with Max Gurney at the Cadaver Club I learnt something new. Seton was proposing to use virtually all his capital to endow a literary prize. Having given up hope of personal fame he was proposing to buy a vicarious immortality. He wasn't skimping the price, either. Incidentally I have an idea now how Seton was killed but as it's going to be virtually impossible to prove, I don't think Reckless will thank me for it. I suppose I'd better phone him as soon as we get back."

He spoke without enthusiasm. Jane Dalgliesh cast a glance at him but asked no questions, and quickly turned her face away in case he should see, and be irritated by, her obvious concern.

"Did Digby know that he was likely to be done out of his inheritance?" she asked.

"Apparently no one knew except Max. The odd thing is that Seton wrote to him about it and typed the letter himself by the look of it. Yet Reckless didn't find the carbon at Seton House. He would certainly have mentioned it if he had. And he would certainly have questioned Sylvia Kedge and Digby to find out whether they knew."

"If Maurice wanted to keep his intention secret, wouldn't he have typed the letter without taking a carbon?" suggested Miss Dalgliesh.

"He took a carbon, all right. The bottom edge of the carbon got turned in when he put the paper into the machine and the last few words appear on the back of the letter. There's also a faint smear of carbon on the top edge. He might have

decided later to destroy the copy but he was meticulous about his affairs and it doesn't seem likely. Incidentally, this isn't the only mystery about carbons. Seton is supposed to have typed that passage about his hero's visit to the Cortez Club while he was staying in London. But the servant at the Cadaver Club says that there were no carbon copies found in his room. So what happened to them?"

His aunt thought for a moment. This was the first time he had ever discussed a case with her and she was intrigued and a little flattered until she remembered that it wasn't, of course, his case. Reckless was the one responsible. It was Reckless who would have to decide the significance, if any, of those missing carbons at the Cadaver. But she was surprised at her own interest in the problem. She said:

"There are several possibilities, I suppose. Perhaps Seton didn't take carbons. In view of his meticulous habits I think that unlikely. Or perhaps he, or someone who had access to his room, destroyed them. Or perhaps the manuscript which Sylvia produced wasn't the one Seton actually sent her. I expect that Reckless has checked with the postman that a long, buff envelope was delivered to her but we've only her word that it contained the manuscript. And, if it did, presumably someone who knew that Seton was staying at the Club could have substituted one set of papers for another sometime between the sticking down of the envelope and its posting. Or could they? Do we know if Seton put the envelope out for posting where other people could see it? Or did he take it immediately to the post himself?"

"This was one of the things I asked Plant. No one at the Cadaver posted anything for Seton. But the envelope could have been left in his room long enough for someone to get at it. Or he could have handed it to someone else to post. But surely no one could have relied on that? And we know that this wasn't an unpremeditated killing. At least, I know it. I've yet to convince Reckless that it was a killing at all."

His aunt said: "Isn't there another possibility? We know that Seton couldn't have posted the second manuscript, the one describing the body drifting to shore. He was dead by

then. And we've no reason to suppose that he even wrote it. We've only got Sylvia Kedge's word that it was his work."

"I think he wrote it," said Dalgliesh. "When Max Gurney showed me Seton's letter I recognized the typing. The same man typed the second manuscript."

As he spoke they were moving instinctively out of the bite of the wind into the shelter of the sunken lane which ran between the sand dunes and the bird sanctuary. Some twenty yards further on was the third in a series of small observation hides which overlooked the sanctuary. This particular hide made a natural turning point to their beach walks and Dalgliesh did not need to ask his aunt whether they should go in. To spend ten minutes scanning the reed beds through his aunt's binoculars and sheltering from the bitter east coast winds had become one of those rituals which were part of an autumn visit to Monksmere. The hide was typical of its kind, a rough wooden shelter, reed thatched, with a bench high enough to support tired thighs along the back wall and a slit at eye level giving a wide view over the marshes. In summer it smelt strongly of sun-baked wood, moist earth and lush grasses. Even in the cold months, this warmth lingered, as if all the heat and smells of summer were trapped within its wooden walls.

They had reached the hide and Miss Dalgliesh was about to step first through the narrow entrance when Dalgliesh suddenly said:

"No! Wait!" A minute earlier he had been strolling along almost in a dream. Now, suddenly, his brain awoke to the significance of the signs which his trained senses had subconsciously noted: the single line of male footprints leading from the sand dusted lane to the hide entrance, a trace on the wind of a sick stench which had nothing to do with the smell of earth or grasses. As his aunt paused he slipped in front of her and stood in the entrance of the hide.

His tall body blocked most of the light from the narrow entrance so that he smelt death before he saw it. The stench of sour vomit, blood and diarrhoea stung his nostrils as if the air of the little hut was saturated with corruption and evil. The

smell was not unfamiliar to him but, as always, he had to fight against a momentary and intolerable urge to be sick. Then he bent down, the light streamed in behind him and he saw the body clearly for the first time.

Digby Seton had crawled like a dog into the corner of the hut to die and he had not died easily. The pathetic body, rigid and cold, was huddled along the far wall, the knees drawn up almost to the chin, the head twisted upwards as if the glazed eyes had made one last despairing effort to catch the light. In his agony he had bitten his bottom lip almost in two and a stream of blood, blackened now, had mixed with the vomit which encrusted his chin and the lapels of the once smart Melton overcoat. He had dug in the earth of the hut with torn and bleeding hands, smearing it over his face and hair and stuffing it even into his mouth as if in a last delirious craving for coolness and water. Six inches from his body lay his hip flask, the top unscrewed.

Dalgliesh heard his aunt's calm voice.

"Who is it, Adam?"

"Digby Seton. No, don't come in. There's nothing we can do for him. He's been dead for twelve hours at least; from some irritant poison by the look of it, poor devil."

He heard her sigh and she muttered something that he could not catch. Then she said:

"Shall I go for Inspector Reckless or would you rather I stayed here?"

"You go, if you will. I'll keep an eye on this place."

It was possible that he could have saved ten or fifteen minutes by going himself but there was nothing that anyone could do now to help Seton and he had no intention of leaving her alone in this stinking place of death. And she was a fast and strong walker; there would be little time wasted.

She set off at once and he watched her until a turn in the lane hid her from sight. Then he made his way to the top of the sand dunes and found a sheltered hollow in which to sit, his back wedged against a clump of marram grass. From this point of vantage he could keep the hide under observation and could see on his right the whole sweep of the beach and

on his left the sunken lane. From time to time he caught a glimpse of his aunt's tall striding figure. She seemed to be making excellent time but it would be at least three quarters of an hour before Reckless and his men, laden with stretcher and their paraphernalia, came into view. There was no spot closer to the beach to bring an ambulance than Pentlands and no shorter way to the hide than by the lane. Burdened with their equipment, they would have a hard time of it against the wind.

Dalgliesh had spent only a few minutes in the hide but every detail was sharp and clear in his mind. He had no doubt that Digby Seton had been murdered. Although he had not searched the body—that was a job for Reckless—nor even touched it except to verify briefly that it was cold and that rigor mortis was well established, he had little doubt that no suicide note would be found. Digby Seton, that facile, uncomplicated, rather stupid young man, as pleased with his fortune as a child with a new toy and full of happy plans for bigger and brighter night clubs, was hardly a likely suicide risk. And even Digby had sense enough to know that there were easier ways of dying than to have one's stomach and guts burnt away with poison. There had been no bottle near the body except the hip flask. Almost certainly that had contained the stuff. The dose must have been very large. Dalgliesh's mind ranged over the possibilities. Arsenic? Antimony? Mercury? Lead? All could produce those signs. But this was mere speculation. In time the pathologists would have all the answers; the name of the poison, the dose, the time it had taken for Seton to die. And the rest would be for Reckless.

But assuming that the stuff had been put in the hip flask, who was a likely suspect? Someone who had access both to the poison and the flask. That was obvious. Someone who knew the victim well; knew that Digby, alone and bored, wouldn't be able to resist taking a pull at the flask before facing the bitter wind and the long walk home. And that implied someone who could persuade him to a rendezvous at the hide. Why else should he have gone there? No one at

Monksmere had ever known Digby Seton to be interested in bird watching or in walking. And he had not been dressed for either activity. Nor had he carried binoculars. This was murder all right. Even Reckless would hardly suggest that Digby Seton had died naturally or that someone with a perverted sense of humour had put his corpse in the hide with the object of inconveniencing Adam Dalgliesh and his aunt.

Dalgliesh had no doubt that the two murders were related but he was struck with their dissimilarity. It was as if two different minds were at work. The killing of Maurice Seton had been almost unnecessarily complicated. Although it might still be difficult to prove that the crime was indeed murder in face of the pathologist's report of death from natural causes, there was little else natural about it. The difficulty was not lack of clues. There were too many. It was as if the murderer had needed to demonstrate his cleverness as much as he had needed to kill Seton. But this new killing was simpler, more direct. There could be no possibility here of a verdict of death from natural causes. This murderer was not trying any double bluff. There hadn't even been an attempt to make it look like suicide, to suggest that Digby had killed himself in a fit of remorse over his brother's death. Admittedly it wouldn't have been easy to fake a suicide but Dalgliesh thought it significant that no attempt had been made. And he was beginning to understand why. He could think of one vital reason why this killer should want to avoid any suggestion that Digby had killed himself through remorse or had been in any way concerned in his brother's death.

Dalgliesh was surprisingly warm and comfortable in the shelter of the marram grass. He could hear the wind whistling in the dunes and the insistent thudding of the tide. But the tall clumps of grass shielded him so effectively that he had an odd sense of isolation as if the roar of wind and sea was coming from far away. Through the thin screen of grasses he could see the hide, a familiar, ordinary, primitive hut outwardly no different from half a dozen others which fringed the bird sanctuary. He could almost persuade himself that

it was no different. Touched by this sense of isolation and unreality he had to resist an absurd impulse to see if Seton's body were really there.

Jane Dalgliesh must have made good time. It was less than forty-five minutes before he caught the first glimpse of approaching figures in the lane. The straggling group came briefly into view and then they were hidden again behind the dunes. The second time he glimpsed them they seemed no nearer. Then, unexpectedly, they turned the last bend in the lane and were with him. He saw a windblown, incongruous little group, burdened with equipment and having the air of a badly organized and slightly demoralized expedition. Reckless was there, of course, grim-faced and rigid with anger, the ubiquitous raincoat buttoned to his chin. He had with him his sergeant, the police surgeon, a photographer and two young detective constables, carrying a stretcher and a rolled canvas shield. Few words were exchanged. Dalgliesh bellowed his report in the Inspector's ear and then went back to his shelter in the dunes and left them to it. This wasn't his job. There was no sense in having an extra pair of feet churning up the moist sand around the hide. The men got to work. There was much shouting and gesticulating. The wind, as if in spite, had risen to a crescendo on their arrival and even in the comparative shelter of the lane, it was hard to make oneself heard. Reckless and the doctor disappeared into the hide. There at least, thought Dalgliesh, it would be sheltered enough. Sheltered, airless and stinking of death. They were welcome to it. After about five minutes they reappeared and the photographer, tallest of the group, bent nearly double and edged his equipment through the opening. Meanwhile the two constables were making ineffective efforts to get up a screen around the hide. The canvas leaped and whirled in their hands and whipped around their ankles with every gust of wind. Dalgliesh wondered why they bothered. There were hardly likely to be many sightseers on this lonely shore nor were the sandy approaches to the hide likely to yield further clues. There were only three sets of prints lead-

ing to the door; his own, those of his aunt, and the third set which were presumably Digby Seton's. They had already been measured and photographed and soon, no doubt, the flying sand would obliterate them completely.

It was half an hour before they got the corpse out of the hide and placed on the stretcher. As the constables struggled to hold down the mackintosh covers while the straps were applied, Reckless came over to Dalgliesh. He said:

"A friend of yours telephoned me yesterday afternoon. A Mister Max Gurney. It appears he's been keeping to himself some interesting information about Maurice Seton's Will."

It was an unexpected opening. Dalgliesh said:

"I lunched with him and he asked me whether he ought to get in touch with you."

"So he said. You'd imagine he would be capable of thinking it out for himself. Seton was found dead with marks of violence on the body. It stands to reason we'd be interested in the money side."

"Perhaps he shares your view that it was a natural death," suggested Dalgliesh.

"Maybe. But that's hardly his business. Anyway, he's told us now and it was news to me. There was no record of it at Seton House."

Dalgliesh said:

"Seton took a carbon of the letter. Gurney will be posting the original to you and you'll find the carbon markings on the back. Someone destroyed the copy, presumably."

Reckless said gloomily:

"Someone. Perhaps Seton himself. I haven't changed my mind yet about that killing, Mr. Dalgliesh. But you could be right. Especially in view of this." He jerked his head towards the stretcher which the two policemen squatting at the poles, were now bracing themselves to raise. "There's no doubt about this one. This is murder, all right. So we take our choice. One murderer and one unpleasant practical joker. Or one murderer and two crimes. Or two murderers."

Dalgliesh suggested that this last was unlikely in such a small community.

"But possible, Mr. Dalgliesh. After all, the two deaths haven't much in common. There's nothing particularly subtle or ingenious about this killing. Just a whacking great dose of poison in Seton's hip flask and the knowledge that, sooner or later, he'd take a swig at it. All the murderer had to do was ensure that he wasn't too close to medical help when it happened. Not that it would have done him much good by the look of it."

Dalgliesh wondered how the killer had succeeded in luring Seton to the hide. Had it been done by persuasion or by threats? Was Seton expecting to meet a friend or an enemy? If the latter, was he the sort of man to go alone and undefended? But suppose it were a different kind of assignation? For how many people at Monksmere would Digby Seton have been ready to walk two miles over rough ground on a cold autumn day and in the teeth of a rising gale?

The stretcher was moving forward now. One of the constables had apparently been instructed to stay on guard at the hide. The rest of the party fell into line behind the corpse like an escort of shabby and ill-assorted mourners. Dalgliesh and Reckless walked together and in silence. Ahead, the shrouded lump on the stretcher swayed gently from side to side as the bearers picked their way over the ridges in the lane. The edges of the canvas flapped rhythmically like a sail in the wind and overhead a sea bird hovered over the corpse, screaming like a soul in pain, before rising in a wide curve to disappear over the marshes.

2

It was early evening before Dalgliesh saw Reckless alone. The Inspector had spent the afternoon interviewing his suspects and checking on Digby Seton's movements during the past few days. He arrived at Pentlands just before six o'clock, ostensibly to ask Miss Dalgliesh again if she had seen anyone walking along the shore towards Sizewell on the previous day and whether she had any idea what could have induced Digby Seton to visit the hide. Both questions had been answered earlier when Dalgliesh and his aunt had met Reckless at the Green Man to give their formal account of the finding of the body. Jane Dalgliesh had stated that she had spent the whole of Monday evening at Pentlands and had seen no one. But then, as she had pointed out, it would be possible for Digby—or indeed, anyone else—to have walked to the hide by the sunken lane behind the sand dunes or by way of the beach, and this path for most of its length wasn't visible from Pentlands.

"All the same," said Reckless obstinately, "he must have come past your cottage to get into the lane. Would that really be possible without you seeing him?"

"Oh perfectly, provided he kept close in to the cliffs. There is a strip of about twenty yards between my access to the beach and the beginning of the lane when I might have glimpsed him. But I didn't. Perhaps he wanted to avoid notice and chose his moment to slip past."

Reckless muttered as if thinking aloud.

"And that suggests a secret assignation. Well, we suspect that. He wasn't the man to go bird watching on his own. Besides, it must have been dusk before he set off. Miss

Kedge said that he got his own tea at Seton House yesterday. She found the dirty tea things waiting for her to wash up this morning."

"But no supper?" enquired Miss Dalgliesh.

"No supper, Miss Dalgliesh. It looks as if he died before he had his evening meal. But the P.M. will tell us more, of course."

Jane Dalgliesh made her excuses and went into the kitchen to prepare dinner. Dalgliesh guessed that she thought it tactful to leave him alone with Reckless. As soon as the door closed behind her, he asked:

"Who saw him last?"

"Latham and Bryce. But nearly everyone admits to having spent some time yesterday with him. Miss Kedge saw him shortly after breakfast when she went up to the house to do her chores. He has kept her on as a kind of secretary-housemaid. Making use of her rather as his half-brother did, I imagine. Then he lunched with Miss Calthrop and her niece at Rosemary Cottage and left shortly after three. He called in on Bryce on his way home to Seton House to gossip about the return of your aunt's chopper and to try to find out what you were doing in London. That little trip seems to have aroused general interest. Latham was with Bryce at the time and the three of them were together until Seton left shortly after four."

"What was he wearing?"

"The clothes he was found in. He could have carried his flask in his jacket, trousers or overcoat pocket. He took the coat off, of course, at Rosemary Cottage and Miss Calthrop hung it in the hall cupboard. At Bryce's place he slung it over a chair. No one admits to seeing the flask. As I see it, any of them could have put in the poison, Kedge, Calthrop, Marley, Bryce or Latham. Any of them. And it needn't have been yesterday." He did not, Dalgliesh noted, add Miss Dalgliesh's name; but that didn't mean that she wasn't on the list. Reckless went on:

"I can't make much headway, of course, until I get the P.M. and know what the poison was. Then we shall get mov-

ing. It shouldn't be too difficult to prove possession. This wasn't the kind of stuff you get prescribed on E.C.10 or buy over the chemist's counter."

Dalgliesh thought he could guess what the poison was and where it had come from. But he said nothing. There had already been too much theorizing in advance of the facts and he judged it wiser to wait for the post-mortem. But if he were right, Reckless wasn't going to find it so easy to prove possession. Nearly everyone at Monksmere had access to this particular source. He began to feel rather sorry for the Inspector.

They sat together in silence for a minute. It wasn't a companionable silence. Dalgliesh could sense the stress between them. He couldn't guess what Reckless was feeling, he could only recognize with a kind of hopeless irritation his own awkwardness and dislike. He looked across at the Inspector's face with detached interest, building up the features in his mind as he might an identikit picture, observing the flatness of the wide cheekbones, the patch of white smooth-looking skin at each side of the mouth, the downward fold at the corners of the eyes and the little rhythmic twitch at the upper lid which was the only sign that the man had nerves. The face was uncompromising in its ordinariness, its anonymity. And yet, sitting there in that grubby raincoat, his face grey with tiredness, he still had force and personality. It might not be a personality which others found appealing. But it was there.

Suddenly Reckless, as if making up his mind to something, said harshly. "The Chief Constable wants to call in the Yard. He's sleeping on it. But I think he's already made up his mind. And there are those who will say it's none too soon."

Dalgliesh could find nothing appropriate to say to this. Reckless, still not looking at him, added:

"He seems to take your view, that the two crimes are connected."

Dalgliesh wondered whether he was being accused of trying to influence the Chief Constable. He couldn't recall

expressing this view to Reckless but it seemed to him obvious. He said so and added:

"When I was in London yesterday it came to me how Maurice Seton could have been killed. It's little more than conjecture at present and God knows how you'll be able to prove it. But I think I know how it was done."

Briefly he outlined his theory, morbidly sensitive to every inflection in his own voice which the Inspector might interpret as criticism or self-congratulation. His story was received in silence. Then Reckless said:

"What put you on to that, Mr. Dalgliesh?"

"I'm not altogether sure. A number of small things I suppose. The terms of Seton's Will; the way he behaved at that basement table in the Cortez Club, his insistence on having one particular room whenever he stayed at the Cadaver Club; the architecture of his house even."

Reckless said:

"It's possible, I suppose. But without a confession I'll never prove it unless someone panics."

"You could look for the weapon."

"A funny kind of weapon, Mr. Dalgliesh."

"But a weapon and a lethal one."

Reckless drew an ordnance map from his pocket and spread it out on the table. Together they bent their heads over it, the Inspector's pencil hovering above the twenty mile radius around Monksmere.

"Here?" he asked.

"Or here. If I were the killer I'd look for deep water."

Reckless said:

"Not the sea, though. It might get washed up while we could still identify it. Not that I think it likely anyone would have connected it with the crime."

"But you might have. And the murderer couldn't risk that. Better get rid of it where there was every chance it wouldn't be found, or would be found too late. Failing an old mine shaft I'd have looked for a sluice or river."

The pencil came down and Reckless made three small crosses.

"We'll try here first Mr. Dalgliesh. And I hope to God you're right. Otherwise with this second death on our hands, it's all going to be a waste of time."

Without another word, he folded the map and was gone.

3

After dinner there was more company. Celia Calthrop, her niece, Latham and Bryce arrived within a short time of each other, driving or fighting their way through the rising storm to seek a spurious safety at Jane Dalgliesh's fireside. Perhaps, thought Dalgliesh, they could neither bear their own company nor feel at ease with each other. This at least was neutral ground, offering the comforting illusion of normality, the age-old protection of light and a warm fire against the darkness and enmity of the night. It certainly wasn't a time for the nervous or imaginative to be alone. The wind was alternately howling and moaning across the headland and a fast running tide was thundering up the beach driving the shingle in ridges before it. Even from the sitting room at Pentlands he could hear its long withdrawing sigh. From time to time a fitful moon cast its dead light over Monksmere so that the storm became visible and he could see, from the cottage windows, the stunted trees writhing and struggling as if in agony and the whole wilderness of sea lying white and turbulent under the sky.

The uninvited guests, their heads down, fought their way up the path to Miss Dalgliesh's door with the desperation of a fugitive band.

By half-past eight they had all arrived. No one had troubled to fetch Sylvia Kedge, but apart from her the little company of five nights earlier was met again. And Dalgliesh was struck by the difference in them. Analysing it, he realized that they looked ten years older. Five nights ago they had been only mildly concerned and a little intrigued by Seton's disappearance. Now they were anxious and shaken, possessed by images of blood and death from which they had little hope of shaking

free. Behind the brave assumptions of ease, the rather desperate attempts at normality, he could smell fear.

Maurice Seton had died in London and it was still theoretically possible to believe that he had died naturally or that someone in London was responsible for his murder if not for the mutilation of his body. But Digby's death was on home ground and no one could pretend that there had been anything natural about it. But Celia Calthrop, apparently, was still prepared to try. She was squatting in the fireside chair, knees gracelessly splayed, her hands restless in the heavy lap.

"It's the most terrible tragedy. Poor boy! I don't suppose we shall ever know what drove him to it. And he had everything to live for: youth, money, talent, looks, charm."

This startlingly unrealistic assessment of Digby Seton was received in silence. Then Bryce said:

"I grant you he had money, Celia. Or the prospect of it anyway. Otherwise one did tend to think of poor Digby as a whey-faced, ineffectual, conceited, vulgar little twit. Not that one bore him the least ill-will. Nor, incidently, does one believe that he killed himself."

Latham burst out impatiently:

"Of course he didn't! And Celia doesn't even believe it either! So why not be honest for a change, Celia? Why not admit that you're as scared as the rest of us?"

Celia said with dignity:

"I'm not in the least scared."

"Oh, but you ought to be!" Bryce's gnome-like face was creased with mischief, his eyes sparkled up at her. He looked suddenly less harassed, less like a tired old man.

"After all, you're the one who gains by his death. There should be a nice little sum left even after double death duties. And Digby's been a fairly regular visitor to you recently hasn't he? Didn't he lunch with you yesterday? You must have had plenty of opportunities to slip a little something into his flask. You were the one who told us that he always carried it. In this very room. Remember?"

"And where am I supposed to have got hold of arsenic?"

"Ah—but we don't know yet that it was arsenic Celia!

That's exactly the kind of remark that you shouldn't make. It doesn't matter in front of Oliver and me but the Inspector may get wrong ideas. I do hope you haven't been talking to him about arsenic."

"I haven't been talking to him about anything. I've merely answered his questions as fully and honestly as I can. I suggest you and Oliver do the same. And I don't know why you're so keen to prove Digby was murdered. It's this morbid love you both have for looking on the dark side."

Latham said dryly:

"Just a morbid love of looking facts in the face."

But Celia was undaunted:

"Well, if it were murder, all I can say is that Jane Dalgliesh was very lucky to have Adam with her when she found the body. Otherwise people might begin to think. But a C.I.D. Superintendent—well, naturally he knows how important it is not to disturb anything or tamper with the evidence."

Dalgliesh, too fascinated by the enormity of the remark and Celia's capacity for self-deception to make his protest, wondered whether she had forgotten that he was there. The others seemed to have forgotten too.

"What might people begin to think?" asked Latham quietly; Bryce laughed.

"You can't seriously suspect Miss Dalgliesh, Celia! If so you're shortly going to be faced with the delicate problem of etiquette. Your hostess is at this moment preparing coffee for you with her own hand. Do you drink it gracefully, or pour it surreptitiously into the flower vase?"

Suddenly Eliza Marley swung round at them:

"For God's sake shut up, both of you! Digby Seton's dead and he died horribly. You may not have liked him but he was a human being. What's more he knew how to enjoy life in his own way. It may not have been your way but what of it? He was happy planning his horrible nightclubs and deciding how to spend his money. You may despise that but he wasn't doing you any harm. And now he's dead. And one of us murdered him. I don't happen to find that amusing."

"My dear, don't distress yourself." Celia's voice had taken

on the vibrant, emotional tone which she now almost unconsciously assumed when dictating the more highly-
charged passages in her novels.

"We're all used to Justin by now. Neither he nor Oliver
cared one whit for Maurice or Digby so it's no use expecting
them to behave with ordinary decency, let alone respect. I'm
afraid they care for no one but themselves. It's pure selfishness, of course. Selfishness and envy. Neither of them has
ever forgiven Maurice for being a creative writer when all
they're fit for is to criticise other people's work and batten
on other men's talent. You see it every day; the envy of the
literary parasite for the creative artist. Remember what
happened to Maurice's play. Oliver killed it because he
couldn't bear to see it succeed."

"Oh that!" Latham laughed. "My dear Celia, if Maurice
wanted to indulge in emotional catharsis he should have consulted a psychiatrist, not inflicted it on the public in the guise
of a play. There are three essentials for any play-wright, and
Maurice Seton hadn't one of them. He must be able to write
dialogue, he must understand what is meant by dramatic conflict, and he must know something about stage-craft."

This was no more than Latham's professional theme song
and Celia was unimpressed.

"Please don't talk to me about craftsmanship, Oliver. When
you have produced a work which shows the slightest sign of
original creative talent there will be some point in discussing
craftsmanship. And that goes for you too Justin."

"What about my novel?" demanded Bryce, affronted.

Celia cast him a long-suffering look and sighed deeply. She
was obviously not prepared to comment on Bryce's novel.
Dalgliesh recalled the work in question; a short exercise in
sensitivity which had been well received but which Bryce
had apparently never found the energy to repeat. He heard
Eliza Marley's laugh.

"Isn't that the book the reviewers said had the intensity and
the sensitivity of a short story? Hardly surprising when
essentially that was all it was. Even I could keep the sensitivity
going for a hundred and fifty pages."

Dalgliesh did not wait to hear more than Bryce's first protesting wail. Predictably the argument was degenerating into literary abuse. He wasn't surprised, having noticed this tendency before in his writing friends; but he had no wish to get involved. At any moment now they would be canvassing his opinion and his own verse no doubt would be subject to the devastating candour of the young. True, the argument appeared to be taking their minds from the subject of murder but there were more agreeable ways of getting through the evening.

Holding the door open for his aunt as she came in with the tray of coffee, he took the opportunity to slip away. It was perhaps a little unkind to abandon her just at this moment to the contentions of her guests but he didn't doubt her capacity to survive. He was less sure of his own.

His room was still and very quiet, insulated by sound building and oak boards from the jabber of the dissenting voices below. He unlatched the window on the seaward wall and forced it open with both hands against the blast of the gale. The wind rushed into the room swirling the bed cover into folds, sweeping the papers from his desk and rustling the pages of his bedside Jane Austen like a giant hand. It took his breath away so that he leaned gasping against the window ledge, welcoming the sting of spray on his face and tasting the salt drying on his lips. When he closed the window the silence seemed absolute. The thundering surf receded and faded like the far-away moaning on another shore.

The room was cold. He hitched his dressing gown around his shoulders and switched on one bar of the electric fire. Then he gathered up the scattered sheets of paper and replaced them with obsessive care, sheet on sheet, on the small writing table. The square white pages seemed to reproach him and he remembered that he hadn't written to Deborah. It wasn't that he had been too indolent, too busy or too preoccupied with the problem of Seton's murder. He knew perfectly well what had held him back. It was a cowardly reluctance to commit himself further by even one word until he had made up his mind about the future. And he was

no nearer that tonight than he had been on the first day of the holiday. He had known when they said goodbye on his last evening that she understood and accepted that this break was in some way crucial for them, that he wasn't driving alone to Monksmere solely to escape from London or recover from the strain of his last case. There was no reason, otherwise, why she shouldn't have come with him. She wasn't as tied to her job as all that. But he hadn't suggested it and she had said nothing except that last "Remember me at Blythburgh." She had been at school near Southwold and knew and loved Suffolk. Well, he had remembered, and not only at Blythburgh. Suddenly he longed for her. The need was so intense that he no longer cared whether it were wise to write. In the face of this craving to see her again, to hear her voice, all his uncertainties and self-distrust seemed as unimportant and ludicrously unreal as the morbid legacy of a nightmare, fading in the light of day. He longed to talk to her, but with the sitting room filled with people there would be no chance of telephoning tonight. Switching on the desk lamp he sat at the table and unscrewed his pen. The words, as sometimes happened, came simply and easily. He wrote them down without pausing to think too much or even to wonder whether he was being sincere.

> *Remember me, you said, at Blythburgh,*
> *As if you were not always in my mind*
> *And there could be an art to bend more sure*
> *A heart already wholly you inclined.*
> *Of you, the you enchanted mind bereave*
> *More clearly back your image to receive,*
> *And in this unencumbered holy place*
> *Recall again an unforgotten grace.*
> *I you possessed must needs remember still*
> *At Blythburgh my love, or where you will.*

"This metaphysical conceit, like most minor verse, comes to you with an ulterior motive. I don't need to tell you what. I won't say that I wish you here. But I wish I were with you. This place is full of death and disagreeableness and I

don't know which is worse. But God and the Suffolk C.I.D. willing I shall be back in London by Friday evening. It would be good to know that you might be at Queenhithe."

Writing this note must have taken longer than he thought for his aunt's knock on the door surprised him. She said:

"They're going, Adam. I don't know whether you feel the need to say goodnight."

He went down with her. They were, indeed, going and he was surprised to see that the clock said twenty past eleven. No one spoke to him and they seemed as unconcerned at his reappearance as they had been at his going. The fire had been let die and was now little more than a heap of white ash. Bryce was helping Celia Calthrop into her coat and Dalgliesh heard her say:

"It's naughty of us to be so late. And I've got to be up so early. Sylvia phoned me from Seton House late this afternoon and asked me to drive her to the Green Man first thing to-morrow. There's something urgent she has to tell Reckless."

Latham, already at the door, spun round.

"What does she mean—something urgent to tell him?"

Miss Calthrop shrugged.

"My dear Oliver, how can I know? She more or less hinted that she knew something about Digby but I imagine it's just Sylvia trying to make herself important. You know how she is. But one can hardly refuse to take her."

"But didn't she give you any idea what it's all about?"

Latham was sharply insistent.

"No she didn't. And I certainly wasn't going to give her the satisfaction of asking. And I'm not going to hurry myself. If this wind continues I shall be lucky to get much sleep to-night."

Latham looked as if he would like to have questioned further but Celia had already pushed past him. Murmuring a final and abstracted goodnight to his hostess, he followed the others into the storm. A few minutes later straining his ears against the howling of the wind, Dalgliesh heard the slamming of doors and the faint row of the departing cars.

4

The wind woke Dalgliesh just before three o'clock. As he
drifted into consciousness he heard the three chimes of the
sitting room clock and his first waking thought was a drowsy
wonder that so sweet and uninsistent a sound could strike so
clearly through the bedlam of the night. He lay awake and
listened. Drowsiness gave way to pleasure, then to a faint
excitement. He had always enjoyed a storm at Monksmere.
The pleasure was familiar and predictable; the frisson of
danger; the illusion of being poised on the very edge of
chaos; the contrast between the familiar comfort of his
bed and the violence of the night. He wasn't worried. Pentlands had stood for four hundred years against the Suffolk
seas. It would stand tonight. The sounds he was hearing now
hadn't changed with the years. For over four hundred years
men had lain awake in this room and listened to the sea.
One storm was very like another, all impossible to describe
except in clichés. He lay still and listened to the familiar
noises; the wind hurling itself against the walls like a demented animal; the perpetual background surge of the sea, the
hiss of rain heard as the gusts abated; and, in the momentary
calm, the trickle of falling shingle from roof and window sills.
At about twenty to four the storm seemed to be dying away.
There was one moment of complete peace in which Dalgliesh
could hear his own breathing. Shortly afterwards he must
have drifted again into sleep.

Suddenly he woke again to a gust so violent that the cottage
seemed to rock, the sea roared as if it were about to break over
the roof. He had never known anything like this before, even
at Monksmere. It was impossible to sleep through such fury.
He had an uncomfortable urge to be up and dressed.

He switched on his bedside lamp and, at that moment, his aunt appeared in the doorway, close buttoned into her old plaid dressing gown and with one heavy plait of hair hanging over her shoulder. She said:

"Justin is here. He thinks we ought to see if Sylvia Kedge is all right. We may have to get her out of that cottage. He says that the sea's coming in fast."

Dalgliesh reached for his clothes.

"How did he get here? I didn't hear him."

"Well, that isn't surprising, is it? You were probably asleep. He walked. He says we can't get the car to the road because of flooding. So it looks as if we'll have to go across the headland. He tried to telephone the coastguards but the line is down."

She disappeared and Dalgliesh hurriedly pulled on his clothes, cursing gently.

It was one thing to lie in warm security analysing the noises of the storm; it was another to fight one's way over the highest point of the headland on an adventure which could appeal only to tne young, the energetic or the incurably romantic.

He felt unreasonably irritated with Sylvia Kedge as if she were somehow responsible for her own danger. Surely to God the girl knew whether the cottage was safe in a storm! It might, of course, be that Bryce was fussing unnecessarily. If Tanner's Cottage had stood through the 1953 flood disaster it would stand tonight. But the girl was a cripple. It was right to make sure. All the same it was hardly an enterprise to be welcomed. At best it would be uncomfortable, exhausting and embarrassing. At worst, especially with Bryce in tow, it had all the elements of farce.

His aunt was already in the sitting room when he went down. She was packing a thermos and mugs into a rucksack and was fully dressed. She must have been wearing most of her clothes under her dressing gown when she called him. It struck Dalgliesh that Bryce's call was not altogether unexpected and that Sylvia Kedge's danger might be more real than he knew. Bryce, wearing a heavy oilskin which reached to his ankles topped with an immense sou'wester, stood dripping and glistening in the middle of the room, like an animated

advertisement for sardines. He was clutching a coil of heavy rope with every appearance of knowing what to do with it and had the air of a man dedicated to action.

He said:

"If there's any swimming to be done, my dear Adam, one must leave it to you. One has one's asthma, alas." He gave Dalgliesh a sly elliptical glance and added deprecatingly, "Also, one cannot swim."

"Of course," said Dalgliesh faintly. Did Bryce seriously believe that anyone could swim on a night like this? But there was no point in arguing. Dalgliesh felt like a man committed to an enterprise which he knows to be folly but which he can't summon up the energy to resist.

Bryce went on:

"I didn't call for Celia or Liz. No point in having a crowd. Besides, the lane is flooded so they wouldn't be able to get through. But I did try to get Latham. However, he wasn't at home. So we must just manage on our own." He was apparently unconcerned at Latham's absence. Dalgliesh bit back his questions. There was enough on hand without taking on fresh problems. But what on earth could Latham be doing on a night like this? Had the whole of Monksmere gone mad?

Once they had climbed out of the shelter of the lane and had mounted the headland there was energy for nothing but the effort of moving forward and Dalgliesh let the problem of Latham drop from his mind. It was impossible to walk upright and they clawed onwards like crouched beasts until aching thighs and stomach muscles forced them to kneel, palms pressed against the turf, to recover breath and energy. But the night was warmer than Dalgliesh had expected and the rain, less heavy now, dried softly on their faces. From time to time they gained the shelter of scrub and bushes and, released from the weight of the wind, trod lightly as disembodied spirits through the warm, green-smelling darkness.

Emerging from the last of these refuges they saw Priory House to sea-ward, the windows ablaze with light so that the house looked like a great ship riding the storm. Bryce drew

them back into the shelter of the bushes and shouted:

"I suggest that Miss Dalgliesh calls Sinclair and his housekeeper to help. By the look of it they're up and about. And we shall need a long stout ladder. Our best plan is for you, Adam, to wade across Tanner's Lane if the water isn't too high and get to the house as soon as possible. The rest of us will move inland until we can cross the lane and approach the house from the north bank. We ought to be able to reach you with the ladder from that side."

Before he had finished expounding this unexpectedly lucid and positive plan Miss Dalgliesh without a word set off towards Priory House. Dalgliesh, cast without his consent in the role of hero, was intrigued by the change in Bryce. The little man obviously had a concealed passion for action. Even his affectations had fallen away. Dalgliesh had the novel and not disagreeable sensation of being under command. He was still unconvinced that there was any real danger. But if there were, Bryce's plan was as good as any.

But when they reached Tanner's Lane and stood sheltering in the slope of the south bank and looking down on Tanner's Cottage, the danger was apparent. Under a racing moon the lane shone white, a turbulent sheet of foam which had already covered the garden path and was sucking at the cottage door. The downstairs lights were on. From where they stood the squat, ugly doll's house looked strangely lonely and threatened. But Bryce apparently found the situation more hopeful than he had expected. He hissed in Dalgliesh's ear:

"It's not very high. You ought to be able to get across with the rope. Funny, I thought it would be well up by now. This may be as far as it will get. Not much danger really. Still, you'd better go in, I suppose." He sounded almost disappointed.

The water was incredibly cold. Dalgliesh was expecting it but the shock still took his breath away. He had stripped off his oilskin and jacket and was wearing only his slacks and jersey. One end of the rope was around his waist. The other, hitched around the trunk of a sapling, was being plied out inch by inch through Bryce's careful hands. The swift current was already armpit high and Dalgliesh had to fight hard to

keep upright. Occasionally his feet stumbled into a rut in the lane's surface and he lost his footing. Then, for a desperate moment, it was a struggle to keep his head above water as he fought on the end of the rope like a hooked fish. It was hopeless to try to swim against this tide. The cottage lights were still on as he gained the door and braced his back against it. The sea was boiling around his ankles, each wave carrying it higher. Panting to get back his breath he signalled to Bryce to release the rope. In response the bulky little figure on the far bank flailed its arms enthusiastically but made no move to unhitch the rope from the tree. Probably his exuberant gestures were no more than a congratulatory acknowledgement that Dalgliesh had gained his objective. Dalgliesh cursed his folly in not having agreed with Bryce who should keep the rope before plunging to his task with such spectacular fervour. Any shouted communication between them was impossible. If he were not to remain tethered to the tree indefinitely—and his situation was already uncomfortably close to burlesque—he had better let Bryce have the rope. He released the bowline and the rope whipped free from his waist. Immediately Bryce began to coil it in with wide sweeps of his arms.

The wind had dropped a little but he could hear no sounds from inside the cottage and there was no answer to his shout. He pushed against the door but it was stuck. Something was wedged against it. He pushed harder and felt the obstruction shift as if a heavy sack were sliding across the floor. Then there was a gap wide enough for him to squeeze through and he saw that the sack was the body of Oliver Latham.

He had fallen across the narrow hall, his body blocking the sitting room doorway and his head resting face upward on the first stair. It looked as if he had struck the banister. There was a gash behind the left ear from which the blood was still oozing and another over the right eye. Dalgliesh knelt over him. He was alive and already regaining consciousness. At the feel of Dalgliesh's hand he groaned, twisted his head to one side and was neatly sick. The grey eyes opened, tried to focus, then closed again.

Dalgliesh looked across the brightly lit sitting room to the still figure sitting bolt upright on the divan bed. The face was an oval, deathly pale against the heavy swathes of hair. The black eyes were immense. They stared across at him, watchful, speculative. She seemed utterly unaware of the swirling water spreading now in waves across the floor.

"What happened?" Dalgliesh asked.

She said calmly:

"He came to kill me. I used the only weapon I had. I threw the paper weight at him. He must have caught his head when he fell. I think I've killed him."

Dalgliesh said briefly:

"He'll live. There's not much wrong with him. But I've got to get him upstairs. Stop where you are. Don't try to move. I'll come back for you."

She gave a little shrug of the shoulders and asked:

"Why can't we get across the lane? You came that way."

Dalgliesh answered brutally:

"Because the water's already up to my armpits and running in a torrent. I can't swim across burdened with a cripple and a semi-conscious man. We'll get upstairs. If necessary we'll have to get on the roof."

He edged his shoulder under Latham's body and braced himself for the lift. The staircase was steep, ill-lit and narrow but its very narrowness was an advantage. Once he had Latham balanced across his shoulders it was possible to pull himself up by both banisters. Luckily there were no corners. At the top he felt for the switch and the top landing was flooded with light. He paused for a moment recalling where the skylight was. Then he pushed open the door to his left and groped round again for a light. It took him a few seconds to find. As he stood in the doorway grasping Latham's body with his left hand and running his right over the wall the smell of the room came out at him, musty, airless and sickly sweet like a faint stench of decay. Then his fingers found the switch and the room became visible, lit by a single unshaded bulb hanging from the centre of the ceiling. It had obviously been Mrs. Kedge's bedroom and looked he thought as it must

have done when she last slept in it. The furniture was heavy and ugly. The great bed, still made up, occupied almost all the back of the room. It smelt of damp and decay. Dalgliesh dumped Latham gently on it and looked up at the slope of the roof. He had been right about the skylight. But there was only the one tiny square window and this faced the lane. If they were to get out of the cottage it would have to be by the roof.

He went back to the sitting room to fetch the girl. The water was waist high and she was standing on the divan bed and holding on to the mantelshelf for support. Dalgliesh noticed that she had a small plastic sponge bag hanging around her neck. Presumably it contained such valuables as she possessed. As he entered she gazed round the room as if to ensure that there was nothing else which she wished to take. He fought his way over to her, feeling the strength of the tide even in this tiny confined space and wondering how long the foundations of the cottage could stand against it. It was easy to comfort oneself with the thought that the cottage had survived earlier floods. But the tide and the wind were unpredictable. The water may have risen further in earlier years but it could hardly have burst in with greater force. Even as he struggled across to the waiting figure he thought he could hear the walls shake.

He came up to her and without a word, lifted her in his arms. She was surprisingly light. True, he could feel the downward drag of the heavy leg irons but the upper part of her body was so buoyant that it might have been boneless, sexless even. He was almost surprised to feel the rib cage under his hands and the firmness of her high breasts. She lay passively in his arms as he carried her sideways up the narrow stairs and into her mother's room. It was only then that he remembered her crutches. He felt a sudden embarrassment, a reluctance to speak of them. As if reading his thoughts she said:

"I'm sorry. I should have remembered. They're hitched on to the end of the mantelshelf."

That meant another trip downstairs but it was hardly

avoidable. It would have been difficult to manage both the girl and her crutches in one journey up those narrow stairs. He was about to carry her over to the bed when she looked at Latham's writhing body and said with sudden vehemence. "No! Not there! Leave me here." He slid her gently from his arms and she leaned back against the wall. For a moment their eyes were level and they gazed at each other, wordlessly. It seemed to Dalgliesh that in that moment some kind of communication passed but whether those black eyes held a warning or an appeal he was never afterwards able to decide.

He had no difficulty in retrieving the crutches. The water in the sitting room had now covered the mantelshelf and as Dalgliesh reached the bottom of the stairs they floated through the sitting room door. He grasped them by the rubber grips of the hand pieces and drew them over the banisters. As he retreated again up the stairs a great wave broke through the shattered front door and hurled him to his feet. The pedestal of the banisters broke free, spun as if in a whirlpool and was dashed into splinters against the wall. And this time there could be no doubt about it: he felt the cottage shake.

The skylight was about ten feet above the floor, impossible to reach without something to stand on. It was useless to try shifting the heavy bed, but there was a square substantial looking commode by the side of it and he dragged this across and positioned it under the skylight.

The girl said: "If you can push me through first I'll be able to help with . . . him."

She looked across at Latham who had now dragged himself upright and was sitting, head in hands, on the edge of the bed. He was groaning audibly.

She added: "I've got strong hands and shoulders."

And she held out the ugly hands towards him like a suppliant. This in fact had been Dalgliesh's plan. Getting Latham on to the roof was the trickiest part of the business. Without her help he doubted whether it would be possible.

The skylight, encrusted with dirt and festooned with grey cobwebs, looked as if it might be hard to shift. But when Dalgliesh punched at the frame he heard the splinter of

rotting wood. The skylight jerked upwards and was immediately whirled away into the storm. Night came bursting into the close little room sweeping it with welcome gusts of cold, sweet air. At that moment the lights failed and they saw as from the bottom of a pit the small grey square of turbulent sky and the reeling moon.

Latham came lurching across the room towards them.

"What the hell . . . ? Someone's put out the bloody light."

Dalgliesh guided him back to the bed.

"Stay here and save your strength. You're going to need it. We've got to get out on the roof."

"You can. I'm staying here. Get me a doctor. I want a doctor. Oh God, my head!"

Dalgliesh left him rocking in lachrymose self-pity on the edge of the bed and went back to the girl.

Jumping from the chair he grasped the outer frame of the skylight and drew himself up. As he had recalled, the crown of the slated roof was only a few feet away. But the slope was steeper than he had expected and the chimney stack, which would afford them some shelter and support, was at least five feet to the left. He dropped again to the floor and said to the girl:

"See if you can get astride the roof and work your way back to the chimney. If you're in trouble, stay absolutely still and wait for me. I'll manage Latham once we're both out but I shall need you to help pull him up. But I won't shove him through until you're properly balanced. Give me a shout when you're ready. Do you want your crutches?"

"Yes," she said calmly. "I want my crutches. I can hook them on to the roof top and they may be useful."

He hoisted her through the skylight by the irons which braced both her legs from thigh to ankles. Their rigid strength made it easy for him to push her high on to the crown of the roof. She grasped it and swung one leg to the other side then crouched down low against the fury of the storm, her hair streaming in the wind. He saw her nod vigorously as a sign that she was ready. Then she leaned towards him and held out both her hands.

It was at that moment that he sensed a warning, the unmistakable instinct for danger. It was as much part of his detective's equipment as his knowledge of firearms, his nose for an unnatural death. It had saved him time and time again and he acted on it instinctively. There was no time now for argument or analysis. If the three of them were to survive they had to get out on that roof. But he knew that Latham and the girl mustn't be up there alone together.

It wasn't easy getting Latham through the skylight. He was only just conscious and even the swirls of water spreading now over the bedroom floor couldn't rouse him to a sense of danger. He craved only to be allowed to sink on to the pillows of the bed and fight his nausea in comfort. But at least he could cooperate to some extent. He wasn't yet a dead weight. Dalgliesh took off his own and Latham's shoes then urged him on to the chair and hoisted him through the skylight. Even when the girl's hands had caught Latham under his armpits he didn't let go but immediately swung himself through the hole bracing himself against the wind, his back to the flooded lane and his legs dangling into the room. Together they pulled and pushed the half-conscious man until his hands grasped the roof top and he pulled himself up and lay astride it, motionless. The girl released her hands and taking up her elbow crutches, edged herself backward until she was leaning against the chimney stack. Dalgliesh swung himself up to join Latham.

It was then that it happened. In the second when Dalgliesh weakened his hold on Latham she struck. It was so instantaneous that he hardly saw the vicious kick of the armoured legs. But the irons caught Latham's hands and, immediately, they loosed their hold of the roof and his body slipped. Dalgliesh shot out his hands and caught Latham's wrists. There was a sudden intolerable jerk and he took the full weight of Latham's body as it hung spread-eagled over the roof. Then she struck again and again. And now it was Dalgliesh's hands. They were too numb to feel the pain but he experienced the sudden scalding gush of blood and knew that it couldn't be long before the wrists were fractured and Latham slid out of

his powerless hands. And then it would be his turn. She was braced securely against the chimney stack and armed with her crutches and those deadly irons. No one on the bank could see them. They were the wrong side of the roof and the night was dark. To those anxious watchers if indeed they were there they could be nothing more than crouched silhouettes against the sky. And when his and Latham's bodies were found there would be no injuries which couldn't be explained by the fury of the rocks and sea. There was only one chance for him and that was to let Latham go. Alone he could probably wrest the crutches from her. Alone he would have more than an even chance. But she knew of course that he wouldn't let Latham go. She had always known just how her adversary would act. He hung on doggedly; and still the blows fell.

They had both discounted Latham. Perhaps the girl thought he was unconscious. But suddenly a slate, dislodged by his fall, fell from the roof and his feet found a hold. Some desperate instinct for survival awoke in him. He lurched forward twisting his left hand from Dalgliesh's weakening hold and clutched with sudden force at her leg irons. Surprised she lost her balance and, at that moment, a gust of wind tore at the roof. Latham pulled again and she fell. Dalgliesh shot out his hand towards her and caught at the string of the little bag around her neck. The cord snapped and the body rolled past him. The clumsy surgical boots could find no hold and the rigid legs, powerless in their heavy irons rolled her over and over inexorably towards the edge. Then she hit the gutter and bounced into space, turning like a mechanical doll, her legs splayed against the sky. They heard the one wild cry and then nothing. Dalgliesh stuffed the little bag into his pocket and then lay motionless, his head resting on his bleeding hands. And it was then that he felt the ladder nudging his back.

Uninjured, the journey to the bank would have been re-latively easy. But Dalgliesh's hands were now almost useless. The pain had started and he could hardly bear to flex the fingers. And there was no grip left. Latham's last effort seemed to have exhausted him. He seemed about to lapse again

into unconsciousness. It took some minutes before Dalgliesh, shouting in his ear, could urge him on the ladder.

Dalgliesh went first, working his way backward and supporting Latham as best as he could with his hooked arms. Latham's face, beaded with sweat, was within inches of his own. Dalgliesh could smell his breath, the sweet-sour trace of too much drinking, too much high living. He wondered bitterly whether his last conscious discovery before they were hurled into the vortex was to be this realization that Latham had mild halitosis. There were more significant discoveries and there were pleasanter ways of dying. Surely Latham could make some effort! Why the hell couldn't the man keep himself in decent physical condition? Dalgliesh muttered alternate curses and encouragement under his breath and Latham, as if catching them, roused himself to a fresh effort, grasped the next rung with both hands and drew himself forward a few painful inches. Suddenly the rung bent, then snapped from the ladder. It spun from Latham's hand in a wide arch and disappeared, soundlessly, below the waves. For a sickening moment both their heads dropped through the gap and hung, wide-eyed above the boiling water only twenty feet below. Then Latham lifted his head to rest it on the edge of the ladder and grunted at Dalgliesh:

"You'd better get back. This ladder won't stand two. No sense in both of us getting wet."

"Save your breath," said Dalgliesh. "And keep moving."

He braced his elbows under Latham's armpit and lifted him forward a few rungs. The ladder creaked and bent. They lay immobile after the effort then tried again. This time Latham managed to grip a rung with his feet and lurched forward with such unexpected force that Dalgliesh was nearly thrown off his balance. The ladder, caught by a sudden gust, swung sideways. They could feel it shift on the roof. Neither dared move until the wild swing steadied. Then they inched forward again. They were nearing the bank now. Below they could see the dark shapes of tangled trees. Dalgliesh thought that they must be within earshot of the headland but there was no sound except the howling of the storm. He guessed

that the little group was waiting in silence, terrified to break their fearful concentration even with shouts of encouragement. Suddenly it was all over. He felt a strong grip on his ankles. Someone was pulling him to safety.

He wasn't conscious of relief, only of intense weariness and self-disgust. There was no strength left in his body but his mind was clear enough and his thoughts were bitter. He had underestimated the difficulties, had allowed himself to be drawn by Bryce into the amateurish farce in a tolerant contempt of the danger, had behaved like an impulsive fool. They had set out like a couple of Boy Scouts to save the girl from drowning. And, as a result, the girl had drowned. All that had been necessary was to wait quietly in that upstairs bedroom until the water began to drop. The storm was already abating. By morning they could have been rescued in comfort, cold possibly, but unharmed.

And then, as if in answer to his thought, he heard the rumbling. It grew into a roar and the little group on the bank watched fascinated as the cottage with a kind of awkward grace curtseyed slowly into the sea. The roar reverberated around the headland and the waves, dashing against the dam of bricks, leaped and thundered. The spume rose dancing into the night sky, and floated into their eyes. And then the rumbling died away. The last Tanner's Cottage was under the sea.

The headland was peopled with black shapes. They crowded around him blotting out the storm. Their mouths opened and shut but he could hear nothing they said. He had one vivid picture of R. B. Sinclair's white hair streaming against the moon and he could hear Latham demanding a doctor with the querulous insistence of a child. Dalgliesh longed intolerably to sink down to the soft turf and lie there quietly until the pain had gone from his hands and this dreadful aching from his body. But someone was holding him up. He supposed it must be Reckless. The hands braced under his armpits were unexpectedly firm and he could smell the strong pungent smell of wet gaberdine and feel its harshness against his face. Then the mouths,

opening and shutting like the jaws of puppets, began to make sounds. They were asking if he was all right and someone, he thought it was Alice Kerrison, was suggesting that they all go back to Priory House. Someone else mentioned the Landrover. It could probably get through the lane to Pentlands if Miss Dalgliesh would prefer to take Adam home. For the first time Dalgliesh noticed the Landrover, a dark shape on the outskirts of the group. It must be the one belonging to Bill Coles and that bulky figure in yellow oilskins must be Coles himself. How in the devil had he got here? The white blur of faces seemed to be expecting him to make up his mind to something. He said: "I want to go home."

He shook off their helping hands and hoisted himself by his elbows into the back of the Landrover. On the floor was a cluster of storm lanterns which cast their yellow light on the row of sitting figures. For the first time he saw his aunt. She had one arm round Latham's shoulders and he was leaning against her. He looked, thought Dalgliesh, like the romantic lead in a Victorian melodrama with his long pale face, his closed eyes, and the white handkerchief which someone had bound around his brow already showing a stain of blood. Reckless got in last and sat against Dalgliesh. As the Landrover lurched off across the headland Dalgliesh held out his torn hands like a surgeon waiting to be gloved. He said to Reckless:

"If you can get your hand into my pocket there's a plastic bag there which will interest you. I tore it from Sylvia Kedge's neck. I can't touch anything myself."

He shifted his body so that Reckless, bouncing violently with the shaking of the Landrover, could slide his hand into the pocket. He drew out the little bag, untied the cord and edging his thumb into the neck worked it open. Then he spilled the contents out on to his lap. There was a small faded photograph of a woman in an oval silver frame, a reel of recording tape, a folded wedding certificate and a plain gold ring.

5

Brightness was pressing painfully against Dalgliesh's eyeballs. He swam up through a kaleidoscope of whirling reds and blues and forced open his eyelids, gummed with sleep, to blink at the bright day. It must be long after his normal waking hour; already shafts of sunlight lay warm across his face. He lay for a moment, cautiously stretching his legs and feeling the ache return almost pleasurably to his sore muscles. His hands felt heavy. Drawing them from under the bedclothes he turned the two white cocoons slowly before his eyes, focussing on them with the strained intentness of a child. Presumably these professional looking bandages had been applied by his aunt but he had no clear recollection of her doing so. She must have used some ointment too. He could feel a disagreeable slipperiness inside the encasing gauze. He was becoming aware now that his hands still hurt but he could move the joints, and the tips of his three middle fingers, the only parts visible, looked normal enough. Apparently no bones were broken.

He wriggled his arms into his dressing gown and walked across to the window. Outside the morning was calm and bright, bringing an immediate memory of the first day of his holiday. For a moment the fury of the night seemed as remote and legendary as any of the great storms of the past. But the evidence was before him. The tip of headland visible from his eastward window was ravaged and raw as if an army had clumped across it littering its way with torn boughs and uprooted gorse. And, although the wind had died to a breeze so that the litter of the headland scarcely stirred, the sea was still turbulent, slopping in great sluggish waves to the horizon as if weighted with sand. It was the colour of mud, too turbid and violent to reflect the blue translucence of the sky.

Nature was at odds with itself, the sea in the last throes of a private war, the land lying exhausted under a benign sky.

He turned from the window and looked round the room as if seeing it for the first time. There was a folded blanket across the back of the easy chair by the window and a pillow resting on the arm. His aunt must have spent the night sleeping there. It could hardly have been because of concern for him. He remembered now. They had brought Latham back to Pentlands with them; his aunt must have given up her room. The realization irritated him and he wondered whether he was being petty enough to resent his aunt's concern for a man he had never liked. Well, what of it? The dislike was mutual if that were any justification and the day threatened to be traumatic enough without beginning it in a mood of morbid self-criticism. But he could have done without Latham. The events of the night were too raw in the memory to relish the prospect of exchanging small talk over breakfast with his partner in folly.

As he made his way downstairs he could hear a murmur of voices from the kitchen. There was the familiar morning smell of coffee and bacon but the sitting room was empty. His aunt and Latham must be breakfasting together in the kitchen. He could hear Latham's high arrogant voice more clearly now although his aunt's softer replies were inaudible. He found himself treading softly so that they might not hear him, tiptoeing across the sitting room like an intruder. Soon, inevitably, he would have to face Latham's excuses and explanations, even—horrible thought—his gratitude. Before long the whole of Monksmere would arrive to question, argue, discuss and exclaim. Little of the story would be news to him, and he had long outgrown the satisfaction of being proved right. He had known who for a long time now and since Monday night he had known how. But to the suspects the day would bring a gratifying vindication and they could be expected to make the most of it. They had been frightened, inconvenienced and humiliated. It would be churlish to grudge them their fun. But for the moment he trod warily, as if reluctant to waken the day.

There was a small fire burning in the sitting room, its thin flame flickering wanly in the brightness of the sun. He saw that it was after eleven o'clock and the post had already arrived. There was a letter for him propped on the mantelpiece. Even across the room he could recognize Deborah's large, sloping handwriting. He felt in his dressing gown pocket for his own unposted letter to her, and with difficulty propped it up beside that other envelope, his small and upright hand looking obsessionally neat beside her generous scrawl. Hers was a thin envelope. That meant one page at the most. Suddenly he knew just what Deborah could have written on no more than one quarto page and the letter became infected with the menace of the day, opening it a chore which could reasonably be postponed. As he stood there, angry at his own indecision and trying to force himself to that one simple action he heard the approaching car. So they were coming already, avid no doubt with curiosity and pleasurable anticipation. But when the car drew nearer he recognized the Ford which Reckless used and, moving to the window, could see that the Inspector was alone. A minute later the car door slammed and Reckless paused, as if bracing himself to approach the cottage. Under his arm he carried Celia Calthrop's tape recorder. The day had begun.

Five minutes later the four of them listened together to the murderer's confession. Reckless sat beside the tape recorder frowning at it constantly with the anxious, slightly peeved look of a man who expects it at any moment to break down. Jane Dalgliesh sat in her usual chair on the left of the fire, motionless, hands folded in her lap, listening as intently as if to music. Latham displayed himself against the wall, one arm drooping from the chimney piece, his bandaged head resting against the grey stones. He looked, thought Dalgliesh, like a slightly passé actor posing for a publicity photograph. He, himself, sat opposite his aunt balancing a tray on his knees, spearing with a fork the small cubes of buttered toast which she had prepared for him or cupping his hands, comfortably insulated, round a steaming beaker of coffee.

The voice of the dead girl spoke to them, not with the familiar irritating submissiveness, but clear, confident and controlled. Only from time to time was there a trace of excitement quickly restrained. This was her paean of triumph, yet she told her dreadful story with the assurance and detachment of a professional broadcaster reading a book at bedtime.

"This is the fourth time I've dictated my confession and it won't be the last. The tape can be used over and over again. One can always improve. Nothing need be final. Maurice Seton used to say that, working away at his pathetic books as if they were worth writing, as if anyone cared what word he used. And as likely as not it would be my word in the end, my suggestion, breathed oh so tentatively and quietly so that he wouldn't notice that it was a human being who spoke. I wasn't ever that to him. Just a machine who could take shorthand, type, mend his clothes, wash up, even do a little cooking. Not a really efficient machine, of course, I hadn't the use of my legs. But that made it easier for him in some ways. It meant that he didn't even have to think of me as female. He never saw me as a woman, of course. That was to be expected. But after a time I wasn't even female. I could be asked to work late, stay the night, share his bathroom. No one would talk. No one would care. There was never any scandal. Why should there be? Who would want to touch me? Oh, he was safe enough with me in the house. And, God knows, I was safe enough with him.

"He would have laughed if I had told him that I could make him a good wife. No, not laughed. He would have been disgusted. It would have seemed like mating with a half-wit, or an animal. Why should deformity be disgusting? Oh, he wasn't the only one. I've seen that look in other faces. Adam Dalgliesh. Why should I instance him? He can hardly bear to look at me. It's as if he's saying, 'I like women to be lovely. I like women to be graceful. I'm sorry for you but you offend me'. I offend myself Superintendent. I offend myself. But I mustn't waste tape on preliminaries. My first confessions were too long, imperfectly balanced. By the end they even

bored me. But there will be time to get the story right, to tell it perfectly so that I can play the tape over and over for the rest of my life and yet feel the first keen pleasure. Then, perhaps, one day I shall clean it all away. But not yet. Perhaps never. It would be amusing to leave it for posterity. The only drawback to planning and carrying out a perfect murder is that no one else can appreciate it. I may as well have the satisfaction, however childish, of knowing that I shall make the headlines after my death.

"It was a complicated plot, of course, but that made it all the more satisfying. After all, there is nothing difficult about killing a man. Hundreds of people do it every year and have their brief moment of notoriety before they are as forgotten as yesterday's news. I could have killed Maurice Seton any day I chose, especially after I got my hands on those five grains of white arsenic. He took them from the Cadaver Club museum, substituting a bottle of baking powder, at the time he was writing *Death in the Pot*. Poor Maurice, he was obsessed by this urge for verisimilitude. He couldn't even write about an arsenical poisoning without handling the stuff, smelling it, seeing how quickly it would dissolve, enjoying the thrill of playing with death. This absorption in detail, this craving for vicarious experience, was central to my plot. It led him, the predestined victim, to Lily Coombs and the Cortez Club. It led him to his murderer. He was an expert in vicarious death. I should like to have been there to see how he enjoyed the real thing. He meant to put the stuff back, of course; it was only borrowed. But before he could do so I did some substituting of my own. The baking powder in the show case at the Club was replaced by Maurice with baking powder—again. I thought that the arsenic might come in handy. And it will. It will shortly come in very handy indeed. There will be no problem for me in putting it into that flask which Digby always carries. And then what? Wait for the inevitable moment when he is alone and can't face the next minute without a drink? Or tell him that Eliza Marley has discovered something about Maurice's death and wants to meet him secretly far along the beach? Any method will

do. The end will be the same. And once he is dead, what can anyone prove? After a little time I shall ask to see Inspector Reckless and tell him that Digby has been complaining recently about indigestion and that I have seen him at Maurice's medicine chest. I shall explain how Maurice borrowed some arsenic once from the Cadaver Club but he assured me that he had replaced it. But suppose he didn't? Suppose he couldn't bring himself to part with it? That would be typical of Maurice. Everyone will say so. Everyone will know about *Death in the Pot*. The powder in the museum show case will be tested and found to be harmless. And Digby Seton will have died by a tragic accident but through his half-brother's fault. I find that very satisfying. It is a pity that Digby, who despite his stupidity, has been very appreciative of so many of my ideas, has to be kept ignorant of this final part of the plan.

"I could have used that arsenic for Maurice just as easily and seen him die in agony any day I chose. It would have been easy. Too easy. Easy and unintelligent. Death by poison wouldn't have satisfied any of the necessary conditions of Maurice's murder. It was those conditions which made the crime so interesting to plan and so satisfying to execute. Firstly, he had to die from natural causes. Digby, as his heir, would be the natural suspect and it was important to me that nothing should jeopardise Digby's inheritance. Then he had to die away from Monksmere; there must be no danger of anyone suspecting me. On the other hand I wanted the crime to be connected with the Monksmere community; the more they were harassed, suspected and frightened the better, I had plenty of old scores to be settled. Besides, I wanted to watch the investigation. It wouldn't have suited me to have it treated as a London crime. Apart from the fun of watching the reactions of the suspects I thought it important that the police work should be under my eye. I must be there to watch and, if necessary, to control. It didn't work out altogether as I had planned, but on the whole very little has happened which I haven't known about. Ironically, I have been less skilful at times than I hoped at controlling my own emotions, but everyone else has behaved strictly according to my plan.

"And then there was Digby's requirement to be met. He wanted the murder to be associated with L. J. Luker and the Cortez Club. His motive was different, of course. He didn't particularly want Luker to be suspected. He just wanted to show him that there were more ways than one of committing murder and getting away with it. What Digby wanted was a death which the police would have to accept as natural—because it would be natural—but which Luker would know had been murder. That's why he insisted on sending Luker the severed hands. I took most of the flesh off them first with acid—it was an advantage to have a dark room in the cottage and the acid available—but I still didn't like the idea. It was a stupid, an unnecessary risk. But I gave in to Digby's whim. A condemned man, by tradition, is pampered. One tries to gratify his more harmless requests.

"But before I describe how Maurice died there are two extraneous matters to get out of the way. Neither of them is important but I mention them because both had an indirect part in Maurice's murder and both were useful in throwing suspicion on Latham and Bryce. I can't take much credit for Dorothy Seton's death. I was responsible, of course, but I didn't intend to kill her. It would have seemed a waste of effort to plan to kill a woman so obviously bent on self destruction. It couldn't, after all, have been long. Whether she took an overdose of her drugs, fell over the cliff on one of her half-doped nocturnal wanderings, got killed with her lover on one of their wild drives around the country, or merely drank herself to death, it could only be a matter of time. I wasn't even particularly interested. And then, soon after she and Alice Kerrison had left for that last holiday at Le Touquet I found the manuscript. It was a remarkable piece of prose. It's a pity that people who say that Maurice Seton couldn't write will never have the chance to read it. When he cared, he could write phrases that scorched the paper. And he cared. It was all there; the pain, the sexual frustration, the jealousy, the spite, the urge to punish. Who better than I could know how he felt? It must have given him the greatest satisfaction to write it all down. There could be no typewriter, no mechanical keys

between this pain and its expression. He needed to see the words forming themselves under his hand. He didn't mean to use it, of course. I did that; merely steaming open one of his weekly letters to her and including it with that. Looking back, I'm not even sure what I expected to happen. I suppose it was just that the sport was too good to miss. Even if she didn't destroy the letter and confronted him with it he could never be absolutely sure that he himself hadn't inadvertently posted it. I knew him so well, you see. He was always afraid of his own subconscious, persuaded that it would betray him in the end. Next day I enjoyed myself watching his panic, his desperate searching, his anxious glances at me to see whether I knew. When he asked whether I had thrown away any papers I answered calmly that I had only burnt a small quantity of scrap. I saw his face lighten. He chose to believe that I had thrown away the letter without reading it. Any other thought would have been intolerable to him so that was what he chose to believe until the day he died. The letter was never found. I have my own idea what happened to it. But the whole of Monksmere believes that Maurice Seton was largely responsible for his wife's suicide. And who could have a better motive for revenge in the eyes of the police than her lover, Oliver Latham?

"It is probably unnecessary to explain that it was I who killed Bryce's cat. That would have been obvious to Bryce at the time if he hadn't been so desperate to cut down the body that he failed to notice the slip knot. If he had been in any condition to examine the rope and the method he would have realized that I could have strung up Arabella without lifting myself more than an inch or two in my chair. But, as I had anticipated, he neither acted rationally nor thought coolly. It never occurred to him for a second that Maurice Seton might not be the culprit. It may seem strange that I waste time discussing the killing of a cat but Arabella's death had its place in my scheme. It ensured that the vague dislike between Maurice and Bryce hardened into active enmity so that Bryce, like Latham, had a motive for revenge. The death of a cat may be a poor motive for the death of a man

and I thought it unlikely that the police would waste much time with Bryce. But the mutilation of the body was a different matter. Once the post-mortem showed that Maurice had died from natural causes the police would concentrate on the reasons for hacking off the hands. It was, of course, vital that they should never suspect why this mutilation was necessary and it was convenient that there should be at least two people at Monksmere, both spiteful, both aggrieved, both with an obvious motive. But there were two other reasons why I killed Arabella. Firstly I wanted to. She was a useless creature. Like Dorothy Seton she was kept and petted by a man who believed that beauty has a right to exist, however stupid, however worthless, because it is beauty. It took only two twitching seconds on the end of a clothes line to dispose of that nonsense. And then, her death was to some extent a dress rehearsal. I wanted to try out my acting ability, to test myself under strain. I won't waste time now describing what I discovered about myself. I shall never forget it; the sense of power, the outrage, the heady mixture of fear and excitement. I have felt that again many times since. I am feeling it now. Bryce gives a graphic account of my distress, my tiresomely uncontrolled behaviour after the body was cut down, and not all of it was acting.

"But to return to Maurice. It was by a lucky chance that I discovered the one fact about him that was crucial for my purpose—that he suffered badly from claustrophobia. Dorothy must have known of course. After all there were nights when she condescended to let him share her bedroom. He must have woken her sometimes with his recurring nightmare just as he woke me. I often wonder how much she knew and whether she told Oliver Latham before she died. That was a risk I had to take. But what if she did? No one can prove that I knew. Nothing can change the fact that Maurice Seton died from natural causes.

"I remember that night, over two years ago, very clearly. It was a wet, blustery day in mid-September and the evening grew wilder as darkness fell. We had been working together since ten o'clock that morning and it wasn't going well.

Maurice was trying to finish a series of short stories for an evening paper. It wasn't his métier and he knew it; he was working against time and he hated that. I had broken off only twice, to cook us a light lunch at one-thirty and again at eight o'clock when I prepared sandwiches and soup. By nine o'clock when we had finished our meal, the wind was howling around the house and I could hear a high tide pounding on the beach. Even Maurice could hardly expect me to get home in my wheelchair once darkness had fallen and he never offered to drive me home. That, after all, would put him to the trouble of fetching me again next day. So he suggested that I should stay the night. He didn't ask me if I were willing. It didn't occur to him that I might object or that I might perhaps prefer my own toothbrush or toilet things or even my own bed. The ordinary courtesies of life didn't apply to me. But he told me to put sheets on the bed in his wife's old room and he came himself to look for a nightdress for me. I don't know why. I think it may have been the first time since her death that he had brought himself to open her drawers and cupboards and that my presence was both an opportunity for breaking a taboo and a kind of support. Now that I can wear any of her underclothes or can rip them to shreds just as the fancy takes me, I can bring myself to smile at the memory of that night. Poor Maurice! He hadn't remembered that those wisps of chiffon, those bright transparencies in nylon and silk would be so pretty, so delicate, so very unsuitable for my twisted body. I saw the look on his face as his hands hovered over them. He couldn't bear to think of her clothes against my flesh. And then he found what he wanted. It was there at the bottom of the drawer, an old woollen nightdress which had belonged to Alice Kerrison. Dorothy had worn it once at Alice's insistance when she had been ill with influenza and was sweating with rigor. And it was this nightdress which Maurice handed to me. Would his fate have been any different, I wonder, if he had acted otherwise that night? Probably not. But it pleases me to think that his hands, hesitating over the layers of gaudy nonsense, were choosing between life and death.

"It was shortly after three o'clock when I was awoken by his scream. At first I thought it was a sea bird screeching. Then it came again and again. I fumbled for my crutches and went in to him. He was leaning, half dazed, against the bedroom window and had the last disorientated look of a man who has been sleep walking. I managed to coax him back into bed. It wasn't difficult. He took my hand like a child. As I drew the sheets up under his chin he suddenly seized my arm and said, 'Don't leave me! Don't go yet! It's my nightmare. It's always the same. I dream I'm being buried alive. Stay with me till I'm asleep.' So I stayed. I sat there with his hand in mine until my fingers were stiff with cold and my whole body ached. There were a great many things which he told me in the darkness about himself, about his great consuming fear, before his fingers relaxed, the muttering ceased and he dropped into peaceful sleep. His jaw had fallen open so that he looked stupid and ugly and vulnerable. I had never seen him asleep before. I was pleased to see his ugliness, his helplessness and I felt a sense of power which was so pleasurable that it almost frightened me. And, sitting there beside him, listening to that quiet breathing, I pondered how I might use this new knowledge to my advantage. I began to plan how I might kill him.

"He said nothing to me next morning about the events of the night. I was never sure whether he had completely forgotten his nightmare and my visit to his room. But I don't think so. I believe he remembered well enough but put it out of his thoughts. After all, he didn't have to apologize or explain to me. One doesn't need to justify one's weakness either to a servant or an animal. That's why it is so satisfying, so convenient to have a tame one in the house.

"There was no hurry over the planning, no time limit in which he had to die, and this in itself added to the interest and allowed me to develop a more complicated and sophisticated murder than would have been possible were I working against the clock. I share Maurice's view here. No one can do his best work in a hurry. Towards the end, of course, there was some urgency when I found, and destroyed, the carbon

of the letter to Max Gurney announcing that Maurice was thinking of changing his Will. But, by then, my final plans had been ready for over a month.

"I knew from the beginning that I should need an accomplice and who that accomplice should be. The decision to use Digby Seton to destroy firstly his half-brother and then himself was so magnificent in its boldness that at times I was frightened at my own daring. But it wasn't as foolhardy as it appears. I knew Digby, I knew precisely his weaknesses and his strengths. He is less stupid and far greedier than people realize, more practical but less imaginative, not particularly brave but obstinate and persistent. Above all, he is fundamentally weak and vain. My plan made use of his abilities as well as his defects. I have made very few mistakes in my handling of him and if I underestimated him in some important respects this has proved less catastrophic than I might have feared. He is becoming a liability as well as a nuisance now, of course, but he won't be worrying me for long. If he had proved less irritating to me and more reliable I might have considered letting him live for a year or so. I should prefer to have avoided death duties on Maurice's estate. But I have no intention of letting greed trap me into folly.

"In the beginning I did nothing so crude as to present Digby with a plan for killing Maurice. What I suggested to him was no more than a complicated practical joke. He didn't, of course, believe this for long but then he wasn't required to. During all the preliminary planning, neither of us mentioned the word murder. He knew and I knew, but neither of us spoke. We conscientiously kept up the fiction that we were engaged in an experiment, not perhaps without some danger but completely without malice, to prove to Maurice that it was possible to transport a man from London to Monksmere secretly and without his knowledge or cooperation. That was to be our alibi. If the plot failed and we were discovered with the body on our hands our story was ready and no one would be able to disprove it. Mr. Seton had wagered us that we couldn't kidnap him and take him back to Monksmere with-

out being discovered. He wanted to introduce such a scheme into his new book. There would be plenty of witnesses to testify that Maurice loved to experiment, that he was meticulous about detail. And if he should unexpectedly die of a heart attack during the journey, how could we be blamed? Manslaughter? Possibly. But murder, never.

"I think that Digby almost believed the fiction for a time. I did my best to keep it going. There are few men with the courage or the strength of mind to plan murder in cold blood and Digby certainly isn't one of them. He likes his unpleasant facts gift-wrapped. He prefers to shut his eyes to reality. He has always shut his eyes to the truth about me.

"Once he had convinced himself that it was all a cosy little game with easy rules, no personal risk and a prize of £200,000, he quite enjoyed planning the details. I gave him nothing to do which wasn't well within his peculiar capabilities and he wasn't pressed for time. Firstly, he had to find a second-hand motor cycle and long torpedo-shaped side car. He had to buy them separately and for cash in a part of London where he wasn't known. He had to rent or buy a flat with reasonable privacy and access to a garage, and keep his new address secret from Maurice. All this was relatively simple and I was pleased on the whole with the efficient way in which my creature coped. This was almost the most trying time for me. There was so little I personally could do to control events. Once the body had been brought to Monksmere I should be here to organize and direct. Now I had to rely on Digby to carry out instructions. It was Digby alone who must manage the business at the Cortez Club, and I had never been particularly happy about his plan to lure Maurice to the Mews Cottages. It seemed to me unnecessarily complicated and dangerous. I could think of safer and easier ways. But Digby insisted on bringing the Cortez Club into the plot. He had this need to involve and impress Luker. So I let him have his way—after all the plot couldn't incriminate me—and I admit that it worked admirably. Digby confided to Lily Coombs the fiction about the experiment to kidnap his half-brother and told her that Maurice had wagered a couple

of thousand that it couldn't be done. Lily was paid a hundred in cash for her help. All she had to do was to watch out for Maurice, spin him a yarn about the dope traffic and direct him to Carrington Mews for any further information he wanted. If he didn't take the bait nothing would be lost. I had other plans for luring him to Carrington Mews and one of those could be used. But, of course, he took the bait. It was in the service of his art and he had to go. Digby had been carefully hinting about Lily Coombs and the Cortez Club on each of his visits and Maurice had typed out the inevitable little white reference card for future use. Once Maurice had arrived in London for his regular autumn visit it was as certain that he would show himself one night at the Cortez as it was that he would stay in his usual room at the Cadaver Club, the room which he could reach without having to use that small claustrophobic lift. Digby could even predict to Lily Coombe the night on which he would appear. Oh yes, Maurice took the bait all right! He would have walked into hell in the service of his writing. And that, of course, was what he did.

"Once Maurice appeared at the door of the Carrington Mews cottage Digby's part was relatively simple. The swift knock out blow, too slight to leave a mark but heavy enough to be effective, wasn't difficult for a man who had once been a boxing champion. The adaptations to the side car to convert it into a travelling coffin had been an easy matter for one who had built Sheldrake singlehanded. The side car was ready and waiting and there was access to the garage from the house. The slight body, unconscious and breathing stertorously—for Lily had done her part well and Maurice had drunk far more wine than was good for him—was slid into the side car and the top nailed in place. There were, of course, air holes in the sides. It was no part of my plan that he should suffocate. Then Digby drank his half bottle of whisky and set out to provide himself with his alibi. We couldn't know precisely when it would be required, of course, and this was a slight worry. It would be a pity if Maurice died too soon. That he would die, and die in torment, was certain. It was merely a

231

question of how long that torment would last and when it would begin. But I instructed Digby to get himself arrested as soon as he was a safe distance from home.

"Later next morning, as soon as he was released, Digby set out with the motor cycle and side car for Monksmere. He didn't look at the body. I had instructed him not to open the side car but I doubt whether he was tempted. He was still living in the comfortable, imaginary world of the plot which I had created for him. I couldn't foresee how remarkably he would react when he could no longer pretend to believe in it. But when he set out secretly from Carrington Mews that morning I have no doubt that he felt as innocently excited as a schoolboy whose practical joke is going well. There was no trouble on the journey. The black plastic driving suit, the helmet and goggles were a perfect disguise as I had known they would be. He had a single ticket to Sax-mundham from Liverpool Street in his pocket and before leaving the West End he posted to Seton House my description of the Cortez Club. It seems almost unnecessary to say that a typing style can easily be disguised but not the type-writer used. I had typed the passage some weeks earlier on Maurice's machine wearing a glove on my right hand and with bandaged left fingers. The passage about the mutilated body floating out to sea had been typed by Maurice and was taken by me from his papers. Using it was one of the small but agreeable refinements which I had incorporated into my plan when I learned about Miss Calthrop's idea for an effective opening for one of Maurice's books. It was in every sense a gift to me as well as to Maurice. To a large extent it determined the whole shape of the murder plot, and I made use of it brilliantly.

"But there was one vital part of my plot which I haven't yet mentioned. Strangely enough, although I expected it to be the most difficult, it was the easiest of all. I had to make Digby Seton marry me. I thought that bringing him to this might take weeks of skilful persuasion. And I didn't have those weeks. All the planning had to be done in those rare weekends when he was at Monksmere. I let him write to me

because I could be sure that the letters would be burnt, but I never wrote to him and we never telephoned each other. But persuading him to this disagreeable and yet essential part of the plan wasn't the kind of thing I could do by post. I even wondered whether this would be the rock on which the whole scheme would be wrecked. But I misjudged him. He wasn't entirely stupid. If he had been I would never have risked making him a partner in his own destruction. He could recognize the inevitable. And after all, it was in his own interest. He had to marry to get his hands on the money. There was no one else he wanted. He certainly wasn't keen on a wife who would make demands on him or interfere in his life, a wife who might even want to sleep with him. And he knew that he had to marry me for one overriding reason. No one would be able to prove that we killed Maurice unless one of us talked. And a wife can't be made to give evidence against her own husband. It was arranged, of course, that we would divorce after a reasonable time and I was very generous about the marriage settlement. Not suspiciously generous. Just very very reasonable. I could afford to be. He had to marry me to keep me quiet and collect the cash. I had to marry him because I wanted the whole of his fortune. As his widow.

"We married by licence on 15th March at a London Registry Office. He hired a car and called for me early. No one saw us leaving the cottage. How could they? Celia Calthrop was away so there was no chance of her calling for me. Oliver Latham and Justin Bryce were in London. I neither knew nor cared whether Jane Dalgliesh was at home. I telephoned Maurice to say that I wasn't well enough to report for work. He was irritated but he wasn't concerned, and I had no fear that he might call at the cottage to see how I was. Maurice hated illness. He would care if his dog were sick. But then, he was fond of his dog. I find it very satisfying that he might be alive now if only he had cared enough to call at Tanner's Cottage that day, to wonder where I had gone—why I had lied.

"But time and this tape are running out. I have settled my account with Maurice Seton. This is my triumph not my justification and there is still much to be told.

"Digby, driving the motor cycle and side car, arrived at Tanner's Cottage just before six o'clock on Wednesday. It was dark by then and there was no one about. There never is once dusk has fallen on this coast. Maurice was dead, of course, Digby's face was very white under the helmet as he prised off the lid of the side car. I think he had expected to see his victim's face contorted into a grimace of horror, the dead eyes glaring accusingly. Unlike me he hadn't read Maurice's text-books on forensic medicine. He didn't know about the relaxing of muscles after death. The calm face, so ordinary, so vacuous, so completely without the power to be either frightening or pathetic seemed to reassure him. But I had forgotten to explain about rigor mortis. He hadn't expected that we should need to break the rigor in the knees so that the body could be fitted into my wheel chair and taken down to the shore. He didn't enjoy that necessary bit of business. I can still hear his high nervous giggle at the sight of Maurice's thin legs, clad in those ridiculous trousers and sticking straight out like the broomstick legs of a guy. Then Digby hit them and the rigor broke and they dangled and swung above the foot rest like the legs of a child. That small act of personal violence to the body did something to Digby. I was perfectly ready to take off the hands myself. I wanted to bring that chopper down. But Digby took it from me and waited without speaking while I laid out the hands ready for him on the thwart. I might have made a neater job of it. I doubt whether I would have enjoyed it any more than he. Afterwards I took the hands from him and put them in my mackintosh toilet bag. Digby had a use for them; he was determined to send them to Luker. But there were things I had to do to them first in the privacy of my dark room. In the meantime I slung the bag around my neck and enjoyed the feel of those dead hands, seeming to creep against my flesh.

"Last of all Digby pushed the dinghy out on the ebb tide, wading deep into the sea. I wasn't worried about bloodstains. The dead bleed slowly if they bleed at all. If there was spotting on the cycling suit the sea would wash it away. Digby waded back to me, glistening out of the darkness, hands clasped

above his head, like someone who has been ritually cleansed. He did not speak as he wheeled me back to the cottage. As I have said, in some ways I under-estimated him, and it was only on that silent journey back through the narrow lane that it struck me he could be dangerous.

"The rest of the night's work should have been the simplest. The plan was for Digby to drive as fast as he could to Ipswich. On the way he would stop at a lonely place on the bank of the Sizewell Sluice, detach the side car and sink it into the deep water. Once in Ipswich he would take the number plates off the motor cycle and abandon it in a side street. It was an old machine and it was unlikely that anyone would bother to trace the owner. And, even if it were traced to Digby and the side car found, we still had our second line of defence: the story of the experiment to kidnap Maurice, the innocent wager that went so tragically wrong. And we should have Lily Coombs to corroborate our story.

"My instructions to Digby were very clear. After abandoning the cycle he would first post Maurice's manuscript describing the handless body drifting out at sea. Then he would go to the station, still wearing his overalls, and would take a platform ticket. I didn't want the ticket collector to note the passenger who was joining his train at Ipswich with a ticket issued in London. Digby would push through the barrier when there was a convenient crowd, join the Saxmundham train, change his overalls in the lavatory, put them in a small hold-all, and arrive at Saxmundham at eight-thirty. He would then take a cab to Seton House where I would be waiting for him in the darkness to check that all had gone according to plan and to give him any instructions for the future. As I have said, it was the easiest part of the night's work and I expected no trouble. But Digby was beginning to sense his power. He did two very stupid things. He couldn't resist the temptation to detach the side car and drive at top speed around the village, even showing himself to Bryce. And he invited Liz Marley to meet him at Saxmundham. The first was no more than childish exhibitionism; the second could have been fatal. I was physically very tired by

now and emotionally unprepared to deal with this insubordination. As I heard Miss Marley's car drive up and was watching them both from the shadow of the curtains, the telephone rang. I know now that it was only Plant making a routine enquiry for Mr. Seton. At the time it shook me. Two unforeseen things were happening together and I was prepared for neither. If I had been given time to take myself in hand I should have coped with the situation better. As it was, I quarrelled violently with Digby. There is no point in wasting time with what either of us said, but it ended with Digby driving off furiously into the night with the intention, he said, of going back to London. I didn't believe him. He had too much at stake to throw in his hand now. This was no more than another childish gesture of independence provoked by the quarrel and intended simply to frighten me. But I waited until the early hours for the return of the Vauxhall, sitting there in the darkness since I dare not put on a light, wondering whether one moment of temper was to undo all my careful planning, and scheming how the situation might yet be retrieved. It was two in the morning before I made my way home. Next morning I was back at Seton House early. Still no sign of the car. It was not until Thursday night when the telephone call came through to Pentlands that I knew what had happened. By then I had no need to simulate shock. It is good to know that Digby Seton will soon be paying for what he did to me during those twenty-four hours. He was surprisingly resourceful about it all. His story about the false telephone call was very clever. It would explain any hints about Maurice's death which he may have let out during the periods of babbling semi-consciousness. It strengthened his alibi. It made things even more uncomfortable for the Monksmere community. I had to admire his ingenuity, his inventiveness. And I wondered how long it would be before he began thinking about ridding himself of me.

"There is little more to say. The return of the chopper to Jane Dalgliesh was no more difficult than stealing it had been. The plastic cycling suit was cut into shreds and floated out

on the ebb tide. I took the flesh off the knuckles of Maurice's hands with acid from the dark room and Digby posted his parcel. It was all quite simple. All according to plan. And now there is only the last chapter. In a few days' time I shall be able to dictate this again. I feel no particular hatred for Digby. I shall be glad when he is dead but I am quite happy to picture his agony without wanting to see it. But I wish I could have been there when Maurice Seton died.

"And that reminds me of the last explanation of all. Why wasn't I content for his dead body to be left in London, a bundle of flesh and clothes in a Paddington gutter? The reason is simple. We had to take off his hands. Those tell-tale hands with the knuckles torn to the bone where he had battered them against his coffin lid."

The voice had finished. For a few seconds the tape ran on. Then Reckless leant across and it clicked to a stop. Without speaking he bent to pull out the cord. Jane Dalgliesh got up from her chair and with a murmured word to Latham went out to the kitchen. Almost at once Dalgliesh heard the splash of running water and the chink of a kettle lid. What was she doing, he wondered. Getting on with preparing the lunch? Making fresh coffee for her visitors? What was she thinking? Now that it was all over was she even interested in that tumult of hate which had destroyed and disrupted so many lives including her own? One thing was certain. If she did later talk about Sylvia Kedge she wouldn't indulge in sentimental regrets of "If only we had known! If only we could have helped her!" To Jane Dalgliesh people were as they were. It was as pointlessly presumptious to try to change them as it was impertinent to pity them. Never before had his aunt's uninvolvement struck him so forcibly; never before had it seemed so frightening.

Latham slowly released himself from his self-conscious pose in front of the fire and sank down into the empty chair. He laughed uncertainly. "Poor devil! Killed because of his choice of a nightdress. Or was it because of his choice of bedroom?"

Reckless didn't answer. Carefully he curled the flex of the

237

tape recorder then tucked the machine under his arm. Turning at the door he spoke to Dalgliesh.

"We've dredged up the side car. It was within twenty yards of the spot you marked. Another lucky guess, Mr. Dalgliesh."

Dalgliesh could picture the scene. It would be pleasant on the bank of the lonely sluice in the early morning sun, a green peace broken only by the distant rumble of traffic, the singing water, the deep voices of the men as they bent to the tackle, the squelch of mud as the waders sucked at the river bed. And then the thing they sought would break surface at last, shaped like a gigantic striped marrow, the black hull festooned with weeds and glistening as the gouts of mud slipped away. He had no doubt that it looked very small to the band of toiling policemen as they urged and steadied it towards the bank. But then, Maurice Seton had been a small man.

When Reckless had left, Latham said belligerently:

"I must thank you for saving my life."

"Must you? I should have thought it was the other way round. It was you who kicked her off the roof."

The reply was quick, defensive.

"That was an accident. I never meant her to fall."

Of course not, thought Dalgliesh. It had to be an accident. Latham was the last man to live with the thought that he had killed a woman, even in self defence. Well, if that was the way he had decided to remember it, he might as well begin now as later. And what the hell did it matter anyway? He wished that Latham would go. The thought of gratitude between them was ridiculous and embarrassing, and he was too sore in mind and body to relish a morning of small talk. But there was something he needed to know. He said:

"I've been wondering why you went to Tanner's Cottage last night. You saw them I suppose—Digby and Kedge?"

The two square envelopes propped side by side were starkly white against the grey stones of the chimney piece. He would have to open Deborah's letter soon. It was ridiculous and humiliating this urge to throw it into the fire unread, as if one could with a single assertive gesture burn away all the past. He heard Latham's voice:

"Of course. The first evening I arrived. I lied about the time, incidentally. I was here soon after six. Soon afterwards, I walked along the cliff and saw the two figures with the boat. I recognized Sylvia and I thought that the man was Seton although I couldn't be sure. It was too dark to see what they were up to but it was obvious that they were shoving the dinghy out to sea. I couldn't see what the bundle was in the bottom of it, but afterwards I could guess. It didn't worry me. Maurice had it coming to him as far as I was concerned. As you seem to have guessed, Dorothy Seton sent me that last letter he wrote to her. I suppose she expected me to avenge her. I'm afraid she mistook her man. I've seen too many second-rate actors make fools of themselves in that role to fancy playing it myself. I hadn't any objection to letting someone else do the job, but when Digby was murdered I thought it was time I found out what Kedge was playing at. Celia told us that Sylvia was planning to see Reckless this morning; it seemed prudent to get in first."

It would be futile, of course, to point out that Latham could have saved Digby's life by speaking sooner. And was it even true? The murderers had their story ready: the bet with Seton; the experiment that went horribly wrong; the panic when they discovered that Maurice was dead; the decision to take off the battered hands in an attempt to cover up. Would it really have been possible without a confession to prove that Maurice Seton hadn't died a natural death?

He gripped Deborah's letter between his left thumb and rigidly bandaged palm and tried to insinuate the tips of his right hand fingers under the flap; but the tough paper resisted him. Latham said impatiently:

"Here, let me do it!"

Under his long nicotine-stained fingers the envelope ripped open. He handed it to Dalgliesh:

"Don't mind me."

"It's all right," said Dalgliesh. "I know what's in it. It can wait." But he was unfolding the sheet as he spoke. There were only eight lines. Deborah had never been verbose even in her love letters but there was a brutal economy

about these final staccato sentences. And why not? Theirs was a basic human dilemma. You could either spend a lifetime together laboriously exploring it, or you could dispose of it in eight lines. He found himself counting and recounting them, calculating the number of words, noticing with unnatural interest the spread of the lines, the details of the handwriting. She had decided to accept the job offered to her at the firm's American house. By the time he received this she would be in New York. She could no longer bear to loiter about on the periphery of his life waiting for him to make up his mind. She thought it unlikely that they would ever see each other again. It was better for them both that way. The sentences were conventional, almost trite. It was a goodbye without panache or originality, even without dignity. And if it had been written in pain there was no sign of it in that confident hand.

He could hear Latham's high arrogant voice running on in the background, saying something about an appointment at an Ipswich Hospital to have his head X-rayed, suggesting that Dalgliesh might go with him and have his hand examined, speculating spitefully on what Celia would have to pay in lawyer's fees before she could get her hands on the Seton fortune, attempting once more with the clumsiness of a school-boy to justify himself for the death of Sylvia Kedge. Dalgliesh turned his back on him and taking his own letter from the mantelpiece, laid the twin envelopes together and tore at them impatiently. But they were too strong for him and, in the end, he had to throw them whole into the fire. They took a long time to burn, each separate sheet charring and curling as the ink faded so that, at last, his own verses shone up at him, silver on black, obstinately refusing to die, and he could not even grasp the poker to beat them into dust.

SHROUD FOR A
NIGHTINGALE

FOR
J.M.C.

Contents

Chapter One

Demonstration of Death

I

On the morning of the first murder Miss Muriel Beale, Inspector of Nurse Training Schools to the General Nursing Council, stirred into wakefulness soon after 6 o'clock and into a sluggish early morning awareness that it was Monday, 12th January, and the day of the John Carpendar Hospital inspection. Already she had half-registered the first familiar sounds of a new day: Angela's alarm silenced almost before she was conscious of hearing it; Angela herself padding and snuffling about the flat like a clumsy but benevolent animal; the agreeably anticipatory tinklings of early tea in preparation. She forced open her eyelids, resisting an insidious urge to wriggle down into the enveloping warmth of the bed and let her mind drift again into blessed unconsciousness. What on earth had prompted her to tell Matron Taylor that she would arrive shortly after 9 a.m. in time to join the third-year students' first teaching session of the day? It was ridiculously, unnecessarily early. The hospital was in Heatheringfield on the Sussex/Hampshire border, a drive of nearly fifty miles, some of which would have to be done before daybreak. And it was raining, as it had rained with dreary insistence for the past week. She could hear the faint hiss of car tyres on the Cromwell Road and an occasional spatter against the window-pane. Thank God she had taken the trouble to check the map of Heatheringfield to find out exactly where the hospital lay. A developing market town, particularly if it were unfamiliar, could be a time-wasting maze to the motorist in the snarl of commuter traffic on a wet Monday morning. She felt instinctively that it was going to be a difficult day and stretched out under the bedclothes as if bracing herself to meet it. Extending her

cramped fingers, she half-relished the sharp momentary ache of her stretched joints. A touch of arthritis there. Well, it was to be expected. She was forty-nine after all. It was time she took life a little more gently. What on earth had led her to think she could get to Heatheringfield before half past nine?

The door opened, letting in a shaft of light from the passage. Miss Angela Burrows jerked back the curtains, surveyed the black January sky and the rain-spattered window and jerked them together again. "It's raining," she said with the gloomy relish of one who has prophesied rain and who cannot be held responsible for the ignoring of her warning. Miss Beale propped herself on her elbow, turned on the bedside lamp, and waited. In a few seconds her friend returned and set down the early morning tray. The tray cloth was of starched embroidered linen, the flowered cups were arranged with their handles aligned, the four biscuits on the matching plate were precisely placed, two of a kind, the teapot gave forth a delicate smell of freshly made Indian tea. The two women had a strong love of comfort and an addiction to tidiness and order. The standards which they had once enforced in the private ward of their teaching hospital were applied to their own comfort, so that life in the flat was not unlike that in an expensive and permissive nursing home.

Miss Beale had shared a flat with her friend since they had both left the same training school twenty-five years ago. Miss Angela Burrows was the Principal Tutor at a London teaching hospital. Miss Beale had thought her the paradigm of nurse tutors and, in all her inspections, subconsciously set her standard by her friend's frequent pronouncements on the principles of sound nurse teaching. Miss Burrows, for her part, wondered how the General Nursing Council would manage when the time came for Miss Beale to retire. The happiest marriages are sustained by such comforting illusions and Miss Beale's and Miss Burrows's very different, but essentially innocent, relationship was similarly founded. Except in this capacity for mutual but unstated admiration they were very different. Miss Burrows was sturdy, thick-set and formidable, hiding a vulnerable sensitivity under an air of blunt common sense. Miss Beale was small and birdlike, precise in speech and movement

and threatened with an out-of-date gentility which sometimes brought her close to being thought ridiculous. Even their physiological habits were different. The heavy Miss Burrows awoke to instantaneous life at the first sound of her alarm, was positively energetic until teatime, then sank into sleepy lethargy as the evening advanced. Miss Beale daily opened her gummed eyelids with reluctance, had to force herself into early morning activity and became more brightly cheerful as the day wore on. They had managed to reconcile even this incompatibility. Miss Burrows was happy to brew the early morning tea and prepare breakfast and Miss Beale washed up after dinner and made the nightly cocoa.

Miss Burrows poured out both cups of tea, dropped two lumps of sugar in her friend's cup and took her own to the chair by the window. Early training forbade Miss Burrows to sit on the bed. She said: "You need to be off early. I'd better run your bath. When does it start?"

Miss Beale muttered feebly that she had told Matron that she would arrive as soon as possible after nine o'clock. The tea was blessedly sweet and reviving. The promise to start out so early was a mistake but she began to think that she might after all make it by 9.15.

"That's Mary Taylor, isn't it? She's got quite a reputation considering she's only a provincial matron. Extraordinary that she's never come to London. She didn't even apply for our job when Miss Montrose retired." Miss Beale muttered incomprehensibly which, since they had had this conversation before, her friend correctly interpreted as a protest that London wasn't everybody's choice and that people were too apt to assume that nothing remarkable ever came out of the provinces.

"There's that, of course," conceded her friend. "And the John Carpendar's in a very pleasant part of the world. I like that country on the Hampshire border. It's a pity you're not visiting it in summer. Still, it's not as if she's matron of a major teaching hospital. With her ability she easily could be; she might have become one of the Great Matrons." In their student days she and Miss Beale had suffered at the hands of one of the Great Matrons but they never ceased to lament the passing of that terrifying breed.

"By the way, you'd better start in good time. The road's up just before you strike the Guildford by-pass."

Miss Beale did not inquire how she knew that the road was up. It was the sort of thing Miss Burrows invariably did know. The hearty voice went on:

"I saw Hilda Rolfe, their Principal Tutor, in the Westminster Library this week. Extraordinary woman! Intelligent, of course, and reputedly a first-class teacher, but I imagine she terrifies the students."

Miss Burrows frequently terrified her own students, not to mention most of her colleagues on the teaching staff, but would have been amazed to be told it. Miss Beale asked:

"Did she say anything about the inspection?"

"Just mentioned it. She was only returning a book and was in a hurry so we didn't talk long. Apparently they've got a bad attack of influenza in the school and half her staff are off with it."

Miss Beale thought it odd that the Principal Tutor should find time to visit London to return a library book if staffing problems were so difficult, but she didn't say so. Before breakfast Miss Beale reserved her energy for thought rather than speech. Miss Burrows came round the bed to pour out the second cups. She said:

"What with this weather and with half the training staff off sick, it looks as if you're in for a pretty dull day."

As the two friends were to tell each other for years to come, with that cosy predilection for re-stating the obvious which is one of the pleasures of long intimacy, she could hardly have been more wrong. Miss Beale, expecting nothing worse of the day than a tedious drive, an arduous inspection, and a possible tussle with those members of the Hospital Nurse Education Committee who took the trouble to attend, dragged her dressing-gown around her shoulders, stubbed her feet into her bedroom slippers and shuffled off to the bathroom. She had taken the first steps on her way to witness a murder.

II

Despite the rain, the drive was less difficult than Miss Beale had feared. She made good time and was in Heatheringfield just before

250

9 o'clock in time to meet the last surge of the morning rush to work. The wide Georgian high street was blocked with vehicles. Women were driving their commuter husbands to the station or their children to school, vans were delivering goods, buses were discharging and loading their passengers. At the three sets of traffic lights the pedestrians streamed across the road, umbrellas slanted against the soft drizzle. The young had the spruce, over-uniformed look of the private-school child; the men were mostly bowler-hatted and carrying briefcases; the women were casually dressed with that nice compromise between town smartness and country informality, typical of their kind. Watching for the lights, the pedestrian crossings and the signpost to the hospital, Miss Beale had only a brief chance to notice the elegant eighteenth-century guildhall, the carefully preserved row of timber-fronted houses and the splendid crocketed spire of Holy Trinity church, but she gained an impression of a prosperous community which cared about preserving its architectural heritage even if the row of modern chain stores at the end of the high street suggested that the caring might well have begun thirty years earlier.

But here at last was the signpost. The road to the John Carpendar Hospital led upward from the High Street between a broad avenue of trees. To the left was a high stone wall which bounded the hospital grounds.

Miss Beale had done her homework. Her briefcase, plump on the back seat of the car, contained a comprehensive note on the hospital's history as well as a copy of the last General Nursing Council Inspector's report and the comments of the Hospital Management Committee on how far it had been possible to implement the inspector's optimistic recommendations. As she knew from her researches, the hospital had a long history. It had been founded in 1791 by a wealthy merchant who had been born in the town, had left it in youthful penury to seek his fortune in London, and had returned there in his retirement to enjoy patronizing and impressing his neighbours. He could have purchased fame and ensured his salvation by succouring the widows and fatherless or by re-building the church. But the age of science and reason was succeeding the age of faith and it had become fashionable to endow a hospital for

the sick poor. And so, with the almost obligatory meeting in a local coffee house, the John Carpendar Hospital was born. The original house, of some architectural interest, had long since been replaced, first by a solid Victorian monument to ostentatious piety and then by the more functional gracelessness of the twentieth century.

The hospital had always flourished. The local community was predominantly middle-class and prosperous, with a well-developed charitable sense and too few objects on which to indulge it. Just before the Second World War a well-equipped private patients' wing had been added. Both before and after the advent of the National Health Service it had attracted wealthy patients, and consequently eminent consultants, from London and further afield. Miss Beale reflected that it was all very well for Angela to talk about the prestige of a London teaching hospital, but the John Carpendar had its own reputation. A woman might well think there were worse jobs than being Matron of a developing district general hospital, well thought of by the community it served, agreeably placed and fortified by its own local traditions.

She was at the main gates now. There was a porter's lodge on the left, an ornate doll's house in tessellated brick, a relic of the Victorian hospital, and—on the right—the doctors' car park. Already a third of the marked plots were occupied by the Daimlers and the Rolls. It had stopped raining and the dawn had given way to the grey normality of a January day. The lights were full on in the hospital. It lay before her like a great ship at anchor, brightly lit, latent with activity and power. To the left stretched the low glass-fronted buildings of the new out-patient department. Already a thin stream of patients was making its dispirited way to the entrance.

Miss Beale drew up alongside the inquiry hatch of the lodge, wound down the car window, and announced herself. The porter, ponderous and uniformed in self-importance, deigned to come out to present himself.

"You'll be the General Nursing Council, Miss," he stated grandiloquently. "What a pity you decided to come in this gate. The Nurse Training School is in Nightingale House, only a 100 yards or so from the Winchester Road entrance. We always use the back entrance for Nightingale House."

He spoke with reproachful resignation, as if deploring a singular lack of judgement which would cost him dear in extra work.

"But presumably I can get to the school this way?"

Miss Beale had no stomach for a return to the confusion of the High Street or intention of circling the hospital grounds in search of an elusive back entrance.

"Well you can, Miss." The porter's tone implied that only the wilfully obstinate would try, and he settled himself against the car door as if to deliver confidential and complicated directions. They proved, however, remarkably simple. Nightingale House was in the hospital grounds at the rear of the new out-patient department.

"Just take this road to the left, Miss, and keep straight on past the mortuary till you get to the resident medical quarters. Then turn to the right. There's a signpost where the road forks. You can't miss it."

For once this notoriously unpropitious assertion seemed justified. The grounds of the hospital were extensive and well wooded, a mixture of formal garden, grass, and clumped unkempt trees which reminded Miss Beale of the grounds of an old mental hospital. It was rare to find a general hospital so well endowed with space. But the several roads were well signposted and only one led to the left of the new out-patient department. The mortuary was easily identi-fied, a squat, ugly little building tactfully sited among the trees and made more sinister by its strategic isolation. The medical officers' residence was new and unmistakable. Miss Beale had time to indulge her usual, frequently quite unjustified, resentment that Hospital Management Committees were always more ready to rehouse their doctors than to provide adequate accommodation for the nurse training school, before noting the promised sign. A white painted board pointed to the right and read "Nightingale House, Nurse Training School".

She changed gear and turned carefully. The new road was nar-row and winding, banked high on each side with sodden leaves so that there was barely room for the single car. Everywhere was dampness and desolation. The trees grew close to the path and knitted themselves above it, ribbing the dark tunnel with their strong black boughs. From time to time a gust of wind brought

down a spatter of raindrops on the car roof or flattened a falling leaf against the windscreen. The grass verge was scarred with flower beds, regular and oblong as graves and spiked with stunted bushes. It was so dark under the trees that Miss Beale switched on her side lamps. The road shone before her like an oiled ribbon. She had left the car window down and could smell, even above the inevitable car smell of petrol and warm vinyl, a sweet fungoid stench of decay. She felt strangely isolated in the dim quietness and suddenly she was touched with an irrational unease, a bizarre sensation of journeying out of time into some new dimension, borne onwards towards an uncomprehended and inescapable horror. It was only a second's folly and she quickly shook it off, reminding herself of the cheerful bustle of the High Street less than a mile away and the nearness of life and activity. But it had been an odd and disconcerting experience. Angry at herself at this lapse into morbid folly, she wound up the car window and stepped on the accelerator. The little car leaped forward.

Suddenly she found she had turned the last corner and Nightingale House was before her. She nearly stood on the brakes in surprise. It was an extraordinary house, an immense Victorian edifice of red brick, castellated and ornate to the point of fancy, and crowned with four immense turrets. It was brightly lit in the dark January morning and after the gloom of the road it blazed at her like the castle from some childhood mythology. An immense conservatory was grafted onto the right side of the house, looking, thought Miss Beale, more appropriate to Kew Gardens than to what had obviously once been a private residence. It was less brightly lit than the house but through the faintly luminous glass she could discern the sleek green leaves of aspidistras, the harsh red of poinsettias and the yellow and bronze blobs of chrysanthemums.

Miss Beale's recent moment of panic under the trees was completely forgotten in her amazement at Nightingale House. Despite her normal confidence in her own taste, she was not entirely immune to the vagaries of fashion and she wondered uneasily whether in certain company it might not be proper to admire it. But it had become a habit with her to look at every building with an eye to its

suitability as a nurse training school—she had once, on a Paris holiday, found herself to her horror rejecting the Elysée Palace as unworthy of further notice—and as a nurse training school Nightingale House was obviously quite impossible. She had only to look at it for the objections to spring to mind. Most of the rooms would be far too large. Where, for instance, would one find cosy offices for the principal tutor, clinical instructor or school secretary? Then the building would be extremely difficult to heat adequately and those oriel windows, picturesque no doubt if one liked that sort of thing, would keep out a great deal of light. Worse still, there was something forbidding, even frightening, about the house. When the Profession (Miss Beale, in defiance of an unfortunate comparison, always thought of it with a capital P) was climbing so painfully into the twentieth century, kicking away the stones of outworn attitudes and methods—Miss Beale was frequently required to make speeches and certain pet phrases tended to stick in her mind—it really was a pity to house young students in this Victorian pile. It would do no harm to incorporate a strong comment about the need for a new school in her report. Nightingale House was rejected even before she set foot in it.

But there was nothing to criticize in her welcome. As she reached the top step, the heavy door swung open letting out a gust of warm air and a smell of fresh coffee. A uniformed maid stood deferentially aside and behind her down the wide oak staircase, gleaming against the dark panelling like a Renaissance portrait in grey and gold, came the figure of Matron Mary Taylor, hand outstretched. Miss Beale assumed her bright professional smile, compounded of happy expectation and general reassurance, and stepped forward to meet her. The ill-fated inspection of the John Carpendar Training School had begun.

III

Fifteen minutes later, four people made their way down the main staircase to the demonstration room on the ground floor where they were to watch the first teaching session of the day. Coffee had been served in Matron's sitting-room in one of the turret blocks where

Miss Beale had been introduced to the principal tutor, Miss Hilda Rolfe, and to a senior consultant surgeon, Mr. Stephen Courtney-Briggs. She knew both by reputation. Miss Rolfe's presence was necessary and expected, but Miss Beale was a little surprised that Mr. Courtney-Briggs was prepared to devote so much of his morning to the inspection. He had been introduced as Vice-Chairman of the Hospital Nurse Education Committee and she would normally have expected to meet him with other members of the committee for the summing-up discussion at the end of the day. It was unusual for a senior surgeon to sit in at a teaching session and it was gratifying that he took such a personal interest in the school.

There was room for three to walk abreast in the wide wood-panelled corridors and Miss Beale found herself escorted by the tall figures of Matron and Mr. Courtney-Briggs rather, she felt, like a diminutive delinquent. Mr. Courtney-Briggs, stoutly impressive in the formal striped trousers of a consultant, walked on her left. He smelt of after-shave lotion. Miss Beale could discern it even above the pervading smell of disinfectant, coffee and furniture cream. She thought it surprising but not disagreeable. The Matron, tallest of the three, walked in serene silence. Her formal dress of grey gaberdine was buttoned high to the neck with a thin band of white linen around the throat and cuffs. Her corn-gold hair, almost indistinguishable in colour from her skin, was combed back from the high forehead and bound tight by an immense triangle of muslin, its apex reaching nearly to the small of her back. The cap reminded Miss Beale of those worn during the last war by Sisters of the Army Nursing Service. She had seldom seen it since. But its simplicity suited Miss Taylor. That face, with its high cheekbones and large, slightly protuberant eyes—they reminded Miss Beale irreverently of pale veined gooseberries—could have looked grotesque under the fripperies of a more orthodox head-dress. Behind the three of them Miss Beale could sense the disturbing presence of Sister Rolfe, uncomfortably close on their heels.

Mr. Courtney-Briggs was talking:

"This influenza epidemic has been a thorough nuisance. We've had to defer taking the next set off the wards and we thought at one time that this set would have to go back. It was a close thing."

"It would be," thought Miss Beale. Whenever there was a crisis in the hospital the first people to be sacrificed were the student nurses. Their training programme could always be interrupted. It was a sore point with her, but now was hardly the time to protest. She made a vaguely acquiescent noise. They started down the last staircase. Mr. Courtney-Briggs continued his monologue:

"Some of the training staff have gone down with it too. The demonstration this morning is being taken by our clinical instructor, Mavis Gearing. We've had to recall her to the school. Normally, of course, she would be doing nothing but ward teaching. It's a comparatively new idea that there should be a trained instructor to teach the girls on the wards, using the patients as clinical material. Ward sisters just haven't the time these days. Of course the whole idea of the block system of training is relatively new. When I was a medical student the probationers, as we called them then, were taught entirely on the wards with occasional lectures in their own free time from the medical staff. There was little formal teaching and certainly no taking them off the wards each year for a period in the nurse training school. The whole concept of nurse training has altered."

Miss Beale was the last person to require an explanation of the function and duties of a clinical instructor or the development of nurse training methods. She wondered whether Mr. Courtney-Briggs had forgotten who she was. This elementary instruction was more suitable for new members of a Hospital Management Committee, who were generally as ignorant of nurse training as they were of anything else to do with hospitals. She had the feeling that the surgeon had something on his mind. Or was this merely the aimless chatter, unrelated to its hearer, of an egotist who could not tolerate even a moment without the comforting resonance of his own voice? If so, the sooner he got back to his out-patient session or ward round and let the inspection proceed without the benefit of his presence, the better for all concerned.

The little procession passed across the tessellated hall to a room at the front of the building. Miss Rolfe slipped forward to open the door and stood aside as the others entered. Mr. Courtney-Briggs ushered Miss Beale in before him. Immediately she was at home.

Despite the anomalies of the room itself—the two great windows with their spatter of coloured panes, the immense fireplace of carved marble with its draped figures supporting the chimney-piece, the high moulded ceiling desecrated with the three tubes of fluorescent light—it was happily evocative of her own student days, an utterly acceptable and familiar world. Here was all the para-phernalia of her profession; the rows of glass-fronted cabinets, with their instruments placed in shining precision; the wall charts show-ing in lurid diagram the circulation of the blood and the improbable processes of digestion; the wall-mounted blackboard smeared with the dust of past lecture notes imperfectly erased; the demonstration trolleys with their linen-covered trays; the two demonstration beds, one containing a life-sized doll propped among the pillows; the inevitable skeleton hanging from its gibbet in forlorn decrepitude. Pervading all was the astringent and potent smell of disinfectant. Miss Beale breathed it in like an addict. Whatever faults she might later find with the room itself, the adequacy of the teaching equip-ment, the lighting or the furniture, she never felt other than at home in this intimidating atmosphere.

She bestowed on students and teacher her brief smile of re-assurance and encouragement and perched herself on one of the four chairs placed ready at the side of the room. Matron Taylor and Miss Rolfe seated themselves on each side of her as quietly and unobtrusively as possible in the face of Mr. Courtney-Briggs's determination to be fussily gallant over pulling out the ladies' chairs. The arrival of the little party, however tactfully arranged, seemed temporarily to have disconcerted the nurse tutor. An in-spection was hardly a natural teaching situation, but it was always interesting to see how long it took a tutor to re-establish *rapport* with her class. A first-class teacher, as Miss Beale knew from per-sonal experience, could hold a class's interest even through a heavy bombing raid let alone the visit of a General Nursing Council In-spector; but she did not feel that Mavis Gearing was likely to prove one of that rare and dedicated band. The girl—or woman rather—lacked authority. She had a propitiatory air; she looked as though she might easily simper. And she was a great deal too heavily made up for a woman who should have her mind on less ephemeral arts.

But she was, after all, merely the clinical instructor, not a qualified nurse tutor. She was taking the session at short notice and under difficulties. Miss Beale made a mental resolution not to judge her too harshly.

The class, she saw, were to practise feeding a patient by intra-gastric tube. The student who was to act as patient was already in one of the demonstration beds, her check dress protected by a mackintosh bib, her head supported by the back rest and a bank of pillows. She was a plain girl with a strong, obstinate and oddly mature face, her dull hair drawn back unbecomingly from a high nobbly forehead. She lay there immobile under the harsh strip lighting, looking a little ridiculous but strangely dignified as if concentrating on some private world and dissociating herself from the whole procedure by an effort of will. Suddenly it occurred to Miss Beale that the girl might be frightened. The thought was ridiculous but it persisted. She found herself suddenly unwilling to watch that resolute face. Irritated by her own unreasonable sensitivity, she turned her attention to the nurse tutor.

Sister Gearing cast an apprehensive and interrogative glance at the Matron, received a confirmatory nod and resumed her lesson.

"Nurse Pearce is acting the part of our patient this morning. We have just been going through her history. She is Mrs. Stokes, the fifty-year-old mother of four children, wife of a council refuse collector. She has had a larynectomy for the treatment of cancer." She turned to a student sitting on her right.

"Nurse Dakers, will you please describe Mrs. Stokes's treatment so far."

Nurse Dakers dutifully began. She was a pale, thin girl who blushed unbecomingly as she spoke. It was difficult to hear her but she knew her facts and presented them well. A conscientious little thing, thought Miss Beale, not outstandingly intelligent, perhaps, but hard working and reliable. It was a pity that no one had done anything about her acne. She retained her air of bright professional interest whilst Nurse Dakers propounded the fictional medical history of Mrs. Stokes and took the opportunity of a close look at the remaining students in the class, making her customary private assessment of their characters and ability.

The influenza epidemic had certainly taken its toll. There was a total of seven girls only in the demonstration room. The two who were standing one on each side of the demonstration bed made an immediate impression. They were obviously identical twins, strong, ruddy-faced girls, with copper-coloured hair clumped in a thick fringe above remarkable blue eyes. Their caps, the pleated crowns as small as saucers, were perched well forward, the two immense wings of white linen jutting behind. Miss Beale, who knew from her own student days what could be done with a couple of white-tipped hat pins, was nevertheless intrigued by the art which could so firmly attach such a bizarre and unsubstantial edifice on such a springing bush of hair. The John Carpendar uniform struck her as interestingly out of date. Nearly every hospital she visited had replaced these old-fashioned winged caps with the smaller American-type which were easier to wear, quicker to make up, and cheaper to buy and launder. Some hospitals, to Miss Beale's regret, were even issuing disposable paper caps. But a hospital's nurse uniform was always jealously defended and changed with reluctance and the John Carpendar was obviously wedded to tradition. Even the uniform dresses were slightly old fashioned. The twins' plump and speckled arms bulged from sleeves of check pink gingham which reminded Miss Beale of her own student days. Their skirt lengths paid no concession to modern fashion and their sturdy feet were planted in low-heeled black lace-up shoes.

She glanced quickly at the remaining students. There was a calm, bespectacled girl with a plain intelligent face. Miss Beale's immediate reaction was that she would be glad to have her on any ward. Next to her sat a dark, sulky-looking girl, rather over-made-up and assuming an air of careful disinterest in the demonstration. Rather common, thought Miss Beale. Miss Beale, to her superiors' occasional embarrassment, was fond of such unfashionable adjectives, used them unashamedly and knew precisely what she meant by them. Her dictum "Matron recruits a very nice type of girl" meant that they came of respectable middle-class families, had received the benefit of grammar school education, wore their skirts knee length or longer, and were properly aware of the privilege and responsibilities of being a student nurse. The last student in the class

was a very pretty girl, her blonde hair worn in a fringe as low as her eyebrows above a pert, contemporary face. She was attractive enough for a recruiting poster, thought Miss Beale, but somehow it was the last face one would choose. While she was wondering why, Nurse Dakers came to the end of her recital.

"Right, Nurse," said Sister Gearing. "So we are faced with the problem of a post-operative patient, already seriously under-nourished and now unable to take food by mouth. That means what? Yes, Nurse?"

"Intra-gastric or rectal feeding, Sister."

It was the dark sulky-looking girl who answered, her voice care-fully repressing any note of enthusiasm or even interest. Certainly not an agreeable girl, thought Miss Beale.

There was a murmur from the class. Sister Gearing raised an interrogative eyebrow. The spectacled student said:

"Not rectal feeding, Sister. The rectum can't absorb sufficient nourishment. Intra-gastric feeding by the mouth or nose."

"Right, Nurse Goodale, and that's what the surgeon has ordered for Mrs. Stokes. Will you carry on please, Nurse. Explain what you are doing at each step."

One of the twins drew the trolley forward and demonstrated her tray of requirements: the gallipot containing sodium bicarbonate mixture for cleaning mouth or nostrils; the polythene funnel and eight inches of tubing to fit it; the connector; the lubricant; the kidney bowl with the tongue spatula, tongue forceps and gag. She held up the Jacques oesophageal tube. It dangled from her freckled hand obscenely like a yellow snake.

"Right, Nurse," encouraged Sister Gearing. "Now the feed. What are you giving her?"

"Actually, it's just warm milk, Sister."

"But if we were dealing with a real patient?"

The twin hesitated. The spectacled student said with calm authority: "We could add soluble protein, eggs, vitamin prepara-tions and sugar."

"Right. If tube feeding is to continue for more than forty-eight hours we must ensure that the diet is adequate in calories, protein and vitamins. At what temperature are you giving the feed, Nurse?"

"Body temperature, Sister, 38° C."

"Correct. And as our patient is conscious and able to swallow we are giving her this feed by mouth. Don't forget to reassure your patient, Nurse. Explain simply to her what you are going to do and why. Remember this, girls, never begin any nursing procedure without telling your patient what is to happen."

They were third-year students, thought Miss Beale. They should know this by now. But the twin, who no doubt would have coped easily enough with a real patient, found it embarrassingly difficult to explain her procedure to a fellow student. Suppressing a giggle she muttered a few words at the rigid figure in the bed and almost thrust the oesophageal tube at her. Nurse Pearce, still gazing fixedly ahead, felt for the tube with her left hand and guided it into her mouth. Then shutting her eyes she swallowed. There was a convulsive spasm of the throat muscles. She paused to take breath, and then swallowed again. The tube shortened. It was very silent in the demonstration room. Miss Beale was aware that she felt unhappy but was unsure why. It was a little unusual perhaps for gastric feeding to be practised on a student in this way but it was not unknown. In a hospital it might be more usual for a doctor to pass the tube but a nurse might well have to take the responsibility; it was better to learn on each other than on a seriously ill patient and the demonstration doll wasn't really a satisfactory substitute for a living subject. She had once acted as the patient in her own training school and had found swallowing the tube unexpectedly easy. Watching the convulsive movements of Nurse Pearce's throat and swallowing in an unconscious sympathy she could almost recall, after thirty years, the sudden chill as the tube slid over the soft palate and the faint shock of surprise at the ease of it all. But there was something pathetic and disturbing about that rigid white-faced figure on the bed, eyes tight closed, bibbed like a baby, the thin tube dragging and wriggling like a worm from the corner of her mouth. Miss Beale felt that she was watching gratuitous suffering, that the whole demonstration was an outrage. For a second she had to fight an urge to protest.

One of the twins was now attaching a 20-ml. syringe to the end of the tube, ready to aspirate some of the gastric juices to test that

the end of the tube had reached the stomach. The girl's hands were quite steady. Perhaps it was just Miss Beale's imagination that the room was preternaturally silent. She glanced across at Miss Taylor. The Matron had her eyes fixed on Nurse Pearce. She was frowning slightly. Her lips moved and she shifted in her seat. Miss Beale wondered if she were about to expostulate. But the Matron made no sound. Mr. Courtney-Briggs was leaning forward in his chair, his hands clasping his knees. He was gazing intently, not at Nurse Pearce, but at the drip as if mesmerized by the gentle swing of the tubing. Miss Beale could hear the heavy rasp of his breathing. Miss Rolfe sat bolt upright, her hands folded loosely in her lap, her black eyes expressionless. But Miss Beale saw that they were fixed, not on the girl in the bed, but on the fair pretty student. And for a fleeting second the girl looked back at her, equally expressionless.

The twin who was administering the feed, obviously satisfied that the end of the oesophageal tube was safely in the stomach, lifted the funnel high over Nurse Pearce's head and began slowly to pour the milky mixture down the tube. The class seemed to be holding its breath. And then it happened. There was a squeal, high-pitched, horribly inhuman, and Nurse Pearce precipitated herself from the bed as if propelled by an irresistible force. One second she was lying, immobile, propped against her mound of pillows, the next she was out of bed, teetering forward on arched feet in a parody of a ballet dancer, and clutching ineffectually at the air as if in frantic search of the tubing. And all the time she screamed, perpetually screamed, like a stuck whistle. Miss Beale, aghast, had hardly time to register the contorted face, the foaming lips, before the girl thudded to the floor and writhed there, doubled like a hoop, her forehead touching the ground, her whole body twitching in agony.

One of the students screamed. For a second no one moved. Then there was a rush forward. Sister Gearing tugged at the tube and tore it from the girl's mouth. Mr. Courtney-Briggs moved resolutely into the mêlée, his arms wide. Matron and Sister Rolfe bent over the twitching figure hiding her from view. Then Miss Taylor rose and looked round at Miss Beale.

"The students . . . could you look after them please? There's an empty room next door. Keep them together."

She was trying to keep calm but urgency made her voice sharp. "Quickly please."

Miss Beale nodded. The Matron bent again over the convulsed figure. The screaming had stopped now. It was succeeded by a piteous moaning and a dreadful staccato drumming of heels on the wooden floor. Mr. Courtney-Briggs took off his coat, threw it to one side, and began to roll up his sleeves.

IV

Muttering gentle encouragement, Miss Beale shepherded the little group of students across the hall. One of them, she was not sure which, said in a high-pitched voice: "What happened to her? What happened? What went wrong?" But no one replied. They moved in a shocked daze into the room next door. It was at the back of the house, a small, odd-shaped room which had obviously been partitioned from the original high-ceilinged drawing-room and which now served as the Principal Tutor's office. Miss Beale's first glance took in a business-like desk, a bank of green steel filing cabinets, a crowded notice board, a small pegboard fitted with hooks from which hung a variety of keys, and a chart along the whole of one wall showing the teaching programme and the progress of each individual student. The partition wall cut the mullioned window in half so that the office, unpleasing in its proportions, was also inconveniently dark. One of the students clicked down the switch and the central bar of fluorescence began to flicker into light. Really, thought Miss Beale, her mind clutching desperately at the comfort of its normal preoccupations, it was a most unsuitable room for a Principal Tutor, or for any other tutor, come to that.

This brief remembrance of the purpose of her visit brought a second's comfort. But almost immediately the awful reality of the moment reasserted itself. The students—a pathetic and disorganized little bunch—had crowded together in the middle of the room as if incapable of action. Glancing quickly around, Miss Beale saw that there were only three chairs. For a moment she felt as embarrassed and nonplussed as a hostess who is not sure how she is going to seat

all her guests. The concern wasn't altogether irrelevant. She would have to get the girls comfortable and relaxed if there were to be any chance of keeping their minds off what was happening next door; and they might be incarcerated for a long time.

"Come along," she said brightly. "Let's move Sister's desk back against the wall, then four of you can perch there. I'll take the desk chair and two of you can have the easy chairs."

At least it was activity. Miss Beale saw that the thin, fair student was shaking. She helped her into one of the easy chairs and the dark, sulky-looking girl promptly took the other. Trust her to look after number one, thought Miss Beale. She busied herself helping the other students to clear the desk and push it back against the wall. If only she could send one of them to make some tea! Despite her intellectual assent to more modern methods of combating shock, Miss Beale still put her faith in warm strong sweet tea. But there wasn't a chance of any. It wouldn't do to upset and alert the kitchen staff.

"Now suppose we introduce ourselves," she said encouragingly. "My name is Miss Muriel Beale. There's no need to tell you I'm a G.N.C. Inspector. I know some of your names but I am not really sure who is who."

Five pairs of eyes gazed at her with startled incomprehension. But the efficient student—as Miss Beale still thought of her—quietly identified them.

"The twins are Maureen and Shirley Burt. Maureen is the elder by about two minutes and has the most freckles. Otherwise we don't find it easy to tell them apart. Next to Maureen is Julia Pardoe. Christine Dakers is in one armchair and Diane Harper in the other. I'm Madeleine Goodale."

Miss Beale, never good at remembering names, made her customary mental recapitulation. The Burt twins. Bonny and bouncing. It would be easy enough to remember their name, although impossible to decide which was which. Julia Pardoe. An attractive name for an attractive girl. Very attractive if one liked that blonde, rather feline prettiness. Smiling into the unresponsive violet-blue eyes, Miss Beale decided that some people, and not all of them men, might like it very much indeed. Madeleine Goodale. A good sen-

sible name for a good sensible girl. She thought she would have no difficulty in remembering Goodale. Christine Dakers. Something very wrong there. The girl had looked ill throughout the brief demonstration and now seemed close to collapse. She had a poor skin, unusually so for a nurse. It was now drained of colour so that the spots around the mouth and over the forehead stood out in an angry rash. She was huddled deep into the armchair, her thin hands alternately smoothing and plucking at her apron. Nurse Dakers was certainly the most affected of all the group. Perhaps she had been a particular friend of Nurse Pearce. Miss Beale superstitiously made a quick mental amendment of tense. Perhaps she was a particular friend. If only they could get the girl some hot reviving tea!

Nurse Harper, her lipstick and eye shadow garish on the whitened face said suddenly: "There must have been something in the feed."

The Burt twins turned to her simultaneously. Maureen said: "Of course there was! Milk."

"I mean something beside the milk." She hesitated. "Poison."

"But there couldn't be! Shirley and I took a fresh bottle of milk out of the kitchen fridge first thing this morning. Miss Collins was there and saw us. We left it in the demo room and didn't pour it into the measuring jug until just before the demonstration, did we, Shirley?"

"That's right. It was a fresh bottle. We took it at about 7 o'clock."

"And you didn't add anything by mistake?"

"Like what? Of course we didn't."

The twins spoke in unison, sounding sturdily confident, almost unworried. They knew exactly what they had done and when, and no one, Miss Beale saw, was likely to shake them. They weren't the type to be tormented by unnecessary guilt or fretted by those irrational doubts which afflict less stolid, more imaginative personalities. Miss Beale thought that she understood them very well.

Julia Pardoe said: "Perhaps someone else mucked about with the feed."

She looked round at her fellow students from under lowered lids, provocative, a little amused.

Madeleine Goodale said calmly: "Why should they?"

Nurse Pardoe shrugged and pursed her lips into a little secret smile. She said: "By accident. Or it might have been a practical joke. Or perhaps it was done on purpose."

"But that would be attempted murder!" It was Diane Harper who spoke. She sounded incredulous. Maureen Burt laughed.

"Don't be daft, Julia. Who would want to murder Pearce?"

No one replied. The logic was apparently unassailable. It was impossible to imagine anyone wanting to murder Pearce. Pearce, Miss Beale realized, was either of the company of the naturally inoffensive or was too negative a personality to inspire the tormenting hatred which can lead to murder. Then Nurse Goodale said drily: "Pearce wasn't everyone's cup of tea."

Miss Beale glanced at the girl, surprised. It was an odd remark to come from Nurse Goodale, a little insensitive in the circumstances, disconcertingly out of character. She noted, too, the use of the past tense. Here was one student who didn't expect to see Nurse Pearce alive again.

Nurse Harper reiterated stoutly: "It's daft to talk about murder. No one would want to kill Pearce."

Nurse Pardoe shrugged: "Perhaps it wasn't meant for Pearce. Jo Fallon was supposed to act as patient today, wasn't she? It was Fallon's name next on the list. If she hadn't been taken ill last night, it would have been Fallon in that bed this morning."

They were silent. Nurse Goodale turned to Miss Beale.

"She's right. We take it in strict turn to act as patient; it wasn't really Pearce's turn this morning. But Josephine Fallon was taken into the sick bay last night—you've probably heard that we have an influenza epidemic—and Pearce was next on the list. Pearce was taking Fallon's place."

Miss Beale was momentarily at a loss. She felt that she ought to put a stop to the conversation, that it was her responsibility to keep their minds off the accident, and surely it could only have been an accident. But she didn't know how. Besides, there was a dreadful fascination in getting at the facts. For her, there always had been. Perhaps, too, it was better that the girls should indulge this detached, investigatory interest, rather than sit there making unnatural and

ineffective conversation. Already she saw that shock was giving way to that half-ashamed excitement which can follow tragedy, so long, of course, as it is someone else's tragedy.

Julia Pardoe's composed, rather childish voice went on: "So if the victim was really meant to be Fallon, it couldn't have been one of us, could it? We all knew that Fallon wouldn't be acting the patient this morning."

Madeleine Goodale said: "I should think that everyone knew. Everyone at Nightingale House anyway. There was enough talk about it at breakfast."

They were silent again, considering this new development. Miss Beale noted with interest that there were no protestations that no one would want to murder Fallon. Then Maureen Burt said:

"Fallon can't be all that sick. She was back here in Nightingale House this morning, just after eight-forty. Shirley and I saw her slipping out of the side door just before we went into the demo room after breakfast."

Nurse Goodale asked sharply: "What was she wearing?" Maureen was unsurprised at this apparently irrelevant question.

"Slacks. Her top coat. That red headscarf she wears. Why?"

Nurse Goodale, obviously shaken and surprised, made an attempt to conceal it. She said:

"She slipped those on before we took her to the sick bay last night. I suppose she came back to fetch something she wanted from her room. But she shouldn't have left the ward. It was stupid. She had a temperature of 103·8 when she was warded. Lucky for her that Sister Brumfett didn't see her."

Nurse Pardoe said maliciously: "Funny though, isn't it?" No one replied. It was indeed funny, thought Miss Beale. She recalled her long damp drive from the hospital to the nurse training school. The road was a winding one; obviously there would be a short cut through the trees. But it was a strange journey for a sick girl to make on an early January morning. There must have been some compelling reason to bring her back to Nightingale House. After all, if she did want something from her room there was nothing to prevent her asking for it. Any of the students would gladly have taken it across to the sick bay. And this was the girl who should

268

have played the patient that morning, who should, logically, be lying next door among the tangle of tubes and linen.

Nurse Pardoe said: "Well, there's one person who knew that Fallon wouldn't be acting patient this morning. Fallon herself."

Nurse Goodale, white-faced, looked across at her.

"If you want to be stupid and malicious I suppose I can't stop you. But, if I were you, I would stop short of slander."

Nurse Pardoe looked unconcerned, even a little pleased. Catching sight of her sly, gratified smile, Miss Beale decided that it was time this talking stopped. She was searching for a change of topic when Nurse Dakers said faintly from the depths of her chair: "I feel sick."

There was immediate concern. Only Nurse Harper made no move to help. The rest gathered around the girl, glad of the chance to be doing something. Nurse Goodale said: "I'll take her to the downstairs cloakroom."

She supported the girl out of the room. To Miss Beale's surprise Nurse Pardoe went with her, their recent antagonism apparently forgotten as they supported Nurse Dakers between them. Miss Beale was left with the Burt twins and Nurse Harper. Another silence fell. But Miss Beale had learned her lesson. She had been unforgivably irresponsible. There was to be no more talk of death or murder. While they were here and in her charge they might as well work. She gazed sternly at Nurse Harper and invited her to describe the signs, symptoms and treatment of pulmonary collapse.

Ten minutes later the absent three returned. Nurse Dakers still looked pale but was composed. It was Nurse Goodale who looked worried. As if unable to keep it to herself, she said:

"The bottle of disinfectant is missing from the lavatory. You know the one I mean. It's always kept there on the little shelf. Pardoe and I couldn't find it."

Nurse Harper interrupted her bored but surprisingly competent recital and said:

"You mean that bottle of milky-looking mixture? It was there after supper last night."

"That's a long time ago. Has anyone been in that loo this morning?"

Apparently no one had. They looked at each other in silence.

It was then that the door opened. Matron came quietly in and shut it behind her. There was a creak of starched linen as the twins slipped from the desk and stood to attention. Nurse Harper rose gracelessly from her chair. All of them turned towards Miss Taylor.

"Children," she said, and the unexpected and gentle word told them the truth before she spoke.

"Children, Nurse Pearce died a few minutes ago. We don't yet know how or why, but when something inexplicable like this happens we have to call the police. The Hospital Secretary is doing that now. I want you to be brave and sensible as I know you will be. Until the police arrive, I think it would be better if we don't talk about what has happened. You will collect your textbooks and Nurse Goodale will take you to wait in my sitting-room. I shall be ordering some strong hot coffee and it will be brought up to you soon. Is that understood?"

There was a subdued murmur of, "Yes, Matron."

Miss Taylor turned to Miss Beale.

"I'm so very sorry, but it will mean your waiting here too."

"Of course, Matron, I quite understand."

Across the heads of the students their eyes met in bewildered speculation and wordless sympathy.

But Miss Beale was a little horrified to remember afterwards the banality and irrelevance of her first conscious thought.

"This must be the shortest inspection on record. What on earth will I say to the General Nursing Council?"

v

A few minutes earlier the four people in the demonstration room had straightened up and looked at each other, white-faced, utterly exhausted. Heather Pearce was dead. She was dead by any criteria, legal or medical. They had known it for the last five minutes but had worked on, doggedly and without speaking, as if there were still a chance that the flabby heart would pulse again into life. Mr. Courtney-Briggs had taken off his coat to work on the girl and the front of his waistcoat was heavily stained with blood. He stared at

270

the thickening stain, brow creased, nose fastidiously wrinkled, almost as if blood were an alien substance to him. The heart massage had been messy as well as ineffectual. Surprisingly messy for Mr. Courtney-Briggs, the Matron thought. But surely the attempt had been justified? There hadn't been time to get her over to the theatre. It was a pity that Sister Gearing had pulled out the oesophageal tube. It had, perhaps, been a natural reaction but it might have cost Pearce her only chance. While the tube was in place they could at least have tried an immediate stomach wash-out. But an attempt to pass another tube by the nostril had been frustrated by the girl's agonized spasms and, by the time these had ceased, it was too late and Mr. Courtney-Briggs had been forced to open the chest wall and try the only measure left to him. Mr. Courtney-Briggs's heroic efforts were well known. It was only a pity that they left the body looking so pathetically mangled and the demonstration room stinking like an abattoir. These things were better conducted in an operating theatre, shrouded and dignified by the paraphernalia of ritual surgery.

He was the first to speak.

"This wasn't a natural death. There was something other than milk in that feed. Well, that's obvious to all of us I should have thought. We'd better call the police. I'll get on to the Yard. I know someone there, as it happens. One of the Assistant Commissioners."

He always did know someone, thought the Matron. She felt the need to oppose him. Shock had left an aftermath of irritation and, irrationally, it focused on him. She said calmly:

"The local police are the ones to call and I think that the Hospital Secretary should do it. I'll get Mr. Hudson on the house telephone now. They'll call in the Yard if they think it necessary. I can't think why it should be. But that decision is for the Chief Constable, not for us."

She moved over to the wall telephone, carefully walking round the crouched figure of Miss Rolfe. The Principal Tutor was still on her knees. She looked, thought the Matron, rather like a character from a Victorian melodrama with her smouldering eyes in a deathly white face, her black hair a little dishevelled under the frilly cap,

and those reeking hands. She was turning them over slowly and studying the red mass with a detached, speculative interest as if she, too, found it difficult to believe that the blood was real. She said:

"If there's a suspicion of foul play ought we to move the body?" Mr. Courtney-Briggs said sharply: "I have no intention of moving the body."

"But we can't leave her here, not like this!" Miss Gearing was almost weeping in protest. The surgeon glared at her.

"My dear woman, the girl's dead! Dead! What does it matter where we leave the body? She can't feel. She can't know. For God's sake don't start being sentimental about death. The indignity is that we die at all, not what happens to our bodies."

He turned brusquely and went over to the window. Sister Gearing made a movement as if to follow him, and then sank into the nearest chair and began to cry softly like a snuffling animal. No one took any notice of her. Sister Rolfe got stiffly to her feet. Holding her hands raised in front of her in the ritual gesture of an operating theatre nurse she walked over to a sink in the corner, nudged on the tap with her elbow, and began to wash her hands. At the wall-mounted telephone the Matron was dialling a five-digit number. They heard her calm voice.

"Is that the Hospital Secretary's office? Is Mr. Hudson there? It's Matron." There was a pause. "Good morning, Mr. Hudson. I am speaking from the ground floor demonstration room in Nightingale House. Could you please come over immediately? Yes. Very urgent. I'm afraid something tragic and horrible has happened and it will be necessary for you to telephone the police. No, I'd rather not tell you on the telephone. Thank you." She replaced the receiver and said quietly: "He's coming at once. He'll have to put the Vice-Chairman in the picture, too—it's unfortunate that Sir Marcus is in Israel—but the first thing is to get the police. And now I had better tell the other students."

Sister Gearing was making an attempt to control herself. She blew loudly into her handkerchief, replaced it in her uniform pocket, and raised a blotched face.

"I'm sorry. It's the shock, I suppose. It's just that it was all so horrible. Such an appalling thing to happen. And the first time

272

I've taken a class too! And everyone sitting and watching it like that. The other students as well. Such a horrible accident."

"Accident, Sister?" Mr. Courtney-Briggs turned from the window. He strode over to her and bent his bull-like head close to hers. His voice was harsh, contemptuous as he almost spat the words into her face. "Accident? Are you suggesting that a corrosive poison found its way into that feed by accident? Or that a girl in her right mind would choose to kill herself in that particularly horrible way? Come, come, Sister, why not be honest for once? What we've just witnessed was murder!"

Chapter Two

Cease Upon the Midnight

I

It was late in the evening of Wednesday, 28th January, sixteen days after the death of Nurse Pearce and, in the students' sitting-room on the first floor of Nightingale House, Nurse Dakers was writing her mid-week letter to her mother. It was usual for her to finish it in time for the Wednesday evening post but, this week, she had lacked the energy and inclination to settle down to the task. Already the waste-paper basket at her feet held the screwed-up copies of the first two rejected drafts. And now she was trying again.

She was sitting at one of the twin writing-desks in front of the window, her left elbow almost brushing the heavy curtains which shut out the dank blackness of the night, her forearm curled protectively around the writing-pad. Opposite to her, the desk lamp shone on the bent head of Madeleine Goodale, so close that Nurse Dakers could see the clean white scalp at the hair parting and smell the almost imperceptible antiseptic tang of shampoo. Two text-books were open before Goodale and she was making notes. Nothing, thought Nurse Dakers with resentful envy, was worrying her; nothing in the room or beyond it could disturb her quiet concentration. The admirable and secure Goodale was making sure that the John Carpendar Gold Medal for top marks in the final examination would eventually be pinned on her immaculate apron.

Frightened by the strength of this sudden and shaming antagonism, which she felt must communicate itself to Goodale, Nurse Dakers slid her eyes from the bent head so disconcertingly close to hers and gazed around the room. It was so familiar to her after nearly three years of training that normally she hardly noticed the

274

details of architecture or furnishing. But tonight she saw it with an unexpected clarity, as if it had nothing to do with her or with her life. It was too large to be cosy and was furnished as if it had acquired odd items over the years and taken them to itself. It must once have been an elegant drawing-room, but the walls had long since lost their paper and were now painted and scruffy, due—it was rumoured—for redecoration when money allowed. The ornate fireplace of carved marble and surrounding oak was fitted with a large gas stove, old and ugly in design but still remarkably efficient, hissing a strong heat even into the dark corners of the room. The elegant mahogany table against the far wall with its jumble of magazines might have been bequeathed by John Carpendar himself. But it was scratched and dull now, dusted regularly but rarely polished, its surface scarred and ringed. To the left of the fireplace, in incongruous contrast, stood a large, modern television set, the gift of the Hospital League of Friends. In front of it was an immense cretonne-covered sofa with sagging springs, and a single matching armchair. The rest of the chairs were similar to those in the hospital out-patient department but were now too old and shabby to be tolerated for the use of patients. The arm-rests of pale wood were grubby; the coloured vinyl seats were stretched and dented and now smelt unpleasantly in the heat from the fire. One of the chairs was empty. It was the red-seated one which Nurse Pearce had invariably used. Scorning the intimacy of the sofa, she would sit there, a little apart from the huddle of students around the television set, watching the screen with careful disinterest as if it were a pleasure she could easily forgo. Occasionally she would drop her eyes to a book in her lap as if the folly presented for her entertainment had become too much to bear. Her presence, thought Nurse Dakers, had always been a little unwelcome and oppressive. The atmosphere of the students' sitting-room had always been lighter, more relaxed without that upright and censorious figure. But the empty chair, the dented seat, was almost worse. Nurse Dakers wished that she had the courage to walk over to it, to swing it into line with the other chairs around the television set and settle herself nonchalantly into its sagging curves, exorcizing once and for all that oppressive ghost. She wondered if the other students felt

the same. It was impossible to ask. Were the Burt twins, bunched together in the depths of the sofa, really as absorbed as they appeared by the old gangster film they were watching? They were each knitting one of the heavy sweaters which they invariably wore in winter, their fingers clicking away, their eyes never leaving the screen. Beside them Nurse Fallon lolled in the armchair, one trousered leg swung casually over the arm. It was her first day back in the school after her sick leave and she still looked pale and drawn. Was her mind really on the sleek-haired hero with his tall wide-ribboned and ridiculous trilby, his over-padded shoulders, whose raucous voice, punctuated with gunshots, filled the room? Or was she, too, morbidly conscious of that empty red chair, the dented seat, the rounded ends of the arm-rests polished by Pearce's hand?

Nurse Dakers shivered. The wall clock showed that it was already after nine-thirty. Outside the wind was rising. It was going to be a wild night. In the rare intervals of quiet from the television set she could hear the creaking and sighing of the trees and could picture the last leaves falling softly on grass and path, isolating Nightingale House in a sludge of silence and decay. She forced herself to pick up her pen. She really must get on! Soon it would be time for bed and, one by one, the students would say their good nights and disappear, leaving her to brave alone the poorly-lit staircase and the dark corridor beyond. Jo Fallon would still be here of course. She never went to bed until the television programme closed for the night. Then she would make her lonely way upstairs to prepare her nightly hot whisky and lemon. Everyone knew Fallon's invariable habit. But Nurse Dakers felt that she could not face being left alone with Fallon. Hers was the last company she would choose, even in that lonely, frightening walk from the sitting-room to bed.

She began writing again.

"Now please, Mummy, don't keep on worrying about the murder."

The impossibility of the sentence struck her as soon as she saw the words on the paper. Somehow she must avoid the use of that emotive, blood-stained word. She tried again. "Now please,

Mummy, don't start worrying about the things you read in the papers. There really isn't any need. I'm perfectly safe and happy and no one really believes that Pearce was deliberately killed."

It wasn't true of course. Some people must think that Pearce had been deliberately killed or why would the police be here? And it was ridiculous to suppose that the poison could have got into the feed by accident or that Pearce, the god-fearing, conscientious and essentially dull Pearce, would have chosen to kill herself in that agonizing and spectacular way. She wrote on:

"We still have the local C.I.D. here, but they don't come in so often now. They have been very kind to us students and I don't think they suspect anyone. Poor Pearce wasn't very popular, but it's ridiculous to think that anyone here would want to harm her."

Had the police really been kind, she wondered? They had certainly been very correct, very polite. They had produced all the usual reassuring platitudes about the importance of co-operating with them in solving this terrible tragedy, telling the truth at all times, keeping nothing back however trivial and unimportant it might seem. Not one of them had raised his voice; not one had been aggressive or intimidating. And all of them had been frightening. Their very presence in Nightingale House, masculine and confident, had been, like the locked door of the demonstration room, a constant reminder of tragedy and fear. Nurse Dakers had found Inspector Bailey the most frightening of them all. He was a huge, ruddy, moon-faced man whose encouraging and avuncular voice and manner were in unnerving contrast to his cold pig-like eyes. The questioning had gone on and on. She could still recall the interminable sessions, the effort of will necessary to meet that probing gaze.

"Now I'm told that you were the most upset of them all when Nurse Pearce died. She was a particular friend of yours perhaps?"

"No. Not really. Not a particular friend. I hardly knew her."

"Well, there's a surprise! After nearly three years of training with her? Living and working so closely together, I should have thought that you all got to know each other pretty well."

She had struggled to explain.

"In some ways we do. We know each other's habits. But I

277

didn't really know what she was like; as a person, I mean." A silly reply. How else could you know anyone except as a person? And it wasn't true. She had known Pearce. She had known her very well.

"But you got on well together? There hadn't been a quarrel or anything like that? No unpleasantness?"

An odd word. Unpleasantness. She had seen again that grotesque figure, teetering forward in agony, fingers scrabbling at the ineffectual air, the thin tubing stretching the mouth like a wound. No, there had been no unpleasantness.

"And the other students? They got on well with Nurse Pearce, too? There had been no bad blood as far as you know?"

Bad blood. A stupid expression. What was the opposite she wondered? Good blood? There was only good blood between us. Pearce's good blood. She had answered:

"She hadn't any enemies as far as I know. And if anyone did dislike her, they wouldn't kill her."

"So you all tell me. But someone did kill her, didn't they? Unless the poison wasn't intended for Nurse Pearce. She only played the part of the patient by chance. Did you know that Nurse Fallon had been taken ill that night?"

And so it had gone on. Questions about every minute of that last terrible demonstration. Questions about the lavatory disinfectant. The empty bottle, wiped clean of finger-prints, had been quickly found by the police lying among the bushes at the back of the house. Anyone could have thrown it from a bedroom window or bathroom window in the concealing darkness of that January morning. Questions about her movements from the moment of first awakening. The constant reiteration in that minatory voice that nothing should be held back, nothing concealed.

She wondered whether the other students had been as frightened. The Burt twins had seemed merely bored and resigned, obeying the Inspector's sporadic summons with a shrug of the shoulders and a weary, "Oh, God, not again!" Nurse Goodale had said nothing when she was called for questioning and nothing afterwards. Nurse Fallon had been equally reticent. It was known that Inspector Bailey had interviewed her in the sick bay as soon as she was

278

well enough to be seen. No one knew what had happened at that interview. It was rumoured that Fallon had admitted returning to Nightingale House early in the morning of the crime but had refused to say why. That would be very like Fallon. And now she had returned to Nightingale House to rejoin her set. So far she hadn't even mentioned Pearce's death. Nurse Dakers wondered if and when she would; and, morbidly sensitive to the hidden meaning in every word, struggled on with her letter:

"We haven't used the demonstration room since Nurse Pearce's death but otherwise the set is continuing to work according to plan. Only one of the students, Diane Harper, has left the school. Her father came to fetch her two days after Nurse Pearce died and the police didn't seem to mind her leaving. We all thought it was silly of her to give up so near to her finals but her father has never been keen on her training as a nurse and she is engaged to be married anyway, so I suppose she thought it didn't matter. No one else is thinking of leaving and there really isn't the slightest danger. So please, darling, do stop worrying about me. Now I must tell you about tomorrow's programme."

There was no need to go on drafting now. The rest of the letter would be easy. She read over what she had written and decided that it would do. Taking a fresh sheet of paper from the pad she began to write the final letter. With any luck she would just get it finished before the film ended and the twins put away their knitting and went to bed.

She scribbled quickly on and, half an hour later, her letter finished, saw with relief that the film had come to the last holocaust and the final embrace. At the same moment Nurse Goodale removed her reading spectacles, looked up from her work, and closed her book. The door opened and Julia Pardoe appeared.

"I'm back," she announced, and yawned. "It was a lousy film. Anyone making tea?" No one answered but the twins stubbed their knitting-needles into the balls of wool and joined her at the door, switching off the television on their way. Pardoe would never bother to make tea if she could find someone else to do it and the twins usually obliged. As she followed them out of the sitting-room Nurse Dakers looked back at the silent, immobile figure of Fallon

279

alone now with Madeleine Goodale. She had a sudden impulse to speak to Fallon, to welcome her back to the school, to ask after her health, or simply to say good night. But the words seemed to stick in her throat, the moment passed, and the last thing she saw as she closed the door behind her was Fallon's pale and individual face, blank eyes still fixed on the television set as if unaware that the screen was dead.

II

In a hospital, time itself is documented, seconds measured in a pulse beat, the drip of blood or plasma; minutes in the stopping of a heart; hours in the rise and fall of a temperature chart, the length of an operation. When the events of the night of 28th–29th January came to be documented there were few of the protagonists at the John Carpendar Hospital who were unaware what they had been doing or where they were at any particular moment of their waking hours. They might not choose to tell the truth, but at least they knew where the truth lay.

It was a night of violent but erratic storm, the wind varying in intensity and even in direction from hour to hour. At ten o'clock it was little more than a sobbing *obbligato* among the elms. An hour later it suddenly reached a crescendo of fury. The great elms around Nightingale House cracked and groaned under the onslaught, while the wind screamed among them like the cachinnation of devils. Along the deserted paths, the banks of dead leaves, still heavy with rain, shifted sluggishly then broke apart into drifts and rose in wild swirls like demented insects, to glue themselves against the black barks of the trees. In the operating theatre at the top of the hospital Mr. Courtney-Briggs demonstrated his imperturbability in the face of crisis by muttering to his attendant registrar that it was a wild night before bending his head again to the satisfying contemplation of the intriguing surgical problem which throbbed between the retracted lips of the wound. Below him in the silent and dimly lit wards the patients muttered and turned in their sleep as if conscious of the tumult outside. The radiographer, who had been called from home to take urgent X-rays of Mr. Courtney-Briggs's

patient, replaced the covers on the apparatus, switched out the lights and wondered whether her small car would hold the road. The night nurses moved silently among their patients testing the windows, drawing the curtains more closely as if to keep out some threatening and alien force. The porter on duty in the main gate lodge shifted uneasily in his chair then rose cramped to his feet and put a couple more chunks of coal on the fire. He felt in need of warmth and comfort in his isolation. The little house seemed to shake with every gust of the wind.

But shortly before midnight the storm abated, as if sensing the approach of the witching hour, the dead of night when the pulse of man beats slowest and the dying patient slips most easily into the last oblivion. There was an eerie silence for about five minutes, succeeded by a soft rhythmic moaning as the wind swooped and sighed among the trees as if exhausted by its own fury. Mr. Courtney-Briggs, the operation completed, peeled off his gloves and made his way into the surgeons' changing room. As soon as he was disrobed he made a telephone call from the wall instrument to the Sisters' floor at Nightingale House and asked Sister Brumfett, the Sister in charge of the private ward, to return to the ward to supervise the care of his patient for the first critical hour. He noted with satisfaction that the wind had dropped. She could make her own way through the grounds as she had done at his bidding countless times before. He need feel under no obligation to fetch her in his car.

Less than five minutes later Sister Brumfett plodded resolutely through the trees, her cloak folded around her like a flag whipped close to a flag pole, her hood drawn down over the frilly Sister's cap. It was curiously peaceful in this brief interlude of the storm. She moved silently over the sodden grass, feeling the pull of the rain-soaked earth through the thick soles of her shoes while, from time to time, a thin branch, torn by the storm, broke loose from its last thread of bark and thudded with gentle inadvertence at her feet. By the time she had gained the peace of the private ward and was helping the third-year student make up the post-operative bed and prepare the stand ready for the blood drip, the wind was rising again. But Sister Brumfett, absorbed in her task, no longer noticed it.

Shortly after half past twelve Albert Colgate, the porter on night duty in the main lodge, who was nodding over his evening paper, was jerked into consciousness by a band of light sweeping across the lodge window and the purr of an approaching car. It must, he thought, be Mr. Courtney-Briggs's Daimler. So the operation was over. He expected the car to sweep out of the main gate but unexpectedly it stopped. There were two peremptory hoots on the horn. Muttering, the porter thrust his arms into his overcoat and made his way out of the lodge door. Mr. Courtney-Briggs wound down the window and shouted at him through the wind.

"I tried to get out of the Winchester gate but there's a tree down across the path. I thought I'd better report it. Get it seen to as soon as you can."

The porter thrust his head through the car window encountering an immediate and luxurious smell of cigar smoke, after-shave lotion and leather. Mr. Courtney-Briggs recoiled slightly from his nearness. The porter said:

"That'll be one of those old elms no doubt, sir. I'll report it first thing in the morning. There's nothing I can do tonight, sir, not in this storm."

Mr. Courtney-Briggs began to wind up the window. Colgate's head made a sudden withdrawal.

The surgeon said: "There's no need to do anything tonight. I've tied my white scarf on one of the boughs. I doubt whether anyone else will use that road until the morning. If they do, they'll see the scarf. But you might warn anyone who drives in this way. Good night, Colgate."

The large car purred out of the front gate and Colgate made his way back into the lodge. Meticulously he noted the time by the wall clock over the fireplace and made a record in his book. "12.32 Mr. Courtney-Briggs reports fallen tree across the Winchester Road path."

He had settled again into his chair and taken up his paper before the thought struck him that it was odd that Mr. Courtney-Briggs should have tried to drive out through the Winchester gate. It wasn't on his quickest route home and it was a road he seldom used.

Mr. Courtney-Briggs invariably used the front entrance. Presumably, thought Colgate, he had a key to the Winchester Road gate. Mr. Courtney-Briggs had a key to most parts of the hospital. But it was odd all the same.

Just before 2 o'clock on the silent second floor of Nightingale House, Maureen Burt stirred in her sleep, muttered incoherently through her moist pursed lips and awoke to the disagreeable awareness that three cups of tea before bed had been two too many. She lay still for a moment, sleepily aware of the groaning of the storm, wondered whether she might not after all manage to get to sleep again, realized that her discomfort was too great to be reasonably borne and felt for the switch of her bedside lamp. The light was instantaneous and blinding, shocking her into full consciousness. She wriggled her feet into her bedroom slippers, threw her dressing-gown around her shoulders and padded out into the corridor. As she quietly closed her bedroom door behind her a sudden gust of wind billowed out the curtains at the far corridor window. She went across to shut it. Through the agitated tracery of boughs and their leaping shadows on the window-pane she could see the hospital riding the storm like a great ship at anchor, the ward windows only faintly luminous in comparison with the vertical line of brightly lit eyes marking the Sisters' offices and ward kitchens. She shut down the window carefully and, reeling slightly with sleep, felt her way down the passage to the cloakroom. Less than a minute later she came out again into the corridor, pausing momentarily to accustom her eyes to the gloom. From the confusion of shadows at the top of the stairs a deeper shadow detached itself, moved forward and was revealed as a cloaked and hooded figure. Maureen was not a nervous girl and in her somnolent state was conscious only of surprise that someone else should be awake and about. She saw at once that it was Sister Brumfett. Two piercing bespectacled eyes peered at her through the gloom. The Sister's voice was unexpectedly sharp.

"It's one of the Burt twins, isn't it? What are you doing here? Is anyone else up?"

"No, Sister. At least I don't think so. I've just been to the lavatory."

"Oh I see. Well, as long as everyone's all right. I thought that the

storm might have disturbed you all. I've just come back from my ward. One of Mr. Courtney-Briggs's patients had a relapse and he had to operate urgently."

"Yes, Sister," said Nurse Burt, uncertain what else was expected of her. She was surprised that Sister Brumfett should bother to explain her presence to a mere student nurse, and she watched a little uncertainly as the Sister drew her long cloak more firmly around her and stumped briskly down the corridor towards the far stairs. Her own room was on the floor above, immediately next to Matron's flat. When she reached the bottom of the stairs, Sister Brumfett turned and seemed about to speak. It was at that moment that Shirley Burt's door opened slowly, and a tousled red head appeared.

"What's up?" it inquired sleepily.

Sister Brumfett walked towards them.

"Nothing, Nurse. I'm just on my way back to bed. I've come from my ward. And Maureen had to get up to go to the lavatory. There's nothing to worry about."

Shirley gave no impression that she was or ever had been worried. She now trotted out on to the landing, pulling her dressing-gown around her. Resigned and a little complacent, she said:

"When Maureen wakes up I do too. We've always been like that ever since we were babies. You ask Mum!" A little unsteady with sleep but not ungratified that the family theurgy still worked, she closed her bedroom door behind her with the finality of one who, being up, intends to stay up.

"No use trying to get off again in this wind. I'm going to brew some cocoa. Can we bring you up a mug, Sister. It'd help you to sleep?"

"No thank you, Nurse. I don't think I shall have any trouble in sleeping. Be as quiet as you can. You don't want to disturb the others. And don't get cold." She turned again towards the stairs. Maureen said: "Fallon's awake. At least her bedside lamp's still on."

The three of them looked down the corridor to where an eye of light from Nurse Fallon's keyhole pierced the darkness and threw a small luminous shadow on the linenfold panelling opposite.

Shirley said: "We'll take her a mug then. She's probably awake and reading. Come on, Maureen! Good night, Sister."

They shuffled off together down the corridor to the small utility room at the end. After a second's pause Sister Brumfett, who had been looking steadily after them, her face rigid and expressionless, turned finally towards the stairs and made her way up to bed.

Exactly one hour later but unheard and unrecorded by anyone in Nightingale House, a weakened pane of glass in the conservatory which had rattled spasmodically throughout the night, fell inwards to explode into splinters on the tessellated floor. The wind rushed in through the aperture like a questing animal. Its cold breath rustled the magazines on the wicker tables, lifted the fronds of the palms and sent the fern leaves gently waving. Finally it found the long white cupboard centred under the plant shelves. Early in the evening, the door had been left ajar by the desperate and hurried visitor who had last thrust a hand into the cupboard depths. All night the door had stayed open, motionless on its hinges. But now the wind set it gently swinging to and fro, then as if wearying of the game, finally closed it with a soft, decisive thud.

And everything living under the roof of Nightingale House, slept.

III

Nurse Dakers was awoken by the whirr of the bedside alarm clock. The faintly luminous dial showed the time as 6.15. Even with the curtains drawn back the room was still completely dark. The square of faint light came, as she knew, not from the door but from the distant lights of the hospital where already the night staff would be taking round the first morning cups of tea. She lay still for a moment, adjusting to her own wakefulness, putting out tentative feelers to the day. She had slept well despite the storm of which she had been only briefly aware. She realized with a spring of joy that she could actually face the day with confidence. The misery and apprehension of the previous evening, of the previous weeks, seemed to have lifted. It seemed now no more than the effect of tiredness and temporary depression. She had passed down a

tunnel of misery and insecurity since Pearce's death but this morning, miraculously, she had come out into daylight again. It was like Christmas morning in childhood. It was the beginning of a summer holiday from school. It was waking refreshed at the end of a febrile illness with the comfortable knowledge that Mummy was there and that all the solaces of convalescence lay ahead. It was familiar life restored.

The day shone before her. She catalogued its promises and pleasures. In the morning there would be the materia-medica lecture. This was important. She had always been weak on drugs and dosages. Then, after the coffee break, Mr. Courtney-Briggs would give his third year surgery seminar. It was a privilege that a surgeon of his eminence should take so much trouble with the student nurse training. She was a little afraid of him, particularly of his sharp staccato questions. But this morning she would be brave and speak up confidently. Then in the afternoon the hospital bus would take the set to the local maternity and child welfare clinic to watch the local authority staff at work. This, too, was important to someone who hoped in time to become a district nurse. She lay for a few moments contemplating this gratifying programme then she got out of bed, shuffled her feet into her slippers, struggled into her cheap dressing-gown and made her way along the passage to the students' utility room.

The Nightingale nurses were called promptly at seven each morning by one of the maids, but most students, accustomed to early waking when on the wards, set their alarm clocks at 6.30 to give themselves time for tea-making and gossip. The early arrivals were already there. The little room was brightly lit, cheerfully domestic, smelling, as always, of tea, boiled milk and detergent. The scene was reassuringly normal. The Burt twins were there, faces still puffy from sleep, each twin stoutly cocooned into a bright red dressing-gown. Maureen was carrying her portable wireless tuned to Radio 2 and was gently jerking hips and shoulders to the rhythm of the B.B.C.'s early morning syncopation. Her twin was setting their two immense mugs on a tray and rummaging in a tin for biscuits. The only other student present was Madeleine Goodale who, clad in an ancient plaid dressing-gown, was watching,

teapot in hand, for the first spurt of steam from the kettle. In her mood of optimism and relief, Nurse Dakers could have hugged them all.

"Where's Fallon this morning?" asked Maureen Burt with no great interest.

Nurse Fallon was a notoriously late riser, but she was usually one of the first to make tea. It was her habit to carry it back to enjoy at leisure in bed, where she would stay until the last possible moment consistent with presenting herself at breakfast on time. But this morning her personal teapot and the matching cup and saucer were still on the cupboard shelf beside the canister of china tea which Fallon preferred to the strong brown brew which the rest of the set considered necessary before they could face the day.

"I'll give her a call," suggested Nurse Dakers, happy to be of use and longing to celebrate her release from the strain of the last few weeks by general benevolence.

"Wait a moment, then you can take her a cuppa out of my pot," suggested Maureen.

"She won't like Indian tea. I'll see if she's awake and just let her know the kettle's on the boil."

For a moment it occurred to Nurse Dakers to make Fallon's tea for her. But the impulse faded. It was not that Fallon was particularly temperamental or unpredictable, but somehow people did not interfere with her personal things nor expect her to share them. She had few possessions but they were expensive, elegant, carefully chosen and so much part of her *persona* that they seemed sacrosanct.

Nurse Dakers almost ran along the passage to Fallon's room. The door was unlocked. That did not surprise her. Ever since one of the students had been taken ill in the night some years ago and had been too weak to creep across the room to unlock the door, there had been a rule forbidding girls to lock themselves in at night. Since Pearce's death one or two had taken to turning their keys, and if the Sisters suspected it they said nothing. Perhaps they, too, slept more soundly behind locked doors. But Fallon had not been afraid.

The curtains were closely drawn. The bedside lamp was on but

with the adjustable shade tilted so that it threw a pale moon on the far wall and left the bed in shadow. There was a tangle of black hair on the pillow. Nurse Dakers felt along the wall for the light switch and paused before clicking it on. Then she pressed it down very gently as if it were possible softly and gradually to illuminate the room and spare Fallon that first fierce wakening. The room blazed into light. She blinked in the unexpected glare. Then she moved very quietly across to the bed. She didn't scream or faint. She stood absolutely still for a moment looking down at Fallon's body, and smiling a little as if surprised. She had no doubt that Fallon was dead. The eyes were still wide open but they were cold and opaque, like the eyes of dead fish. Nurse Dakers bent down and stared into them as if willing them into brightness or seeking in vain some trace of her own reflection. Then she slowly turned and left the room, switching off the light and closing the door behind her. She swayed like a sleep-walker along the passage, steadying her hands against the wall.

At first the students didn't notice her return. Then three pairs of eyes were suddenly fixed on her, three figures stood frozen in a tableau of puzzled inquiry. Nurse Dakers leaned against the door post and opened her mouth soundlessly. The words wouldn't come. Something seemed to have happened to her throat. Her whole jaw was trembling uncontrollably and her tongue was stuck to the roof of her mouth. Her eyes pleaded with them. It seemed minutes while they watched her struggle. When the words did come she sounded calm, gently surprised.

"It's Fallon. She's dead."

She smiled like someone waking from a dream, patiently explaining: "Someone's murdered Fallon."

The room emptied. She wasn't aware of their concerted dash down the corridor. She was alone. The kettle was screeching now, the lid rattling under the force of the steam. Carefully she turned down the gas, frowning with concentration. Very slowly, like a child entrusted with a precious task, she took down the canister, the elegant teapot, the matching cup and saucer, and humming gently to herself, made Fallon's early morning tea.

Chapter Three

Strangers in the House

I

"The pathologist is here, sir."

A detective constable put his cropped head round the bedroom door and raised an interrogative eyebrow.

Chief Superintendent Adam Dalgliesh turned from his examination of the dead girl's clothes, his six feet two inches uncomfortably trapped between the foot of the bed and the wardrobe door. He looked at his watch. It was eight minutes past ten. Sir Miles Honeyman, as always, had made good time.

"Right, Fenning. Ask him to be good enough to wait for a moment, will you? We'll be finished in here in a minute. Then some of us can clear out and make room for him."

The head disappeared. Dalgliesh closed the wardrobe door and managed to squeeze himself between it and the foot of the bed. Certainly there was no room for a fourth person at present. The huge bulk of the finger-print man occupied the space between the bedside table and the window as, bent almost double, he brushed charcoal carefully on to the surface of the whisky bottle, turning it by its cork. Beside the bottle stood a glass plate bearing the dead girl's prints, the whorls and composites plainly visible.

"Anything there?" asked Dalgliesh.

The print man paused and peered more closely.

"A nice set of prints coming up, sir. They're hers all right. Nothing else, though. It looks as if the chap who sold it gave the bottle the usual wipe over before wrapping. It'll be interesting to see what we get from the beaker."

He cast a jealously possessive glance at it as it lay where it had fallen from the girl's hand, lightly poised in a curve of the counter-

pane. Not until the last photograph had been taken would it be yielded up for his examination.

He bent again to his task on the bottle. Behind him the Yard photographer manœuvred his tripod and camera—a new Cambo monorail, Dalgliesh noticed—to the right-hand foot of the bed. There was a click, an explosion of light, and the image of the dead girl leapt up at them and lay suspended in air, burning itself on Dalgliesh's retina. Colour and shape were intensified and distorted in that cruel, momentary glare. The long black hair was a tangled wig against the whiteness of the pillows; the glazed eyes were exophthalmic marbles, as if rigor mortis were squeezing them out of their sockets; the skin was very white and smooth, looking repulsive to the touch, an artificial membrane, tough and impermeable as vinyl. Dalgliesh blinked, erasing the image of a witch's plaything, a grotesque puppet casually tossed against the pillow. When he next looked at her she was again a dead girl on a bed; no more and no less. Twice more the distorted image leapt up at him and lay petrified in air as the photographer took two pictures with the Polaroid Land camera to give Dalgliesh the immediate prints for which he always asked. Then it was over. "That was the last. I'm through, sir," said the photographer. "I'll let Sir Miles in now." He put his head around the door while the print man, grunting with satisfaction, lovingly lifted the drinking beaker from the counterpane with a pair of forceps and set it alongside the whisky bottle.

Sir Miles must have been waiting on the landing for he trotted in immediately, a familiar rotund figure with his immense head of black curling hair and eager beady eyes. He brought with him an air of music hall *bonhommie* and, as always, a faint smell of sour sweat. He was unfretted by the delay. But then Sir Miles, God's gift to forensic pathology or an amateur mountebank as you chose to take him, did not easily take offence. He had gained much of his reputation and also, possibly, his recent knighthood by adhering to the principle that you should never willingly offend anyone, however humble. He greeted the departing photographer and the finger-print officer as if they were old friends, and Dalgliesh by his Christian name. But the socialities were perfunctory; his pre-

occupation preceded him like a miasma as he wriggled up close to the bed.

Dalgliesh despised him as a ghoul; hardly, he admitted, a rational cause for dislike. In a perfectly organized world, foot fetishists would, no doubt, become chiropodists; hair fetishists, hairdressers; and ghouls, morbid anatomists. It was surprising that so few of them did. But Sir Miles laid himself open to the implication. He approached each new corpse with eagerness, almost with glee; his macabre jokes had been heard at half the dining clubs in London; he was an expert in death who obviously enjoyed his work. Dalgliesh felt inhibited in his company by the consciousness of his dislike for the man. Antipathy seemed to crackle from him. But Sir Miles was oblivious of it. He liked himself too well to conceive that other men might find him less lovable, and this endearing naïvety gave him a kind of charm. Even those colleagues who most deplored his conceit, his publicity seeking, and the irresponsibility of most of his public utterances, found it hard to dislike him as much as they felt they should. Women were said to find him attractive. Perhaps he had a morbid fascination for them. Certainly his was the infectious good nature of a man who necessarily finds the world an agreeable place since it contains himself.

He always tut-tutted over a body. He did so now, plucking back the sheet with a curiously mincing gesture of his pudgy fingers. Dalgliesh walked over to the window and gazed out at the tracery of boughs through which the distant hospital, still lit up, gleamed like an insubstantial palace suspended in air. He could hear the faint rustling of bed linen. Sir Miles would only be making a preliminary examination, but even to think of those pudgy fingers insinuating themselves into the body's tender orifices was enough to make one hope for a peaceful death in one's own bed. The real job would be done later on the mortuary table, that aluminium sink with its grim accessories of drains and sprays on which Josephine Fallon's body would be systematically dismembered in the cause of justice, or science, or curiosity, or what you will. And afterwards, Sir Miles's mortuary attendant would earn his guinea by stitching it up again into a decent semblance of humanity so that the family could view it without trauma. If there were a family. He wondered

who, if anyone, would be Fallon's official mourners. Superficially there was nothing in her room—no photographs, no letters—to suggest that she had close ties with any living soul.

While Sir Miles sweated and muttered, Dalgliesh made a second tour of the room, carefully avoiding watching the pathologist. He knew this squeamishness to be irrational and was half ashamed of it. Post mortem examinations did not upset him. It was this impersonal examination of the still warm female body which he couldn't stomach. A few short hours ago she would have been entitled to some modesty, to her own choice of doctor, free to reject those unnaturally white and eagerly probing fingers. A few hours ago she was a human being. Now she was dead flesh.

It was the room of a woman who preferred to be unencumbered. It contained the necessary basic comforts and one or two carefully chosen embellishments. It was as if she had itemized her needs and provided for them expensively but precisely and without extravagance. The thick rug by the bed was not, he thought, the kind provided by the Hospital Management Committee. There was only one picture but that was an original water colour, a charming landscape by Robert Hills, hung where the light from the window lit it most effectively. On the window-sill stood the only ornament, a Staffordshire pottery figure of John Wesley preaching from his pulpit. Dalgliesh turned it in his hands. It was perfect; a collector's piece. But there were none of the small trivial impedimenta which those living in institutions often dispose about them to provide comfort or reassurance.

He walked over to the bookcase beside the bed and again examined the books. They, too, seemed chosen to minister to predictable moods. A collection of modern poetry, his own last volume included; a complete set of Jane Austen, well worn but in a leather binding and printed on India paper; a few books on philosophy nicely balanced between scholarship and popular appeal; about two dozen paper-backs of modern novels, Greene, Waugh, Compton Burnett, Hartley, Powell, Cary. But most of the books were poetry. Looking at them, he thought, we shared the same tastes. If we had met we should at least have had something to say to each other. "Everyman's death diminishes me." But, of

course, Doctor Donne. The over-exploited dictum had become a fashionable catch phrase in a crowded world where non-involvement was practically a social necessity. But some deaths still held their power to diminish more than others. For the first time in years he was conscious of a sense of waste, of a personal irrational loss.

He moved on. At the foot of the bed was a wardrobe with a chest of drawers attached, a bastard contraption in pale wood, designed, if anyone had consciously designed an object so ugly, to provide the maximum of space in the minimum of room. The top of the chest was meant to serve as a dressing-table and held a small looking-glass. In front of it were her brush and comb. Nothing else.

He opened the small left-hand drawer. It held her make-up, the jars and tubes neatly arranged on a small papiermâché tray. There was a great deal more than he had expected to find: cleansing cream, a box of tissues, foundation cream, pressed powder, eye shadow, mascara. She had obviously made up with care. But there was only one of each item. No experiments, no impulse buying, no half used and discarded tubes with the make-up congealed round the stopper. The collection said: "This is what suits me. This is what I need. No more and no less."

He opened the right-hand drawer. It held nothing but a concertina file, each compartment indexed. He thumbed through the contents. A birth certificate. A certificate of baptism. A post office savings account book. The name and address of her solicitor. There were no personal letters. He tucked the file under his arm.

He moved on to the wardrobe and examined again the collection of clothes. Three pairs of slacks. Cashmere jumpers. A winter coat in bright red tweed. Four well-cut dresses in fine wool. They all spoke of quality. It was an expensive wardrobe for a student nurse.

He heard a final satisfied grunt from Sir Miles and turned round. The pathologist was straightening himself and peeling off his rubber gloves. They were so thin that it looked as if he were shedding his epidermis. He said:

"Dead, I should say, about ten hours. I'm judging mainly by rectal temperature and the degree of rigor in the lower limbs. But

it's no more than a guess, my dear fellow. These things are chancy, as you know. We'll have a look at the stomach contents; that may give us a clue. At present, and on the clinical signs, I should say she died about midnight give or take an hour. Taking a common sense view, of course, she died when she drank that nightcap."

The finger-print officer had left the whisky bottle and beaker on the table and was working now on the door handle. Sir Miles trotted round to them and without touching the beaker bent his head and placed his nose close to the rim.

"Whisky. But what else? That's what we're asking ourselves, my dear fellow. That's what we're asking ourselves. One thing, it wasn't a corrosive. No carbolic acid this time. I didn't do the P.M. on that other girl by the way. Rikki Blake did that little job. A bad business. I suppose you're looking for a connection between the two deaths?"

Dagliesh said: "It's possible."

"Could be. Could be. This isn't likely to be a natural death. But we'll have to wait for the toxicology. Then we may learn something. There's no evidence of strangulation or suffocation. No external marks of violence come to that. By the way, she was pregnant. About three months gone, I'd say. I got a nice little *ballottement* there. Haven't found that sign since I was a student. The P.M. will confirm it of course."

His little bright eyes searched the room. "No container for the poison apparently. If it were poison, of course. And no suicide note?"

"That's not conclusive evidence," said Dalgliesh.

"I know. I know. But most of them leave a little *billet doux*. They like to tell the tale, my dear fellow. They like to tell the tale. The mortuary van's here by the way. I'll take her away if you're finished with her."

"I've finished," said Dalgliesh.

He waited and watched while the porters manœuvred their stretcher into the room and with brisk efficiency dumped the dead weight onto it. Sir Miles fretted around them with the nervous anxiety of an expert who has found a particularly good specimen and must carefully supervise its safe transport. It was odd that the

removal of that inert mass of bone and tightening muscle, to which each in his different way had been ministering, should have left the room so empty, so desolate. Dalgliesh had noticed it before when the body was taken away; this sense of an empty stage, of props casually disposed and bereft of meaning, of a drained air. The recently dead had their own mysterious *charisma*; not without reason did men talk in whispers in their presence. But now she was gone, and there was nothing further for him to do in the room. He left the finger-print man annotating and photographing his finds, and went out into the passage.

II

It was now after eleven o'clock but the corridor was still very dark, the one clear window at the far end discernible only as a square haze behind the drawn curtains. Dalgliesh could at first just make out the shape and colour of the three red fire buckets filled with sand and the cone of a fire extinguisher gleaming against the carved oak panelling of the walls. The iron staples, driven brutally into the woodwork, on which they were supported, were in incongruous contrast to the row of elegant light fittings in convoluted brass which sprang from the centres of the quatrefoil carvings. The fittings had obviously originally been designed for gas, but had been crudely adapted without imagination or skill to the use of electricity. The brass was unpolished and most of the delicate glass shades, curved in a semblance of flower petals, were missing or broken. In each of the deflowered clusters a single socket was now monstrously budded with one grubby and low-powered bulb whose faint and diffused light threw shadows across the floor and served only to accentuate the general gloom. Apart from the one small window at the end of the corridor there was little other natural light. The huge window over the well of the staircase, a pre-Raphaelite representation in lurid glass of the expulsion from Eden, was hardly functional.

He looked into the rooms adjacent to that of the dead girl. One was unoccupied, with the bed stripped, the wardrobe door ajar and the drawers, lined with fresh newspaper, all pulled out as if to

demonstrate the room's essential emptiness. The other was in use but looked as if it had been hurriedly left; the bedclothes were carelessly thrown back and the bedside rug was rumpled. There was a little pile of textbooks on the bedside table and he opened the flyleaf of the first to hand and read the inscription, "Christine Dakers". So this was the room of the girl who had found the body. He inspected the wall between the two rooms. It was thin, a light partition of painted hardboard which trembled and let out a soft boom as he struck it. He wondered whether Nurse Dakers had heard anything in the night. Unless Josephine Fallon had died instantly and almost soundlessly some indication of her distress must surely have penetrated this insubstantial partition. He was anxious to interview Nurse Christine Dakers. At present she was in the nurses' sick bay suffering, so he was told, from shock. The shock was probably genuine enough, but even if it were not, there was nothing he could do about it. Nurse Dakers was for the moment effectively protected by her doctors from any questioning by the police.

He explored a little further. Opposite the row of nurses' bedrooms was a suite of bathroom cubicles and lavatories leading out of a large square cloakroom fitted with four wash-basins, each surrounded by a shower curtain. Each of the bath cubicles had a small sash window fitted with opaque glass, inconveniently placed but not difficult to open. They gave a view of the back of the house and of the two short wings, each built above a brick cloister, which were incongruously grafted on to the main building. It was as if the architect, having exhausted the possibilities of Gothic revival and baroque, had decided to introduce a more contemplative and ecclesiastical influence. The ground between the cloisters was an overgrown jungle of laurel bushes and untended trees which grew so close to the house that some of the branches seemed to scrape the downstairs windows. Dalgliesh could see dim figures searching among the bushes and could hear the faint mutter of voices. The discarded bottle of disinfectant which had killed Heather Pearce had been found among these bushes and it was possible that a second container, its contents equally lethal, might also have been hurled in the dark hours from the same window. There was a nail

brush on the bath rack and, reaching for it, Dalgliesh hurled it in a wide arc through the window and into the bushes. He could neither see nor hear its fall but a cheerful face appeared among the parted leaves, a hand was waved in salute and the two searching constables moved back deeper into the undergrowth.

He next made his way along the passage to the nurses' utility room at the far end. Detective Sergeant Masterson was there with Sister Rolfe. Together they were surveying a motley collection of objects laid out before them on the working surface rather as if they were engaging in a private Kim's game. There were two squeezed lemons; a bowl of granulated sugar; an assortment of mugs containing cold tea, the surface of the liquid mottled and puckered; and a delicate Worcester teapot with matching cup and saucer and milk jug. There was also a crumpled square of thin white wrapping paper bearing the words "Scunthorpe's Wine Stores, 149, High Street, Heatheringfield" and a scribbled receipt smoothed out and held flat by a couple of tea canisters.

"She bought the whisky yesterday morning, sir," Masterson said. "Luckily for us, Mr. Scunthorpe is punctilious about receipts. That's the bill and that's the wrapping paper. So it looks as if she first opened the bottle when she went to bed yesterday."

Dalgliesh asked: "Where was it kept?"

It was Sister Rolfe who replied. "Fallon always kept her whisky in her bedroom."

Masterson laughed.

"Not surprising with the stuff costing nearly three quid a bottle."

Sister Rolfe looked at him with contempt.

"I doubt whether that would worry Fallon. She wasn't the type to mark the bottle."

"She was generous?" asked Dalgliesh.

"No, merely unconcerned. She kept her whisky in her room because Matron asked her to."

But brought it in here yesterday to prepare her late night drink, thought Dalgliesh. He stirred the sugar gently with his finger.

Sister Rolfe said: "That's innocent. The students tell me that they all used it when they made their morning tea. And the Burt twins, at least, drank some of theirs."

"But we'll send it and the lemon to the lab just the same," said Dalgliesh.

He lifted the lid from the little teapot and looked inside. Answering his unspoken question, Sister Rolfe said:

"Apparently Nurse Dakers made early tea in it. The pot is Fallon's of course. No one else has early tea in antique Worcester."

"Nurse Dakers made tea for Nurse Fallon before she knew that the girl was dead?"

"No, afterwards. It was a purely automatic reaction, I imagine. She must have been in shock. After all, she had just seen Fallon's body. She could hardly expect to cure rigor mortis with hot tea, even with the best China blend. I suppose you'll want to see Dakers, but you'll have to wait. She's in the sick bay at the moment. I think they told you. It's part of the private wing and Sister Brumfett is looking after her. That's why I'm here now. Like the police, we're a hierarchical profession and when Matron isn't in Nightingale House, Brumfett is next in the pecking order. Normally she would be dancing attendance on you, not I. You've been told, of course, that Miss Taylor is on her way back from a conference in Amsterdam. She had to deputise unexpectedly for the Chairman of the Area Nurse Training Committee, luckily for her. So at least there's one senior member of the staff with an alibi."

Dalgliesh had been told, and more than once. The absence of the Matron seemed to be a fact which everyone he had met, however briefly, had found it necessary to mention, explain or regret. But Sister Rolfe was the first to make a snide reference to the fact that it gave Miss Taylor an alibi, at least for the time of Fallon's death.

"And the rest of the students?"

"They're in the small lecture room on the floor below. Sister Gearing, our clinical instructor, is taking them for a private study period. I don't suppose they're doing much reading. It would have been better to set them something more active but it's not easy at a moment's notice. Will you see them there?"

"No, later. And in the demonstration room where Nurse Pearce died."

She glanced at him and then turned her eyes away quickly, but not so quickly that he missed the look of surprise and, he thought,

disapproval. She had expected him to show more sensitivity, more consideration. The demonstration room had not been used since Nurse Pearce's death. To interview the students there so soon after this second tragedy would reinforce memory with fresh horror. If any of them were ready to be unnerved, this might do it and he had never considered using any other room. Sister Rolfe, he thought, was like all the rest of them. They wanted their murderers caught but only by the most gentlemanly means. They wanted them punished, but only if the punishment did not outrage their own sensibility.

Dalgliesh asked: "How is this place locked at night?"

"Sister Brumfett, Sister Gearing, and myself take responsibility for a week at a time. It's Gearing's turn this week. We're the only three Sisters who are resident here. We lock and bolt the front door and the kitchen door at eleven o'clock promptly. There's a small side door with a Yale lock and an inside bolt. If any student or member of the staff has a late pass she is issued with a key to that door and bolts it when she comes in. Sisters have a key in their possession permanently. There's only one other door and that leads from Matron's flat on the third floor. She has a private staircase and, of course, her own key. Apart from that, there are the fire escape doors but they are all kept locked on the inside. The place wouldn't be difficult to break into. I imagine that few institutions are. But we've never had a burglar so far as I know. Incidentally, there's a pane of glass out in the conservatory. Alderman Kealey, the Vice-Chairman, seems to think that Fallon's murderer got in that way. He's a great man for finding comfortable explanations for all life's embarrassing problems. It looks to me as if the pane blew in with the wind, but you'll no doubt form your own opinion."

She's talking too much, he thought. Loquacity was one of the commonest reactions to shock or nervousness and one which any interrogating officer made the most of. Tomorrow she would despise herself for it, and become that much more difficult, that much less co-operative. In the meantime she was telling him more than she realized.

The broken pane would, of course, have to be looked at, the woodwork examined for marks of entry. But he thought it unlikely

that Nurse Fallon's death had been the work of any intruder. He asked: "How many people slept here last night?"

"Brumfett, Gearing and myself. Brumfett was out for part of the night. I understand she was recalled to the ward by Mr. Courtney-Briggs. Miss Collins was here. She's the housekeeper. And there were five student nurses: Nurse Dakers, the Burt twins, Nurse Goodale, and Nurse Pardoe. And Fallon slept here of course. That is, if Fallon had time to sleep! Incidentally, her bedside light was on all night. The Burt twins were up brewing cocoa shortly after two and nearly took a cup in to Fallon. If they'd done so you might have got a clearer idea of the time of death. But it occurred to them that she might have fallen asleep with the light on and wouldn't exactly welcome being woken, even to the sight and smell of cocoa. The twins' invariable solace is food and drink, but at least they've lived long enough to realize that not everyone shares their pre-occupation and that Fallon, in particular, might prefer sleep and privacy to cocoa and their company."

"I shall be seeing the Burt twins. What about the hospital grounds? Are they left open at night?"

"There's always a porter on duty at the front lodge. The main gates aren't locked because of the accident ambulances but he keeps an eye on anyone else who comes in or leaves. Nightingale House is much closer to the rear entrance to the grounds, but we don't usually go that way by foot because the path is ill-lit and rather frightening. Besides, it leads into the Winchester Road which is almost two miles from the main part of the town. The back gate is locked at dusk summer and winter by one of the porters but all the Sisters and Matron have keys."

"And the nurses with late passes?"

"They're expected to use the front gate and walk along the main path which skirts the hospital. There's a much shorter cut through the trees which we use in the daytime—it's only about two hundred yards—but not many people choose to come that way at night. I daresay Mr. Hudson, he's the Hospital Secretary, can let you have a plan of the grounds and of Nightingale House. Incidentally, he and the Vice-Chairman are waiting for you now in the library. The Chairman, Sir Marcus Cohen, is in Israel. Even so, it's quite a re-

ception committee. Even Mr. Courtney-Briggs has deferred his out-patient session to welcome the Yard to Nightingale House."

"Then," said Dalgliesh, "perhaps you'll be good enough to let them know that I'll be with them shortly."

It was a dismissal. Sergeant Masterson, as if to soften it, said suddenly and loudly: "Sister Rolfe has been very helpful."

The woman gave a guttural snort of derision.

"Helping the police! Isn't there a sinister connotation about that phrase? Anyway, I don't think I can be particularly helpful. I didn't kill either of them. And last night I was at a film at the new arts cinema here. They're showing an Antonioni series. This week it's *L'Avventura*. I didn't get in until just before eleven and went straight to bed. I didn't even see Fallon."

Dalgliesh asked: "Did you go to the cinema alone?"

Sister Rolfe hesitated for a second and said curtly: "Yes."

Dalgliesh recognized with weary resignation the first lie and wondered how many more, important and unimportant, would be spoken before the investigation was complete. But this wasn't the time to interrogate Sister Rolfe. She wasn't going to be an easy witness. She had answered his questions fully but with undisguised resentment. He wasn't sure whether it was he or his job which she disliked, or whether any man would have provoked this tone of angry contempt. Her face matched her personality, rebarbative and defensive. It was strong and intelligent but without softness or feminity. The deep-set and very dark eyes might have been attractive but they were set under a pair of perfectly straight black eyebrows, so dark and bushy that they gave to the face a faint suggestion of deformity. Her nose was large and open pored, her lips a thin uncompromising line. It was the face of a woman who had never learnt to come to terms with life, and had, perhaps, given up trying. He thought suddenly that, if she proved to be a murderess and her photograph were at last published, other women, avidly searching that uncompromising mask for the marks of depravity, would profess themselves unsurprised. Suddenly he felt sorry for her with a mixture of irritation and compassion one might feel for the inadequate or the physically deformed. He turned quickly away so that she should not catch that sudden spasm of pity. To her it

would, he knew, be the ultimate insult. And when he turned again
to thank her formally for her help, he saw that she had gone.

III

Sergeant Charles Masterson was six feet three inches tall and
broad shouldered. He carried his bulk easily and all his movements
were surprisingly controlled and precise for such an assertively
masculine and heavy man. He was generally considered handsome,
particularly by himself, and with his strong face, sensual lips and
hooded eyes looked remarkably like a well-known American film
actor of the guts-and-guns school. Dalgliesh occasionally suspected
that the sergeant, aware, as he could hardly fail to be, of the resemblance, was helping it along by assuming a trace of an American
accent.

"All right, Sergeant. You've had a chance to look at the place,
you've talked to some of the people. Tell me about it."

This invitation had been known to strike terror into the hearts of
Dalgliesh's subordinates. It meant that the Superintendent now
expected to hear a brief, succinct, accurate, elegantly phrased but
comprehensive account of the crime which would give all the salient
facts so far known to someone who came to it freshly. The ability
to know what you want to say and to say it in the minimum of
appropriate words is as uncommon in policemen as in other members
of the community. Dalgliesh's subordinates were apt to complain
that they hadn't realized that a degree in English was the new
qualification for joining the C.I.D. But Sergeant Masterson was less
intimidated than most. He had his weaknesses, but lack of confidence was not one of them. He was glad to be working on the case.
It was well known at the Yard that Superintendent Dalgliesh
couldn't tolerate a fool and that his definition of folly was individual
and precise. Masterson respected him because Dalgliesh was one
of the Yard's most successful detectives and for Masterson success
was the only real criteria. He thought him very able, which is not to
say that he thought Adam Dalgliesh as able as Charles Masterson.
Most of the time, and for reasons which it seemed to him unprofitable to explore, he disliked him heartily. He suspected that the

302

antipathy was mutual, but this didn't particularly worry him. Dalgliesh wasn't a man to prejudice a subordinate's career because he disliked him and was known to be meticulous, if judicious, in ascribing credit where it was due. But the situation would need watching, and Masterson intended to watch it. An ambitious man on his carefully planned climb to senior rank was a fool if he didn't early recognize that it was bloody daft to antagonize a senior officer. Masterson had no intention of being that kind of a fool. But a little co-operation from the Super in this campaign of mutual goodwill wouldn't be unwelcome. And he wasn't sure he was going to get it. He said:

"I'll deal with the two deaths separately, sir. The first victim. . . ."

"Why talk like a crime reporter, Sergeant? Let's be sure we have a victim before we use that word."

Masterton began: "The first deceased . . . the first girl to die was a twenty-one-year-old student nurse, Heather Pearce." He went on to recite the facts of both girls' deaths, as far as they were known, taking care to avoid the more blatant examples of police jargon, to which he knew his Super to be morbidly sensitive, and resisting the temptation to display his recently acquired knowledge of intra-gastric feeding about which he had taken trouble to extract from Sister Rolfe a comprehensive, if grudging, explanation. He ended: "So we have, sir, the possibilities that one or both of the deaths was suicide, that one or both was accidental, that the first was murder but that the wrong victim was killed, or that there were two murders with two intended victims. An intriguing choice, sir."

Dalgliesh said: "Or that Fallon's death was due to natural causes. Until we get the toxicology report we're theorizing in advance of the facts. But for the present we treat both deaths as murder. Well, let's go to the library and see what the Vice-Chairman of the Hospital Management Committee has to say to us."

IV

The library, easily identified by a large painted sign above the door, was a pleasant high-ceilinged room on the first floor, next to the student nurses' sitting-room. One wall was entirely taken up

303

with three ornate oriel windows, but the other three were book-lined to the ceiling, leaving the centre of the room bare. It was furnished with four tables ranged in front of the windows and two shabby sofas, one on each side of the stone fireplace, where now an ancient gas fire hissed its sinister welcome. In front of it, under the two strips of fluorescent lighting, a group of four men, muttering together conspiratorially, turned in one movement at the entrance of Dalgliesh and Masterson and watched them with wary curiosity. It was a familiar moment to Dalgliesh, compounded as always of interest, apprehension and hope—this first confrontation of the protagonists in a murder case with the outsider, the alien expert in violent death who has come among them, an unwelcome guest, to demonstrate his invidious talents.

Then the silence broke, the rigid figures relaxed. The two men Dalgliesh had already met—Stephen Courtney-Briggs and Paul Hudson, the Hospital Secretary—moved forward with formal welcoming smiles. Mr. Courtney-Briggs, who apparently took charge of any situation dignified by his presence, made the introductions. The Group Secretary, Raymond Grout, shook hands damply. He had a gently lugubrious face, puckered now with distress like that of the child on the verge of crying. His hair lay in strands of silver silk over a high-domed forehead. He was probably younger than he appeared, thought Dalgliesh, but even so, he must be very near retirement.

Beside the tall, stooped figure of Grout, Alderman Kealey looked as perky as a terrier. He was a ginger-haired, foxy little man, bandy as a jockey and wearing a plaid suit, the awfulness of its pattern emphasized by the excellence of its cut. It gave him an anthropomorphic appearance, like an animal in a child's comic; and Dalgliesh almost expected to find himself shaking a paw.

"It was good of you to come, Superintendent, and so promptly," he said.

The folly of the remark apparently struck him as soon as he had made it, for he darted a keen glance from under spiky ginger eyebrows at his companions, as if defying them to smirk. No one did, but the Group Secretary looked as humiliated as if the solecism had been his, and Paul Hudson turned his face away to hide an embar-

rassed grin. He was a personable young man who, on Dalgliesh's first arrival at the hospital, had shown himself as both efficient and authoritative. Now, however, the presence of his Vice-Chairman and the Group Secretary seemed to have inhibited his speech and he had the apologetic air of a man present on sufferance. Mr. Courtney-Briggs said:

"It's too much to hope for any news yet, I suppose? We saw the mortuary van leaving, and I had a few words with Miles Honeyman. He couldn't commit himself at this stage, of course, but he'll be surprised if this was a natural death. The girl killed herself. Well, I should have thought that was obvious to anyone."

Dalgliesh said: "Nothing is obvious yet."

There was a silence. The Vice-Chairman seemed to find it embarrassing for he cleared his throat noisily and said:

"You'll want an office, of course. The local C.I.D. worked from the police station here. They were really very little trouble to us. We hardly knew they were in the place." He looked with faint optimism at Dalgliesh, as if hardly sanguine that the flying squad would be equally accommodating. Dalgliesh replied shortly:

"We shall want a room. Is it possible to make one available in Nightingale House? That would be the most convenient."

The request seemed to disconcert them. The Group Secretary said tentatively: "If Matron were here . . . it's difficult for us to know what's free. She shouldn't be long now."

Alderman Kealey grunted. "We can't let everything wait for Matron. The Superintendent wants a room. Find him one."

"Well there's Miss Rolfe's office on the ground floor, just next to the demonstration room." The Group Secretary bent his sad eyes on Dalgliesh. "You've met Miss Rolfe, our Principal Tutor, of course. Now if Miss Rolfe can move temporarily into her secretary's room . . . Miss Buckfield is off with flu, so it's free. It's rather cramped, only a cupboard really, but if Matron . . ."

"Get Miss Rolfe to move out any of her things she'll need. The porters can shift the filing cabinets." Alderman Kealey turned and barked at Dalgliesh: "Will that do?"

"If it's private, reasonably soundproof, has a lock on the door, is large enough to take three men and has a direct telephone to the

exchange, it will do. If it also has running water, so much the better."

The Vice-Chairman, chastened by this formidable list of requirements, said tentatively: "There's a small cloakroom and lavatory on the ground floor opposite Miss Rolfe's room. That could be put at your disposal."

Mr. Grout's misery deepened. He glanced across at Mr. Courtney-Briggs as if seeking an ally but the surgeon had been unaccountably silent for the last few minutes and seemed reluctant to meet his eyes. Then the telephone rang. Mr. Hudson, apparently glad of a chance of activity, sprang to answer it. He turned to his Vice-Chairman.

"It's the *Clarion*, sir. They're asking for you personally."

Alderman Kealey grasped the receiver resolutely. Having decided to assert himself he was apparently ready to take command of any situation, and this one was well within his capabilities. Murder might be outside his normal preoccupations but dealing tactfully with the local Press was something he understood.

"Alderman Kealey here. The Vice-Chairman of the Management Committee. Yes, we've got the Yard here. The victim? Oh, I don't think we want to talk about a victim. Not yet anyway. Fallon. Josephine Fallon. Age?" He placed his hand over the mouthpiece and turned to the Group Secretary. Oddly enough, it was Mr. Courtney-Briggs who replied.

"She was thirty-one years, ten months," he said. "She was precisely twenty years younger than me to the day."

Alderman Kealey, unsurprised by the gratuitous information, returned to his listener.

"She was thirty-one. No, we don't know yet how she died. No one knows. We are awaiting the post mortem report. Yes, Chief Superintendent Dalgliesh. He's here now but he's too busy to talk. I hope to issue a Press statement this evening. We ought to have the autopsy report by then. No, there's no reason to suspect murder. The Chief Constable has called in the Yard as a precautionary measure. No, as far as we're aware, the two deaths aren't connected in any way. Very sad. Yes, very. If you care to telephone about six I may have some more information. All we know at present is that

306

Nurse Fallon was found dead in her bed this morning shortly after seven. It could very well have been a heart attack. She was just recovering from flu. No, there wasn't a note. Nothing like that."

He listened for a moment then again placed his hand over the mouthpiece and turned to Grout.

"They're asking about relatives. What do we know about them?"

"She hadn't any. Fallon was an orphan." Again it was Mr. Courtney-Briggs who replied.

Alderman Kealey passed on this information and replaced the receiver. Smiling grimly he gave Dalgliesh a look of mingled self-satisfaction and warning. Dalgliesh was interested to hear that the Yard had been called in as a precautionary measure. It was a new conception of the flying squad's responsibilities and one which he felt was unlikely to deceive the local Press boys, still less the London reporters who would soon be on the scent. He wondered how the hospital was going to cope with the publicity. Alderman Kealey was going to need some advice if the inquiry were not to be hampered. But there was plenty of time for that. Now all he wanted was to get rid of them, to get started with the investigation. These social preliminaries were always a time-consuming nuisance. And soon there would be a Matron to propitiate, to consult, possibly even to antagonize. From the Group Secretary's unwillingness to move a step without her consent, it looked as if she were a strong personality. He didn't relish the prospect of making it clear to her, tactfully, that there would be room for only one strong personality in this investigation.

Mr. Courtney-Briggs, who had been standing at the window, staring out at the storm-wrecked garden, turned, shook himself free of his preoccupations and said:

"I'm afraid I can't spare any more time now. I have a patient to see in the private wing and then a ward round. I was due to lecture to the students here later this morning but that'll have to be cancelled now. You'll let me know, Kealey, if there's anything I can do."

He ignored Dalgliesh. The impression given, and no doubt intended, was that he was a busy man who had already wasted too much time on a triviality. Dalgliesh resisted the temptation to delay

him. Agreeable as it would be to tame Mr. Courtney-Briggs's arrogance, it was an indulgence which he couldn't afford at present. There were more pressing matters.

It was then that they heard the sound of a car. Mr. Courtney-Briggs returned to the window and looked out, but did not speak. The rest of the little group stiffened and turned as if pulled by a common force to face the door. A car door slammed. Then there was silence for a few seconds followed by the clip of hurried footsteps on a tessellated floor. The door opened and Matron came in.

Dalgliesh's first impression was of a highly individual yet casual elegance and a confidence that was almost palpable. He saw a tall slender woman, hatless, with pale honey-gold skin and hair of almost the same colour, drawn back from a high forehead and swathed into an intricate coil at the nape of her neck. She was wearing a grey tweed coat with a bright green scarf knotted at her neck and carrying a black handbag and a small travelling case. She came into the room quietly and, placing her case on the table, drew off her gloves and surveyed the little party silently. Almost instinctively, as if watching a witness, Dalgliesh noticed her hands. The fingers were very white, long and tapering but with unusually bony joints. The nails were clipped short. On the third finger of the right hand an immense sapphire ring in an ornate setting gleamed against the knuckle. He wondered irrelevantly whether she took it off when she was on duty and, if so, how she forced it over those nodular joints.

Mr. Courtney-Briggs, after a brief, "Good morning, Matron," made his way to the door and stood there like a bored guest, demonstrating his anxiety to make a quick get-away. But the others crowded around her. There was an immediate sense of relief. Muttered introductions were made.

"Good morning, Superintendent." Her voice was deep, a little husky, a voice as individual as herself. She seemed hardly aware of him, yet he was conscious of a swift appraisal from the green exophthalmic eyes. Her handshake was firm and cool, but so momentary that it seemed a fleeting meeting of palms, nothing more.

The Vice-Chairman said: "The police will want a room. We thought perhaps Miss Rolfe's office?"

"Too small, I think, and not private enough, so close to the main hall. It would be better if Mr. Dalgliesh had the use of the visitors' sitting-room on the first floor and the cloakroom next door to it. The room has a key. There's a desk with lockable drawers in the general office and that can be moved up. That way the police will get some privacy and there'll be a minimum of interference with the work of the school."

There was a murmur of assent. The men looked relieved. The Matron said to Dalgliesh: "Will you need a bedroom? Do you want to sleep in the hospital?"

"That won't be necessary. We shall be staying in the town. But I would prefer to work from here. We shall probably be here late every night so that it would be helpful if we could have keys."

"For how long?" asked the Vice-Chairman suddenly. It was on the face of it, a stupid question, but Dalgliesh noticed that all their faces turned to him as if it were one he could be expected to answer. He knew his reputation for speed. Did they perhaps know it too?

"About a week," he said. Even if the case dragged on for longer, he would learn all he needed from Nightingale House and its occupants within seven days. If Nurse Fallon had been murdered— and he believed she had—the circle of suspects would be small. If the case didn't break within a week it might never break. He thought there was a small sigh of relief.

Matron said: "Where is she?"

"They took the body to the mortuary, Matron."

"I didn't mean Fallon. Where is Nurse Dakers? I understood it was she who found the body."

Alderman Kealey replied. "She's being nursed in the private ward. She was pretty shaken up so we asked Dr. Snelling to take a look at her. He's given her a sedative and Sister Brumfett's looking after her."

He added: "Sister Brumfett was a little concerned about her. On top of that she's got rather a sick ward. Otherwise she would have met you at the airport. We all felt rather badly about your arriving with no one to meet you, but the best thing seemed to be to telephone a message for you, asking you to ring us here as soon as you

309

landed. Sister Brumfett thought that the shock would be less if you learnt it in that way. On the other hand it seemed wrong not to have someone there. I wanted to send Grout but. . . ."

The husky voice broke in with its quiet reproof: "I should have thought that sparing me shock was the least of your worries." She turned to Dalgliesh:

"I shall be in my sitting-room here on the third floor in about forty-five minutes' time. If it's convenient for you, I should be glad to have a word with you then."

Dalgliesh, resisting the impulse to reply with a docile, "Yes, Matron," said that it would. Miss Taylor turned to Alderman Kealey.

"I'm going to see Nurse Dakers now. Afterwards the Superintendent will want to interview me and then I shall be in my main office in the hospital if you or Mr. Grout want me. I shall, of course, be available all day."

Without a further word or look she gathered up her travelling case and handbag and went out of the room. Mr. Courtney-Briggs perfunctorily opened the door for her, then prepared to follow. Standing in the open doorway, he said with jovial belligerence:

"Well, now that Matron's back and the important matter of accommodation for the police has been settled, perhaps the work of the hospital can be permitted to continue. I shouldn't be late for your interview if I were you, Dalgliesh. Miss Taylor isn't accustomed to insubordination."

He shut the door behind him. Alderman Kealey looked for a moment perplexed, then he said:

"He's upset, of course. Well, naturally. Wasn't there some kind of rumour. . . ."

Then his eyes lit on Dalgliesh. He checked himself suddenly, and turned to Paul Hudson:

"Well, Mr. Hudson, you heard what Matron said. The police are to use the visitors' sitting-room on this floor. Get on with it, my dear fellow. Get on with it!"

Miss Taylor changed into uniform before she went over to the private ward. At the time it seemed an instinctive thing to do, but, wrapping her cloak tightly around her as she walked briskly along the small footpath leading from Nightingale House to the hospital, she realized that the instinct had been prompted by reason. It was important to the hospital that Matron was back, and important that she should be seen to be back.

The quickest way to the private wing was through the out-patients' hall. The department was already buzzing with activity. The circles of comfortable chairs, carefully disposed to give an illusion of informality and relaxed comfort, were filling quickly. Volunteers from the ladies' committee of the League of Friends were already presiding at the steaming urn, serving tea to those regular patients who preferred to attend an hour before their appointments for the pleasure of sitting in the warmth, reading the magazines and chatting to their fellow habitués. As Matron passed she was aware of heads turning to watch her. There was a brief silence, followed by the customary murmur of deferential greeting. She was conscious of the white-coated junior medical staff standing briefly to one side as she passed, of the student nurses pressing themselves back against the wall.

The private ward was on the second floor of what still was called the new building, although it had been completed in 1945. Miss Taylor went up by the lift, sharing it with two radiographers and a young houseman. They murmured their formal, "Good morning, Matron," and stood in unnatural silence until the lift stopped, then stood back while she went out before them.

The private ward consisted of a suite of twenty single rooms, opening each side of a wide central corridor. The Sister's office, the kitchen, and the utility room were just inside the door. As Miss Taylor entered, a young first-year student nurse appeared from the kitchen. She flushed when she saw Matron and muttered something about fetching Sister.

"Where is Sister, Nurse?"

"In room 7 with Mr. Courtney-Briggs, Matron. His patient isn't too well."

"Don't disturb them: just tell Sister when she appears that I've come to see Nurse Dakers. Where is she?"

"In room 3, Matron." She hesitated.

"It's all right, Nurse, I'll find my own way. Get on with what you are doing."

Room 3 was at the far end of the corridor, one of six single rooms, usually reserved for sick nurses. Only when these rooms were all occupied were the staff nursed in the side rooms of the wards. It was not, Miss Taylor noted, the room in which Josephine Fallon had been nursed. Room 3 was the sunniest and most pleasant of the six rooms reserved for nurses. A week ago it had been occupied by a nurse with pneumonia, a complication of influenza. Miss Taylor, who visited every ward in the hospital once a day and who received daily reports on every sick nurse, thought it unlikely that Nurse Wilkins was fit enough yet to be discharged. Sister Brumfett must have moved her to make room 3 available for Nurse Dakers. Miss Taylor could guess why. The one window gave a view of the lawns and smoothly forked flower beds at the front of the hospital; from this side of the ward it was impossible to glimpse Nightingale House even through the bare tracery of the winter trees. Dear old Brumfett! So unprepossessingly rigid in her views, but so imaginative when it came to the welfare and comfort of her patients. Brumfett, who talked embarrassingly of duty, obedience, loyalty, but who knew exactly what she meant by those unpopular terms and lived by what she knew. She was one of the best ward sisters that the John Carpendar had, or ever would have. But Miss Taylor was glad that devotion to duty had kept Sister Brumfett from meeting the plane at Heathrow. It was bad enough to come home to this further tragedy without the added burden of Brumfett's doglike devotion and concern.

She drew the stool from under the bed and seated herself beside the girl. Despite Dr. Snelling's sedative, Nurse Dakers was not asleep. She was lying very still on her back gazing at the ceiling. Now her eyes turned to look at Matron. They were blank with misery. On the bedside locker there was a copy of a textbook, *Materia Medica for Nurses*. The Matron picked it up.

"This is very conscientious of you, Nurse, but just for the short time you are in here, why not have a novel from the Red Cross trolley or a frivolous magazine? Shall I bring one in for you?"

She was answered by a flood of tears. The slim figure twisted convulsively in the bed, buried her head in the pillow and clasped it with shaking hands. The bed shook with the paroxysm of grief. The Matron got up, moved over to the door and clicked across the board which covered the nurses' peephole. She returned quickly to her seat and waited without speaking, making no move except to place her hand on the girl's head. After a few minutes the dreadful shaking ceased and Nurse Dakers grew calmer. She began to mutter, her voice hiccuping with sobs, half muffled by the pillow:

"I'm so miserable, so ashamed."

The Matron bent her head to catch the words. A chill of horror swept over her. Surely she couldn't be listening to a confession of murder? She found herself praying under her breath.

"Dear God, please not. Not this child! Surely not this child?"

She waited, not daring to question. Nurse Dakers twisted herself round and gazed up at her, her eyes reddened and swollen like two amorphous moons in a face blotched and formless with misery.

"I'm wicked, Matron, wicked. I was glad when she died."

"Nurse Fallon?"

"Oh no, not Fallon! I was sorry about Fallon. Nurse Pearce."

The Matron placed her hands on each of the girl's shoulders, pressing her back against the bed. She held the trembling body firmly and looked down into the drowned eyes.

"I want you to tell me the truth, Nurse. Did you kill Nurse Pearce?"

"No, Matron."

"Or Nurse Fallon?"

"No, Matron."

"Or have anything at all to do with their deaths?"

"No, Matron."

Miss Taylor let out her breath. She relaxed her hold on the girl and sat back.

"I think you'd better tell me all about it."

So, calmly now, the pathetic story came out. It hadn't seemed

313

like stealing at the time. It had seemed like a miracle. Mummy had so needed a warm winter coat and Nurse Dakers had been saving thirty shillings from her monthly salary cheque. Only the money had taken so long to save and the weather was getting colder; and Mummy, who never complained, and never asked her for anything, had to wait nearly fifteen minutes for the bus some mornings and caught cold so easily. And if she did catch cold she couldn't stay away from work because Miss Arkwright, the buyer in the department store, was only waiting for an opportunity to get her sacked. Serving in a store wasn't really the right job for Mummy, but it wasn't easy to find a job when you were over fifty and unqualified, and the young assistants in the department weren't very kind. They kept hinting that Mummy wasn't pulling her weight, which wasn't true. Mummy might not be as quick as they were but she really took trouble with the customers.

Then Nurse Harper had dropped the two crisp new £5 notes almost at her feet. Nurse Harper who had so much pocket money from her father that she could lose £10 without really worrying about it. It had happened about four weeks ago. Nurse Harper had been walking with Nurse Pearce from the Nurses' Home to the hospital dining-room for breakfast, and Nurse Dakers had been following a few feet behind. The two notes had fallen out of Nurse Harper's cape pocket and had lain there fluttering gently. Her first instinct had been to call after the other two students, but something about the sight of the money had stopped her. The notes had been so unexpected, so unbelievable, so beautiful in their pristine crispness. She had just stood looking at them for a second, and then she had realized that she was really looking at Mummy's new coat. And, by then, the other two students had passed almost out of sight, the notes were folded in her hand, and it was too late.

The Matron asked: "How did Nurse Pearce know that you had the notes?"

"She said that she'd seen me. She just happened to glance round when I was bending to pick up the notes. It meant nothing to her at the time, but when Nurse Harper told everyone that she'd lost the money and that the notes must have fallen out of her cape pocket on the way over to breakfast, Nurse Pearce guessed what

had happened. She and the twins went with Nurse Harper to search the path to see if they could find the money. I expect that was when she remembered about my stooping down."

"When did she first talk to you about it?"

"A week later, Matron, a fortnight before our set came into block. I expect she couldn't bring herself to believe it before then. She must have been trying to make up her mind to speak to me."

So Nurse Pearce had waited. The Matron wondered why. It couldn't have taken her a whole week to clarify her suspicions. She must have recalled seeing Dakers stoop to pick up the notes as soon as she heard that they were missing. So why hadn't she tackled the girl at once? Had it perhaps been more satisfying to her twisted ego to wait until the money was spent and the culprit safely in her power?

"Was she blackmailing you?" she demanded.

"Oh no, Matron!" The girl was shocked.

"She only took back five shillings a week, and that wasn't blackmail. She sent the money every week to a society for discharged prisoners. She showed me the receipts."

"And did she, incidentally, explain why she wasn't re-paying it to Nurse Harper?"

"She thought it would be difficult to explain without involving me and I begged her not to do that. It would have been the end of everything, Matron. I want to take a district nurse training after I'm qualified so that I can look after Mummy. If I could get a country district we could have a cottage together and perhaps even a car. Mummy will be able to give up the store. I told Nurse Pearce about that. Besides, she said that Harper was so careless about money that it wouldn't hurt her to learn a lesson. She sent the payments to the society for discharged prisoners because it seemed appropriate. After all, I might have gone to prison if she hadn't shielded me."

The Matron said drily: "That, of course, is nonsense and you should have known it was nonsense. Nurse Pearce seems to have been a very stupid and arrogant young woman. Are you sure that she wasn't making any other demands on you? There is more than one kind of blackmail."

"But she wouldn't do that, Matron!" Nurse Dakers struggled to lift her head from the pillow. "Pearce was . . . well, she was good." She seemed to find the word inadequate and puckered her brow as if desperately anxious to explain.

"She used to talk to me quite a lot and she gave me a card with a passage out of the Bible which I had to read every day. Once a week she used to ask me about it."

The Matron was swept by a sense of moral outrage so acute that she had to find relief in action. She got up from the stool and walked over to the window, cooling her flaring face against the pane. She could feel her heart bumping and noticed with almost clinical interest that her hands were shaking. After a moment she came back again to the bedside.

"Don't talk about her being good. Dutiful, conscientious, and well-meaning if you like, but not good. If ever you meet real goodness you will know the difference. And I shouldn't worry about being glad that she is dead. In the circumstances you wouldn't be normal if you felt differently. In time you may be able to pity her and forgive her."

"But Matron, it's me who ought to be forgiven. I'm a thief." Was there a suggestion of masochism in the whine of the voice, the perverse self-denigration of the born victim? Miss Taylor said briskly:

"You're not a thief. You stole once; that's a very different thing. Every one of us has some incident in our lives that we're ashamed and sorry about. You've recently learned something about yourself, about what you're capable of doing, which has shaken your confidence. Now you have to live with that knowledge. We can only begin to understand and forgive other people when we have learned to understand and forgive ourselves. You won't steal again. I know that, and so do you. But you did once. You are capable of stealing. That knowledge will save you from being too pleased with yourself, from being too self-satisfied. It can make you a much more tolerant and understanding person and a better nurse. But not if you go on indulging in guilt and remorse and bitterness. Those insidious emotions may be very enjoyable but they aren't going to help you or anyone else."

The girl looked up at her.

"Will the police have to know?"

That, of course, was the question. And there could be only one answer.

"Yes. And you will have to tell them, just as you've told me. But I shall have a word first with the Superintendent. He's a new detective, from Scotland Yard this time, and I think he's an intelligent and understanding man."

Was he? How could she possibly tell? That first meeting had been so brief, merely a glance and a touching of hands. Was she merely comforting herself with a fleeting impression that here was a man with authority and imagination who might be able to solve the mystery of both deaths with a minimum of harm to the innocent and guilty alike. She had felt this instinctively. But was the feeling rational? She believed Nurse Dakers's story; but then she was disposed to believe it. How would it strike a police officer faced with a multiplicity of suspects but no other discernible motive? And the motive was there all right. It was Nurse Dakers's whole future, and that of her mother. And Dakers had behaved rather oddly. True she had been most distressed of all the students when Pearce had died, but she had pulled herself together remarkably quickly. Even under intense police questioning she had kept her secret safe. What then had precipitated this disintegration into confession and remorse? Was it only the shock of finding Fallon's body? And why should Fallon's death be so cataclysmic if she had had no hand in it?

Miss Taylor thought again about Pearce. How little one really knew about any of the students. Pearce, if one thought about her at all, had typified the dull, conscientious, unattractive student who was probably using nursing to compensate for the lack of more orthodox satisfactions. There was usually one such in every nurse training school. It was difficult to reject them when they applied for training since they offered more than adequate educational qualifications and impeccable references. And they didn't on the whole make bad nurses. It was just that they seldom made the best. But now she began to wonder. If Pearce had possessed such a secret craving for power that she could use this child's guilt and distress

as fodder for her own ego, then she had been far from ordinary or ineffective. She had been a dangerous young woman.

And she had worked it all out very cleverly. By waiting a week until she could be reasonably certain that the money had been spent, she had left Dakers no option. The child could hardly claim then that she had yielded to a sudden impulse but intended to return the money. And even if Dakers had decided to confess, perhaps to the Matron, Nurse Harper would have had to be told: Pearce would have seen to that. And only Harper could decide whether or not to prosecute. It might have been possible to influence her, to persuade her to mercy. But suppose it had not been possible? Nurse Harper would almost certainly have confided in her father, and the Matron couldn't see Mr. Ronald Harper showing mercy to anyone who had helped herself to his money. Miss Taylor's acquaintance with him had been brief but revealing. He had arrived at the hospital two days after Pearce's death, a large, opulent-looking and aggressive man, top heavy in his fur-lined motoring coat. Without preliminaries or explanation he had launched into his prepared tirade, addressing Matron as if she were one of his garage hands. He wasn't going to let his girl stay another minute in a house with a murderer at large, police or no police. This nurse training had been a damn fool idea in the first place, and now it was going to stop. His Diane didn't need a career anyway. She was engaged, wasn't she? A bloody good match too! His partner's son. They could put the marriage forward instead of waiting until the summer and, in the meantime, Diane could stay at home and help in the office. He was taking her away with him now, and he'd like to see anyone try to stop him.

No one had stopped him. The girl had made no objection. She had stood meekly in the Matron's office overtly demure, but smiling a little as if gratified by all the fuss, by her father's assertive masculinity. The police could not prevent her leaving, nor had they seemed concerned to try. It was odd, thought the Matron, that no one had seriously suspected Harper; and if the two deaths were the work of one hand, their instinct had been right. She had last seen the girl stepping into her father's immense and ugly car, legs spindly beneath the new fur coat he had bought her to compensate

for her disappointment at cutting short her training, and turning to wave good-bye to the rest of the set like a film star condescending to her assembled fans. No, not a particularly attractive family: Miss Taylor would be sorry for anyone who was in their power. And yet, such were the vagaries of personality, Diane Harper had been an efficient nurse, a better nurse in many ways than Pearce.

But there was one more question which had to be asked, and it took her a second to summon the courage to ask it.

"Did Nurse Fallon know about this business?"

The girl answered at once, confident, a little surprised.

"Oh no, Matron! At least I don't think so. Pearce swore that she wouldn't tell a soul, and it wasn't as if she was particularly friendly with Fallon. I'm sure she wouldn't have told Fallon."

"No," said the Matron. "I don't suppose she would."

Gently she lifted Nurse Dakers's head and smoothed the pillows.

"Now I want you to try and get some sleep. You'll feel a great deal better when you wake up. And try not to worry."

The girl's face relaxed. She smiled up at the Matron and, putting out her hand, briefly touched Miss Taylor's face. Then she snuggled down into the sheets as if resolute for sleep. So that was all right. But of course it was. It always worked. How easy and how insidiously satisfying was this doling out of advice and comfort, each portion individually flavoured to personal taste! She might be a Victorian vicar's wife presiding over a soup kitchen. To each according to her need. It happened in the hospital every day. A ward Sister's brightly professional voice. "Here's Matron to see you, Mrs. Cox. I'm afraid Mrs. Cox isn't feeling quite so well this morning, Matron." A tired pain-racked face smiling bravely up from the pillow, mouth avid for its morsel of affection and re-assurance. The Sisters bringing their problems, the perpetual un-solvable problems over work and incompatible personalities.

"Are you feeling happier about it now, Sister?"

"Yes, thank you, Matron. Much happier."

The Group Secretary, desperately coping with his own inade-quacies.

"I should feel better if we could have just a word about the problem, Matron." Of course he would! They all wanted to have

just a word about the problem. They all went away feeling better. Hear what comfortable words our Matron saith. Her whole working life seemed a blasphemous liturgy of reassurance and absolution. And how much easier both to give and to accept was this bland milk of human kindness than the acid of truth. She could imagine the blank incomprehension, the resentment with which they would greet her private credo.

"I haven't anything to offer. There isn't any help. We are all alone, all of us from the moment of birth until we die. Our past is our present and our future. We have to live with ourselves until there isn't any more time left. If you want salvation look to yourself. There's nowhere else to look."

She sat for a few more minutes and then quietly left the room. Nurse Dakers gave a brief valedictory smile. As she entered the corridor she saw Sister Brumfett and Mr. Courtney-Briggs coming out of his patient's room. Sister Brumfett bustled up.

"I'm sorry, Matron. I didn't know you were on the ward."

She always used the formal title. They might spend the whole of their off-duty together driving or golfing; they might visit a London show once a month with the cosy, boring regularity of an old married couple; they might drink their early morning tea and late night hot milk together in indissoluble tedium. But in the hospital Brumfett always called her Matron. The shrewd eyes searched hers.

"You've seen the new detective, the man from the Yard?"

"Only briefly. I'm due for a session with him as soon as I get back."

Mr. Courtney-Briggs said: "I know him as a matter of fact; not well but we have met. You'll find him reasonable and intelligent. He's got quite a reputation of course. He's said to work very quickly. As far as I'm concerned, that's a considerable asset. The hospital can stand only so much disruption. He'll want to see me I suppose, but he'll have to wait. Let him know that I'll pop across to Nightingale House when I've finished my ward round, will you Matron?"

"I'll tell him if he asks me," replied Miss Taylor calmly. She turned to Sister Brumfett.

"Nurse Dakers is calmer now, but I think it would be better if she were not disturbed by visitors. She'll probably manage to get some sleep. I'll send over some magazines for her and some fresh flowers. When is Dr. Snelling due to see her?"

"He said he would come in before lunch, Matron."

"Perhaps you would ask him to be good enough to have a word with me. I shall be in the hospital all day."

Sister Brumfett said: "I suppose that Scotland Yard detective will want to see me too. I hope he isn't going to take too long about it. I've got a very sick ward."

The Matron hoped that Brum wasn't going to be too difficult. It would be unfortunate if she thought she could treat a Chief Superintendent of the Metropolitan Police as if he were a recalcitrant House Surgeon. Mr. Courtney-Briggs, no doubt, would be his usual arrogant self, but she had a feeling that Superintendent Dalgliesh would be able to cope with Mr. Courtney-Briggs.

They walked to the door of the ward together. Miss Taylor's mind was already busy with fresh problems. Something would have to be done about Nurse Dakers's mother. It would be some years before the child was fully qualified as a district nurse. In the meantime she must be relieved of the constant anxiety about her mother. It might be helpful to have a word with Raymond Grout. There might be a clerical job somewhere in the hospital which would suit her. But would that be fair? One couldn't indulge one's own urge to help at someone else's expense. Whatever problems of staff recruitment the hospital service might have in London, Grout had no difficulty in filling his clerical jobs. He had a right to expect efficiency; and the Mrs. Dakers of this world, dogged by their own inadequacy as much as by ill-luck, could seldom offer that. She supposed she would have to telephone the woman; the parents of the other students too. The important thing was to get the girls out of Nightingale House. The training schedule couldn't be disrupted; it was tight enough as it was. She had better arrange with the House Warden for them to sleep in the Nurses' Home—there would be room enough with so many nurses in the sick bay—and they could come over each day to use the library and lecture room. And then there would be the Vice-Chairman of the Hospital Management

Committee to consult and the Press to cope with, the inquest to attend and the funeral arrangements to be discussed. People would be wanting to get in touch with her continually. But first, and most important, she must see Superintendent Dalgliesh.

Chapter Four

Questions and Answers

I

The Matron and the Sisters had their living-quarters on the third
floor of Nightingale House. When he reached the top of the staircase Dalgliesh saw that the south-west wing had been cut off from
the rest of the landing by a specially constructed partition in white-
painted wood in which a door, meanly proportioned and insubstantial in contrast to the high ceiling and oak-lined walls, bore the
legend 'Matron's Flat'. There was a push bell, but before pressing
it he briefly explored the corridor. It was similar to the one below
but fitted with a red carpet which, although faded and scuffed, gave
an illusion of comfort to the emptiness of this upper floor.

Dalgliesh moved silently from door to door. Each bore a hand-
written name card slotted into the brass holder. He saw that Sister
Brumfett occupied the room immediately adjacent to Matron's flat.
Next was a bathroom, functionally divided into three mean cubicles,
each with its bath and lavatory. The slot on the next door bore
Sister Gearing's name; the next two rooms were empty. Sister
Rolfe was at the north end of the corridor immediately next to the
kitchen and utility room. Dalgliesh had no authority to enter any
of the bedrooms but he tentatively turned the handles on each of
the doors. As he expected, they were locked.

The Matron herself opened the door of her flat to him within
seconds of his ring, and he followed her into the sitting-room. Its
size and magnificence caught the breath. It occupied the whole of
the south-west turret, an immense white-painted octagonal room,
the ceiling starred in patterns of gold and pale blue, and with two
huge windows facing out towards the hospital. One of the walls
was lined from ceiling to floor with white bookcases. Dalgliesh

resisted the impertinence of walking casually towards them in the hope of assessing Mary Taylor's character by her taste in literature. But he could see from where he stood that there were no textbooks, no bound official reports or sloping banks of files. This was a living-room, not an office.

An open fire burnt in the grate, the wood still crackling with its recent kindling. It had as yet made no impression on the air of the room which was cold and very still. Matron was wearing a short scarlet cape over her grey dress. She had taken off her head-dress and the huge coil of yellow hair lay like a burden on the frail, etiolated neck.

She was fortunate, he thought, to have been born in an age which could appreciate individuality of feature and form, owing everything to bone structure and nothing to the gentle nuances of femininity. A century ago she would have been called ugly, even grotesque. But today most men would think her interesting, and some might even describe her as beautiful. For Dalgliesh she was one of the most beautiful women he had ever met.

Placed precisely in the middle of the three windows was a sturdy oak table bearing a large black-and-white telescope. Dalgliesh saw that this was no amateur's toy but an expensive and sophisticated instrument. It dominated the room. The Matron saw his eyes upon it and said:

"Are you interested in astronomy?"

"Not particularly."

She smiled. "'Le silence éternel de ces espaces infinis m'affraie'?"

"Discomforts rather than terrifies. It's probably my vanity. I can't interest myself in anything which I not only don't understand but know that I have no prospect of ever understanding."

"That for me is the attraction. It's a form of escapism, even of voyeurism, I suppose—this absorption in an impersonal universe which I can't do anything to influence or control and, better still, which no one expects me to. It's an abdication of responsibility. It restores personal problems to their proper proportion."

She motioned Dalgliesh towards the black leather sofa in front of the fire. Before it, a low table held a tray with a coffee percolator, hot milk, crystal sugar and two cups.

324

As he seated himself, he smiled and said: "If I want to indulge in humility or speculate on the incomprehensible, I prefer to look at a primrose. The expense is nugatory, the pleasure is more immediate, and the moral just as valid."

The mobile mouth mocked him.

"And at least you restrict your indulgence in these dangerous philosophical speculations to a few short weeks in the spring."

This conversation is, he thought, a verbal pavane. If I'm not careful I shall begin to enjoy it. I wonder when she will get down to business. Or is she expecting me to make the first move? And why not? It is I who am the suppliant, the intruder.

As if reading his thoughts, she said suddenly:

"It's odd that they should both have been such friendless girls, both orphans. It makes my task less onerous. There aren't any desolated parents to be comforted, thank God. Nurse Pearce only had the grandparents who brought her up. He's a retired miner and they live in some poverty in a cottage just outside Nottingham. They belong to a very puritanical religious sect and their only re-action to the child's death was to say, 'God's Will be Done.' It seemed an odd response to a tragedy which was so obviously the will of man."

"So you think Nurse Pearce's death was murder then?"

"Not necessarily. But I don't accuse God of tampering with the intra-gastric drip."

"And Nurse Fallon's relatives?"

"None, as far as I know. She was asked for her next of kin when she first became a student and told us she was an orphan with no blood relations living. There was no reason to question it. It was probably true. But her death will be in the papers tomorrow and if there are any relatives or friends no doubt we shall be hearing from them. You've spoken to the students, I expect?"

"I've just had a preliminary talk with them as a group. I saw them in the demonstration room. It's been useful in giving me a background to the case. They've all agreed to be finger-printed and that's being done now. I shall need the prints of everyone who was in Nightingale House last night and this morning, if only for eli-mination purposes. And I shall, of course, need to interview every-

one separately. But I'm glad of this chance to see you first. After all, you were in Amsterdam when Nurse Fallon died. That means there's one less suspect for me to worry about."

He saw with surprise her knuckles whiten around the handle of the coffee pot. Her face flushed. She closed her eyes and he thought he heard her sigh. He watched her a little disconcerted. What he had said must surely be obvious to a woman of her intelligence. He hardly knew why he had bothered to say it. If this second death were murder, then anyone with an alibi covering the whole of yesterday evening and night must be free of suspicion. As if sensing his surprise, she said:

"I'm sorry. I must seem obtuse. I know it's foolish to feel such relief at not being under suspicion when one knows anyway that one is innocent. Perhaps it's because none of us is innocent in any real sense. A psychologist could explain it, I'm sure. But ought you to be so confident? Couldn't the poison—if it were poison—have been put into Fallon's whisky bottle any time after she bought it, or another and poisoned bottle substituted for the one she purchased? That could have been done before I left for Amsterdam on Tuesday evening."

"I'm afraid you must resign yourself to innocence. Miss Fallon bought this particular bottle of whisky from Scunthorpe's wine shop in the High Street yesterday afternoon, and took her first and only drink from it on the night she died. The bottle is still almost full, the whisky remaining is perfectly good whisky as far as we know, and the only prints on the bottle are Miss Fallon's own."

"You've worked very fast. So the poison was put either into the glass after she'd poured her hot drink or into the sugar?"

"If she were poisoned. We can't be sure of anything till we get the P.M. report and perhaps not even then. The sugar is being tested but that is really only a formality. Most of the students helped themselves from that bowl when they had their early morning tea and at least two of the girls drank theirs. So that leaves us with the beaker of whisky and hot lemon. Miss Fallon made it very easy for a murderer. Apparently the whole of Nightingale House knew that, if she didn't go out in the evening, she watched the television until the programme closed down. She was a poor sleeper

326

and never went to bed early. When the television ended she would go to her room and undress. Then in her bedroom slippers and dressing-gown she would go to the little pantry on the second floor and make her nightcap. She kept the whisky in her room but she couldn't make the drink there because there's no water laid on and no means of heating it. So it was her habit to take the insulated tumbler with the whisky poured out ready and add the hot lemon in the pantry. A supply of lemons was kept there in the cupboard with the cocoa, coffee, chocolate and other items with which the nurses used to make their late night drinks. Then she would take the tumbler back to her room and leave it on the bedside locker while she had her bath. She always bathed quickly and she liked to get into bed immediately afterwards while she was still warm. I expect that's why she made her drink before she went into the bathroom. By the time she got back to her room and into bed, the drink was at precisely the right temperature. And apparently the routine never varied."

The Matron said: "It's rather frightening how much people get to know about each other's habits in a small closed community like this. But, of course, it's inevitable. There's no real privacy. How can there be? I knew about the whisky, of course, but it hardly seemed my business. The girl certainly wasn't an incipient alcoholic and she wasn't handing it out to the younger students. At her age she was entitled to her own choice of nightcap."

Dalgliesh asked how the Matron had learned about the whisky.

"Nurse Pearce told me. She asked to see me and gave me the information in a spirit of 'I don't want to tell tales but I think you ought to know'. Drink and the devil were one and the same to Nurse Pearce. But I don't think Fallon made any secret of the whisky drinking. How could she? As I said, we know about each other's little habits. But there are some things, of course, that we don't know. Josephine Fallon was a very private person. I can't give you any information about her life outside the hospital and I doubt whether anyone here can."

"Who was her friend here? She must have had someone she confided in, surely? Isn't that necessary for any woman in this kind of closed community?"

327

She looked at him a little strangely.

"Yes. We all need someone. But I think Fallon needed a friend less than most. She was remarkably self-sufficient. If she confided in anyone it would be Madeleine Goodale."

"The plain one with the round face and large spectacles?"

Dalgliesh recalled her. It was not an unattractive face, mainly because of the good skin and the intelligence of those large grey eyes behind the thick horn rims. But Nurse Goodale could never be other than plain. He thought he could picture her future; the years of training willingly endured, the success in examinations; the gradually increasing responsibility until, at last, she too was a Matron. It was not unusual for such a girl to be friendly with a more attractive woman. It was one way of gaining at least a vicarious share in a more romantic, less dedicated life. As if reading his thoughts, Miss Taylor said:

"Nurse Goodale is one of our most efficient nurses. I was hoping that she would stay on after her training to take a post as staff nurse. But that is hardly likely. She's engaged to our local vicar and they want to marry next Easter."

She glanced across at Dalgliesh a little maliciously.

"He is considered a most eligible young man. You seem surprised, Superintendent."

Dalgliesh laughed: "After over twenty years as a policeman I should have learnt not to make superficial judgements. I think I had better see Nurse Goodale first. I understand the room you're making available isn't ready yet. I suppose we could go on using the demonstration room. Or are you likely to be needing it?"

"I would prefer you to see the girls somewhere else if you would. That room has very unhappy and dramatic memories for them. We're not even using it yet for teaching demonstrations. Until the small visitors' room on the first floor is ready I'd be happy for you to interview the students here."

Dalgliesh thanked her. He replaced his coffee cup on the table. She hesitated, then said:

"Mr. Dalgliesh, there's one thing I want to say. I feel—I am— *in loco parentis* to my students. If ever any question . . . if you should begin to suspect that any one of them is involved, I can

328

rely on you to let me know? They would then need protection. There would surely be the question of getting a solicitor." She hesitated again:

"Please forgive me if I'm being offensive. One has so little experience in these matters. It's just that I shouldn't like them . . ."

"To be trapped?"

"To be rushed into saying things which might quite wrongly incriminate them or other members of the staff."

Dalgliesh found himself unreasonably irritated.

"There are rules laid down, you know," he said.

"Oh, rules! I know there are rules. But I'm sure you are both too experienced and too intelligent to let them hinder you over much. I'm just reminding you that these girls are less intelligent and in such matters not experienced at all."

Fighting his irritation, Dalgliesh said formally:

"I can only tell you that the rules are there and that it's in our interests to keep them. Can't you imagine what a gift to the defending counsel any infringement would be? A young unprotected girl, a student nurse, bullied by a senior police officer with years of experience in trapping the unwary. Enough difficulties are placed in the path of the police in this country; we don't voluntarily add to them."

She flushed and he was interested to see the wave of colour sweep from her neck over the pale honey glowing skin making her look momentarily as if the veins ran with fire. Then, instantaneously, it passed. The change was so sudden that he couldn't be sure that he had actually seen that tell-tale metamorphosis. She said composedly:

"We both have our responsibilities. We must hope that they don't conflict. In the meantime you must expect me to be as concerned with mine as you are with yours. And that brings me to some information which I have to give you. It concerns Christine Dakers, the student who discovered Nurse Fallon's body."

She described briefly and succinctly what had happened during her visit to the private ward. Dalgliesh noted with interest that she made no comment, offered no opinion, and attempted no justification of the girl. He didn't ask her whether she believed the story. She was a highly intelligent woman. She must know that what she

had handed him was the first motive. He asked when he would be able to interview Nurse Dakers.

"She's sleeping now. Dr. Snelling, who is in charge of the nurses' health, is to see her later this morning. He will then report to me. If he agrees, it should be possible for you to see her this afternoon. And now I'll send for Nurse Goodale. That is, if there is nothing more I can tell you?"

"I shall need a great deal of information about people's ages, backgrounds and the time they've been at the hospital. Won't that be on their personal records? It would be helpful if I could have those."

The Matron thought. Dalgliesh noticed that when she did so her face fell into absolute repose. After a moment she said:

"All the staff here have personal dossiers, of course. Legally these are the property of the Hospital Management Committee. The Chairman won't be back from Israel until tomorrow evening but I'll consult the Vice-Chairman. I imagine that he will ask me to look through the records, and if they contain nothing private which is irrelevant to your inquiry, to pass them over."

Dalgliesh decided that it would be prudent not to press for the moment the question of who should decide what was irrelevant to his inquiry.

He said: "There are personal questions I shall have to ask, of course. But it would be a great deal more convenient and would save time if I could get the routine information from the records."

It was strange that her voice could be so agreeable and yet so obstinate.

"I can see that it would be a great deal more convenient; it would also be a check on the truth of what you are told. But the records can only be handed over under the conditions I have just stated."

So she was confident that the Vice-Chairman would accept and endorse her view of what was right. And undoubtedly he would. Here was a formidable woman. Faced with a tricky problem she had given the matter thought, come to a decision and had stated it firmly without apology or wavering. An admirable woman. She would be easy to deal with as long, of course, as all her decisions were as acceptable as this.

He asked if he might use the telephone; recalled Sergeant Masterson from his supervision of the preparation of the small visitors' room to serve as an office; and prepared himself for the long tedium of the individual interviews.

<h2 style="text-align:center">II</h2>

Nurse Goodale was summoned by telephone and arrived within two minutes looking unhurried and composed. Miss Taylor seemed to think that neither explanation nor reassurance was necessary to this self-possessed young woman but simply said:

"Sit down, Nurse. Superintendent Dalgliesh wants to talk to you."

Then she took up her cloak from the chair, swung it over her shoulders, and went out without another glance at either of them. Sergeant Masterson opened his notebook. Nurse Goodale seated herself in an upright chair at the table but when Dalgliesh motioned her to an armchair before the fire, moved without demur. She sat stiffly on the very edge of the chair, her back straight, her surprisingly shapely and elegant legs planted modestly side by side. But the hands lying in her lap were perfectly relaxed and Dalgliesh, seated opposite, found himself confronting a pair of disconcertingly intelligent eyes. He said:

"You were probably closer to Miss Fallon than anyone else in the hospital. Tell me about her."

She showed no surprise at the form of his first question, but paused for a few seconds before replying as if marshalling her thoughts. Then she said:

"I liked her. She tolerated me better than she did most of the other students but I don't think her feeling for me was much stronger than that. She was thirty-one after all, and we must all have seemed rather immature to her. She had a rather sarcastic tongue which didn't help, and I think some of the girls were rather afraid of her.

"She seldom spoke to me about her past but she did tell me that both her parents were killed in 1944 in a bombing raid on London. She was brought up by an elderly aunt and educated at one of those

boarding-schools where they take children from an early age and keep them until they're ready to leave. Provided the fees are paid of course, but I got the impression that there wasn't any difficulty about that. She always wanted to be a nurse but she got tuberculosis after she left school and had to spend two years in a sanatorium. I don't know where. After that, two hospitals turned her down on grounds of health, so she took a number of temporary jobs. She told me soon after we began our training that she had once been engaged but that it didn't work out."

"You never asked her why?"

"I never asked her anything. If she had wanted to tell me she would have done so."

"Did she tell you that she was pregnant?"

"Yes. She told me two days before she went sick. She must have suspected before then but the confirming report came that morning. I asked her what she intended doing about it and she said that she would get rid of the baby."

"Did you point out that this was probably illegal?"

"No. She didn't care about legality. I told her that it was wrong."

"But she still intended to go ahead with the abortion?"

"Yes, she said that she knew a doctor who would do it and that there wouldn't be any real risk. I asked her if she needed money and she said that she would be all right, that money was the least of her problems. She never told me who she was going to, and I didn't ask."

"But you were prepared to help her with money had she needed it, even though you disapproved of getting rid of the baby?"

"My disapproval wasn't important. What was important was that it was wrong. But when I knew that she had made up her mind I had to decide whether to help her. I was afraid that she might go to some unqualified back street abortionist and risk her life and health. I know that the law has changed, that it's easier now to get a medical recommendation, but I didn't think she would qualify. I had to make a moral decision. If you are proposing to commit a sin it is as well to commit it with intelligence. Otherwise you are insulting God as well as defying Him, don't you think?"

332

Dalgliesh said gravely: "It's an interesting theological point which I'm not competent to argue. Did she tell you who was the father of the child?"

"Not directly. I think it may have been a young writer she was friendly with. I don't know his name or where you can find him but I do know that Jo spent a week with him in the Isle of Wight last October. She had seven days' holiday due and she told me that she'd decided to walk in the island with a friend. I imagine he was the friend. It certainly wasn't anyone from here. They went during the first week and she told me that they'd stayed in a small inn about five miles south of Ventnor. That's all she did tell me. I suppose it's possible that she became pregnant during that week?"

Dalgliesh said: "The dates would fit. And she never confided in you about the father of the child?"

"No. I asked her why she wouldn't marry the father and she said that it would be unfair to the child to burden it with two irresponsible parents. I remember her saying: 'He would be horrified at the idea, anyway, unless he had a sudden urge to experience fatherhood just to see what it was like. And he might like to see the baby born so that he could write a lurid account of childbirth some day. But he really isn't committed to anyone but himself.' "

"But did she care for him?"

The girl paused a full minute before replying. Then she said:

"I think she did. I think that may have been why she killed herself."

"What makes you think that she did?"

"I suppose because the alternative is even more unlikely. I never thought that Jo was the type to kill herself—if there is a type. But I really didn't know her. One never does really know another human being. Anything is possible for anyone. I've always believed that. And it's surely more likely that she killed herself than that someone murdered her. That seems absolutely incredible. Why should they?"

"I was hoping you might be able to tell me."

"Well, I can't. She hadn't any enemies at the John Carpendar as far as I know. She wasn't popular. She was too reserved, too solitary. But people didn't dislike her. And even if they did, murder

333

surely suggests something more than ordinary dislike. It seems so much more probable that she came back to duty too soon after influenza, was overcome by psychological depression, felt she couldn't cope with getting rid of the baby, and yet couldn't face up to having an illegitimate child and killed herself on impulse."

"You said when I questioned you all in the demonstration room that you were probably the last person to see her alive. What exactly happened while you were together last night? Did she give you any idea that she might be thinking of suicide?"

"If she had, I should hardly have left her to go to bed alone. She said nothing. I don't think we exchanged more than half a dozen words. I asked her how she felt and she replied that she was all right. She obviously wasn't in the mood to chat so I didn't make myself a nuisance. After about twenty minutes I went up to bed. I never saw her again."

"And she didn't mention her pregnancy?"

"She mentioned nothing. She looked tired, I thought, and rather pale. But then, Jo always was rather pale. It's distressing for me to think that she might have needed help and that I left her without speaking the words that might have saved her. But she wasn't a woman to invite confidences. I stayed behind when the others left because I thought she might want to talk. When it was plain that she wanted to be alone, I left."

She talked about being distressed, thought Dalgliesh, but she neither looked nor sounded it. She felt no self-reproach. Why indeed should she? He doubted whether she felt particular grief. She had been closer to Josephine Fallon than any of the students. But she had not really cared. Was there anyone in the world who had? He asked:

"And Nurse Pearce's death?"

"I think that was essentially an accident. Someone put the poison in the feed as a joke or out of vague malice without realizing that the result would be fatal."

"Which would be odd in a third-year student nurse whose programme of lectures presumably included basic information on corrosive poisons."

"I wasn't suggesting that it was a nurse. I don't know who it was.

I don't think you'll ever find out now. But I can't believe that it was wilful murder."

That was all very well, thought Dalgliesh, but surely it was a little disingenuous in a girl as intelligent as Nurse Goodale. It was, of course, the popular, almost the official view. It exonerated everyone from the worst crime and indicted no one of anything more than malice and carelessness. It was a comforting theory, and unless he were lucky it might never be disproved. But he didn't believe it himself, and he couldn't accept that Nurse Goodale did. But it was even harder to accept that here was a girl to comfort herself with false theories or deliberately to shut her eyes to unpalatable facts.

Dalgliesh then asked her about her movements on the morning of Pearce's death. He already knew them from Inspector Bailey's notes and her previous statement and was not surprised when Nurse Goodale confirmed them without hesitation. She had got up at 6.45 and had drunk early morning tea with the rest of the set in the utility room. She had told them about Fallon's influenza since it was to her room that Nurse Fallon had come when she was taken ill in the night. None of the students had expressed particular concern but they had wondered how the demonstration would go now that the set was so decimated and had speculated, not without malice, how Sister Gearing would acquit herself in the face of a G.N.C. inspection. Nurse Pearce had drunk her tea with the rest of the set and Nurse Goodale thought that she remembered Pearce saying:

"With Fallon ill, I suppose I shall have to act the patient." Nurse Goodale couldn't recall any comment or discussion about this. It was well accepted that the next student on the list substituted for anyone who was ill.

After she had drunk her tea, Nurse Goodale had dressed and had then made her way to the library to revise the treatment of larynectomy in preparation for the morning's session. It was important that there should be a quick and lively response to questions if the seminar were to be a success. She had settled herself to work at about 7.15 and Nurse Dakers had joined her shortly afterwards, sharing a devotion to study which, thought Dalgliesh, had at least been rewarded by an alibi for most of the time before breakfast.

335

She and Dakers had said nothing of interest to each other while they had been working and had left the library at the same time and gone into breakfast together. That had been at about ten minutes to eight. She had sat with Dakers and the Burt twins, but had left the breakfast room before them. That was at 8.15. She had returned to her bedroom to make the bed, and then gone to the library to write a couple of letters. That done, she had paid a brief visit to the cloakroom and had made her way to the demonstration room just before a quarter to nine. Only Sister Gearing and the Burt twins were already there, but the rest of the set had joined them shortly afterwards; she couldn't remember in what order. She thought that Pearce had been one of the last to arrive.

Dalgliesh asked: "How did Nurse Pearce seem?"

"I noticed nothing unusual about her, but then I wouldn't expect to. Pearce was Pearce. She made a negligible impression."

"Did she say anything before the demonstration began?"

"Yes, she did as a matter of fact. It's odd that you should ask that. I haven't mentioned it before, I suppose because Inspector Bailey didn't ask. But she did speak. She looked round at us—the set had all assembled by then—and asked if anyone had taken anything from her bedroom."

"Did she say what?"

"No. She just stood there with that accusing rather belligerent look she occasionally had and said: 'Has anyone been to my room this morning or taken anything from it?' "

"No one replied. I think we just all shook our heads. It wasn't a question we took particularly seriously. Pearce was apt to make a great fuss about trifles. Anyway, the Burt twins were busy with their preparations and the rest of us were chatting. Pearce didn't get a great deal of attention paid to her question. I doubt whether half of us heard her even."

"Did you notice how she reacted? Was she worried or angry or distressed?"

"None of those things. It was odd really. I remember now. She looked satisfied, almost triumphant, as if something she suspected had been confirmed. I don't know why I noticed that, but I did. Sister Gearing then called us to order and the demonstration began."

336

Dalgliesh did not immediately speak at the end of this recital and, after a little time, she took his silence for dismissal and rose to go. She got out of the chair with the same controlled grace as she had seated herself, smoothed her apron with a scarcely discernible gesture, gave him a last interrogatory glance and walked to the door. Then she turned as if yielding to an impulse.

"You asked me if anyone had a reason to kill Jo. I said I knew of no one. That is true. But I suppose a legal motive is something different. I ought to tell you that some people might think I had a motive."

Dalgliesh said: "Had you?"

"I expect you'll think so. I am Jo's heir, at least I think I am. She told me about three months ago that she had made her will and that she was leaving me all she had. She gave me the name and address of her solicitor. I can let you have the information. They haven't yet written to me but I expect they will, that is if Jo really made her will. But I expect she did. She wasn't a girl to make promises she didn't fulfil. Perhaps you would prefer to get in touch with the solicitors now? These things take time, don't they?"

"Did she say why she was making you her legatee?"

"She said that she had to leave her money to someone and that I would probably do most good with it. I didn't take the matter very seriously and neither, I think, did she. After all she was only thirty-one. She wasn't expecting to die. And she warned me that she'd probably change her mind long before she got old enough to make the legacy a serious prospect for me. After all she'd probably marry. But she felt she ought to make a will and I was the only person at the time who she cared to remember. I thought that it was only a formality. It never occurred to me that she might have much to leave. It was only when we had our talk about the cost of an abortion that she told me how much she was worth."

"And was it—is it—much?"

The girl answered calmly: "About £16,000 I believe. It came from her parents' insurances."

She smiled a little wryly.

"Quite worth having you see, Superintendent. I should think it would rank as a perfectly respectable motive, wouldn't you? We

shall be able to put central heating in the vicarage now. And if you saw my fiancé's vicarage—twelve rooms, nearly all of them facing north or east—you would think I had quite a motive for murder."

III

Sister Rolfe and Sister Gearing were waiting with the students in the library; they had moved from the nurses' sitting-room in order to occupy the waiting time with reading and revision. How much the girls were really taking in was problematic but the scene certainly looked peaceful and studious enough. The students had seated themselves at the desks in front of the window and sat, books open before them, in apparent absorption. Sister Rolfe and Sister Gearing, as if to emphasize their seniority and solidarity, had withdrawn to the sofa in front of the fire and were seated side by side. Sister Rolfe was marking with green biro a pile of first-year students' exercises, picking up each notebook from a stack on the floor at her feet, and adding it, when dealt with, to the growing pile which rested against the back of the sofa. Sister Gearing was ostensibly making notes for her next lecture, but seemed unable to keep her eyes from her colleague's decisive hieroglyphics.

The door opened and Madeleine Goodale returned. Without a word she went back to her desk, took up her pen and resumed work.

Sister Gearing whispered: "Goodale seems calm enough. Odd, considering she was supposed to be Fallon's best friend."

Sister Rolfe did not raise her eyes. She said drily:

"She didn't really care about Fallon. Goodale has only a limited emotional capital and I imagine she expends it all on that extraordinarily dull parson she's decided to marry."

"He's good-looking, though. Goodale's lucky to get him, if you ask me."

But the subject was of a secondary interest to Sister Gearing and she didn't pursue it. After a minute she said peevishly:

"Why haven't the police sent for someone else?"

"They will." Sister Rolfe added another exercise book, liberally embellished in green, to a completed pile by her side. "They're probably still discussing Goodale's contribution."

"They ought to have seen us first. After all, we're Sisters. Matron should have explained. And why isn't Brumfett here? I don't see why she should be treated any differently from us."

Sister Rolfe said: "Too busy. Apparently a couple of the second-year students on the ward have now gone down with flu. She sent over some sort of note to Mr. Dalgliesh by a porter, presumably giving information about her movements last night. I met him bringing it in. He asked me where he could find the gentlemen from Scotland Yard."

Sister Gearing's voice became petulant:

"That's all very well, but she ought to be here. God knows, we're busy too! Brumfett lives in Nightingale House; she had as much opportunity to kill Fallon as anyone."

Sister Rolfe said quietly: "She had more chance."

"What do you mean, more chance?"

Sister Gearing's sharp voice cut into the silence and one of the Burt twins lifted her head.

"She's had Fallon in her power in the sick bay for the last ten days."

"But surely you don't mean. . . ? Brumfett wouldn't!"

"Precisely," said Sister Rolfe coldly. "So why make stupid and irresponsible remarks?"

There was a silence broken only by the rustle of paper and the hiss of the gas fire. Sister Gearing fidgeted.

"I suppose if Brumfett's lost another two nurses with flu she'll be pressing Matron to recall some of this block. She's got her eyes on the Burt twins, I know."

"Then she'll be unlucky. This set have had their training disrupted enough already. After all, it's their last block before their finals. Matron won't let it be cut short."

"I shouldn't be too sure. It's Brumfett, remember. Matron doesn't usually say no to her. Funny though, I did hear a rumour that they aren't going on holiday together this year. One of the pharmacists' assistants had it from Matron's secretary that Matron plans to motor in Ireland on her own."

My God, thought Sister Rolfe. Isn't there any privacy in this place? But she said nothing, only shifting a few inches from the restless figure at her side.

It was then that the wall telephone rang. Sister Gearing leapt up and went across to answer it. She turned to the rest of the group, her face creased with disappointment.

"That was Sergeant Masterson. Superintendent Dalgliesh would like to see the Burt twins next please. He's moved to the visitors' sitting-room on this floor."

Without a word and with no signs of nervousness, the Burt twins closed their books and made for the door.

IV

It was half an hour later and Sergeant Masterson was making coffee. The visitors' sitting-room had been provided with a miniature kitchen, a large recess fitted with a sink and Formica covered cupboard, on which stood a double gas-ring. The cupboard had been cleared of all its paraphernalia except for four large beakers, a canister of sugar and one of tea, a tin of biscuits, a large earthenware jug and strainer, and three transparent air-tight packets of fresh-ground coffee. By the side of the sink were two bottles of milk. The cream-line was easily discernible, but Sergeant Masterson prised the cap away from one of the bottles and sniffed at the milk suspiciously before heating a quantity in a saucepan. He warmed the earthenware jug with hot water from the tap, dried it carefully in the tea towel which hung by the side of the sink, spooned in a generous quantity of coffee and stood waiting for the kettle's first burst of steam. He approved of the arrangements that had been made. If the police had to work in Nightingale House this room was as convenient and comfortable as any and the coffee was an unexpected bonus which mentally, he credited to Paul Hudson. The Hospital Secretary had struck him as an efficient and imaginative man. His couldn't be an easy job. The poor devil probably had one hell of a life, sandwiched between those two old fools, Kealey and Grout, and that high-handed bitch of a Matron.

He strained the coffee with meticulous care and carried a beaker over to his chief. They sat and drank companionably together, eyes straying to the storm-wrecked garden. Both of them had a strong

dislike of badly cooked food or synthetic coffee and Masterson thought that they never got closer to liking each other than when they were eating and drinking together, deploring the inadequacies of the meals at the inn, or as now, rejoicing in good coffee. Dalgliesh comforted his hands around the beaker and thought that it was typical of Mary Taylor's efficiency and imagination to ensure that they had real coffee available. Hers couldn't be an easy job. That ineffectual couple, Kealey and Grout, wouldn't be much help to anyone, and Paul Hudson was too young to give much support.

After a moment of appreciative sipping, Masterson said:

"That was a disappointing interview, sir."

"The Burt twins? Yes, I must say I had hoped for something more interesting. After all, they were at the centre of the mystery; they administered the fatal drip; they glimpsed the mysterious Nurse Fallon on her way out of Nightingale House; they met Sister Brumfett on her perambulations in the early hours. But we knew all that already. And we don't know any more now."

Dalgliesh thought about the two girls. Masterson had drawn up a second chair on their entrance and they had sat there side by side, freckled hands ritualistically disposed in their laps, legs modestly crossed, each girl a mirror image of her twin. Their polite anti-phonal answers to his questions, spoken in a West Country burr, were as agreeable to the ear as their shining good health to the eye. He had rather taken to the Burt twins. He might, of course, have been facing a couple of experienced accomplices in evil. Anything was possible. Certainly they had had the best opportunity to poison the drip and as good a chance as anyone in Nightingale House to doctor Fallon's nightcap. Yet they had seemed perfectly at ease with him, a little bored perhaps at having to repeat much of their story, but neither frightened nor particularly worried. From time to time they had gazed at him with a gentle speculative concern rather as if he were a difficult patient whose condition was beginning to give rise to some anxiety. He had noticed this intent and compassionate regard on the faces of the other nurses during their first encounter in the demonstration room and had found it disconcerting.

"And you noticed nothing odd about the milk?"

They had answered almost in unison, rebuking him in the calm voice of common sense.

"Oh no! Well, we wouldn't have gone ahead with the drip if we had, would we?"

"Can you remember taking the cap off the bottle; was it loose?"

Two pairs of blue eyes looked at each other, almost as if in signal. Then Maureen replied:

"We don't remember that it was. But even if it had been, we wouldn't have suspected that someone had been at the milk. We would just have thought that the dairy put it on like that."

Then Shirley spoke on her own:

"I don't think we would have noticed anything wrong with the milk anyway. You see, we were concentrating on the procedures for giving the drip, making sure that we had all the instruments and equipment we needed. We knew that Miss Beale and Matron would arrive at any minute."

That, of course, was the explanation. They were girls who had been trained to observe, but their observation was specific and limited. If they were watching a patient they would miss nothing of his signs or symptoms, not a flicker of the eyelids or a change of pulse; anything else happening in the room, however dramatic, would probably be unnoticed. Their attention had been on the demonstration, the apparatus, the equipment, the patient. The bottle of milk presented no problems. They had taken it for granted. And yet they were farmer's daughters. One of them—it had been Maureen—had actually poured the stuff from the bottle. Could they really have mistaken the colour, the texture, the smell of milk?

As if reading his thoughts Maureen said:

"It wasn't as if we could smell the carbolic. The whole demo room stinks of disinfectant. Miss Collins throws the stuff around as if we're all lepers."

Shirley laughed: "Carbolic isn't effective against leprosy!"

They looked at each other, smiling in happy complicity.

And so the interview had gone on. They had no theories to propound, no suggestions to offer. They knew no one who could wish Pearce or Fallon dead, and yet both deaths—since they had

occurred—seemed to cause them no particular surprise. They could recall every word of the conversation between Sister Brumfett and themselves in the small hours of that morning, yet the encounter apparently had made little impression on them. When Dalgliesh asked if the Sister had seemed unusually worried or distressed, they gazed at him simultaneously, brows creased in perplexity, before replying that Sister had seemed just the same as usual.

As if following his chief's thoughts, Masterson said:

"Short of asking them outright if Sister Brumfett looked as if she'd just come straight from murdering Fallon you couldn't have put it much plainer. They're an odd uncommunicative couple."

"At least they're sure of the time. They took that milk shortly after seven o'clock and went straight into the demonstration room with it. They stood the bottle unopened on the instrument trolley while they made preliminary preparations for the demonstration. They left the demonstration room at seven twenty-five for breakfast and the bottle was still on the trolley when they returned at about twenty-to-nine to complete their preparations. They then stood it, still unopened, in a jug of hot water to bring it to blood heat and it remained there until they poured the milk from the bottle into a measuring jug about two minutes before Miss Beale and Matron's party arrived. Most of the suspects were at breakfast together from eight until eight twenty-five, so that the mischief was either done between seven twenty-five and eight o'clock or in the short period between the end of breakfast and the twins' return to the demonstration room."

Masterson said: "I still find it strange that they noticed nothing odd about that milk."

"They may have noticed more than they realize at present. After all, this is the umpteenth time they've told their story. During the weeks since Pearce's death, their first statements have become fixed in their minds as the immutable truth. That's why I haven't asked them the crucial question about the milk bottle. If they gave me the wrong answer now they'd never change it. They need to be shocked into total recall. They're not seeing anything that happened with fresh eyes. I dislike reconstructions of the crime; they always make

me feel like a fictional detective. But I think there may be a case for reconstruction here. I shall have to be in London early tomorrow, but you and Greeson can see to it. Greeson will probably enjoy himself."

He told Masterson briefly what he proposed and ended:

"You needn't bother to include the Sisters. I expect you can get a supply of the disinfectant from Miss Collins. But for God's sake keep an eye on the stuff and chuck it away afterwards. We don't want another tragedy."

Sergeant Masterson took up the two beakers and carried them over to the sink. He said:

"Nightingale House does seem to be touched with ill-luck, but I can't see the killer having another go while we're around."

It was to prove a singularly unprophetic remark.

v

Since her encounter with Dalgliesh in the nurses' utility room earlier that morning Sister Rolfe had had time to recover from shock and to consider her position. As Dalgliesh had expected she was now far less forthcoming. She had already given to Inspector Bailey a clear and unambiguous statement about the arrangements for the demonstration and the intra-gastric feeding and about her own movements on the morning that Nurse Pearce died. She confirmed the statement accurately and without fuss. She agreed that she had known that Nurse Pearce was to act the part of the patient and pointed out sarcastically that there would be little point in denying the knowledge since it was she whom Madeleine Goodale had called when Fallon was taken ill.

Dalgliesh asked: "Did you have any doubt of the genuineness of her illness?"

"At the time?"

"Then or now."

"I suppose you're suggesting that Fallon could have feigned influenza to ensure that Pearce took her place, and then sneaked back to Nightingale House before breakfast to doctor the drip? I don't know why she did come back, but you can put any idea that

she was pretending to be ill out of your head. Even Fallon couldn't simulate a temperature of 103·8, a minor rigor and a racing pulse. She was a very sick girl that night, and she remained sick for nearly ten days."

Dalgliesh pointed out that it was all the more odd that she should have been well enough to make her way back to Nightingale House next morning. Sister Rolfe replied that it was so odd that she could only assume that Fallon had had an imperative need to return. Invited to speculate on what that need could have been she replied that it wasn't her job to propound theories. Then, as if under a compulsion, she added:

"But it wasn't to murder Pearce. Fallon was highly intelligent, easily the most intelligent of her year. If Fallon came back to put the corrosive in the feed she would know perfectly well that there was a considerable risk of her being seen in Nightingale House even if she weren't missed on the ward, and she'd have taken good care to have a story ready. It wouldn't have been difficult to think of something. As it is, I gather she merely declined to give Inspector Bailey any explanation."

"Perhaps she was clever enough to realize that this extraordinary reticence would strike another intelligent woman in exactly that way."

"A kind of double bluff? I don't think so. It would be banking too heavily on the intelligence of the police."

She admitted calmly that she had no alibi for any of the time from seven o'clock when the twins had collected the bottle of milk from the kitchen until ten minutes to nine when she had joined the Matron and Mr. Courtney-Briggs in Miss Taylor's sitting-room to await the arrival of Miss Beale, except for the period from eight to eight twenty-five when she had breakfasted at the same table as Sister Brumfett and Sister Gearing. Sister Brumfett had left the table first and she had followed at about eight twenty-five. She had gone first to her office next door to the demonstration room, but finding Mr. Courtney-Briggs in occupation, had made her way at once to her bed-sitting-room on the third floor.

When Dalgliesh asked whether Sister Gearing and Sister Brumfett had appeared their usual selves at breakfast she replied drily that they exhibited no signs of impending homicidal mania if that

was what he meant. Gearing had read the *Daily Mirror* and Brumfett the *Nursing Times*, if that were of any significance, and the conversation had been minimal. She regretted she could offer no witnesses to her own movements before or after the meal but that was surely understandable; for some years now she had preferred to wash and go to the lavatory in private. Apart from that, she valued the free time before the day's work and preferred to spend it alone.

Dalgliesh asked: "Were you surprised to find Mr. Courtney-Briggs in your office when you went there after breakfast?"

"Not particularly. I took it for granted that he had spent the night in the medical officers' quarters and had come over early to Nightingale House to meet the G.N.C. Inspector. He probably wanted somewhere to write a letter. Mr. Courtney-Briggs assumes the right to use any room in the John Carpendar as his private office if the fancy takes him."

Dalgliesh asked her about her movements the previous night. She repeated that she had been to the cinema alone but added this time that she had met Julia Pardoe on the way out and that they had walked back to the hospital together. They had come in through the Winchester Road gate to which she had a key and had got back to Nightingale House shortly after eleven. She had gone immediately to her room and had seen no one. Nurse Pardoe, she assumed, had either gone straight to bed or had joined the rest of the set in the student nurses' sitting-room.

"So you have nothing to tell me, Sister? Nothing that can help?"

"Nothing."

"Not even why, unnecessary surely, you lied about going to the cinema alone?"

"Nothing. And I shouldn't have thought my private affairs were any concern of yours."

Dalgliesh said calmly: "Miss Rolfe, two of your students are dead. I'm here to find out how and why they died. If you don't want to co-operate, say so. You don't have to answer my questions. But don't try to tell me what questions I am to ask. I'm in charge of this investigation. I do it my way."

"I see. You make up the rules as you go along. All we can do is

say when we don't want to play. Yours is a dangerous game, Mr. Dalgliesh."

"Tell me something about these students. You're the Principal Nurse Tutor; you must have a good many girls through your hands. I think you're a good judge of character. We'll start with Nurse Goodale."

If she felt surprise or relief at his choice she concealed it.

"Madeleine Goodale is confidently expected to take the Gold Medal as the best nurse of her year. She is less intelligent than Fallon—than Fallon was—but she's hard working and extremely conscientious. She's a local girl. Her father is well known in the town, an extremely successful estate agent who inherited a long established family business. He's a member of the Town Council and was on the Hospital Management Committee for a number of years. Madeleine went to the local grammar school and then came to us. I don't think she ever considered any other nurse training school. The whole family has a strong local loyalty. She is engaged to the young vicar of Holy Trinity and I understand they plan to marry as soon as she completes her training. Another good career lost to the profession, but she knows her own priorities I suppose."

"The Burt twins?"

"Good sensible kindly girls, with more imagination and sensitivity than they are usually credited with. Their people are farmers near Gloucester. I'm not sure why they chose this hospital. I have an idea a cousin trained here and was happy enough. They are the kind of girls who would choose a training school on that kind of family basis. They aren't particularly intelligent but they aren't stupid. We don't have to take stupid girls here, thank God. Each of them has a steady boy friend and Maureen is engaged. I don't think either of them looks on nursing as a permanent job."

Dalgliesh said: "You're going to have trouble finding leaders for the profession if this automatic resignation on marriage becomes the rule."

She said drily: "We're having trouble now. Who else are you interested in?"

"Nurse Dakers."

"Poor kid! Another local girl, but with a very different back-

347

ground from Goodale. Father was a minor local government officer who died of cancer when she was twelve. Mother has been struggling on ever since with a small pension. The girl was educated at the same school as Goodale but they were never friendly as far as I know. Dakers is a conscientious hard-working student with a great deal of ambition. She'll do all right but she won't do better than all right. She tires easily, isn't really robust. People think of her as timid and highly strung, whatever that euphemism means. But Dakers is tough enough. She's a third-year student, remember. A girl doesn't get this far with her training if she's fundamentally weak, physically or mentally."

"Julia Pardoe?"

Sister Rolfe had herself well under control now and there was no change in her voice as she went on.

"The only child of divorced parents. Mother is one of those pretty but selfish women who find it impossible to stay long with one husband. She's on her third now, I believe. I'm not sure that the girl really knows which is her father. She hasn't been often at home. Mother sent her off to a prep. school when she was five. She had a stormy school career and came here straight from the sixth form of one of those independent girls' boarding-schools, where the girls are taught nothing but manage to learn a great deal. She first applied to one of the London teaching hospitals. She didn't quite measure up to their standard of acceptance either socially or academically but the Matron referred her here. Schools like ours have this kind of arrangement with the teaching hospitals. They get a dozen applications for every place. It's mostly snobbery and the hope of catching a husband. We're quite happy to take a number of their rejects; I suspect that they often make better nurses than the girls they accept. Pardoe was one of them. An intelligent but untrained mind. A gentle and considerate nurse."

"You know a great deal about your students."

"I make it my business to. But I take it I'm not expected to give an opinion of my colleagues."

"Sister Gearing and Sister Brumfett? No. But I'd be glad of your opinion of Nurse Fallon and Nurse Pearce."

"I can't tell you much about Fallon. She was a reserved, almost

348

a secretive girl. Intelligent, of course, and more mature than the majority of students. I think I only had one personal conversation with her. That was at the end of her first year when I called her for an interview and asked her for her impressions of nursing. I was interested to know how our methods here struck a girl who was so different from the ordinary run of the straight-from-school student. She said that it wasn't fair to judge while one was still an apprentice and treated as if one were a sub-normal kitchen maid but that she still thought nursing was her job. I asked her what had attracted her to the profession and she said that she wanted to acquire a skill which would make her independent anywhere in the world, a qualification which would always be in demand. I don't think she had any particular ambition to get on in the profession. Her training was just a means to an end. But I could be wrong. As I said, I never really knew her."

"So you can't say whether she had enemies?"

"I can't say why anyone should want to kill her, if that's what you mean. I should have thought that Pearce was a much more likely victim."

Dalgliesh asked her why.

"I didn't take to Pearce. I didn't kill her, but then I'm not given to murdering people merely because I dislike them. But she was a strange girl, a mischief maker and a hypocrite. It's no use asking me how I know. I haven't any real evidence and, if I had, I doubt whether I should give it to you."

"So you didn't find it surprising that she should have been murdered?"

"I found it astonishing. But I never for one moment thought her death was suicide or an accident."

"And who do you suppose killed her?"

Sister Rolfe looked at him with a kind of grim satisfaction.

"You tell me, Superintendent. You tell me!"

VI

"So you went to the cinema last night and on your own?"

"Yes, I told you."

349

"To see a revival of *L'Avventura*. Perhaps you felt that the subtleties of Antonioni could best be experienced without a companion? Or perhaps you couldn't find anyone willing to go with you?"

She couldn't, of course, resist that.

"There are plenty of people to take me to the movies if I want them to."

The movies. It had been the flicks when Dalgliesh was her age. But the generation chasm was deeper than a matter of mere semantics, the alienation more complete. He simply didn't understand her. He hadn't the slightest clue to what was going on behind that smooth and childish forehead. The remarkable violet blue eyes, set wide apart under curved brows, gazed at him, wary but unconcerned. The cat's face with its small rounded chin and wide cheek bones expressed nothing but a vague distaste for the matter in hand. It was difficult, Dalgliesh thought, to imagine finding a prettier or more agreeable figure than Julia Pardoe beside one's sick bed; unless, of course, one happened to be in real pain or distress when the Burt twins' sturdy common sense or Madeleine Goodale's calm efficiency would be a great deal more acceptable. It might be a personal prejudice, but he couldn't imagine any man willingly exposing his weakness or physical distress to this pert and self-absorbed young woman. And what precisely, he wondered, was she getting out of nursing? If the John Carpendar had been a teaching hospital he could have understood it. That trick of widening the eyes when she spoke so that the hearer was treated to a sudden blaze of blue, of slightly parting moist lips above the neat eburnean teeth would go down very well with a gaggle of medical students.

It was not, he noticed, without its effect on Sergeant Masterson.

But what was it that Sister Rolfe had said of her?

"An intelligent but untrained mind; a gentle and considerate nurse."

Well, it could be. But Hilda Rolfe was prejudiced. And so, in his own way, was Dalgliesh.

He pressed on with his interrogation, resisting the impulse to sarcasm, to the cheap jibes of antipathy.

"Did you enjoy the film?"

"It was all right."

"And you returned to Nightingale House from this all right film when?"

"I don't know. Just before eleven, I suppose. I met Sister Rolfe outside the cinema and we walked back together. I expect she's told you."

So they must have talked since this morning. This was their story and the girl was repeating it without even the pretence that she cared whether she were believed. It could be checked of course. The girl in the cinema box office might remember whether they had arrived together. But it was hardly worth the trouble of inquiry. Why indeed should it matter, unless they had spent the evening concocting murder as well as imbibing culture? And if they had, here was one partner in iniquity who wasn't apparently worried.

Dalgliesh asked: "What happened when you got back?"

"Nothing. I went to the nurses' sitting-room and they were all watching the telly. Well, actually they switched it off as I came in. The Burt twins came to make tea in the nurses' kitchen and we took it into Maureen's room to drink it. Dakers came with us. Madeleine Goodale was left with Fallon. I don't know what time they came up. I went to bed as soon as I'd had my tea. I was asleep before twelve."

So she might have been. But this had been a very simple murder. There had been nothing to prevent her waiting, perhaps in one of the lavatory cubicles, until she heard Fallon running her bath. Once Fallon was in the bathroom, Nurse Pardoe would know what all the other students knew; that a beaker of whisky and lemon would be waiting on Fallon's bedside table. How simple to slip into her room and add something to the drink. Add what? It was maddening, this working in the dark with its inevitable tendency to theorize in advance of the facts. Until the autopsy was completed and the toxicology result available he couldn't even be sure that he was investigating a murder.

He suddenly changed tack, reverting to a previous course of questioning.

"Are you sorry about Nurse Pearce's death?"

Again the wide opened eyes, the little *moue* of consideration, the suggestion that it was really rather a silly question.

"Of course." A little pause. "She never did me any harm."

"Did she do anyone any harm?"

"You'd better ask them." Another pause. Perhaps she felt that she had been imprudently foolish and rude. "What harm could Pearce do to anyone?"

It was spoken with no tinge of contempt, almost with disinterest, a mere statement of fact.

"Someone killed her. That doesn't suggest that she was innocuous. Someone must have hated her enough to want her out of the way."

"She could have killed herself. When she swallowed that tube she knew what was coming to her all right. She was terrified. Anyone watching her could see that."

Julia Pardoe was the first student to have mentioned Nurse Pearce's fear. The only other person present to have noticed it had been the General Nursing Council Inspector who, in her statement, had stressed the girl's look of apprehension, almost of endurance. It was interesting and surprising that Nurse Pardoe should have been so perceptive. Dalgliesh said:

"But do you really believe that she put a corrosive poison into the feed herself?"

The blue eyes met his. She gave her little secret smile.

"No. Pearce was always terrified when she had to act as patient. She hated it. She never said anything, but anyone could see what she was feeling. Swallowing that tube must have been particularly bad for her. She told me once that she couldn't bear the thought of a throat examination or operation. She'd had her tonsils out as a child and the surgeon—or it may have been a nurse—was rough with her and hurt her badly. Anyway, it had been a horrible experience and had left her with this phobia about her throat. Of course, she could have explained to Sister Gearing and one of us would have taken her place. She didn't have to act the patient. No one was forcing her. But I suppose Pearce thought it was her duty to go through with it. She was a great one for duty."

So anyone present could have seen what Pearce was feeling. But in fact, only two of them had seen. And one of them had been this apparently insensitive young woman.

Dalgliesh was intrigued, but not particularly surprised, that Nurse Pearce should have chosen to confide in Julia Pardoe. He had met it before, this perverse attraction which the pretty and popular often held for the plain and despised. Sometimes it was even reciprocated; an odd mutual fascination which, he suspected, formed the basis of many friendships and marriages that the world found inexplicable. But if Heather Pearce had been making a pathetic bid for friendship or sympathy by a recital of childhood woes she had been unlucky. Julia Pardoe respected strength, not weakness. She would be impervious to a plea for pity. And yet—who knew?—Pearce might have got something from her. Not friendship, or sympathy, or pity even; but a modicum of understanding.

He said on a sudden impulse:

"I think you probably knew more about Nurse Pearce than anyone else here, probably understood her better. I don't believe her death was suicide, neither do you. I want you to tell me everything about her which would help me to a motive."

There was a second's pause. Was it his imagination or was she really making up her mind to something? Then she said in her high, unemphatic, childish voice:

"I expect she was blackmailing someone. She tried it with me once."

"Tell me about it."

She looked up at him speculatively as if assessing his reliability or wondering whether the story was worth the trouble of telling. Then her lips curved in a little reminiscent smile. She said calmly:

"My boy friend spent a night with me about a year ago. Not here; in the main nurses' home. I unlocked one of the fire escape doors and let him in. We did it for a lark really."

"Was he someone from the John Carpendar?"

"Um, um. One of the surgical registrars."

"And how did Heather Pearce find out about it?"

"It was the night before our preliminary—the first examination for State Registration. Pearce always got a stomach-ache before exams. I suppose she was prowling down the corridor to the loo and saw me letting Nigel in. Or she may have been on her way back to

353

bed and listened at the door. Perhaps she heard us giggling or something. I expect she listened as long as she could. I wonder what she made of it. No one has ever wanted to make love to Pearce so I suppose she got a thrill just out of listening to someone else in bed with a man. Anyway, she tackled me about it next morning and then threatened to tell Matron and have me chucked out of the nurse training school."

She spoke without resentment, almost with a touch of amusement. It hadn't bothered her at the time. It didn't bother her now.

Dalgliesh asked: "And what price was she asking for her silence?"

He had no doubt that, whatever the price, it hadn't been paid.

"She said she hadn't made up her mind about that; she would have to think about it. It would have to be appropriate. You should have seen her face. It was all mottled and red like a disgusted turkey cock. I don't know how I kept a straight face. I pretended to be terribly worried and contrite and asked if we should talk about it that night. That was just to give me time to get in touch with Nigel. He lived with his widowed mother just outside the town. She adores him and I knew she wouldn't make any difficulty about swearing that he spent the night at home. She wouldn't even mind that we'd been together. She thinks that her precious Nigel's entitled to take just what he likes. But I didn't want Pearce to talk before I got that fixed up. When I saw her that evening I told her that both of us would deny the story absolutely and that Nigel would back it up with an alibi. She'd forgotten about his mother. There was something else she'd forgotten too. Nigel is Mr. Courtney-Briggs's nephew. So if she talked, all that would happen would be that Mr. Courtney-Briggs would get her chucked out, not me. Pearce was terribly stupid, really."

"You seem to have coped with admirable efficiency and composure. So you never learned what punishment Pearce had in store for you?"

"Oh yes I did! I let her talk about that before I told her. It was more amusing that way. It wasn't a question of punishment; it was more like blackmail. She wanted to come in with us, be one of my crowd."

"Your crowd?"

"Well, me, Jennifer Blain and Diane Harper really. I was going with Nigel at the time and Diane and Jennifer had his friends. You haven't met Blain; she's one of the students who are off with flu. Pearce wanted us to fix her up a man for her so that she could make up a fourth."

"Didn't you find that surprising? From what I've heard of her, Heather Pearce wasn't exactly the type to be interested in sex."

"Everyone is interested in sex, in their own way. But Pearce didn't put it like that. She made out that the three of us weren't to be trusted and that we ought to have someone reliable to keep an eye on us. No prizes for guessing who! But I knew what she really wanted. She wanted Tom Mannix. He was the paediatric registrar at the time. He was spotty and rather a drip really, but Pearce fancied him. They both belonged to the hospital Christian Fellowship and Tom was going to be a missionary or something after his two years here were up. He'd have suited Pearce all right, and I daresay I could have made him go out with her once or twice if I'd pressed him. But it wouldn't have done her any good. He didn't want Pearce; he wanted me. Well, you know how it is."

Dalgliesh did know. This, after all, was the commonest, the most banal of personal tragedies. You loved someone. They didn't love you. Worse still, in defiance of their own best interests and to the destruction of your peace, they loved another. What would half the world's poets and novelists do without this universal tragicomedy? But Julia Pardoe was untouched by it. If only, thought Dalgliesh, her voice had held a trace of pity, or even interest! But Pearce's desperate need, the longing for love which had led her to this pathetic attempt at blackmail, provoked in her victim nothing, not even an amused contempt. She couldn't even be bothered to ask him to keep the story a secret. And then, as if reading his thoughts, she told him why.

"I don't mind your knowing about it now. Why should I? After all, Pearce is dead. Fallon too. I mean, with two murders in the place, Matron and the Hospital Management Committee have something more important to worry about than Nigel and me in bed together. But when I think of that night! Honestly, it was hilarious. The bed was far too narrow and it kept creaking and

Nigel and I were giggling so much we could hardly. . . . And then to think of Pearce with one eye to the keyhole!"

And then she laughed. It was a peal of spontaneous and reminiscent joy, innocent and infectious. Looking up at her, Masterson's heavy face coruscated into a wide indulgent grin and, for one extraordinary second, he and Dalgliesh had to restrain themselves from laughing aloud with her.

VII

Dalgliesh hadn't summoned the members of the little group in the library in any particular order and it wasn't with malice aforethought that he had left Sister Gearing to the last. But the long wait had been unkind to her. She had obviously found time, earlier in the morning, to make up her face with lavish care; an instinctive preparation, no doubt, for whatever traumatic encounters the day might bring. But the make-up had worn badly. The mascara had run and was now smudged into the eye shadow, there were beads of sweat along the forehead and a trace of lipstick in the cleft of the chin. Perhaps she had been unconsciously fiddling with her face. Certainly, she was finding it difficult now to keep her hands still. She sat twisting her handkerchief through her fingers and crossing and recrossing her legs in fidgety discomfort. Without waiting for Dalgliesh to speak she broke into a high frenetic chatter.

"You and your sergeant are staying with the Maycrofts at the Falconer's Arms, aren't you? I hope they're making you comfortable. Sheila's a bit of a drag but Bob's good value when you get him on his own."

Dalgliesh had taken very good care not to get Bob on his own. He had chosen the Falconer's Arms because it was small, convenient, quiet, and half empty; it had not taken long to understand why. Group Captain Robert Maycroft and his wife were more concerned to impress visitors with their own gentility than to minister to the comfort of their guests, and Dalgliesh fervently hoped to be out of the place by the end of the week. In the meantime he had no intention of discussing the Maycrofts with Sister Gearing and he guided her politely but firmly towards more relevant subjects.

Unlike the other suspects she found it necessary to waste the first five minutes in expressing her horror at the deaths of the two girls. It had been all too horrible, tragic, awful, ghastly, beastly, unforgettable, inexplicable. The emotion, thought Dalgliesh, was real enough even if its expression wasn't original. The woman was genuinely distressed. He suspected that she was also very frightened.

He took her through the events of Monday, 12th January. She had little new of interest to say and her account tallied with that already on the file. She had woken very late, dressed in a hurry, and had only just managed to get down to the dining-room by eight o'clock. There she had joined Sister Brumfett and Sister Rolfe for breakfast and had first heard from them that Nurse Fallon had been taken ill in the night. Dalgliesh asked her if she remembered which of the Sisters had given her the news.

"Well, I can't say I do really. I think it was Rolfe but I can't be sure. I was in a bit of a tizzy that morning what with one thing and another. It hadn't helped oversleeping like that, and I was naturally a bit nervous about the General Nursing Council inspection. After all, I'm not a qualified Sister Tutor. I was only deputizing for Sister Manning. And it's bad enough taking the first demonstration of a set without Matron and the G.N.C. Inspector, Mr. Courtney-Briggs and Sister Rolfe all sitting there with their beady eyes on every move you make. It struck me that with Fallon absent, there would only be about seven students left in the set. Well, that suited me all right; the fewer the better as far as I was concerned. I only hoped the little beasts would answer up and show some intelligence."

Dalgliesh asked her who had left the dining-room first.

"Brumfett did. Dead keen as usual to get back to her ward, I suppose. I left next. I took my papers through into the conservatory with a cup of coffee and sat down for ten minutes' read. Christine Dakers, Diane Harper and Julia Pardoe were there. Harper and Pardoe were chatting together and Dakers was sitting on her own reading a magazine. I didn't stay long and they were still there when I left. I went up to my room at about half past eight, collecting my post on the way, and then came down again and went straight into the demonstration room just before quarter to nine.

The Burt twins were already there finishing their preparations and Goodale arrived almost immediately. The rest of the set came in together at about ten to nine, except Pearce, who didn't arrive until last. There was the usual girlish chatter before we got down to work but I can't remember any of it. The rest you know."

Dalgliesh did know. But although he thought it unlikely that there was anything new to learn from Sister Gearing he took her again through the events of that traumatic demonstration. But she had nothing fresh to reveal. It had all been too awful, terrible, ghastly, frightful, unbelievable. She would never forget it as long as she lived.

Dalgliesh then turned to the death of Fallon. But here Sister Gearing had a surprise for him. She was the first suspect to produce an alibi, or what she obviously hoped was one, and she put it forward with understandable satisfaction. From eight o'clock until after midnight she had been entertaining a friend in her room. She gave Dalgliesh his name with coy reluctance. He was Leonard Morris, the chief pharmacist of the hospital. She had invited him to dinner, had produced a simple meal of spaghetti bolognaise in the Sisters' kitchen on the third floor and had served it in her sitting-room at eight o'clock, shortly after his arrival. They had been together for the whole of the four hours except for the few minutes when she had fetched the supper dish from the kitchen, and for a couple of minutes at about midnight when he had visited the lavatory, and a similar period earlier in the evening when she had left him for the same purpose. Apart from that they had never been out of each other's sight. She added eagerly that Len—Mr. Morris that was—would be only too happy to confirm her story. Len would remember the times perfectly well. Being a pharmacist he was precise and accurate about details. The only difficulty was that he wasn't in the hospital this morning. He had telephoned the pharmacy just before nine to say that he was sick. But he would be back at work tomorrow, she was sure of it. Len hated taking time off.

Dalgliesh asked at what hour he had actually left Nightingale House.

"Well, it couldn't have been long after midnight. I remember that when my clock struck twelve Len said that it was really time

358

he was off. We went out about five minutes later, down the back staircase, the one leading from Matron's flat. I left the door open: Len collected his bicycle from where he'd left it and I walked with him to the first turn in the path. It wasn't exactly a night for a stroll but we'd still one or two matters about the hospital to discuss —Len lectures in pharmacology to the second-year students—and I thought I could do with a breath of air. Len didn't like to leave me to walk back alone so he came back as far as the door. I suppose it was about twelve fifteen when we finally parted. I came in through Matron's door and locked it behind me. I went straight back to my room, took the supper things into the kitchen to wash them up, went to the bathroom, and was in bed by a quarter to one. I didn't see Fallon all the evening. The next thing I knew was Sister Rolfe dashing in to wake me up with the news that Dakers had found Fallon dead in bed."

"So you went out and returned through Miss Taylor's flat. Was her door left unlocked then?"

"Oh, yes! Matron usually leaves it open when she's away. She knows we find it convenient and more private to use her staircase. After all we're grown women. We're not exactly forbidden to entertain friends in our rooms and it isn't particularly nice to have to show them out through the main house with every little student watching with her eyes out on stalks. Matron's awfully good like that. I think she even leaves her sitting-room unlocked when she's not in Nightingale House. I suppose that's so that Sister Brumfett can use it if she feels inclined. Brumfett, in case you hadn't heard, is Matron's spaniel. Most Matrons keep a little dog you know. Mary Taylor has Brumfett."

The note of bitter cynicism was so unexpected that Masterson's head came up from his note-taking with a jerk and he looked at Sister Gearing as if she were an unpromising candidate who had suddenly revealed unexpected potentialities. But Dalgliesh let it pass. He asked:

"Was Sister Brumfett using Miss Taylor's flat last night?"

"At midnight! Not Brumfett! She goes to bed early unless she's in town gallivanting with Matron. She's usually brewing her last cuppa by ten-fifteen. Anyway, she was called out last night. Mr.

Courtney-Briggs rang her to go over to the private ward and receive one of his patients back from the theatre. I thought everyone knew. That was just before twelve."

Dalgliesh asked if Sister Gearing had seen her.

"No, but my friend did. Len, I mean. He popped his head out of the door to see if the coast was clear to go to the loo before we left and saw Brumfett wrapped in her cloak, carrying that old bag of hers, disappearing down the staircase. It was obvious that she was going out, and I guessed that she had been called back to the ward. That's always happening to Brumfett. Mind you, it's partly her own fault. There's such a thing as being too conscientious."

It was not, thought Dalgliesh, a fault to which Sister Gearing was likely to be prone. It was difficult to imagine her tramping through the grounds at midnight in the depth of winter at the casual summons of any surgeon, however eminent. But he felt rather sorry for her. She had given him a depressing glimpse into the stultifying lack of privacy, and of the small pettinesses and subterfuges with which people living in unwelcome proximity try to preserve their own privacy or invade that of others. The thought of a grown man peeping surreptitiously around the door before coming out, of two adult lovers creeping furtively down a back staircase to avoid detection, was grotesque and humiliating. He remembered the Matron's words. "We do get to know things here; there's no real privacy." Even poor Brumfett's choice of nightcap and her usual hour for bed were common knowledge. Small wonder that Nightingale House bred its own brand of neurosis, that Sister Gearing felt it necessary to justify a walk with her lover in the grounds, their obvious and natural wish to prolong the final good night, with unconvincing twaddle about the need to discuss hospital business. He found it all profoundly depressing and he wasn't sorry when it was time to let her go.

VIII

Dalgliesh rather enjoyed his half hour with the housekeeper, Miss Martha Collins. She was a thin, brown-skinned woman, brittle and nobbly as a dead branch who looked as if the sap had

long since dried in her bones. She gave the appearance of having gradually shrunk in her clothes without having noticed it. Her working overall of thick fawn cotton hung in long creases from her narrow shoulders to mid-calf and was bunched around her waist by a schoolboy's belt of red and blue stripes clasped with a snake buckle. Her stockings were a concertina around her ankles, and either she preferred to wear shoes at least two sizes too large, or her feet were curiously disproportionate to the rest of her body. She had appeared as soon as summoned, had plonked herself down opposite Dalgliesh, her immense feet planted firmly astride, and had eyed him with anticipatory malevolence as if about to interview a particularly recalcitrant housemaid. Throughout the interview she didn't once smile. Admittedly there was nothing in the situation to provoke amusement but she seemed incapable of raising even the briefest smile of formal recognition. But despite these inauspicious beginnings the interview hadn't gone badly. Dalgliesh wondered whether her acidulated tone and perversely unattractive appearance were part of a calculated *persona*. Perhaps some forty years earlier she had decided to become a hospital character, the beloved tyrant of fiction, treating everyone from the matron to the junior maid with equal irreverence, and had found the characterization so successful and satisfying that she had never managed to drop it. She grumbled incessantly but it was without malice, a matter of form. He suspected that, in fact, she enjoyed her work and was neither as unhappy nor discontented as she chose to appear. She would hardly have stayed in the job for forty years if it were as intolerable as she made it sound.

"Milk! Don't talk to me about milk. There's more trouble about milk in this house than about the rest of the catering put together and that's saying something. Fifteen pints a day we're getting through even with half the house down with the flu. Don't ask me where it's all going. I've stopped being responsible for it and so I told Matron. There's a couple of bottles go up first thing each morning to the Sisters' floor so that they can make their own early tea. Two bottles between three I send up. You'd think that'd be enough for everyone. Matron's is separate, of course. She gets a pint and not a drop grudged. But the trouble that milk causes! The

first Sister to get at it takes all the cream, I suppose. Not very considerate, and so I told Matron. They're lucky to get a bottle or two of Channel Island milk; no one else in the house does. There's nothing but complaints. Sister Gearing going on because it's too watery for her and Sister Brumfett because it's not all Channel Island and Sister Rolfe wanting it sent up in half-pint bottles which she knows as well as I do you can't get any more. Then there's the milk for the students' early tea and that cocoa and stuff they brew themselves at night. They're supposed to sign for the bottles which they take from the fridge. The stuff isn't grudged, but that's the rule. Well, you take a look at the record book yourself! Nine times out of ten they can't be troubled. And then there are the empties. They're supposed to rinse them out and return them to the kitchen. You wouldn't think that would be too much bother. Instead they leave the bottles about the house, in their rooms, in the cupboards, and in the utility room—half-rinsed too—until the place stinks. My girls have got enough to do without running around after the students and their empties, and so I told Matron.

"What do you mean, was I in the kitchen when the Burt twins took their pint? You know I was. I said so to the other policeman. Where else would I be at that hour of the day? I'm always in my kitchen by quarter to seven and it was nearly three minutes past when the Burt twins came in. No, I didn't hand the bottle to them. They helped themselves from the fridge. It's not my job to wait hand and foot on the students and so I told Matron. But there was nothing wrong with that milk when it left my kitchen. It wasn't delivered until six thirty and I've got enough to do before breakfast without messing about putting disinfectant into the milk. Besides, I've got an alibi. I was with Mrs. Muncie from six forty-five onwards. She's the daily woman who comes in from the town to lend a hand when I'm short. You can see her any time you like but I don't suppose you'll get much out of her. The poor soul hasn't got much between the ears. Come to think of it, I doubt whether she'd notice if I spent the whole morning poisoning the milk. But she was with me for what it's worth. And I was with her all the time. No popping out every other minute to the lavatory for me, thank you. I do all that sort of thing at the proper time.

362

"The lavatory disinfectant? I thought you'd be asking about that. I fill up the bottles myself from the big tin they send over once a week from the main hospital store. It's not really my job but I don't like to leave it to the housemaids. They're so careless. They'd only get the stuff slopped all over the lavatory floors. I refilled that bottle in the downstairs W.C. the day before Nurse Pearce died so it must have been nearly full. Some of the students bother to put a little down the bowl when they've finished with the lavatory but most of them don't. You'd think student nurses would be particular about little things like that, but they're no better than other young people. The stuff is mostly used by the maids when they've cleaned the W.C. bowl. All the lavatories get cleaned once a day. I'm very particular about having clean lavatories. The downstairs one was due to be cleaned by Morag Smith after lunch, but Nurse Goodale and Nurse Pardoe noticed that the bottle was missing before then. I'm told that the other policeman found it empty among the bushes at the back of the house. And who put it there, I'd like to know?

"No, you can't see Morag Smith. Didn't they tell you? She's on a day's leave. She went off after tea yesterday, lucky for her. They can't pin this latest spot of bother on Morag. No. I don't know whether she went home. I didn't inquire. The maids are enough responsibility when they're under my nose in Nightingale House. I don't concern myself with what they do on their days off. Just as well from some of the things I hear. She'll be back late tonight more than likely and Matron has left instructions that she's to move to the Resident Staff Hostel. This place is too dangerous for us now apparently. Well, no one's shifting me. I don't know how I'm supposed to manage in the mornings if Morag doesn't show her face until just before breakfast. I can't control my staff if they're not under my eyes and so I told Matron. Not that Morag's much bother. She's as obstinate as they come but she's not a bad worker once you get her started. And if they try to tell you that Morag Smith interfered with the dripfeed, don't you believe them. The girl may be a bit dense but she's not a raving lunatic. I'll not have my staff slandered without cause.

"And now I'll tell you something, Mr. Detective." She raised her

thin rump from her chair, leaned forward across the desk and fixed
Dalgliesh with her beady eyes. He willed himself to meet them
without blinking and they stared at each other like a couple of
wrestlers before a bout.

"Yes, Miss Collins?"

She stuck out a lean nodular finger and prodded him sharply in
the chest. Dalgliesh winced.

"No one had any right to take that bottle out of the lavatory
without my permission or to use it for any other purpose except for
cleaning the lavatory bowl. Nobody!"

It was apparent where in Miss Collins's eyes the full enormity of
the crime had lain.

IX

At twenty minutes to one, Mr. Courtney-Briggs appeared. He
knocked briskly at the door, came in without waiting for an invitation, and said curtly:

"I can give you a quarter of an hour now, Dalgliesh, if it's convenient."

His tone assumed that it would be. Dalgliesh assented and indicated the chair. The surgeon looked across at Sergeant Masterson
sitting impassively with his notebook at the ready, hesitated, then
turned the chair so that its back was to the sergeant. Then he seated
himself and slipped his hand into his waistcoat pocket. The
cigarette case he drew out was of finely tooled gold and so slim that
it looked hardly functional. He offered a cigarette to Dalgliesh but
not to Masterson and seemed neither surprised nor particularly
interested at the Superintendent's refusal. He lit his own. The
hands cupped around the lighter were large, square-fingered; not
the sensitive hands of a fictional surgeon, but strong carpenter's
hands, beautifully cared for.

Dalgliesh, overtly busy with his papers, observed the man. He
was big but not yet fat. The formal suit fitted him almost too well,
containing a sleek well-fed body and enhancing the effect of latent
power only imperfectly controlled. He could still be called handsome. His long hair brushed straight back from a high forehead

was strong and dark, except for one single white strand. Dalgliesh wondered whether it were bleached. His eyes were too small for the large, rather florid face, but were well shaped and set wide apart. They gave nothing away.

Dalgliesh knew that it had been Mr. Courtney-Briggs who had been mainly responsible for the Chief Constable calling in the Yard. From Inspector Bailey's somewhat bitter account during their brief colloquy when Dalgliesh had taken over the case, it was easy to understand why. The surgeon had made himself a nuisance from the beginning and his motives, if they were capable of rational explanation, raised interesting speculations. At first he had asserted vigorously that Nurse Pearce had obviously been murdered, that it was unthinkable that anyone connected with the hospital could have been concerned with the crime, and that the local police had a duty to proceed on this assumption and to find and arrest the killer with a minimum of delay. When their investigations yielded no immediate results, he became restive. He was a man used to exercising power and he was certainly not without it. There were eminent people in London who owed their lives to him and some of them had considerable nuisance value. Telephone calls, some tactful and half-apologetic, others frankly critical, were made both to the Chief Constable and to the Yard. As the Inspector in charge of the investigation became more convinced that Nurse Pearce's death was the result of a practical joke which had tragically misfired, so Mr. Courtney-Briggs and his co-agitators proclaimed more loudly that she had been murdered, and pressed more strongly for the case to be handed over to the Yard. And then Nurse Fallon had been found dead. It could be expected that the local C.I.D. would be galvanized into fresh activity, that the diffuse light which had played over the first crime would sharpen and focus on this second death. And it was at this moment that Mr. Courtney-Briggs had chosen to telephone the Chief Constable to announce that no further activity was necessary, that it was obvious to him that Nurse Fallon had committed suicide, that this could only have been in remorse at the tragic result of the practical joke which had killed her colleague, and that it was now in the hospital's interest to close the case with the minimum of fuss before nurse

recruitment and indeed the whole future of the hospital was jeopardized. The police are not unused to these sudden quirks of temperament, which is not to say that they welcome them. Dalgliesh thought that it must have been with considerable satisfaction that the Chief Constable decided that, in all the circumstances, it would be prudent to call in the Yard to investigate both the deaths.

During the week following Nurse Pearce's death, Courtney-Briggs had even rung up Dalgliesh, who had been his patient three years earlier. It had been a case of uncomplicated appendicitis, and although Dalgliesh's vanity was gratified by the smallness and neatness of the resultant scar, he felt that the surgeon's expertise had been adequately rewarded at the time. He had certainly no wish to be used for Courtney-Briggs's private ends. The telephone call had been embarrassing and he had resented it. He was interested to see that the surgeon had apparently decided that this was an incident it would be advisable for both of them to forget.

Without lifting his eyes from his papers, Dalgliesh said:

"I understand that you take the view that Miss Fallon killed herself?"

"Of course. It's the obvious explanation. You're not suggesting that someone else put stuff into her whisky? Why should they?"

"There's the problem, isn't there, of the missing container? That is, if it were poison. We shan't know until we get the autopsy report."

"What problem? There's no problem. The beaker was opaque, heat insulated. She could have put the stuff into it earlier that evening. No one would have noticed. Or she could have carried a powder in a slip of paper and flushed it down the lavatory. The container's no problem. Incidentally, it wasn't a corrosive this time. That much was evident when I saw the body."

"Were you the first doctor on the scene?"

"No. I wasn't in the hospital when they found her. Dr. Snelling saw her. He's the general physician who looks after the nurses here. He realized at once that there was nothing to be done. I went across to have a look at the body as soon as I heard the news. I arrived at the hospital just before nine. By then the police had arrived, of course. The local people, I mean. I can't think why they weren't

left to get on with it. I rang the Chief Constable to make my views known. Incidentally, Miles Honeyman tells me that she died about midnight. I saw him just as he was leaving. We were at medical school together."

"So I understand."

"You were wise to call him in. I gather that he's generally considered to be the best."

He spoke complacently, success condescending to recognize success. His criteria were hardly subtle, thought Dalgliesh. Money, prestige, public recognition, power. Yes, Courtney-Briggs would always demand the best for himself, confident of his ability to pay for it.

Dalgliesh said: "She was pregnant. Did you know?"

"So Honeyman told me. No, I didn't know. These things happen, even today when birth control is reliable and easily obtained. But I should have expected a girl of her intelligence to be on the Pill."

Dalgliesh remembered the scene that morning in the library when Mr. Courtney-Briggs had known the girl's age to a day. He asked his next question without apology.

"Did you know her well?"

The implication was plain and the surgeon did not reply for a moment. Dalgliesh had not expected him to bluster or threaten and he did neither. There was an increased respect in the sharp look which he gave his interrogator.

"For a time, yes." He paused. "You could say I knew her intimately."

"Was she your mistress?"

Courtney-Briggs looked at him, impassive, considering. Then he said:

"That's putting it rather formally. We slept together fairly regularly during her first six months here. Are you objecting?"

"It's hardly for me to object if she didn't. Presumably she was willing?"

"You could say that."

"When did it end?"

"I thought I told you. It lasted until the end of her first year. That's a year and a half ago."

"Did you quarrel?"

"No. She decided she'd, shall we say, exhausted the possibilities. Some women like variety. I do myself. I wouldn't have taken her on if I'd thought she was the type to make trouble. And don't get me wrong. I don't make it a practice to sleep with student nurses. I'm reasonably fastidious."

"Wasn't it difficult to keep the affair secret? There's very little privacy in a hospital."

"You have romantic ideas, Superintendent. We didn't kiss and cuddle in the sluice room. When I said I slept with her I meant just that. I don't use euphemisms for sex. She came to my Wimpole Street flat when she had a night off and we slept there. I haven't a resident man there and my house is near Selborne. The porter at Wimpole Street must have known, but he can keep his mouth shut. There wouldn't be many tenants left in the building if he couldn't. There wasn't any risk, provided that she didn't talk, and she wasn't a talker. Not that I would have minded particularly. There are certain areas of private behaviour in which I do as I like. You too no doubt."

"So it wasn't your child?"

"No. I'm not careless. Besides the affair was over. But if it hadn't been I should hardly have killed her. That kind of solution causes more embarrassment than it prevents."

Dalgliesh asked: "What would you have done?"

"That would have depended on the circumstances. I should have had to be sure it was my child. But this particular problem is hardly uncommon and not insoluble if the woman is reasonable."

"I've been told that Miss Fallon planned to get an abortion. Did she approach you?"

"No."

"She might have done?"

"Certainly she might have done. But she didn't."

"Would you have helped her if she had?"

The surgeon looked at him.

"That question is hardly within your terms of reference, I should have thought."

Dalgliesh said: "That's for me to judge. The girl was pregnant;

she apparently intended to get an abortion; she told a friend that she knew someone who would help her. I'm naturally interested to know who she had in mind."

"You know the law. I'm a surgeon not a gynaecologist. I prefer to stick to my own speciality and to practice it legally."

"But there are other kinds of help. Referring her to an appropriate consultant, helping with the fees."

A girl with £16,000 to bequeath was hardly likely to want help with the fees for an abortion. But Miss Goodale's legacy was not being made public and Dalgliesh was interested to learn whether Courtney-Briggs knew about Fallon's capital. But the surgeon gave no sign.

"Well, she didn't come to me. She may have had me in mind but she didn't come. And if she had, I wouldn't have helped. I make it my business to assume my own responsibilities; but I don't take on other people's. If she chose to look elsewhere for her satisfaction she could look elsewhere for her help. I didn't impregnate her. Someone did. Let him look after her."

"That would have been your response?"

"Certainly it would. And rightly."

His voice held a note of grim satisfaction. Looking at him, Dalgliesh saw that his face was flushed. The man was controlling his emotion with difficulty. And Dalgliesh had little doubt of the nature of that emotion. It was hate. He went on with his interrogation.

"Were you in the hospital last night?"

"Yes. I was called to operate on an emergency. One of my patients relapsed. It wasn't altogether unexpected, but very serious. I finished operating at eleven forty-five p.m. The time will be noted in the theatre register. Then I rang Sister Brumfett at Nightingale House to ask her to be good enough to return to her ward for an hour or so. My patient was a private patient. After that I rang my home to say that I would be returning that night instead of sleeping here in the medical officers' quarters as I do occasionally after a late operation. I left the main building shortly after twelve. I intended driving out by the Winchester Road gate. I have my own key. However, it was a wild night, as you probably noticed,

and I discovered that there was an elm down over the path. I was lucky not to drive into it. I got out of the car and knotted my white silk scarf round one of the branches to warn anyone else who might be driving that way. It wasn't likely that anyone would, but the tree was an obvious danger and there was no chance of getting it moved before daylight. I reversed the car and left by the main entrance, reporting the fallen tree to the gate porter on my way out."

"Did you notice the time then?"

"I didn't. He may have done. But, at a guess, it was probably about twelve fifteen, maybe later. I wasted a bit of time at the tree."

"You would have had to drive past Nightingale House to reach the back gate. You didn't go in?"

"I had no reason to go in and I didn't go in, either to poison Nurse Fallon or for any other reason."

"And you saw no one in the grounds?"

"After midnight and in the middle of a storm? No, I saw no one."

Dalgliesh switched his questioning.

"You saw Nurse Pearce die, of course. I suppose there was never a real chance of saving her?"

"Never, I should say. I took pretty vigorous measures, but it isn't easy when you don't know what you're treating."

"But you knew it was poison?"

"Pretty soon. Yes. But I didn't know what. Not that it would have made any difference. You've seen the post-mortem report. You knew what that stuff did to her."

Dalgliesh asked: "You were in Nightingale House from eight o'clock onwards on the morning that she died?"

"You know perfectly well that I was if, as I assume, you've taken the trouble to read my original statement. I arrived in Nightingale House shortly after eight. My contract here is for six notional half-days a week; I'm in the hospital all day on Monday, Thursday and Friday; but it's not uncommon for me to be called in to operate on an emergency, particularly if it's a private patient, and I occasionally do a Saturday morning session in the theatre if the lists are long. I'd been called out shortly after eleven o'clock on Sunday night for

an emergency appendicectomy—one of my private patients—and it was convenient to spend the night in the medical officers' quarters."

"Which are where?"

"In that deplorably designed new building near the out-patients' department. They serve breakfast at the ungodly hour of seven thirty."

"You were here rather early surely. The demonstration wasn't due to begin until nine."

"I wasn't here merely for the demonstration, Superintendent. You're really rather ignorant of hospitals, aren't you? The Senior Consultant Surgeon doesn't normally attend nurse training sessions unless he's actually lecturing the students. I only attended on January 12th because the G.N.C. Inspector was to be there and I'm Vice-Chairman of the Nurse Education Committee. It was a courtesy to Miss Beale to be here to meet her. I came in early because I wanted to work on some clinical notes which I had left in Sister Rolfe's office after a previous lecture. I also wanted to have a chat with Matron before the inspection began and to be sure that I was there in time to receive Miss Beale. I went up to Matron's flat at eight thirty-five and found her finishing breakfast. And, if you're thinking that I could have put the corrosive in the milk bottle any time between eight and eight thirty-five, you're perfectly right. As it happens, I didn't."

He looked at his watch.

"And now if there's nothing else you need to ask I must get my lunch. I've another out-patients' session this afternoon and time's pressing. If it's really necessary, I can probably give you a few more minutes before I leave but I hope it won't be. I've already signed one statement about Pearce's death and I've nothing to add or to alter. I didn't see Fallon yesterday. I didn't even know she was discharged from the sick-bay. She wasn't carrying my child, and even if she had been, I shouldn't have been foolish enough to kill her. Incidentally, what I told you about our previous relationship was naturally in confidence."

He looked across meaningly at Sergeant Masterson.

"Not that I care whether it's made public. But, after all, the girl is dead. We may as well try to protect her reputation."

371

Dalgliesh found it difficult to believe that Mr. Courtney-Briggs was interested in anyone's reputation but his own. But, gravely, he gave the necessary assurance. He saw the surgeon leave without regret. An egotistical bastard whom it was agreeable, if childish, to provoke. But a murderer? He had the hubris, the nerve and the egotism of a killer. More to the point, he had had the opportunity. And the motive? Hadn't it been a little disingenuous of him to have confessed so readily to his relationship with Josephine Fallon? Admittedly he couldn't have hoped to keep his secret for long; a hospital was hardly the most discreet of institutions. Had he been making a virtue of necessity, ensuring that Dalgliesh heard the version of the affair before the inevitable gossip reached his ears? Or had it been merely the candour of conceit, the sexual vanity of a man who wouldn't trouble to conceal any exploit which proclaimed his attraction and virility?

Putting his papers together, Dalgliesh became aware that he was hungry. He had made an early start to the day and it had been a long morning. It was time to turn his mind from Stephen Courtney-Briggs and for him and Masterson to think about luncheon.

Chapter Five

Table Talk

I

The resident Sisters and students from Nightingale House took only their breakfast and afternoon tea in the dining-room at the school. For their main midday and evening meal they joined the rest of the staff in the hospital cafeteria where all but the consultants ate in institutionalized and noisy proximity. The food was invariably nourishing, adequately cooked, and as varied as was compatible with the need to satisfy the differing tastes of several hundred people, avoid outraging their religious or dietary susceptibilities, and keep within the catering officer's budget. The principles governing the menu planning were invariable. Liver and kidneys were never served on the days when the urinary surgeon operated, and the nurses were not faced with the same menu as that which they had just served to the patients.

The cafeteria system had been introduced at the John Carpendar hospital against strong opposition from all grades of staff. Eight years ago there had been separate dining-rooms for the Sisters and nurses, one for the administrative and lay professional staff, and a canteen for the porters and artisans. The arrangements had suited everyone as making a proper distinction between grades and ensuring that people are in reasonable quietness and in the company of those with whom they preferred to spend their lunch break. But now only the senior medical staff enjoyed the peace and privacy of their own dining-room. This privilege, jealously defended, was under perpetual attack from Ministry auditors, Government catering advisers and work study experts who, armed with costing statistics, had no difficulty in proving that the system was uneconomical. But so far the doctors had won. Their strongest argu-

ment was their need to discuss the patients in privacy. This suggestion that they never stopped working, even for meals, was greeted with some scepticism but was difficult to refute. The need to keep the patients' affairs confidential touched on that area of patient-doctor relationship which the doctors were always quick to exploit. Before this mystique even the Treasury auditors were powerless to prevail. Furthermore, they had had the support of Matron. Miss Taylor had made it known that she considered it eminently reasonable that the senior medical staff should continue to have their own dining-room. And Miss Taylor's influence over the Chairman of the Hospital Management Committee was so obvious and of such long standing that it had almost ceased to excite comment. Sir Marcus Cohen was a wealthy and personable widower and the only surprise now was that he and Matron hadn't married. This, it was generally accepted, was either because Sir Marcus, an acknowledged leader of the country's Jewish community, chose not to marry outside his faith or because Miss Taylor, wedded to her vocation, chose not to marry at all.

But the extent of Miss Taylor's influence over the Chairman and thus over the Hospital Management Committee was beyond speculation. It was known to be particularly irritating to Mr. Courtney-Briggs since it considerably diminished his own. But in the matter of the consultants' dining-room it has been exercised in his favour and had proved decisive.

But if the rest of the staff had been forced into proximity they had not been forced into intimacy. The hierarchy was still apparent. The immense dining-room had been divided into smaller dining areas separated from each other by screens of lattice work and troughs of plants, and in each of these alcoves the atmosphere of a private dining-room was re-created.

Sister Rolfe helped herself to plaice and chips, carried her tray to the table which, for the past eight years, she had shared with Sister Brumfett and Sister Gearing, and looked around at the denizens of this strange world. In the alcove nearest the door were the laboratory technicians in their stained overalls, noisily animated. Next to them was old Fleming, the out-patient pharmacist, rolling bread pellets like pills in his nicotine-stained fingers. At the next

374

table were four of the medical stenographers in their blue working overalls. Miss Wright, the senior secretary, who had been at the John Carpendar for twenty years, was eating with furtive speed as she always did, avid to get back to her typewriter. Behind the adjacent screen was a little clutch of the lay professional staff—Miss Bunyon the head radiographer, Mrs. Nethern, the head medical social worker and two of the physiotherapists, carefully preserving their status by an air of calm unhurried efficiency, an apparent total disinterest in the food they were eating and the choice of a table as far removed as possible from that of the junior clerical staff.

And what were they all thinking about? Fallon probably. There couldn't be anyone in the hospital from the consultants to the ward maids who didn't know by now that a second Nightingale student had died in mysterious circumstances and that Scotland Yard had been called in. Fallon's death was probably the subject of gossip at most of the tables this morning. But it didn't prevent people from eating their lunch or from getting on with their job. There was so much to do; there were so many other pressing concerns; there was even so much fresh gossip. It wasn't just that life had to go on; in hospital that cliché had particular relevance. Life did go on, carried forward by the imperative momentum of birth and death. New booked admissions came in; ambulances daily disgorged the emergencies; operation lists were posted; the dead were laid out and the healed discharged. Death, even sudden and unexpected death, was more familiar to these young fresh-faced students than it was to even the most experienced senior detective. And there was a limit to its power to shock. You either came to terms with death in your first year, or you gave up being a nurse. But murder? That was different. Even in this violent world, murder still held its macabre and primitive power to shock. But how many people in Nightingale House really believed that Pearce and Fallon had been murdered? It would take more than the presence of the Yard's wonder boy and his retinue to give credence to such an extraordinary idea. There were too many other possible explanations, all of them simpler and more believable than murder. Dalgliesh might believe as he chose; proving it would be another matter.

Sister Rolfe bent her head and began unenthusiastically to dis-

sect her plaice. She felt no particular hunger. The strong smell of food was heavy on the air, stifling appetite. The noise of the cafeteria beat against her ears. It was ceaseless and inescapable, a confused continuum of discord in which individual sounds were scarcely distinguishable.

Next to her, her cloak folded neatly at the back of her chair and the shapeless tapestry bag which accompanied her everywhere dumped at her feet, Sister Brumfett was eating steamed cod and parsley sauce with belligerent intensity as if she resented the need to eat and was venting her irritation on the food. Sister Brumfett invariably chose steamed fish; and Sister Rolfe felt suddenly that she couldn't face another lunch hour of watching Brumfett eat cod.

She reminded herself that there was no reason why she should. There was nothing to prevent her sitting somewhere else, nothing except this petrification of the will which made the simple act of carrying her tray three feet to a different table seem impossibly cataclysmic and irrevocable. On her left, Sister Gearing toyed with her braised beef, and chopped her wedge of cabbage into neat squares. When she actually began to eat she would shove the food in avidly like a greedy schoolgirl. But always there were these finicky and salivatory preliminaries. Sister Rolfe wondered how many times she had resisted the urge to say, "For God's sake Gearing, stop messing about and eat it!" One day, no doubt, she would say it. And another middle-aged and unlikeable Sister would be pronounced "getting very difficult. It's probably her age".

She had considered living out of the hospital. It was permissible and she could afford it. The purchase of a flat or small house would be the best investment for her retirement. But Julia Pardoe had disposed of that idea in a few half-interested, destructive comments dropped like cold pebbles into the deep pool of her hopes and plans. Sister Rolfe could still hear that high, childish voice.

"Live out. Why should you want to do that? We shouldn't see so much of each other."

"But we should, Julia. And in much greater privacy and without all this risk and deceit. It would be a comfortable and agreeable little house. You'd like it."

"It wouldn't be as easy as slipping upstairs to see you when I feel like it."

When she felt like it? Felt like what? Sister Rolfe had desperately fought off the question she never dared to let herself ask.

She knew the nature of her dilemma. It wasn't, after all, peculiar to herself. In any relationship there was one who loved and one who permitted himself or herself to be loved. This was merely to state the brutal economics of desire; from each according to his ability, to each according to his need. But was it selfish or presumptuous to hope that the one who took knew the value of the gift; that she wasn't wasting love on a promiscuous and perfidious little cheat who took her pleasure wherever she chose to find it? She had said:

"You could probably come twice or three times a week, perhaps more often. I wouldn't move far."

"Oh, I don't see how I could manage that. I don't see why you want the work and bother of a house. You're all right here."

Sister Rolfe thought: "But I'm not all right here. This place is souring me. It isn't only the long-stay patients who become institutionalized. It's happening to me. I dislike and despise most of the people I'm required to work with. Even the job is losing its hold. The students get more stupid and worse educated with every intake. I'm not even sure any more of the value of what I'm supposed to be doing."

There was a crash near the counter. One of the maids had dropped a tray of used crockery. Looking instinctively across, Sister Rolfe saw that the detective had just come in and taken up his tray at the end of the line. She watched the tall figure, disregarded by the chattering queue of nurses, as he began to move slowly down the line between a white-coated houseman and a pupil midwife, helping himself to roll and butter, waiting for the girl to hand out his choice of main course. She was surprised to see him there. It had never occurred to her that he would eat in the hospital dining-hall or that he would be on his own. Her eyes followed him as he reached the end of the line, handed over his meal ticket and turned to look for a vacant seat. He seemed utterly at ease and almost oblivious of the alien world around him. She thought that he was probably a man who could never imagine himself at a disadvantage in any

company since he was secure in his private world, possessed of that core of inner self-esteem which is the basis of happiness. She wondered what kind of a world his was, then bent her head to her plate irritated at this unusual interest he aroused in her. Probably he would be thought handsome by most women, with that lean bony face, at once arrogant and sensitive. It was probably one of his professional assets, and being a man he would make the most of it. No doubt it was one of the reasons why he had been given this case. If dull Bill Bailey could make nothing of it, let the Yard's wonder boy take over. With a house full of women and three middle-aged spinsters as his chief suspects, no doubt he fancied his chances. Well, good luck to him!

But she was not the only one at the table to notice his arrival. She felt rather than saw Sister Gearing stiffen and a second later heard her say:

"Well, well. The handsome sleuth! He'd better feed with us or he may find himself in a gaggle of students. Someone should have told the poor man how the system works."

And now, thought Sister Rolfe, she'll give him one of her street corner come-hither looks and we shall be burdened with him for the rest of the meal. The look was given and the invitation not refused. Dalgliesh, carrying his tray nonchalantly and apparently completely at ease, threaded his way across the room and came up to their table. Sister Gearing said:

"What have you done with that handsome sergeant of yours? I thought policemen went about in pairs like nuns."

"My handsome sergeant is studying reports and lunching on sandwiches and beer in the office while I enjoy the fruits of seniority with you. Is this chair taken?"

Sister Gearing moved her own chair closer to Sister Brumfett and smiled up at him:

"It is now."

II

Dalgliesh sat down, well aware that Sister Gearing wanted him, that Sister Rolfe didn't, and that Sister Brumfett, who had acknowledged his arrival with a brief nod, didn't care whether he joined

378

them or not. Sister Rolfe looked across at him unsmilingly and said to Sister Gearing:

"Don't imagine Mr. Dalgliesh is sharing our table for the sake of your *beaux yeux*. The Superintendent plans to take in information with his braised beef."

Sister Gearing giggled: "My dear, it's no use warning me! I couldn't keep a thing to myself if a really attractive man set his mind to wangle it out of me. It would be quite useless for me to commit a murder. I haven't the brain for it. Not that I think for one moment that anyone has—committed murder I mean. Anyway, let's leave the grisly subject during lunch. I've had my grilling, haven't I, Superintendent?"

Dalgliesh disposed his cutlery around the plate of braised beef and tilting back his chair to save himself the trouble of rising, added his used tray to the stack on the nearby stand. He said:

"People here seem to be taking Nurse Fallon's death calmly enough."

Sister Rolfe shrugged: "Did you expect them to be wearing black arm bands, talking in whispers, and refusing their lunch? The job goes on. Anyway, only a few will have known her personally, and still fewer knew Pearce."

"Or liked her apparently," said Dalgliesh.

"No, I don't think they did on the whole. She was too self-righteous, too religious."

"If you can call it religious," said Sister Gearing.

"It wasn't my idea of religion. *Nil nisi* and all that, but the girl was just a prig. She always seemed to be a damn sight more concerned with other people's shortcomings than she was with her own. That's why the other kids didn't like her. They respect genuine religious conviction. Most people do, I find. But they didn't like being spied on."

"Did she spy on them?" asked Dalgliesh.

Sister Gearing seemed half to regret what she had said.

"Perhaps that's putting it a bit strongly. But if anything went wrong in the set you can bet Nurse Pearce knew all about it. And she usually managed to bring it to the notice of authority. Always with the best motives, no doubt."

379

Sister Rolfe said drily: "She had an unfortunate habit of interfering with other people for their own good. It doesn't make for popularity."

Sister Gearing pushed her plate to one side, drew a bowl of plums and custard towards her and began to extract the stones from the fruit as carefully as if it were a surgical operation. She said:

"She wasn't a bad nurse, though. You could rely on Pearce. And the patients seemed to like her. I suppose they found that holier than thou attitude reassuring."

Sister Brumfett looked up from her plate and spoke for the first time.

"You're not in a position to give an opinion on whether she was a good nurse. Nor is Rolfe. You only see the girls in the training school. I see them on the wards."

"I see them on the wards too. I'm the clinical instructor remember. It's my job to teach them on the ward."

Sister Brumfett was unrepentant.

"Any student teaching that's done on my ward is done by me, as you know very well. Other ward Sisters can welcome the clinical instructor if they like. But on the private ward I do the teaching. And I prefer it that way when I see some of the extraordinary ideas you seem to put into their heads. And, by the way, I happen to know—Pearce told me, as a matter of fact—that you visited my ward when I was off duty on 7th January and conducted a teaching session. In future, please consult me before using my patients as clinical material."

Sister Gearing flushed. She tried to laugh but her amusement sounded artificial. She glanced across at Sister Rolfe as if enlisting her aid but Sister Rolfe kept her eyes firmly on her plate. Then, belligerently and rather like a child determined to have the last word, she said with apparent irrelevance:

"Something happened to upset Pearce while she was on your ward."

Sister Brumfett's sharp little eyes glared up at her.

"On my ward? Nothing upset her on my ward!"

The sturdy assertion conveyed unmistakedly that no nurse worthy of the name could be upset by anything that happened on

the private ward; that upsetting things just weren't permitted when Sister Brumfett was in charge.

Sister Gearing shrugged.

"Well, something upset her. It could have been something totally unconnected with the hospital, I suppose, but one never quite believes that poor Pearce had any real life outside these walls. It was the Wednesday of the week before this block went into school. I visited the chapel just after five o'clock to do the flowers—that's how I remember which day it was—and she was sitting there alone. Not kneeling or praying, just sitting. Well, I did what I had to do and then went out without speaking to her. After all, the chapel's open for rest and meditation and if one of the students wants to meditate that's all right by me. But when I went back nearly three hours later because I'd left my scissors in the sacristy she was still there, sitting perfectly still and in the same seat. Well, meditation's all very well, but four hours is a bit excessive. I don't think that the kid could have had any supper. She looked pretty pale too, so I went up to her and asked her if she was all right, if there was anything I could do for her. She didn't even look at me as she replied. She said: 'No thank you, Sister. There was something troubling me which I had to think over very carefully. I did come here for help but not from you.'"

For the first time during the meal Sister Rolfe sounded amused.

She said: "Caustic little beast! Meaning, I suppose, that she'd come to consult a higher power than the clinical instructor."

"Meaning mind your own business. So I did."

Sister Brumfett said, as if feeling that her colleague's presence at a place of worship needed some explanation:

"Sister Gearing is very good at arranging flowers. That's why Matron asked her to look after the chapel. She sees to the flowers every Wednesday and Saturday. And she does very charming arrangements for the Annual Sisters' Dinner." Sister Gearing stared at her for a second and then laughed.

"Oh, little Mavis isn't just a pretty face. But thanks for the compliment."

A silence fell. Dalgliesh addressed himself to his braised beef. He wasn't disconcerted by the lack of conversation and had no in-

tention of helping them out by introducing a fresh subject. But Sister Gearing seemed to feel that silence was reprehensible in the presence of a stranger. She said brightly:

"I see from the minutes that the Hospital Management Committee have agreed to introduce the Salmon Committee proposals. Better late than never. I suppose that means that Matron will be head of the nursing services over all the hospitals in the group. Chief Nursing Officer! It'll be a big thing for her, but I wonder how C.B. will take it. If he had his way, Matron would be given less authority not more. She's a big enough thorn in his flesh as it is."

Sister Brumfett said: "It's time something was done to wake up the psychiatric hospital and the geriatric units. But I don't know why they want to change the title. If Matron was good enough for Florence Nightingale it's good enough for Mary Taylor. I don't suppose she particularly wants to be called Chief Nursing Officer. It sounds like an army rank. Ridiculous."

Sister Rolfe shrugged her thin shoulders.

"Don't expect me to get enthusiastic about the Salmon Report. I'm beginning to wonder what's happening to nursing. Every report and recommendation seems to take us further away from the bedside. We have dieticians to see to the feeding, physiotherapists to exercise the patients, medical social workers to listen to their troubles, ward orderlies to make the beds, laboratory technicians to take blood, ward receptionists to arrange the flowers and interview the relatives, operating theatre technicians to hand the surgeon the instruments. If we're not careful nursing will become a residual skill, the job which is left when all the technicians have had their turn. And now we have the Salmon Report with all its talk of first, second and third tiers of management. Management for what? There's too much technical jargon. Ask yourself what is the function of the nurse today. What exactly are we trying to teach these girls?"

Sister Brumfett said: "To obey orders implicitly and be loyal to their superiors. Obedience and loyalty. Teach the students those and you've got a good nurse."

She sliced a potato in two with such viciousness that the knife rasped the plate. Sister Gearing laughed.

"You're twenty years out of date, Brumfett. That was good enough for our generation, but these kids ask whether the orders are reasonable before they start obeying and what their superiors have done to deserve their respect. A good thing too on the whole. How on earth do you expect to attract intelligent girls into nursing if you treat them like morons? We ought to encourage them to question established procedures, even to answer back occasionally."

Sister Brumfett looked as if she, for one, would willingly dispense with intelligence if its manifestations were so disagreeable.

"Intelligence isn't the only thing. That's the trouble nowadays. People think it is."

Sister Rolfe said: "Give me an intelligent girl and I'll make a good nurse of her whether she thinks she has a vocation or not. You can have the stupid ones. They may minister to your ego but they'll never make good professional women." She looked at Sister Brumfett as she spoke and the undertone of contempt was unmistakable. Dalgliesh dropped his eyes to his plate and pretended more interest than he could feel in the careful separation of meat from fat and gristle. Sister Brumfett reacted predictably:

"Professional women! We're talking about nurses. A good nurse thinks of herself as a nurse first and last. Of course she's a professional woman! I thought we'd all accepted that by now. But there's too much thinking and talking of status nowadays. The important thing is to get on with the job."

"But what job exactly? Isn't that precisely what we're asking ourselves?"

"You may be. I'm perfectly clear what I'm doing. Which, at the moment, is coping with a very sick ward."

She pushed her plate to one side, flicked her cloak around her shoulders with brisk expertise, gave them a valedictory nod which was as much a warning as a good-bye, and strutted out of the dining-room with her brisk ploughman's waddle, the tapestry bag swinging at her side. Sister Gearing laughed and watched her go.

"Poor old Brum! According to her, she's always got a very sick ward."

Sister Rolfe said drily: "She invariably has."

383

They finished the meal almost in silence. Then Sister Gearing left, first murmuring something about a clinical teaching session on the E.N.T. ward. Dalgliesh found himself walking back to Nightingale House with Sister Rolfe. They left the dining-room together and he retrieved his coat from the rack. They then passed down a long corridor and through the out-patients' department. It had obviously only recently been opened and the furniture and decoration were still bright and new. The large waiting-hall with its groups of formica-topped tables and easy chairs, its troughs of pot plants and unremarkable pictures was cheerful enough, but Dalgliesh had no wish to linger. He had the healthy man's dislike and disgust of hospitals, founded partly on fear and partly on repugnance, and he found this atmosphere of determined cheerfulness and spurious normality unconvincing and frightening. The smell of disinfectant, which to Miss Beale was the elixir of life, infected him with the gloomier intimations of mortality. He did not think that he feared death. He had come close to it once or twice in his career and it had not unduly dismayed him. But he did grievously fear old age, mortal illness and disablement. He dreaded the loss of independence, the indignities of senility, the yielding up of privacy, the abomination of pain, the glimpses of patient compassion in the faces of friends who knew that their indulgences would not be claimed for long. These things might have to be faced in time unless death took him quickly and easily. Well, he would face them. He was not arrogant enough to suppose himself secure from the lot of other men. But in the meantime, he preferred not to be reminded.

The out-patients' department was next to the casualty department entrance and as they passed it a stretcher was wheeled in. The patient was an emaciated old man; his moist lips spewed feebly above the rim of a vomit bowl, his immense eyes rolled uncomprehendingly in the skull-like head. Dalgliesh became aware that Sister Rolfe was looking at him. He turned his head in time to catch her glance of speculation and, he thought, contempt.

"You don't like this place, do you?" she asked.

"I'm not very happy in it, certainly."

"Neither am I at present, but I suspect for very different reasons."

They walked on for a minute in silence. Then Dalgliesh asked if Leonard Morris lunched in the staff dining-room when he was in the hospital.

"Not often. I believe he brings sandwiches and eats them in the pharmacy office. He prefers his own company."

"Or that of Sister Gearing?"

She laughed contemptuously.

"Oh, you've got on to that have you? But of course! She was entertaining him last night, I hear. Either the food or the subsequent activity seems to have been rather more than the little man could take. What thorough little scavengers the police are! It must be a strange job, sniffing around for evil like a dog round trees."

"Isn't evil a strong word for Leonard Morris's sexual preoccupations?"

"Of course. I was just being clever. But I shouldn't let the Morris-Gearing affair worry you. It's been hiccuping on for so long now that it's become almost respectable. It isn't even good for a gossip. She's the kind of woman who must have someone in tow, and he likes someone to confide in about the awfulness of his family and the beastliness of the hospital medical staff. They don't exactly take him at his own evaluation as an equal professional man. He's got four children, by the way. I imagine that if his wife decided to divorce him and he and Gearing were free to marry nothing would disconcert them more. Gearing would like a husband no doubt, but I don't think she's cast poor little Morris for the role. It's more likely . . ."

She broke off. Dalgliesh asked:

"You think she has a more eligible candidate in mind?"

"Why not try asking her? She doesn't confide in me."

"But you are responsible for her work? The clinical instructor comes under the senior nurse tutor?"

"I'm responsible for her work not her morals."

They had reached the far door of the casualty department and as Sister Rolfe put out her hand to push it open Mr. Courtney-Briggs

385

swept in. He was followed by a half-dozen chattering junior staff, white-coated and with stethoscopes slung round their necks. The two on each side of him were nodding in deferential attention as the great man spoke. Dalgliesh thought that he had the conceit, the patina of vulgarity and the slightly coarse *savoir-faire* which he associated with one type of successful professional man. As if reading his thoughts, Miss Rolfe said:

"They're not all alike, you know. Take Mr. Molravey, our ophthalmic surgeon. He reminds me of a dormouse. Every Tuesday morning he patters in and stands for five hours in the theatre without speaking an unnecessary word, whiskers twitching and picking away with fastidious little paws at a succession of patients' eyes. Then he thanks everyone formally down to the most junior theatre nurse, peels off his gloves and patters away again to play with his collection of butterflies."

"A modest little man, in fact."

She turned towards him and he detected again in her eyes that uncomfortable elliptical flicker of contempt.

"Oh no! Not modest! He gives a different performance, that's all. Mr. Molravey is just as convinced as is Mr. Courtney-Briggs that he's a very remarkable surgeon. They are both vain in a professional sense. Vanity, Mr. Dalgliesh, is a surgeon's besetting sin as subservience is a nurse's. I've never yet met a successful surgeon who wasn't convinced that he ranked only one degree lower than Almighty God. They're all infected with hubris." She paused:

"Isn't that supposed to be true also of murderers?"

"Of one type of murderer. You must remember that murder is a highly individual crime."

"Is it? I should have thought that the motives and the means would be monotonously familiar to you. But you, of course, are the expert."

Dalgliesh said: "You have little respect for men apparently, Sister?"

"A great deal of respect. I just don't happen to like them. But you have to respect a sex that has brought selfishness to such an art. That's what gives you your strength, this ability to devote yourselves entirely to your own interest."

Dalgliesh said, a little maliciously, that he was surprised that Miss Rolfe, since she obviously resented the subservience of her job, hadn't chosen a more masculine occupation. Medicine perhaps?

She laughed bitterly.

"I wanted to do medicine but I had a father who didn't believe in educating women. I'm forty-six, remember. When I was at school we didn't have universal free grammar school education. Father earned too much for me to get a free place, so he had to pay. He stopped paying as soon as he decently could, when I was sixteen."

Dalgliesh found nothing appropriate to say. The confidence surprised him. She was hardly the woman, he would have thought, to expose a personal grievance to a stranger and he didn't flatter himself that she found him sympathetic. She would find no man sympathetic. The outburst was probably a spontaneous release of pent up bitterness, but whether against her father, men in general or the limitations and subservience of her job it was hard to say.

They had left the hospital now and were passing along the narrow path which led to Nightingale House. Neither of them spoke another word until the house was reached. Sister Rolfe wrapped her long cloak tightly around her and pulled up her hood as if it could protect her from more than the bite of the wind. Dalgliesh was immersed in his private thoughts. And thus, with the width of the path between them, they paced together in silence under the trees.

IV

In the office Detective Sergeant Masterson was typing a report. Dalgliesh said:

"Immediately before she came into the school, Nurse Pearce was working on the private ward under Sister Brumfett. I want to know if anything significant happened there. And I want a detailed account of her last week's duty and an hour-by-hour account of what she did on her last day. Find out who the other nursing staff were, what her duties were, when she was off duty, how she appeared to the other staff. I want the names of the patients who were on the ward while she was nursing there and what happened

387

to them. Your best plan is to talk to the other nurses and to work from the nursing reports. They're bound to keep a book which is written up daily."

"Shall I get it from Matron?"

"No. Ask Sister Brumfett for it. We deal directly with her, and for God's sake be tactful. Have you those reports ready yet?"

"Yes, sir. They've been typed. Do you want to read them now?"

"No. Tell me if there's anything I ought to know. I'll look at them tonight. I suppose it's too much to expect that any of our suspects has a police record?"

"If they have, sir, it isn't noted on the personal dossiers. There's remarkable little information in most of them. Julia Pardoe was expelled from school, though. She seems to be the only delinquent among them."

"Good God! What for?"

"Her dossier doesn't say. Apparently it was something to do with a visiting maths master. Her headmistress felt it right to mention it when she sent Matron a reference before the girl started here. It isn't very specific. She writes that Julia was more sinned against than sinning and that she hoped the hospital would give her the chance of training for the only career she has ever shown any interest in, or signs of being suited for."

"A nice double edged comment. So that's why the London teaching hospitals wouldn't take her. I thought Sister Rolfe was being a little disingenuous about the reasons. Anything about the others? Any previous connections between them?"

"Matron and Sister Brumfett trained together in the north at Nethercastle Royal Infirmary, did their midwifery training at the Municipal Maternity Hospital there and came here fifteen years ago, both as ward Sisters. Mr. Courtney-Briggs was in Cairo during 1946–7 and so was Sister Gearing. He was a major in the R.A.M.C. and she was a nursing sister in the Q.A.R.N.S. There's no sugges-tion that they knew each other there."

"If they did, you'd hardly expect to find the fact recorded on their personal records. But they probably did. Cairo in '46 was a chummy place, so my army friends tell me. I wonder if Miss Taylor

served in the Q.A.R.N.S. That's an army nursing service cap which she wears."

"If she did, sir, it isn't on her dossier. The earliest document is her reference from her training school when she came here as a Sister. They thought very highly of her at Nethercastle."

"They think very highly of her here. Have you checked on Courtney-Briggs?"

"Yes, sir. The lodge porter makes a note of every car in and out after midnight. Mr. Courtney-Briggs left at twelve thirty-two a.m."

"Later than he led us to believe. I want a check on his schedule. The precise time he finished the operation will be in the operating theatre book. The junior doctor assisting him will probably know when he left—Mr. Courtney-Briggs is the kind of man who gets escorted to his car. Then drive over the route and time him. They will have moved the tree by now but it should be possible to see where it came down. He can't have wasted more than a few minutes at the most tying on his scarf. Find out what happened to that. He'd hardly lie about something so easily disproved, but he's arrogant enough to think he can get away with anything, including murder."

"Constable Greeson can do the checking, sir. He likes these reconstruction jobs."

"Tell him to curb his urge for verisimilitude. There's no need for him to don an operating gown and go into the theatre. Not that they'd let him. Is there any news yet from Sir Miles or the lab?"

"No, sir, but we've got the name and address of the man Nurse Fallon spent that week in the Isle of Wight with. He's a G.P.O. night telephonist and lives in North Kensington. The local people got on to them almost at once. Fallon made it very easy for them. She booked in her own name and they had two single rooms."

"She was a woman who valued her privacy. Still, she hardly got pregnant by staying in her own room. I'll see the man tomorrow morning after I've visited Miss Fallon's solicitor. Is Leonard Morris in the hospital yet, do you know?"

"Not yet, sir. I checked at the pharmacy that he telephoned this morning and said he wasn't well. Apparently he suffers from a duodenal ulcer. They assume that it's playing him up again."

"It will play him up a great deal worse if he doesn't come back soon and get the interview over. I don't want to embarrass him by visiting his house, but we can't wait indefinitely to get Sister Gearing's story verified. Both these murders, if they were murders, hinge on the question of timing. We must know everyone's movements, if possible, to the minute. Time is crucial."

Masterson said: "That's what surprises me about the poisoned drip. The carbolic couldn't have been added to the milk without a great deal of care, particularly in replacing the bottle seal and making sure that the concentration was right and that the stuff had the texture and colour of milk. It couldn't have been done in a hurry."

"I've no doubt a great deal of care and time were taken. But I think I know how it was done."

He described his theory. Sergeant Masterson, cross with himself for having missed the obvious, said:

"Of course. It must have been done that way."

"Not must, Sergeant. It was probably done that way."

But Sergeant Masterson had seen an objection and voiced it.

Dalgliesh replied: "But that wouldn't apply to a woman. A woman could do it easily and one woman in particular. But I admit it would be more difficult for a man."

"So the assumption is that the milk was doctored by a woman?"

"The probability is that both girls were murdered by a woman. But it's still only a probability. Have you heard yet whether Nurse Dakers is well enough to be interviewed? Dr. Snelling was supposed to be seeing her this morning."

"Matron rang just before lunch to say that the girl is still asleep, but that she'll probably be fit enough once she wakes up. She's under sedation, so God knows when that'll be. Shall I take a look at her while I'm in the private wing?"

"No. I'll see her later. But you might check on this story that Fallon returned to Nightingale House on the morning of 12th January. Someone might have seen her leave. And where were her clothes kept while she was warded? Could anyone have got hold of them and impersonated her? It seems unlikely but it ought to be checked."

"Inspector Bailey did check, sir. No one saw Fallon leave but they admit that she could have got out of the ward undetected. They were very busy and she had a private room. If it were found empty they would probably have assumed that she'd gone to the bathroom. Her clothes were hung in the wardrobe in her room. Anyone who had a right to be in the ward could have got at them, provided, of course, that Fallon was asleep or out of the room. But no one thinks it likely that anyone did."

"Nor do I. I think I know why Fallon came back to Nightingale House. Nurse Goodale told us that Fallon had received the pregnancy confirmation only two days before she went sick. It's possible that she didn't destroy it. If so, it's the one possession in her room which she wouldn't want to leave for someone else to find. It certainly isn't among her papers. My guess is that she came back to retrieve it, tore it up, and flushed it down the lavatory."

"Couldn't she have telephoned Nurse Goodale and asked her to destroy it?"

"Not without exciting suspicion. She couldn't be sure that she'd get Goodale herself when she rang and she wouldn't want to give anyone else a message. This insistence to speak to one particular nurse and the reluctance to accept help from anyone else would look rather odd. But it's no more than a theory. Is the search of Nightingale House completed?"

"Yes, sir. They've found nothing. No trace of poison and no container. Most of the rooms contain bottles of aspirin and Sister Gearing, Sister Brumfett and Miss Taylor all have a small supply of sleeping tablets. But surely Fallon didn't die of hypnotic or soporific poisoning?"

"No. It was quicker than that. We shall just have to possess ourselves in patience until we get the laboratory report."

V

At two thirty-four p.m. precisely, in the largest and most luxurious of the private rooms, Sister Brumfett lost a patient. She always thought of death in that way. The patient was lost; the battle was over; she, Sister Brumfett, had been personally defeated.

The fact that so many of her battles were foredoomed to failure, that the enemy even if repulsed in the present skirmish, was always assured of final victory, never mitigated her sense of failure. Patients did not come into Sister Brumfett's ward to die; they came in to get better, and with Sister's indomitable will to fortify them, they usually did get better, often to their own surprise and occasionally despite their own wishes.

She had hardly expected to win this particular battle but it was only when Mr. Courtney-Briggs lifted his hand to turn off the blood drip that she accepted failure. The patient had certainly fought well; a difficult patient, a demanding patient, but a good fighter. He had been a wealthy business man whose meticulous plans for his future certainly didn't include dying at forty-two. She recalled the look of wild surprise, almost of outrage, with which he had greeted the realization that death was something neither he nor his accountant could fix. Sister Brumfett had seen too much of his young widow on that lady's daily visits to suppose that she would suffer much grief or inconvenience. The patient was the only one who would have been furious at the failure of Mr. Courtney-Briggs's heroic and expensive efforts to save him, and happily for the surgeon, the patient was the one person in no position to demand either explanation or excuse.

Mr. Courtney-Briggs would see the widow and offer her his customary carefully phrased condolences, his assurance that everything humanly possible had been done. In this case, the size of the bill would be a guarantee of that and a powerful antidote, no doubt, to the inevitable guilt of bereavement. Courtney-Briggs was really very good with the widows; and to do him justice, the poor as well as the rich received the consolation of his hand on their shoulder, of the stereotyped phrases of comfort and regret.

She drew the fold of the sheet up over the suddenly vacant face. Closing the dead eyes with practised fingers, she felt the eyeballs still warm under the wrinkled lids. She was conscious neither of grief nor anger. There was only, as always, this dragging weight of failure tugging like a physical load at the tired muscles of her stomach and back.

They turned away from the bed together. Glancing at the sur-

geon's face, Sister Brumfett was struck by his look of weariness. For the first time he, too, appeared threatened with failure and with age. It was, of course, unusual for a patient to die when he was there to see it happen. Still less frequently did they die on the operating table, even if the scramble from the theatre to the ward was sometimes a little undignified. But, unlike Sister Brumfett, Mr. Courtney-Briggs did not have to watch over his patients to the last gasp. All the same, she did not believe that this particular death had depressed him. It was, after all, not unexpected. He had nothing with which to reproach himself even if he had been given to self-criticism. She felt that he was stressed by some subtler worry, and she wondered whether it was something to do with Fallon's death. He's lost some of his bounce, thought Sister Brumfett. He looks suddenly ten years older.

He preceded her down the passage to her office. As they neared the ward kitchen there was the sound of voices. The door was open. A student nurse was setting a trolley with the afternoon tea trays. Sergeant Masterson was leaning against the sink and watching her with the air of a man completely at home. As the Sister and Mr. Courtney-Briggs appeared in the doorway the girl flushed, muttered a low "good afternoon, sir" and pushed her trolley past them into the corridor with clumsy haste. Sergeant Masterson gazed after her with tolerant condescension, then transferred his level gaze to the Sister. He appeared not to notice Mr. Courtney-Briggs.

"Good afternoon, Sister, could I have a word with you?"

Baulked of the initiative, Sister Brumfett said repressively:

"In my office if you please, Sergeant. That is where you should have waited in the first place. People do not wander in and out of my ward just as they please, and that includes the police."

Sergeant Masterson, unchastened, looked slightly gratified at this speech as if it confirmed something to his satisfaction. Sister Brumfett bustled into her office, tight-lipped and ready for battle. Rather to her surprise Mr. Courtney-Briggs followed.

Sergeant Masterson said: "I wonder, Sister, if I could see the ward report book covering the period when Nurse Pearce was on this ward? I'm particularly interested in her last week here."

Mr. Courtney-Briggs broke in roughly:

"Aren't they confidential medical records, Sister? Surely the police will have to apply for a subpoena before they can make you produce them?"

"Oh, I don't think so, sir." Sergeant Masterson's voice, quiet, almost too respectful, yet held a tinge of amusement which wasn't lost on his hearer. "Ward nursing records surely aren't medical documents in the proper sense. I merely want to see who was being nursed here during that period and whether anything happened which might be of interest to the Superintendent. It's been suggested that something occurred to upset Nurse Pearce while she was nursing on your ward. She went from here straight to the school, remember."

Sister Brumfett, mottled and shaking with an anger which left small room for fear, found her voice.

"Nothing happened on my ward. Nothing! It's all stupid, malicious gossip. If a nurse does her job properly and obeys orders there's no need for her to be upset. The Superintendent is here to investigate a murder not to interfere with my ward."

Mr. Courtney-Briggs broke in blandly:

"And even if she were—upset is the word I think you used, Sergeant—I don't see what relevance that has to her death."

Sergeant Masterson smiled at him as if humouring a wilfully obstinate child.

"Anything that happened to Nurse Pearce in the week immediately before she was killed may have relevance, sir. That's why I'm asking to see the ward report book."

As neither Sister Brumfett nor the surgeon made any move to comply, he added:

"It's only a matter of confirming information we already have. I know what she was doing on the ward during that week. I'm told she was devoting all her time to nursing one particular patient. A Mr. Martin Dettinger. 'Specializing' him, I think you call it. My information is that she seldom left his room while she was on duty here during the last week of her life."

So, thought Sister Brumfett, he had been gossiping with the student nurses. But of course! That was how the police worked. It was pointless to try to keep anything private from them. Everything,

even the medical secrets of her ward, the nursing care of her own patients, would be nosed out by this impertinent young man and reported to his superior officer. There was nothing in the ward report book which he couldn't find out by more devious means; discover, magnify, misinterpret and use to make mischief. Inarticulate with anger and something close to panic she heard Mr. Courtney-Briggs's bland and reassuring voice.

"Then you'd better hand the book over, Sister. If the police insist on wasting their own time there's no need for us to encourage them to waste ours."

Without another word, Sister Brumfett went to her desk and, bending down, opened the deep right-hand drawer and took out a large, hard-backed book. Silently and without looking at him, she handed it to Sergeant Masterson. The Sergeant thanked her profusely and turned to Mr. Courtney-Briggs:

"And now, sir, if the patient's still with you, I'd like to have a word with Mr. Dettinger."

Mr. Courtney-Briggs made no attempt to keep the satisfaction out of his voice.

"I think that is likely to challenge even your ingenuity, Sergeant. Mr. Martin Dettinger died on the day Nurse Pearce left this ward. If I remember rightly, she was with him when he died. So both of them are safely out of reach of your inquisition. And now, if you'd be good enough to excuse us, Sister and I have work to do."

He held open the door and Sister Brumfett strutted out before him. Sergeant Masterson was left alone, holding the ward record book in his hand.

"Bloody bastard," he said aloud.

He stood for a moment, thinking. Then he went in search of the medical record department.

VI

Ten minutes later he was back in the office. Under his arm was the ward report book and a buff-coloured file, stamped with a warning in black capital letters that it was not to be handed to the patient, and bearing the name of the hospital and Martin Dettinger's

395

medical record number. He placed the book on the table and handed the file to Dalgliesh.

"Thank you. You got it without trouble?"

"Yes, sir," said Masterson. He saw no reason to explain that the Medical Records Officer had been out of his department and that he had half persuaded, half bullied the junior clerk on duty into handing over the file on the grounds, which he didn't for a moment believe, that the rules about the confidentiality of medical records no longer applied when the patient was dead and that when a Superintendent of the Yard asked for a thing he was entitled to get it without fuss and without delay. They studied the file together. Dalgliesh said:

"Martin Dettinger. Aged forty-six. Gave his address as his London Club. C. of E. Divorced. Next-of-kin, Mrs. Louise Dettinger, 23 Saville Mansions, Marylebone. Mother. You had better see the lady, Masterson. Make an appointment for tomorrow evening. I shall need you here during the day while I'm in town. And take trouble with her. She must have visited her son pretty frequently when he was in hospital. Nurse Pearce was specializing him. The two women probably saw quite a lot of each other. Something happened to upset Pearce while she was working on the private ward during the last week of her life and I want to know what it was."

He turned back to the medical record.

"There's a lot of paper here. The poor chap seems to have had a stormy medical history. He suffered from colitis for the past ten years, and before that there's a record of long spells of undiagnosed ill health, perhaps a forerunner of the condition which killed him. He was in hospital for three periods during his army service, including a spell of two months in an army hospital in Cairo in 1947. He was invalided out of the army in 1952 and emigrated to South Africa. That doesn't seem to have done him much good. There are notes here from a hospital in Johannesburg. Courtney-Briggs wrote for them; he certainly takes trouble. His own notes are pretty copious. He took over the case a couple of years ago and seems to have been acting as a kind of general practitioner to Dettinger as well as his surgeon. The colitis became acute about a month ago,

and Courtney-Briggs operated to remove a large part of the bowel on Friday, 2nd January. Dettinger survived the operation, although he was in a pretty bad state by then, and made some progress until the early morning of Monday, 5th January, when he relapsed. After that he was seldom conscious for long, and he died at five thirty p.m. on Friday, 9th January."

Masterson said: "Nurse Pearce was with him when he died."

"And apparently she nursed him almost single-handed for the last week of his life. I wonder what the nursing record tells us."

But the nursing record was far less informative than the medical file. Nurse Pearce had entered in her careful schoolgirl's hand the details of her patient's temperature, respiration and pulse, his restlessness and brief hours of sleep, his medication and food. It could not be faulted as a meticulous record of nursing care. Beyond that it told them nothing.

Dalgliesh closed the book.

"You'd better return this to the ward and the medical folder to the proper department. We've learnt all we can from them. But I feel in my bones that Martin Dettinger's death has something to do with this case."

Masterson did not reply. Like all detectives who had worked with Dalgliesh, he had a healthy respect for the old man's hunches. Inconvenient, perverse and far-fetched they might seem, but they had been proved right too often to be safely ignored. And he had no objection to an evening trip to London. Tomorrow was Friday. The time-table on the hall notice-board showed that the students' sessions ended early on Friday. They would be free soon after five. He wondered whether Julia Pardoe would fancy a drive to town. After all, why not? Dalgliesh wouldn't be back by the time he was due to set out. It could be arranged with care. And there were some suspects it would be a positive pleasure to interview on their own.

VII

Just before half past four Dalgliesh, in defiance of convention and prudence, took tea alone with Sister Gearing in her bed-sitting-room. She had met him casually passing across the ground floor

hall as the students were filing out of the lecture room after the last seminar of the day. She had given the invitation spontaneously and without coyness, although Dalgliesh noted that Sergeant Masterson was not included. He would have accepted the invitation even had it been delivered on highly scented and pink writing-paper and accompanied by the most blatant of sexual innuendoes. What he wanted after the formal interrogation of the morning was to sit in comfort and listen to a flow of artless, candid and slightly malicious gossip; to listen with the surface of his mind soothed, uninvolved, even a little cynically amused, but with the sharp claws of the intelligence sharpened for their pickings. He had learned more about the Nightingale House Sisters from their conversation at luncheon than he had in all his formal interviews, but he couldn't spend all his time tagging along behind the nursing staff, picking up scraps of gossip like so many dropped handkerchiefs. He wondered whether Sister Gearing had something to tell or something to ask. Either way he didn't expect an hour in her company to be wasted.

Dalgliesh hadn't yet been in any of the rooms on the third floor except Matron's flat and he was struck by the size and pleasant proportions of Sister Gearing's room. From here, even in winter, the hospital couldn't be seen, and the room had a calm of its own, remote from the frenetic life of wards and departments. Dalgliesh thought that in summer it must be very pleasant with nothing but a curdle of tree tops breaking the view of the far hills. Even now, with the curtains drawn against the fading light and the gas fire giving out a merry hiss, it was welcoming and warm. Presumably the divan bed in the corner with its cretonne cover and carefully arranged bank of cushions had been provided by the Hospital Management Committee, as had the two comfortable armchairs similarly covered and the rest of the uninteresting but functional furniture. But Sister Gearing had imposed her own personality on the room. There was a long shelf along the far wall on which she had arranged a collection of dolls in different national costumes. On another wall was a smaller shelf holding an assortment of china cats of different sizes and breeds. There was one particularly repulsive specimen in spotted blue, bulging of eye and adorned with a bow of blue ribbon; and propped beside it was a greetings card. It

showed a female robin, the sex denoted by a frilly apron and flowered bonnet, perched on a twig. At her feet, a male robin was spelling out the words "Good luck" in worms. Dalgliesh hastily averted his eyes from this abomination and continued his tactful examination of the room.

The table in front of the window was presumably intended as a desk but about half a dozen photographs in silver frames effectively took up most of the working space. There was a record player in a corner with a cabinet of records beside it and a poster of a recent pop idol pinned on the wall above. There was a large number of cushions of all sizes and colours, three pouffes of unattractive design, an imitation tiger rug in brown-and-white nylon, and a coffee table on which Sister Gearing had set out the tea. But the most remarkable object in the room, in Dalgliesh's eyes, was a tall vase of winter foliage and chrysanthemums, beautifully arranged, standing on a side table. Sister Gearing was reputably good with flowers, and this arrangement had a simplicity of colour and line which was wholly pleasing. It was odd, he thought, that a woman with such an instinctive taste in flower arrangement should be content to live in this vulgarly over-furnished room. It suggested that Sister Gearing might be a more complex person than one would at first suppose. On the face of it, her character was easily read. She was a middle-aged, uncomfortably passionate spinster, not particularly well educated or intelligent, and concealing her frustrations with a slightly spurious gaiety. But twenty-five years as a policeman had taught him that no character was without its complications, its inconsistencies. Only the young or the very arrogant imagined that there was an identikit to the human mind.

Here in her own place Sister Gearing was less overtly flirtatious than she was in company. Admittedly she had chosen to pour the tea while curled on a large cushion at his feet, but he guessed from the number and variety of these cushions plumped around the room that this was her usual comfortable habit, rather than a kittenish invitation for him to join her. The tea was excellent. It was hot and freshly brewed, and accompanied by lavishly buttered crumpets with anchovy paste. There was an admirable absence of doilys and sticky cakes, and the cup handle could be comfortably

held without dislocating one's fingers. She looked after him with quiet efficiency. Dalgliesh thought that Sister Gearing was one of those women who, when alone with a man, consider it their duty to devote themselves entirely to his comfort and the flattering of his ego. This may arouse fury in other less dedicated women, but it is unreasonable to expect a man to object.

Relaxed by the warmth and comfort of her room and stimulated by tea, Sister Gearing was obviously in a mood for talk. Dalgliesh let her chatter on, only occasionally throwing in a question. Neither of them mentioned Leonard Morris. The artless confidences for which Dalgliesh hoped would hardly spring from embarrassment or restraint.

"Of course, what happened to that poor kid Pearce is absolutely appalling, however it was caused. And with the whole set looking on like that! I'm surprised that it hadn't upset their work completely, but the young are pretty tough these days. And it isn't as if they liked her. But I can't believe any one of them put that corrosive into the feed. After all, these are third-year students. They know that carbolic acid taken straight into the stomach in that concentration is lethal. Damn it all, they had a lecture about poisons in their previous block. So it couldn't have been a practical joke that misfired."

"All the same, that seems to be the general view."

"Well, it's natural, isn't it? No one wants to believe that Pearce's death was murder. And if this were a first-year block I might believe it. One of the students might have tampered with the feed on impulse, perhaps with the idea that lysol is an emetic and that the demonstration might be enlivened by Pearce sicking up all over the G.N.C. Inspector. An odd idea of humour, but the young can be pretty crude. But these kids must have known what that stuff would do to the stomach."

"And what about Nurse Fallon's death?"

"Oh, suicide I should think. After all, the poor girl was pregnant. She probably had a moment of intense depression and didn't see the point of going on. Three years of training wasted and no family to turn to. Poor old Fallon! I don't think she was really the suicidal type, but it probably happened on impulse. There has been a cer-

tain amount of criticism about Dr. Snelling—he looks after the students' health—letting her come back to the block so soon after her influenza. But she hates being off and it isn't as if she were on the wards. This is hardly the time of the year to send people away for convalescence. She was as well off in school as anywhere. Still, the flu couldn't have helped. It probably left her feeling pretty low. This epidemic is having some pretty nasty after-effects. If only she'd confided in someone. It's awful to think of her putting an end to herself like that with a houseful of people who would have been glad to help if only she'd asked. Here, let me give you another cup. And try one of those shortbreads. They're home made. My married sister sends me them from time to time."

Dalgliesh helped himself to a piece of shortbread from the proffered tin and observed that there were those who thought that Nurse Fallon might have had another reason for suicide, apart from her pregnancy. She could have put the corrosive in the feed. She had certainly been seen in Nightingale House at the crucial time.

He put forward the suggestion slyly, awaiting her reaction. It wouldn't, of course, be new to her; it must have occurred to everyone in Nightingale House. But she was too simple to be surprised that a senior detective should be discussing his case so frankly with her, and too stupid to ask herself why.

She dismissed this theory with a snort.

"Not Fallon! It would have been a foolish trick and she was no fool. I told you, any third-year nurse would know that the stuff was lethal. And if you're suggesting that Fallon intended to kill Pearce —and why on earth should she?—I'd say that she was the last person to suffer remorse. If Fallon decided to do murder she wouldn't waste time repenting afterwards, let alone kill herself in remorse. No, Fallon's death is understandable enough. She had post-flu depression and she felt she couldn't cope with the baby."

"So you think they both committed suicide?"

"Well, I'm not so sure about Pearce. You'd have to be pretty crazy to choose that agonizing way of dying, and Pearce seemed sane enough to me. But it's a possible explanation, isn't it? And I can't see you proving anything else however long you stay."

He thought he detected a note of smug complacency in her voice and glanced at her abruptly. But the thin face showed nothing but its usual look of vague dissatisfaction. She was eating shortbread, nibbling at it with sharp, very white teeth. He could hear them rasping against the biscuits. She said:

"When one explanation is impossible, the improbable must be true. Someone said something like that. G. K. Chesterton wasn't it? Nurses don't murder each other. Or anyone else for that matter."

"There was Nurse Waddingham," said Dalgliesh.

"Who was she?"

"An unprepossessing and unpleasant woman who poisoned with morphine one of her patients, a Miss Baguley. Miss Baguley had been so ill advised as to leave Nurse Waddingham her money and property in turn for life-long treatment in the latter's nursing home. She struck a poor bargain. Nurse Waddingham was hanged."

Sister Gearing gave a frisson of simulated distaste.

"What awful people you do get yourself mixed up with! Anyway, she was probably one of those unqualified nurses. You can't tell me that Waddingham was on the General Nursing Council's Register."

"Come to think of it, I don't believe she was. And I wasn't mixed up with it. It happened in 1935."

"Well, there you are then," Sister Gearing said as if vindicated.

She stretched across to pour him a second cup of tea, then wriggled herself more comfortably into her cushion and leaned back against the arm of his chair, so that her hair brushed his knee. Dalgliesh found himself examining with mild interest the narrow band of darker hair each side of the parting where the dye had grown out. Viewed from above, her foreshortened face looked older, the nose sharper. He could see the latent pouch of skin under the bottom eyelashes and a spatter of broken veins high on the cheekbones, the purple threads only half disguised by make-up. She was no longer a young woman; that he knew. And there was a great deal more about her that he had gleaned from her dossier. She had trained at a hospital in the East End of London after a variety of unsuccessful and unprofitable office jobs. Her

nursing career had been chequered and her references were suspiciously non-committal. There had been doubt about the wisdom of seconding her for training as a clinical instructor, a suggestion that she had been motivated less by a desire to teach than by the hope of an easier job than that of ward Sister. He knew that she was having difficulty with the menopause. He knew more about her than she realized, more than she would think he had any right to know. But he didn't yet know whether she was a murderess. Intent for a moment on his private thoughts, he hardly caught her next words.

"It's odd your being a poet. Fallon had your last volume of verse in her room, didn't she? Rolfe told me. Isn't it difficult to reconcile poetry with being a policeman?"

"I've never thought of poetry and police work as needing to be reconciled in that ecumenical way."

She laughed coyly.

"You know very well what I mean. After all it is a little unusual. One doesn't think of policemen as poets."

He did, of course, know what she meant. But it wasn't a subject he was prepared to discuss. He said:

"Policemen are individuals like people in any other job. After all, you three nursing Sisters haven't much in common have you? You and Sister Brumfett could hardly be more different personalities. I can't see Sister Brumfett feeding me on anchovy crumpets and home-made shortbread."

She reacted at once, as he had known she would.

"Oh, Brumfett's all right when you get to know her. Of course she's twenty years out of date. As I said at lunch, the kids today aren't prepared to listen to all that guff about obedience and duty and a sense of vocation. But she's a marvellous nurse. I won't hear a word against Brum. I had an appendicectomy here about four years ago. It went a bit wrong and the wound burst. Then I got an infection which was resistant to antibiotics. The whole thing was a mess. Not one of our Courtney-Briggs's most successful efforts. Anyway I felt like death. One night I was in ghastly pain and couldn't sleep and I felt absolutely sure I wouldn't see the morning. I was terrified. It was sheer funk. Talk about the fear of death! I

403

knew what it meant that night. Then Brumfett came round. She was looking after me herself; she wouldn't let the students do a thing for me when she was on duty. I said to her: 'I'm not going to die, am I?' She looked down at me. She didn't tell me not to be a fool or give me any of the usual comforting lies. She just said in that gruff voice of hers: 'Not if I can help it you aren't.' And immediately the panic stopped. I knew that if Brumfett was fighting on my side I'd win through. It sounds a bit daft and sentimental put like that, but that's what I thought. She's like that with all the really sick patients. Talk about confidence! Brumfett makes you feel that she'd drag you back from the edge of the grave by sheer will-power, even if all the devils in hell were tugging the other way; which in my case they probably were. They don't make them like that any more."

Dalgliesh made appropriately assenting noises and paused briefly before picking up the references to Mr. Courtney-Briggs. He asked rather naïvely whether many of the surgeon's operations went so spectacularly wrong. Sister Gearing laughed:

"Lord, no! Courtney-Briggs's operations usually go the way he wants. That's not to say they go the way the patient would choose if he knew the whole of it. C.B. is what they call a heroic surgeon. If you ask me, most of the heroism has to be shown by the patients. But he does an extraordinary good job of work. He's one of the last remaining great general surgeons. You know, take anything on, the more hopeless the better. I suppose a surgeon is rather like a lawyer. There's no glory to be had in getting someone off if he's obviously innocent. The greater the guilt the greater the glory."

"What is Mrs. Courtney-Briggs like? I presume he's married. Does she show herself at the hospital?"

"Not very often, although she's supposed to be a member of the League of Friends. She gave the prizes away last year when the Princess couldn't come at the last moment. Blonde, very smart. Younger than C.B. but beginning to wear a bit now. Why do you ask? You don't suspect Muriel Courtney-Briggs surely? She wasn't even in the hospital the night Fallon died. Probably tucked up in bed in their very nice little place near Selborne. And she certainly hadn't any motive for killing poor Pearce."

So she did have a motive for getting rid of Fallon. Mr. Courtney-Briggs's liaison had probably been more noticed than he had realized. Dalgliesh wasn't surprised that Sister Gearing should know about it. Her sharp nose would be adept at smelling out sexual scandal.

He said: "I wondered if she were jealous."

Sister Gearing, unaware of what she had told, rambled happily on.

"I don't suppose she knew. Wives don't usually. Anyway, C.B. wasn't going to break up his marriage to wed Fallon. Not him! Mrs. C.B. has plenty of money of her own. She's the only child of Price of Price and Maxwell, the building firm—and what with C.B.'s earnings and Daddy's ill-gotten gains, they're very comfortable. I don't think Muriel worries much what he does as long as he behaves himself properly to her and the money keeps rolling in. I know I wouldn't. Besides, if rumour's correct, our Muriel doesn't exactly qualify for the League of Purity."

"Anyone here?" asked Dalgliesh.

"Oh no, nothing like that. It's just that she goes around with quite a smart set. She usually gets her picture in every third issue of the social glossies. And they're in with the theatrical crowd too. C.B. had a brother who was an actor, Peter Courtney. He hanged himself about three years ago. You must have read about it."

Dalgliesh's job gave him few opportunities to see a play and theatre going was one of the pleasures he missed most. He had seen Peter Courtney act only once but it had been a performance not easily forgotten. He had been a very young Macbeth, as introspective and sensitive as Hamlet, in thrall sexually to a much older wife, and whose physical courage was compounded of violence and hysteria. It had been a perverse but interesting interpretation, and it had very nearly succeeded. Thinking of the performance now, Dalgliesh imagined that he could detect a likeness between the brothers, something to do with the set of the eyes perhaps. But Peter must have been the younger by nearly twenty years. He wished he knew what the two men, so widely separated in age and talent, had made of each other.

Suddenly and irrelevantly Dalgliesh asked:

"How did Pearce and Fallon get on together?"

"They didn't. Fallon despised Pearce. I don't mean she hated her or would have harmed her; she just despised her."

"Was there any particular reason?"

"Pearce took it upon herself to tell Matron about Fallon's little tipple of whisky at nights. Self-righteous little beast. Oh, I know she's dead and I ought not to have said that. But really, Pearce could be insufferably self-righteous. Apparently what happened was that Diane Harper—she's left the training school now—had a bad cold about a fortnight before the set came into the block, and Fallon fixed her a hot whisky and lemon. Pearce could smell the stuff half-way along the corridor and concluded that Fallon was now attempting to seduce her juniors with the demon drink. So she appeared in the utility room—they were in the main nurses' home then, of course—in her dressing-gown, sniffing the air like an avenging angel, and threatened to report Fallon to Matron unless she promised more or less on her knees never to touch the stuff again. Fallon told her where to go and what to do with herself when she got there. She had a picturesque turn of phrase when roused, had Fallon. Nurse Dakers burst into tears, Harper lost her temper and the general noise brought the House Sister on to the scene. Pearce reported it to Matron all right, but no one knows with what result, except that Fallon started keeping her whisky in her own room. But the whole thing caused a great deal of feeling in the third year. Fallon was never popular with the set, she was too reserved and sarcastic. But they liked Pearce a damn sight less."

"And did Pearce dislike Fallon?"

"Well, it's difficult to say. Pearce never seemed to concern herself with what other people thought of her. She was an odd girl, pretty insensitive too. For example, she might disapprove of Fallon and her whisky-drinking but that didn't prevent her from borrowing Fallon's library ticket."

"When did this happen?"

Dalgliesh leaned across and replaced his teacup on the tray. His voice was level, unconcerned. But he felt again that spring of excitement and anticipation, the intuitive sense that something important had been said. It was more than a hunch; it was, as

always, a certainty. It might happen several times during a case if he were lucky, or not at all. He couldn't will it to happen and he was afraid to examine its roots too closely since he suspected that it was a plant easily withered by logic.

"Just before she came into block, I think. It must have been the week before Pearce died. The Thursday, I think. Anyway, they hadn't yet moved into Nightingale House. It was just after supper time in the main dining-room. Fallon and Pearce were walking out of the door together and I was just behind them with Goodale. Then Fallon turned to Pearce and said: 'Here's the library token I promised you. I'd better give it to you now as I don't suppose we'll see each other in the morning. You'd better take the reader's ticket too, or they may not let you have the book.' Pearce mumbled something and grabbed the token rather ungraciously I thought, and that was that. Why? It isn't important, is it?"

"I can't think why it should be," said Dalgliesh.

VIII

He sat through the next fifteen minutes in exemplary patience. Sister Gearing couldn't have guessed from his courteous attention to her chattering and the leisurely way in which he drank his third and last cup of tea, that every moment was now grudged. When the meal was over, he carried the tray for her into the small Sisters' kitchen at the end of the corridor while she fretted at his heels, bleating her protests. Then he said, "Thank you," and left.

He went at once to the cell-like bedroom which still held nearly all the possessions Nurse Pearce had owned at the John Carpendar. It took him a moment to select the correct key from the heavy bunch in his pocket. The room had been locked after her death and was still locked. He went in, switching on the light. The bed was stripped and the whole room was very tidy and clean as if it, too, had been laid out for burial. The curtains were drawn back so that, from outside, the room would look no different from any other. The window was open but the air held a faint tang of disinfectant as if someone had tried to obliterate the memory of Pearce's death by a ritual purification.

He had no need to refresh his memory. The detritus of this particular life was pathetically meagre. But he went through her leavings again, turning them in careful hands as if the feel of cloth and leather could transmit their own clues. It didn't take long. Nothing had altered since his first inspection. The hospital wardrobe, identical to that in Nurse Fallon's room, was more than adequate for the few woollen dresses, unexciting in colour and design, which, under his questing hands, swung from their padded hangers and gave out a faint smell of cleaning fluid and mothballs. The thick winter coat in fawn was of good quality but obviously old. He sought once more in the pockets. There was nothing except the handkerchief which had been there on his first examination, a crumpled ball of white cotton smelling of sour breath.

He moved to the chest of drawers. Here again the space provided had been more than sufficient. The two top drawers were filled with underclothes, strong sensible vests and knickers, comfortably warm no doubt for an English winter but with no concessions to glamour or fashion. The drawers were lined with newspaper. The sheets had been taken out once already, but he ran his hand under them and felt nothing but the gritty surface of bare unpolished wood. The remaining three drawers held skirts, jumpers and cardigans; a leather handbag, carefully wrapped in tissue paper; a pair of best shoes in a string bag; an embroidered handkerchief sachet with a dozen handkerchiefs carefully folded; an assortment of scarves; three pairs of identical nylon stockings still in their wrappers.

He turned again to the bedside locker and the small shelf fixed above it. The locker held a bedside lamp, a small alarm clock in a leather case which had long since run down, a packet of paper handkerchiefs with one crumpled tissue half-pulled through the slit, and an empty water carafe. There was also a leather-bound Bible and a writing-case. Dalgliesh opened the Bible at the flyleaf and read again the inscription in careful copper plate. "Awarded to Heather Pearce for attendance and diligence. St. Mark's Sunday School." Diligence. An unfashionable, intimidating word, but one, he felt, of which Nurse Pearce would have approved.

He opened the writing-case, but with little hope of finding what

408

he sought. Nothing had changed since his first examination. Here still was the half-finished letter to her grandmother, a dull recital of the week's doings written as impersonally as a ward report, and a quarto-sized envelope, posted to her on the day of her death and obviously slipped into the writing-case by someone who, having opened it, couldn't think of what else to do with it. It was an illustrated brochure on the work of a home in Suffolk for German war refugees apparently sent in the hope of a donation.

He turned his attention to the small collection of books on the wall shelf. He had seen them before. Then, as now, he was struck by the conventionality of her choice and by the meagreness of this personal library. A school prize for needlework. *Lamb's Tales from Shakespeare*. Dalgliesh had never believed that any child read them and there was no evidence that Nurse Pearce had done so. There were two travel books, *In the Steps of St. Paul* and *In the Steps of the Master*. In both the girl had carefully inscribed her name. There was a well-known but out-of-date edition of a nursing textbook. The date on the flyleaf was nearly four years old. He wondered whether she had bought it in anticipation of her training, only to find that its advice on applying leeches and administering enemas had become out of date. There was a copy of Palgrave's *Golden Treasury*, also a school prize, but this time inappropriately for deportment. This, too, showed little sign of having been read. Lastly there were three paper-backs—novels by a popular woman writer, each advertised as "The Book of the Film"—and a fictional and highly sentimental account of the wanderings across Europe of a lost dog and cat which Dalgliesh remembered had been a bestseller some five years previously. This was inscribed, "To Heather, with love from Auntie Edie, Christmas 1964." The whole collection told him little about the dead girl, except that her reading had apparently been as restricted as her life. And nowhere he found what he was seeking.

He didn't go again to look in Nurse Fallon's room. The scene-of-crime officer had searched every inch of it, and he himself could have described the room in minute detail and given an accurate inventory of all its contents. Wherever the library ticket and the token were, he could be sure that they weren't there. Instead he

ran lightly up the wide staircase to the floor above where he had noticed a wall-mounted telephone when carrying Sister Gearing's tea tray to the utility room. A card listing the internal extensions hung beside it and, after a moment's thought, he rang the nurses' sitting-room. Maureen Burt answered. Yes, Nurse Goodale was still there. Almost immediately Dalgliesh heard her voice and he asked her to come up to see him in Nurse Pearce's room.

She came so promptly that he had hardly reached the door before he saw the self-assured, uniformed figure at the top of the stairs. He stood aside and she moved into the room before him and silently surveyed the stripped bed, the silent bedside clock, the closed Bible, letting her gaze rest briefly on each object with gentle un-inquisitive interest. Dalgliesh moved to the window and, both standing, they regarded each other wordlessly across the bed. Then he said:

"I'm told that Nurse Fallon lent a library ticket to Nurse Pearce sometime during the week before she died. You were leaving the dining-room with Sister Gearing at the time. Can you remember what happened?"

Nurse Goodale was not given to showing surprise.

"Yes, I think so. Fallon had told me earlier that day that Pearce wanted to visit one of the London libraries and had asked to borrow her reader's ticket and the token. Fallon was a member of the Westminster library. They've got a number of branches in the City but you aren't really supposed to belong unless you either live or work in Westminster. Fallon had a flat in London before she became a student here and had kept her reader's card and token. It's an excellent library, much better than we've got here, and it's useful to be able to borrow books. I think Sister Rolfe is a member too. Fallon took her reader's ticket and one of the tokens across to lunch and handed them to Pearce as we were leaving the dining-room."

"Did Nurse Pearce say why she wanted them?"

"Not to me. She may have told Fallon. I don't know. Any of us could borrow one of Fallon's tokens if we wanted to. Fallon didn't require an explanation."

"What precisely are these tokens like?"

410

"They're small oblongs of pale blue plastic with the City Arms stamped on them. The library usually gives four to every reader and you hand one in every time you take out a book, but Jo only had three. She may have lost the fourth. There's also the reader's ticket. That's the usual small piece of cardboard with the name, address and date of expiry. Sometimes the assistant asks to see the reader's ticket and I suppose that's why Jo handed it over with the token."

"Do you know where the other two are?"

"Yes, in my room. I borrowed them about a fortnight ago when I went up to town with my fiancé to attend a special service in the Abbey. I thought we might have time to visit the Great Smith Street branch to see whether they had the new Iris Murdoch. However, we met some friends from Mark's theological college after the service and never got to the library. I meant to return the tokens to Jo but I slipped them in my writing-case and forgot about them. She didn't remind me. I can show them to you if it would be helpful."

"I think it would. Did Heather Pearce use her token, do you know?"

"Well, I assume she did. I saw her waiting for the Green Line bus to town that afternoon. We were both off duty so it must have been the Thursday. I imagine that she had it in mind to visit the library."

She looked puzzled.

"Somehow I feel quite sure that she did take out a library book but I can't think why I should be so certain."

"Can't you? Think very hard."

Nurse Goodale stood silently, her hands folded composedly as if in prayer over the white stiffness of her apron. He did not hurry her. She gazed fixedly ahead then turned her eyes to the bed and said quietly:

"I know now. I saw her reading a library book. It was the night when Jo was taken ill, the night before Pearce herself died. I went into her bedroom just after half past eleven to ask her to go and look after Jo while I fetched Sister. She was sitting up in bed with her hair in two plaits and she was reading. I remember now. It was a large book, bound in a dark colour, dark blue I think, and with a

reference number stamped in gold at the foot of the spine. It looked an old and rather heavy book. I don't think it was fiction. She was holding it propped up against her knees I remember. When I appeared she closed it quickly and slipped it under her pillow. It was a strange thing to do but it didn't mean anything to me at the time. Pearce was always oddly secretive. Besides, I was too concerned about Jo. But I remember it now."

She stood again in silence for a few moments. Dalgliesh waited. Then she said quietly:

"I know what's worrying you. Where's that book now? It wasn't among her things when Sister Rolfe and I tidied her room and made a list of her belongings after her death. The police were with us and we didn't find a book anything like it. And what happened to the ticket? It wasn't among Fallon's things either."

Dalgliesh asked:

"What exactly happened that night? You said you went in to Nurse Fallon shortly after eleven thirty. I thought she didn't go to bed before midnight."

"She did that night. I suppose it was because she wasn't feeling well and hoped that an early bed would put her right. She didn't tell anyone she was ill. Jo wouldn't. And I didn't go in to her. She came into me. Shortly after eleven thirty she woke me up. She looked ghastly. She was obviously in a high fever and she could hardly stand. I helped her back to her bed, went in to ask Pearce to stay with her, and then rang Sister Rolfe. She's generally responsible for us when we're in Nightingale House. Sister came to look at Jo and then telephoned the private wing and asked for an ambulance to come over for her. Then she rang Sister Brumfett to let her know what had happened. Sister Brumfett likes to know what's happening on her ward even when she's off duty. She wouldn't have been pleased to arrive in the hospital next morning and find that Jo had been warded without her being told. She came down to have a look at Jo but didn't go over in the ambulance with her. It wasn't really necessary."

"Who did accompany her?"

"I did. Sister Rolfe and Sister Brumfett went back to their rooms and Pearce returned to hers."

So the book could hardly have been removed that night, thought Dalgliesh. Pearce would certainly have noticed its absence. Even if she had decided not to continue reading it, she would hardly settle to sleep with a heavy book under her pillow. So the probability was that someone had taken it after her death. One thing was certain. A particular book had been in her possession late on the night before she died yet was not in her room when the police, Miss Rolfe and Nurse Goodale examined it for the first time at about ten past ten the next morning. Whether or not that book had come from Westminster library, it was missing, and if the book wasn't from the library, then what had happened to the token and the reader's ticket? Neither was among her things. And if she had decided not to use them and handed them back to Fallon, why weren't they among Fallon's possessions?

He asked Nurse Goodale what had happened immediately after Nurse Pearce's death.

"Matron sent us students up to her sitting-room and asked us to wait there. Sister Gearing joined us after about half an hour and then some coffee came and we drank that. We stayed there together talking and trying to read until Inspector Bailey and Matron arrived. That must have been about eleven o'clock, perhaps a little earlier."

"And were you all together in that room for the whole of that time?"

"Not all the time. I went out to the library to fetch a book I wanted and was away about three minutes. Nurse Dakers left the room too. I'm not sure why but I think she muttered something about going to the lavatory. Otherwise, as far as I can remember, we all stayed together. Miss Beale, the G.N.C. Inspector, was with us."

She paused.

"You think that this missing library book has something to do with Pearce's death, don't you? You think it's important."

"I think that it may be. That's why I want you to say nothing about our conversation."

"Of course, if that's what you want." She paused.

"But couldn't I try to find out what has happened to the book?

I could ask the other students quite casually if they had the ticket and token. I could pretend that I wanted to use them."

Dalgliesh smiled: "Leave the detecting to me. I'd much prefer you to say nothing."

He saw no reason to suggest to her that in a murder investigation too much knowledge could be dangerous. She was a sensible girl. She would think it out for herself soon enough. Taking his silence for dismissal she turned to go. When she reached the door she hesitated and turned:

"Superintendent Dalgliesh, forgive me if I'm interfering. I can't believe that Pearce was murdered. But if she was, then surely the library book could have been taken from her room any time after five to nine when Pearce went into the demo room. The murderer would know that she wouldn't come out of that room alive and that it would be safe for him, or her, to remove it. If the book were taken after Pearce's death it could have been taken by anyone and for a perfectly innocent reason. But if it were taken before she died then it was taken by her killer. That would be true even if the book itself had nothing to do with the reason why she was killed. And Pearce's question to us all about something missing from her room suggests that the book was taken before she died. And why should the murderer bother to remove it if it wasn't in some way connected with the crime?"

"Exactly," said Dalgliesh. "You're a very intelligent young woman."

For the first time he saw Nurse Goodale disconcerted. She blushed, looking at once as pink and pretty as a young bride, then smiled at him, turned quickly and was gone. Dalgliesh, intrigued by the metamorphosis, decided that the local vicar had shown much sense and discernment in choosing his wife. What the parochial church council would make of her uncompromising intelligence was another matter. And he hoped that he wouldn't have to arrest her for murder before they had a chance to make up their minds.

He followed her into the corridor. As usual it was gloomily obscure, lit only by the two bulbs high in a cluster of entwined brass. He had reached the top of the staircase when instinct made him pause and then retrace his steps. Switching on his torch he

bent low and moved the beam slowly over the surface of sand in the two fire buckets. The nearer one was caked and grey with dust; it had obviously not been disturbed since it was filled. But the surface of the second one bore a fresher look. Dalgliesh put on his thin cotton searching gloves, fetched from Nurse Pearce's bedroom a sheet of newspaper from one of the drawers, spread it on the corridor floor and slowly tipped out the sand in a rising pyramid. He found no hidden library ticket. But there tumbled out a squat, screw-topped tin, with a stained label. Dalgliesh brushed off the grains of sand to reveal the black print of a skull and the word POISON in capitals. Underneath were the words: "Plant Spray. Death to Insects, Harmless to Plants. Use carefully in accordance with instructions."

He did not need to read the instructions to know what he had found. This stuff was almost pure nicotine. The poison which had killed Nurse Fallon was at last in his hands.

Chapter Six

Long Day's Ending

I

Five minutes later Dalgliesh, having spoken to the forensic science laboratory director and to Sir Miles Honeyman, looked up at a sulkily defensive Sergeant Masterson.

"I'm beginning to see why the Force is so keen on training civilian searchers. I told the scene-of-crime officer to stick to the bedroom, that we'd see to the rest of the house. I thought for some reason that policemen could use their eyes."

Sergeant Masterson, the more furious because he knew the rebuke to be justified, controlled himself with difficulty. He found any criticism difficult to take; from Dalgliesh it was almost impossible. He stiffened to attention like an old soldier on a charge, knowing full well that Dalgliesh would be exasperated rather than mollified by this punctilio, and contrived to sound at the same time both aggrieved and contrite.

"Greeson is a good searcher. I haven't known Greeson miss anything before. He can use his eyes all right, sir."

"Greeson has excellent eyesight. The trouble is that there's no connection between his eyes and his brain. And that's where you come in. The damage is done now. There's no point in holding a post mortem. We don't know whether this tin was in the bucket or not when Fallon's body was discovered this morning. But at least we've found it now. The laboratory has the viscera by the way. Sir Miles called in with it about an hour ago. They're already putting some of the stuff through the gas chromatograph. Now that they know what they're looking for it should speed things. We'd better get this tin off to them as soon as possible. But we'll have a look at it first."

416

He went over to his murder bag for the finger-print powder, insufflator and lens. The squat little tin became sooty under his careful hands. But there were no prints, only a few amorphous smudges on the faded label.

"Right," he said. "Find the three Sisters, will you Sergeant? They're the ones most likely to know where this tin came from. They live here. Sister Gearing is in her sitting-room. The others should be somewhere around. And if Sister Brumfett is still on her ward she'll have to leave it. Anyone who dies in the next hour must do so without her assistance."

"Do you want to see them separately or together?"

"Either. It doesn't matter. Just get them. Gearing's the one most likely to help. She looks after the flowers."

Sister Gearing arrived first. She came in jauntily, her face perked with curiosity and flushed with the lingering euphoria of a successful hostess. Then her eyes lit on the tin. The transformation was so immediate and startling that it was almost comic. She gasped, "Oh, no!", shot her hand to her mouth and sank into the chair opposite Dalgliesh, deadly pale.

"Where did you. . . ? Oh my God! You're not telling me that Fallon took nicotine?"

"Took, or was given. You recognize this tin, Sister?"

Sister Gearing's voice was almost inaudible.

"Of course. It's my . . . isn't it the tin of rose spray? Where did you find it?"

"Somewhere about the place. Where and when did you see it last?"

"It's kept in that white cupboard under the shelf in the conservatory, just to the left of the door. All my gardening stuff is there. I can't remember when I saw it last."

She was on the edge of tears; happy confidence completely dissolved.

"Honestly, it's just too awful! It's frightful! I feel dreadful about it. I really do. But how was I to tell that Fallon would know the stuff was there and use it? I didn't even remember about it myself. If I had, I'd have gone to check that it was still there. I suppose there's no doubt about it? She did die of nicotine poisoning?"

"There's a great deal of doubt until we get the toxicology report. But taking the common-sense view, it looks as if this stuff killed her. You bought it when?"

"Honestly, I can't remember. Sometime early last summer, just before the roses were due. One of the other Sisters might remember. I'm responsible for most of the plants in the conservatory here. At least, I'm not really responsible; it's never been an official arrangement. But I like flowers and there's no one else to bother so I do what I can. I was trying to establish a small rose bed outside the dining-room, too, and I needed the stuff to kill pests. I bought it from Bloxham's Nurseries on the Winchester Road. Look, you can see the address stamped on the label. And I kept it with my other gardening things, gloves and string and the watering cans and trowels and so on, in the corner cupboard in the conservatory."

"Can you remember when you last saw it?"

"Not really. But I went to the cupboard for my gloves last Saturday morning. We had a special service at the chapel on Sunday and I wanted to do the flowers. I thought I might be able to find some interesting boughs, bits of autumn foliage or seed pods in the garden to help the decoration. I don't remember seeing the tin there on Saturday but I think I might have noticed if it were actually missing. But I'm not sure. I haven't used it for months."

"Who else knew that it was there?"

"Well, anyone could have known. I mean, the cupboard isn't locked and there was nothing to stop people looking inside. I suppose I ought to have locked it but one doesn't expect . . . I mean if people are going to kill themselves they'll find a way somehow. I feel absolutely awful but I won't be made to feel responsible. I won't! It isn't fair! She could have used anything. Anything!"

"Who could?"

"Well, Fallon. If Fallon did kill herself. Oh, I don't know what I'm saying."

"Did Nurse Fallon know about the nicotine?"

"Not unless she looked in the cupboard and found it. The only people I can say for certain who did know are Brumfett and Rolfe. I remember that they were sitting in the conservatory when I put the tin into the cupboard. I held it up and said something daft

about having enough poison there to kill the lot of them, and Brumfett told me that I ought to lock it up."

"But you didn't?"

"Well, I put it straight away in the cupboard. There isn't a lock
so I couldn't do anything about it. Anyway, the tin's labelled
clearly enough. Anyone can see that it's poison. And one doesn't
expect people to kill themselves. Besides, why the nicotine? Nurses
have plenty of opportunity to get hold of drugs. It's not fair to
blame me. After all, the disinfectant which killed Pearce was just
as lethal. No one complained because that was left in the lavatory.
You can't run a nurse training school like a psychiatric unit. I'm
not going to be blamed. People here are supposed to be sane, not
homicidal maniacs. I won't be made to feel guilty. I won't!"

"If you didn't use the stuff on Nurse Fallon there's no reason
why you should feel guilty. Did Sister Rolfe say anything when
you brought in the tin?"

"I don't think so. Just looked up from her book. But I can't
really remember. I can't even tell you exactly when it was. But it
was a warm sunny day. I do remember that. I think it was probably
in late May or early June. Rolfe may remember, and Brumfett
certainly will."

"We'll ask them. In the meantime I'd better have a look at this
cupboard."

He left the tin of nicotine for Masterson to pack for despatch to
the laboratory, told him to send Sister Brumfett and Sister Rolfe
to the conservatory, and followed Sister Gearing out of the room.
She led him down to the ground floor, still muttering her indignant
protests. They passed into the empty dining-room. The discovery
that the door into the conservatory was locked shook Sister Gearing
from her mood of frightened resentment.

"Damn! I'd forgotten. Matron thought we'd better keep it
locked after dark because some of the glass isn't too secure. You
remember that a pane fell out during the storm? She's afraid someone could get in this way. Usually we don't bother to lock it until
we do the final locking up last thing at night. The key will be on
the board in Rolfe's office. Wait here. I won't be a jiffy."

She returned almost immediately and fitted the large old-

fashioned key into the lock. They passed into the warm fungoid smell of the conservatory. Sister Gearing unerringly reached for the switch, and the two long tubes of fluorescent light, suspended from the high concave ceiling, flickered erratically, then burst into brilliance, revealing the arboreal jungle in all its lushness. The conservatory was a remarkable sight. Dalgliesh had thought so on his first tour of the house, but now, dazzled by the fierce glare on leaves and glass, he blinked in wonder. Around him a minor forest of greenery twined, sprouted, crept and burst in menacing profusion while, outside, its pale reflection hung in the evening air and stretched, motionless and insubstantial, into a green infinity.

Some of the plants looked as if they had flourished in the conservatory since the day it was built. They sprang like mature if miniature palm trees from ornate urns, spreading a canopy of glistening leaves under the glass. Others, more exotic, sprouted bursts of foliage from their scarred and dentate stalks or, like giant cacti, lifted rubber lips, spongy and obscene, to suck the humid air. Between them the ferns sprayed a green shadow, their fragile fronds moving in the draught from the door. Around the sides of the great room were white shelves on which stood pots of the more domestic and agreeable plants which were Sister Gearing's care— red, pink and white chrysanthemums, and African violets. The conservatory should have evoked a tender scene of Victorian domesticity, of fluttering fans and whispered confidences behind the palms. But for Dalgliesh, no corner of Nightingale House was free of the oppressive atmosphere of evil; the very plants seemed to be sucking their manna from a tainted air.

Mavis Gearing went straight over to a low, four-foot-long cupboard in white-painted wood, fitted underneath the wall shelf to the left of the door and hardly visible behind the curtain of waving ferns. It had one inadequate door fitted with a small knob and no lock. Together they crouched to look in it. Although the overhead fluorescent lights were unpleasantly garish, the recesses of the cupboard were dim and their view obstructed by the shadow of their heads. Dalgliesh switched on his torch. Its beam revealed the usual paraphernalia of the indoor gardener. He made a mental inventory. There were balls of green twine, a couple of watering cans, a small

spray, packets of seed, some opened and half-used with their tops pressed back, a small plastic bag of potting compost and one of fertilizer, about two dozen flower pots of varying sizes, a small stack of seed trays, pruning shears, a trowel and small fork, a disorderly pile of seedmen's catalogues, three clothbound books on gardening, their covers stained and dirty, an assortment of flower vases, and bundles of tangled wire.

Mavis Gearing pointed to a space in the far corner.

"That's where it was. I put it well back. It couldn't have been a temptation to anyone. You wouldn't even notice it, just opening the door. It was quite hidden really. Look, that's the space—you can see where it was."

She spoke with urgent self-justification, as if the empty space acquitted her of all responsibility. Then her voice changed. It dropped a tone and became huskily pleading like an amateur actress playing a seduction scene.

"I know it looks bad. First, I was in charge of the demonstration when Pearce died. And now this. But I haven't touched the stuff since I used it last summer. I swear I haven't! I know some of them won't believe me. They'll be glad—yes glad—and relieved if suspicion falls on me and Len. It'll let them out. Besides they're jealous. They've always been jealous. It's because I've got a man and they haven't. But you believe me don't you? You've got to believe me!"

It was pathetic and humiliating. She pressed her shoulder against his, as they knelt huddled together in a ridiculous parody of prayer. He could feel her breath against his cheek. Her right hand, the fingers twitching nervously, crept across the floor towards his hand.

Then her mood broke. They heard Sister Rolfe's cold voice from the door.

"The Sergeant told me to meet you here. Am I interrupting anything?"

Dalgliesh felt the pressure on his shoulder immediately released, and Sister Gearing scrambled gracelessly to her feet. He got up more slowly. He neither felt nor looked embarrassed, but he was not sorry that Miss Rolfe had chosen that moment to appear.

Sister Gearing broke into explanation:

"It's the rose spray. That stuff containing nicotine. Fallon must have taken it. I feel absolutely ghastly about it, but how was I to know? The Superintendent has found the tin."

She turned to Dalgliesh.

"You didn't say where?"

"No," Dalgliesh said. "I didn't say where." He spoke to Miss Rolfe.

"Did you know the stuff was kept in this cupboard?"

"Yes, I saw Gearing put it there. Some time last summer wasn't it?"

"You didn't mention this to me."

"I didn't think of it until now. It never occurred to me that Fallon might have taken nicotine. And, presumably, we don't yet know that she did."

Dalgliesh said: "Not until we get the toxicology report."

"And even then, Superintendent, can you be sure that the drug came from this tin? There are other sources of nicotine at the hospital surely? This could be a blind."

"Of course, although it seems to me highly unlikely. But the forensic science laboratory should be able to tell us that. This nicotine is mixed with a proportion of concentrated detergent. It will be identifiable by gas chromatography."

She shrugged.

"Well, that should settle it then."

Mavis Gearing cried out: "What do you mean, other sources of supply? Who are you getting at? Nicotine isn't kept in the pharmacy, as far as I know. And anyway Len had left Nightingale House before Fallon died."

"I wasn't accusing Leonard Morris. But he was on the spot when both of them died, remember, and he was here in this room when you put the nicotine in the cupboard. He's a suspect like the rest of us."

"Was Mr. Morris with you when you bought the nicotine?"

"Well, he was as a matter of fact. I'd forgotten it or I would have told you. We'd been out together that afternoon and he came back here to tea."

She turned angrily to Sister Rolfe.

"It's nothing to do with Len, I tell you! He hardly knew Pearce or Fallon. Pearce hadn't anything on Len."

Hilda Rolfe said calmly: "I wasn't aware that she had anything on anyone. I don't know whether you're trying to put ideas into Mr. Dalgliesh's head, but you're certainly putting them into mine."

Sister Gearing's face disintegrated into misery. Moaning, she jerked her head from side to side as if desperately seeking help or asylum. Her face, sickly and surrealist, was suffused with the green light of the conservatory.

Sister Rolfe gave Dalgliesh one sharp look, then ignoring him, moved over to her colleague and said with unexpected gentleness:

"Look Gearing, I'm sorry. Of course I'm not accusing Leonard Morris or you. But the fact that he was here would have come out anyway. Don't let the police fluster you. It's how they work. I don't suppose the Superintendent cares a damn whether you or I or Brumfett killed Pearce and Fallon so long as he can prove someone did. Well, let him get on with it. Just answer his questions and keep calm. Why not get on with your job and let the police get on with theirs?"

Mavis Gearing wailed like a child seeking reassurance:

"But it's all so awful!"

"Of course it is! But it won't last for ever. And in the meantime, if you must confide in a man, find yourself a solicitor, a psychiatrist or a priest. At least you can be reasonably sure that they'll be on your side."

Mavis Gearing's worried eyes moved from Dalgliesh to Rolfe. She looked like a child hesitating to decide where her allegiance lay. Then the two women moved imperceptibly together and gazed at Dalgliesh, Sister Gearing in puzzled reproach and Sister Rolfe with the tight satisfied smile of a woman who has just brought off a successful piece of mischief.

II

At that moment Dalgliesh caught the sound of approaching foot-steps. Someone was moving across the dining-room. He turned to

the door, expecting to find that Sister Brumfett had at last come to be interviewed. The conservatory door opened but, instead of her squat figure, he saw a tall bare-headed man wearing a belted raincoat and with a gauze patch taped across his left eye. A peevish voice spoke from the doorway:

"What's happened to everyone? This place is like a morgue."

Before anyone could reply, Miss Gearing had darted forward and seized his arm. Dalgliesh saw with interest his frown and twitch of involuntary recoil.

"Len, what is it? You're hurt! You never told me! I thought it was your ulcer. You never said anything about hurting your head!"

"It was my ulcer. But this didn't help it."

He spoke directly to Dalgliesh:

"You must be Chief Superintendent Dalgliesh of New Scotland Yard. Miss Gearing told me that you wanted to see me. I'm on my way to my general practitioner's surgery but I'm at your disposal for half an hour."

But Sister Gearing was not to be diverted from her concern.

"But you never said anything about an accident! How did it happen? Why didn't you tell me about it when I rang?"

"Because we had other things to discuss and because I didn't want you to fuss."

He shook off her detaining arm and sat himself down in a wicker chair. The two women and Dalgliesh moved in close to him. There was a silence. Dalgliesh revised his unreasonably preconceived notions of Miss Gearing's lover. He should have looked ridiculous, sitting there in his cheap raincoat with his patched eye and bruised face and speaking in that grating sarcastic voice. But he was curiously impressive. Sister Rolfe had somehow conveyed the impression of a little man, nervous, ineffectual and easily intimidated. This man had force. It might be only the manifestation of pent-up nervous energy; it might be the obsessive resentment born of failure or unpopularity. But his was certainly not a comfortable or negligible personality.

Dalgliesh asked: "When did you learn that Josphine Fallon was dead?"

"When I rang my pharmacy office just after nine thirty this

424

morning to say that I wouldn't be in. My assistant told me. I suppose the news was all over the hospital by then."

"How did you react to the news?"

"React? I didn't react. I hardly knew the girl. I was surprised, I suppose. Two deaths in the same house and so close together in time; well, it's unusual to say the least of it. It's shocking really. You could say I was shocked."

He spoke like a successful politician condescending to express an attributable opinion to a cub reporter.

"But you didn't connect the two deaths?"

"Not at the time. My assistant just said that another Nightingale —we call the students Nightingales when they are in block—that another Nightingale student, Jo Fallon, had been found dead. I asked how and he said something about a heart attack following influenza. I thought it was a natural death. I suppose that's what everyone thought at first."

"When did you think otherwise?"

"I suppose when Miss Gearing rang me about an hour later to say that you were here."

So Sister Gearing had telephoned Morris at his home. She must have wanted to reach him urgently to have risked that. Was it perhaps to warn him, to agree their story? While Dalgliesh was wondering what excuse, if any, she had given to Mrs. Morris, the pharmacist answered the unspoken question.

"Miss Gearing doesn't usually ring me at home. She knows that I like to keep my professional and my private life absolutely separate. But she was naturally anxious about my health when she rang the laboratory after breakfast and was told that I wasn't in. I suffer from a duodenal ulcer."

"Your wife, no doubt, was able to reassure her."

He replied calmly but with a sharp glance at Sister Rolfe, who had moved to the periphery of the group:

"My wife takes the children to her mother's all day on Fridays."

As Mavis Gearing would no doubt have known. So they had, after all, had a chance to consult each other, to decide on their story. But if they were concocting an alibi, why fix it for midnight? Because they knew for the best or worse of reasons that Fallon had

425

died at that hour? Or because, knowing her habits, they judged that midnight was the most likely time? Only the killer, and perhaps not even he, could know precisely when Fallon had died. It could have been before midnight. It could have been as late as two thirty. Even Miles Honeyman with his thirty years' experience couldn't time the death precisely from clinical signs alone. The only certain thing was that Fallon was dead and that she had died almost immediately after drinking her whisky. But when exactly had that been? It was her usual habit to prepare her late night drink as soon as she went upstairs to bed. But no one admitted to having seen her after she left the nurses' sitting-room. Fallon could, just possibly, have been alive when Sister Brumfett and the Burt twins saw her light shining through the keyhole just after two a.m. And if she had been alive then what had she been doing between midnight and two o'clock? Dalgliesh had been concentrating on those people who had access to the school. But suppose Fallon had left Nightingale House that night, perhaps to keep an assignation. Or suppose she had deferred making her nightly drink of whisky and lemon because she was expecting a visitor. The front and back doors of Nightingale House had been found bolted in the morning, but Fallon could have let her visitor out any time during the night and bolted the door behind him.

But Mavis Gearing was still preoccupied with her lover's damaged head and bruised face.

"What happened to you, Len? You've got to tell me. Did you come off your bicycle?"

Sister Rolfe laughed unkindly. Leonard Morris bestowed on her a measured glance of intimidating contempt, then turned to Sister Gearing.

"If you must know Mavis, yes I did. It happened after I left you last night. There was one of the big elms down across the path and I cycled right into it."

Sister Rolfe spoke for the first time.

"Surely you could see it in the light of your bicycle lamp?"

"My bicycle lamp, Sister, not unreasonably, is fixed to shine on the road. I saw the tree trunk. What I didn't see in time was one of the high jutting boughs. I was lucky not to lose an eye."

Sister Gearing, predictably, gave an anguished yelp.

Dalgliesh asked: "What time did this happen?"

"I've just told you. Last night after I had left Nightingale House. Oh, I see! You're asking what time precisely? As it happens I can answer that. I came off my bicycle under the impact and was afraid that my watch had been broken. Fortunately it hadn't. The hands stood at twelve seventeen a.m. precisely."

"Wasn't there some warning—a white scarf—tied to the branch?"

"Of course not, Superintendent. If there had been I should hardly have ridden straight into it."

"If it were tied high up on a bough you might not have noticed it."

"It wasn't there to notice. After I'd picked up my bicycle and recovered a little from the shock I inspected the tree carefully. My first thought was that I might be able to shift it at least slightly and leave part of the road clear. That was obviously impossible. The job was going to need a tractor and tackle. But there was no scarf on any part of that tree at twelve seventeen a.m."

"Mr. Morris," said Dalgliesh, "I think it's time you and I had a little talk."

But Sister Brumfett was waiting for him outside the interview room. Before Dalgliesh could speak she said accusingly:

"I was summoned to see you in this room. I came promptly at some inconvenience to my ward. When I arrive I'm told that you're not in your room and will I please go down to the conservatory. I don't propose to chase around Nightingale House for you. If you want to see me I can spare you half an hour now."

"Miss Brumfett," said Dalgliesh, "you seem determined by your behaviour to give me the impression that you killed these girls. It's possible you did. I shall come to a conclusion about that as soon as I reasonably can. In the meantime, please curb your enthusiasm for antagonizing the police and wait until I can see you. That will be when I've finished talking to Mr. Morris. You can wait here outside the office or go to your own room, whichever suits you. But I shall want you in about thirty minutes and I, too, have no intention of chasing over the house to find you."

He had no idea how she would take this rebuke. Her reaction was surprising. The eyes behind the thick spectacles softened and twinkled. Her face broke into a momentary grin and she gave a satisfied little nod as if she had at least succeeded in provoking a particularly docile student into showing a flash of spirit.

"I'll wait here." She plonked herself down on the chair outside the office door then, nodded towards Morris.

"And I shouldn't let him do all the talking or you'll be lucky to be through in half an hour."

III

But the interview took less than thirty minutes. The first couple were spent by Morris in making himself comfortable. He took off his shabby raincoat, shaking it and smoothing down the folds as if it had somehow become contaminated in Nightingale House, then folded it with fussy precision over the back of his chair. Then he seated himself opposite Dalgliesh and took the initiative.

"Please don't fire questions at me, Superintendent. I don't like being interrogated. I prefer to tell my story in my own way. You needn't worry about it being accurate. I'd hardly be chief pharmacist of an important hospital if I hadn't the head for detail and a good memory for facts."

Dalgliesh said mildly: "Then could I have some facts please, starting perhaps with your movements last night."

Morris continued as if he hadn't heard this eminently reasonable request.

"Miss Gearing has given me the privilege of her friendship for the past six years. I've no doubt that certain people here, certain women living in Nightingale House, have placed their own interpretation on that friendship. That is to be expected. When you get a community of middle-aged spinsters living together you're bound to get sexual jealousy."

"Mr. Morris," said Dalgliesh gently. "I'm not here to investigate your relationship with Miss Gearing or hers with her colleagues. If those relationships have anything to do with the deaths of these

428

two girls, then tell me about them. Otherwise let's leave out the amateur psychology and get down to the material facts."

"My relationship with Miss Gearing is germane to your inquiry in that it has brought me into this house at about the time Nurse Pearce and Nurse Fallon died."

"All right. Then tell me about those two occasions."

"The first was the morning when Nurse Pearce died. You are, no doubt, aware of the details. Naturally I reported my visit to Inspector Bailey since he caused a notice to be appended to all the hospital notice-boards inquiring the names of people who had visited Nightingale House on the morning on which Nurse Pearce died. But I have no objection to repeating the information. I called in here on my way to the pharmacy to leave Miss Gearing a note. It was in fact a card, one of those 'good luck' cards which it is customary to send friends before some important event. I knew that Miss Gearing would have to take the first demonstration of the day, indeed the first demonstration of this school, as Sister Manning, who is Miss Rolfe's first assistant, is sick with flu. Miss Gearing was naturally nervous, particularly as the General Nursing Council Inspector was to be present. Unfortunately I missed the previous evening's post. I was anxious for her to get my card before she went into the demonstration so I decided to slip it into her cubby hole myself. I came to work especially early, arrived at Nightingale House shortly after eight, and left almost immediately. I saw no one. Presumably the staff and students were at breakfast. I certainly didn't enter the demonstration room. I wasn't particularly keen to draw attention to myself. I merely inserted the card in its envelope into Miss Gearing's cubby hole and withdrew. It was rather an amusing card. It showed two robins, the male bird forming the words 'good luck' in worms at the feet of the female. Miss Gearing may well have kept the card; she has a fancy for such trifles. No doubt she would show it to you on request. It would corroborate my story of what I was doing in Nightingale House."

Dalgliesh said gravely: "I have already seen the card. Did you know what the demonstration would be about?"

"I knew that it was on intra-gastric feeding but I didn't know

that Nurse Fallon had been taken ill in the night or who was to act the part of the patient."

"Have you any idea at all how the corrosive poison got into the drip?"

"If you would just let me take my own time. I was about to tell you. I have none. The most likely explanation is that someone was playing a stupid joke and didn't realize that the result would be fatal. That, or an accident. There are precedents. A new-born baby was killed in the maternity wing of a hospital—not happily one of ours—only three years ago when a bottle of disinfectant was mistaken for milk. I can't explain how the accident here could have occurred or who in Nightingale House could have been so ignorant and stupid as to think that the result of putting a corrosive poison in the milk feed would entertain anyone."

He paused as if defying Dalgliesh to interrupt with another question. Meeting only a bland interrogatory gaze, he went on:

"So much for Nurse Pearce's death. I can't help you further there. It's rather a different matter with Nurse Fallon."

"Something that happened last night; someone you saw?"

The irritation snapped out: "Nothing to do with last night, Superintendent, Miss Gearing has already told you about last night. We saw no one. We left her room immediately after twelve o'clock and went out down the back stairs through Miss Taylor's flat. I retrieved my bicycle from the bushes at the rear of the house —I see no reason why my visits here should be advertised to every mean-minded female in the neighbourhood—and we walked together to the first turn in the path. Then we paused to talk and I escorted Miss Gearing back to Nightingale House and watched her in through the back door. She had left it open. I finally rode off and, as I have told you, got to the fallen elm at twelve seventeen a.m. If anyone passed that way after me and fixed a white scarf to a branch, I can only say that I didn't see him. If he came by car it must have been parked at the other side of Nightingale House. I saw no car."

Another pause. Dalgliesh made no sign, but Masterson permitted himself a sigh of weary resignation as he rustled over a page of his note pad.

"No, Superintendent, the event which I am about to relate took

430

place last spring when this present set of students, including Nurse Fallon, were in their second-year block. As was customary, I gave them a lecture on poisons. At the end of my talk all the students except Nurse Fallon had gathered up their books and left. She came up to the desk and asked me for the name of a poison which could kill painlessly and instantaneously and which an ordinary person might be able to obtain. I thought it an unusual question but saw no reason why I should refuse to answer it. It never occurred to me for one moment that the question had any personal application and, in any case, it was information she could have obtained from any book in the hospital library on materia medica or forensic medicine."

Dalgliesh said: "And what exactly did you tell her, Mr. Morris?"

"I told her that one such poison was nicotine and that it could be obtained from an ordinary rose spray."

Truth or a lie? Who could tell? Dalgliesh fancied that he could usually detect lying in a suspect; but not this suspect. And if Morris stuck to his story, how could it ever be disproved? And if it were a lie, its purpose was plain—to suggest that Josephine Fallon had killed herself. And the obvious reason why he should wish to do that was to protect Sister Gearing. He loved her. This slightly ridiculous, pedantic man; that silly, flirtatious, ageing woman— they loved each other. And why not? Love wasn't the prerogative of the young and desirable. But it was a complication in any investigation—pitiable, tragic or ludicrous, as the case might be, but never negligible. Inspector Bailey, as he knew from the notes on the first crime, had never fully believed in the story of the greetings card. It was in his opinion a foolish and childish gesture for a grown man, and particularly out of character for Morris; therefore he distrusted it. But Dalgliesh thought differently. It was one with Morris's lonely, unromantic cycle rides to visit his mistress; the machine hidden ignominiously in the bushes behind Nightingale House; the slow walk together through the cold of a January midnight prolonging those last precious minutes; his clumsy but strangely dignified defence of the woman he loved. And this last statement, true or false, was inconvenient to say the least. If he stuck to it it would be a powerful argument for those who preferred to believe that Fallon

had died by her own hand. And he would stick to it. He looked at Dalgliesh now with the steadfast, exalted gaze of a prospective martyr, holding his adversary's eyes, daring him to disbelieve. Dalgliesh sighed:

"All right," he said. "We won't waste time in speculation. Let's go once again over the timing of your movements last night."

IV

Sister Brumfett, true to her promise, was waiting outside the door when Masterson let Leonard Morris out. But her previous mood of cheerful acquiescence had vanished and she settled herself down opposite Dalgliesh as if to do battle. Before that matriarchal glare he felt something of the inadequacy of a junior student nurse newly arrived on the private ward; and something stronger and horribly familiar. His mind traced the surprising fear unerringly to its source. Just so had the Matron of his prep. school once looked at him, producing in the homesick eight-year-old the same inadequacy, the same fear. And for one second he had to force himself to meet her gaze.

It was the first opportunity he had had to observe her closely and on her own. It was an unattractive and yet an ordinary face. The small shrewd eyes glared into his through steel spectacles, their bridge half embedded in the deep fleshy cleft above the mottled nose. Her iron grey hair was cut short, framing in ribbed waves the plump marsupial cheeks and the obstinate line of the jaw. The elegant gophered cap which on Mavis Gearing looked as delicate as a meringue of spun lace and which flattered even Hilda Rolfe's androgynous features was bound low on Sister Brumfett's brow like a pie frill circling a particularly unappetizing crust. Take that symbol of authority away and replace it by an undistinguished felt hat, cover the uniform with a shapeless fawn coat, and you would have the prototype of a middle-aged suburban housewife strutting through the supermarket, shapeless bag in hand, eyes shrewd for this week's bargain. Yet here, apparently, was one of the best ward Sisters John Carpendar had ever had. Here, more surprisingly, was Mary Taylor's chosen friend.

Before he could begin to question her, she said:

"Nurse Fallon committed suicide. First she killed Pearce and then herself. Fallon murdered Pearce. I happen to know that she did. So why don't you stop worrying Matron and let the work of the hospital go on? There's nothing you can do to help either of them now. They're both dead."

Spoken in that authoritative and disconcertingly evocative tone the statement had the force of a command. Dalgliesh's reply was unreasonably sharp. Damn the woman! He wouldn't be intimidated.

"If you know that for certain, you must have some proof. And anything you know ought to be told. I'm investigating murder, Sister, not the theft of a bedpan. You have a duty not to withhold evidence."

She laughed; a sharp, derisive hoot like an animal coughing.

"Evidence! You wouldn't call it evidence. But I know!"

"Did Nurse Fallon speak to you when she was being nursed on your ward? Was she delirious?"

It was no more than a guess. She snorted her derision.

"If she did, it wouldn't be my duty to tell you. What a patient lets out in delirium isn't gossip to be bandied about. Not on my ward anyway. It isn't evidence either. Just accept what I tell you and stop fussing. Fallon killed Pearce. Why do you think she came back to Nightingale House that morning, with a temperature of 103? Why do you think she refused to give the police a reason? Fallon killed Pearce. You men like to make things so complicated. But it's all so simple really. Fallon killed Pearce, and there's no doubt she had her reasons."

"There are no valid reasons for murder. And even if Fallon did kill Pearce, I doubt whether she killed herself. I've no doubt your colleagues have told you about the rose spray. Remember that Fallon hadn't been in Nightingale House since that tin of nicotine was placed in the conservatory cupboard. Her set haven't been in Nightingale House since the spring of last year and Sister Gearing bought the rose spray in the summer. Nurse Fallon was taken ill on the night that this block began and didn't return to Nightingale House until the evening before she died. How do you account for the fact that she knew where to find the nicotine?"

433

Sister Brumfett looked surprisingly disconcerted. There was a moment's silence and then she muttered something unintelligible. Dalgliesh waited. Then she said defensively:

"I don't know how she got hold of it. That's for you to discover. But it's obvious that she did."

"Did you know where the nicotine had been put?"

"No. I don't have anything to do with the garden or the conservatory. I like to get out of the hospital on my free days. I usually play golf with Matron or we go for a drive. We try to arrange our off duty together."

Her tone was smug with satisfaction. She made no attempt to hide her complacency. What was she trying to convey, he wondered. Was this reference to the Matron her way of telling him that she was teacher's pet, to be treated with deference?

He said: "Weren't you in the conservatory that evening last summer when Miss Gearing came in with the stuff?"

"I don't remember."

"I think you'd better try to remember, Sister. It shouldn't be difficult. Other people remember perfectly well."

"If they say I was there, I probably was."

"Miss Gearing says that she showed you all the bottle and made a facetious remark about being able to poison the whole school with a few drops. You told her not to be childish and to make sure the tin was locked away. Do you remember now?"

"It's the sort of silly remark Mavis Gearing would make and I daresay I did tell her to be careful. It's a pity she didn't take notice of me."

"You take these deaths very calmly, Sister."

"I take every death very calmly. If I didn't I couldn't do my job. Death is happening all the time in a hospital. It's probably happening now on my ward as it did this afternoon to one of my patients!"

She spoke with sudden and passionate protest, stiffening as if in outrage that the dread finger could touch anyone for whom she was responsible. Dalgliesh found the sudden change of mood disconcerting. It was as if this thickening, unattractive body housed the temperament of a *prima donna*, passionate and irrational. At one moment the eyes, small and unremarkable behind their thick

434

lenses, met his in dull resentment, the obstinate little mouth snapped out its grievances. And then, suddenly, there was this metamorphosis. She blazed at him, her face flaming with indignation so that it came fiercely alive. He had a glimpse of that fervent and possessive love with which she encompassed those in her care. Here was a woman, outwardly unremarkable, who had dedicated her life to a single aim with formidable determination. If something —or someone—got in the way of what she regarded as the greater good, how far would that determination carry her? She seemed to Dalgliesh a fundamentally unintelligent woman. But murder was frequently the last resort of the unintelligent. And were these murders, for all their complexity, the work of a clever woman? A bottle of disinfectant quickly seized; a tin of nicotine readily available. Didn't both these deaths speak of a sudden uncontrolled impulse, an unthinking reliance on the easiest means? Surely in a hospital there were more subtle methods of disposal?

The shrewd eyes were regarding him with watchful dislike. The whole interrogation was an outrage to her. It was hopeless to try to propitiate such a witness and he had no stomach to try. He said:

"I want to go through your movements on the morning Nurse Pearce died, and last night."

"I've already told Inspector Bailey about the morning Pearce died. And I've sent you a note."

"I know. Thank you for it. Now I want you to tell me yourself."

She made no further protest but recited the sequence of her movements and actions as if they were a railway time-table.

Her account of her movements on the morning of Heather Pearce's death agreed almost exactly with the written statement she had already given to Inspector Bailey. She described only her own actions, put forward no theories, gave no opinion. After that first revealing outburst she had apparently decided to stick to facts.

She had woken at six thirty on the Monday the twelfth of January, and had then joined the Matron for early morning tea which it was their habit to drink together in Miss Taylor's flat. She had left Matron at seven fifteen and had then bathed and dressed. She had stayed in her own room until about ten minutes to eight when she had collected her paper from the rack in the hall and had

gone in to breakfast. She had seen no one on the stairs or in the hall. Sister Gearing and Sister Rolfe had joined her in the dining-room and they had breakfasted together. She had finished her breakfast and had left the room first; she was unable to say precisely when but it was probably not later than twenty-past eight, had returned briefly to her sittingroom on the third floor, and had then walked over to the hospital where she had arrived on her ward shortly before nine o'clock. She had known about the General Nursing Council Inspection since, obviously, Matron had talked to her about it. She had known about the demonstration since details of the nurse training programme were on the hall notice-board. She had known about Josephine Fallon's illness since Sister Rolfe had telephoned her during the night. She had not, however, known that Nurse Pearce was to take Fallon's place. She agreed that she could have discovered this easily by a glance at the notice-board, but she had not troubled to look. There was no reason why she should be concerned. Taking an interest in the general nurse training programme was one thing, bothering to check on who was to act as the patient was quite another.

She had not known that Nurse Fallon had returned to Nightingale House that morning. Had she done so, she would have reprimanded the girl severely. By the time she had reached the ward Nurse Fallon was in her room and in bed. No one in the ward had noticed her absence. Apparently the Staff Nurse had thought she was in the bathroom or the lavatory. It was reprehensible of the Staff Nurse not to have checked, but the ward was particularly busy and one did not expect patients, particularly student nurses, to behave like idiots. Nurse Fallon had probably only left the ward for about twenty minutes. Her walk through the dark morning had apparently done her no harm. She had made a quick recovery from the influenza and there had been no complications. She had not seemed particularly depressed while she was in the ward, and if there was anything worrying her, she had not confided in Sister Brumfett. In Sister Brumfett's opinion, the girl had been perfectly well enough on discharge from the ward to rejoin her set in Nightingale House.

Next she went through her movements on the previous night, in the same dull, unemphatic voice. Matron had been in Amsterdam

at the International Conference so she had spent the evening alone watching television in the Sisters' sitting-room. She had gone to bed at ten p.m. and had been awakened at about quarter to twelve by Mr. Courtney-Briggs's telephone call. She had made her way across to the hospital by a short cut through the trees and had helped the student nurse on duty to prepare the bed for the patient's return. She had stayed with her patient until satisfied that the oxygen and drip were being satisfactorily administered and that his general condition was as good as could be expected. She had returned to Nightingale House shortly after two a.m. and on her way up to her room had seen Maureen Burt coming out of the lavatory. The other twin had appeared almost immediately and she had had a brief conversation with them. She had declined their offer to make her cocoa and had gone straight up to her room. Yes, there was a light shining through Fallon's keyhole at that time. She had not gone into Fallon's room and had no way of knowing whether the girl was alive or dead. She had slept well and had awoken just after seven o'clock when Sister Rolfe had come rushing in with the news that Fallon's body had been discovered. She hadn't seen Fallon since the girl was discharged from her ward after supper on the Tuesday.

At the end of the recital there was a silence, then Dalgliesh asked:

"Did you like Nurse Pearce, Sister? Or Nurse Fallon?"

"No. I didn't dislike them either. I don't believe in having personal relationships with the student nurses. Like and dislike don't come into it. They're either good nurses or they aren't."

"And were they good nurses?"

"Fallon was better than Pearce. She had more intelligence and more imagination. She wasn't an easy colleague but the patients liked her. Some people thought her callous but you wouldn't find a patient who said so. Pearce tried too hard. She went about looking like a young Florence Nightingale, or so she thought. Always thinking of the impression she was making. A silly girl fundamentally. But you could rely on her. She always did what was correct. Fallon did what was right. That takes instinct as well as training. Wait until you're dying, my good man. You'll know the difference."

So Josephine Fallon had been both intelligent and imaginative. He could believe it. But these were the last two qualities he would have expected Sister Brumfett to praise. He recalled the conversation at luncheon, her insistence on the need for unquestioning obedience. He said carefully:

"I'm surprised that you should rank imagination among the virtues of a student nurse. I thought that you valued absolute obedience above all. It's difficult to reconcile imagination, which is surely individual, even iconoclastic, with the submission to authority of the good subordinate. I'm sorry if I sound presumptuous. This conversation hasn't much to do with my business here, I know. But I'm curious."

It had a great deal to do with his business there; his curiosity wasn't irrelevant. But she wasn't to know that. She said gruffly:

"Obedience to rightful authority comes first. You're in a disciplined service; you shouldn't need telling. It's only when the obedience is automatic, when the discipline is accepted and even welcomed, that one learns the wisdom and courage that can safely step outside the rules when the moment comes. Imagination and intelligence are dangerous in nursing if they aren't founded on discipline."

So she wasn't as simple or as obstinately conformist as she appeared, or chose to appear to her colleagues. And she, too, had imagination. Was this the Brumfett, he wondered, that Mary Taylor knew and valued. And yet, he was convinced that his first impressions hadn't been wrong. Fundamentally, she wasn't an intelligent woman. Was she, even now, voicing the theory, the very words perhaps, of another? "The wisdom and courage to step outside the rules." Well, someone in Nightingale House had stepped outside them, someone hadn't lacked the courage. They looked at each other. He was beginning to wonder if Nightingale House had put some kind of spell on him, if its threatening atmosphere had begun to affect his judgement. For behind the thick spectacles he thought he saw the eyes change, thought he detected an urgency to communicate, to be understood, even a plea for help. And then the illusion passed. He was facing again the most ordinary, the most uncompromising, the least complex of all his suspects. And the interview was at an end.

It was now after nine o'clock but Dalgliesh and Masterson were still together in the office. There were at least a couple of hours' work ahead before they could break for the night, checking and comparing statements, searching for the tell-tale discrepancy, planning tomorrow's activity. Dalgliesh decided to let Masterson get on with it and dialling the internal number of Matron's flat, he asked if she could give him twenty minutes of her time. Courtesy and policy both dictated that he should keep her informed, but there was another reason for seeing her before he left Nightingale House.

She had left the door of the flat open for him and he passed straight down the corridor to the sitting-room, knocked and entered. He walked into peace, quietness, light. And coldness. The room was surprisingly chilly. A bright fire was burning in the grate but its warmth hardly reached the far corners of the room. As he went across to her he saw that she was appropriately dressed, her long legs encased in brown velvet slacks topped by a high necked cashmere sweater in pale fawn, the sleeves pushed back from brittle wrists. A silk scarf in bright green was knotted around her throat.

They sat down together on the sofa. Dalgliesh saw that she had been working. There was an open briefcase propped against the leg of the coffee table and a spread of papers across its surface. A coffee pot stood in the grate, and the comforting scent of warm wood and coffee pervaded the room.

She offered him coffee or whisky; nothing else. He accepted the coffee and she rose to fetch a second cup. When she had returned, the coffee poured, he said:

"They've told you, I expect, that we've found the poison."

"Yes. Gearing and Rolfe both came to see me after you'd finished questioning them. I suppose this means that it must be murder?"

"I think so, unless Nurse Fallon hid the tin herself. But somehow that seems unlikely. To make a deliberate mystery of suicide with the object of causing the maximum of trouble would be the action

of an exhibitionist or a neurotic. This girl seems to me to have been neither, but I wanted your view."

"I agree with you. Fallon, I would have said, was essentially a rational person. If she decided to kill herself it would be for reasons which seemed good to her at the time and I would expect her to leave a brief but lucid note explaining them. A great many suicides kill themselves to make trouble for other people. But not Fallon."

"That would be my assessment, but I wanted to ask someone who had actually known her."

She asked: "What does Madeleine Goodale say?"

"Nurse Goodale thinks that her friend killed herself; but that was before we found the nicotine."

He didn't say where and she didn't ask. He had no intention of telling anyone in Nightingale House where the tin had been found. But one person would know where it had been hidden and with luck might inadvertently reveal their guilty knowledge.

He went on: "There is another matter. Miss Gearing tells me she entertained a friend in her room last night; she says that she let him out through your door. Does that surprise you?"

"No. I leave the flat open when I'm not here so that the Sisters can use the back staircase. It gives them at least the illusion of privacy."

"At the cost, surely, of your own?"

"Oh, I think it's understood that they don't come into the flat. I trust my colleagues. Even if I didn't, there's nothing here to interest them. I keep all official papers in my office over at the hospital."

She was right of course. There was nothing here to interest anyone except him. The sitting-room for all its individuality was almost as plain as his own flat high above the Thames at Queenhithe. Perhaps that was one reason why he felt so at home. Here were no photographs to invite speculation; no bureau bursting with its accumulated hoard of trivia; no pictures to betray a private taste; no invitations to advertise the diversity, the existence even, of a social life. He held his own flat inviolate; it would have been intolerable to him to think that people could walk in and out at will.

440

But here was an even greater reticence; the self-sufficiency of a woman so private that even her personal surroundings were permitted to give nothing away.

He said: "Mr. Courtney-Briggs tells me that he was Josephine Fallon's lover for a short period during her first year. Did you know that?"

"Yes. I knew it in the same way that I know Mavis Gearing's visitor yesterday was almost certainly Leonard Morris. In a hospital, gossip spreads by a kind of osmosis. One can't always remember being told the latest scandal; one just gets to know."

"And is there much to know?"

"More perhaps than in less sensational institutions. Is that so very surprising? Men and women who have to watch daily what the body can suffer in agony and degradation aren't likely to be too scrupulous about availing themselves of its solace."

When, and with whom, he wondered, did she find her consolation? In her job; in the power which that job undoubtedly gave her? In astronomy, tracing through long nights the paths of the movable stars? With Brumfett? Surely to God not with Brumfett!

She said: "If you're thinking that Stephen Courtney-Briggs might have killed to protect his reputation, well, I don't believe it. I got to know about the affair. So did half the hospital, I've no doubt. Courtney-Briggs isn't particularly discreet. Besides, such a motive would only apply to a man vulnerable to public opinion."

"Every man is vulnerable in some way to public opinion."

She gave him a sudden keen glance from those extraordinary exophthalmic eyes.

"Of course. No doubt Stephen Courtney-Briggs is as capable of killing to prevent personal disaster or public disgrace as any of us. But not, I think, to prevent people knowing that a young and attractive woman was willing to go to bed with him; or that, middle-aged as he may be, he is still able to take his sexual pleasure where he finds it."

Was there a trace of contempt, of resentment almost, in her voice? For a moment he caught an echo of Sister Rolfe.

"And Hilda Rolfe's friendship with Julia Pardoe? You knew about that?"

441

She smiled a little bitterly.

"Friendship? Yes, I know, and I think that I understand. But I'm not sure that you do. The orthodox reaction, if the affair became known, would be that Rolfe is corrupting Pardoe. But if that young woman has been corrupted, I suspect that it happened before she came to the John Carpendar. I don't propose to interfere. The affair will settle itself. Julia Pardoe should qualify as a State Registered Nurse in a few months' time. I happen to know that she has plans for her future and they certainly don't include staying on here. I'm afraid there is a great deal of unhappiness ahead for Sister Rolfe. But we must meet that when it comes."

Her voice told him that she knew, that she was watching, that she had the situation under control. And that it was not a matter for further discussion.

He finished his coffee in silence, then rose to go. There was nothing else he needed to ask at present and he found himself disagreeably sensitive to every nuance in her voice, every silence which might imply that his presence was irksome. It could hardly be welcome, he knew that. He was used to being the harbinger, at best of ill news, at worst of disaster. But at least he could avoid forcing his company on her a minute more than was necessary.

As she rose to accompany him to the door he made a casual reference to the architecture of the house and asked how long it had been in the possession of the hospital. She said:

"It's a tragic and rather horrible story. The place was built in 1880 by a Thomas Nightingale, a local string and rope manufacturer who had come up in the world and wanted a house to dignify his new position. The name is fortuitously appropriate; it has nothing to do with Florence or with the bird. Nightingale lived here with his wife, they had no children, until 1886. In the January of that year the body of one of the maidservants, a nineteen-year-old girl called Nancy Gorringe, who had been taken by Mrs. Nightingale from an orphanage, was found hanging from one of the trees in the grounds. When the body was cut down it was apparent that she had been systematically ill-treated, beaten, tortured even, over a period of months. It had been calculated sadism. One of the most horrible features of the case was that the other

members of the staff must have had some idea what was going on, but did nothing. They were apparently well treated; they paid touching tribute at the trial to Nightingale as a just and considerate master. It must have been similar to some of these modern cases of child cruelty where only one member of the family is singled out for violence and neglect and the others acquiesce in the ill treatment. A taste for vicarious sadism, I suppose, or just the desperate hope of preserving their own safety. And yet it's odd. Not one of them turned against Nightingale, not even when local feeling was at its height in the weeks following the trial. He and his wife were both convicted and spent many years in prison. I have an idea that they died there. Anyway, they never returned to Nightingale House. It was sold to a retired boot manufacturer who lived here for only two years before deciding that he didn't like it. He sold it to one of the governors of the hospital who spent the last twelve years of his life here and bequeathed it to the John Carpendar. It has always been something of an embarrassment to the hospital; no one has been quite sure what to do with it. It's not really suitable as a nurse training school, but it's difficult to see what exactly it would be suitable for. There's a story that Nancy Gorringe's ghost can be heard weeping in the grounds after dark at this time of year. I've never heard her and it's a tale we try to keep from the students. But it's never been a happy house."

And it was less happy than ever now, thought Dalgliesh, as he made his way back to the office. Now there were two murders to add to the history of the violence and hate.

He told Masterson that he could go off duty, then settled down for a last solitary study of the papers. Hardly had the Sergeant left when the outside telephone rang. It was the director of the forensic science laboratory to say that the tests were complete. Josephine Fallon had died of nicotine poisoning and the nicotine had come from the tin of rose spray.

VI

It was two hours before he finally locked the side door of Nightingale House behind him and set out to walk back to the Falconer's Arms.

443

The path was lit by the old-fashioned type of street lamp, but the lamps were widely spaced and dim so that for most of the time he walked in darkness. He met no one and could well believe that this lonely path was unpopular with the students once night had fallen. The rain had stopped but the wind was rising, shaking down the last drops from the interlocking branches of the elms. He could feel them spitting against his face and seeping under the collar of his coat, and felt a momentary regret that he had decided that morning not to use his car. The trees grew very close to the path, separated from it by a narrow verge of sodden turf. It was a warm night despite the rising wind, and a light mist moved among the trees and coiled around the lamps. The pathway was about ten feet wide. It must have been once a main drive to Nightingale House, but it wound inconsequently among the clumps of elms and birch as if the original owner of the house had hoped to increase his self-importance by the length of his drive.

As he walked he thought about Christine Dakers. He had seen the girl at three forty-five p.m. The private ward had been very quiet at that time and, if Sister Brumfett were about, she had taken care to keep out of his way. The Staff Nurse had received him and had shown him into Nurse Dakers's room. The girl had been sitting up against the pillows looking as flushed and triumphant as a newly-delivered mother and had welcomed him as if she expected congratulations and an offering of flowers. Someone had already supplied her with a vase of daffodils and there were two pots of chrysanthemums beside the tea tray on the overbed table, and a spatter of magazines strewn over the bed cover.

She had tried to appear unconcerned and contrite as she told her story but the acting had been unconvincing. In truth she had been radiant with happiness and relief. And why not? Matron had visited her. She had confessed and had been forgiven. She was filled now with the sweet euphoria of absolution. More to the point, he thought, the two girls who might have menaced her had gone for good. Diane Harper had left the hospital. And Heather Pearce was dead.

And to what exactly had Nurse Dakers confessed? Why this extraordinary liberation of spirit? He wished he knew. But he had

come out of her room little wiser than when he went in. But at least, he thought, she had confirmed Madeleine Goodale's evidence of their study time together in the library. Unless there was collusion, which seemed unlikely, they had given each other an alibi for the time before breakfast. And, after breakfast, she had taken her final cup of coffee into the conservatory where she had sat reading the *Nursing Mirror* until it was time to join the demonstration. Nurse Pardoe and Nurse Harper had been with her. The three girls had left the conservatory at the same time, had paid a brief visit to the bathroom and lavatories on the second floor, and had then made their way straight to the demonstration room. It was very difficult to see how Christine Dakers could have poisoned the feed.

Dalgliesh had covered about fifty yards when he stopped in mid-stride, frozen into immobility by what, for one unbelievable second, he thought was the sound of a woman crying. He stood still, straining to distinguish that desperate alien voice. For a moment all was silent, even the wind seemed to have dropped. Then he heard it again, this time unmistakably. This wasn't the night cry of an animal or the figment of a tired but over-stimulated brain. Somewhere in the cluster of trees to his left a woman was howling in misery.

He was not superstitious, but he had the imaginative man's sensitivity to atmosphere. Standing alone in the darkness and hearing that human voice wailing in descant to the rising wind he felt a frisson of awe. The terror and helplessness of that nineteenth-century maidservant touched him briefly as if with her own cold finger. He entered for one appalling second into her misery and hopelessness. The past fused with the present. The terror was eternal. The last desperate act was here and now. Then the moment passed. This was a real voice, a living woman. Pressing on his torch, he turned from the path into the utter darkness of the trees.

About twenty yards from the edge of the turf he could see a wooden hut about twelve feet square, its one dimly lit window casting a square of light on the bark of the nearest elm. He strode over to it, his feet soundless on the sodden earth, and pushed open the door. The warm, rich smell of wood and of paraffin wafted out to meet him. And there was something else. The smell of human

life. Sitting huddled in a broken wicker chair, with a storm lantern on the upturned box beside her, was a woman.

The impression of an animal trapped in its lair was immediate and inevitable. They gazed at each other soundlessly. Despite her wild crying, cut off instantaneously at his entrance as if it had been simulated, the eyes which peered keenly into his were unclouded and bright with menace. This animal might be in distress but it was on its own ground and all its senses were alert. When she spoke she sounded gloomily belligerent but with no trace of curiosity or fear.

"Who are yer?"

"My name's Adam Dalgliesh. What's yours?"

"Morag Smith."

"I've heard about you, Morag. You must have got back to the hospital this evening."

"That's right. And told by Miss Collins to report to the resident staff hostel if yer please. I asked to go back to the medical officers' quarters if I couldn't stay in Nightingale House. But oh no! No bloody fear! Got on too well with the doctors I did. So it's off to the 'ostel. They bugger you about properly in this place, they do. I asked to see Matron but Sister Brumfett said she wasn't to be worried."

She paused in her recital of woes to fiddle with the wick of the lantern. The light increased. She screwed up her eyes at him.

"Adam Dalgliesh. Funny name. You're new around 'ere, aren't yer?"

"I only arrived this morning. I expect they've told you about Nurse Fallon. I'm a detective. I'm here to find out how she and Nurse Pearce died."

At first he thought that the news was going to precipitate another bout of wailing. She opened her mouth wide but then, thinking better of it, gave a little gasp and closed it sharply again. She said gruffly:

"I never killed 'er."

"Nurse Pearce? Of course not. Why should you?"

"That's not what the other one thought."

"What other one?"

446

"That Inspector, Inspector bloody Bill Bailey. I could see what 'e was thinking. Asking all them questions, and his eyes fixed on yer all the bleeding time. What were yer doing from the moment you got up? What the 'ell did he think I was doing? Working! That's what I was doing. Did you like Nurse Pearce? Was she ever unkind to you? I'd 'ave like to see 'er try. Anyway, I never even knew 'er. Well, I 'adn't been over Nightingale 'ouse for more than a week. But I could see what 'e was after. It's always the same. Blame the poor bloody maid."

Dalgliesh moved into the hut and seated himself on a bench against the wall. He would have to question Morag Smith and this seemed as good a time as any. He said:

"I think you're wrong, you know. Inspector Bailey didn't suspect you. He told me so."

She gave a derisive snort.

"Yer don't want to believe everything the police tell yer. Blimey, didn't yer dad tell yer that? 'e suspected me all right. Bloody Bugger Bailey. My God, my dad could tell you some things about the police."

No doubt the police could tell a lot about dad, thought Dalgliesh, but rejected that line of conversation as unlikely to be profitable. The inspector's name lent itself to alliterative abuse and Morag was in the mood to relish it. Dalgliesh hastened to defend his colleague.

"Inspector Bailey was only doing his job. He didn't mean to upset you. I'm a policeman too, and I shall have to ask questions. We all do. I shan't get anywhere unless you help. If Nurse Pearce and Nurse Fallon were killed, then I'm going to find out who did it. They were young, you know. Nurse Pearce was about your age. I don't suppose they wanted to die."

He was not sure how Morag would react to this nicely judged appeal to justice and sentiment but he could see the sharp little eyes probing through the semi-darkness.

" 'elp yer!" Her voice was full of scorn. "Don't kid me. Your sort don't need 'elp. Yer know 'ow the milk got into the coconut all right."

Dalgliesh considered this startling metaphor and decided, in the

absence of contrary evidence, that it was intended as a compliment. He balanced his torch upright on the bench so that it threw one bright pool of light on the roof, wriggled his thighs more firmly against the wall, and cushioned his head against a thick bundle of raffia which hung from a nail above him. He was surprisingly comfortable. He asked conversationally:

"Do you come here often?"

"Only when I'm upset." Her tone suggested that this was an eventuality for which any reasonable woman would make provision.

"It's private 'ere." She added defensively: "It used to be private, anyway."

Dalgliesh felt rebuked.

"I'm sorry. I won't come here again."

"Oh, I don't mind you. You can come again if you like."

The voice might be ungracious but the compliment was unmistakable. They sat for a moment in curiously companionable silence.

The stout walls of the hut enclosed them, insulating them in an unnatural silence from the moaning of the wind. Inside, the air was cold but musty, smelling pungently of wood, paraffin and humus. Dalgliesh looked around him. The place was not uncomfortable. There was a bale of straw in the corner, a second old cane chair similar to that in which Morag was curled, and an upturned packing-case covered with oilcloth which served as a table. On it he could just make out the shape of a primus oil stove. One of the wall shelves held a white aluminium teapot and a couple of mugs. He guessed that the gardener had once used the place as a comfortable retreat from the ardours of work as well as a potting and storage shed. In spring and summer, isolated in the quiet of the trees and surrounded by bird song, it must, Dalgliesh thought, be an agreeable hiding place. But this was mid-winter. He said:

"Forgive my asking, but wouldn't it be more comfortable to be upset in your own room? And more private?"

"It isn't cosy over in Nightingale 'ouse. And it isn't cosy in the resident staff 'ostel either. I like it 'ere. It smells like my dad's shed on the allotment. And nobody comes after dark. They're all afraid of the ghost."

"And you aren't?"

"I don't believe in 'em."

It was, thought Dalgliesh, the ultimate vindication of sturdy scepticism. You didn't believe in a thing, therefore it didn't exist. Untortured by imagination, you could enjoy the reward of your own certainty even if it were only the undisputed possession of a garden shed when you were feeling upset. He found this admirable. He wondered whether he ought to inquire the cause of her grief, suggest perhaps that she should confide in Matron. Had that wild crying really been caused by nothing more than Bill Bailey's passionately resented attentions? Bailey was a good detective, but not particularly subtle with people. One couldn't afford to be critical. Every detective, however competent, knew what it was unwittingly to antagonize a witness. Once this happened it was the devil to get anything useful out of her—and it usually was a woman—even if the antipathy were partly subconscious. Success in a murder investigation depended largely on making people want to help you, getting them to talk. Bill Bailey had singularly failed with Morag Smith. Adam Dalgliesh, too, had failed in his time.

He remembered what Inspector Bailey, in that brief hour's colloquy when the case had been handed over, had told him about the two maids.

"They're out of it. The old one, Miss Martha Collins, has been at the hospital for forty years and if she had homicidal tendencies would have shown them before now. She's mainly concerned about the theft of the lavatory disinfectant. Seems to regard it as a personal affront. Probably takes the view that the lavatory is her responsibility and the murder isn't. The young girl, Morag Smith, is half dotty if you ask me, and as obstinate as an army mule. She might have done it, I suppose, but I can't for the life of me see why. Heather Pearce hadn't done anything to upset her as far as I know. And in any case she hardly had the time. Morag was only transferred from the doctors' residence to Nightingale House on the day before Pearce died. I gather that she wasn't too pleased about the change, but that's scarcely a motive for starting to kill off the student nurses. Besides, the girl isn't frightened. Obstinate, but not frightened. If she did it, I doubt whether you'll ever prove it."

They sat on in silence. He wasn't anxious to probe into her grief

and suspected that she had been indulging an irrational need for a good cry. She had chosen her secret place for it and was entitled to emotional privacy even if her physical privacy had been invaded. He was too reticent himself to have any stomach for the emotional prying which gives so many people the comforting illusion that they care. He seldom did care. Human beings were perpetually interesting to him, and nothing about them surprised him any more. But he didn't involve himself. He wasn't surprised that she should like the shed, smelling as it did of home.

He became aware of a confused background mumbling. She had returned to a recital of her grievance.

"Kept looking at me all the time 'e did. And asking the same old thing over and over again. Stuck up too. You could see that he fancied himself."

Suddenly she turned to Dalgliesh.

"You feeling sexy?"

Dalgliesh gave the question serious attention.

"No. I'm too old to feel sexy when I'm cold and tired. At my age you need the creature comforts if you're to perform with any pleasure to your partner or credit to yourself."

She gave him a look in which disbelief struggled with commiseration.

"You're not that old. Thanks for the 'anky anyway."

She gave one last convulsive blow before handing it back. Dalgliesh slipped it quickly into his pocket, resisting the temptation to drop it unobtrusively behind the bench. Stretching his legs ready to move, he only half heard her next words.

"What did you say?" he asked, careful to keep his voice level, uninquisitorial.

She answered sulkily.

"I said that 'e never found out about me drinking the milk anyway, bugger 'im. I never told 'im."

"Was that the milk used for the demonstration feed? When did you drink it?"

He tried to sound conversational, only mildly interested. But he was aware of the silence in the hut and the two sharp eyes staring at him. Could she really be unaware of what she was telling him?

"It was at eight o'clock, maybe a minute before. I went into the demo room to see if I'd left my tin of polish there. And there was this bottle of milk on the trolley and I drank some of it. Just a bit off the top."

"Just out of the bottle?"

"Well, there wasn't any cup 'andy was there? I was thirsty and I saw the milk and I just fancied a bit. So I took a swig."

He asked the crucial question.

"You just had the cream off the top?"

"There wasn't no cream. It wasn't that kind of milk."

His heart leapt.

"And what did you do then?"

"I didn't do nothing."

"But weren't you afraid that Sister Tutor would notice that the bottle wasn't full?"

"The bottle was full. I filled it up with water from the tap. Anyway, I only took a couple of gulps."

"And replaced the seal on top of the bottle?"

"That's right. Careful like so as they wouldn't notice."

"And you never told anyone?"

"No one asked me. That Inspector asked me if I'd been in the demo room and I said only before seven o'clock when I did a bit of cleaning. I wasn't going to tell 'im nothing. It wasn't 'is bloody milk anyway; 'e never paid for it."

"Morag, are you quite, quite sure of the time?"

"Eight o'clock. The demo clock said eight anyway. I looked at it because I was supposed to help serve the breakfasts, the dining-room maids being off with flu. Some people think you can be in three places at once. Anyway, I went into the dining-room where the Sisters and the students had all started eating. Then Miss Collins gave me one of 'er looks. Late again Morag! So it must 'ave been eight. The students always start breakfast at eight."

"And were they all there?"

"Of course they was all there! I told yer! They was at their breakfast."

But he knew that they had been there. The twenty-five minutes from eight until eight twenty-five was the only time in which all the

female suspects had been together, eating under the eye of Miss Collins and full in each other's gaze. If Morag's story were true, and he didn't for one moment doubt it, then the scope of the inquiry had been dramatically narrowed. There were only six people who had no firm alibi for the whole of the period from eight o'clock until the class assembled at eight forty. He would have to check the statements of course, but he knew what he would find. This was the sort of information he had been trained to recall at will and the names came obediently to mind. Sister Rolfe, Sister Gearing, Sister Brumfett, Nurse Goodale, Leonard Morris and Stephen Courtney-Briggs.

He pulled the girl gently to her feet.

"Come on, Morag, I'm going to see you back to the hostel. You're a very important witness and I don't want you to get pneumonia before I've had a chance to take your statement."

"I don't want to write nothing down. I'm no scholar."

"Someone will write it down for you. You'll only have to sign it."

"I don't mind doing that. I'm not daft. I can sign my name I 'ope."

And he would have to be there to see that she did. He had a feeling that Sergeant Masterson would be no more successful than Inspector Bailey in dealing with Morag. It would be safer to take her statement himself even if it meant a later start than he had planned for his journey to London.

But it would be time well spent. As he turned to pull the shed door firmly closed behind them—it had no lock—he felt happier than at any time since the finding of the nicotine. Now he was making progress. On the whole, it hadn't been too bad a day.

Chapter Seven

Danse Macabre

I

It was five minutes to seven the next morning. Sergeant Masterson and Detective Constable Greeson were in the kitchen at Nightingale House with Miss Collins and Mrs. Muncie. It seemed like the middle of the night to Masterson, dark and cold. The kitchen smelt agreeably of new baked bread, a country smell, nostalgic and comforting. But Miss Collins was no prototype of the buxom and welcoming country cook. She watched, lips tight and arms akimbo, as Greeson placed a filled milk bottle in the front of the middle shelf of the refrigerator, and said:

"Which one are they supposed to take?"

"The first bottle to hand. That's what they did before, didn't they?"

"So they say. I had something better to do than sit and watch them. I've got something better to do now."

"That's okay by us. We'll do the watching."

Four minutes later the Burt twins came in together. No one spoke. Shirley opened the refrigerator door and Maureen took out the first bottle to hand. Followed by Masterson and Greeson the twins made their way to the demonstration room through the silent and echoing hall. The room was empty and the curtains drawn. The two fluorescent lights blazed down on a semicircle of vacant chairs and on the high narrow bed where a grotesque demonstration doll, round mouthed, nostrils two black and gaping apertures, was propped against the pillows. The twins set about their preparations in silence. Maureen set down the bottle on the trolley, then dragged out the drip-feed apparatus and positioned it by the side of the bed.

453

Shirley collected instruments and bowls from the various cupboards and set them out on the trolley. The two policemen watched. After twenty minutes Maureen said:

"That's as much as we did before breakfast. We left the room just like it is now."

Masterson said: "Okay. Then we'll put forward our watches to eight forty when you came back here. There's no point in hanging about. We can call the rest of the students in now."

Obediently the twins adjusted their pocket watches while Greeson rang the library where the remaining students were waiting. They came almost immediately and in the order of their original appearance. Madeleine Goodale first, followed by Julia Pardoe and Christine Dakers who arrived together. No one made any attempt to talk and they took their places silently on the semicircle of chairs, shivering a little as if the room were cold. Masterson noticed that they kept their eyes averted from the grotesque doll in the bed. When they had settled themselves he said:

"Right, Nurse. You can go ahead with the demonstration now. Start heating the milk."

Maureen looked at him puzzled.

"The milk? But no one's had a chance to ..." Her voice died away.

Masterson said: "No one's had a chance to poison it? Never mind. Just go ahead. I want you to do precisely what you did last time."

She filled a large jug with hot water from the tap then stood the unopened bottle in it for a few seconds to warm the milk. Receiving Masterson's impatient nod to get on with it, she prised the cap off the bottle and poured the liquid into a glass measuring jug. Then she took a glass thermometer from the instrument trolley and checked the temperature of the liquid. The class watched in fascinated silence. Maureen glanced at Masterson. Receiving no sign, she took up the oesophageal tube and inserted it into the rigid mouth of the doll. Her hand was perfectly steady. Lastly she lifted a glass funnel high over her head and paused. Masterson said:

"Go ahead, Nurse. It isn't going to hurt the doll to get a bit damp. That's what it's made for. A few ounces of warm milk isn't going to rot its guts."

Maureen paused. This time the fluid was visible and all their eyes were on the white curving stream. Then suddenly the girl paused, arm still poised high, and stood motionless, like a model awkwardly posed.

"Well," said Masterson: "Is it or isn't it?"

Maureen lowered the jug to her nostrils, then without a word passed it to her twin. Shirley sniffed and looked at Masterson.

"This isn't milk, is it? It's disinfectant. You wanted to test whether we really could tell!"

Maureen said: "Are you telling us that it was disinfectant last time; that the milk was poisoned before we took the bottle out of the fridge?"

"No. Last time the milk was all right when you took it out of the fridge. What did you do with the bottle once the milk had been poured into the measuring jug?"

Shirley said: "I took it over to the sink in the corner and rinsed it out. I'm sorry I forgot. I should have done that earlier."

"Never mind. Do it now."

Maureen had placed the bottle on the table by the side of the sink, its crumpled cap at its side. Shirley picked it up. Then she paused. Masterson said very quietly:

"Well?"

The girl turned to him, perplexed.

"There's something different, something wrong. It wasn't like this."

"Wasn't it? Then think. Don't worry yourself. Relax. Just relax and think."

The room was preternaturally silent. Then Shirley swung round to her twin.

"I know now, Maureen! It's the bottle top. Last time we took one of the homogenized bottles from the fridge, the kind with the silver cap. But when we came back into the demonstration room after breakfast it was different. Don't you remember? The cap was gold. It was Channel Island milk."

Nurse Goodale said quietly from her chair: "Yes. I remember too. The only cap I saw was gold."

Maureen looked across at Masterson in puzzled inquiry.

"So someone must have changed the cap?"

Before he had a chance to reply they heard Madeleine Goodale's calm voice.

"Not necessarily the cap. Somebody changed the whole bottle."

Masterson did not reply. So the old man had been right! The solution of disinfectant had been made up carefully and at leisure and the lethal bottle substituted for the one from which Morag Smith had drunk. And what had happened to the original bottle? Almost certainly it had been left in the small kitchen on the Sisters' floor. Wasn't it Sister Gearing who had complained to Miss Collins that the milk was watery?

II

Dalgliesh's business at the Yard was quickly completed and by eleven o'clock he was in North Kensington.

Number 49 Millington Square, W.10, was a large dilapidated Italianate house fronted with crumbling stucco. There was nothing remarkable about it. It was typical of hundreds in this part of London. It was obviously divided into bed-sitting-rooms since every window showed a different set of curtains, or none, and it exuded that curious atmosphere of secretive and lonely over-occupation which hung over the whole district. Dalgliesh saw that there was no bank of bell pushes in the porch and no neat list of the tenants. The front door was open. He pushed through the glass panelled door which led to the hall and was met at once by a smell of sour cooking, floor polish and unwashed clothes. The walls of the hall had been papered with a thick encrusted paper, now painted dark brown, and glistening as if it exuded grease and perspiration. The floor and staircase were laid with a patterned linoleum, patched with a brighter newer design where the tears would have been dangerous, but otherwise torn and unmended. The paintwork was an institutional green. There was no sign of life but, even at this time of the day, he felt its presence behind the tightly closed and numbered doors as he made his way unchallenged to the upper floors.

Number 14 was on the top floor at the back. As he approached

456

the door he heard the sharp staccato clatter of typing. He knocked loudly and the sound stopped. There was a wait of more than a minute before the door half opened and he found himself facing a pair of suspicious and unwelcoming eyes.

"Who are you? I'm working. My friends know not to call in the mornings."

"But I'm not a friend. May I come in?"

"I suppose so. But I can't spare you much time. And I don't think it'll be worth your while. I don't want to join anything; I haven't the time. And I don't want to buy anything because I haven't the money. Anyway, I've got everything I need." Dalgliesh showed his card.

"I'm not buying or selling; not even information which is what I'm here for. It's about Josephine Fallon. I'm a police officer and I'm investigating her death. You, I take it, are Arnold Dowson."

The door was opened wider.

"You'd better come in." No sign of fear but perhaps a certain wariness in the grey eyes.

It was an extraordinary room, a small attic with a sloping roof and a dormer window, furnished almost entirely with crude and unpainted wooden boxes, some still stencilled with the name of the original grocer or wine merchant. They had been ingeniously fitted together so that the walls were honeycombed from floor to ceiling with pale wooden cells, irregular in size and shape and containing all the impedimenta of daily living. Some were stacked close with hard-backed books; others with orange paperbacks. Another framed a small two-bar electric fire, perfectly adequate to heat so small a room. In another box was a neat pile of clean but unironed clothes. Another held blue-banded mugs and other crockery, and yet another displayed a group of *objets trouvés*, sea-shells, a Staffordshire dog, a small jam jar or bird feathers. The single bed, blanket-covered, was under the window. Another upturned box served as a table and desk. The only two chairs were the folding canvas type sold for picnicking. Dalgliesh was reminded of an article once seen in a Sunday colour supplement on how to furnish your bed-sitting-room for under £50. Arnold Dowson had probably done it for half the price. But the room was not unpleasing. Every-

457

thing was functional and simple. It was perhaps too claustrophobic for some tastes and there was something obsessional in the meticulous tidiness and the way in which every inch of space had been used to the full which prevented it from being restful. It was the room of a self-sufficient, well-organized man who, as he had told Dalgliesh, plainly had everything he wanted.

The tenant suited the room. He looked almost excessively tidy. He was a young man, probably not much over twenty, Dalgliesh thought. His fawn polo-neck sweater was clean, with each cuff neatly turned back to match its fellow, and the collar of a very white shirt visible at the neck. His blue jeans were faded but unstained and had been carefully washed and ironed. There was a crease down the centre of each leg and the ends had been turned up and stitched carefully into place. It gave an oddly incongruous effect to such an informal outfit. He wore leather sandals of the buckled style normally seen on children, and no socks. His hair was very fair and was brushed into a helmet which framed his face in the manner of a medieval page. The face beneath the sleek fringe was bony and sensitive, the nose crooked and too large, the mouth small and well shaped with a hint of petulance. But his most remarkable feature were his ears. They were the smallest Dalgliesh had ever seen on a man, and were without colour even at the tips. They looked as if they were made of wax. Sitting on an upturned orange box with his hands held loosely between his knees and his watchful eyes on Dalgliesh, he looked like the centrepiece of a surrealist painting; singular and precise against the multi-cellular background. Dalgliesh pulled out one of the boxes and seated himself opposite the boy. He said:

"You knew that she was dead, of course?"

"Yes. I read about it in this morning's papers."

"Did you know that she was pregnant?"

This at least produced emotion. The boy's tight face whitened. His head jerked up and he stared at Dalgliesh silently for a moment before replying.

"No. I didn't know. She didn't tell me."

"She was nearly three months' pregnant. Could it have been your child?"

Dowson looked down at his hands.

"It could have been, I suppose. I didn't take any precautions, if that's what you mean. She told me not to worry, that she'd see to that. After all, she was a nurse. I thought she knew how to take care of herself."

"That was something I suspect she never did know. Hadn't you better tell me about it?"

"Do I have to?"

"No. You don't have to say anything. You can demand to see a solicitor and make any amount of fuss and trouble and cause a great deal of delay. But is there any point? No one is accusing you of murdering her. But someone did. You knew her and presumably you liked her. For some of the time, anyway. If you want to help you can best do it by telling me everything you knew about her."

Dowson got slowly to his feet. He seemed as slow-moving and clumsy as an old man. He looked round as if disoriented. Then he said:

"I'll make some tea."

He shuffled over to a double gas ring, fitted to the right of the meagre and unused fireplace, lifted the kettle as if testing by weight that it held sufficient water, and lit the gas. He took down two of the mugs from one of the boxes and set them out on a further box which he dragged between himself and Dalgliesh. It held a number of neatly folded newspapers which looked as if they hadn't been read. He spread one over the top of the box and set out the blue mugs and a bottle of milk as formally as if they were about to drink from Crown Derby. He didn't speak again until the tea was made and poured. Then he said:

"I wasn't her only lover."

"Did she tell you about the others?"

"No, but I think one of them was a doctor. Perhaps more than one. That wouldn't be surprising in the circumstances. We were talking once about sex and she said that a man's nature and character were always completely revealed when he made love. That if he were selfish or insensitive or brutal he couldn't conceal it in bed whatever he might do with his clothes on. Then she said that she had once slept with a surgeon and it was only too apparent that

most of the bodies he came into contact with had been anaesthe-
tized first; that he was so busy admiring his own technique that it
never occurred to him that he was in bed with a conscious woman.
She laughed about it. I don't think she minded very much. She
laughed about a great many things."

"But you don't think she was happy?"

He appeared to be considering. Dalgliesh thought: And for
God's sake don't answer, "who is?"

"No, not really happy. Not for most of the time. But she did
know how to be happy. That was the important thing."

"How did you meet her?"

"I'm learning to be a writer. That's what I want to be and I've
never wanted to be anything else. I have to earn some money to live
while I get my first novel finished and published, so I work at night
as a continental telephone operator. I know enough French to make
it possible. The pay isn't bad. I don't have many friends because
there isn't time and I never went to bed with any woman until I
met Jo. Women don't seem to like me. I met her last summer in St.
James's Park. She was there on one of her off-duty days and I was
there to watch the ducks and see what the park looked like. I wanted
to set one of the scenes in my book in St. James's Park in July, and
I went there to make some notes. She was lying on her back on the
grass staring at the sky. She was quite alone. One of the pages of
my notebook got detached and blew across the grass into her face.
I went after it and apologized, and we chased it together."

He was holding the mug of tea looking at it as if staring again
into the summer surface of the lake.

"It was an odd day—very hot, sunless and blustery. The wind
blew in warm gusts. The lake looked heavy like oil."

He paused for a moment, and when Dalgliesh didn't speak, went
on:

"So we met and talked, and I asked her to come back for tea. I
don't know what I expected. After tea we talked more and she made
love to me. She told me weeks later that she didn't have that in mind
when she came here but I don't know. I don't even know why she
came back. Perhaps she was bored."

"Did you have it in mind?"

460

"I don't know that either. Perhaps. I know that I wanted to make love to a woman. I wanted to know what it was like. That's one experience you can't write about until you know."

"And sometimes not even then. And how long did she continue to provide you with copy?"

The boy seemed unaware of the irony. He said:

"She used to come here about once a fortnight on her day off. We never went out together except to a pub occasionally. She would bring in some food and cook a meal and afterwards we would talk and go to bed."

"What did you talk about?"

"I suppose I did most of the talking. She didn't tell me much about herself, only that both her parents had been killed while she was a child and that she had been brought up in Cumberland by an elderly aunt. The aunt is dead now. I don't think Jo had a very happy childhood. She always wanted to be a nurse but she got T.B. when she was seventeen. It wasn't very bad and she spent eighteen months in a sanitorium in Switzerland and was cured. But the doctors advised her not to train as a nurse. So she did a number of other jobs. She was an actress for about three years; but that wasn't much of a success. Then she was a waitress and a shop assistant for a time. Then she became engaged but nothing came of it. She broke it off."

"Did she say why?"

"No, except that she found something out about the man which made it impossible to marry him."

"Did she say what it was or who the man was?"

"No, and I didn't ask. But I think he may have been some kind of sexual pervert."

Seeing Dalgliesh's face he added quickly:

"I don't really know. She never told me. Most of the things I know about Jo just came up casually in conversation. She never really talked about herself for long. It's just an idea I have. There was a kind of bitter hopelessness about the way she spoke of her engagement."

"And after that?"

"Well, apparently she decided that she might as well go back to

her original idea of being a nurse. She thought she could get through the medical examination with luck. She chose the John Carpendar Hospital because she wanted to be near London but not actually in it, and thought that a small hospital would be less arduous. She didn't want her health to break down, I suppose."

"Did she talk about the hospital?"

"Not much. She seemed happy enough there. But she spared me the intimate details of the bedpan rounds."

"Do you know whether she had an enemy?"

"She must have had, mustn't she, if somebody killed her? But she never told me about it. Perhaps she didn't know."

"Do these names mean anything to you?"

He went through the names of all the people, students, sisters, surgeon, pharmacist, who had been in Nightingale House the night Josephine Fallon had died.

"I think she mentioned Madeleine Goodale to me. I've a feeling they were friendly. And the Courtney-Briggs name seems familiar. But I can't remember any details."

"When did you last see her?"

"About three weeks ago. She came on her night off and cooked supper."

"How did she seem then?"

"She was restless and she wanted to make love rather badly. Then just before she left she said that she wouldn't see me again. A few days later I got a letter. It merely said, 'I meant what I said. Please don't try to get in touch. It's nothing you've done so don't worry. Good-bye and thank you. Jo.'"

Dalgliesh asked if he had kept the letter.

"No. I only keep important papers. I mean, there isn't room here to hoard letters."

"And did you try to get in touch with her again?"

"No. She'd asked me not to and there didn't seem much point in it. I suppose if I'd known about the child I might have done. But I'm not sure. There's nothing I could have done. I couldn't have had a child here. Well, you can see that. How could I? She wouldn't want to marry me and I never considered marrying her.

I don't want to marry anyone. But I don't think she killed herself because of the baby. Not Jo."

"All right. You don't think she killed herself. Tell me why."

"She wasn't the type."

"Oh, come now! You can do better than that."

The boy said belligerently: "It's true enough. I've known two people in my life who killed themselves. One was a boy in my last year at school when we were sitting for our G.C.E. The other was a manager of a dry cleaning firm I worked for. I drove the delivery van. Well, in both cases, everyone said all the usual things about how dreadful and how surprising it was. But I wasn't really surprised. I don't mean that I was expecting it or anything like that. I just wasn't really surprised. When I thought about both deaths I could believe that they had actually done it."

"Your sample is too small."

"Jo wouldn't kill herself. Why should she?"

"I can think of reasons. She hadn't made much success of her life so far. She hadn't any relatives to care about her, and very few friends. She didn't sleep easily at night, wasn't really happy. She had at last succeeded in training to be a nurse and was within a few months of her final examination. And then she finds herself pregnant. She knows that her lover won't want the child, that it's no use looking to him for comfort or support."

Dowson cried out in vehement protest.

"She never looked to anyone for comfort or support! That's what I'm trying to tell you! She slept with me because she wanted to. I'm not responsible for her. I'm not responsible for anyone. Anyone! I'm only responsible for myself. She knew what she was doing. It wasn't as if she were a young, inexperienced girl who needed kindness and protection."

"If you believe that only the young and innocent need comfort and protection you're thinking in clichés. And if you begin by thinking in clichés you end by writing them."

The boy said sullenly: "Maybe. But that's what I believe."

Suddenly he got up and went over to the wall. When he came back to the centre box Dalgliesh saw that he held a large smooth stone. It fitted snugly into his curved palm, a perfect ovoid. It was

463

a pale grey, flecked like an egg. Dowson let it slide from his hand on to the table where it rocked gently into stillness. Then he sat down again and bent forward, his head in his hands. Together they looked at the stone. Dalgliesh did not speak. Suddenly the boy said:

"She gave it to me. We found it together on the beach at Ventnor, in the Isle of Wight. We went there together last October. But of course you know. That must have been how you traced me. Lift it. It's surprisingly heavy."

Dalgliesh took the stone in his hands. It was satisfying to touch, smooth and cool. He took pleasure in the sea-washed perfection of its shape, in the hard unyielding roundness of it which yet fitted with such gentleness into the palm of his hand.

"I never had a holiday by the sea when I was a boy. Dad died before I was six and the old woman hadn't the money. So I missed out on the seaside. Jo thought it would be fun to go there together. It was very warm last October. Remember? We took the ferry from Portsmouth and there were only half a dozen people on it besides ourselves. The island was empty too. We could walk from Ventnor to St. Catherine's Lighthouse without meeting a soul. It was warm enough and deserted enough to bathe naked. Jo found this stone. She thought it would do as a paper-weight. I wasn't going to tear my pocket carrying that weight home but she did. Then, when we got back here, she gave it to me as a keepsake. I wanted her to have it but she said that I'd forget the holiday long before she did. Don't you see? She knew how to be happy. I'm not sure that I do. But Jo did. If you're like that you don't kill yourself. Not when you know how marvellous living can be. Colette knew about that. She wrote about 'a compelling fierce and secret *rapport* with the earth and everything that gushes from its breasts'." He looked at Dalgliesh.

"Colette was a French writer."

"I know. And you believe that Josephine Fallon could feel that?"

"I know she could. Not for long. Not often. But when she was happy she was marvellous. If you once know that kind of happiness you don't kill yourself. While you live there's a hope it could happen again. So why cut yourself off from the hope of it for ever?"

Dalgliesh said: "You cut yourself off from the misery too. That

might seem more important. But I think you're right. I don't believe Josephine Fallon killed herself. I believe she was murdered. That's why I'm asking if there's anything else you can tell me."

"No. I was on duty at the Exchange the night she died. I had better give you the address. I suppose you'll want to check."

"There are reasons why it's extremely unlikely to have been anyone who wasn't familiar with Nightingale House. But we shall check."

"Here's the address then."

He tore a corner from the newspaper covering the table and taking a pencil from his trouser pocket, wrote down the address in a crabbed hand, his head nearly touching the paper. Then he folded it as if the message were secret, and pushed it across the table.

"Take the stone too. I'd like you to have it. No, take it. Please take it. You think I'm heartless, that I'm not grieving for her. But I am. I want you to find out who killed her. It won't do any good to her or to the man, but I want you to find out. And I am sorry. It's just that I can't let myself feel too much. I can't let myself get involved. You understand?"

Dalgliesh took the stone in his hand and rose to go.

"Yes," he said: "I understand."

III

Mr. Henry Urquhart of Messrs. Urquhart, Wimbush and Portway was Josephine Fallon's solicitor. Dalgliesh's appointment with him was for twelve twenty-five p.m., a time disobligingly chosen, he felt, to intimate that every minute of the solicitor's time was valuable and that he was prepared to spare the police no more than half an hour before lunch. Dalgliesh was admitted immediately. He doubted whether a detective sergeant would have been received so promptly. This was one of the minor advantages for his passion for doing the job himself, for resisting the pressures to make him into a desk detective, controlling the investigation from his office with a small army of detective constables, scenes-of-crime men, photographers, finger-print experts and scientists ministering to his ego and effectively cutting him off from all but the main protagonists of

the crime. He knew that he had a reputation for solving his cases very fast, but he never grudged time on jobs which some of his colleagues thought more appropriate to a detective constable. As a result he was sometimes given information which a less experienced interrogator would have missed. He hardly expected this happy bonus from Mr. Henry Urquhart. This interview was likely to be little more than the formal and punctilious exchange of relevant facts. But it had been necessary for him to visit London. There were matters which he had to attend to at the Yard. And it was always a pleasure to visit on foot and in the fitful sunlight of a winter morning these secluded corners of the City.

Messrs. Urquhart, Wimbush and Portway were one of the most respected and successful of the City's firms of solicitors. Dalgliesh felt that few of Mr. Urquhart's clients could have been mixed up in a murder investigation. They might have their little difficulties from time to time with the Queen's proctor; they might, against all advice, indulge in imprudent litigation or obstinately persist in devising unwise wills; they might require their solicitor's services to devise technical defences to the drink and driving laws; it might indeed be necessary to extricate them from all manner of folly and imprudence. But their killing would be done legally.

The room into which he was shown could have served as a stage set for a successful solicitor's office. The coal fire was banked high in the grate. From above the mantel shelf the portrait of the founder gazed down in approval on his great grandson. The desk at which the great grandson sat was of the same period as the portrait and displayed the same qualities of durability, fitness for the task in hand, and a sturdy opulence which stopped just short of ostentation. On the other wall there was a small oil. Dalgliesh thought that it looked very like a Jan Steen. It proclaimed to the world that the firm knew a good picture when it saw one and could afford to display it on the wall.

Mr. Urquhart, tall, ascetic, discreetly grey at the temples and with the air of a reserved dominie, was well cast for the role of a successful solicitor. He was wearing an exceedingly well-cut suit, but in lovat tweed as if the more orthodox pin stripe would have verged on caricature. He received Dalgliesh without apparent

curiosity or concern but the Superintendent noted with interest that Miss Fallon's box was already on the table before him. Dalgliesh stated his business briefly and ended:

"Can you tell me anything about her? In a murder inquiry anything we can learn about the past life and personality of the victim is helpful."

"And this, you are now confident, is murder?"

"She was killed by taking nicotine in her late night beaker of whisky. As far as we know, she wasn't aware that the tin or rose spray was in the conservatory cupboard, and if she knew and it occurred to her to use it, I doubt whether she would subsequently have hidden the tin."

"I see. And there is, too, the suggestion that the poison administered to the first victim—Heather Pearce wasn't it—was intended for my client?"

Mr. Urquhart sat for a moment finger to finger with his head slightly bent as if consulting either his own subconscious, a higher power, or the ghost of his former client before divulging what he knew. Dalgliesh thought that he could have saved the time. Urquhart was a man who knew perfectly well how far he was prepared to go, professionally or otherwise. The pantomime was unconvincing. And his story, when it came, did nothing to clothe the dry bones of Josephine Fallon's life. The facts were there. He consulted the papers in front of him, and presented them logically, unemotionally, lucidly. The time and place of her birth; the circumstances of her parents' death; her subsequent upbringing by an elderly aunt, who together with him had been a trustee until Miss Fallon's majority; the date and circumstance of that aunt's death from cancer of the uterus; the money left to Josephine Fallon and the exact way in which it had been invested; the girl's movements after her twenty-first birthday in so far, as he pointed out dryly, she had troubled to inform him of them.

Dalgliesh said: "She was pregnant. Did you know?"

It could not be said that this news disconcerted the solicitor although his face creased into the vaguely pained look of a man who can never quite reconcile himself to the messiness of the world.

"No. She didn't tell me. But then I would not expect her to do

467

so, unless, of course, she was thinking of applying for an affiliation order. I gather that was not in question."

"She told her friend, Madeleine Goodale, that she intended to have an abortion."

"Indeed. An expensive and to my mind, despite the recent legislation, a dubious business. I speak morally, of course, not legally. The recent legislation . . ."

Dalgliesh said: "I am aware of the recent legislation. So there is nothing else you can tell me?"

The solicitor's tone held a tinge of reproof.

"I have already told you a great deal about her background and financial position in so far as they were known to me. I am afraid I can't supply you with any more recent or intimate information. Miss Fallon consulted me seldom. Indeed she had no reason to do so. The last time was about her will. You are, I believe, already appraised of its terms. Miss Madeleine Goodale is the sole legatee. The estate is likely to amount to approximately twenty thousand pounds."

"Was there a previous will?"

Was it Dalgliesh's imagination, or did he detect the slight stiffening of facial muscles, the almost imperceptible frown which greeted an unwelcome question.

"There were two, but the second of these was never signed. The first, made soon after her majority, left everything to medical charities, including cancer research. The second she proposed to execute on the occasion of her marriage. I have the letter here."

He handed this across to Dalgliesh. It was addressed from a flat in Westminster and was written in a confident upright and unfeminine hand.

"Dear Mr. Urquhart, This is to let you know that I shall be married on 14th March at St. Marylebone Registry Office to Peter Courtney. He is an actor; you may have heard of him. Will you please draw up a will for me to sign on that date. I shall leave everything to my husband. His full name incidentally is Peter Albert Courtney Briggs. No hyphen. I expect you'll need to know that to draw up the will. We shall be living at this address.

"I shall also need some money. Could you please ask Warranders

468

to make two thousand pounds available to me by the end of the month? Thank you. I hope that you and Mr. Surtees are keeping well. Yours sincerely, Josephine Fallon."

A cool letter, thought Dalgliesh. No explanations. No justification. No expressions of happiness or hope. And come to that, no invitation to the wedding.

Henry Urquhart said: "Warranders were her stockbrokers. She always dealt with them through us, and we kept all her official papers. She preferred us to do so. She said she preferred to travel unencumbered."

He repeated the phrase, smiling complacently as if he found it in some way remarkable, and glanced at Dalgliesh as if expecting him to comment.

He went on: "Surtees is my clerk. She always asked after Surtees."

He seemed to find that fact more puzzling than the terms of the letter itself.

Dalgliesh said: "And Peter Courtney subsequently hanged himself."

"That is so, three days before the wedding. He left a note for the coroner. It wasn't read out at the inquest, I'm thankful to say. It was quite explicit. Courtney wrote that he had planned to marry to extricate himself from certain financial and personal difficulties, but at the last moment had found he couldn't face it. He was a compulsive gambler apparently. I am informed that uncontrolled gambling is, in fact, a disease akin to alcoholism. I know little of the syndrome but can appreciate that it could be tragic in its consequences, particularly for an actor whose earnings, although large, are erratic. Peter Courtney was very heavily in debt and totally unable to extricate himself from a compulsion which daily made that debt worse."

"And the personal difficulties? I believe he was a homosexual. There was gossip about it at the time. Do you know whether your client knew?"

"I have no information. It seems unlikely that she should not have known since she committed herself so far as to become engaged. She may, of course, have been so sanguine or so unwise as to suppose that she could help to cure him. I should have advised her

against the marriage had she consulted me, but as I have said she did not consult me."

And shortly afterwards, thought Dalgliesh, a matter of months only, she had begun her training at the John Carpendar and was sleeping with Peter Courtney's brother. Why? Loneliness? Boredom? A desperate need to forget? Payment for services rendered? What services? Simple sexual attraction, if physical need were ever simple, for a man who physically was a coarse edition of the fiancé she had lost? The need to reassure herself that she could attract heterosexual desire? Courtney-Briggs himself had suggested that it was she who had taken the initiative. It was certainly she who had brought the affair to an end. There had been no mistaking the surgeon's bitter resentment of a woman who had had the temerity to reject him before he had chosen to reject her.

As he rose to go Dalgliesh said: "Peter Courtney's brother is a consultant surgeon at the John Carpendar Hospital. But perhaps you knew?"

Henry Urquhart smiled his tight, unamused smile.

"Oh yes, I know. Stephen Courtney-Briggs is a client of mine. Unlike his brother, he has acquired a hyphen to his name and a more permanent success." He added with apparent irrelevance:

"He was holidaying in a friend's yacht in the Mediterranean when his brother died. He came home immediately. It was, of course, a great shock as well as being a considerable embarrassment."

It must have been, thought Dalgliesh. But Peter dead was decidedly less embarrassing than Peter living. It would no doubt have suited Stephen Courtney-Briggs to have had a well-known actor in the family, a younger brother who, without competing in his own field, would have added his lustre to the patina of success and given Courtney-Briggs an entrée to the extravagantly egotistical world of the stage. But the asset had become a liability; the hero an object of derision or, at best, of pity. It was a failure his brother would find hard to forgive.

Five minutes later Dalgliesh shook hands with Urquhart and left. As he passed through the hall the girl at the switchboard, hearing his footsteps, glanced round, flushed, and paused in

momentary confusion, plug in hand. She had been well trained but not quite well enough. Unwilling to embarrass her further, Dalgliesh smiled and passed swiftly out of the building. He had no doubt that, on Henry Urquhart's instructions, she was ringing Stephen Courtney-Briggs.

IV

Saville Mansions was a block of late Victorian flats close to Marylebone Road, respectable, prosperous but neither ostentatious nor opulent. Masterson had the expected trouble in finding a vacant lot to park his car and it was after seven thirty before he entered the building. The entrance hall was dominated by a grille-encased lift of ornate design and a reception desk presided over by a uniformed porter. Masterson, who had no intention of stating his business, nodded to him casually and ran lightly up the stairs. Number 23 was on the second floor. He pressed the bell and prepared for a brief wait.

But the door opened immediately and he found himself almost embraced by an extraordinary apparition, painted like the caricature of a stage whore and wearing a short evening dress of flame-coloured chiffon which would have looked incongruous on a woman half her age. The bodice was so low that he could glimpse the fold between the sagging breasts bunched high into the cups of her brassière, and could see where the powder lay caked in the cracks of dry yellow skin. Her lashes were weighted with mascara; the brittle hair, dyed an improbable blonde, was dressed in lacquered swathes around the raddled face; her carmine-painted mouth hung open in incredulous dismay. Their surprise was mutual. They stared at each other as if unable to believe their eyes. The change in her face from relief to disappointment was almost comic.

Masterson recovered first and announced himself:

"You remember", he said, "I telephoned early this morning and made an appointment?"

"I can't see you now. I'm just going out. I thought you were my dancing partner. You said you'd come early in the evening."

A shrill nagging voice made sharper by disappointment. She

looked as if she might close the door in his face. Quickly he slid one foot across the threshold.

"I was unavoidably detained. I'm sorry."

Unavoidably detained. Too right, he had been. That frantic but ultimately satisfying interlude in the back of the car had occupied more of the evening than he had anticipated. It had taken longer, too, to find a sufficiently secluded spot even on a dark winter's evening. The Guildford Road had offered few promising turnings into open country with its prospect of grass verges and unfrequented lanes. Julia Pardoe had been fussy too. Every time he slowed the car at a likely spot he had been met with her quiet, "not here". He had first seen her as she was about to step off the pavement on to the pedestrian crossing which led to the entrance of Heatheringfield station. He had slowed the car for her but, instead of waving her on, had leaned over and opened the passenger door. She had paused for only a second before walking over to him, coat swinging above the knee-length boots, and had slipped into the seat beside him without a word or glance. He had said:

"Coming up to town?"

She had nodded and had smiled secretively, eyes fixed on the windscreen. It had been as simple as that. She had hardly spoken a dozen words throughout the drive. The tentative or more overt preliminaries which he felt the game demanded of him had met with no response. He might have been a chauffeur with whom she was driving in unwelcome proximity. In the end, pricked by anger and humiliation, he had begun to wonder whether he could have been mistaken. But there had been the reassurance of that concentrated stillness, the eyes which, for minutes at a time, had watched with blue intensity his hands stroking the wheel or busy with the gears. She had wanted it all right. She had wanted it as much as he. But you could hardly call it a quick lay. One thing, surprisingly, she had told him. She was on her way to meet Hilda Rolfe; they were going to a theatre together after an early dinner. Well, either they would have to go without dinner or miss the first act; she was apparently unconcerned either way.

Amused and only slightly curious he had asked:

472

'How are you going to explain your lateness to Sister Rolfe? Or won't you bother now to turn up?"

She had shrugged.

"I shall tell her the truth. It might be good for her." Seeing his sudden frown she had added with contempt:

"Oh, don't worry! She won't sneak to Mr. Dalgliesh. Hilda isn't like that."

Masterson hoped she was right. This was something Dalgliesh wouldn't forgive.

"What will she do?" he had asked.

"If I tell? Chuck in her job I imagine; leave the John Carpendar. She's pretty fed up with the place. She only stays on because of me."

Wrenching his mind from the memory of that high, merciless voice into the present, Masterson forced himself to smile at the very different woman now confronting him and said in a propitiatory tone:

"The traffic you know. . . . I had to drive from Hampshire. But I shan't keep you long."

Holding out his warrant card with that slightly furtive air inseparable from the gesture he edged himself into the flat. She didn't try to stop him. But her eyes were blank, her mind obviously elsewhere. As she closed the door, the telephone rang. Without a murmur she left him standing in the hall and almost ran into a room to the left. He could hear her voice rising in protest. It seemed to be expostulating, then pleading. Then there was a silence. He moved quietly up the hall and strained his ears to hear. He thought he detected the clicking of the dial. Then she was speaking again. He couldn't hear the words. This time the conversation was over in seconds. Then came another click of the dial. Another wail. In all she rang four numbers before she reappeared in the hall.

"Is anything wrong?" he asked. "Can I help?"

She screwed up her eyes and regarded him intently for a second like a housewife assessing the quality and price of a piece of beef. Her reply when it came was peremptory and astonishing.

"Can you dance?"

"I was the Met. police champion for three years running," he

473

lied. The Force, not surprisingly, held no dancing championships but he thought it unlikely that she would know this and the lie, like most of his lies, came easily and spontaneously.

Again that speculative, intent gaze.

"You'll need a dinner-jacket. I've still got Martin's things here. I'm going to sell them but the man hasn't come yet. He promised he'd come this afternoon but he didn't. You can't rely on anyone these days. You look about the same size. He was quite broad before his illness."

Masterson resisted the temptation to laugh aloud. He said gravely:

"I'd like to help you out if you're in a difficulty. But I'm a policeman. I'm here to get information not to spend the night dancing."

"It isn't the whole night. The ball stops at eleven thirty. It's the Delaroux Dancing Medal Ball at the Athenaeum Ballroom off the Strand. We could talk there."

"It would be easier to talk here." Her sullen face set in obstinacy.

"I don't want to talk here."

She spoke with the peevish insistence of a whining child. Then her voice hardened for the ultimatum.

"It's the ball or nothing."

They faced one another in silence. Masterson considered. The idea was grotesque, of course, but he wasn't going to get anything out of her tonight unless he agreed. Dalgliesh had sent him to London for information and his pride wouldn't let him return to Nightingale House without it. But would his pride permit him to spend the rest of the evening escorting this painted hag in public? There was no difficulty about the dancing. That was one of the skills, although not the most important, that Sylvia had taught him. She had been a randy blonde, ten years older than himself, with a dull bank manager husband whom it had been a positive duty to cuckold. Sylvia had been crazy on ballroom dancing and they had progressed together through a series of bronze, silver and gold medal competitions before the husband had become inconveniently menacing, Sylvia had begun to hint about divorce, and Masterson had prudently decided that the relationship had outlasted its useful-

474

ness, not to say his capacity for indoor exercise, and that the police service offered a reasonable career for an ambitious man who was looking for an excuse for a period of comparative rectitude. Now his taste in women and dancing had changed and he had less time for either. But Sylvia had had her uses. As they told you at Detective Training School, no skill is ever wasted in police work.

No, there would be no difficulty about the dancing. Whether she was equally expert was another matter. The evening would probably be a fiasco and whether he went with her or not she would probably talk in time. But when would that be? Dalgliesh liked to work fast. This was one of those cases where the number of suspects was limited to a small, closed community and he didn't normally expect to spend more than a week on them. He wouldn't exactly thank his subordinate for a wasted evening. And then there was that time in the car to be accounted for somehow. It wouldn't be a good night to return empty-handed. And what the hell! It would make a good story for the boys. And if the evening became too impossible he could always ditch her. He'd better remember to take his own clothes in the car in case he needed to make a quick escape.

"All right," he said. "But it's got to be worth my while."

"It will be."

Martin Dettinger's dinner-jacket fitted him better than he had feared. It was strange, this ritual of dressing up in another man's clothes. He found himself searching in the pockets as if they too could hold some kind of clue. But he found nothing. The shoes were too small and he made no effort to force them on his feet. Luckily he was wearing black shoes with leather soles. They were too heavy for dancing and looked incongruous with the dinner-jacket but they would have to do. He bundled his own suit in a cardboard box reluctantly provided by Mrs. Dettinger and they set off.

He knew that there would be little chance of finding a space for the car in or near the Strand so drove over the South Bank and parked next to County Hall. Then they walked to Waterloo Station and hired a taxi. That part of the evening wasn't too bad. She had wrapped herself in a voluminous, old-fashioned fur coat. It smelt

strong and sour as if a cat had got at it, but at least it was concealing. For the whole of the journey neither of them spoke a word.

The dance had already started when they arrived shortly after eight and the great hall was unpleasantly full. They made their way to one of the few remaining empty tables under the balcony. Masterson noticed that each of the male instructors sported a red carnation; the women a white one. There was a great deal of promiscuous kissing and caressing pats of shoulders and arms. One of the men minced up to Mrs. Dettinger with little bleats of welcome and congratulation.

"You're looking marvellous Mrs. D. Sorry to hear that Tony's ill. But I'm glad you found a partner."

The glance at Masterson was perfunctorily curious. Mrs. Dettinger received this greeting with a clumsy jerk of the head and a slight leer of gratification. She made no attempt to introduce Masterson.

They sat out the next two dances and Masterson contented himself with looking round the hall. The whole atmosphere was drearily respectable. A huge bunch of balloons hung from the ceiling, ready no doubt to descend for some orgiastic climax to tonight's festivities. The band wore red jackets with gold epaulettes and had the gloomily resigned look of men who have seen it all before. Masterson looked forward to an evening of cynical uninvolvement, the gratification of observing the folly of others, the insidious pleasure of disgust. He recalled the description of a French diplomat of the English dancing "avec les visages si tristes, les derrières si gais". Here the bottoms were positively staid, but the faces were fixed in grins of stimulated delight so unnatural that he wondered whether the school had taught the approved facial expression with the correct steps. Away from the dance floor all the women looked worried, their expressions ranging from slight apprehension to almost frantic anxiety. They greatly outnumbered the men and some of them were dancing together. The majority were middle-aged or older and the style of dress was uniformly old-fashioned, the bodices tight and low cut, the immense circular skirts studded with sequins.

The third dance was a quick step. She turned to him suddenly

476

and said, "We'll dance this." Unprotesting, he led her on to the floor and clasped her rigid body with his left arm. He resigned himself to a long and exhausting evening. If this old harpy had anything useful to tell—and the old man seemed to think she had—then, by God, she would tell it even if he had to jangle her round this bloody floor until she dropped. The notion was pleasing and he indulged it. He could picture her, disjointed as a puppet loosed from its cords, the brittle legs sprawled awkwardly, the arms swinging into the final exhaustion. Except that he would probably drop first. That half-hour with Julia Pardoe hadn't been the best possible preparation for a night on the dance floor. But the old bitch had plenty of life in her. He could taste and feel the beads of sweat tickling the corners of his mouth, but she was hardly breathing faster and her hands were cool and dry. The face close to his was intent, the eyes glazed, the lower lip sagging open. It was like dancing with an animated bag of bones.

The music crashed to a stop. The conductor swung round and flashed his artificial smile over the floor. The players relaxed, permitting themselves a brief smile. The kaleidoscope of colour in the middle of the floor coalesced then flowed into new patterns as the dancers disengaged and minced back to their tables. A waiter was hovering for orders. Masterson crooked his finger.

"What will you have?"

He sounded as ungracious as a miser forced into standing his round. She asked for a gin and tonic and when it came accepted it without thanks or apparent gratification. He settled for a double whisky. It was to be the first of many. Spreading the flame-coloured skirt around her chair, she began to survey the hall with that look of disagreeable intensity which he was beginning to know so well. He might not have been there. Careful, he thought, don't get impatient. She wants to keep you here. Let her.

"Tell me about your son," he said quietly, careful to keep his voice even and unemphatic.

"Not now. Some other evening. There's no hurry."

He nearly shouted aloud with exasperation. Did she really think that he planned to see her again? Did she expect him to dance with her for ever on the half promise of a titbit of information? He pic-

tured them, capering grotesquely through the years, involuntary participants in a surrealist charade. He put down his glass.

"There won't be another time. Not unless you can help me. The Superintendent isn't keen on spending public money when there's nothing to be learned. I have to justify every minute of my time."

He instilled into his voice the right degrees of resentment and self-righteousness. She looked at him for the first time since they had sat down.

"There might be something to be learned. I never said there wasn't. What about the drinks?"

"The drinks?" He was momentarily nonplussed.

"Who pays for the drinks?"

"Well, normally they are on expenses. But when it's a question of entertaining friends, like tonight for example, naturally I pay myself."

He lied easily. It was one of the talents which he thought helped most in his job.

She nodded as if satisfied. But she didn't speak. He was wondering whether to try again when the band crashed into a cha-cha. Without a word she rose and turned towards him. They took the floor again.

The cha-cha was succeeded by a mamba, the mamba by a waltz, the waltz by a slow fox-trot. And still he had learned nothing. Then there was a change in the evening's programme. The lights suddenly dimmed and a sleek man, glistening from head to toe as if he had bathed in hair oil, appeared in front of the microphone and adjusted it for his height. He was accompanied by a languid blonde, her hair elaborately dressed in a style already five years out of date. The spotlight played upon them. She dangled a chiffon scarf negligently from her right hand and surveyed the emptying dance floor with a proprietorial air. There was an anticipatory hush. The man consulted a list in his hand.

"And now, ladies and gentlemen, the moment we have all been waiting for. The exhibition dances. Our medalists for the year will demonstrate for our delight the dances which won them their awards. We begin with our silver medallist, Mrs. Dettinger, dancing"—he consulted the list—"dancing the tango."

He swept a chubby hand around the floor. The band crashed into a discordant fanfare. Mrs. Dettinger rose, dragging Masterson with her. Her claw was like a vice round his wrist. The spotlight swung round and settled on them. There was a little burst of applause. The sleek man continued:

"Mrs. Dettinger is dancing with—could we have the name of your new partner Mrs. Dettinger?" Masterson called out loudly:

"Mr. Edward Heath."

The sleek man paused, then decided to take it at its face value. Forcing enthusiasm into his voice, he proclaimed:

"Mrs. Dettinger, silver medallist, dancing the tango with Mr. Edward Heath."

The cymbals clashed, there was a further spatter of applause. Masterson led his partner on to the floor with exaggerated courtesy. He was aware that he was slightly drunk and was glad of it. He was going to enjoy himself.

He clasped his hand to the small of her back and assumed an expression of lecherous expectancy. It won an immediate giggle from the nearest table. She frowned and he watched fascinated while an unbecoming crimson flowed over her face and neck. He realized with delight that she was intensely nervous, that this pathetic charade actually mattered to her. It was for this moment that she had dressed so carefully, painted her raddled face. The Delaroux Medal Ball. The demonstration tango. And then her partner had failed her. Lost courage probably, the poor sap. But fate had provided her with a personable and competent substitute. It must have seemed like a miracle. It was for this moment that he had been enticed to the Athenaeum Hall, kept dancing here hour after tedious hour. The knowledge was exhilarating. By God, he had her now. This was to be her big moment. He would see that she didn't forget it in a hurry.

The slow rhythm began. He noted with irritation that it was the same old tune for this dance that they had played most of the evening. He hummed the words in her ear. She whispered:

"We're supposed to be dancing the Delaroux tango."

"We're dancing the Charles Masterson tango, sweetheart."

Clasping her tightly he marched her belligerently across the floor

479

in a strutting parody of the dance, swung her viciously around so that her laquered hair nearly brushed the floor and he heard her bones cracking, and held her in the pose while he bestowed a smile of surprised gratification on the party at the nearest table. The giggle was louder now, more prolonged. As he jerked her upright and waited for the next beat she hissed:

"What do you want to know?"

"He recognized someone, didn't he? Your son. When he was in the John Carpendar Hospital. He saw someone he knew?"

"Will you behave yourself and dance properly?"

"Perhaps."

They were moving again in an orthodox tango. He could feel her relaxing a little in his arms, but he still kept a firm hold on her.

"It was one of the Sisters. He'd seen her before."

"Which Sister?"

"I don't know, he didn't tell me."

"What did he tell you?"

"After the dance."

"Tell me now if you don't want to end on the floor. Where had he seen her before?"

"In Germany. She was in the dock. It was a war trial. She got off but everybody knew she was guilty."

"Where in Germany?"

He mouthed the words through lips stretched into the fatuous smile of a professional dancing partner.

"Felsenheim. It was a place called Felsenheim."

"Say it again. Say that name again!"

"Felsenheim."

The name meant nothing to him but he knew he would remember it. With luck he would get the details later but the salient facts must be torn from her now while he had her in his power. It might not be true, of course. None of it might be true. And if true it might not be relevant. But this was the information he had been sent to get. He felt a surge of confidence and good humour. He was even in danger of enjoying the dance. He decided that it was time for something spectacular and led her into a complicated routine beginning with a progressive link and ending with a close promenade

that took them diagonally across the hall. It was faultlessly executed and the applause was loud and sustained. He asked:

"What was her name?"

"Irmgard Grobel. She was only a young girl then, of course. Martin said that was why she got off. He never had any doubt she was guilty."

"Are you sure he didn't tell you which Sister it was?"

"No. He was very ill. He told me about the trial when he came home from Europe, so I already knew about it. But he was unconscious most of the time in hospital. And when he wasn't he was mostly delirious."

So he could have made a mistake, thought Masterson. It was an unlikely enough story. And surely it would be hard to recognize a face after over twenty-five years; except that he must have watched that particular face with fascinated intensity all through the trial. It must have made an impression on a young and probably sensitive man. Enough, perhaps, for him to relive it in his delirium and delude himself that one of the faces bending over him in those few moments of consciousness and lucidity was the face of Irmgard Grobel. But supposing, just supposing, he had been right. If he had told his mother he might well have told his special nurse or blurted it out in his delirium. And what use had Heather Pearce made of her knowledge?

He whispered softly into her ear: "Who else have you told?"

"Nobody. I haven't told anybody. Why should I?"

Another rock swing. Then an over swing. Very nice. More applause. He tightened his hold on her and made his voice husky with menace beneath the fixed grin.

"Who else? You must have told someone."

"Why should I?"

"Because you're a woman."

It was a lucky reply. The mulish obstinacy on her face softened. She glanced up at him for a second, then fluttered her sparse mascara-coated eyelashes in a travesty of flirtation. Oh God, he thought, she's going to be coy.

"Oh well . . . perhaps I did tell just one person."

"I know bloody well you did. I'm asking who?"

Again the deprecatory glance, the little move of submission. She had decided to enjoy this masterful man. For some reason, perhaps the gin, perhaps the euphoria of the dance, her resistance had crumbled. It was going to be hunky-dory from now on.

"I told Mr. Courtney-Briggs, Martin's surgeon. Well, it seemed only right."

"When?"

"Last Wednesday. The Wednesday of last week, I mean. At his consulting rooms in Wimpole Street. He had just left the hospital on the Friday when Martin died so I couldn't see him earlier. He's only at the John Carpendar on Monday, Thursday and Friday."

"Did he ask to see you?"

"Oh no! The staff nurse who was taking Sister's place said that he would be very glad to have a talk with me if I thought it would be helpful and that I could phone Wimpole Street to make an appointment. I didn't then. What was the use? Martin was dead. But then I got his bill. Not very nice, I thought, so soon after Martin had passed away. Two hundred guineas! I thought it was monstrous. After all, it's not as if he did any good. So I thought I'd just pop into Wimpole Street and see him and mention what I knew. It wasn't right for the hospital to employ a woman like that. A murderess really. And then to charge all that money. There was a second bill from the hospital for his maintenance you know, but it wasn't anything like Mr. Courtney-Briggs's two hundred guineas."

The sentences were disjointed. She spoke them close into his ear as opportunity offered. But she was neither breathless nor incoherent. She had plenty of energy for both the dance and the talk. And it was Masterson who was feeling the strain. Another progressive link leading into the *doré* and ending with a close promenade. She didn't put a foot wrong. The old girl had been well taught even if they couldn't give her grace or *élan*.

"So you trotted along to tell him what you knew and suggested that he took a slice off his profits?"

"He didn't believe me. He said that Martin was delirious and mistaken and that he could personally vouch for all the Sisters. But he took £50 off the bill."

She spoke with grim satisfaction. Masterson was surprised. Even

482

if Courtney-Briggs had believed the story there was no reason why he should deduct a not inconsiderable amount from his bill. He wasn't responsible for recruiting or appointing the nursing staff. He had nothing to worry about. Masterson wondered whether he had believed the story. He had obviously said nothing, either to the Chairman of the Hospital Management Committee or to the Matron. Perhaps it was true that he could vouch personally for all the Sisters and the £50 deduction had merely been a gesture to keep a tiresome woman quiet. But Courtney-Briggs hadn't struck Masterson as the kind of man to submit himself to blackmail or to relinquish a penny of what he thought was due to him.

It was at that moment that the music crashed to a finish. Masterson smiled benevolently on Mrs. Dettinger, and led her back to their table. The applause lasted until they reached it and then was cut off abruptly as the sleek man announced the next dance. Masterson looked around for the waiter and beckoned.

"Well, now," he said to his partner, "that wasn't so bad, was it? If you behave yourself nicely for the rest of the evening I might even take you home."

He did take her home. They left early but it was well past midnight before he finally left the Baker Street flat. By then he knew that he had as much of the story as she could tell him. She had grown maudlin after their return, a reaction, he felt, to triumph and gin. He had kept her supplied with the latter through the rest of the evening, not enough to make her unmanageably drunk but sufficient to keep her talkative and pliable. But the journey home had been a nightmare, not made easier by the cab driver's glances of mingled amusement and contempt as he drove them from the hall to the South Bank car park, and by the disapproving superciliousness of the hall porter when they arrived at Saville Mansions. Once in the flat he had coaxed, comforted and bullied her into coherence, making black coffee for them both in the unbelievably squalid kitchen—a slut's kitchen he thought, glad of one more reason to despise her—and giving it to her with promises that, of course, he wouldn't leave her, that he would call for her again the following Saturday, that they would be permanent dancing partners. By midnight he had got out of her all he wanted to know about Martin

483

Dettinger's career and his stay in the John Carpendar Hospital. There wasn't a great deal to be learned about the hospital. She hadn't visited often during the week he was there. Well, what was the point of it? There wasn't anything she could do for him. He was unconscious most of the time and didn't really know her even when he woke. Except that once, of course. She had hoped then for a little word of comfort and appreciation, but all she had got was that odd laugh and the talk about Irmgard Grobel. He had told her that story years before. She was tired of hearing it. A boy ought to be thinking of his mother when he was dying. It had been a terrible effort to sit there watching. She was a sensitive person. Hospitals upset her. The late Mr. Dettinger hadn't understood how sensitive she was.

There was apparently a great deal that the late Mr. Dettinger hadn't understood, his wife's sexual needs among them. Masterson listened to the story of her marriage without interest. It was the usual story of an unsatisfied wife, a henpecked husband and an unhappy and sensitive child. Masterson heard it without pity. He wasn't particularly interested in people. He divided them into two broad groups, the law-abiding and the villains and the ceaseless war which he waged against the latter fulfilled, as he knew, some inarticulate need of his own nature. But he was interested in facts. He knew that, when anybody visited the scene of a crime, some evidence was left behind or some was taken away. It was the detective's job to find that evidence. He knew that finger-prints hadn't yet been known to lie and that human beings did frequently, irrationally, whether they were innocent or guilty. He knew that facts stood up in court and people let you down. He knew that motive was unpredictable although he had honesty enough sometimes to recognize his own. It had struck him at the very moment of entering Julia Pardoe that his act, in its anger and exaltation, was in some way directed against Dalgliesh. But it never occurred to him to ask why. That would have seemed profitless speculation. Nor did he wonder whether, for the girl also, it had been an act of malice and private retribution.

"You'd think a boy would want his mother when he was dying. It was terrible to sit there and hear that dreadful breathing, first

soft and then dreadfully loud. Of course he had a private room. That's why the hospital was able to charge. He wasn't National Health. But the other patients must have heard the noise all over the ward."

"Cheyne-Stoke's breathing," said Masterson. "It comes before the death rattle."

"They should have done something about it. It upset me dreadfully. That special nurse he had should have done something about it. The plain one. I suppose she was doing her duty, but she never gave a thought to me. After all, the living need some attention. There wasn't anything else she could do for Martin."

"That was Nurse Pearce. The one who died."

"Yes, I remember you told me. So she's dead too. I hear of nothing but death. It's all around me. What did you call that breathing?"

"Cheyne Stoke's. It means that you're going to die."

"They should have done something about it. That girl should have done something about it. Did she breathe like that before she died?"

"No, she screamed. Someone poured disinfectant into her stomach and burned it out."

"I don't want to hear about it! I don't want to hear about it any more! Tell me about the dance. You will come back next Saturday, won't you?"

And so it had gone on. It had been tedious and exhausting and, in the end, almost frightening. The triumphant glow of getting what he wanted had faded before midnight and he was aware only of hatred and disgust. While he listened to her babblings he toyed with imagined violence. It was easy to see how these things happened. A handy poker. The silly face smashed into pulp. Blow on blow on blow. The bones splintering. A gush of blood. An orgasm of hatred. Imagining it, he found it hard to keep his breathing even. He took her hand gently.

"Yes," he said. "Yes, I'll come again. Yes. Yes."

The flesh was dry and hot now. She might have been in a fever. The painted nails were ridged. On the back of the hand the veins stood out like purple cords. He traced with a caressing finger the brown stains of age.

Shortly after midnight her voice burbled into incoherency, her head sank forward, and he saw that she was asleep. He waited for a moment, then disengaged his hand and tiptoed into the bedroom. It took him only a couple of minutes to change his clothes. Then he tiptoed into the bathroom and washed his face and the hand which had touched hers, washed them over and over again. Finally he left the flat, shutting the door quietly behind him as if afraid to wake her, and went out into the night.

v

Fifteen minutes later, Masterson's car passed the flat where Miss Beale and Miss Burrows, cosily dressing-gowned, were sipping their late night cocoa before the dying fire. They heard it as one brief crescendo in the intermittent flow of traffic, and broke off their chatter to speculate with desultory interest on what brought people out in the small hours of the morning. It was certainly unusual for them to be still up at this hour, but tomorrow was Saturday and they could indulge their fondness for late-night conversation in the comforting knowledge that they could lie in next morning.

They had been discussing the visit that afternoon of Chief Superintendent Dalgliesh. Really, they agreed, it had been a success, almost a pleasure. He had seemed to enjoy his tea. He had sat there, deep in their most comfortable armchair, and the three of them had talked together as if he were as harmless and familiar as the local vicar.

He had said to Miss Beale: "I want to see Nurse Pearce's death through your eyes. Tell me about it. Tell me everything you saw and felt from the moment you drove through the hospital gates."

And Miss Beale had told him, taking a shameful pleasure in her half-hour of importance, in his obvious appreciation that she had observed so carefully and could describe with such clarity. He was a good listener, they conceded. Well, that was part of his job. He was clever, too, at making people talk. Even Angela, who had sat in watchful silence for most of the time, couldn't explain why she had felt drawn to mention her recent encounter with Sister Rolfe

in the Westminster library. And his eyes had flickered with interest, interest which had faded into disappointment when she told him the date. The friends agreed that they couldn't have been mistaken. He had been disappointed. Sister Rolfe had been seen in the library on the wrong day.

VI

It was after eleven o'clock when Dalgliesh turned the key in his desk drawer, locked the office behind him and let himself out of the side door of Nightingale House to walk back to the Falconer's Arms. At the turn of the path where it narrowed before losing itself in the dark shadows of the trees, he looked back at the gaunt pile of the house, enormous and sinister, with its four turrets black against the night sky. The house was in almost total darkness. There was only one lighted window and it took him a minute to identify the room. So Mary Taylor was in her bedroom but not yet asleep. The light was merely a faint glow, perhaps from a bedside lamp, and as he watched it went out.

He made his way towards the Winchester Gate. The trees here were very close to the path. Their black boughs arched over his head shutting out the faint light from the nearest lamp. For about fifty yards he walked in absolute darkness, treading swiftly and silently over the mush of dead leaves. He was in that state of physical tiredness when the mind and body seem detached, the body, conditioned to reality, moving half consciously in the familiar physical world, while the liberated mind swings into uncontrolled orbit in which fantasy and fact show an equally ambiguous face. Dalgliesh was surprised that he was so tired. This job was no more arduous than any other. He was working long hours, but then a sixteen-hour day was normal for him when he was on a case. And this extraordinary weariness wasn't the exhaustion of frustration or failure. The case would break by tomorrow morning. Later tonight Masterson would be back with another piece of the jigsaw and the picture would be complete. In two days at the latest he would have left Nightingale House. In two days' time he would have seen the last of that gold and white room in the south-west turret.

487

Moving like an automaton he heard, too late, the sudden muted footfall at his back. Instinctively, he threw himself round to face his adversary and felt the blow glance from his left temple to his shoulder. There was no pain, only a crack as if his whole cranium had split, a numbness of his left arm, and after a second which seemed an eternity, the warm, almost comforting, gush of blood. He gave one gasp and crumpled forward. But he was still conscious. Blinded by blood and fighting against nausea, he tried to rise, feeling for the earth with both hands, willing himself to get up and fight. But his feet scrabbled ineffectively in the moist earth and there was no strength in his arms. His eyes were blinded by his own blood. The suffocating smell of damp humus pressed against his nose and mouth, pungent as an anaesthetic. He lay there, helplessly retching, waking pain with every spasm, and waited in angry impotence for the final annihilating blow.

But nothing happened. He sank, unresisting, into unconsciousness. A few seconds later he was recalled to reality by a hand gently shaking his shoulder. Someone was bending over him. He heard a woman's voice.

"It's me. What's 'appened? Somebody cosh yer?"

It was Morag Smith. He struggled to answer, to warn her to get away quickly. The two of them would be no match for a determined killer. But his voice seemed incapable of forming words. He was aware that somewhere very close a man was groaning, then realized with bitter humour, that the voice was his. He seemed to have no control over it. He was aware of hands moving around his head. Then she shuddered like a child.

"Ugh! Yer all over blood!"

Again he tried to talk. She bent her head nearer. He could see the dark strands of hair and the white face hovering in front of him. He struggled to rise and this time managed to get to his knees.

"Did you see him?"

"Not really—'e 'eard me coming through. Made off towards Nightingale 'ouse. Blimey, you don't 'alf look a bloody mess. 'ere, lean on me."

"No. Leave me and get help. He may be back."

"Not 'im. Anyway, we're better together. I don't fancy going it

488

alone. Ghosts is one thing, bloody murderers is another. Come on, I'll give yer a 'and."

He could feel the sharp bones in her thin shoulders, but the fragile body was remarkably wiry and she stood his weight well. He forced himself to his feet and stood there swaying. He asked:

"Man or woman?"

"Didn't see. Could've been either. Never mind about that now. Think yer can make it to Nightingale 'ouse? That'd be the nearest."

Dalgliesh felt remarkably better now that he was on his legs. He could scarcely see the path but he took a few tentative steps forward, his hand supported by her shoulder.

"I think so. The back door would be the nearest. It can't be more than fifty yards. Ring the bell of Matron's flat. I know she's there."

Together they shuffled slowly along the path obliterating, as Dalgliesh realized bitterly, any footprints as he might have otherwise have hoped to find next morning. Not that these sodden leaves would yield many clues. He wondered what had happened to the weapon. But this was pointless speculation. He could do nothing until it was light. He felt a wave of gratitude and affection for the tough little person whose brittle arm lay weightless as a child's around his hip. We must look an odd pair, he thought. He said:

"You probably saved my life, Morag. He only ran off because he heard you coming."

He, or was it she? If only Morag had been in time to glimpse whether it were a man or a woman. He could scarcely catch her reply.

"Don't talk bloody daft."

He heard, without surprise, that she was crying. She made no attempt to suppress or check her sobbing and it didn't impede their progress. Perhaps, to Morag, crying was almost as natural as walking. He made no effort to comfort her except to press on her shoulders. She took that as a plea for more support and tightened her arm around his hips, leaning against him, helping him on his way. And thus incongruously entwined they passed under the shadows of the trees.

The light in the demonstration room was bright, too bright. It pierced even his gummed eyelids and he moved his head restlessly from side to side to escape the shaft of pain. Then his head was being steadied by cool hands. Mary Taylor's hands. He heard her speaking to him, telling him that Courtney-Briggs was in the hospital. She had sent for Courtney-Briggs. Then the same hands were taking off his tie, undoing the buttons of his shirt, slipping his arms out of his jacket with practised skill.

"What happened?"

It was Courtney-Briggs's voice, harsh and masculine. So the surgeon had arrived. What had he been doing in the hospital? Another emergency operation? Courtney-Briggs's patients seemed curiously prone to relapse. What alibi had he for the last half-hour? Dalgliesh said:

"Someone was lying in wait for me. I've got to check who's in Nightingale House."

A firm grip was on his arm. Courtney-Briggs was pressing him back into his chair. Two swinging blobs of grey hovered over him. Her voice again.

"Not now. You can hardly stand. One of us will go."

"Go now."

"In a minute. We've locked all the doors. We shall know if anyone returns. Rely on us. Just relax."

So reasonable. Rely on us. Relax. He gripped metal arms on the chair, taking hold on reality.

"I want to check for myself."

Half blinded by blood, he sensed rather than saw their mutual glance of concern. He knew that he sounded like a petulant child, beating his insistence against the implacable calm of the grown-ups. Maddened with frustration, he tried to rise from the chair. But the floor tipped sickeningly, then rose up to meet him through whorls of screaming colour. It was no good. He couldn't stand.

"My eyes," he said. Courtney-Briggs's voice, annoyingly reasonable:

"In one moment. I must look first at your head."

"But I want to see!"

His blindness infuriated him. Were they doing this to him deliberately? He put up a hand and began to pick at the caked eyelids. He could hear them talking together, low voiced, in the muttered idiom of their craft from which he, the patient, was excluded. He was conscious of new sounds, the hiss of a sterilizer, a jingle of instruments, the closing of a metal lid. Then the smell of disinfectant sharpened. Now she was cleaning his eyes. A pad, deliciously cool, was wiped across each lid, and he opened them blinking to see more clearly the sheen of her dressing-gown and the long plait of hair falling over her left shoulder. He spoke to her directly.

"I must know who's in Nightingale House. Could you check now, please?"

Without another word or a further glance at Courtney-Briggs, she slipped out of the room. As soon as the door was closed, Dalgliesh said:

"You didn't tell me that your brother was once engaged to Josephine Fallon."

"You didn't ask me."

The surgeon's voice was deliberate, uninterested, the response of a man with his mind on his job. There was a snip of scissors, a momentary chill of steel against the skull. The surgeon was clipping Dalgliesh's hair around the wound.

"You must have known that I should be interested."

"Oh, interested! You'd be interested all right. Your kind have an infinite capacity for taking an interest in other people's affairs. But I confined myself to satisfying your curiosity only so far as the deaths of these two girls were concerned. You can't complain that I've held anything relevant back. Peter's death isn't relevant—merely a private tragedy."

Not so much a private tragedy thought Dalgliesh as a public embarrassment. Peter Courtney had violated his brother's first principle, the necessity of being successful. Dalgliesh said:

"He hanged himself."

"As you say, he hanged himself. Not a very dignified or pleasant way to go, but the poor boy hadn't my resources. The day when

they make my final diagnosis I shall have more appropriate measures available than doing myself to death on the end of a rope."

His egotism, thought Dalgliesh, was astounding. Even his brother's death had to be seen in relationship to himself. He stood complacently secure at the hub of his private universe while other people—brother, mistress, patient—revolved round that central sun existing by virtue of its warmth and light, obedient to its centripetal force. But wasn't that how most people saw themselves? Was Mary Taylor less self-absorbed? Was he himself? Wasn't it merely that she and he pandered more subtly to their essential egotism?

The surgeon moved over to his black instrument case and took out a mirror mounted on a metal band which he clipped around his head. He came back to Dalgliesh, ophthalmoscope in hand and settled himself into a chair opposite his patient. They sat confronting each other, foreheads almost touching. Dalgliesh could sense the metal of the instrument against his right eye. Courtney-Briggs commanded:

"Look straight ahead."

Dalgliesh stared obediently at the pinpoint of light. He said:

"You left the main hospital building at about midnight. You spoke to the porter at the main gate at twelve thirty-eight a.m. Where were you between those times?"

"I told you. There was a fallen elm blocking the back path. I spent some minutes examining the scene and making sure that other people didn't injure themselves on it."

"One person did precisely that. That was at twelve seventeen a.m. There was no warning scarf tied on the branches at that time."

The ophthalmoscope moved to the other eye. The surgeon's breathing was perfectly regular.

"He was mistaken."

"He doesn't think so."

"So you deduce that I arrived at the fallen tree later than twelve seventeen a.m. It may have been so. As I wasn't concocting an alibi, I didn't check the time every two minutes."

"But you're not suggesting that it took you over seventeen

minutes to drive from the main hospital to that particular place."

"Oh, I think I could make out quite a case for the delay, don't you know. I could claim that I needed, in your deplorable police jargon, to obey a call of nature and left my car to meditate among the trees."

"And did you?"

"I may have done. When I've dealt with your head, which incidentally is going to need about a dozen stitches, I'll give some thought to the matter. You'll forgive me if I concentrate now on my own job."

The matron had quietly returned. She took up her stance next to Courtney-Briggs like an acolyte waiting for orders. Her face was very white. Without waiting for her to speak the surgeon handed her the ophthalmoscope. She said:

"Everyone who should be in Nightingale House is in her room."

Courtney-Briggs was running his hands over Dalgliesh's left shoulder causing pain with every thrust of the strong probing fingers. He said:

"The collar-bone seems all right. Badly bruised but not fractured. Your attacker must have been a tall woman. You're over six feet yourself."

"If it were a woman. Or she may have had a long weapon, a golf club perhaps."

"A golf club. Matron, what about your clubs? Where do you keep them?"

She answered dully: "In the hall at the bottom of my staircase. The bag is usually left just inside the door."

"Then you'd better check them now."

She was gone for less than two minutes and they waited her return in silence. When she came back she spoke directly to Dalgliesh.

"One of the irons is missing."

The news seemed to hearten Courtney-Briggs. He said almost jovially:

"Well, there's your weapon for you! But there's not much point in searching for it tonight. It'll be lying about somewhere in the grounds. Your men can find it and do everything necessary to it tomorrow; test it for finger-prints, look for blood and hair, all the

usual tricks. You're not in any fit state to bother yourself tonight. We've got to get this wound sutured. I shall have to get you over to the out-patient theatre. You'll need an anaesthetic."

"I don't want an anaesthetic."

"Then I can give you a local. That just means a few injections around the wound. We could do this here, Matron."

"I don't want any anaesthetic. I just want it stitched."

Courtney-Briggs explained patiently as if to a child.

"It's a very deep cut and it's got to be sutured. It's going to hurt badly if you won't accept an anaesthetic."

"I tell you I don't want one. And I don't want a prophylactic injection of penicillin or anti-tetanus. I just want it sutured."

He felt them look at each other. He knew that he was being obstinately unreasonable but he didn't care. Why couldn't they get on with it? Then Courtney-Briggs spoke, curiously formal:

"If you'd prefer another surgeon. . . ."

"No, I just want you to get on with it."

There was a moment's silence. Then the surgeon spoke:

"All right. I'll be as quick as I can."

He was aware that Mary Taylor had moved behind him. She drew his head back against her breast, supported it between cold, firm hands. He shut his eyes like a child. The needle felt immense, an iron rod simultaneously ice cold and red hot which pierced his skull time and time again. The pain was an abomination, made bearable only by anger and by his obstinate determination not to betray weakness. He set his features into a rigid mask. But it was infuriating to feel the involuntary tears seeping under his eyelids.

After an eternity he realized that it was over. He heard himself say:

"Thank you. And now I'd like to get back to my office. Sergeant Masterson has instructions to come on here if I'm not in the hotel. He can drive me home."

Mary Taylor was winding a crêpe bandage around his head. She didn't speak. Courtney-Briggs said:

"I'd prefer you to go straight to bed. We can let you have a room in the Medical Officers' quarters for tonight. I'll arrange for an X-ray first thing in the morning. Then I'd like to see you again."

"You can arrange what you like for tomorrow. Just now I'd like to be left alone."

He got up from the chair. She put a hand on his arm, supporting him. But he must have made some kind of gesture for she dropped her arm. He felt surprisingly light on his feet. It was odd that such an insubstantial body could support the weight of so heavy a head. He put up an exploring hand and felt the scope of the bandage; it seemed an immense distance from his skull. Then, focusing his eyes carefully, he walked unhindered across the room to the door. As he reached it, he heard Courtney-Briggs's voice.

"You will want to know where I was at the time of the attack. I was in my room in the Medical Officers' quarters. I'm staying there for tonight ready for an early operating session. I'm sorry I can't oblige you with an alibi. I can only hope that you realize that, if I want to put anyone out of the way, I have subtler methods at my disposal than a golf iron."

Dalgliesh didn't reply. Without looking round and without a further word he left them and closed the door of the demonstration room quietly behind him. The stairs looked a formidable climb and, at first, he was afraid that he wouldn't be able to make it. But he grasped the banister resolutely and, step by careful step, made his way back to the office and settled down to wait for Masterson.

Chapter Eight

A Circle of Burnt Earth

It was nearly two in the morning when the gate porter waved Masterson through the main entrance of the hospital. The wind was rising steadily as he drove along the twisting path to Nightingale House between an avenue of black rumbustious trees. The house was in darkness except for the one lit window where Dalgliesh was still working. Masterson scowled at it. It had been irritating and disconcerting to discover that Dalgliesh was still at Nightingale House. He expected to have to give his report on the day's activities; the prospect wasn't unpleasing since he was fortified by success. But it had been a long day. He hoped that they weren't in for one of the Superintendent's all-night sessions.

Masterson let himself in at the side door, double locking it behind him. The silence of the vast entrance hall received him, eerie and portentous. The house seemed to be holding its breath. He smelt again the alien but now familiar amalgam of disinfectant and floor polish, unwelcoming and faintly sinister. As if afraid to stir the sleeping house—half empty as it was—he did not switch on the light but made his way across the hall by the beam of his electric torch. The notices on the hall board gleamed white reminding him of mourning cards in the vestibule of some foreign cathedral. Of your charity pray for the soul of Josephine Fallon. He found himself tiptoeing up the stairs as if afraid to wake the dead.

In the first-floor office Dalgliesh was sitting at his desk with the file open before him. Masterson stood stock-still in the doorway, concealing his surprise. The Superintendent's face was drawn and grey under an immense cocoon of white crêpe bandage. He was sitting bolt upright, forearms resting on the desk, palms spread lightly

496

each side of the page. The pose was familiar. Masterson reflected, not for the first time, that the Superintendent had remarkable hands and knew how to display them to advantage. He had long decided that Dalgliesh was one of the proudest men he knew. This essential conceit was too carefully guarded to be generally recognized, but it was gratifying to catch him out in one of the lesser vanities. Dalgliesh looked up without smiling.

"I expected you back two hours ago, Sergeant. What were you doing?"

"Extracting information by unorthodox means, sir."

"You look as if the unorthodox means have been used on you."

Masterson bit back the obvious retort. If the old man chose to be mysterious about his injury he wasn't going to give him the gratification of showing curiosity.

"I was dancing until nearly midnight, sir."

"At your age that shouldn't be too exhausting. Tell me about the lady. She seems to have made an impression on you. You had an agreeable evening?"

Masterson could have retorted with reason that he had had one hell of an evening. He contented himself with an account of what he had learned. The exhibition tango was prudently forgotten. Instinct warned him that Dalgliesh might think it neither funny nor clever. But he gave an otherwise accurate account of the evening. He tried to keep it factual and unemotional but became aware that he was enjoying some of the telling. His description of Mrs. Dettinger was concise but caustic. Towards the end he hardly troubled to conceal his contempt and disgust of her. He felt that he was making rather a good job of it.

Dalgliesh listened in silence. His cocooned head was still bent over the file and Masterson got no hint of what he was feeling. At the end of the recital Dalgliesh looked up:

"Do you enjoy your work, Sergeant?"

"Yes sir, for most of the time."

"I thought you might say that."

"Was the question intended as a rebuke, sir?"

Masterson was aware that he was entering on dangerous ground but was unable to resist this first tentative step.

497

Dalgliesh didn't answer the question. Instead he said:

"I don't think it's possible to be a detective and remain always kind. But if you ever find that cruelty is becoming pleasurable in itself, then it's probably time to stop being a detective."

Masterson flushed and was silent. This from Dalgliesh! Dalgliesh who was so uncaring about his subordinates' private life as to seem unaware that they had any; whose caustic wit could be as devastating as another man's bludgeon. Kindness! And how kind exactly was he himself? How many of his notable successes had been won with kindness? He would never be brutal, of course. He was too proud, too fastidious, too controlled, too bloody inhuman in fact for anything so understandable as a little down-to-earth brutality. His reaction to evil was a wrinkle of the nose not a stamp of the foot. But kindness! Tell that to the boys, thought Masterson.

Dalgliesh went on talking as if he said nothing remarkable.

"We'll have to see Mrs. Dettinger again, of course. And we'll want a statement. Did you think she was telling the truth?"

"It's difficult to tell. I can't think why she should lie. But she's a strange woman and she wasn't feeling too pleased with me at the time. It might give her some kind of perverse satisfaction to mislead us. She might have substituted Grobel's name for one of the other defendants, for example."

"So that the person her son recognized on the ward could have been any one of the Felsenheim defendants, those who are still alive and unaccounted for. What exactly did her son tell her?"

"That's the problem, sir. Apparently he gave her to understand that this German woman, Irmgard Grobel, was employed at the John Carpendar but she can't recall his exact words. She thinks he said something like:

"'This is a funny kind of hospital, ma, they've got Grobel here, working as one of the Sisters.'"

Dalgliesh said: "Suggesting that it wasn't the Sister who was actually nursing him, otherwise he'd presumably have said so. Except, of course, that he was unconscious most of the time and may not have seen Sister Brumfett previously or appreciated that she was in charge of the ward. He wasn't in any state to recognize

the niceties of the hospital hierarchy. According to his medical record he was either delirious or unconscious most of the time, which would make his evidence suspect even if he hadn't inconveniently died. Anyway, his mother at first didn't apparently take the story too seriously. She didn't mention it to anyone at the hospital? Nurse Pearce, for example?"

"She says not. I think at the time Mrs. Dettinger's main concern was to collect her son's belongings and the death certificate and claim on the insurance."

"Bitter, Sergeant?"

"Well, she's paying nearly £2,000 a year for dancing lessons and she'd come to the end of her capital. These Delaroux people like payment in advance. I heard all about her finances when I took her home. Mrs. Dettinger wasn't out to make trouble. But then she received Mr. Courtney-Briggs's bill, and it occurred to her that she might use her son's story to get a reduction. And she got one too. Fifty quid."

"Which suggests that Mr. Courtney-Briggs is either more charitable than we had supposed or thought that the information was worth the money. Did he pay it over at once?"

"She says not. She first visited him at his Wimpole Street consulting rooms on the evening of Wednesday, January twenty-first. She didn't get much joy on that occasion so she rang him up last Saturday morning. The receptionist told her that Mr. Courtney-Briggs was out of the country. She intended to ring again on the Monday but the cheque for fifty pounds came by the first post. There was no letter and no explanation, merely his compliment slip. But she got the message all right."

"So he was out of the country last Saturday. Where, I wonder? Germany? That's something to check, anyway."

Masterson said, "It all sounds so unlikely, sir. And it doesn't really fit."

"No. We're pretty certain who killed both those girls. Logically all the facts point to one person. And as you say, this new evidence doesn't really fit in. It's disconcerting when you scramble around in the dirt for a missing piece of the jigsaw and then find it's part of a different puzzle."

"So you don't think it's relevant, sir? I should hate to think that my evening's exertions with Mrs. Dettinger were in vain."

"Oh, it's relevant. It's exceedingly relevant. And we've found some corroboration. We've traced the missing library book. Westminster City Library were very helpful. Miss Pearce went to the Marylebone Branch on the afternoon of Thursday, 8th January, when she was off duty and asked if they had a book dealing with German war trials. She said she was interested in a trial at Felsenheim in November 1945. They couldn't find anything in stock but they said they would make inquiries of other London libraries and suggested that she should come back or telephone them in a day or two. She telephoned on the Saturday morning. They told her that they'd been able to trace a book which dealt with the Felsenheim trial among others, and she called in for it that afternoon. On each visit she gave her name as Josephine Fallon and presented Fallon's ticket and the blue token. Normally, of course, they wouldn't have noticed the name and address. They did so because the book had to be specially obtained from another library."

"Was the book returned, sir?"

"Yes, but anonymously, and they can't say exactly when. It was probably on the Wednesday after Pearce died. Someone left it on the non-fiction trolley. When the assistant went to fill up the trolley with recently returned books she recognized it and took it back to the counter to be registered and put on one side ready for return to its parent library. No one saw who returned it. The library is particularly busy and people come in and out at will. Not everyone has a book to return or calls at the counter. It would be easy enough to bring in a book in a basket or a pocket and slip it among the others on the trolley. The assistant who found it had been on counter duty for most of the morning and afternoon and one of the junior staff had been replenishing the trolley. The girl was getting behind with the work so her senior went to give a hand. She noticed the book at once. That was at four thirty approximately. But it could have been put there at any time."

"Any prints, sir?"

"Nothing helpful. A few smudges. It had been handled by quite a number of the library staff and God knows how many of the

public. And why not? They weren't to know that it was part of the evidence in a murder inquiry. But there's something interesting about it. Have a look."

He opened one of the desk drawers and brought out a stout book bound with a dark blue cloth and embossed with a library catalogue number on the spine. Masterson took it and laid it on the table. He seated himself and opened it carefully, taking his time. It was an account of various war trials held in Germany from 1945 onwards, apparently carefully documented, unsensational in treatment and written by a Queen's Counsel who had once been on the staff of the Judge Advocate General. There were only a few plates and of these only two related to the Felsenheim trial. One showed a general view of the Court with an indistinct glimpse of the doctor in the dock, and the other was a photograph of the camp commandant. Dalgliesh said:

"Martin Dettinger is mentioned, but only briefly. During the war he served in the King's Wiltshire Light Infantry and in November 1945 he was appointed as a member of a military Court set up in West Germany to try four men and one woman accused of war crimes. These Courts were established under a Special Army Order of June 1945 and this one consisted of a President who was a Brigadier of the Grenadier Guards, four army officers of whom Dettinger was one, and the Judge Advocate appointed by the Judge Advocate General to the Forces. As I said, they had the job of trying five people who, it was alleged—you'll find the indictment on page 127—'acting jointly and in pursuance of a common intent and acting for and on behalf of the then German Reich did on or about 3rd September 1944 wilfully, deliberately and wrongfully aid, abet and participate in the killing of 31 human beings of Polish and Russian nationality'."

Masterson was not surprised that Dalgliesh should be able to quote the indictment word for word. This was an administrator's trick, this ability to memorize and present facts with accuracy and precision. Dalgliesh could do it better than most, and if he wanted to exercise his technique it was hardly for his Sergeant to interrupt. He said nothing. He noticed that the Superintendent had taken up a large grey stone, a perfect ovoid, and was rolling it slowly be-

tween his fingers. It was something that had caught his eye in the grounds, presumably, and which he had picked up to serve as a paper-weight. It certainly hadn't been on the office desk that morning. The tired, strained voice went on.

"These 31 men, women and children were Jewish slave workers in Germany and were said to have been suffering from tuberculosis. They were sent to an institution in Western Germany which was originally designed to care for the mentally sick but which since the summer of 1944 had been dedicated, not to curing, but to the business of killing. There is no evidence to how many German mentally ill patients were done to death there. The staff had been sworn to secrecy about what went on, but there were plenty of rumours in the neighbouring districts. On the 3rd September 1944, a transport of Polish and Russian nationals were sent to the institution. They were told they were to receive treatment for tuberculosis. That night they were given lethal injections—men, women and children—and by the morning they were dead and buried. It was for this crime, not for the murder of the German nationals, that the five accused were on trial. One was the head doctor Max Klein, one a young pharmacist Ernst Gumbmann, one the chief male nurse Adolf Straub, and one a young, untrained female nurse aged 18, Irmgard Grobel. The head doctor and the chief male nurse were found guilty. The doctor was condemned to death and the male nurse to twenty-three years' imprisonment. The pharmacist and the woman were acquitted. You can find what her counsel said on page 140. You had better read it out."

Surprised, Masterson took up the book in silence and turned to page 140. He began reading. His voice sounded unnaturally loud.

"This court is not trying the defendant Irmgard Grobel for participation in the death of German nationals. We know now what was happening at Steinhoff Institution. We know, too, that it was in accordance with German law as proclaimed by Adolf Hitler alone. In accordance with orders handed down from the highest authority, many thousands of insane German people were put to death with perfect legality from 1940 onward. On moral grounds one can judge this action as one pleases. The question is not whether the staff at Steinhoff thought it wrong or whether they thought it

merciful. The question is whether they thought it was lawful. It has been proved by witnesses that there was such a law in existence. Irmgard Grobel, if she were concerned with the deaths of these people, acted in accordance with this law.

"But we are not concerned with the mentally ill. From July 1944 this same law was extended to cover incurably tubercular foreign workers. It might be contended that the accused would be in no doubt of the legality of such killings when she had seen German nationals put out of their misery in the interests of the State. But that is not my contention. We are not in a position to judge what the accused thought. She was not implicated in the only killings which are the concern of this Court. The transport of Russians and Poles arrived at Steinhoff on 3rd September 1944 at half past six in the evening. On that day Irmgard Grobel was returning from her leave. The Court has heard how she entered the nurses' quarters at half past seven and changed into her uniform. She was on duty from nine o'clock. Between the time of entering the Institution and arriving in the nurses' duty room in E Block she spoke only to two other nurses, witnesses Willig and Rohde. Both these women have testified that they did not tell Grobel of the arrival of the transport. So Grobel enters the duty room. She had had a difficult journey and is tired and sick. She is hesitating whether or not to seek permission to go off duty. It is then that the telephone rings and Doctor Klein speaks to her. The Court has heard the evidence of witnesses to this conversation. Klein asks Grobel to look in the drug store and tell him how much evipan and phenol there is in stock. You have heard how the evipan was delivered in cartons, each carton containing 25 injections and each injection consisting of one capsule of evipan in powder form and one container of sterile water. The evipan and phenol, together with other dangerous drugs, were kept in the nurses' duty room. Grobel checks the amounts and reports to Klein that there are two cartons of evipan and about 150 c.c. of liquid phenol in stock. Klein then orders her to have all the available evipan and phenol ready to hand over to male nurse Straub who will fetch it. He also orders her to hand over twelve 10 c.c. syringes and a quantity of strong needles. The accused claimed that at no time did he state for what purpose these drugs were

required and you have heard from the accused Straub that he, also, did not enlighten her.

"Irmgard Grobel did not leave the duty room until she was carried back to her quarters at nine twenty that night. The Court has heard how Nurse Rohde coming late on duty found her in a faint on the floor. For five days she was confined to her bed with acute vomiting and fever. She did not see the Russians and Poles enter E Block, she did not see their bodies carried out in the early hours of 4th September. When she returned to duty the corpses had been buried.

"Mr. President, this Court has heard witnesses who have testified to the kindness of Irmgard Grobel, to her gentleness with the child patients, to her skill as a nurse; I would remind the Court that she is young, hardly more than a child herself. But I do not ask for an acquittal on the grounds of her youth nor her sex but because she, alone of the accused, is manifestly innocent of this charge. She had no hand in the deaths of these 31 Russians and Poles. She did not even know that they existed. The Defence has nothing further to add."

Dalgliesh's bitter voice broke in on the silence.

"The usual Teutonic plea of legality you note, Sergeant. They didn't waste much time with their killings did they? Admitted at seven thirty and injected soon after nine. And why evipan? They couldn't be sure that death would be instantaneous unless they injected a heavy dose. I doubt whether less than 20 c.c. would kill immediately. Not that it would worry them. What saved Grobel was being on leave until late that evening. The Defence claimed that she was never told that the foreign prisoners had arrived, that no one knew until the morning of the fourth. That same plea gave the pharmacist his freedom. Technically they were both innocent, if you can use that word of anyone who worked at Steinhoff."

Masterson was silent. It was all so long ago. Grobel had been a girl. Ten years younger than he was now. The war was old history. It had no more relevance to his life than had the Wars of the Roses, less since it did not even evoke the faintly romantic and chivalrous overtones of the history learned in his boyhood. He had no particular feelings about the Germans, or indeed about any race other

than the few he regarded as culturally and intellectually inferior. The Germans were not among these. Germany to him meant clean hotels and good roads, *rippchen* eaten with the local wine at the Apfel Wine Struben Inn, the Rhine curving below him like a silver ribbon, the excellence of the camping ground at Koblenz.

And if any of the accused from Felsenheim were alive they would be well into middle age now. Irmgard Grobel herself would be forty-three. It was all such old history. It had relevance only because it touched this present case. He said:

"It happened so long ago. Is a secret like that worth killing to preserve? Who really cares now? Isn't the official policy to forgive and forget?"

"We English are good at forgiving our enemies; it releases us from the obligation of liking our friends. Take a look at this book, Masterson. What do you notice?"

Masterson let the pages fall apart, shook them gently, lifted the book to eye level and examined the binding. Then he replaced it on the table and pressed back the middle pages. There, embedded deep in the folds were a few grains of sand.

Dalgliesh said: "We've sent a sample to the lab for analysis, but the result isn't much in doubt. It's almost certainly from one of the fire buckets in Nightingale House."

"So that's where it was hidden until he, or she, could return it to the library. The same person hid the book and the tin of rose spray. It all hangs together very neatly, sir."

"A little too neatly, don't you think?" said Dalgliesh.

But Sergeant Masterson had remembered something else.

"That brochure, the one we found in Pearce's room! Wasn't it about the work of a Suffolk Refuge for Fascist War Victims? Suppose Pearce sent for it? Is this another example of making the punishment fit the crime?"

"I think so. We'll get in touch with the place in the morning and find out what, if anything, she promised them. And we'll talk again to Courtney-Briggs. He was in Nightingale House at about the time Fallon died. When we know who he came to see and why, we shall be close to solving this case. But all that must wait for tomorrow."

Masterson stifled a yawn. He said: "It's been tomorrow, sir, for nearly three hours."

II

If the night porter of the Falconer's Arms was surprised at the return of the two guests in the small hours of the morning, one obviously ill and with his head ostentatiously bandaged, he was trained not to show it. His inquiry whether there was anything he could get for the gentlemen was perfunctory; Masterson's reply barely civil. They climbed the three flights of stairs to their floor since the old-fashioned lift was erratic and noisy. Dalgliesh, obstinately determined not to betray his weakness to his Sergeant, made himself take each step without grasping the banister. He knew it to be a foolish vanity and by the time he had gained his room he was paying for it. He was so weak that he had to lean against the closed door for a minute before weaving his unsteady way over to the wash-basin. Grasping the taps for support, he retched painfully and ineffectually, his forehead resting on his forearms. Without lifting his head he twisted on the right-hand tap. There was a gush of ice-cold water. He swilled it over his face and gulped it down from cupped hands. Immediately he felt better.

He slept fitfully. It was difficult to rest his cocooned head comfortably on the pillows, and loss of blood seemed to have left his mind preternaturally active and lucid, militating against sleep. When he did doze it was only to dream. He was walking in the grounds of the hospital with Mavis Gearing. She was skipping girlishly between the trees, brandishing her garden shears and saying kittenishly:

"It's wonderful what you can find to make a show even in this dead time of the year."

It didn't strike him as incongruous that she was snipping full blown red roses from the dead branches, or that neither of them remarked on the body of Mary Taylor, white neck encircled by the hangman's noose, as she swung gently from one of the boughs.

Towards morning he slept more deeply. Even so, the harsh incessant ring of the telephone woke him to instant consciousness.

The illuminated dial of his travelling clock showed 5.49 a.m. He shifted his head with difficulty from the hollowed pillow and felt for the receiver. The voice was instantly recognizable. But then he knew that he could have distinguished it from any other woman's voice in the world.

"Mr. Dalgliesh? This is Mary Taylor. I'm sorry to disturb you but I thought you'd prefer me to ring. We have a fire here. Nothing dangerous; it's only in the grounds. It seems to have started in a disused gardener's hut about fifty yards from Nightingale House. The house itself isn't in any danger but the fire spread very quickly among the trees."

He was surprised how clearly he could think. His wound no longer ached. He felt literally light-headed and it was necessary to touch the rough gauze of the bandage to reassure himself that it was still there. He said:

"Morag Smith. Is she all right? She used that hut as a kind of refuge."

"I know. She told me so this evening after she'd brought you in. I gave her a bed here for the night Morag is safe. That was the first thing I checked."

"And the others in Nightingale House?"

There was a silence. Then she spoke, her voice sharper.

"I'll check now. It never occurred to me. . . ."

"Of course not. Why should it? I'll come over."

"Is that necessary? Mr. Courtney-Briggs was insistent that you should rest. The fire brigade have things under control. At first they were afraid that Nightingale House was threatened but they've axed some of the nearer trees. The blaze should be out in half an hour. Couldn't you wait till morning?"

"I'm coming over now," he said.

Masterson was lying flat on his back, drugged with tiredness, his heavy face vacant with sleep, his mouth half-open. It took nearly a minute to rouse him. Dalgliesh would have preferred to leave him there in his stupor, but he knew that, in his present weakened state, it wouldn't be safe for him to drive. Masterson, shaken at last into wakefulness, listened to his Superintendent's instructions without comment, then pulled on his clothes in resentful silence.

He was too prudent to question Dalgliesh's decision to return to Nightingale House, but it was obvious by his sullen manner that he thought the excursion unnecessary, and the short drive to the hospital was spent in silence.

The fire was visible as a red glow on the night sky long before they came in sight of the hospital, and as they drove through the open Winchester Road gate they could hear the staccato crackle of burning trees and could smell the rich evocative scent of smouldering wood, strong and sweet on the cold air. It broke Masterson's mood of sullen resentment. He breathed it in with noisy enjoyment and said in happy candour:

"I like that smell, sir. It reminds me of boyhood, I suppose. Summer camps with the Boy Scouts. Huddled in a blanket around the camp fire with the sparks soaring off into the night. Bloody marvellous when you're thirteen and being patrol leader is more power and glory than you're ever likely to feel again. You know, sir."

Dalgliesh didn't know. His solitary and lonely boyhood had been devoid of these tribal delights. But it was an interesting and curiously touching glimpse into Masterson's character. Patrol leader in the Boy Scouts! Well, why not? Given a different heritage, a different twist of fate and he could have easily been a leader in a street gang, his essential ambition and ruthlessness channelled into less conformist paths.

Masterson drove the car under the trees at a safe distance and they walked towards the blaze. As if by unspoken consent, they halted and stood together in the shadow of the trees watching in silence. No one appeared to notice them and no one approached. The firemen were getting on with their job. There was only one appliance and they were apparently running the hose from Nightingale House. The fire was by now well under control but it was still spectacular. The shed had gone completely with nothing but a ring of black earth to show where it had once stood, and the surrounding trees were blackened gibbets, stunted and twisted as if with the agony of their burning. On the periphery a few saplings still burned fiercely, crackling and spluttering in the jets from the fire hose. A single flame, writhing and twisting in the stiff breeze,

leapt from tree top to tree top and burned there with the clear incandescent light of a candle before it was scotched by one un-erring jet from the hose. As they watched a tall conifer burst into instantaneous fire and exploded in a shower of golden needles. There was a soft gasp of appreciation, and Dalgliesh saw that a little group of black-cloaked students who had been watching at a distance had crept imperceptibly forward into the light of the fire. It shone momentarily on their faces and he thought he recognized Madeleine Goodale and Julia Pardoe. Then he saw the tall un-mistakable figure of Matron move across to them. She spoke a few words and the little group turned and reluctantly melted into the trees. It was then that she saw Dalgliesh. For a moment she stood absolutely still. Wrapped in her long black cloak, the hood thrown back, she stood against a single sapling like a victim at the stake, the fire glow dancing behind her and the light flaming her pale skin. Then she walked slowly across to him. He saw then that her face was very white. She said:

"You were right. She wasn't in her room. She's left me a letter."

Dalgliesh didn't reply. His mind was so clear that it seemed to be operating outside his own volition, not so much ranging over all the clues of the crime, but seeing it as if from a great height; a land-scape without shadows spread out beneath him, comprehensible, familiar, unambiguous. He knew it all now. Not just how the two girls had been murdered; not just when and why; not just by whom. He knew the essential truth of the whole crime, for it was one crime. He might never be able to prove it; but he knew.

Half an hour later the fire was out. The spent hoses crept and thudded on the blackened earth as they were wound in, sending up little spurts of acrid smoke. The last of the onlookers had melted away and the cacophony of fire and wind was replaced by a gentle background hiss broken only by the orders of the fire officer and the blurred voices of his men. Even the wind had died a little and its touch on Dalgliesh's face was gentle and warm as it passed over the steaming earth. Everywhere there hung the reek of charred wood. The headlights of the fire engine were turned on the smoking circle where the hut had stood. Dalgliesh walked over to it, Masterson on his left, Mary Taylor on his right. The heat struck uncomfortably

through the soles of his shoes. There was little to be seen; a grotesquely twisted piece of metal which might once have been part of a stove; the charred shape of a metal teapot—one kick would disintegrate it beyond recognition. And there was something else, a shape, nothing more, which even in death's extreme desecration, was still horribly human. They stood looking down in silence. It took them a few minutes to identify the few details; the pelvic girdle ridiculously small when denuded of its animate wrapping of muscle and flesh; the skull upturned and innocent as a chalice; the stain where the brain had burst away.

Dalgliesh said: "Get a screen around this place and see that it's kept guarded, then ring Sir Miles Honeyman."

Masterson said: "There's a pretty problem of identification for him here, sir."

"Yes," replied Dalgliesh, "if we didn't know already who it was."

III

They went by tacit consent and without exchanging a word through the quiet house to the Matron's flat. No one followed them. As they entered the sitting-room the carriage clock on the mantelpiece struck half past six. It was still very dark and in contrast to the fire-warmed air of the grounds the room was bitterly cold. The curtains had been drawn back and the casement window left open. Matron went quickly across to close it, drew the curtains together with a swift defensive sweep of her arms and turned to look at Dalgliesh steadily and compassionately, as if seeing him for the first time.

"You look desperately tired and cold. Come over to the fire and sit down."

He walked over and leaned against the fireplace, fearing that if he once sat down he might never be able to get up again. But the mantelpiece felt unstable, the marble slippery as ice. He let himself down into the armchair and watched while she knelt on the hearth rug and added the dry sticks of kindling to the still warm ashes of the previous evening's fire. The sticks blazed into life. She added a few nuggets of coal, holding out her hands to the blaze. Then

without getting up she reached into the pocket of her cloak and handed him a letter.

A pale blue envelope unsealed and addressed in a round, childish but firm hand "to whom it may concern". He took out the letter. Cheap, blue paper, perfectly ordinary, unruled, but with the lines of writing so straight that she must have used the ruled sheet as a guide.

"I killed Heather Pearce and Josephine Fallon. They had discovered something about my past, something which was no concern of theirs, and were threatening to blackmail me. When Sister Gearing rang to tell me Fallon had been taken ill and was warded I knew that Nurse Pearce would act the patient in her place. I collected the bottle of disinfectant very early that morning and filled one of the empty milk bottles from the Sisters' utility room. I replaced the cap carefully and took the bottle with me to breakfast in my tapestry bag. All I had to do was to slip into the demonstration room after I had finished breakfast and substitute the bottle of poison for the bottle of milk on the trolley. If anyone had been in the room I should have made an excuse and tried another time and in another way. But the room was empty. I took the bottle of milk upstairs to the Sisters' utility room and threw the empty bottle of disinfectant out of one of the bathroom windows.

"I was in the conservatory when Sister Gearing produced her tin of nicotine rose spray and I thought of it when it came to killing Fallon. I knew where the key to the conservatory was kept and I wore surgical gloves so that there would be no finger-prints. It was an easy matter to pour the poison into Fallon's beaker of lemon and whisky while she was in the bathroom and the drink was cooling on her bedside table. Her nightly routine never varied. I intended to keep the tin, then place it on her bedside table later that night so that it would look as if she had killed herself. I knew it would be important to impress her finger-prints on the tin but that wouldn't be difficult. I had to change my plan because Mr. Courtney-Briggs telephoned shortly before twelve to call me back to my ward. I couldn't keep the tin in my possession since it wouldn't be possible to have my bag always with me on the ward and I didn't think it would be safe to leave it in my room. So I hid it in the sand bucket

opposite Nurse Fallon's room with the intention of retrieving it and placing it on her bedside table when I returned to Nightingale House. That plan, too, proved impossible. As I got to the top of the stairs the Burt twins came out of their rooms. There was a light shining through Nurse Fallon's keyhole and they said they would take her some cocoa. I expected the body to be discovered that night. There was nothing I could do but to go upstairs to bed. I lay there waiting, expecting every minute to hear the alarm raised. I wondered if the twins had changed their plan and if Fallon had fallen asleep before drinking her whisky and lemon. But I didn't dare to go down and see. If I had been able to place the tin of nicotine by Fallon's bed no one would ever have suspected that she was murdered and I should have committed two perfect crimes.

"There is nothing else to say except that no one knew what I intended to do and no one helped me.

Ethel Brumfett."

Mary Taylor said: "It's her handwriting, of course. I found it on her mantelshelf when I came back after I had telephoned you to check that everyone was safe. But is it true?"

"Oh yes, it's true. She killed both of them. Only the murderess could have known where the tin of nicotine was hidden. It was obvious that the second death was meant to look like suicide. Why then wasn't the tin left on the bedside table? It could only have been because the killer was interrupted in her plan. Sister Brumfett was the one person in Nightingale House who was called out that night and who was prevented on her return from going into Fallon's room. But she was always the first suspect. The bottle of poison must have been prepared at leisure and by someone who had access to milk bottles and to the disinfectant and who could carry the lethal bottle about with her undetected. Sister Brumfett went nowhere without that large tapestry bag. It was bad luck for her that she happened to choose a bottle with the wrong coloured cap. I wonder if she even noticed. Even if she did, there wouldn't be time to change it. The whole plan depended on a substitution which would take merely a second. She would have to hope that no one noticed. And, in fact, no one did. And there is one way in which she was unique among the suspects. She was the only one

who wasn't present to witness either of the deaths. She couldn't lift a hand against Fallon while the girl was her patient. That would have been impossible for her. And she preferred to watch neither murder. It takes a psychopathic killer or a professional willingly to watch their victim die."

She said: "We know that Heather Pearce was a potential blackmailer. I wonder what pathetic incident from poor Brumfett's dreary past she'd raked up for her entertainment?"

"I think you know that, just as I know. Heather Pearce had found out about Felsenheim."

She seemed to freeze into silence. She was curled on the edge of the armchair at his feet, her face turned away from him. After a moment she turned and looked at him.

"She wasn't guilty, you know. Brumfett was conforming, authoritarian, trained to think of unquestioning obedience as a nurse's first duty. But she didn't kill her patients. The verdict of that court at Felsenheim was just. And even if it wasn't, it was the verdict of a properly constituted court of law. She is officially innocent."

Dalgliesh said: "I'm not here to question the verdict at Felsenheim."

As if he had not spoken she went on eagerly, as if willing him to believe.

"She told me about it when we were both students together at Nethercastle General Infirmary. She lived in Germany most of her childhood but her grandmother was English. After the trial she naturally went free and eventually in 1944 married an English sergeant, Ernest Brumfett. She had money and it was a marriage of convenience only, a way of getting out of Germany and into England. Her grandmother was dead by now but she still had some ties with this country. She went to Nethercastle as ward orderly and was so efficient that, after eighteen months, there was no difficulty in getting the Matron to take her on as a student. It was a clever choice of hospital. They weren't likely to delve too carefully into anyone's past, particularly into the past of a woman who had proved her worth. The hospital is a large Victorian building, always busy, chronically understaffed. Brumfett and I finished our

training together, went together to the local maternity hospital to train as midwives, came south together to the John Carpendar. I've known Ethel Brumfett for nearly twenty years. I've watched her pay over and over again for anything that happened at the Steinhoff Institution. She was a girl then. We can't know what happened to her during those childhood years in Germany. We can only know what the grown woman did for this hospital and for her patients. The past has no relevance."

Dalgliesh said: "Until the thing which she must always have subconsciously dreaded happened at last. Until someone from that past recognized her."

She said: "Then all the years of work and striving would come to nothing. I can understand that she felt it necessary to kill Pearce. But why Fallon?"

"For four reasons. Nurse Pearce wanted some proof of Martin Dettinger's story before she spoke to Sister Brumfett. The obvious way to get it seemed to be to consult a record of the trial. So she asked Fallon to lend her a library ticket. She went up to the Westminster library on the Thursday and again on the Saturday when the book was produced. She must have shown it to Sister Brumfett when she spoke to her, must have mentioned where she got the ticket. Sooner or later Fallon would want that ticket back. It was essential that no one ever found out why Nurse Pearce had wanted it or the name of the book she had borrowed from the library. That was one of several significant facts which Sister Brumfett chose to omit from her confession. After she had substituted the bottle of poison for the one of milk, she came upstairs, took the library book from Nurse Pearce's room, and hid it in one of the fire buckets until she had an opportunity to return it anonymously to the library. She knew only too well that Pearce would never come out of that demonstration room alive. It was typical of her to choose the same hiding place later for the tin of nicotine. Sister Brumfett wasn't an imaginative woman.

"But the problem of the library book wasn't the main reason for killing Nurse Fallon. There were three others. She wanted to confuse the motives, to make it look as if Fallon were the intended victim. If Fallon died there would always be the probability that

Pearce had been killed by mistake. It was Fallon who was listed to act as patient on the morning of the inspection. Fallon was a more likely victim. She was pregnant; that alone might provide a motive. Sister Brumfett had nursed her and could have known or guessed about the pregnancy. I don't think there were many signs or symptoms that Sister Brumfett missed in her patients. Then there was the possibility that Fallon would be held responsible for Pearce's death. After all, she had admitted returning to Nightingale House on the morning of the murder and had refused to give any explanation. She could have put the poison in the drip. Then afterwards, tormented by remorse perhaps, she killed herself. That explanation would dispose very neatly of both mysteries. It's an attractive theory from the hospital's point of view and quite a number of people preferred to believe it."

"And the last reason? You said there were four. She wanted to avoid inquiries about the library ticket; she wanted to suggest that Fallon had been the intended victim; alternatively she wanted to implicate Fallon in Pearce's death. What was the fourth motive?"

"She wanted to protect you. She always wanted that. It wasn't easy with the first murder. You were in Nightingale House; you had as much opportunity as anyone to interfere with the drip feed. But at least she could ensure that you had an alibi for the time of Fallon's death. You were safely in Amsterdam. You couldn't possibly have killed the second victim. Why, therefore, should you have killed the first? From the beginning of this investigation I decided that the two murders were connected. It was too much of a coincidence to postulate two killers in the same house at the same time. And that automatically excluded you from the list of suspects."

"But why should anyone suspect me of killing either girl?"

"Because the motive we've imputed to Ethel Brumfett doesn't make sense. Think about it. A dying man came momentarily out of unconsciousness and saw a face bending over him. He opened his eyes and through his pain and delirium he recognized a woman. Sister Brumfett? Would you recognize Ethel Brumfett's face after twenty-five years? Plain, ordinary, inconspicuous Brumfett? There's only one woman in a million who has a face so beautiful and so individual that it can be recognized even in a fleeting glance

across twenty-five years of memory. Your face. It was you and not Sister Brumfett who was Irmgard Grobel."

She said quietly: "Irmgard Grobel is dead."

He went on as if she had not spoken.

"It's not surprising that Nurse Pearce never suspected for one moment that Grobel could be you. You're the Matron, protected by a quasi-religious awe from the taint of human weakness, let alone human sin. It must have been psychologically impossible for her to think of you as a killer. And then, there were the words used by Martin Dettinger. He said it was one of the Sisters. I think I know how he made that mistake. You visit every ward in the hospital once a day, speak to nearly all the patients. The face he saw bending over him was not only clearly the face of Irmgard Grobel. He saw a woman wearing what to him was a Sister's uniform, the short cape and wide triangular cap of the army nursing service. To his drug-muddled mind that uniform meant a Sister. It still means a Sister to anyone who has been nursed in an army hospital, and he had spent months in them."

She said again quietly: "Irmgard Grobel is dead."

"So he told Nurse Pearce much the same as he told his own mother. Mrs. Dettinger wasn't particularly interested. Why should she be? And then she received a hospital account and thought that there might be a way of saving herself a few pounds. If Mr. Courtney-Briggs hadn't been greedy I doubt whether she would have taken it any further. But she did, and Courtney-Briggs was given an intriguing piece of information which he thought it worth taking some time and trouble to verify. We can guess what Heather Pearce thought. She must have experienced much the same triumph and sense of power as when she saw Nurse Dakers stooping to pick up those pound notes fluttering on the path in front of her. Only this time someone a great deal more important and interesting than a fellow student would be in her power. It never occurred to her that the patient could be referring to a woman other than the Sister nursing him. But she knew she had to get proof, or at least assure herself that Dettinger, who after all was a dying man, wasn't deluded or hallucinated. So she spent her half-day on Thursday visiting the Westminster library and asked them

for a book about the Felsenheim trial. They had to borrow it for her from another branch and she returned for it on Saturday. I think she learned enough from that book to convince herself that Martin Dettinger knew what he was talking about. I think that she spoke to Sister Brumfett on the Saturday night and that the Sister didn't deny the charge. I wonder what price Pearce was asking? Nothing as commonplace or understandable or as reprehensible as direct payment for her silence. Pearce liked to exercise power; but even more she enjoyed indulging in moral rectitude. It must have been on Sunday morning that she wrote to the Secretary of the League for the Assistance of Fascist Victims. Sister Brumfett would be made to pay, but the money would go in regular instalments to the League. Pearce was a great one for making the punishment fit the crime."

This time she was silent, sitting there with her hands folded gently in her lap and looking expressionless into some unfathomable past. He said gently:

"It can all be checked, you know. We haven't much of her body left but we don't need it while we have your face. There will be records of the trial, photographs, the record of your marriage to a Sergeant Taylor.

She spoke so quietly that he had to bend his head to hear:

"He opened his eyes very wide and looked at me. He didn't speak. There was a wildness, a desperation about that look. I thought that he was becoming delirious, or perhaps that he was afraid. I think he knew in that moment that he was going to die. I spoke to him a little and then his eyes closed. I didn't recognize him. Why should I?

"I'm not the same person as that child in Steinhoff. I don't mean I think of Steinhoff as if it happened to someone else. It did happen to someone else. I can't even remember now what exactly happened in that court at Felsenheim; I can't recall a single face."

But she had had to tell someone. That must have been part of becoming another person, of putting Steinhoff out of her thoughts. So she had told Ethel Brumfett. They had both been young student nurses at Nethercastle and Dalgliesh supposed that Brumfett represented something to her: kindness, reliability, devotion. Other-

wise, why Brumfett? Why on earth choose her as a confidante? He must have been speaking his words aloud because she said eagerly as if it were important to make him understand:

"I told her because she was so ordinary. There was a security about her ordinariness. I felt that, if Brumfett could listen and believe me and still like me, then nothing that had happened was so very terrible after all. You wouldn't understand that."

But he did understand. There had been a boy in his prep. school like that, so ordinary, so safe, that he was a kind of talisman against death and disaster. Dalgliesh remembered the boy. Funny, but he hadn't thought of him now for over thirty years. Sproat Minor with his round, pleasant, spectacled face, his ordinary conventional family, his unremarkable background, his blessed normality. Sproat Minor, protected by mediocrity and insensitivity from the terrors of the world. Life could not be wholly frightening while it held a Sproat Minor. Dalgliesh wondered briefly where he was now.

He said: "And Brumfett had stuck to you ever since. When you came here she followed. That impulse to confide, the need to have at least one friend who knew all about you, put you in her power. Brumfett, the protector, adviser, confidante. Theatres with Brumfett; morning golf with Brumfett; holidays with Brumfett; country drives with Brumfett; early morning tea and last night drinks with Brumfett. Her devotion must have been real enough. After all, she was willing to kill for you. But it was blackmail all the same. A more orthodox blackmailer, merely demanding a regular tax-free income, would have been infinitely preferable to Brumfett's intolerable devotion."

She said sadly: "It's true. It's all true. How can you possibly know?"

"Because she was essentially a stupid and dull woman and you are not."

He could have added: "Because I know myself."

She cried out in vehement protest.

"And who am I to despise stupidity and dullness? What right had I to be so particular? Oh, she wasn't clever! She couldn't even kill for me without making a mess of it. She wasn't clever enough to

518

deceive Adam Dalgliesh, but when is that to be the criteria for intelligence? Have you ever seen her doing her job? Seen her with a dying patient or a sick child? Have you ever watched this stupid and dull woman, whose devotion and company it is apparently proper for me to despise, working all night to save a life?"

"I've seen the body of one of her victims and read the autopsy report on the other. I'll take your word for her kindness to children."

"Those weren't her victims. They were mine."

"Oh no," he said. "There has only been one victim of yours in Nightingale House and she was Ethel Brumfett."

She rose to her feet in one swift movement and stood facing him, those astonishing green eyes, speculative and unwavering, gazed into his. Part of his mind knew that there were words he ought to speak. What were they, those over-familiar phrases of statutory warning, the professional spiel which came almost unbidden to the lips at the moment of confrontation? They had slipped away, a meaningless irrelevancy, into some limbo of his mind. He knew that he was a sick man, still weak from loss of blood, and that he ought to stop now, to hand over the investigation to Masterson, and get to his bed. He, the most punctilious of detectives, had already spoken as if none of the rules had been formulated, as if he were facing a private adversary. But he had to go on. Even if he could never prove it, he had to hear her admit what he knew to be the truth. As if it were the most natural question in the world he asked quietly:

"Was she dead when you put her into the fire?"

IV

It was at that moment that someone rang the doorbell of the flat. Without a word Mary Taylor swung her cape around her shoulders and went to open it. There was a brief murmur of voices; then Stephen Courtney-Briggs followed her into the sitting-room. Glancing at the clock, Dalgliesh saw that the hands stood at 7.24 a.m. The working day had almost begun.

Courtney-Briggs was already dressed. He showed no surprise at

Dalgliesh's presence and no particular concern at his obvious weakness. He spoke to them both impartially:

"I'm told there was a fire in the night. I didn't hear the engines."

Mary Taylor, her face so white that Dalgliesh thought she might faint, said calmly:

"They came in at the Winchester Road entrance and kept the bells silent so as not to wake the patients."

"And what's this rumour that they found a burnt body in the ashes of the garden shed? Whose body?"

Dalgliesh said: "Sister Brumfett's. She left a note confessing to the murders of Nurse Pearce and Nurse Fallon."

"Brumfett killed them! Brumfett!"

Courtney-Briggs looked at Dalgliesh belligerently, his large handsome features seeming to disintegrate into irritated disbelief.

"Did she say why? Was the woman mad?"

Mary Taylor said: "Brumfett wasn't mad and no doubt she believed that she had a motive."

"But what's going to happen to my ward today? I start operating at nine o'clock. You know that, Matron. And I've got a very long list. Both the staff nurses are off with flu. I can't trust dangerously sick patients to first and second-year students."

The Matron said calmly: "I'll see to it at once. Most of the day nurses should be up by now. It isn't going to be easy but, if necessary, we'll have to withdraw someone from the school."

She turned to Dalgliesh: "I prefer to do my telephoning from one of the Sisters' sitting-rooms. But don't worry. I realize the importance of our conversation. I shall be back to complete it."

Both men looked after her as she went out of the door and closed it quietly behind her. For the first time Courtney-Briggs seemed to notice Dalgliesh. He said brusquely:

"Don't forget to go over to the radiography department and get that head X-rayed. You've no right to be out of bed. I'll examine you as soon as I've finished my list this morning." He made it sound like a tedious chore which he might find time to attend to.

Dalgliesh asked: "Who did you come to visit in Nightingale House the night Josephine Fallon was murdered?"

"I told you. No one. I never entered Nightingale House."

"There are at least ten minutes unaccounted for, ten minutes when the back door leading to the Matron's flat was unlocked. Sister Gearing had let her friend out that way and was walking with him in the grounds. So you thought that the Matron must be in despite the absence of lights and made your way up the stairs to her flat. You must have spent some time there. Why, I wonder? Curiosity? Or were you searching for something?"

"Why should I visit the Matron? She wasn't there. Mary Taylor was in Amsterdam that night."

"But you didn't know that at the time, did you? Miss Taylor wasn't accustomed to attending International Conferences. For reasons we can guess she didn't want her face to be too widely known. This reluctance to undertake public duties was thought becomingly modest in a woman so able and so intelligent. She was only asked late on Tuesday to go to Amsterdam to deputize for the Chairman of the Area Nurse Training Committee. Your sessions are on Mondays, Thursdays and Fridays. Then, on Wednesday night, you were called to operate on a private patient. I don't suppose that the operating-theatre staff, busy with an emergency, thought to mention that the Matron wasn't in the hospital. Why should they?" He paused.

Courtney-Briggs said: "And why am I supposed to have planned to visit the Matron at midnight? You're not supposing that I would have been a welcome visitor? You're not suggesting that she was expecting me?"

"You came to see Irmgard Grobel."

There was a moment's silence. Then Courtney-Briggs said: "How do you know about Irmgard Grobel?"

"From the same person who told you, Mrs. Dettinger."

Another silence. Then he said with the obstinate finality of a man who knows he won't be believed:

"Irmgard Grobel is dead."

"Is she?" asked Dalgliesh. "Didn't you expect to find her in the Matron's flat? Wasn't this your first opportunity to confront her with what you knew? And you must have been looking forward to it. The exercise of power is always pleasurable, isn't it?"

Courtney-Briggs said calmly: "You should know that."

They stood looking at each other in silence. Dalgliesh asked: "What had you in mind?"

"Nothing. I didn't connect Grobel with the deaths of Pearce or Fallon. Even if I had, I doubt whether I should have spoken. This hospital needs Mary Taylor. As far as I'm concerned Irmgard Grobel doesn't exist. She was tried once and found not guilty. That was good enough for me. I'm a surgeon, not a moral theologian. I should have kept her secret."

Of course he would, thought Dalgliesh. Its value would be lost to him once the truth were known. This was very special, very important information, gained at some cost, and he would use it in his own way. It put Mary Taylor for ever in his power. The Matron who so frequently and irritatingly opposed him; whose power was increasing; who was about to be appointed Director of Nursing Services over all the hospitals in the Group; who influenced the Chairman of the Hospital Management Committee against him. Sir Marcus Cohen. How much influence would she retain with that dedicated Jew once he learned about the Steinhoff Institution? It had become fashionable to forget these things. But would Sir Marcus Cohen forgive?

He thought of Mary Taylor's words. There are more ways than one of blackmail. Heather Pearce and Ethel Brumfett both knew that. And perhaps the most subtly pleasurable was the blackmail which made no financial demands but enjoyed its secret knowledge under the cloak of generosity, kindness, complicity or moral superiority. Sister Brumfett hadn't asked much after all, only a room next to her idol; the prestige of being known as the Matron's friend; a companion for her off-duty hours. Poor stupid Pearce had asked only a few shillings a week and a verse or two of scripture. But how they must have relished their power. And how infinitely more gratifying would Courtney-Briggs have found his. No wonder that he had been determined to keep the secret to himself, that he hadn't welcomed the thought of the Yard descending on Nightingale House.

Dalgliesh said: "We can prove that you flew to Germany last Friday night. And I think I can guess why. It was a quicker and

surer way of getting the information you wanted than pestering the Judge Advocate's Department. You probably consulted the newspaper files and the record of the trial. That's what I would have done. And, no doubt, you have useful contacts. But we can find out where you went and what you did. You can't slip in and out of the country anonymously, you know."

Courtney-Briggs said: "I admit that I knew. I admit, too, that I came to Nightingale House to see Mary Taylor on the night Fallon died. But I've done nothing illegal, nothing which could put me in jeopardy."

"I can believe that."

"Even if I'd spoken earlier I should have been too late to save Pearce. She was dead before Mrs. Dettinger came to see me. I've nothing with which to reproach myself."

He was beginning to defend himself clumsily like a schoolboy. Then they heard the soft footfall and looked round. Mary Taylor had returned. She spoke directly to the surgeon.

"I can let you have the Burt twins. I'm afraid it means the end of this block but there's no choice. They'll have to be recalled to the wards."

Courtney-Briggs said grudgingly: "They'll do. They're sensible girls. But what about a Sister?"

"I thought that Sister Rolfe might take over temporarily. But I'm afraid that's impossible. She's leaving the John Carpendar."

"Leaving! But she can't do that!"

"I don't see how I can prevent her. But I don't think I shall be given the opportunity to try."

"But why is she leaving? What's happened?"

"She won't say. I think something about the police investigation has upset her."

Courtney-Briggs swung round at Dalgliesh.

"You see! Dalgliesh, I realize that you're only doing your job, that you were sent here to clear up these girls' deaths. But, for God's sake, doesn't it ever occur to you that your interference makes things a bloody sight worse?"

"Yes," said Dalgliesh. "And in your job? Does it ever occur to you?"

She went with Courtney-Briggs to the front door. They didn't linger. She was back in less than a minute, and walking briskly over to the fire, she slipped her cloak from her shoulders and laid it tidily over the back of the sofa. Then, kneeling, she took up a pair of brass tongs and began to build up the fire, coal carefully disposed on coal, each licking flame fed with its gleaming nugget. Without looking up at Dalgliesh, she said:

"We were interrupted in our conversation, Superintendent. You were accusing me of murder. I have faced that charge once before, but at least the court at Felsenheim produced some evidence. What evidence have you?"

"None."

"Nor will you ever find any."

She spoke without anger or complacency but with an intensity, a quiet finality that had nothing to do with innocence. Looking down at the gleaming head burnished by the firelight Dalgliesh said:

"But you haven't denied it. You haven't lied to me yet and I don't suppose you'll trouble to begin now. Why should she have killed herself in that way? She liked her comfort. Why be uncomfortable in death? Suicides seldom are unless they're too psychotic to care. She had access to plenty of pain-killing drugs. Why not use one of them? Why trouble to creep away to a cold dark garden shed to immolate herself in lonely agony? She wasn't even fortified by the gratifications of a public show."

"There are precedents."

"Not many in this country."

"Perhaps she was too psychotic to care."

"That will be said of course."

"She may have realized that it was important not to leave an identifiable body if she wanted to convince you that she was Grobel. Faced with a written confession and a heap of charred bones, why should you bother any further? There was no point in killing herself to protect me if you could confirm her real identity without trouble."

"A clever and far-sighted woman might argue like that. She was neither. But you are. It must have seemed just worth a try. And even if we never found out about Irmgard Grobel and Felsenheim, it had become important to get rid of Brumfett. As you've said, she couldn't even kill without making a mess of it. She had already panicked once when she tried to murder me. She might easily panic again. She had been an encumbrance for years; now she had become a dangerous liability. You hadn't asked her to kill for you. It wasn't even a reasonable way out of the difficulty. Pearce's threats could have been dealt with if Sister Brumfett had only kept her head and reported the matter to you. But she had to demonstrate her devotion in the most spectacular way she knew. She killed to protect you. And those two deaths bound you and she together indissolubly for life. How could you ever be free or secure while Brumfett lived?"

"Aren't you going to tell me how I did it?"

They might, Dalgliesh thought, be two colleagues talking over a case together. Even through his weakness he knew that this bizarre conversation was dangerously unorthodox, that the woman kneeling at his feet was an enemy, that the intelligence opposed to his was inviolate. She had no hope now of saving her reputation, but she was fighting for freedom, perhaps even for her life. He said:

"I can tell you how I would have done it. It wasn't difficult. Her bedroom was the one nearest the door of your flat. I suppose she asked for that room, and nothing Sister Brumfett wanted could be denied. Because she knew about the Steinhoff Institution? Because she had a hold over you? Or merely because she had lumbered you with the weight of her devotion and you hadn't the ruthlessness to break free? So she slept close to you.

"I don't know how she died. It could have been a tablet, an injection, something you administered on the pretence that it would help her to sleep. She had already, at your request, written the confession. I wonder how you persuaded her to do that? I don't suppose she thought for one moment that it was going to be used. It isn't addressed to me or to any particular person. I imagine you told her that there ought to be something in writing just in case anything happened to her or to you and it was necessary sometime

in the future to have a record of what really happened, proof that would protect you. So she wrote that plain note, probably at your dictation. It has a directness and lucidity that has little, I imagine, to do with Sister Brumfett.

"And so she dies. You have only to carry her body two yards to gain the safety of your door. Even so, this is the most risky part of your plan. Suppose Sister Gearing or Sister Rolfe should appear? So you prop open Sister Brumfett's door and the door of your flat and listen carefully to make sure that the corridor is clear. Then you hoist the body over your shoulder and move swiftly into your flat. You lay the body on the bed and go back to shut her bedroom door and to shut and lock your own front door. She was a plump but short woman. You are tall and strong and have been trained to lift helpless patients. That part wasn't so difficult.

"But now you must move her to your car. It's convenient having access to your garage from the downstairs hall and a private stairway. With both the outside and inside doors of the flat locked you can work without fear of interruption. The body is hoisted into the back of your car and covered with a travelling rug. Then you drive out through the grounds and reverse the car under the trees, as close as possible to the garden shed. You keep the engine running. It is important to make a quick getaway, be back in your flat before the fire is seen. This part of the plan is a little risky but the Winchester Road path is seldom used after dark. The ghost of Nancy Gorringe sees to that. It would be inconvenient but not catastrophic if you were seen. After all, you are the Matron, there is nothing to prevent you taking a night drive. If anyone passes, you will have to drive on and choose another place or another time. But no one does pass. The car is deep under the trees; the lights are out. You carry the body to the shed. Then there is a second journey with the can of petrol. And after that there is nothing to do but souse the body and the surrounding furniture and piles of wood and throw in a lighted match from the open doorway.

"It takes only a moment to restart the car and to drive straight back through the garage doors. Once they are closed behind you, you are safe. Certainly you know that the fire will burn with such fierceness that it will be seen almost at once. But by then you are

back in your own flat, ready to receive the telephone call which tells you that the fire engine is on its way, ready to ring me. And the suicide note which she left in your charge, perhaps never to be used, is ready to be handed over."

She asked quietly: "And how will you prove it?"

"Probably never. But I know that is how it happened."

She said: "But you will try to prove it, won't you? After all, failure would be intolerable for Adam Dalgliesh. You will try to prove it no matter what the cost to yourself or anyone else. And after all, there is a chance. There isn't much hope of finding tyre marks under the trees of course. The effects of the fire, the wheels of the fire engine, the trampling of the men, will have obliterated any clues on the ground. But then you will examine the inside of the car surely, particularly the rug. Don't neglect the car rug, Superintendent. There may be fibres from the clothes, even a few hairs, perhaps. But that wouldn't be surprising. Miss Brumfett often drove with me; the car rug actually belongs to her; it's probably covered with her hairs. But what about clues in my flat? If I carried her body down that narrow back staircase surely there will be marks on the walls where they were grazed by her shoes? Unless, of course, the woman who killed Brumfett had sufficient sense to remove her victim's shoes and carry them separately, perhaps slung by the laces around her neck. They couldn't be left in the flat. You might check on the number of pairs that Brumfett owned. After all, someone in Nightingale House could tell you. We have so little privacy from each other. And no woman would walk through the woods barefoot to her death.

"And the other clues in the flat? If I killed her, ought there not to be a syringe, a bottle of pills, something to indicate how I did it? But her medicine cupboard and mine both contain a supply of aspirin and sleeping tablets. Suppose I gave her those? Or simply stunned or suffocated her? Any method would be as good as another provided it didn't make a mess. How can you possibly prove how she died when all you have for the autopsy are a few charred bones? And there's the suicide note, a note in her own handwriting and containing facts which only the killer of Pearce and Fallon could have known. Whatever you may choose to believe, Super-

intendent, are you going to tell me that the Coroner won't be satisfied that Ethel Brumfett intended that note as a confession before burning herself to death?"

Dalgliesh knew that he could no longer stay upright. He was fighting sickness now as well as weakness. The hand which grasped the mantelshelf for support was colder than the marble and slippery with sweat, and the marble itself was soft and yielding as putty. His wound was beginning to throb painfully, and the dull headache which up to now had been little more than vague discomfort was sharpening and localizing into needles of pain behind his left eye. To drop in a faint at her feet would be unforgettably humiliating. He reached out his arm and found the back of the nearest chair. Then gently he lowered himself into it. Her voice seemed to be coming from a long way off, but at least he could hear the words and knew that his own voice was still steady.

She said: "Suppose I told you that I could manage Stephen Courtney-Briggs, that no one but the three of us need ever know about Felsenheim? Would you be willing to leave my past out of your report so that at least those girls need not have died entirely in vain? It is important for this hospital that I stay on as Matron. I'm not asking you for mercy. I'm not concerned for myself. You will never prove that I killed Ethel Brumfett. Aren't you going to make yourself look ridiculous if you try? Isn't the most courageous and sensible course to forget that this conversation ever took place, to accept Brumfett's confession for the truth which it is, and to close the case?"

He said: "That's not possible. Your past is part of the evidence. I can't suppress evidence or omit relevant facts from my report because I don't choose to like them. If I once did that I should have to give up my job. Not just this particular case, my job. And for always."

"And you couldn't do that, of course. What would a man like you be without his job, this particular job? Vulnerable like the rest of us. You might even have to begin living and feeling like a human being."

"You can't touch me like that. Why humiliate yourself trying? There are regulations, orders, and an oath. Without them no one

could safely do police work. Without them Ethel Brumfett wouldn't be safe, you wouldn't be safe, an Irmgard Grobel wouldn't be safe."

"Is that why you won't help me?"

"Not altogether. I don't choose to."

She said sadly: "That's honest, anyway. And you haven't any doubts?"

"Of course I have. I'm not as arrogant as that. There are always doubts." And so there were. But they were intellectual and philosophical doubts, untormenting and uninsistent. It had been many years since they had kept him awake at night.

"But there are the regulations, aren't there? And the orders. An oath even. They're very convenient shields to shelter behind if the doubts become troublesome. I know. I sheltered behind them once myself. You and I are not so very different after all, Adam Dalgliesh."

She took up her cloak from the back of the chair and threw it around her shoulders. She came over and stood in front of him smiling. Then, seeing his weakness, she held out both her hands and grasping his, helped him to his feet. They stood there facing each other. Suddenly there was the ring of her front door and almost simultaneously the harsh insistent burr of the telephone. For both of them the day had begun.

Chapter Nine

Summer Epilogue

I

It was shortly after nine o'clock when the call came through to him, and Dalgliesh walked out of the Yard and across Victoria Street through an early morning haze, a sure harbinger of yet another hot August day. He found the address without difficulty. It was a large red brick building between Victoria Street and Horseferry Road, not particularly sordid but depressingly dull, a functional oblong with the front punctuated with meanly proportioned windows. There was no lift and he walked unchallenged up the three linoleum-covered flights of stairs to the top floor.

The landing smelt of sour sweat. Outside the flat a grossly fat middle-aged woman in a flowered apron was expostulating to the police constable on duty in an adenoidal whine. As Dalgliesh approached she turned on him, spieling forth a flood of protest and recrimination. What was Mr. Goldstein going to say? She wasn't really allowed to sub-let a room. She had only done it to oblige the lady. And now this. People had no consideration.

He passed her without speaking and went into the room. It was a square box, stuffy and smelling of furniture polish, and over-furnished with the heavy prestige symbols of an earlier decade. The window was open and the lace curtains drawn back but there was little air. The police surgeon and the attendant constable, both large men, seemed to have used all there was.

One corpse more to be viewed; only this one wasn't his responsibility. He need only glance, as if verifying a memory, at the stiffening body on the bed, noting with detached interest that the left arm hung loosely over the side, long fingers curled, and that the hypodermic syringe was still attached to the underarm, a metallic insect

530

with its fang deep embedded in the soft flesh. Death hadn't robbed her of individuality, not yet anyway. That would come soon enough with all the grotesque indignities of decay.

The police surgeon, shirt-sleeved and sweating, was apologetic as if concerned that he might have done the wrong thing. As he turned from the bed Dalgliesh was aware that he was speaking:

"And as New Scotland Yard is so close and the second note was addressed personally to you" . . . he paused uncertainly.

"She injected herself with evipan. The first note is quite explicit. It's a clear case of suicide. That's why the constable didn't want to ring you. He thought it wasn't worth your trouble to come. There's really nothing here of interest."

Dalgliesh said: "I'm glad you did ring. And it isn't any trouble."

There were two white envelopes, one sealed and addressed to himself; the other unsealed and bearing the words, "To anyone whom it may concern." He wondered if she had smiled when she wrote that phrase. Watched by the police surgeon and the constable, Dalgliesh opened the letter. The writing was perfectly firm, black and spiky. He realized with a kind of shock that it was the first time he had seen her handwriting.

"They wouldn't believe you but you were right. I killed Ethel Brumfett. It was the first time I had ever killed; it seems important that you should know that. I injected her with evipan, just as I shall shortly do myself. She thought I was giving her a sedative. Poor trusting Brumfett! She would have easily taken nicotine from my hand and it would have been as appropriate.

"I thought it might be possible for me to make some kind of a useful life. It hasn't been, and I haven't the temperament to live with failure. I don't regret what I did. It was best for the hospital, best for her, best for me. I wasn't likely to be deterred because Adam Dalgliesh sees his job as the embodiment of the moral law."

She was wrong, he thought. They hadn't disbelieved him, they had just demanded, reasonably enough, that he find some proof. He had found none, either at the time or later, although he had pursued the case as if it were a personal vendetta, hating himself and her. And she had admitted nothing; not for one moment had she been in any danger of panicking.

531

There had been very little left unexplained at the resumed inquest on Heather Pearce and the inquest on Josephine Fallon and Ethel Brumfett. Perhaps the Coroner felt that there had been enough rumours and speculation. He had sat with a jury and had made no attempt to inhibit their questions to witnesses, or even to control the proceedings. The story of Irmgard Grobel and the Steinhoff Institution had come out, and Sir Marcus Cohen had sat with Dalgliesh at the back of the Court and listened with a face rigid with pain. After the inquest Mary Taylor walked across the room to him, handed him her letter of resignation, and turned away without a word. She had left the hospital the same day. And that, for the John Carpendar, had been the end. Nothing else had come out. Mary Taylor had gone free; free to find this room, this death.

Dalgliesh walked over to the fireplace. The small grate, tiled in bilious green, was filled with a dusty fan and a jam jar of dried leaves. Carefully he moved them out of the way. He was aware of the police surgeon and the uniformed constable watching him expressionlessly. What did they think he was doing? Destroying evidence? Why should they worry? They had their piece of paper ready to be docketed, produced as evidence, filed away for oblivion. This concerned only him.

He shook the note open in the chimney recess and, striking a match, set light to one of the corners. But there was little draught and the paper was tough. He had to hold it, shaking it gently, until the tips of his fingers scorched before the blackened sheet drifted from his grasp, disappeared into the darkness of the chimney recess and was wafted upwards towards the summer sky.

II

Ten minutes later on the same day Miss Beale drove through the front entrance gate of the John Carpendar Hospital and drew up at the porter's lodge. She was greeted by an unfamiliar face, a new youngish porter, shirt-sleeved in his summer uniform.

"The General Nursing Council Inspector? Good morning, miss. I'm afraid this entrance isn't very convenient for the new school of

nursing. It's just a temporary building at present, miss, built on a cleared part of the grounds where we had the fire. It's quite close to where the old school was. If you just take this first turn. . . ."

"It's all right, thank you," said Miss Beale. "I know the way."

There was an ambulance standing at the entrance to the Casualty Department. As Miss Beale drove slowly past, Nurse Dakers, wearing the lace-trimmed cap and blue belt of a staff nurse, came out of the hospital, conferred briefly with the attendants, and stood supervising the transfer of the patient. She seemed to Miss Beale's eyes to have grown in stature and authority. There was no trace of the terrified student nurse about this confident figure. So Nurse Dakers had qualified. Well, that was to be expected. Presumably the Burt twins, equally elevated, were working somewhere in the hospital. But there had been changes. Nurse Goodale had married; Miss Beale had seen the notice in the national Press. And Hilda Rolfe, so Angela reported, was nursing somewhere in Central Africa. There would be a new Principal Tutor to meet this morning. And a new Matron. Miss Beale wondered briefly about Mary Taylor. She would be earning a good living somewhere if not in nursing. The Mary Taylors of the world were natural survivors.

She drove down the familiar path between the parched summer lawns, the flower beds blotched with overblown roses, and turned into the green tunnel of the trees. The air was still and warm, the narrow road chequered with the first bright sunlight of the day. And here was the last remembered corner. Nightingale House, or what was left of it, was before her.

Once again she stopped the car and gazed. The house looked as if it had been clumsily cut in two by a giant's cleaver, a living thing wantonly mutilated, with its shame and its nakedness exposed to every gaze. A staircase, bereft of its banister and brutally hacked, reeled into nothingness; on the second landing a delicate light filament hung by a thread of flex against the cracked panelling; downstairs the front arched windows, empty of glass, were an elegant arcade of carved stone giving a view of faded wallpaper with lighter patches where pictures and mirrors had once hung. From the remaining ceilings, naked wires sprouted like the bristles of a brush. Propped against a tree at the front of the house was a motley

533

collection of fireplaces, mantelshelves, and sections of carved panelling, obviously selected for preservation. On top of what remained of the rear wall, a figure silhouetted against the sky was picking in a desultory way at the loose bricks. They tumbled one by one into the rubble of the interior of the house, sending up small spurts of dust.

In front of the building another workman, naked to the waist and burnt bronze, was operating a tractor mounted with a crane from which hung an immense iron ball and chain. As Miss Beale watched, hands taut on the steering-wheel as if bracing herself against an instinctive recoil of protest, the ball swung forward and crashed against all that remained of the front wall. For a moment there was nothing but the reverberation of hideous noise. Then the wall buckled gently and collapsed inwards with a roar of cascading bricks and mortar, sending up a monstrous cloud of yellow dust through which the lonely figure on the skyline could be seen dimly like some supervising demon.

Miss Beale paused for a moment, then gently let in the clutch and steered the car to the right to where the low, functional, clean-looking lines of the new temporary school could be glimpsed between the trees. Here was normality, sanity, a world she recognized and knew. This emotion, suspiciously like regret, at witnessing the violent destruction of Nightingale House was really too ridiculous. She fought against it resolutely. It was a horrible house; an evil house. It should have been pulled down fifty years ago. And it had never been in the least suitable as a nurse training school.

AN UNSUITABLE JOB
FOR A WOMAN

For Jane and Peter
who kindly allowed two of
my characters to live at
57 Norwich Street.

Author's Note

A crime novelist, by virtue of his unpleasant craft, has the duty to create at least one highly reprehensible character in each book and it is perhaps inevitable that from time to time their sanguinary misdeeds should impinge upon the dwellings of the just. A writer whose characters have chosen to act out their tragicomedy in an ancient university city is in particular difficulty. He can, of course, call it Oxbridge, invent colleges named after improbable saints and send his characters boating on the Camsis, but this timid compromise merely confuses characters, readers and the author alike, with the result that no one knows precisely where he is and two communities are offered opportunities for offence instead of one.

The greater part of this story is unrepentantly set in Cambridge, a city in which, undeniably, there live and work policemen, coroners, doctors, students, college servants, flower sellers, Dons, scientists, and even, no doubt, retired Majors. None of them, to my knowledge, bears the slightest resemblance to his counterpart in this book. All the characters, even the most unpleasant, are imaginary; the city, happily for us all, is not.

P. D. J.

Chapter One

On the morning of Bernie Pryde's death—or it may have been the morning after, since Bernie died at his own convenience, nor did he think the estimated time of his departure worth recording—Cordelia was caught in a breakdown of the Bakerloo Line outside Lambeth North and was half an hour late at the office. She came up from Oxford Circus underground into the bright June sunshine, sped past the early morning shoppers scanning the windows of Dickins and Jones and plunged into the cacophony of Kingly Street threading her way between the blocked pavement and the shining mass of cars and vans which packed the narrow street. The hurry she knew was irrational, a symptom of her obsession with order and punctuality. There were no appointments booked; no clients to be interviewed; no case outstanding; not even a final report to be written. She and Miss Sparshott, the temporary typist, at Cordelia's suggestion were circulating information about the Agency to all the London solicitors in the hope of attracting custom; Miss Sparshott would probably be busy with it now, eyes straying to her watch, tapping out her staccato irritation at every minute of Cordelia's lateness. She was an unprepossessing woman with lips permanently taut as if to prevent the protruding teeth from springing from her mouth, a receding chin with one coarse hair which grew as quickly as it was plucked, and fair hair set in stiff corrugated waves. That chin and mouth seemed to Cordelia the living refutation that all men are born equal and she tried from time to time to like and sympathize with Miss Sparshott, with a life lived in bedsitting rooms, measured in the five-penny pieces fed to the gas stove and circumscribed by fell seams and hand hemming. For Miss Sparshott was a skilled dressmaker, an assiduous attender at the G.L.C. evening classes. Her clothes were beautifully made but so dateless that they were never actually in

fashion; straight skirts in grey or black which were exercises in how to sew a pleat or insert a zip fastener; blouses with mannish collars and cuffs in insipid pastel shades on which she distributed without discretion her collection of costume jewellery; intricately cut dresses with hems at the precise length to emphasize her shapeless legs and thick ankles.

Cordelia had no premonition of tragedy as she pushed open the street door which was kept perpetually on the latch for the convenience of the secretive and mysterious tenants and their equally mysterious visitors. The new bronze plaque to the left of the door gleamed brightly in the sun in incongruous contrast to the faded and dirt-encrusted paint. Cordelia gave it a short glance of approval:

Pryde's Detective Agency
(*Props:* Bernard G. Pryde   Cordelia Gray)

It had taken Cordelia some weeks of patient and tactful persuasion to convince Bernie that it would be inappropriate to append the words "ex-C.I.D. Metropolitan Police" to his name or prefix "Miss" to hers. There had been no other problem over the plaque since Cordelia had brought no qualifications or relevant past experience to the partnership and indeed no capital, except her slight but tough twenty-two-year-old body, a considerable intelligence which Bernie, she suspected, had occasionally found more disconcerting than admirable, and a half exasperated, half pitying affection for Bernie himself. It was obvious very early to Cordelia that in some undramatic but positive way life had turned against him. She recognized the signs. Bernie never got the enviable front left hand seat in the bus; he couldn't admire the view from the train window without another train promptly obscuring it; the bread he dropped invariably fell buttered side downwards; the Mini, reliable enough when she drove it, stalled for Bernie at the busiest and most inconvenient intersections. She sometimes wondered whether, in accepting his offer of a partnership in a fit of depression or of perverse masochism, she was voluntarily embracing his ill-luck. She certainly never saw herself as powerful enough to change it.

The staircase smelt as always of stale sweat, furniture polish and disinfectant. The walls were dark green and were invariably damp whatever the season as if they secreted a miasma of desperate respectability and defeat. The stairs, with their ornate wrought-iron balustrade, were covered with split and stained linoleum patched by the landlord in various and contrasting colours only when a tenant complained. The Agency was on the third floor. There was no clatter of typewriter keys as Cordelia entered and she saw that Miss Sparshott was engaged in cleaning her machine, an ancient Imperial which was a constant cause of justified complaint. She looked up, her face blotched with resentment, her back as rigid as the space bar.

"I've been wondering when you would turn up, Miss Gray. I'm concerned about Mr. Pryde. I think he must be in the inner office but he's quiet, very quiet, and the door's locked."

Cordelia, chill at heart, wrenched at the door handle:

"Why didn't you do something?"

"Do what, Miss Gray? I knocked at the door and called out to him. It wasn't my place to do that, I'm only the temporary typist, I've no authority here. I should have been placed in a very embarrassing position if he had answered. After all, he's entitled to use his own office I suppose. Besides, I'm not even sure if he's there."

"He must be. The door's locked and his hat is here."

Bernie's trilby, the stained brim turned up all round, a comedian's hat, was hanging on the convoluted hatstand, a symbol of forlorn decrepitude. Cordelia was fumbling in her shoulder bag for her own key. As usual, the object most required had fallen to the bottom of the bag. Miss Sparshott began to clatter on the keys as if to disassociate herself from impending trauma. Above the noise she said defensively:

"There's a note on your desk."

Cordelia tore it open. It was short and explicit. Bernie had always been able to express himself succinctly when he had something to say:

"I'm sorry, partner, they've told me it's cancer and I'm taking the easy way out. I've seen what the treatment does to people and I'm not having any. I've made my will and it's with my

543

solicitor. You'll find his name in the desk. I've left the business
to you. Everything, including *all* the equipment. Good luck
and thank you." Underneath with the inconsiderateness of the
doomed he had scribbled a final unfair plea:

"If you find me alive, for God's sake wait before calling help.
I rely on you for this, partner. Bernie."

She unlocked the door of the inner office and went inside,
closing the door carefully behind her.

It was a relief to see that there was no need to wait. Bernie
was dead. He lay slumped over the desk as if in an extremity of
exhaustion. His right hand was half-clenched and an open
cut-throat razor had slithered over the desk top leaving a thin
trail of blood like a snail's track and had come to rest precariously
poised on the extreme edge of the desk. His left wrist, scored
with two parallel cuts, lay palm upwards in the enamel bowl
which Cordelia used for the washing-up. Bernie had filled it
with water but it was now brimfull with a pale pinky liquid
smelling sickly sweet, through which the fingers, curved as if in
supplication and looking as white and delicate as those of a
child, gleamed as smooth as wax. The blood and water had
overflowed on to the desk and floor soaking the oblong of garish
rug which Bernie had recently bought in the hope of impressing
visitors with his status but which Cordelia privately thought had
only drawn attention to the shabbiness of the rest of the office.
One of the cuts was tentative and superficial but the other had
gone deep as the bone and the severed edges of the wound,
drained of blood, gaped cleanly like an illustration in an anatomy
text book. Cordelia remembered how Bernie had once described
the finding of a prospective suicide when he was first on the beat
as a young constable. It was an old man huddled into a ware-
house doorway who had slashed his wrist with a broken bottle—
but who had later been dragged back to reluctant half-life
because an immense clot of blood had blocked the severed
veins. Bernie, remembering, had taken precautions to ensure that
his blood would not clot. He had, she noticed, taken another
precaution; there was an empty tea cup, the one in which she
served his afternoon tea, on the right of the desk with a grain
or two of powder, aspirin perhaps or a barbiturate, staining the

rim and side. A dried trickle of mucus, similarly stained, hung from the corner of his mouth. His lips were pursed and half open like those of a sleeping child, petulant and vulnerable. She put her head round the office door and said quietly:

"Mr. Pryde is dead; don't come in. I'll ring the police from here."

The telephone message was taken calmly, someone would come round. Sitting beside the body to wait and feeling that she needed to make some gesture of pity and comfort Cordelia laid her hand gently on Bernie's hair. Death had as yet no power to diminish these cold and nerveless cells and the hair felt roughly and unpleasantly alive like that of an animal. Quickly she took her hand away and tentatively touched the side of his forehead. The skin was clammy and very cold. This was death; this was how Daddy had felt. As with him, the gesture of pity was meaningless and irrelevant. There was no more communication in death than there had been in life.

She wondered when exactly Bernie had died. No one now would ever know. Perhaps Bernie himself had not known. There must, she supposed, have been one measurable second in time in which he had ceased to be Bernie and had become this unimportant but embarrassingly unwieldy weight of flesh and bone. How odd that a moment of time so important to him should pass without his knowledge. Her second foster mother, Mrs. Wilkes, would have said that Bernie did know, that there was a moment of indescribable glory, shining towers, limitless singing, skies of triumph. Poor Mrs. Wilkes! Widowed, her only son dead in the war, her small house perpetually noisy with the foster children who were her livelihood, she had needed her dreams. She had lived her life by comfortable maxims stored like nuggets of coal against the winter. Cordelia thought of her now for the first time in years and heard again the tired, determinedly cheerful voice "If the Lord doesn't call on his way out, He'll call on his way back." Well, going or coming, He hadn't called on Bernie.

It was odd but somehow typical of Bernie that he should have retained a dogged and invincible optimism about the business even when they had nothing in the cash box but a few coins

for the gas meter and yet had given up hope of life without even a struggle. Was it perhaps that he had sub-consciously recognized that neither he nor the Agency had any real future and had decided that this way he could yield up both life and livelihood with some honour? He had done it effectively but messily, surprisingly so for an ex-policeman versed in the ways of death. And then she realized why he had chosen the razor and the drugs. The gun. He hadn't really taken the easy way out. He could have used the gun, but he had wanted her to have it; he had bequeathed it to her together with the rickety filing cabinets, the antique typewriter, the scene-of-crime kit, the Mini, his shock-proof and waterproof wrist watch, the blood-soaked rug, the embarrassingly large stock of writing paper with the ornate heading *Pryde's Detective Agency—We take a Pride in our Work.* *All* the equipment; he had underlined all. He must have meant to remind her about the gun.

She unlocked the small drawer at the base of Bernie's desk to which only she and he had a key and drew it out. It was still in the suede draw-string bag which she had made for it, with three rounds of ammunition packed separately. It was a pistol, a .38 semi-automatic; she had never known how Bernie had come by it but she was certain that he had no licence. She had never seen it as a lethal weapon, perhaps because Bernie's boyishly naive obsession with it had reduced it to the impotence of a child's toy. He had taught her to become—at any rate in theory—a creditable shot. They had driven for practice into the depths of Epping Forest and her memories of the gun were linked with dappled shade and the rich smell of decaying leaves. He had fixed a target to a convenient tree; the gun was loaded with blanks. She could still hear the excited staccato orders. "Bend your knees slightly. Feet apart. Arm full length. Now place the left hand against the barrel, cradling it. Keep your eyes on the target. Arm straight, partner, arm straight! Good! Not bad; not bad; not bad at all." "But, Bernie," she had said, "we can never fire it! We haven't a licence." He had smiled, the sly self-satisfied smile of superior knowledge. "If we ever fire in anger it will be to save our lives. In such an eventuality the question of a licence is irrelevant." He had been pleased with this rotund

sentence and had repeated it, lifting his heavy face to the sun like a dog. What, she wondered, had he seen in imagination? The two of them crouching behind a boulder on some desolate moor, bullets pinging against the granite, the gun passed smoking from hand to hand?

He had said: "We'll have to go carefully with the ammunition. Not that I can't get it of course . . ." The smile had become grim, as if at the memory of those mysterious contacts, those ubiquitous and obliging acquaintances whom he had only to summon from their shadow world.

So he had left her the gun. It had been his most prized possession. She slipped it, still shrouded, into the depths of her shoulder bag. It was surely unlikely that the police would examine the drawers of the desk in a case of obvious suicide but it was as well to take no risk. Bernie had meant her to have the gun and she wasn't going to give it up easily. With her bag at her feet she sat down again by the body. She said a brief convent-taught prayer to the God she wasn't sure existed for the soul which Bernie had never believed he possessed and waited quietly for the police.

The first policeman to arrive was efficient but young, not yet experienced enough to hide his shock and distaste at the sight of violent death nor his disapproval that Cordelia should be so calm. He didn't spend long in the inner office. When he came out he meditated upon Bernie's note as if a careful scrutiny could extract some inner meaning from the bald sentence of death. Then he folded it away.

"I'll have to keep this note for the present, Miss. What did he get up to here?"

"He didn't get up to anything. This was his office. He was a private detective."

"And you worked for this Mr. Pryde? You were his secretary?"

"I was his partner. It says so in the note. I'm twenty-two. Bernie was the senior partner; he started the business. He used to work for the Metropolitan Police in the C.I.D. with Superintendent Dalgliesh."

As soon as the words were spoken, she regretted them. They were too propitiatory, too naive a defence of poor Bernie. And

the name Dalgliesh, she saw meant nothing to him. Why should it? He was just one of the local uniformed branch. He couldn't be expected to know how often she had listened with politely concealed impatience to Bernie's nostalgic reminiscences of his time in the C.I.D. before he was invalided out, or to his eulogies on the virtues and wisdom of Adam Dalgliesh. "The Super— well, he was just an Inspector then—always taught us . . . The Super once described a case . . . If there was one thing the Super couldn't stand . . ."

Sometimes she had wondered whether this paragon had actually existed or whether he had sprung impeccable and omnipotent from Bernie's brain, a necessary hero and mentor. It was with a shock of suprise that she had later seen a newspaper picture of Chief Superintendent Dalgliesh, a dark, sardonic face which, on her closer scrutiny, disintegrated into an ambiguity of patterned micro dots, giving nothing away. Not all the wisdom Bernie so glibly recalled was the received gospel. Much, she suspected, was his own philosophy. She in turn had devised a private litany of disdain: supercilious, superior, sarcastic Super; what wisdom, she wondered, would he have to comfort Bernie now.

The policeman had made discreet telephone calls. He now prowled around the outer office, hardly bothering to hide his puzzled contempt at the shabby second-hand furniture, the battered filing cabinet with one drawer half-open to reveal teapot and mugs, the worn linoleum. Miss Sparshott, rigid at an ancient typewriter, gazed at him with fascinated distaste. At last he said:

"Well, suppose you make yourselves a nice cup of tea while I wait for the police surgeon. There is somewhere to make tea?"

"There's a small pantry down the corridor which we share with the other tenants on this floor. But surely you don't need a surgeon? Bernie's dead!"

"He's not officially dead until a qualified medical practitioner says so." He paused: "It's just a precaution."

Against what, Cordelia wondered—judgement, damnation, decay? The policeman went back into the inner office. She followed him and asked softly:

"Couldn't you let Miss Sparshott go? She's from a secretarial agency and we have to pay for her by the hour. She hasn't done any work since I arrived and I doubt whether she will now."

He was, she saw, a little shocked by the apparent callousness of concerning herself with so mercenary a detail while standing within touching distance of Bernie's body, but he said willingly enough:

"I'll just have a word with her, then she can go. It isn't a nice place for a woman."

His tone implied that it never had been.

Afterwards, waiting in the outer office, Cordelia answered the inevitable questions.

"No, I don't know whether he was married. I've a feeling that he was divorced; he never talked about a wife. He lived at 15, Cremona Road, S.E.2. He let me have a bed-sitting room there but we didn't see much of each other."

"I know Cremona Road; my aunt used to live there when I was a kid—one of those streets near the Imperial War Museum."

The fact that he knew the road seemed to reassure and humanize him. He ruminated happily for a moment.

"When did you last see Mr. Pryde alive?"

"Yesterday at about five o'clock when I left work early to do some shopping."

"Didn't he come home last night?"

"I heard him moving around but I didn't see him. I have a gas ring in my room and I usually cook there unless I know he's out. I didn't hear him this morning which is unusual, but I thought he might be lying in. He does that occasionally when it's his hospital morning."

"Was it his hospital morning to-day?"

"No, he had an appointment last Wednesday but I thought that they might have asked him to come back. He must have left the house very late last night or before I woke early this morning. I didn't hear him."

It was impossible to describe the almost obsessional delicacy with which they avoided each other, trying not to intrude, preserving the other's privacy, listening for the sound of flushing

cisterns, tip-toeing to ascertain whether the kitchen or bathroom was empty. They had taken infinite trouble not to be a nuisance to each other. Living in the same small terraced house they had hardly seen each other outside the office. She wondered whether Bernie had decided to kill himself in his office so that the little house would be uncontaminated and undisturbed.

<hr />

At last the office was empty and she was alone. The police surgeon had closed his bag and departed; Bernie's body had been manoeuvred down the narrow staircase watched by eyes from the half-opened doors of other offices; the last policeman had left. Miss Sparshott had gone for good, violent death being a worse insult than a typewriter which a trained typist ought not to be expected to use or lavatory accommodation which was not at all what she had been accustomed to. Alone in the emptiness and silence Cordelia felt the need of physical action. She began vigorously to clean the inner office, scrubbing the blood stains from desk and chair, mopping the soaked rug.

At one o'clock she walked briskly to their usual pub. It occurred to her that there was no longer any reason to patronize the Golden Pheasant but she walked on unable to bring herself to so early a disloyalty. She had never liked the pub or the landlady and had often wished that Bernie would find a nearer house, preferably one with a large bosomy barmaid with a heart of gold. It was, she suspected, a type commoner in fiction than in real life. The familiar lunch-time crowd was clustered around the bar and, as usual, Mavis presided behind it wearing her slightly minatory smile, her air of extreme respectability. Mavis changed her dress three times a day, her hair style once every year, her smile never. The two women had never liked each other although Bernie had galumphed between them like an affectionate old dog, finding it convenient to believe that they were great mates and unaware of or ignoring the almost physical crackle of antagonism. Mavis reminded Cordelia of a librarian known to her in childhood who had secreted the new books

550

under the counter in case they should be taken out and soiled. Perhaps Mavis's barely suppressed chagrin was because she was forced to display her wares so prominently, compelled to measure out her bounty before watchful eyes. Pushing a half pint of shandy and a Scotch egg across the counter in response to Cordelia's order, she said:

"I hear you've had the police round."

Watching their avid faces, Cordelia thought, they know about it, of course; they want to hear the details; they may as well hear them. She said:

"Bernie cut his wrists twice. The first time he didn't get to the vein; the second time he did. He put his arm in water to help the bleeding. He had been told that he had cancer and couldn't face the treatment."

That, she saw, was different. The little group around Mavis glanced at each other, then quickly averted their eyes. Glasses were momentarily checked upon their upward way. Cutting one's wrist was something which other people did but the sinister little crab had his claws of fear into all their minds. Even Mavis looked as if she saw his bright claws lurking among her bottles. She said:

"You'll be looking for a new job, I suppose? After all, you can hardly keep the Agency going on your own. It isn't a suitable job for a woman."

"No different from working behind a bar; you meet all kinds of people."

The two women looked at each other and a snatch of unspoken dialogue passed between them clearly heard and understood by both.

"And don't think, now he's dead, that people can go on leaving messages for the Agency here."

"I wasn't going to ask."

Mavis began vigorously polishing a glass, her eyes still on Cordelia's face.

"I shouldn't think your mother would approve of you staying on alone."

"I only had a mother for the first hour of my life, so I don't have to worry about that."

Cordelia saw at once that the remark had deeply shocked them and wondered again at the capacity of older people to be outraged by simple facts when they seemed capable of accepting any amount of perverse or shocking opinion. But their silence, heavy with censure, at least left her in peace. She carried her shandy and the Scotch egg to a seat against the wall and thought without sentimentality about her mother. Gradually out of a childhood of deprivation she had evolved a philosophy of compensation. In her imagination she had enjoyed a lifetime of love in one hour with no disappointments and no regrets. Her father had never talked about her mother's death and Cordelia had avoided questioning him, fearful of learning that her mother had never held her in her arms, never regained consciousness, never perhaps even known that she had a daughter. This belief in her mother's love was the one fantasy which she could still not entirely risk losing although its indulgence had become less necessary and less real with each passing year. Now, in imagination, she consulted her mother. It was just as she expected: her mother thought it an entirely suitable job for a woman.

The little group at the bar had turned back to their drinks. Between their shoulders she could see her own reflection in the mirror above the bar. Today's face looked no different from yesterday's face; thick, light brown hair framing features which looked as if a giant had placed a hand on her head and the other under her chin and gently squeezed the face together; large eyes, browny-green under a deep fringe of hair; wide cheek bones; a gentle, childish mouth. A cat's face she thought, but calmly decorative among the reflection of coloured bottles and all the bright glitter of Mavis's bar. Despite its look of deceptive youth it could be a secret, uncommunicative face. Cordelia had early learnt stoicism. All her foster parents, kindly and well-meaning in their different ways, had demanded one thing of her—that she should be happy. She had quickly learned that to show unhappiness was to risk the loss of love. Compared with this early discipline of concealment, all subsequent deceits had been easy.

The Snout was edging his way towards her. He settled himself down on the bench, his thick rump in its appalling tweed pressed

close to hers. She disliked the Snout although he had been Bernie's only friend. Bernie had explained that the Snout was a police informer and did rather well. And there were other sources of income. Sometimes his friends stole famous pictures or valuable jewellery. Then the Snout, suitably instructed, would hint to the police where the loot could be found. There was a reward for the Snout to be subsequently shared, of course, among the thieves, and a payoff, too, for the detective, who after all, had done most of the work. As Bernie had pointed out, the insurance company got off lightly, the owners got their property back intact, the thieves were in no danger from the police and the Snout and the detective got their payoff. It was the system. Cordelia, shocked, had not liked to protest too much. She suspected that Bernie too had done some snouting in his time, although never with such expertise or with such lucrative results.

The Snout's eyes were rheumy, his hand around the glass of whisky was shaking.

"Poor old Bernie, I could see he had it coming to him. He'd been losing weight for the last year and he had that grey look to him, the cancer complexion, my dad used to call it."

At least the Snout had noticed; she hadn't. Bernie had always seemed to her grey and sick-looking. A thick, hot thigh edged closer.

"Never had any luck, poor sod. They chucked him out of the C.I.D. Did he tell you? That was Superintendent Dalgliesh, Inspector at the time. Christ, he could be a proper bastard; no second chance from him, I can tell you."

"Yes, Bernie told me," Cordelia lied. She added: "He didn't seem particularly bitter about it."

"No use, is there, in being bitter? Take what comes, that's my motto. I suppose you'll be looking for another job?"

He said it wistfully as if her defection would leave the Agency open for his exploitation.

"Not just yet," said Cordelia. "I shan't look for a new job just yet."

She had made two resolutions: she would keep on Bernie's business until there was nothing left with which to pay the rent,

and she would never come into the Golden Pheasant again as long as she lived.

❧

This resolution to keep the business going survived the next four days—survived discovery of the rent book and agreement which revealed that Bernie hadn't, after all, owned the little house in Cremona Road and that her tenancy of the bedsitting room was illegal and certainly limited; survived learning from the Bank Manager that Bernie's credit balance would barely pay for his funeral and from the garage that the Mini was shortly due for an overhaul; survived the clearing up of the Cremona Road house. Everywhere was the sad detritus of a solitary and mismanaged life.

The tins of Irish stew and baked beans—had he never eaten anything else?—stacked in a carefully arranged pyramid as if in a grocer's window; large tins of floor and metal polish, half-used, with their contents dried or congealed; a drawer of old rags used as dusters but stiff with an amalgam of polish and dirt; a laundry basket unemptied; thick woollen combinations felted with machine washing and stained brown about the crotch—how could he have borne to leave those for discovery?

She went daily to the office, cleaning, tidying, rearranging the filing. There were no calls and no clients and yet she seemed always busy. There was the inquest to attend, depressing in its detached almost boring formality, in its inevitable verdict. There was a visit to Bernie's solicitor. He was a dispirited, elderly man with an office inconveniently situated near Mile End Station who took the news of his client's death with lugubrious resignation as if it were a personal affront, and after a brief search found Bernie's will and pored over it with puzzled suspicion, as if it were not the document he himself had recently drawn up. He succeeded in giving Cordelia the impression that he realized that she had been Bernie's mistress—why else should he have left her the business?—but that he was a man of the world and didn't hold the knowledge against her. He took no part in arranging the funeral except to supply Cordelia with the name

554

of a firm of undertakers; she suspected that they probably gave him a commission. She was relieved after a week of depressing solemnity to find that the funeral director was both cheerful and competent. Once he discovered that Cordelia wasn't going to break down in tears or indulge in the more histrionic antics of the bereaved, he was happy to discuss the relative price and the merits of burial and cremation with conspiratorial candour.

"Cremation every time. There's no private insurance, you tell me? Then get it all over as quickly, easily and cheaply as possible. Take my word, that's what the deceased would want nine times out of ten. A grave's an expensive luxury these days—no use to him—no use to you. Dust to dust, ashes to ashes; but what about the process in between? Not nice to think about, is it? So why not get it over as quickly as possible by the most reliable modern methods? Mind you, Miss, I'm advising you against my own best interests."

Cordelia said:

"It's very kind of you. Do you think we ought to have a wreath?"

"Why not, it'll give it a bit of tone. Leave it to me."

So there had been a cremation and one wreath. The wreath had been a vulgarly inappropriate cushion of lilies and carnations, the flowers already dying and smelling of decay. The cremation service had been spoken by the priest with carefully controlled speed and with a suggestion of apology in his tone as if to assure his hearers that, although he enjoyed a special dispensation, he didn't expect them to believe the unbelievable. Bernie had passed to his burning to the sound of synthetic music and only just on time, to judge by the impatient rustlings of the cortège already waiting to enter the chapel.

Afterwards Cordelia was left standing in the bright sunlight, feeling the heat of the gravel through the soles of her shoes. The air was rich and heavy with the scent of flowers. Swept suddenly with desolation and a defensive anger on Bernie's behalf, she sought a scapegoat and found it in a certain Superintendent of the Yard. He had kicked Bernie out of the only job he had ever wanted to do; hadn't troubled to find out what happened to him later; and, most irrational indictment of all, he hadn't even

bothered to come to the funeral. Bernie had needed to be a detective as other men needed to paint, write, drink or fornicate. Surely the C.I.D. was large enough to accommodate one man's enthusiasm and inefficiency? For the first time Cordelia wept for Bernie; hot tears blurred and multiplied the long line of waiting hearses with their bright coronets so that they seemed to stretch in an infinity of gleaming chrome and trembling flowers. Untying the black chiffon scarf from her head, her only concession to mourning, Cordelia set off to walk to the tube station.

She was thirsty when she got to Oxford Circus and decided to have tea in the restaurant at Dickins and Jones. This was unusual and an extravagance but it had been an unusual and extravagant day. She lingered long enough to get full value for her bill and it was after a quarter past four when she returned to the office.

She had a visitor. There was a woman waiting, shoulders against the door—a woman who looked cool and incongruous against the dirty paintwork and the greasy walls. Cordelia caught her breath in surprise, her upward rush checked. Her light shoes had made no sound on the stairway and for a few seconds she saw her visitor unobserved. She gained an impression, immediate and vivid, of competence and authority and an intimidating rightness of dress. The woman was wearing a grey suit with a small stand-away collar which showed a narrow band of white cotton at the throat. Her black patent shoes were obviously expensive; a large black bag with patch pockets was slung from her left shoulder. She was tall and her hair, prematurely white, was cut short and moulded to her head like a cap. Her face was pale and long. She was reading *The Times*, the paper folded so that she could hold it in her right hand. After a couple of seconds, she became aware of Cordelia and their eyes met. The woman looked at her wrist watch.

"If you are Cordelia Gray, then you're eighteen minutes late. This notice says that you would return at four o'clock."

"I know, I'm sorry." Cordelia hurried up the last few steps and fitted the Yale key into the lock. She opened the door.

"Won't you come in?"

The woman preceded her into the outer office and turned to face her without giving the room even a glance.

"I was hoping to see Mr. Pryde. Will he be long?"

"I'm sorry; I've just come back from his cremation. I mean . . . Bernie's dead."

"Obviously. Our information was that he was alive ten days ago. He must have died with remarkable speed and discretion."

"Not with discretion. Bernie killed himself."

"How extraordinary!" The visitor seemed to be struck by its extraordinariness. She pressed her hands together and for a few seconds walked restlessly about the room in a curious pantomime of distress.

"How extraordinary!" she said again. She gave a little snort of laughter. Cordelia didn't speak, but the two women regarded each other gravely. Then the visitor said:

"Well, I seem to have had a wasted journey."

Cordelia breathed an almost inaudible "Oh no!" and resisted an absurd impulse to fling her body against the door.

"Please don't go before talking to me. I was Mr. Pryde's partner and I own the business now. I'm sure I could help. Won't you please sit down?"

The visitor took no notice of the offered chair.

"No one can help, no one in the world. However, that is beside the point. There is something which my employer particularly wants to know—some information he requires—and he had decided that Mr. Pryde was the person to get it for him. I don't know if he would consider you an effective substitute. Is there a private telephone here?"

"In here, please."

The woman walked into the inner office, again with no sign that its shabbiness had made any impression on her. She turned to Cordelia.

"I'm sorry, I should have introduced myself. My name is Elizabeth Leaming and my employer is Sir Ronald Callender."

"The conservationist?"

"I shouldn't let him hear you call him that. He prefers to be called a micro-biologist, which is what he is. Please excuse me."

She shut the door firmly. Cordelia, feeling suddenly weak, sat

down at the typewriter. They keys, oddly unfamiliar symbols encircled in black medallions, shifted their pattern before her tired eyes, then at a blink clicked back to normality. She grasped the sides of the machine, cold and clammy to the touch, and talked herself back to calmness. Her heart was thudding.

"I must be calm, must show her that I am tough. This silliness is only the strain of Bernie's funeral and too much standing in the hot sun."

But hope was traumatic; she was angry with herself for caring so much.

The telephone call took only a couple of minutes. The door of the inner office opened; Miss Leaming was drawing on her gloves.

"Sir Ronald has asked to see you. Can you come now?"

Come where, thought Cordelia, but she didn't ask.

"Yes, shall I need my gear?"

The gear was Bernie's carefully designed and fitted out scene-of-crime case with its tweezers, scissors, finger printing equipment, jars to collect specimens; Cordelia had never yet had occasion to use it.

"It depends upon what you mean by your gear, but I shouldn't think so. Sir Ronald wants to see you before deciding whether to offer you the job. It means a train journey to Cambridge but you should get back tonight. Is there anyone you ought to tell?"

"No, there's only me."

"Perhaps I ought to identify myself." She opened her handbag. "Here is an addressed envelope. I'm not a white slaver if they exist and in case you're frightened."

"I'm frightened of quite a number of things but not of white slavers and if I were, an addressed envelope would hardly reassure me. I'd insist on telephoning Sir Ronald Callender to check."

"Perhaps you would like to do so?" suggested Miss Leaming without rancour.

"No."

"Then shall we go?" Miss Leaming led the way to the door. As they went out to the landing and Cordelia turned to lock

the office behind her, her visitor indicated the notepad and pencil hanging together from a nail on the wall.

"Hadn't you better change the notice?"

Cordelia tore off her previous message and after a moment's thought wrote:

I am called away to an urgent case. Any messages pushed through the door will receive my immediate and personal attention on return.

"That," pronounced Miss Leaming, "should reassure your clients." Cordelia wondered if the remark was sarcastic; it was impossible to tell from the detached tone. But she didn't feel that Miss Leaming was laughing at her and was surprised at her own lack of resentment at the way in which her visitor had taken charge of events. Meekly, she followed Miss Leaming down the stairs and into Kingly Street.

They travelled by the Central Line to Liverpool Street and caught the 17.36 train to Cambridge with plenty of time. Miss Leaming bought Cordelia's ticket, collected a portable typewriter and a briefcase of papers from the left luggage department and led the way to a first-class carriage. She said:

"I shall have to work in the train; have you anything to read?"

"That's all right. I don't like talking when I'm travelling either. I've got Hardy's *Trumpet Major*—I always have a paperback in my bag."

After Bishops Stortford they had the compartment to themselves but only once did Miss Leaming look up from her work to question Cordelia.

"How did you come to be working for Mr. Pryde?"

"After I left school I went to live with my father on the continent. We travelled around a good deal. He died in Rome last May after a heart attack and I came home. I had taught myself some shorthand and typing so I took a job with a secretarial agency. They sent me to Bernie and after a few weeks he let me help him with one or two of the cases. He decided to train me and I agreed to stay on permanently. Two months ago he made me his partner."

All that had meant was that Cordelia gave up a regular wage in return for the uncertain rewards of success in the form of an equal share of the profits together with a rent-free bedsitting room

in Bernie's house. He hadn't meant to cheat. The offer of the partnership had been made in the genuine belief that she would recognize it for what it was; not a good conduct prize but an accolade of trust.

"What was your father?"

"He was an itinerant Marxist poet and an amateur revolutionary."

"You must have had an interesting childhood."

Remembering the succession of foster mothers, the unexplained incomprehensible moves from house to house, the changes of school, the concerned faces of Local Authority Welfare Officers and school teachers desperately wondering what to do with her in the holidays, Cordelia replied as she always did to this assertion, gravely and without irony.

"Yes, it was very interesting."

"And what was this training you received from Mr. Pryde?"

"Bernie taught me some of the things he learnt in the C.I.D.: how to search the scene of a crime properly, how to collect exhibits, some elementary self-defence, how to detect and lift finger prints—that kind of thing."

"Those are skills which I hardly feel you will find appropriate to this case."

Miss Leaming bent her head over her papers and did not speak again until the train reached Cambridge.

Outside the station Miss Leaming briefly surveyed the car park and led the way towards a small black van. Standing beside it rigidly as a uniformed chauffeur, was a stockily built young man dressed in an open-necked white shirt, dark breeches and tall boots who Miss Leaming introduced casually and without explanation as "Lunn." He nodded briefly in acknowledgement of the introduction but did not smile. Cordelia held out her hand. His grip was momentary but remarkably strong, crushing her fingers; suppressing a grimace of pain she saw a flicker in the large mud-brown eyes and wondered if he had hurt her deliberately. The eyes were certainly memorable and beautiful, moist calves' eyes heavily lashed and with the same look of

troubled pain at the unpredictability of the world's terrors. But their beauty emphasized rather than redeemed the unattractiveness of the rest of him. He was, she thought, a sinister study in black and white with his thick, short neck and powerful shoulders straining the seams of his shirt. He had a helmet of strong black hair, a pudgy slightly pox-marked face and a moist petulant mouth; the face of a ribald cherub. He was a man who sweated profusely; the underarms of his shirt were stained and the cotton stuck to the flesh emphasizing the strong curve of the back and the obtrusive biceps.

Cordelia saw that the three of them were to sit squashed together in the front of the van. Lunn held open the door without apology except to state:

"The Rover's still in dock."

Miss Leaming hung back so that Cordelia was compelled to get in first and to sit beside him. She thought: "They don't like each other and he resents me."

She wondered about his position in Sir Ronald Callender's household. Miss Leaming's place she had already guessed; no ordinary secretary however long in service, however indispensable, had quite that air of authority or talked of "my employer" in that tone of possessive irony. But she wondered about Lunn. He didn't behave like a subordinate but nor did he strike her as a scientist. True, scientists were alien creatures to her. Sister Mary Magdalen was the only one she had known. Sister had taught what the syllabus dignified as general science, a hotch-potch of elementary physics, chemistry and biology unceremoniously lumped together. Science subjects were in general little regarded at the Convent of the Immaculate Conception, although the arts were well taught. Sister Mary Magdalen had been an elderly and timid nun, eyes puzzled behind her steel-rimmed spectacles, her clumsy fingers permanently stained with chemicals, who had apparently been as surprised as her pupils at the extraordinary explosions and fumes which her activities with test tube and flask had occasionally produced. She had been more concerned to demonstrate the incomprehensibility of the universe and the inscrutability of God's laws than to reveal scientific principles and in this she had

certainly succeeded. Cordelia felt that Sister Mary Magdalen would be no help to her in dealing with Sir Ronald Callender; Sir Ronald who had campaigned in the cause of conservation long before his interest became a popular obsession, who had represented his country at International Conferences on Ecology and been knighted for his services to conservation. All this Cordelia, like the rest of the country, knew from his television appearances and the Sunday Colour Supplements. He was the establishment scientist, carefully uncommitted politically, who personified to everyone's reassurance the poor boy who had made good and stayed good. How, Cordelia wondered, had he come to think of employing Bernie Pryde?

Uncertain how far Lunn was in his employer's or Miss Leaming's confidence, she asked carefully:

"How did Sir Ronald hear about Bernie?"

"John Bellinger told him."

So the Bellinger bonus had arrived at last! Bernie had always expected it. The Bellinger case had been his most lucrative, perhaps his only, success. John Bellinger was the director of a small family firm which manufactured specialized scientific instruments. The previous year his office had been plagued by an outbreak of obscene letters and, unwilling to call in the police, he had telephoned Bernie. Bernie, taken on the staff at his own suggestion as a messenger, had quickly solved a not very difficult problem. The writer had been Bellinger's middle-aged and highly regarded personal secretary. Bellinger had been grateful. Bernie, after anxious thought and consultation with Cordelia, had sent in a bill the size of which had astounded them both and the bill had been promptly paid. It had kept the Agency going for a month. Bernie had said: "We'll get a bonus from the Bellinger case, see if we don't. Anything can happen in this job. He only chose us by picking our name from the telephone directory but now he'll recommend us to his friends. This case could be the beginning of something big."

And now, thought Cordelia, on the day of Bernie's funeral, the Bellinger bonus had arrived.

She asked no more questions and the drive, which took less than thirty minutes, passed in silence. The three of them sat

thigh to thigh, but distanced. She saw nothing of the city. At the end of Station Road by the War Memorial the car turned to the left and soon they were in the country. There were wide fields of young corn, the occasional stretch of tree-lined dappled shade, straggling villages of thatched cottages and squat red villas strung along the road, low uplands from which Cordelia could see the towers and spires of the city, shining with deceptive nearness in the evening sun. Finally, there was another village, a thin belt of elms fringing the road, a long curving wall of red brick and the van turned in through open wrought iron gates. They had arrived.

❖❖❖

The house was obviously Georgian, not perhaps the best Georgian but solidly built, agreeably proportioned and with the look of all good domestic architecture of having grown naturally out of its site. The mellow brick, festooned with wisteria, gleamed richly in the evening sun so that the green of the creeper glowed and the whole house looked suddenly as artificial and unsubstantial as a film set. It was essentially a family house, a welcoming house. But now a heavy silence lay over it and the rows of elegantly proportioned windows were empty eyes.

Lunn, who had driven fast but skilfully, braked in front of the porch. He stayed in his seat while the two women got out then drove the van round the side of the house. As she slid down from the high seat Cordelia could glimpse a range of low buildings, topped with small ornamental turrets, which she took to be stables or garages. Through the wide-arched gateway she could see that the grounds dropped slowly away to give a far vista of the flat Cambridgeshire countryside, patterned with the gentle greens and fawns of early summer. Miss Leaming said:

"The stable block has been converted into laboratories. Most of the east side is now glass. It was a skilful job by a Swedish architect, functional but attractive."

For the first time since they had met her voice sounded interested, almost enthusiastic.

The front door was open. Cordelia came into a wide, panelled hall with a staircase curving to the left, a carved stone fireplace to the right. She was aware of a smell of roses and lavender, of carpets gleaming richly against polished wood, of the subdued ticking of a clock.

Miss Leaming led the way to a door immediately across the hall. It led to a study, a room booklined and elegant, one with a view of wide lawns and a shield of trees. In front of the french windows was a Georgian desk and behind the desk sat a man.

Cordelia had seen his photographs in the press and knew what to expect. But he was at once smaller and more impressive than she had imagined. She knew that she was facing a man of authority and high intelligence; his strength came over like a physical force. But as he rose from his seat and waved her to a chair, she saw that he was slighter than his photographs suggested, the heavy shoulders and impressive head making the body look top-heavy. He had a lined, sensitive face with a high-bridged nose, deep-set eyes on which the lids weighed heavily and a mobile, sculptured mouth. His black hair, as yet unflecked with grey, lay heavily across his brow. His face was shadowed with weariness and, as Cordelia came closer, she could detect the twitch of a nerve in his left temple and the almost imperceptible staining of the veins in the irises of the deep-set eyes. But his compact body, taut with energy and latent vigour, made no concession to tiredness. The arrogant head was held high, the eyes were keen and wary under the heavy lids. Above all he looked successful. Cordelia had seen that look before, had recognized it from the back of crowds as, inscrutable, they had watched the famous and notorious pass on their way—that almost physical glow, akin to sexuality and undimmed by weariness or ill-health, of men who knew and enjoyed the realities of power.

Miss Leaming said:

"This is all that remains of Pryde's Detective Agency—Miss Cordelia Gray."

The keen eyes looked into Cordelia's.

"We take a Pride in our Work. Do you?"

Cordelia, tired after her journey at the end of a momentous day, was in no mood for jokes about poor Bernie's pathetic pun. She said:

"Sir Ronald, I have come here because your secretary said that you might want to employ me. If she's wrong, I would be glad to know so that I can get back to London."

"She isn't my secretary and she isn't wrong. You must forgive my discourtesy; it's a little disconcerting to expect a burly ex-policeman and to get you. I'm not complaining, Miss Gray; you might do very well. What are your fees?"

The question might have sounded offensive but it wasn't; he was completely matter-of-fact. Cordelia told him, a little too quickly, a little too eagerly.

"Five pounds a day and expenses, but we try to keep those as low as possible. For that, of course, you get my sole services. I mean I don't work for any other client until your case is finished."

"And is there another client?"

"Well, not just at present but there very well could be." She went on quickly:

"We have a fair-play clause. If I decide at any stage of the investigation that I'd rather not go on with it, you are entitled to any information I have gained up to that point. If I decide to withhold it from you, then I make no charge for the work already done."

That had been one of Bernie's principles. He had been a great man for principles. Even when there hadn't been a case for a week, he could happily discuss the extent to which they would be justified in telling a client less than the full truth, the point at which the police ought to be brought into an enquiry, the ethics of deception or lying in the service of truth. "But no bugging," Bernie would say "I set my face firmly against bugging. And we don't touch industrial sabotage."

The temptation to either wasn't great. They had no bugging equipment and wouldn't have known how to use it if they had, and at no time had Bernie been invited to touch industrial sabotage.

Sir Ronald said:

"That sounds reasonable but I don't think this case will

present you with any crisis of conscience. It is comparatively simple. Eighteen days ago my son hanged himself. I want you to find out why. Can you do that?"

"I should like to try, Sir Ronald."

"I realize that you need certain basic information about Mark. Miss Leaming will type it out for you, then you can read it through and let us know what else you require."

Cordelia said:

"I should like you to tell me yourself, please."

"Is that necessary?"

"It would be helpful to me."

He settled again into his chair and picked up a stub of pencil, twisting it in his hands. After a minute he slipped it absent-mindedly into his pocket. Without looking at her, he began to speak.

"My son Mark was twenty-one on the 25th April this year. He was at Cambridge reading history at my old college and was in his final year. Five weeks ago and without warning, he left the university and took a job as gardener with a Major Markland, who lives in a house called Summertrees outside Duxford. Mark gave me no explanation of this action either then or later. He lived alone in a cottage in Major Markland's grounds. Eighteen days later he was found by his employer's sister hanging by the neck from a strap knotted to a hook in the sitting-room ceiling. The verdict at the inquest was that he took his life while the balance of his mind was disturbed. I know little of my son's mind but I reject that comfortable euphemism. He was a rational person. He had a reason for his action. I want to know what it was."

Miss Leaming, who had been looking out of the french windows to the garden, turned and said with sudden vehemence:

"This lust always to know! It's only prying. If he'd wanted us to know, he'd have told us."

Sir Ronald said:

"I'm not prepared to go on in this uncertainty. My son is dead. *My* son. If I am in some way responsible, I prefer to know. If anyone else is responsible I want to know that too."

Cordelia looked from one to the other: She asked:

"Did he leave a note?"

"He left a note but not an explanation. It was found in his typewriter."

Quietly Miss Leaming began to speak:

"Down the winding cavern we groped our tedious way, till a void boundless as the nether sky appeared beneath us, and we held by the roots of trees and hung over this immensity; but I said: if you please we will commit ourselves to this void, and see whether providence is here also."

The husky, curiously deep voice came to an end. They were silent. Then Sir Ronald said:

"You claim to be a detective, Miss Gray. What do you deduce from that?"

"That your son read William Blake. Isn't it a passage from *The Marriage of Heaven and Hell?*

Sir Ronald and Miss Leaming glanced at each other. Sir Ronald said:

"So I am told."

Cordelia thought that Blake's gently unemphatic exhortation, devoid of violence or despair, was more appropriate to suicide by drowning or by poison—a ceremonious floating or sinking into oblivion—than to the trauma of hanging. And yet there was the analogy of falling, of launching oneself into the void. But this speculation was indulgent fantasy. He had chosen Blake: he had chosen hanging. Perhaps other and more gentle means were not to hand; perhaps he had acted upon impulse. What was it that the Super always said? "Never theorize in advance of your facts." She would have to look at the cottage.

Sir Ronald said, with a touch of impatience.

"Well, don't you want the job?"

Cordelia looked at Miss Leaming but the woman did not meet her eyes.

"I want it very much. I was wondering whether you really want me to take it."

"I'm offering it to you. Worry about your own responsibilities, Miss Gray, and I'll look after mine."

Cordelia said:

"Is there anything else that you can tell me? The ordinary things. Was your son in good health? Did he seem worried about his work or his love affairs? About money?"

"Mark would have inherited a considerable fortune from his maternal grandfather had he reached the age of twenty-five. In the meantime, he received an adequate allowance from me, but from the date of leaving college he transferred the balance back to my own account and instructed his Bank Manager to deal similarly with any future payments. Presumably he lived on his earnings for the last two weeks of his life. The postmortem revealed no illnesses and his tutor testified that his academic work was satisfactory. I, of course, know nothing of his subject. He didn't confide in me about his love affairs—what young man does to his father? If he had any, I would expect them to be heterosexual."

Miss Leaming turned from her contemplation at the garden. She held out her hands in a gesture which could have been resignation or despair:

"We knew nothing about him, nothing! So why wait until he's dead and then start finding out?"

"And his friends?" asked Cordelia quietly.

"They rarely visited here but there were two I recognized at the inquest and the funeral: Hugo Tilling from his own college and his sister who is a post-graduate student at New Hall, studying philology. Do you remember her name, Eliza?"

"Sophie. Sophia Tilling. Mark brought her here to dinner once or twice."

"Could you tell me something about your son's early life? Where was he educated?"

"He went to a pre-prep school when he was five and to a prep school subsequently. I couldn't have a child here running unsupervised in and out of the laboratory. Later, at his mother's wish—she died when Mark was nine months old—he went to a Woodard Foundation. My wife was what I believe is called a High Anglican and wanted the boy educated in that tradition. As far as I know, it had no deleterious effect on him."

"Was he happy at prep school?"

"I expect he was as happy as most eight-year-olds are, which

means that he was miserable most of the time, interposed with periods of animal spirits. Is all this relevant?"

"Anything could be. I have to try to get to know him, you see."

What was it that the supercilious, sapient, superhuman Super had taught? "Get to know the dead person. Nothing about him is too trivial, too unimportant. Dead men can talk. They can lead you directly to their murderer." Only this time, of course, there wasn't a murderer. She said:

"It would be helpful if Miss Leaming could type out the information you have given to me and add the name of his college and his tutor. And please may I have a note signed by you to authorize me to make enquiries."

He reached down to a left-hand drawer in the desk, took out a sheet of writing paper and wrote on it; then he passed it to Cordelia. The printed heading read: From Sir Ronald Callender, F.R.S., Garforth House, Cambridgeshire. Underneath he had written:

The bearer, Miss Cordelia Gray, is authorized to make enquiries on my behalf into the death on 26th May of my son Mark Callender. He had signed and dated it. He asked:

"Is there anything else?"

Cordelia said:

"You talked about the possibility of someone else being responsible for your son's death. Do you quarrel with the verdict?"

"The verdict was in accordance with the evidence which is all one can expect of a verdict. A court of law is not constituted to establish the truth. I'm employing you to make an attempt at that. Have you everything you need? I don't think we can help you with any more information."

"I should like a photograph." They looked at each other nonplussed. He said to Miss Leaming.

"A photograph. Have we a photograph, Eliza?"

"There is his passport somewhere but I'm not sure where. I have that photograph I took of him in the garden last summer. It shows him fairly clearly, I think. I'll get it." She went out of the room. Cordelia said:

"And I should like to see his room, if I may. I assume that he stayed here during his vacations?"

569

"Only occasionally, but of course he had a room here. I'll show it to you."

The room was on the second floor and at the back. Once inside, Sir Ronald ignored Cordelia. He walked over to the window and gazed out over the lawns as if neither she nor the room held any interest for him. It told Cordelia nothing about the adult Mark. It was simply furnished, a school boy's sanctum, and looked as if little had been changed in the last ten years. There was a low white cupboard against one wall with the usual row of discarded childhood toys; a teddy bear, his fur scuffed with much cuddling and one beady eye hanging loose; painted wooden trains and trucks; a Noah's Ark, its deck a-tumble with stiff-legged animals topped by a round-faced Noah and his wife; a boat with limp dejected sail; a miniature darts board. Above the toys were two rows of books. Cordelia went over to examine them. Here was the orthodox library of the middle-class child, the approved classics handed down from generation to generation, the traditional lore of Nanny and mother. Cordelia had come to them late as an adult; they had found no place in her Saturday comic and television-dominated childhood. She said:

"What about his present books?"

"They're in boxes in the cellar. He sent them here for storage when he left college and we haven't had time to unpack them yet. There hardly seems any point in it."

There was a small round table beside the bed and on it a lamp and a bright round stone intricately holed by the sea, a treasure picked up, perhaps, from some holiday beach. Sir Ronald touched it gently with long tentative fingers then began rolling it under his palm over the surface of the table. Then, apparently without thinking, he dropped it into his pocket. "Well," he said. "Shall we go down now?"

They were met at the foot of the stairs by Miss Leaming. She looked up at them as slowly they came down side by side. There was such controlled intensity in her regard that Cordelia waited almost with apprehension for her to speak. But she turned away, her shoulders drooping as if with sudden fatigue, and all she said was:

"I've found the photograph. I should like it back when you've

570

finished with it, please. I've put it in the envelope with the note. There isn't a fast train back to London until nine thirty-seven, so perhaps you would care to stay for dinner?"

⬦⊃∘⊂⬦

The dinner party which followed was an interesting but rather odd experience, the meal itself a blend of the formal and casual which Cordelia felt was the result of conscious effort rather than chance. Some effect, she felt, had been aimed at but whether of a dedicated band of co-workers meeting together at the end of a day for a corporate meal, or the ritual imposition of order and ceremony on a diverse company, she wasn't sure. The party numbered ten: Sir Ronald Callender, Miss Leaming, Chris Lunn, a visiting American Professor, whose unpronounceable name she forgot as soon as Sir Ronald introduced her, and five of the young scientists. All the men, including Lunn, were in dinner jackets, and Miss Leaming wore a long skirt of patchwork satin below a plain sleeveless top. The rich blues, greens and reds gleamed and changed in the candlelight as she moved, and emphasized the pale silver of her hair and the almost colourless skin. Cordelia had been rather nonplussed when her hostess left her in the drawing room and went upstairs to change. She wished that she had something more competitive than the fawn skirt and green top, being at an age to value elegance more highly than youth.

She had been shown to Miss Leaming's bedroom to wash and had been intrigued by the elegance and simplicity of the furniture and the contrasting opulence of the adjacent bathroom. Studying her tired face in the mirror and wielding her lipstick, she had wished she had some eye shadow with her. On impulse, and with a sense of guilt, she had pulled open a dressing-table drawer. It was filled with a variety of make-up; old lipsticks in colours long out-of-date; half used bottles of foundation cream; eye pencils; moisturizing creams; half-used bottles of scent. She had rummaged, and eventually found, a stick of eye shadow which, in view of the wasteful muddle of discarded items in the drawer, she had had little compunction in using. The effect had been bizarre but striking. She could not compete with Miss

571

Leaming but at least she looked five years older. The disorder in the drawer had surprised her and she had had to resist the temptation to see if the wardrobe and the other drawers were in a similar state of disarray. How inconsistent and how interesting human beings were! She thought it astonishing that such a fastidious and competent woman should be content to live with such a mess.

The dining room was at the front of the house. Miss Leaming placed Cordelia between herself and Lunn, a seating which held little prospect of pleasurable conversation. The rest of the party sat where they wished. The contrast between simplicity and elegance showed in the table arrangements. There was no artificial light and three silver branched candlesticks were placed at regular intervals down the table. Between them were set four wine carafes made of thick green glass with curved lips, such as Cordelia had often seen in cheap Italian restaurants. The place mats were of plain cork, but the forks and spoons were antique silver. The flowers were set in low bowls, not skilfully arranged but looking as if they were casualties of a garden storm, blooms which had snapped off in the wind and which someone had thought it kind to place in water.

The young men looked incongruous in their dinner jackets, not ill at ease since they enjoyed the essential self-esteem of the clever and successful, but as if they had picked up the suits second-hand or at a fancy dress costumier and were participating in a charade. Cordelia was surprised at their youth; she guessed that only one was over thirty. Three were untidy, fast talking, restless young men with loud emphatic voices who took no notice of Cordelia after the first introduction. The other two were quieter and one, a tall black-haired boy with strong irregular features, smiled at her across the table and looked as if he would like to have sat within speaking distance.

The meal was brought in by an Italian manservant and his wife who left the cooked dishes on hot plates on a side table. The food was plentiful and the smell almost intolerably appetizing to Cordelia, who hadn't realized until then just how hungry she was. There was a dish heaped high with glistening rice, a large casserole of veal in a rich mushroom sauce, a bowl of spinach.

Beside it on the cold table was a large ham, a sirloin of beef and an interesting assortment of salads and fruit. The company served themselves, carrying their plates back to the table with whatever combination of food, hot or cold, they fancied. The young scientists piled their plates high and Cordelia followed their example.

She took little interest in the conversation except to notice that it was predominantly about science and that Lunn, although he spoke less than the others, spoke as their equal. He should, she thought, have looked ridiculous in his rather tight dinner jacket but, surprisingly, he looked the most at ease, the second most powerful personality in the room. Cordelia tried to analyse why this was so, but was defeated. He ate slowly, with finicky attention to the arrangement of the food on his plate, and from time to time, smiled secretly into his wine.

At the other end of the table Sir Ronald was peeling an apple and talking to his guest, his head inclined. The green rind slid thinly over his long fingers and curved down towards his plate. Cordelia glanced at Miss Leaming. She was staring at Sir Ronald with such unwavering and speculative concern, that Cordelia uncomfortably felt that every eye present must be irresistibly drawn to that pale disdainful mask. Then, Miss Leaming seemed to become aware of her glance. She relaxed and turned to Cordelia:

"When we were travelling here together you were reading Hardy. Do you enjoy him?"

"Very much. But I enjoy Jane Austen more."

"Then you must try to find an opportunity of visiting the Fitzwilliam Museum in Cambridge. They have a letter written by Jane Austen. I think you'd find it interesting."

She spoke with the controlled, artificial brightness of a hostess trying to find a subject to interest a difficult guest. Cordelia, her mouth full of veal and mushrooms, wondered how she would manage to get through the rest of the meal. Luckily, however, the American professor had caught the word "Fitzwilliam" and now called down the table to enquire about the Museum's collection of majolica in which, apparently, he was interested. The conversation became general.

It was Miss Leaming who drove Cordelia to the station, Audley End this time instead of Cambridge; a change for which no reason was given. They didn't speak about the case during the drive. Cordelia was exhausted with tiredness, food and wine and allowed herself to be firmly taken in hand and placed in the train without attempting to gain any further information. She didn't really think she would have got it. As the train drew out, her tired fingers fumbled with the flap of the strong white envelope which Miss Leaming had handed to her and she drew out and read the enclosed note. It was expertly typed and set out, but told her little more than she had already learnt. With it was the photograph. She saw the picture of a laughing boy, his head half-turned towards the camera, one hand shielding his eyes from the sun. He was wearing jeans and a vest and was half lying on the lawn, a pile of books on the grass beside him. Perhaps he had been working there under the trees when she had come out of the french windows with her camera and called imperiously to him to smile. The photograph told Cordelia nothing except, that for one recorded second at least, he had known how to be happy. She placed it back in the envelope; her hands closed protectively over it. Cordelia slept.

Chapter Two

Next morning Cordelia left Cremona Road before seven o'clock. Despite her tiredness the night before, she had made her major preparations before she went to bed. They hadn't taken long. As Bernie had taught her, she checked systematically the scene-of-crime kit, an unnecessary routine since nothing had been touched since, in celebration of their partnership, he had first set it up for her. She put ready the polaroid camera; sorted into order the road maps from the jumble pushed into the back of his desk; shook out the sleeping bag and rolled it ready; filled a carrier bag with iron rations from Bernie's store of tinned soup and baked beans; considered, and finally decided to take, their copy of Professor Simpson's book on forensic medicine and her own Hacker portable radio; checked the first-aid kit. Finally, she found herself a fresh notebook, headed it *Case of Mark Callender* and ruled up the last few pages ready for her expense account. These preliminaries had always been the most satis-fying part of a case, before boredom or distaste set in, before anticipation crumbled into disenchantment and failure. Bernie's planning had always been meticulous and successful; it was reality which had let him down.

Finally, she considered her clothes. If this hot weather continued her Jaeger suit, bought from her savings after much careful thought to see her through almost any inter-view, would be uncomfortably hot, but she might have to interview the head of a college and the dignified professionalism best exemplified by a suit would be the effect to aim at. She decided to travel in her fawn suede skirt with a short-sleeved jumper and pack jeans and warmer jumpers for any field work. Cordelia enjoyed clothes, enjoyed planning and buying them, a pleasure circumscribed less by poverty than by her obsessive need to be able to pack the whole of her wardrobe

into one medium sized suitcase like a refugee perpetually ready for flight.

Once she had shaken free from the tentacles of north London, Cordelia enjoyed the drive. The Mini purred along and Cordelia thought that it had never run so sweetly. She liked the flat East Anglian countryside, the broad streets of the market towns, the way in which the fields grew unhedged to the edge of the road, the openness and freedom of the far horizons and wide skies. The country matched her mood. She had grieved for Bernie and would grieve for him again, missing his comradeship and his undemanding affection, but this, in a sense, was her first case and she was glad to be tackling it alone. It was one that she thought she could solve. It neither appalled nor disgusted her. Driving in happy anticipation through the sunbathed countryside, the boot of the car carefully packed with her gear, she was filled with the euphoria of hope.

When she finally reached Duxford village she had difficulty at first in finding Summertrees. Major Markland was apparently a man who thought that his importance warranted omitting the name of the road from his address. But the second person she stopped to ask was a villager who was able to point the way, taking infinite trouble over the simple directions as if fearing that a perfunctory answer might have seemed discourteous. Cordelia had to find a suitable place to turn and then drive back a couple of miles, for she had already passed Summertrees.

And this, at last, must be the house. It was a large Victorian edifice of red brick, set well back, with a wide turfed verge between the open wooden gate leading to the drive and the road. Cordelia wondered why anyone should have wanted to build such an intimidatingly ugly house or, having decided to do so, should have set down a suburban monstrosity in the middle of the countryside. Perhaps it had replaced an earlier more agreeable house. She drove the Mini onto the grass but at some distance from the gate and made her way up the drive. The garden suited the house; it was formal to the point of artificiality and too well kept. Even the rock plants burgeoned like morbid excrescences at carefully planned intervals between the terrace paving stones. There were two rectangular beds in the lawn, each planted with

576

red rose trees and edged with alternate bands of lobelia and alyssum. They looked like a patriotic display in a public park. Cordelia felt the lack of a flag pole.

The front door was open, giving a view of a dark, brown-painted hall. Before Cordelia could ring, an elderly woman came round the corner of the house trundling a wheelbarrow full of plants. Despite the heat, she was wearing Wellington boots, a jumper and long tweed skirt and had a scarf tied round her head. When she saw Cordelia she dropped the handle of the wheelbarrow and said:

"Oh, good morning. You've come from the church about the jumble, I expect?"

Cordelia said:

"No, not the jumble. I'm from Sir Ronald Callender. It's about his son."

"Then I expect you've called for his things? We wondered when Sir Ronald was going to send for them. They're all still at the cottage. We haven't been down there since Mark died. We called him Mark, you know. Well, he never told us who he was which was rather naughty of him."

"It isn't about Mark's things. I want to talk about Mark himself. Sir Ronald has engaged me to try to find out why his son killed himself. My name is Cordelia Gray."

This news seemed to puzzle rather than disconcert Mrs. Markland. She blinked at Cordelia rapidly through troubled, rather stupid, eyes and clutched at the wheelbarrow handle as if for support.

"Cordelia Gray? Then we haven't met before, have we? I don't think I know a Cordelia Gray. Perhaps it would be better if you came into the drawing room and talked to my husband and sister-in-law."

She abandoned the barrow where it stood in the middle of the path and led the way into the house, pulling off her head scarf and making ineffective pats at her hair. Cordelia followed her through the sparsely furnished hall, smelling of floor polish, with its clutter of walking sticks, umbrellas and mackintoshes draping the heavy oak hat stand, and into a room at the back of the house.

577

It was a horrible room, ill-proportioned, bookless, furnished not in poor taste but in no taste at all. A huge sofa of repellent design and two armchairs surrounded the fireplace and a heavy mahogany table, ornately carved and lurching on its pedestal, occupied the centre of the room. There was little other furniture. The only pictures were framed groups, pale oblong faces too small to identify posed in straight innominate lines in front of the camera. One was a regimental photograph; the other had a pair of crossed oars above two rows of burly adolescents, all of whom were wearing low peaked caps and striped blazers. Cordelia supposed it to be a school boating club.

Despite the warmth of the day, the room was sunless and cold. The doors of the french windows were open. On the lawn outside were grouped a large swinging sofa with a fringed canopy, three cane chairs sumptuously cushioned in a garish blue cretonne, each with its footrest, and a wooden slatted table. They looked part of a setting for a play in which the designer had somehow failed to catch the mood. All the garden furniture looked new and unused. Cordelia wondered why the family should bother to sit indoors on a summer morning while the lawn was so much more comfortably furnished.

Mrs. Markland introduced Cordelia by sweeping her arm in a wide gesture of abandonment and saying feebly to the company in general:

"Miss Cordelia Gray. It isn't about the Church jumble."

Cordelia was struck by the resemblance that husband and wife and Miss Markland bore to each other. All three reminded her of horses. They had long, bony faces, narrow mouths above strong, square chins, eyes set unattractively close, and grey, coarse-looking hair which the two women wore in thick fringes almost to the eyes. Major Markland was drinking coffee from an immense white cup, much stained about the rim and sides, which had been set on a round tin tray. He held *The Times* in his hands. Miss Markland was knitting, an occupation which Cordelia vaguely felt was inappropriate to a hot summer morning.

The two faces, unwelcoming, only partly curious, regarded her with faint distaste. Miss Markland could knit without

looking at the needles, an accomplishment which enabled her to fix Cordelia with sharp, inquisitive eyes. Invited by Major Markland to sit, Cordelia perched on the edge of the sofa, half expecting the smooth cushion to let out a rude noise as it subsided beneath her. She found it, however, unexpectedly hard. She composed her face into the appropriate expression—seriousness combined with efficiency and a touch of propitiatory humility seemed about right, but she wasn't sure that she managed to bring it off. As she sat there, knees demurely together, her shoulder bag at her feet, she was unhappily aware that she probably looked more like an eager seventeen-year-old facing her first interview than a mature business woman, sole proprietor of Pryde's Detective Agency.

She handed over Sir Ronald's note of authority and said:

"Sir Ronald was very distressed on your account, I mean it was awful for you that it should happen on your property when you'd been so kind in finding Mark a job he liked. His father hopes you won't mind talking about it; it's just that he wants to know what made his son kill himself."

"And he sent you?" Miss Markland's voice was a compound of disbelief, amusement and contempt. Cordelia didn't resent the rudeness. She felt Miss Markland had a point. She gave what she hoped was a credible explanation. It was probably true.

"Sir Ronald thinks that it must have been something to do with Mark's life at university. He left college suddenly, as you may know, and his father was never told why. Sir Ronald thought that I might be more successful in talking to Mark's friends than the more usual type of private detective. He didn't feel that he could trouble the police; after all, this sort of enquiry isn't really their kind of job."

Miss Markland said grimly:

"I should have thought it was precisely their job; that is, if Sir Ronald thinks there's something odd about his son's death ..."

Cordelia broke in:

"Oh no, I don't think there's any suggestion of that! He's quite satisfied with the verdict. It's just that he badly wants to know what made him do it."

Miss Markland said with sudden fierceness:

"He was a drop-out. He dropped out of university, apparently he dropped out of his family obligations, finally he dropped out of life. Literally."

Her sister-in-law gave a little bleat of protest.

"Oh, Eleanor, is that quite fair? He worked really well here. I liked the boy. I don't think——"

"I don't deny that he earned his money. That doesn't alter the fact that he was neither bred nor educated to be a jobbing gardener. He was, therefore, a drop-out. I don't know the reason and I have no interest in discovering it."

"How did you come to employ him?" asked Cordelia.

It was Major Markland who answered.

"He saw my advertisement in the *Cambridge Evening News* for a gardener and turned up here one evening on his bicycle. I suppose he cycled all the way from Cambridge. It must have been about five weeks ago, a Tuesday I think."

Again Miss Markland broke in:

"It was Tuesday, May 9th."

The Major frowned at her as if irritated that he couldn't fault the information.

"Yes, well, Tuesday the 9th. He said that he had decided to leave university and take a job and that he'd seen my advertisement. He admitted that he didn't know much about gardening but said that he was strong and was willing to learn. His inexperience didn't worry me; we wanted him mostly for the lawns and for the vegetables. He never touched the flower garden; my wife and I see to that ourselves. Anyway, I quite liked the look of the boy and I thought I'd give him a chance."

Miss Markland said:

"You took him because he was the only applicant who was prepared to work for the miserable pittance you were offering." The Major, so far from showing offence at this frankness, smiled complacently.

"I paid him what he was worth. If more employers were prepared to do that, the country wouldn't be plagued with this inflation." He spoke as one to whom economics were an open book.

"Didn't you think it was odd, his turning up like that?" asked Cordelia.

580

"Of course I did, damned odd! I thought he had probably been sent down; drinks, drugs, revolution, you know the sort of things they get up to at Cambridge now. But I asked him for the name of his tutor as a referee and rang him, a fellow called Horsfall. He wasn't particularly forthcoming but he did assure me that the boy had left voluntarily and to use his own words, his conduct while in college had been almost boringly irreproachable. I need not fear that the shades of Summertrees would be polluted."

Miss Markland turned her knitting and broke into her sister-in-law's little cry of "What can he have meant by that?" with the dry comment:

"A little more boredom of that kind would be welcome from the city of the plains."

"Did Mr. Horsfall tell you why Mark had left college?" asked Cordelia.

"I didn't enquire. That wasn't my business. I asked a plain question and I got a more or less plain answer, as plain as you can expect from those academic types. We certainly had no complaint about the lad while he was here. I speak as I find."

"When did he move into the cottage?" asked Cordelia.

"Immediately. That wasn't our idea, of course. We never advertised the job as residential. However, he'd obviously seen the cottage and taken a fancy to the place and he asked if we'd mind if he camped out there. It wasn't practicable for him to cycle in from Cambridge each day, we could quite see that, and as far as we knew there was no one in the village who could put him up. I can't say I was keen on the idea; the cottage needs a lot doing to it. Actually we have it in mind to apply for a conversion grant and then get rid of the place. It wouldn't do for a family in its present state but the lad seemed keen on roughing it there, so we agreed."

Cordelia said:

"So he must have inspected the cottage before he came for the job?"

"Inspected? Oh, I don't know. He probably snooped around to see what the property was like before he actually came to

581

the door. I don't know that I blame him, I'd have done the same myself."

Mrs. Markland broke in:

"He was very keen on the cottage, very keen. I pointed out that there was no gas or electricity but he said that that wouldn't worry him; he'd buy a primus stove and manage with lamps. There's water laid on, of course, and the main part of the roof is really quite sound. At least I think it is. We don't go there you know. He seemed to settle in very happily. We never actually visited him, there was no need, but as far as I could see he was looking after himself perfectly well. Of course as my husband said, he was very inexperienced; there were one or two things we had to teach him, like coming up to the kitchen early every morning for the orders. But I liked the boy; he was always working hard when I was in the garden."

Cordelia said:

"I wonder if I might have a look at the cottage?"

The request disconcerted them. Major Markland looked at hi
 wife. There was an embarrassed silence and for a moment Cordelia feared that the answer would be no. Then Miss Markland stabbed her needles into the ball of wool and got to her feet:

"I'll come with you now," she said.

The grounds of Summertrees were spacious. First there was the formal rose garden, the bushes closely planted and grouped according to variety and colour like a market garden, the name tags fixed at precisely the same height from the earth. Next was the kitchen garden cut in two by a gravel path with evidence of Mark Callender's work in the weeded rows of lettuce and cabbages, the patches of dug earth. Finally they passed through a gate into a small orchard of old and unpruned apple trees. The scythed grass, smelling richly of hay, lay in thick swathes round the gnarled trunks.

At the furthest end of the orchard was a thick hedge, so overgrown that the wicket gate into the rear garden of the cottage was at first difficult to see. But the grass around it had been trimmed and the gate opened easily to Miss Markland's hand. On the other side was a thick bramble hedge, dark and

582

impenetrable and obviously allowed to grow wild for a generation. Someone had hacked a way through, but Miss Markland
and Cordelia had to bend low to avoid catching their hair on
its tangled tentacles of thorn.

Once free of this barrier, Cordelia lifted her head and blinked
in the bright sunshine. She gave a little exclamation of pleasure.
In the short time in which he had lived here Mark Callender
had created a little oasis of order and beauty out of chaos and
neglect. Old flower beds had been discovered and the surviving
plants tended; the stone path had been scraped free of grass and
moss; a minute square of lawn to the right of the cottage door
had been cut and weeded. On the other side of the path a patch
about twelve feet square had been partly dug. The fork was still
in the earth, driven deep about two feet from the end of the row.

The cottage was a low, brick building under a slate roof.
Bathed in the afternoon sunshine, and despite its bare, rain-
scoured door, its rotted window frames and the glimpse of
exposed beams in the roof, it had the gentle melancholy charm of
age which hadn't yet degenerated into decay. Just outside the
cottage door, dropped casually side by side, was a pair of heavy
gardening shoes encrusted with earth.

"His?" asked Cordelia.

"Who else's?"

They stood together for a moment contemplating the dug
earth. Neither spoke. Then they moved to the back door. Miss
Markland fitted the key into the lock. It turned easily as if the
lock had been recently oiled. Cordelia followed her into the
sitting-room of the cottage.

The air was cool after the heat of the garden but unfresh,
with a taint of contagion. Cordelia saw that the plan of the
cottage was simple. There were three doors, one straight ahead
obviously led to the front garden but was locked and barred,
the joints hung with cobwebs as if it hadn't been opened for
generations. One to the right led, as Cordelia guessed, to the
kitchen. The third door was ajar and she could glimpse through
it an uncarpeted wooden stairway leading to the first floor. In
the middle of the room was a wooden-topped table, the surface
scarred with much scrubbing, and with two kitchen chairs, one

at each end. In the middle of the table a blue ribbed mug held a posy of dead flowers, black brittle stems bearing sad tatters of unidentifiable plants, their pollen staining the surface of the table like golden dust. Shafts of sunlight cut across the still air; in their beams a myriad of motes, specks of dust and infinitesimal life danced grotesquely.

To the right was a fireplace, an old-fashioned iron range with ovens each side of the open fire. Mark had been burning wood and papers; there was a mound of white ash in the grate and a pile of kindling wood and small logs placed ready for the next cool evening. On one side of the fire was a low wooden slatted chair with a faded cushion and on the other a wheel-backed chair with the legs sawn off, perhaps to make it low enough for nursing a child. Cordelia thought that it must have been a beautiful chair before its mutilation.

Two immense beams, blackened with age, ran across the ceiling. In the middle of one was fixed a steel hook, probably once used for hanging bacon. Cordelia and Miss Markland looked at it without speaking; there was no need for question and answer. After a moment they moved, as if by common consent, to the two fireside chairs and sat down. Miss Markland said:

"I was the one who found him. He didn't come up to the kitchen for the day's orders so after breakfast I walked down here to see if he had overslept. It was nine twenty-three exactly. The door was unlocked. I knocked, but there was no reply so I pushed it open. He was hanging from that hook with a leather belt round his neck. He was wearing his blue cotton trousers, the ones he usually worked in, and his feet were bare. That chair was lying on its side on the floor. I touched his chest. He was quite cold."

"Did you cut him down?"

"No. He was obviously dead and I thought it better to leave the body until the police arrived. But I did pick up the chair and place it so that it supported his feet. That was an irrational action, I know, but I couldn't bear to see him hanging there without releasing the pressure on his throat. It was, as I've said, irrational."

"I think it was very natural. Did you notice anything else about him, about the room?"

"There was a half-empty mug of what looked like coffee on the table and a great deal of ash in the grate. It looked as if he had been burning papers. His portable typewriter was where you see it now, on that side table; the suicide note was still in the machine. I read it, then I went back to the house, told my brother and sister-in-law what had happened and rang the police. After the police arrived I brought them to this cottage, and confirmed what I had seen. I never came in here again until this moment."

"Did you, or Major and Mrs. Markland, see Mark on the night he died?"

"None of us saw him after he stopped work at about six-thirty. He was a little later that evening because he wanted to finish mowing the front lawn. We all saw him putting the mower away, then walking across the garden towards the orchard. We never saw him alive again. No one was at home at Summertrees that night. We had a dinner party at Trumpington—an old army colleague of my brother. We didn't get home until after midnight. By then, according to the medical evidence, Mark must have been dead about four hours."

Cordelia said:

"Please tell me about him."

"What is there to tell? His official hours were eight-thirty to six o'clock, with an hour for lunch and half an hour for tea. In the evenings he would work in the garden here or round the cottage. Sometimes in his lunch hour he would cycle to the village store. I used to meet him there from time to time. He didn't buy much—a loaf of wholemeal bread, butter, the cheapest cut of bacon, tea, coffee—the usual things. I heard him ask about free-range eggs and Mrs. Morgan told him that Wilcox at Grange Farm would always sell him half a dozen. We didn't speak when we met, but he would smile. In the evenings once the light had faded, he used to read or type at that table. I could see his head against the lamplight."

"I thought Major Markland said that you didn't visit the cottage?"

"They don't; it holds certain embarrassing memories for them. I do." She paused and looked into the dead fire.

"My fiancé and I used to spend a great deal of time here before the war when he was at Cambridge. He was killed in 1937, fighting in Spain for the Republican cause."

"I'm sorry," said Cordelia. She felt the inadequacy, the insincerity of her response and yet, what else was there to say? It had all happened nearly forty years ago. She hadn't heard of him before. The spasm of grief, so brief that it was hardly felt, was no more than a transitory inconvenience, a sentimental regret for all lovers who died young, for the inevitability of human loss.

Miss Markland spoke with sudden passion as if the words were being forced out of her:

"I don't like your generation, Miss Gray. I don't like your arrogance, your selfishness, your violence, the curious selectivity of your compassion. You pay for nothing with your own coin, not even for your ideals. You denigrate and destroy and never build. You invite punishment like rebellious children, then scream when you are punished. The men I knew, the men I was brought up with, were not like that."

Cordelia said gently:

"I don't think Mark Callender was like that either."

"Perhaps not. At least the violence he practised was on himself." She looked up at Cordelia searchingly.

"No doubt you'll say I'm jealous of youth. It's a common enough syndrome of my generation."

"It ought not to be. I can never see why people should be jealous. After all, youth isn't a matter of privilege, we all get the same share of it. Some people may be born at an easier time or be richer or more privileged than others, but that hasn't anything to do with being young. And being young is terrible sometimes. Don't you remember how terrible it could be?"

"Yes, I remember. But I remember other things too."

Cordelia sat in silence, thinking that the conversation was strange but somehow inevitable and that, for some reason, she didn't resent it. Miss Markland looked up.

"His girl friend visited him once. At least, I suppose she was

his girl friend or why should she have come? It was about three days after he started work."

"What was she like?"

"Beautiful. Very fair, with a face like a Botticelli angel—smooth, oval, unintelligent. She was foreign, French, I think. She was also rich."

"How could you tell that, Miss Markland?" Cordelia was intrigued.

"Because she spoke with a foreign accent; because she arrived driving a white Renault which I took to be her own car; because her clothes, although odd and unsuitable for the country, weren't cheap; because she walked up to the front door and announced that she wanted to see him with the confident arrogance that one associates with the rich."

"And did he see her?"

"He was working in the orchard at the time, scything the grass. I took her down to him. He greeted her calmly and without embarrassment and took her to sit in the cottage garden until it was time for him to stop work. He seemed pleased enough to see her but not, I thought, either delighted or surprised. He didn't introduce her. I left them together and returned to the house before he had the chance to. I didn't see her again."

Before Cordelia could speak she said suddenly:

"You're thinking of living here for a time, aren't you?"

"Will they mind? I didn't like to ask in case they said no."

"They won't know, and if they did, they wouldn't care."

"But do you mind?"

"No. I shan't worry you and I don't mind." They were talking in whispers as if in church. Then Miss Markland got up and moved to the door. She turned.

"You've taken on this job for the money, of course. Why not? But if I were you I'd keep it that way. It's unwise to become too personally involved with another human being. When that human being is dead, it can be dangerous as well as unwise."

◈⊃◦⊂◈

Miss Markland stumped off down the garden path and disappeared through the wicket gate. Cordelia was glad to see her

go. She was fidgeting with impatience to examine the cottage. This was where it had happened; this was where her job really began.

What was it that the Super had said? "When you're examining a building look at it as you would a country church. Walk round it first. Look at the whole scene inside and out; then make your deductions. Ask yourself what you saw, not what you expected to see or what you hoped to see, but what you saw."

He must be a man then who liked country churches and that at least was a point in his favour; for this, surely, was genuine Dalgliesh dogma. Bernie's reaction to churches, whether country or town, had been one of half-superstitious wariness. Cordelia decided to follow the advice.

She made her way first to the east side of the cottage. Here, discreetly set back and almost smothered by the hedge, was a wooden privy with its latched stable-like door. Cordelia peeped inside. The privy was very clean and looked as if it had been recently repainted. When she pulled the chain, to her relief, the bowl flushed. There was a roll of lavatory paper hanging by a string from the door and nailed beside it a small plastic bag containing a crumpled collection of orange papers and other soft wrappings. He had been an economical young man. Next to the privy was a large dilapidated shed containing a man's bicycle, old but well cared for, a large tin of white emulsion paint with the lid rammed down hard and a clean brush upended in a jam jar beside it, a tin bath, a few clean sacks, and a collection of gardening tools. All were shining clean and were neatly disposed against the wall or supported on nails.

She moved to the front of the cottage. This was in marked contrast to the southern aspect. Here Mark Callender had made no attempt to tackle the waist-high wilderness of nettles and grass which stifled the small front garden and almost obliterated the path. A thick climbing shrub sprinkled with small white flowers had thrust its black and thorned boughs to bar the two ground floor windows. The gate leading to the lane had stuck and would open only wide enough for a visitor to squeeze through. On each side a holly tree stood sentinel, its leaves grey with dust. The front hedge of privet was head-high. Cordelia

could see that on either side of the path there had once been twin flower beds edged with large round stones which had been painted white. Now most of the stones had sunk out of sight among the encroaching weeds and nothing remained of the beds but a tangle of wild and straggling roses.

As she took a last look at the front garden, her eye caught a flash of colour half trodden among the weeds at the side of the path. It was a crumpled page of an illustrated magazine. She smoothed it open and saw that it was a colour photograph of a female nude. The woman had her back to the camera and was bending forward, gross buttocks splayed above booted thighs. She was smiling saucily over her shoulder in a blatant invitation made more grotesque by the long androgynous face which even tactful lighting couldn't make other than repellent. Cordelia noted the date at the top of the page; it was the May edition. So the magazine, or at least the picture, could have been brought to the cottage while he was there.

She stood with it in her hand trying to analyse the nature of her disgust which seemed to her excessive. The picture was vulgar and salacious but no more offensive or indecent than dozens on view in the side streets of London. But as she folded it away in her bag—for it was evidence of a kind—she felt contaminated and depressed. Had Miss Markland been more percipient than she knew? Was she, Cordelia, in danger of becoming sentimentally obsessed with the dead boy? The picture probably had nothing to do with Mark; it could easily have been dropped by some visitor to the cottage. But she wished that she hadn't seen it.

She passed round to the west of the cottage and made one more discovery. Hidden behind a clump of elder bushes was a small well about four feet in diameter. It had no superstructure but was closely fitted with a domed lid made of strong slatted wood and fitted at the top with an iron hoop. Cordelia saw that the cover was padlocked to the wooden rim of the well and the lock, although rusty with age, held firm at her tug. Someone had taken the trouble to see that there was no danger here to exploring children or visiting tramps.

And now it was time to explore the interior of the cottage.

First the kitchen. It was a small room with a window over the sink looking east. It had obviously been recently painted and the large table which took up most of the room had been covered with a red plastic cloth. There was a poky larder containing half a dozen tins of beer, a jar of marmalade, a crock of butter and the mouldy heel of a loaf. It was here in the kitchen that Cordelia found the explanation of the disagreeable smell which had struck her on entering the cottage. On the table was an open bottle of milk about half full, the silver top crumpled beside it. The milk was solid and furred with putrefaction; a bloated fly was sucking at the rim of the bottle and still stuck to its feast as, instinctively, she tried to flick it away. On the other side of the table was a twin-burner paraffin stove with a heavy pot on one burner. Cordelia tugged at the close-fitting lid and it came off suddenly, letting out a rich repulsive smell. She opened the table drawer and stirred the mess with a spoon. It looked like beef stew. Chunks of greenish meat, soapy looking potatoes and unidentifiable vegetables floated up through the scum like drowned and putrefying flesh. Beside the sink was an orange box placed on one side and used as a vegetable store. The potatoes were green, the onions had shrunk and sprouted, the carrots were wrinkled and limp. So nothing had been cleaned up, nothing had been removed. The police had taken away the body and any evidence they required but no one, neither the Marklands nor the boy's family or friends, had bothered to come back to clean up the pathetic leavings of his young life.

Cordelia went upstairs. A cramped landing led to two bedrooms, one obviously unused for years. Here the window frame had rotted, the ceiling plaster had crumbled and a faded paper patterned with roses was peeling away with the damp. The second and larger room was the one in which he had slept. There was a single iron bed with a hair mattress and on it a sleeping bag and a bolster folded in two to make a high pillow. Beside the bed was an old table with two candles, stuck with their own wax to a cracked plate, and a box of matches. His clothes were hung in the single cupboard; a pair of bright-green corduroy trousers, one or two shirts, pullovers and one formal suit. A few underclothes, clean but not ironed, were folded on the

ledge above. Cordelia fingered the pullovers. They were hand knitted in thick wool and intricate patterns and there were four of them. Someone, then, had cared enough about him to take some trouble on his behalf. She wondered who.

She ran her hands over his meagre wardrobe, feeling for pockets. She found nothing except a slim, brown leather wallet in the bottom left-hand pocket of his suit. Excitedly she carried it over to the window hoping that it might contain a clue—a letter, perhaps, a list of names and addresses, a personal note. But the wallet was empty except for a couple of pound notes, his driving licence and a blood donor's card issued by the Cambridge blood transfusion service, which showed his group as B rhesus negative.

The uncurtained window gave a view of the garden. His books were arranged on the window shelf. There were only a few of them: several volumes of the *Cambridge Modern History*; some Trollope and Hardy; a complete William Blake; school text book volumes of Wordsworth, Browning and Donne; two paperbacks on gardening. At the end of the row was a white leather-bound book which Cordelia saw was the Book of Common Prayer. It was fitted with a finely wrought brass clasp and looked much used. She was disappointed in the books; they told her little beyond his superficial tastes. If he had come to this solitary life to study, to write or to philosophize he had come singularly ill-equipped.

The most interesting thing in the room was above the bed. It was a small oil painting about nine inches square. Cordelia studied it. It was certainly Italian and probably, she thought, late fifteenth century. It showed a very young tonsured monk reading at a table, his sensitive fingers enleafed between the pages of his book. The long, controlled face was taut with concentration, the heavy lidded eyes were fixed on the page. Behind him, a view from the open window was a miniature of delight. Cordelia thought that one would never tire of looking at it. It was a Tuscan scene showing a walled city with towers enclosed by cypresses, a river winding like a silver stream, a gaudily clad procession preceded by banners, yoked oxen working in the fields. She saw the picture as a contrast between the worlds

591

of intellect and action and tried to remember where she had seen similar paintings. The comrades—as Cordelia always thought of that ubiquitous band of fellow-revolutionaries who attached themselves to her father—had been very fond of exchanging messages in art galleries and Cordelia had spent hours walking slowly from picture to picture, waiting for the casual visitor to pause beside her and whisper his few words of warning or information. The device had always struck her as a childish and unnecessarily histrionic way of communicating, but at least the galleries were warm and she had enjoyed looking at the pictures. She enjoyed this picture; he had obviously liked it too. Had he also liked that vulgar illustration which she had found in the front garden? Were they both an essential part of his nature?

The tour of inspection over, she made herself coffee using a packet from his store cupboard and boiling the water on the stove. She took a chair from the sitting-room and sat outside the back door with the mug of coffee in her lap, her head stretched back to feel the sun. She was filled with a gentle happiness as she sat there, contented and relaxed, listening to the silence, her half-closed lids impressed with the visage of the sun. But now it was the time to think. She had examined the cottage in accordance with the Super's instructions. What did she now know about the dead boy? What had she seen? What could she deduce?

He had been almost obsessively neat and tidy. His garden tools were wiped after use and carefully put away, his kitchen had been painted and was clean and ordered. Yet he had abandoned his digging less than two feet from the end of a row; had left the uncleaned fork in the earth; had dropped his gardening shoes casually at the back door. He had apparently burnt all his papers before killing himself, yet had left his coffee mug unwashed. He had made himself a stew for his supper which he hadn't touched. The preparation of the vegetables must have been done earlier in the same day, or perhaps the day before, but the stew was clearly intended for supper that night. The pot was still on the stove and was full to the brim. This wasn't a heated-up meal, one left from the evening before. This surely

meant that he had only made the decision to kill himself after the stew had been prepared and had been put on the stove to cook. Why should he trouble to prepare a meal that he knew he wouldn't be alive to eat?

But was it likely, she wondered, that a healthy young man coming in from an hour or two of hard digging and with a hot meal waiting should be in that mood of boredom, accidie, anguish or despair which could lead to suicide? Cordelia could remember times of intense unhappiness, but she couldn't recall that they had followed purposeful outdoor exercise in the sun with a meal in prospect. And why the mug of coffee, the one which the police had taken away to analyse? There were tins of beer in the larder; if he had come in thirsty from his digging, why not open one of those? Beer would have been the quickest, the obvious way of quenching thirst. Surely no one, however thirsty, would brew and drink coffee just before a meal. Coffee came after the food.

But suppose someone had visited him that evening. It wasn't likely to have been someone calling with a casual message as he passed by; it was important enough for Mark to break off his digging even within two feet of the end of a row and invite the visitor into the cottage. It was probably a visitor who didn't like or drink beer—could that mean a woman? It was a visitor who wasn't expected to stay for supper but yet was at the cottage long enough to be offered some refreshment. Perhaps it was someone on his way to his own evening meal. Obviously, the visitor hadn't been invited to supper earlier or why would the two of them have begun the meal by drinking coffee and why would Mark have worked so late in the garden instead of coming in to change? So it was an unexpected visitor. But why was there only one mug of coffee? Surely Mark would have shared it with his guest or, if he preferred not to drink coffee, would have opened a tin of beer for himself. But there was no empty beer can in the kitchen and no second mug. Had it perhaps been washed and put away? But why should Mark wash one mug and not the other? Was it to conceal the fact that he'd had a visitor that evening?

The jug of coffee on the kitchen table was almost empty and

the bottle of milk only half full. Surely more than one person had taken milk and coffee. But perhaps that was a dangerous and unwarranted deduction; the visitor might well have had his mug refilled.

But suppose it wasn't Mark who had wished to conceal the fact that a visitor had called that night; suppose it wasn't Mark who had washed and put away the second mug; suppose it was the visitor who had wished to conceal the fact of his presence. But why should he bother to do that since he couldn't know that Mark was going to kill himself? Cordelia shook herself impatiently. This, of course, was nonsense. Obviously the visitor wouldn't have washed up the mug if Mark were still there and alive. He would only have obliterated the evidence of his visit if Mark were already dead. And if Mark had been dead, had been strung up on that hook before his visitor left the cottage, then could this really be suicide? A word dancing at the back of Cordelia's mind, an amorphous half-formed jangle of letters, came suddenly into focus and, for the first time, spelt out clearly the blood-stained word. Murder.

⇚•⇛

Cordelia sat on in the sun for another five minutes finishing her coffee, then she washed up the mug and hung it back on a hook in the larder. She walked down the lane to the road to where the Mini was still parked on the grass verge outside Summertrees, glad of the instinct that had led her to leave it out of sight of the house. Letting in the clutch gently, she drove it slowly down the lane looking carefully from side to side for a possible parking place; to leave it outside the cottage would only advertise her presence. It was a pity that Cambridge wasn't closer; she could then have used Mark's bicycle. The Mini was necessary to her task but would be inconveniently conspicuous wherever she left it.

But she was lucky. About fifty yards down the lane was the entrance to a field, a wide grass verge with a small copse at one side. The copse looked damp and sinister. It was impossible to believe that flowers could spring from this tainted earth or

bloom among these scarred and mis-shapen trees. The ground was scattered with old pots and pans, the upended skeleton of a pram, a battered and rusty gas stove. Beside a stunted oak a matted heap of blankets were disintegrating into the earth. But there was space for her to drive the Mini off the road and under cover of a kind. If she locked it carefully it would be better here than outside the cottage and at night, she thought, it would be unobserved.

But now, she drove it back to the cottage and began to unpack. She moved Mark's few underclothes to one side of the shelf and set her own beside them. She laid her sleeping bag on the bed over his, thinking that she would be glad of the extra comfort. There was a red toothbrush and half-used tube of toothpaste in a jamjar on the kitchen window ledge; she placed her yellow brush and her own tube beside them. She hung her towel next to his across the cord which he had fixed between two nails under the kitchen sink. Then she made an inventory of the contents of the larder and a list of the things she would need. It would be better to buy them in Cambridge; she would only draw attention to her presence if she shopped locally. The saucepan of stew and the half bottle of milk were a worry. She couldn't leave them in the kitchen to sour the cottage with the stench of decay but she was reluctant to throw the contents away. She considered whether to photograph them but decided against it; tangible objects were better evidence. In the end she carried them out to the shed and shrouded them thickly with a piece of old sacking.

Last of all, she thought about the gun. It was a heavy object to carry with her all the time but she felt unhappy about parting with it, even temporarily. Although the back door of the cottage could be locked and Miss Markland had left her the key, an intruder would have no difficulty in breaking-in through a window. She decided that the best plan would be to secrete the ammunition among her underclothes in the bedroom cupboard but to hide the pistol itself separately in or near the cottage. The exact place cost her a little thought, but then she remembered the thick and twisting limbs of the elder bush by the well; by reaching high, she was able to feel for a convenient hollow near

the fork of a branch and could slip the gun, still shrouded in its draw-string bag, among the concealing leaves.

At last she was ready to leave for Cambridge. She looked at her watch; it was half-past ten; she could be in Cambridge by eleven and there would still be two hours of the morning to go. She decided that her best plan would be to visit the newspaper office first and read the account of the inquest, then to see the police; after that she would go in search of Hugo and Sophia Tilling.

She drove away from the cottage with a feeling very like regret, as if she were leaving home. It was, she thought, a curious place, heavy with atmosphere and showing two distinct faces to the world like facets of a human personality; the north, with its dead thorn-barred windows, its encroaching weeds, and its forbidding hedge of privet, was a numinous stage for horror and tragedy. Yet the rear, where he had lived and worked, had cleared and dug the garden and tied up the few flowers, had weeded the path, and opened the windows to the sun, was as peaceful as a sanctuary. Sitting there at the door she had felt that nothing horrible could ever touch her; she was able to contemplate the night there alone without fear. Was it this atmosphere of healing tranquillity, she wondered, that had attracted Mark Callender? Had he sensed it before he took the job, or was it in some mysterious way the result of his transitory and doomed sojourn there? Major Markland had been right; obviously Mark had looked at the cottage before he went up to the house. Had it been the cottage he wanted or the job? Why were the Marklands so reluctant to come to the place, so reluctant that they obviously hadn't visited it even to clean up after his death? And why had Miss Markland spied on him, for surely such close observation was very close to spying? Had she only confided that story about her dead lover to justify her interest in the cottage, her obsessional preoccupation with what the new gardener was doing? And was the story even true? That ageing body heavy with latent strength, that equine expression of perpetual discontent, could she really once have been young, have lain perhaps with her lover on Mark's bed through the long, warm evenings of long-dead summers? How remote, how impossible and grotesque it all seemed.

Cordelia drove down Hills Road, past the vigorous memorial statue of a young 1914 soldier striding to death, past the Roman Catholic church and into the centre of the city. Again she wished that she could have abandoned the car in favour of Mark's bicycle. Everyone else seemed to be riding one and the air tinkled with bells like a festival. In these narrow and crowded streets even the compact Mini was a liability. She decided to park it as soon as she could find a place and set out on foot in search of a telephone. She had decided to vary her programme and see the police first.

But it didn't surprise her when at last she rang the police station to hear that Sergeant Maskell, who had dealt with the Callender case, was tied up all the morning. It was only in fiction that the people one wanted to interview were sitting ready at home or in their office, with time, energy and interest to spare. In real life, they were about their own business and one waited on their convenience, even if, untypically, they welcomed the attention of Pryde's Detective Agency. Usually they didn't. She hardly expected Sergeant Maskell to welcome it. She mentioned Sir Ronald's note of authority to impress her hearer with the authenticity of her business. The name was not without influence. He went away to enquire. After less than a minute he came back to say that Sergeant Maskell could see Miss Gray at two-thirty that afternoon.

So the newspaper office came first after all. Old files were at least accessible and could not object to being consulted. She quickly found what she wanted. The account of the inquest was brief, couched in the usual formal language of a court report. It told her little that was new, but she made a careful note of the main evidence. Sir Ronald Callender testified that he hadn't spoken to his son for over a fortnight before his death, when Mark had telephoned to tell his father of his decision to leave college and to take a job at Summertrees. He hadn't consulted Sir Ronald before making this decision nor had he explained his reasons. Sir Ronald had subsequently spoken to the Master, and the College authorities were prepared to take his son back for the next academic year if he changed his mind. His son had never spoken to him of suicide and had no health or money

597

worries as far as he was aware. Sir Ronald's testimony was followed by a brief reference to other evidence. Miss Markland described how she had found the body; a forensic pathologist testified that the cause of death was asphyxia due to strangulation; Sergeant Maskell recounted the measures he had thought it proper to take and a report from the forensic science laboratory was submitted which stated that a mug of coffee found on the table had been analysed and found harmless. The verdict was that the deceased died by his own hand while the balance of his mind was disturbed. Closing the heavy file, Cordelia felt depressed. It looked as if the police work had been thorough. Was it really possible that these experienced professionals had overlooked the significance of the unfinished digging, the gardening shoes dropped casually at the back door, the untouched supper?

And now, at mid-day, she was free until half-past two. She could explore Cambridge. She bought the cheapest guide book she could find from Bowes and Bowes, resisting the temptation to browse among the books, since time was short and pleasure must be rationed. She stuffed her shoulder bag with a pork pie and fruit bought from a market stall and entered St. Mary's church to sit quietly and work out her itinerary. Then for an hour and a half she walked about the city and its colleges in a trance of happiness.

She was seeing Cambridge at its loveliest. The sky was an infinity of blue from whose pellucid depths the sun shone in unclouded but gentle radiance. The trees in the college gardens and the avenues leading to the Backs, as yet untouched by the heaviness of high summer, lifted their green tracery against stone and river and sky. Punts shot and curtsied under the bridges, scattering the gaudy water fowl, and by the rise of the new Garret Hostel bridge the willows trailed their pale, laden boughs in the darker green of the Cam.

She included all the special sights in her itinerary. She walked gravely down the length of Trinity Library, visited the Old Schools, sat quietly at the back of King's College Chapel marvelling at the upward surge of John Wastell's great vault spreading into curved fans of delicate white stone. The sunlight poured through the great windows staining the still air, blue,

598

crimson and green. The finely carved Tudor roses, the heraldic beasts supporting the crown, stood out in arrogant pride from the panels. Despite what Milton and Wordsworth had written, surely this chapel had been built to the glory of an earthly sovereign, not to the service of God? But that didn't invalidate its purpose nor blemish its beauty. It was still a supremely religious building. Could a non-believer have planned and executed this superb interior? Was there an essential unity between motive and creation? This was the question which Carl alone among the comrades would have been interested to explore and she thought of him in his Greek prison, trying to shut her mind to what they might be doing to him and wishing his stocky figure at her side.

During her tour she indulged in small particular pleasures. She bought a linen tea cloth printed with a picture of the chapel from the stall near the west door; she lay on her face on the shorn grass above the river by Kings Bridge and let the cold green water eddy round her arms; she wandered among the book stalls in the market place and after careful reckoning bought a small edition of Keats printed on India paper and a cotton kaftan patterned in greens, blues and brown. If this hot weather continued it would be cooler than a shirt or jeans for wear in the evenings.

Finally, she returned to King's College. There was a seat set against the great stone wall which ran from the chapel down to the river bank and she sat there in the sun to eat her lunch. A privileged sparrow hopped across the immaculate lawn and cocked a bright insouciant eye. She threw him scraps from the crust of her pork pie and smiled at his agitated peckings. From the river floated the sound of voices calling across the water, the occasional scrunch of wood on wood, the harsh call of a duckling. Everything about her—the pebbles bright as jewels in the gravel path, the silver shafts of grass at the verge of the lawn, the sparrow's brittle legs—was seen with an extraordinarily and individual intensity as if happiness had cleared her eyes.

Then memory recalled the voices. First her father's:

"Our little fascist was educated by the papists. It accounts for a lot. How on earth did it happen, Delia?"

"You remember, Daddy. They muddled me up with another C. Gray who was a Roman Catholic. We both passed the eleven plus exam the same year. When they discovered the mistake they wrote to you to ask if you minded my staying on at the Convent because I'd settled there."

He hadn't in fact replied. Reverend Mother had tried tactfully to conceal that he hadn't bothered to answer and Cordelia had stayed on at the Convent for the six most settled and happy years of her life, insulated by order and ceremony from the mess and muddle of life outside, incorrigibly Protestant, uncoerced, gently pitied as one in invincible ignorance. For the first time she learned that she needn't conceal her intelligence, that cleverness which a succession of foster mothers had somehow seen as a threat. Sister Perpetua had said:

"There shouldn't be any difficulty over your 'A' Levels if you go on as you are at present. That means that we can plan for university entrance in two years' time from this October. Cambridge, I think. We might as well try for Cambridge, and I really don't see why you shouldn't stand a chance of a scholarship."

Sister Perpetua had herself been at Cambridge before she entered the Convent and she still spoke of the academic life, not with longing or regret, but as if it had been a sacrifice worthy of her vocation. Even the fifteen-year-old Cordelia had recognized that Sister Perpetua was a real scholar and had thought it rather unfair of God to bestow a vocation on one who was so happy and useful as she was. But for Cordelia herself, the future had, for the first time, seemed settled and full of promise. She would go to Cambridge and Sister would visit her there. She had a romantic vision of wide lawns under the sun and the two of them walking in Donne's paradise: "Rivers of knowledge are there, arts and sciences flow from thence; gardens that are walled in; bottomless depths of unsearchable councils are there." By the aid of her own brain and Sister's prayers she would win her scholarship. The prayers occasionally worried her. She had absolutely no doubt of their efficacy since God must necessarily listen to one who at such personal cost had listened to Him. And if Sister's influence gave her an unfair advantage over the

other candidates—well, that couldn't be helped. In a matter of such importance neither Cordelia nor Sister Perpetua had been disposed to fret over theological niceties.

But this time Daddy had replied to the letter. He had discovered a need for his daughter. There were no "A" Levels and no scholarship and at sixteen Cordelia finished her formal education and began her wandering life as cook, nurse, messenger and general camp follower to Daddy and the comrades.

But now by what devious routes and for what a strange purpose she had come at last to Cambridge. The city didn't disappoint her. In her wanderings she had seen lovelier places, but none in which she had been happier or more at peace. How indeed, she thought, could the heart be indifferent to such a city where stone and stained glass, water and green lawns, trees and flowers were arranged in such ordered beauty for the service of learning. But as regretfully she rose at last to go, brushing the few crumbs from her skirt, a quotation, untraced and unsought, came into her mind. She heard it with such clarity that the words might have been spoken by a human voice—a young masculine voice, unrecognized and yet mysteriously familiar: "Then saw I that there was a way to hell even from the gates of heaven."

⋘∘⋙

The police headquarters building was modern and functional. It represented authority tempered with discretion; the public were to be impressed but not intimidated. Sergeant Maskell's office and the Sergeant himself conformed to this philosophy. He was surprisingly young and elegantly dressed, with a square, tough face wary with experience and a long but skilfully cut hair style which, Cordelia thought, could only just have satisfied the Force requirements, even for a plain clothes detective. He was punctiliously polite without being gallant and this reassured her. It wasn't going to be an easy interview, but she had no wish to be treated with the indulgence shown to a pretty but importunate child. Sometimes it helped to play the part of a vulnerable and naive young girl eager for information—this was a role in which Bernie had frequently sought to cast her—but

she sensed that Sergeant Maskell would respond better to an unflirtatious competence. She wanted to appear efficient, but not too efficient. And her secrets must remain her own; she was here to get information, not to give it.

She stated her business concisely and showed him her note of authority from Sir Ronald. He handed it back to her, remarking without rancour:

"Sir Ronald said nothing to me to suggest that he was not satisfied with the verdict."

"I don't think that's in question. He doesn't suspect foul play. If he did, he would have come to you. I think he has a scientist's curiosity to know what made his son kill himself and he couldn't very well indulge that at public expense. I mean, Mark's private miseries aren't really your problem, are they?"

"They could be if the reasons for his death disclosed a criminal offence—blackmail, intimidation—but there was never any suggestion of that."

"Are you personally satisfied that he killed himself?"

The Sergeant looked at her with the sudden keen intelligence of a hunting dog on the scent.

"Why should you ask that, Miss Gray?"

"I suppose because of the trouble you took. I've interviewed Miss Markland and read the newspaper report of the inquest. You called in a forensic pathologist; you had the body photographed before it was cut down; you analysed the coffee left in his drinking mug."

"I treated the case as a suspicious death. That's my usual practice. This time the precautions proved unnecessary, but they might not have been."

Cordelia said:

"But something worried you, something didn't seem right?"

He said, as if reminiscing:

"Oh, it was straightforward enough to all appearances. Almost the usual story. We get more than our share of suicides. Here is a young man who gave up his university course for no apparent reason and went to live on his own in some discomfort. You get the picture of an introspective, rather solitary student, one who doesn't confide in his family or friends. Within three

602

weeks after leaving college he's found dead. There's no sign of a struggle; no disturbance in the cottage; he leaves a suicide note conveniently in the typewriter, much the kind of suicide note you would expect. Admittedly, he took the trouble to destroy all the papers in the cottage and yet left the garden fork uncleaned and his work half-completed, and bothered to cook himself a supper which he didn't eat. But all that proves nothing. People do behave irrationally, particularly suicides. No, it wasn't any of those things which gave me a bit of worry; it was the knot."

Suddenly he bent down and rummaged in the left-hand drawer of his desk.

"Here," he said. "How would you use this to hang yourself, Miss Gray?"

The strap was about five feet long. It was a little over an inch wide and was made of strong but supple brown leather, darkened in places with age. One end was tapered and pierced with a row of metal-bound eye holes, the other was fitted with a strong brass buckle. Cordelia took it in her hands; Sergeant Maskell said:

"That was what he used. Obviously it's meant as a strap, but Miss Leaming testified that he used to wear it wound two or three times round his waist as a belt. Well, Miss Gray, how would you hang yourself?"

Cordelia ran the strap through her hands.

"First of all, of course, I'd slip the tapered end through the buckle to make a noose. Then, with the noose round my neck, I'd stand on a chair underneath the hook in the ceiling and draw the other end of the strap over the hook. I'd pull it up fairly tight and then make two half-hitches to hold it firm. I'd pull hard on the strap to make sure that the knot didn't slip and that the hook would hold. Then I'd kick away the chair."

The Sergeant opened the file in front of him and pushed it across the desk.

"Look at that," he said. "That's a picture of the knot."

The police photograph, stark in black and white, showed the knot with admirable clarity. It was a bowline on the end of a low loop and it hung about a foot from the hook.

Sergeant Maskell said:

"I doubt whether he would be able to tie that knot with his hands above his head, no one could. So he must have made the noose first just as you did and then tied the bowline. But that can't be right either. There were only a few inches of strap between the buckle and the knot. If he'd done it that way, he wouldn't have had sufficient play on the strap to get his neck through the noose. There's only one way he could have done it. He made the noose first, pulled it until the strap fitted his neck like a collar and then tied the bowline. Then he got on the chair, placed the loop over the nail and kicked the chair away. Look, this will show you what I mean."

He turned over a new page of the file and suddenly thrust it towards her.

The photograph, uncompromising, unambiguous, a brutal surrealism in black and white, would have looked as artificial as a sick joke if the body were not so obviously dead. Cordelia felt her heart hammering against her chest. Beside this horror Bernie's death had been gentle. She bent her head low over the file so that her hair swung forward to shield her face and made herself study the pitiable thing in front of her.

The neck was elongated so that the bare feet, their toes pointed like a dancer's, hung less than a foot from the floor. The stomach muscles were taut. Above them the high rib cage looked as brittle as a bird's. The head lolled grotesquely on the right shoulder like a horrible caricature of a disjointed puppet. The eyes had rolled upwards under half-open lids. The swollen tongue had forced itself between the lips.

Cordelia said calmly:

"I see what you mean. There are barely four inches of strap between the neck and the knot. Where is the buckle?"

"At the back of the neck under the left ear. There's a phograph of the identation it made in the flesh later in the file."

Cordelia did not look. Why, she wondered, had he shown her the photograph? It wasn't necessary to prove his argument. Had he hoped to shock her into a realization of what she was meddling in; to punish her for trespassing on his patch; to contrast the brutal reality of his professionalism with her amateurish meddling; to warn her perhaps? But against what? The police had no real

suspicion of foul play; the case was closed. Had it, perhaps, been the casual malice, the incipient sadism of a man who couldn't resist the impulse to hurt or shock? Was he even aware of his own motives?

She said:

"I agree he could only have done it in the way you described, if he did it. But suppose someone else pulled the noose tight about his neck, then strung him up. He'd be heavy, a dead weight. Wouldn't it have been easier to make the knot first and then hoist him on to the chair?"

"Having first asked him to hand over his belt?"

"Why use a belt? The murderer could have strangled him with a cord or a tie. Or would that have left a deeper and identifiable mark under the impression of the strap?"

"The pathologist looked for just such a mark. It wasn't there."

"There are other ways, though; a plastic bag, the thin kind they pack clothes in, dropped over his head and held tight against his face; a thin scarf; a woman's stocking."

"I can see you would be a resourceful murderess, Miss Gray. It's possible, but it would need a strong man and there would have to be an element of surprise. We found no sign of a struggle."

"But it could have been done that way?"

"Of course, but there was absolutely no evidence that it was."

"But if he were first drugged?"

"That possibility did occur to me; that's why I had the coffee analysed. But he wasn't drugged, the P.M. confirmed it."

"How much coffee had he drunk?"

"Only about half a mug, according to the P.M. report and he died immediately afterwards. Sometime between seven and nine p.m. was as close as the pathologist could estimate."

"Wasn't it odd that he drank coffee before his meal?"

"There's no law against it. We don't know when he intended to eat his supper. Anyway, you can't build a murder case on the order in which a man chooses to take his food and drink."

"What about the note he left? I suppose it isn't possible to raise prints from typewriter keys?"

"Not easily on that type of key. We tried but there was nothing identifiable."

605

"So in the end you accepted that it was suicide?"

"In the end I accepted that there was no possibility of proving otherwise."

"But you had a hunch? My partner's old colleague—he's a Superintendent of the C.I.D.—always backed his hunches."

"Ah, well, that's the Met, they can afford to indulge themselves. If I backed all my hunches I'd get no work done; it isn't what you suspect, it's what you can prove that counts."

"May I take the suicide note and the strap?"

"Why not, if you sign for them? No one else seems to want them."

"Could I see the note now, please?"

He extracted it from the file and handed it to her. Cordelia began to read to herself the first half-remembered words:

> *a void, boundless as the nether sky appeared*
> *beneath us . . .*

She was struck, not for the first time, by the importance of the written word, the magic of ordered symbols. Would poetry hold its theurgy if the lines were printed as prose, or prose be so compelling without the pattern and stress of punctuation? Miss Leaming had spoken Blake's passage as if she recognized its beauty yet here, spaced on the page, it exerted an even stronger power.

It was then that two things about the quotation caught at her breath. The first was not something which she intended to share with Sergeant Maskell but there was no reason why she should not comment on the second.

She said:

"Mark Callender must have been an experienced typist. This was done by an expert."

"I didn't think so. If you look carefully you'll see that one or two of the letters are fainter than the rest. That's always the sign of an amateur."

"But the faint letters aren't always the same ones. It's usually the keys on the edges of the keyboard which the inexperienced typist hits more lightly. And the spacing here is good until nearly the end of the passage. It looks as if the typist suddenly realized

that he ought to disguise his competence but hadn't time to retype the whole passage. And it's strange that the punctuation is so accurate."

"It was probably copied direct from the printed page. There was a copy of Blake in the boy's bedroom. The quotation is from Blake, you know, the Tyger Tyger burning bright poet."

"I know. But if he typed it from the book, why bother to return the Blake to his bedroom?"

"He was a tidy lad."

"But not tidy enough to wash up his coffee mug or clean his garden fork."

"That proves nothing. As I said, people do behave oddly when they're planning to kill themselves. We know that the typewriter was his and that he'd had it for a year. But we couldn't compare the typing with his work. All his papers had been burnt."

He glanced at his watch and got to his feet. Cordelia saw that the interview was over. She signed a chit for the suicide note and the leather belt, then shook hands and thanked him formally for his help. As he opened the door for her he said, as if on impulse:

"There's one intriguing detail you may care to know. It looks as if he was with a woman some time during the day on which he died. The pathologist found the merest trace—a thin line only—of purple-red lipstick on his upper lip."

Chapter Three

❧❀❧

New Hall, with its Byzantine air, its sunken court and its shining domed hall like a peeled orange, reminded Cordelia of a harem; admittedly one owned by a sultan with liberal views and an odd predilection for clever girls, but a harem nonetheless. The college was surely too distractingly pretty to be conducive to serious study. She wasn't sure, either, whether she approved of the obtrusive femininity of its white brick, the mannered prettiness of the shallow pools where the goldfish slipped like blood-red shadows between the water lilies, its artfully planted saplings. She concentrated on her criticism of the building; it helped to prevent her being intimidated.

She hadn't called at the Lodge to ask for Miss Tilling, afraid that she might be asked her business or refused admission; it seemed prudent just to walk in and chance to luck. Luck was with her. After two fruitless enquiries for Sophia Tilling's room, a hurrying student called back at her:

"She doesn't live in college but she's sitting on the grass over there with her brother."

Cordelia walked out of the shadow of the court into bright sunlight and over turf as soft as moss towards the little group. There were four of them, stretched out on the warm-smelling grass. The two Tillings were unmistakably brother and sister. Cordelia's first thought was that they reminded her of a couple of pre-Raphaelite portraits with their strong dark heads held high on unusually long necks, and their straight noses above curved, foreshortened upper lips. Beside their bony distinction, the second girl was all softness. If this were the girl who had visited Mark at the cottage, Miss Markland was right to call her beautiful. She had an oval face with a neat slender nose, a small but beautifully formed mouth, and slanted eyes of a strikingly deep blue which gave her whole face an oriental

appearance intriguingly at variance with the fairness of her skin and her long blonde hair. She was wearing an ankle-length dress of fine mauve patterned cotton, buttoned high at the waist but with no other fastening. The gathered bodice cupped her full breasts and the skirt fell open to reveal a pair of tight fitting shorts in the same material. As far as Cordelia could see, she wore nothing else. Her feet were bare and her long, shapely legs were untanned by the sun. Cordelia reflected that those white voluptuous thighs must be more erotic than a whole city of sun-burnt limbs and that the girl knew it. Sophia Tilling's dark good looks were only a foil to this gentler, more entrancing beauty.

At first sight the fourth member of the party was more ordinary. He was a stocky, bearded young man with russet curly hair and a spade-shaped face, and was lying on the grass by the side of Sophie Tilling.

All of them, except the blonde girl, were wearing old jeans and open-necked cotton shirts.

Cordelia had come up to the group and had stood over them for a few seconds before they took any notice of her. She said:

"I'm looking for Hugo and Sophia Tilling. My name is Cordelia Gray." Hugo Tilling looked up:

"What shall Cordelia do, love and be silent."

Cordelia said:

"People who feel the need to joke about my name usually enquire after my sisters. It gets very boring."

"It must do. I'm sorry. I'm Hugo Tilling, this is my sister, this is Isabelle de Lasterie and this is Davie Stevens.

Davie Stevens sat up like a jack-in-the-box and said an amiable "Hi."

He looked at Cordelia with a quizzical intentness. She wondered about Davie. Her first impression of the little group, influenced perhaps by the college architecture, had been of a young sultan taking his ease with two of his favourites and attended by the captain of the guard. But, meeting Davie Stevens's steady intelligent gaze, that impression faded. She suspected that, in this seraglio, it was the captain of the guard who was the dominant personality.

Sophia Tilling nodded and said "Hullo."

Isabelle did not speak but a smile beautiful and meaningless spread over her face. Hugo said:

"Won't you sit down, Cordelia Gray, and explain the nature of your necessities?"

Cordelia knelt gingerly, wary of grass stains on the soft suede of her skirt. It was an odd way to interview suspects—only, of course, these people weren't suspects—kneeling like a suppliant in front of them. She said:

"I'm a private detective. Sir Ronald Callender has employed me to find out why his son died."

The effect of her words was astonishing. The little group, which had been lolling at ease like exhausted warriors, stiffened with instantaneous shock into a rigid tableau as if struck to marble. Then, almost imperceptibly, they relaxed. Cordelia could hear the slow release of held breath. She watched their faces. Davie Stevens was the least concerned. He wore a half-rueful smile, interested but unworried, and gave a quick look at Sophie as if in complicity. The look was not returned; she and Hugo were staring rigidly ahead. Cordelia felt that the two Tillings were carefully avoiding each other's eyes. But it was Isabelle who was the most shaken. She gave a gasp and her hand flew to her face like a second-rate actress simulating shock. Her eyes widened into fathomless depths of violet blue and she turned them on Hugo in desperate appeal. She looked so pale that Cordelia half expected her to faint. She thought:

"If I'm in the middle of a conspiracy, then I know who is its weakest member."

Hugo Tilling said:

"You're telling us that Ronald Callender has employed you to find out why Mark died?"

"Is that so extraordinary?"

"I find it incredible. He took no particular interest in his son when he was alive, why begin now he's dead?"

"How do you know he took no particular interest?"

"It's just an idea I had."

Cordelia said:

"Well, he's interested now even if it's only the scientist's urge to discover truth."

"Then he'd better stick to his microbiology, discovering how to make plastic soluble in salt water, or whatever. Human beings aren't susceptible to his kind of experiment."

Davie Stevens said with casual unconcern:

"I wonder that you can stomach that arrogant fascist."

The gibe plucked at too many chords of memory. Wilfully obtuse, Cordelia said:

"I didn't enquire what political party Sir Ronald favours."

Hugo laughed.

"Davie doesn't mean that. By fascist Davie means that Ronald Callender holds certain untenable opinions. For example, that all men may not be created equal, that universal suffrage may not necessarily add to the general happiness of mankind, that the tyrannies of the left aren't noticeably more liberal or supportable than the tyrannies of the right, that black men killing black men is small improvement on white men killing black men in so far as the victims are concerned and that capitalism may not be responsible for all the ills that flesh is heir to from drug addiction to poor syntax. I don't suggest that Ronald Callender holds all or indeed any of these reprehensible opinions. But Davie thinks that he does."

Davie threw a book at Hugo and said without rancour:

"Shut up! You talk like the *Daily Telegraph*. And you're boring our visitor."

Sophie Tilling asked suddenly:

"Was it Sir Ronald who suggested that you should question us?"

"He said that you were Mark's friends; he saw you at the inquest and funeral."

Hugo laughed:

"For God's sake, is that his idea of friendship?"

Cordelia said:

"But you were there?"

"We went to the inquest—all of us except Isabelle, who, we thought, would have been decorative but unreliable. It was rather dull. There was a great deal of irrelevant medical evidence about the excellent state of Mark's heart, lungs and digestive system. As far as I can see, he would have gone on living for ever if he hadn't put a belt round his neck."

"And the funeral—were you there too?"

"We were, at the Cambridge Crematorium. A very subdued affair. There were only six of us present in addition to the undertaker's men; we three, Ronald Callender, that secretary/housekeeper of his and an old nanny type dressed in black. She cast rather a gloom over the proceedings, I thought. Actually she looked so exactly like an old family retainer that I suspect she was a policewoman in disguise."

"Why should she be? Did she look like one?"

"No, but then you don't look like a private eye."

"You've no idea who she was?"

"No, we weren't introduced; it wasn't a chummy kind of funeral. Now I recall it, not one of us spoke a single word to any of the others. Sir Ronald wore a mask of public grief, the King mourning the Crown Prince."

"And Miss Leaming?"

"The Queen Consort; she should have had a black veil over her face."

"I thought that her suffering was real enough," said Sophie.

"You can't tell. No one can. Define suffering. Define real."

Suddenly Davie Stevens spoke, rolling over onto his stomach like a playful dog.

"Miss Leaming looked pretty sick to me. Incidentally, the old lady was called Pilbeam; anyway, that was the name on the wreath."

Sophie laughed:

"That awful cross of roses with the black-edged card? I might have guessed it came from her; but how do you know?"

"I looked, honey. The undertaker's men took the wreath off the coffin and propped it against the wall so I took a quick butchers. The card read 'With sincere sympathy from Nanny Pilbeam'."

Sophie said:

"So you did, I remember now. How beautifully feudal! Poor old nanny, it must have cost her a packet."

"Did Mark ever talk about a Nanny Pilbeam?" Cordelia asked.

They glanced at each other quickly. Isabelle shook her head. Sophie said "not to me."

Hugo Tilling replied:

"He never talked about her, but I think I did see her once before the funeral. She called at college about six weeks ago—on Mark's twenty-first birthday actually, and asked to see him. I was in the Porter's Lodge at the time and Robbins asked me if Mark was in college. She went up to his room and they were there together for about an hour. I saw her leaving, but he never mentioned her to me either then or later."

And soon afterwards, thought Cordelia, he gave up university. Could there be a connection? It was only a tenuous lead, but she would have to follow it.

She asked out of a curiosity that seemed both perverse and irrelevant.

"Were there any other flowers?"

It was Sophie who replied:

"A simple bunch of unwired garden flowers on the coffin. No card. Miss Leaming, I suppose. It was hardly Sir Ronald's style."

Cordelia said:

"You were his friends. Please tell me about him."

They looked at each other as if deciding who should speak. Their embarrassment was almost palpable. Sophie Tilling was picking at small blades of grass and rolling them in her hands. Without looking up, she said:

"Mark was a very private person. I'm not sure how far any of us knew him. He was quiet, gentle, self-contained, unambitious. He was intelligent without being clever. He was very kind; he cared about people, but without inflicting them with his concern. He had little self-esteem but it never seemed to worry him. I don't think there is anything else we can say about him."

Suddenly Isabelle spoke in a voice so low that Cordelia could hardly catch it. She said:

"He was sweet."

Hugo said with a sudden angry impatience.

"He was sweet and he is dead. There you have it. We can't tell you any more about Mark Callender than that. We none

of us saw him after he chucked college. He didn't consult us before he left, and he didn't consult us before he killed himself. He was, as my sister has told you, a very private person. I suggest that you leave him his privacy."

"Look," said Cordelia, "you went to the inquest, you went to the funeral. If you had stopped seeing him, if you were so unconcerned about him, why did you bother?"

"Sophie went out of affection. Davie went because Sophie did. I went out of curiosity and respect; you mustn't be seduced by my air of casual flippancy into thinking that I haven't a heart."

Cordelia said obstinately:

"Someone visited him at the cottage on the evening he died. Someone had coffee with him. I intend to find out who that person was."

Was it her fancy that this news surprised them? Sophie Tilling looked as if she were about to ask a question when her brother quickly broke in:

"It wasn't any of us. On the night Mark died we were all in the second row of the dress circle of the Arts Theatre watching Pinter. I don't know that I can prove it. I doubt whether the booking clerk has kept the chart for that particular night, but I booked the seats and she may remember me. If you insist on being tediously meticulous, I can probably introduce you to a friend who knew of my intention to take a party to the play; to another who saw some at least of us in the bar in the interval; and to another with whom I subsequently discussed the performance. None of this will prove anything; my friends are an accommodating bunch. It would be simpler for you to accept that I am telling the truth. Why should I lie? We were all four at the Arts Theatre on the night of 26th May."

Davie Stevens said gently:

"Why not tell that arrogant bastard Pa Callender to go to hell and leave his son in peace, then find yourself a nice simple case of larceny?"

"Or murder," said Hugo Tilling.

"Find yourself a nice simple case of murder."

As if in obedience to some secret code, they began getting up, piling their books together, brushing the grass cuttings from

their clothes. Cordelia followed them through the courts and out of college. Still in a silent group they made their way to a white Renault parked in the forecourt.

Cordelia came up to them and spoke directly to Isabelle.

"Did you enjoy the Pinter? Weren't you frightened by that dreadful last scene when Wyatt Gillman is gunned down by the natives?"

It was so easy that Cordelia almost despised herself. The immense violet eyes grew puzzled.

"Oh, no! I did not care about it, I was not frightened. I was with Hugo and the others, you see."

Cordelia turned to Hugo Tilling.

"Your friend doesn't seem to know the difference between Pinter and Osborne."

Hugo was settling himself into the driving seat of the car. He twisted round to open the back door for Sophie and Davie. He said calmly:

"My friend, as you choose to call her, is living in Cambridge, inadequately chaperoned I'm happy to say, for the purpose of learning English. So far her progress has been erratic and in some respects disappointing. One can never be certain how much my friend has understood."

The engine purred into life. The car began to move. It was then that Sophie Tilling thrust her head out of the window and said impulsively:

"I don't mind talking about Mark if you think it will help. It won't, but you can come round to my house this afternoon if you like—57 Norwich Street. Don't be late; Davie and I are going on the river. You can come too if you feel like it."

The car accelerated. Cordelia watched it out of sight. Hugo raised his hand in ironic farewell but not one of them turned a head.

Cordelia muttered the address to herself until it was safely written down: 57, Norwich Street. Was that the address where Sophie lodged, a hostel perhaps, or did her family live in

Cambridge? Well, she would find out soon enough. When ought she to arrive? Too early would look over eager; too late and they might have set out for the river. Whatever motive had prompted Sophie Tilling to issue that belated invitation, she mustn't loose touch with them now.

They had some guilty knowledge; that had been obvious. Why else had they reacted so strongly to her arrival? They wanted the facts of Mark Callender's death to be left undisturbed. They would try to persuade, cajole, even to shame her into abandoning the case. Would they, she wondered, also threaten? But why? The most likely theory was that they were shielding someone. But again, why? Murder wasn't a matter of climbing late into college, a venial infringement of rules which a friend would automatically condone and conceal. Mark Callender had been their friend; to two of them he might have been more than a friend. Someone whom he knew and trusted had pulled a strap tight round his neck, had watched and listened to his agonized choking, had strung his body on a hook like the carcass of an animal. How could one reconcile that appalling knowledge with Davie Stevens' slightly amused and rueful glance at Sophie, with Hugo's cynical calm, with Sophie's friendly and interested eyes? If they were conspirators, then they were monsters. And Isabelle? If they were shielding anyone, it was most likely to be her. But Isabelle de Lasterie couldn't have murdered Mark. Cordelia remembered those frail sloping shoulders, those ineffective hands almost transparent in the sun, the long nails painted like elegant pink talons. If Isabelle were guilty, she hadn't acted alone. Only a tall and very strong woman could have heaved that inert body onto the chair and up to the hook.

Norwich Street was a one-way thoroughfare and, initially, Cordelia approached it from the wrong direction. It took her some time to find her way back to Hills Road, past the Roman Catholic church and down the fourth turning to the right. The street was terraced with small brick houses, obviously early Victorian. Equally obviously, the road was on its way up. Most of the houses looked well cared for; the paint on the identical front doors was fresh and bright; lined curtains had replaced

the draped lace at the single ground-floor windows and the bases of the walls were scarred where a damp course had been installed. Number fifty-seven had a black front door with the house number painted in white behind the glass panel above. Cordelia was relieved to see that there was space to park the Mini. There was no sign of the Renault among the almost continuous row of old cars and battered bicycles which lined the edge of the pavement.

The front door was wide open. Cordelia pressed the bell and stepped tentatively into a narow white hall. The interior of the house was immediately familiar to her. From her sixth birthday she had lived for two years in just such a Victorian terraced cottage with Mrs. Gibson on the outskirts of Romford. She recognized the steep and narrow staircase immediately ahead, the door on the right leading to the front parlour, the second door set aslant which led to the back parlour and through it to the kitchen and yard. She knew that there would be cupboards and a curved alcove on each side of the fireplace; she knew where to find the door under the stairs. Memory was so sharp that it imposed on this clean, sun-scented interior the strong odour of unwashed napkins, cabbage and grease which had permeated the Romford house. She could almost hear the children's voices calling her outlandish name across the rookery of the primary school playground across the road, stamping the asphalt with the ubiquitous Wellington boots which they wore in all seasons, flailing their thin jersied arms: "Cor, Cor, Cor!"

The furthest door was ajar and she could glimpse a room painted bright yellow and spilling over with sunlight. Sophie's head appeared.

"Oh, it's you! Come in. Davie has gone to collect some books from college and to buy food for the picnic. Would you like tea now or shall we wait? I'm just finishing the ironing."

"I'd rather wait, thank you."

Cordelia sat down and watched while Sophie wound the flex around the iron and folded the cloth. She glanced around the room. It was welcoming and attractive, furnished in no particular style or period, a cosy hotch-potch of the cheap and the valuable, unpretentious and pleasing. There was a sturdy oak

617

table against the wall; four rather ugly dining chairs; a Windsor chair with a plump yellow cushion; an elegant Victorian sofa covered with brown velvet and set under the window; three good Staffordshire figures on the mantel shelf above the hooded wrought-iron grate. One of the walls was almost covered with a notice board in dark cork which displayed posters, cards, *aides-mémoire*, and pictures cut from magazines. Two, Cordelia saw, were beautifully photographed and attractive nudes.

Outside the yellow-curtained window the small walled garden was a riot of greenery. An immense and multi-flowered holyhock burgeoned against a tatty looking trellis; there were roses planted in Ali Baba jars and a row of pots of bright-red geraniums lined the top of the wall.

Cordelia said:

"I like this house. Is it yours?"

"Yes, I own it. Our grandmother died two years ago and left Hugo and me a small legacy. I used mine for the down payment on this house and got a local authority grant towards the cost of conversion. Hugo spent all of his laying down wine. He was ensuring a happy middle age; I was ensuring a happy present. I suppose that's the difference between us."

She folded the ironing cloth on the end of the table and stowed it away in one of the cupboards. Sitting opposite to Cordelia, she asked abruptly:

"Do you like my brother?"

"Not very much. I thought he was rather rude to me."

"He didn't mean to be."

"I think that's rather worse. Rudeness should always be intentional, otherwise it's insensitivity."

"Hugo isn't at his most agreeable when he's with Isabelle. She has that affect on him."

"Was she in love with Mark Callender?"

"You'll have to ask her, Cordelia, but I shouldn't think so. They hardly knew each other. Mark was my lover, not hers. I thought I'd better get you here to tell you myself since someone's bound to sooner or later if you go around Cambridge ferreting out facts about him. He didn't live here with me, of course. He had rooms in college. But we were lovers for almost the

618

whole of last year. It ended just after Christmas when I met Davie."

"Were you in love?"

"I'm not sure. All sex is a kind of exploitation, isn't it? If you mean, did we explore our own identities through the personality of the other, then I suppose we were in love or thought that we were. Mark needed to believe himself in love. I'm not sure I know what the word means."

Cordelia felt a surge of sympathy. She wasn't sure either. She thought of her own two lovers; Georges whom she had slept with because he was gentle and unhappy and called her Cordelia, a real name, her name, not Delia, Daddy's little fascist; and Carl who was young and angry and whom she had liked so much that it seemed churlish not to show it in the only way which seemed to him important. She had never thought of virginity as other than a temporary and inconvenient state, part of the general insecurity and vulnerability of being young. Before Georges and Carl she had been lonely and inexperienced. Afterwards she had been lonely and a little less inexperienced. Neither affair had given her the longed-for assurance in dealing with Daddy or the landladies, neither had inconveniently touched her heart. But for Carl she had felt tenderness. It was just as well that he had left Rome before his lovemaking had become too pleasurable and he too important to her. It was intolerable to think that those strange gymnastics might one day become necessary. Lovemaking, she had decided, was over-rated, not painful but surprising. The alienation between thought and action was so complete. She said:

"I suppose I only meant were you fond of each other, and did you like going to bed together?"

"Both of those things."

"Why did it end? Did you quarrel?"

"Nothing so natural or uncivilized. One didn't quarrel with Mark. That was one of the troubles about him. I told him that I didn't want to go on with the affair and he accepted my decision as calmly as if I were just breaking a date for a play at the Arts. He didn't try to argue or dissuade me. And if you're wondering whether the break had anything to do with his death,

well you're wrong. I wouldn't rank that high with anyone, particularly not Mark. I was probably fonder of him than he was of me."

"So why did it end?"

"I felt that I was under moral scrutiny. It wasn't true; Mark wasn't a prig. But that's how I felt, or pretended to myself that I felt. I couldn't live up to him and I didn't even want to. There was Gary Webber, for example. I'd better tell you about him; it explains a lot about Mark. He's an autistic child, one of the uncontrollable, violent ones. Mark met him with his parents and their other two children on Jesus Green about a year ago; the children were playing on the swings there. Mark spoke to Gary and the boy responded to him. Children always did. He took to visiting the family and looking after Gary one evening a week so that the Webbers could get out to the pictures. During his last two vacs he stayed in the house and looked after Gary completely while the whole family went off for a holiday. The Webbers couldn't bear the boy to go to hospital; they'd tried it once and he didn't settle. But they were perfectly happy to leave him with Mark. I used to call in some evenings and see them together. Mark would hold the boy on his lap and rock him backwards and forwards for hours at a time. It was the one way to quieten him. We disagreed about Gary. I thought he would be better dead and I said so. I still think it would be better if he died, better for his parents, better for the rest of the family, better for him. Mark didn't agree. I remember saying:

" 'Oh well, if you think it reasonable that children should suffer so that you can enjoy the emotional kick of relieving them——' After that the conversation became boringly metaphysical. Mark said:

" 'Neither you nor I would be willing to kill Gary. He exists. His family exists. They need help which we can give. It doesn't matter what we feel. Actions are important, feelings aren't.' "

Cordelia said:

"But actions arise out of feelings."

"Oh, Cordelia, don't you start! I've had this particular conversation too many times before. Of course they do!"

They were silent for a moment. Then Cordelia, reluctant to

shatter the tenuous confidence and friendship which she sensed was growing between them, made herself ask:

"Why did he kill himself—if he did kill himself?" Sophie's reply was as emphatic as a slammed door.

"He left a note."

"A note perhaps. But, as his father pointed out, not an explanation. It's a lovely passage of prose—at least I think so—but as a justification for suicide it just isn't convincing."

"It convinced the jury."

"It doesn't convince me. Think, Sophie! Surely there are only two reasons for killing oneself. One is either escaping from something or to something. The first is rational. If one is in intolerable pain, despair or mental anguish and there is no reasonable chance of a cure, then it's probably sensible to prefer oblivion. But it isn't sensible to kill oneself in the hope of gaining some better existence or to extend one's sensibilities to include the experience of death. It isn't possible to experience death. I'm not even sure it's possible to experience dying. One can only experience the preparations for death, and even that seems pointless since one can't make use of the experience afterwards. If there's any sort of existence after death we shall all know soon enough. If there isn't, we shan't exist to complain that we've been cheated. People who believe in an after life are perfectly reasonable. They're the only ones who are safe from ultimate disillusionment."

"You've thought it all out, haven't you. I'm not sure that suicides do. The act is probably both impulsive and irrational."

"Was Mark impulsive and irrational?"

"I didn't know Mark."

"But you were lovers! You slept with him!"

Sophie looked at her and cried out in angry pain.

"I didn't know him! I thought I did, but I didn't know the first thing about him!"

They sat without speaking for almost two minutes. Then Cordelia asked:

"You went to dinner at Garforth House didn't you? What was it like?"

"The food and the wine were surprisingly good, but I don't

621

suppose that's what you had in mind. The dinner party wasn't otherwise memorable. Sir Ronald was amiable enough when he noticed I was there. Miss Leaming, when she could tear her obsessive attention from the presiding genius, looked me over like a prospective mother-in-law. Mark was rather silent. I think he'd taken me there to prove something to me, or perhaps to himself; I'm not sure what. He never talked about the evening or asked me what I thought. A month later Hugo and I both went to dinner. It was then I met Davie. He was the guest of one of the research biologists and Ronald Callender was angling to get him. Davie did a vac job there in his final year. If you want the inside dope on Garforth House, you should ask him."

Five minutes later Hugo, Isabelle and Davie arrived. Cordelia had gone upstairs to the bathroom and heard the car stop and the jabber of voices in the hall. Footsteps passed beneath her towards the back parlour. She turned on the hot water. The gas boiler in the kitchen immediately gave forth a roar as if the little house were powered by a dynamo. Cordelia let the tap run, then stepped out of the bathroom, closing the door gently behind her. She stole to the top of the stairs. It was hard luck on Sophie to waste her hot water, she thought guiltily; but worse was the sense of treachery and shabby opportunism as she crept down the first three stairs and listened. The front door had been closed but the door to the back parlour was open. She heard Isabelle's high unemphatic voice:

"But if this man Sir Ronald is paying her to find out about Mark, why cannot I pay her to stop finding out?"

Then Hugo's voice, amused, a little contemptuous:

"Darling Isabelle, when will you learn that not everyone can be bought?"

"She can't, anyway. I like her."

It was Sophie speaking. Her brother replied:

"We all like her. The question is, how do we get rid of her?"

Then for a few minutes there was a murmur of voices, the words undistinguishable, broken by Isabelle.

"It is not, I think, a suitable job for a woman."

There was the sound of a chair scraping against the floor, a shuffle of feet. Cordelia darted guiltily back into the bathroom and

turned off the tap. She recalled Bernie's complacent admonition when she had asked whether they needed accept a divorce case.

"You can't do our job, partner, and be a gentleman." She stood watching at the half-open door. Hugo and Isabelle were leaving. She waited until she heard the front door close and the car drive away. Then she went down to the parlour. Sophie and Davie were together, unpacking a large carrier bag of groceries. Sophie smiled and said:

"Isabelle has a party tonight. She has a house quite close to here in Panton Street. Mark's tutor, Edward Horsfall, will probably be there and we thought it might be useful for you to talk to him about Mark. The party's at eight o'clock but you can call for us here. Just now we're packing a picnic; we thought we'd take a punt on the river for an hour or so. Do come if you'd like to. It's really much the pleasantest way of seeing Cambridge."

◈〰◦〰◈

Afterwards, Cordelia remembered the river picnic as a series of brief but intensely clear pictures, moments in which sight and sense fused and time seemed momentarily arrested while the sunlit image was impressed on her mind. Sunlight sparkling on the river and gilding the hairs of Davie's chest and forearms; the flesh of his strong upper arms speckled like an egg; Sophie lifting her arm to wipe the sweat from her brow as she rested between thrusts of the punt pole; green-black weeds dragged by the pole from mysterious depths to writhe sinuously below the surface; a bright duck cocking its white tail before disappearing in a flurry of green water. When they had rocked under Silver Street Bridge a friend of Sophie's swam alongside, sleek and snout-nosed like an otter, his black hair laying like blades across his cheeks. He rested his hands on the punt and opened his mouth to be fed chunks of sandwiches by a protesting Sophie. The punts and canoes scraped and jostled each other in the turbulence of white water racing under the bridge. The air rang with laughing voices and the green banks were peopled with half-naked bodies lying supine with their faces to the sun.

623

Davie punted until they reached the higher level of the river and Cordelia and Sophie stretched out on the cushions at opposite ends of the punt. Thus distanced it was impossible to carry on a private conversation; Cordelia guessed that this was precisely what Sophie had planned. From time to time, she would call out snatches of information as if to emphasize that the outing was strictly educational.

"That wedding cake is John's—we're just passing under Clare bridge, one of the prettiest, I think. Thomas Grumbald built it in 1639. They say he was only paid three shillings for the design. You know that view, of course; it's a good view of Queen's, though."

Cordelia's courage failed her at the thought of interrupting this desultory tourist's chat with the brutal demand:

"Did you and your brother kill your lover?"

Here, rocking gently on the sunlit river, the question seemed both indecent and absurd. She was in danger of being lulled into a gentle acceptance of defeat; viewing all her suspicions as a neurotic hankering after drama and notoriety, a need to justify her fee to Sir Ronald. She believed Mark Callender had been murdered because she wanted to believe it. She had identified with him, with his solitariness, his self-sufficiency, his alienation from his father, his lonely childhood. She had even—most dangerous presumption of all—come to see herself as his avenger. When Sophie took over the pole, just past the Garden House Hotel, and Davie edged his way along the gently rocking punt and stretched himself out beside her, she knew that she wouldn't be able to mention Mark's name. It was out of no more than a vague, unintrusive curiosity that she found herself asking:

"Is Sir Ronald Callender a good scientist?" Davie took up a short paddle and began lazily to stir the shining water.

"His science is perfectly respectable, as my dear colleagues would say. Rather more than respectable, in fact. At present the lab is working on ways of expanding the use of biological monitors to assess pollution of the sea and estuaries; that means routine surveys of plants and animals which might serve as indicators. And they did some very useful preliminary work last year on the degradation of plastics. R.C. isn't so hot himself, but then you can't expect much original science from the over

624

fifties. But he's a great spotter of talent and he certainly knows how to run a team if you fancy that dedicated, one for all, band of brothers approach. I don't. They even publish their papers as the Callender Research Laboratory, not under individual names. That wouldn't do for me. When I publish, it's strictly for the glory of David Forbes Stevens and, incidentally, for the gratification of Sophie. The Tillings like success."

"Was that why you didn't want to stay on when he offered you a job?"

"That among other reasons. He pays too generously and he asks too much. I don't like being bought and I've a strong objection to dressing up every night in a dinner jacket like a performing monkey in a zoo. I'm a molecular biologist. I'm not looking for the holy grail. Dad and Mum brought me up as a Methodist and I don't see why I should chuck a perfectly good religion which served me very well for twelve years just to put the great scientific principle or Ronald Callender in its place. I distrust these sacerdotal scientists. It's a bloody wonder that little lot at Garforth House aren't genuflecting three times a day in the direction of the Cavendish."

"And what about Lunn? How does he fit in?"

"Oh, that boy's a bloody wonder! Ronald Callender found him in a children's home when he was fifteen—don't ask me how—and trained him to be a lab assistant. You couldn't find a better. There isn't an instrument made which Chris Lunn can't learn to understand and care for. He's developed one or two himself and Callender has had them patented. If anyone in that lab is indispensable it's probably Lunn. Certainly Ronald Callender cares a damn sight more for him than he did for his son. And Lunn, as you might guess, regards R.C. as God almighty, which is very gratifying for them both. It's extraordinary really, all that violence which used to be expressed in street fights and coshing old ladies, harnessed to the service of science. You've got to hand it to Callender. He certainly knows how to pick his slaves."

"And is Miss Leaming a slave?"

"Well, I wouldn't know just what Eliza Leaming is. She's responsible for the business management and, like Lunn, she's

probably indispensable. Lunn and she seem to have a love-hate relationship, or, perhaps, a hate-hate relationship. I'm not very clever at detecting these psychological nuances."

"But how on earth does Sir Ronald pay for it all?"

"Well, that's the thousand-dollar question, isn't it? It's rumoured that most of the money came from his wife and that he and Elizabeth Leaming between them invested it rather cleverly. They certainly needed to. And then he gets a certain amount from contract work. Even so, it's an expensive hobby. While I was there they were saying that the Wolvington Trust were getting interested. If they come up with something big— and I gather it's below their dignity to come up with anything small—then most of Ronald Callender's troubles should be over. Mark's death must have hit him. Mark was due to come into a pretty substantial fortune in four years' time and he told Sophie that he intended to hand most of it over to Dad."

"Why on earth should he do that?"

"God knows. Conscience money, perhaps. Anyway, he obviously thought it was something that Sophie ought to know."

Conscience money for what, Cordelia wondered sleepily. For not loving his father enough? For rejecting his enthusiasms? For being less than the son he had hoped for? And what would happen to Mark's fortune now? Who stood to gain by Mark's death? She supposed that she ought to consult his grandfather's will and find out. But that would mean a trip to London. Was it really worth it?

She stretched back her face to the sun and trailed one hand in the river. A splash of water from the punt pole stung her eyes. She opened them and saw that the punt was gliding close to the bank and under the shade of overhanging trees. Immediately in front of her a torn branch, cleft at the end and thick as a man's body, hung by a thread of bark and turned gently as the punt passed beneath it. She was aware of Davie's voice; he must have been talking for a long time. How odd that she couldn't remember what he'd been saying!

"You don't need reasons for killing yourself; you need reasons for not killing yourself. It was suicide, Cordelia. I should let it go at that."

Cordelia thought that she must have briefly slept, since he seemed to be answering a question she couldn't remember having asked. But now there were other voices, louder and more insistent. Sir Ronald Callender's: "My son is dead. *My* son. If I am in some way responsible, I'd prefer to know. If anyone else is responsible, I want to know that too." Sergeant Maskell's: "How would you use this to hang yourself, Miss Gray?" The feel of the belt, smooth and sinuous, slipping like a live thing through her fingers.

She sat bolt upright, hands clasped around her knees, with such suddenness that the punt rocked violently and Sophie had to clutch at an overhanging branch to keep her balance. Her dark face, intriguingly fore-shortened and patterned with the shadow of leaves, looked down at Cordelia from what seemed an immense height. Their eyes met. In that moment Cordelia knew how close she had come to giving up the case. She had been suborned by the beauty of the day, by sunshine, indolence, the promise of comradeship, even friendship, into forgetting why she was here. The realization horrified her. Davie had said that Sir Ronald was a good picker. Well, he had picked her. This was her first case and nothing and no one was going to hinder her from solving it.

She said formally:

"It was good of you to let me join you, but I don't want to miss the party tonight. I ought to talk to Mark's tutor and there may be other people there who could tell me something. Isn't it time that we thought about turning back?"

Sophie turned her glance on Davie. He gave an almost imperceptible shrug. Without speaking, Sophie drove the pole hard against the bank. The punt began slowly to turn.

⋘०⋙

Isabelle's party was due to begin at eight o'clock but it was nearly nine when Sophie, Davie and Cordelia arrived. They walked to the house which was only five minutes from Norwich Street; Cordelia never discovered the exact address. She liked the look of the house and wondered how much it was costing

Isabelle's father in rent. It was a long, white, two-storey villa with tall curved windows and green shutters, set well back from the street, with a semi-basement and a flight of steps to the front door. A similar flight led down from the sitting-room to the long garden.

The sitting-room was already fairly full. Looking at her fellow guests, Cordelia was glad that she had bought the kaftan. Most people seemed to have changed although not necessarily, she thought, into something more attractive. What was aimed at was originality; it was preferable to look spectacular, even bizarre, than to appear nondescript.

The sitting-room was elegantly but unsubstantially furnished and Isabelle had impressed on it her own untidy, impractical and iconoclastic femininity. Cordelia doubted whether the owners had provided the ornate crystal chandelier, far too heavy and large for the room, which hung like a sunburst from the middle of the ceiling, or the many silken cushions and curtains which gave the room's austere proportions something of the ostentatious opulence of a courtesan's boudoir. The pictures, too, must surely be Isabelle's. No house owner letting his property would leave pictures of this quality on the walls. One, hanging above the fireplace, was of a young girl hugging a puppy. Cordelia gazed at it in excited pleasure. Surely she couldn't mistake that individual blue of the girl's dress, that marvellous painting of the cheeks and plump young arms, skin which simultaneously absorbed and reflected light—lovely, tangible flesh. She cried out involuntarily so that people turned to look at her:

"But that's a Renoir!"

Hugo was at her elbow. He laughed.

"Yes; but don't sound so shocked, Cordelia. It's only a small Renoir! Isabelle asked Papa for a picture for her sitting-room. You didn't expect him to provide a print of the Haywain or one of those cheap reproductions of Van Gogh's boring old chair."

"Would Isabelle have known the difference?"

"Oh, yes. Isabelle knows an expensive object when she sees one."

Cordelia wondered whether the bitterness, the hard edge of contempt in his voice, was for Isabelle or for himself. They looked

across the room to where she stood, smiling at them. Hugo moved towards her like a man in a dream and took her hand. Cordelia watched. Isabelle had dressed her hair in a high cluster of curls, Grecian style. She was wearing an anke-length dress of cream matt silk, with a very low square neckline and small intricately tucked sleeves. It was obviously a model and should, Cordelia felt, have looked out of place at an informal party. But it didn't. It merely made every other woman's dress look like an improvization and reduced her own, whose colours had seemed muted and subtle when she bought it, to the status of a gaudy rag.

Cordelia was determined to get Isabelle alone some time during the evening but could see that it wasn't going to be easy. Hugo stuck tenaciously to her side, steering her among her guests with one proprietorial hand on her waist. He seemed to be drinking steadily and Isabelle's glass was always filled. Perhaps as the evening wore on they would get careless and there would be a chance to separate them. In the meantime, Cordelia decided to explore the house, and a more practical matter, to find out before she needed it where the lavatory was. It was the kind of party where guests were left to find out these things for themselves.

She went up to the first floor and making her way down the passage pushed gently open the door of the far room. The smell of whisky met her immediately; it was overpowering and Cordelia instinctively slipped into the room and closed the door behind her, afraid that it might permeate the house. The room, which was in an indescribable state of disarray, wasn't empty. On the bed and half covered by the counterpane a woman was lying; a woman with bright ginger hair splayed over the pillow and wearing a pink silk dressing-gown. Cordelia walked up to the bed and looked down at her. She was insensible with drink. She lay there emitting puffs of foul, whisky-laden breath which rose like invisible balls of smoke from the half-open mouth. Her lower lip and jaw were tense and creased, giving the face a look of stern censoriousness as if she disapproved strongly of her own condition. Her thin lips were thickly painted, the strong purple stain had seeped into the cracks around the mouth so that the body looked parched in an extremity of cold. Her hands, the

gnarled fingers brown with nictotine and laden with rings, lay quietly on the counterpane. Two of the talon-like nails were broken and the brick-red varnish on the others was cracked or peeled away.

The window was obstructed by a heavy dressing-table. Averting her eyes from the mess of crumpled tissues, open bottles of face cream, spilt powder and half drunk cups of what looked like black coffee, Cordelia squeezed behind it and pushed open the window. She gulped in lungfulls of fresh, cleansing air. Below her in the garden pale shapes moved silently over the grass and between the trees like the ghosts of long dead revellers. She left the window open and went back to the bed. There was nothing here that she could do but she placed the cold hands under the counterpane and, taking a second and warmer gown from the hook on the door, tucked it around the woman's body. That, at least, would compensate for the fresh air blowing across the bed.

That done, Cordelia slipped back into the passage, just in time to see Isabelle coming out of the room next door. She shot out an arm and half dragged the girl back into the bedroom. Isabelle gave a little cry, but Cordelia planted her back firmly against the door and said in a low, urgent whisper:

"Tell me what you know about Mark Callender."

The violet eyes slewed from door to window as if desperate for escape.

"I wasn't there when he did it."

"When who did what?"

Isabelle retreated towards the bed as if the inert figure, who was now groaning stertorously, could offer support. Suddenly the woman turned on her side and gave a long snort like an animal in pain. Both girls glanced at her in startled alarm. Cordelia reiterated:

"When who did what?"

"When Mark killed himself; I wasn't there."

The woman on the bed gave a little sigh. Cordelia lowered her voice:

"But you were there some days earlier, weren't you? You called at the house and enquired for him. Miss Markland saw

you. Afterwards you sat in the garden and waited until he'd finished work."

Was it Cordelia's imagination that the girl suddenly seemed more relaxed, that she was relieved at the innocuousness of the question?

"I just called to see Mark. They gave me his address at the college Lodge. I went to visit him."

"Why?" The harsh question seemed to puzzle her. She replied simply:

"I wanted to be with him. He was my friend."

"Was he your lover too?" asked Cordelia. This brutal frankness was surely better than asking whether they had slept together, or gone to bed together—stupid euphemisms which Isabelle might not even understand: it was hard to tell from those beautiful but frightened eyes just how much she did understand.

"No, Mark was never my lover. He was working in the garden and I had to wait for him at the cottage. He gave me a chair in the sun and a book until he was free."

"What book?"

"I don't remember, it was very dull. I was dull too until Mark came. Then we had tea with funny mugs that had a blue band, and after tea we went for a walk and then we had supper. Mark made a salad."

"And then?"

"I drove home."

She was perfectly calm now. Cordelia pressed on, aware of the sound of footsteps passing up and down the stairs, of the ring of voices.

"And the time before that? When did you see him before that tea party?"

"It was a few days before Mark left college. We went for a picnic in my car to the seaside. But first we stopped at a town— St. Edmunds town, is it?—and Mark saw a doctor."

"Why? Was he ill?"

"Oh no, he was not ill, and he did not stay long enough for what you call it—an examination. He was in the house a few minutes only. It was a very poor house. I waited for him in the car, but not just ouside the house you understand."

"Did he say why he went there?"

"No, but I do not think he got what he wanted. Afterwards he was sad for a little time, but then we went to the sea and he was happy again."

She, too, seemed happy now. She smiled at Cordelia, her sweet, unmeaning smile. Cordelia thought: it's just the cottage that terrifies her. She doesn't mind talking about the living Mark, it's his death she can't bear to think about. And yet, this repugnance wasn't born of personal grief. He had been her friend; he was sweet; she liked him. But she was getting on very well without him.

There was a knock at the door. Cordelia stood aside and Hugo came in. He lifted an eyebrow at Isabelle and, ignoring Cordelia, said:

"It's your party, ducky; coming down?"

"Cordelia wanted to talk to me about Mark."

"No doubt. You told her, I hope, that you spent one day with him motoring to the sea and one afternoon and evening at Summertrees and that you haven't seen him since."

"She told me," said Cordelia. "She was practically word perfect. I think she's safe to be let out on her own now."

He said easily:

"You shouldn't be sarcastic, Cordelia, it doesn't suit you. Sarcasm is all right for some women, but not for women who are beautiful in the way that you are beautiful."

They were passing down the stairs together to meet the hubbub in the hall. The compliment irritated Cordelia. She said:

"I suppose that woman on the bed is Isabelle's chaperone. Is she often drunk?"

"Mademoiselle de Congé? Not often as drunk as that, but I admit that she is seldom absolutely sober."

"Then oughtn't you to do something about it?"

"What should I do? Hand her over to the twentieth-century Inquisition—a psychiatrist like my father? What has she done to us to deserve that? Besides, she is tediously conscientious on the few occasions when she's sober. It happens that her compulsions and my interest coincide."

Cordelia said severely:

"That may be expedient but I don't think it's very responsible and it isn't kind."

He stopped in his tracks and turned towards her, smiling directly into her eyes.

"Oh, Cordelia, you talk like the child of progressive parents who has been reared by a nonconformist nanny and educated at a convent school. I do like you!"

He was still smiling as Cordelia slipped away from them and infiltrated into the party. She reflected that his diagnosis hadn't been so very wrong.

She helped herself to a glass of wine, then moved slowly round the room listening unashamedly to scraps of conversation, hoping to hear Mark's name mentioned. She heard it only once. Two girls and a very fair, rather insipid young man were standing behind her. One of the girls said:

"Sophie Tilling seems to have recovered remarkably quickly from Mark Callender's suicide. She and Davie went to the cremation, did you know? Typical of Sophie to take her current lover to see the previous one incinerated. I suppose it gave her some kind of a kick."

Her companion laughed.

"And little brother takes over Mark's girl. If you can't get beauty, money and brains, settle for the first two. Poor Hugo! He suffers from a sense of inferiority. Not quite handsome enough; not quite clever enough—Sophie's First must have shaken him—not quite rich enough. No wonder he has to rely on sex to give him confidence."

"And, even there, not quite . . ."

"Darling, you should know."

They laughed and moved away. Cordelia felt her face burning. Her hand shook almost spilling her wine. She was surprised to find how much she cared, how much she had come to like Sophie. But that, of course, was part of the plan, that was Tilling strategy. If you can't shame her into giving up the case, suborn her; take her on the river; be nice to her; get her on our side. And it was true, she was on their side, at least against malicious detractors. She comforted herself with the censorious reflection

that they were as bitchy as guests at a suburban cocktail party. She had never in her life attended one of those innocuous if boring gatherings for the routine consumption of gossip, gin and canapés but, like her father who had never attended one either, she found no difficulty in believing that they were hot beds of snobbery, spite and sexual innuendo.

A warm body was pressing against her. She turned and saw Davie. He was carrying three bottles of wine. He had obviously heard at least part of the conversation, as the girls had no doubt intended, but he grinned amiably.

"Funny how Hugo's discarded women always hate him so much. It's quite different with Sophie. Her ex-lovers clutter up Norwich Street with their beastly bicycles and broken-down cars. I'm always finding them in the sitting-room drinking my beer and confiding to her the awful trouble they're having with their present girls."

"Do you mind?"

"Not if they don't get any further than the sitting-room. Are you enjoying yourself?"

"Not very much."

"Come and meet a friend of mine. He's been asking who you are."

"No thank you, Davie. I must keep myself free for Mr. Horsfall. I don't want to miss him."

He smiled at her, rather pityingly she thought, and seemed about to speak. But he changed his mind and moved away, clutching his bottles to his chest and shouting a cheerful warning as he edged himself through the throng.

Cordelia worked her way around the room, watching and listening. She was intrigued by the overt sexuality; she had thought that intellectuals breathed too rarified air to be much interested in the flesh. Obviously this was a misapprehension. Come to think of it, the comrades, who might have been supposed to live in randy promiscuity, had been remarkably staid. She had sometimes felt that their sexual activities were prompted more by duty than instinct, more a weapon of revolution or a gesture against the bourgeois mores they despised than a response to human need. Their basic energies were all devoted to politics.

634

It was not difficult to see where most of the energies of those present were directed.

She needn't have worried about the success of the kaftan. A number of men showed themselves willing or even eager to detach themselves from their partners for the pleasure of talking to her. With one particularly, a decorative and ironically amusing young historian, Cordelia felt that she could have spent an entertaining evening. To enjoy the sole attention of one agreeable man and no attention at all from anyone else was all she ever hoped from a party. She wasn't naturally gregarious and, alienated by the last six years from her own generation, found herself intimidated by the noise, the underlying ruthlessness and the half-understood conventions of these tribal matings. And she told herself firmly that she wasn't here to enjoy herself at Sir Ronald's expense. None of her prospective partners knew Mark Callender or showed any interest in him, dead or alive. She mustn't get herself tied for the evening to people who had no information to give. When this seemed a danger and the talk became too beguiling, she would murmur her excuses and slip away to the bathroom or into the shadows of the garden where little groups were sitting on the grass smoking pot. Cordelia couldn't be mistaken in that evocative smell. They showed no disposition to chat and here, at least, she could stroll in privacy gaining courage for the next foray, for the next artfully casual question, the next inevitable response.

"Mark Callender? Sorry—we never met. Didn't he go off to sample the simple life and end by hanging himself or something?"

Once she took refuge in Mademoiselle de Congé's room, but she saw that the inert figure had been unceremoniously dumped on a cushion of pillows on the carpet and that the bed was being occupied for quite another purpose.

She wondered when Edward Horsfall would arrive or whether he would arrive at all. And if he did, would Hugo remember or bother to introduce her? She couldn't see either of the Tillings in the hot crush of gesticulating bodies which by now had crammed the sitting-room and spilled into the hall and half-way up the stairs. She was beginning to feel that this would be a wasted evening when Hugo's hand fell on her arm. He said:

"Come and meet Edward Horsfall. Edward, this is Cordelia Gray; she wants to talk about Mark Callender."

Edward Horsfall was another surprise. Cordelia had subconsciously conjured up the picture of an elderly don, a little distrait with the weight of his learning, a benevolent if detached mentor of the young. Horsfall could not have been much over thirty. He was very tall, his hair falling long over one eye, his lean body curved as a melon rind, a comparison reinforced by the pleated yellow shirt front under a jutting bow tie.

Any half acknowledged, half shameful hope which Cordelia may have nourished that he would immediately take to her and be happily ungrudging of his time so long as they were together was quickly dispersed. His eyes were restless, flicking obsessively back to the door. She suspected that he was alone by choice, deliberately keeping himself free from encumbrances until the hoped-for companion arrived. He was so fidgety that it was difficult not to be fretted by his anxiety. She said:

"You don't have to stay with me all the evening you know, I only want some information."

Her voice recalled him to an awareness of her and to some attempt at civility.

"That wouldn't exactly be a penance. I'm sorry. What do you want to know?"

"Anything you can tell me about Mark. You taught him history didn't you? Was he good at it?"

It wasn't a particularly relevant question but one which she felt all teachers might respond to as a start.

"He was more rewarding to teach than some students I'm afflicted with. I don't know why he chose history. He could very well have read one of the sciences. He had a lively curiosity about physical phenomenon. But he decided to read history."

"Do you think that was to disoblige his father?"

"To disoblige Sir Ronald?" He turned and stretched out an arm for a bottle. "What are you drinking? There's one thing about Isabelle de Lasterie's parties, the drink is excellent, presumably because Hugo orders it. There's an admirable absence of beer."

"Doesn't Hugo drink beer then?" asked Cordelia.

"He claims not to. What were we talking about? Oh, yes, disobliging Sir Ronald. Mark said that he chose history because we have no chance of understanding the present without understanding the past. That's the sort of irritating cliché people come out with at interviews, but he may have believed it. Actually, of course, the reverse is true; we interpret the past through our knowledge of the present."

"Was he any good?" asked Cordelia. "I mean, would he have got a First?"

A First, she naively believed, was the ultimate in scholastic achievement, the certificate of pronounced intelligence that the recipient carried unchallenged through life. She wanted to hear that Mark was safe for a First.

"Those are two separate and distinct questions. You seem to be confusing merit with achievement. Impossible to predict his class, hardly a First. Mark was capable of extraordinarily good and original work but he limited his material to the number of his original ideas. The result tended to be rather thin. Examiners like originality but you've got to spew up the accepted facts and orthodox opinions first if only to show that you've learnt them. An exceptional memory and fast legible handwriting; that's the secret of a First. Where are you, incidentally?" He noticed Cordelia's brief look of incomprehension.

"At what college?"

"None; I work. I'm a private detective."

He took this information in his stride.

"My uncle employed one of those once to find out if my aunt was being screwed by their dentist. She was, but he could have found out more easily by the simple expedient of asking them. His way, he lost the services of a wife and of a dentist simultaneously and paid through the nose for information he could have got for nothing. It made quite a stir in the family at the time. I should have thought that the job was——"

Cordelia finished the sentence for him.

"An unsuitable job for a woman?"

"Not at all. Entirely suitable I should have thought, requiring, I imagine, infinite curiosity, infinite pains and a penchant for interfering with other people." His attention was wandering

again. A group near to them were talking and snatches of the conversation came to them.

"——typical of the worst kind of academic writing. Contempt for logic; a generous sprinkling of vogue names; spurious profundity and bloody awful grammar."

The tutor gave the speakers a second's attention, dismissed their academic chat as beneath his notice and condescended to transfer his attention but not his regard back to Cordelia.

"Why are you so interested in Mark Callender?"

"His father has employed me to find out why he died. I was hoping that you might be able to help. I mean, did he ever give you a hint that he might be unhappy, unhappy enough to kill himself? Did he explain why he gave up college?"

"Not to me. I never felt that I got near him. He made a formal goodbye, thanked me for what he chose to describe was my help, and left. I made the usual noises of regret. We shook hands. I was embarrassed, but not Mark. He wasn't I think, a young man susceptible to embarrassment."

There was a small commotion at the door and a group of new arrivals pushed themselves noisily into the throng. Among them was a tall, dark girl in a flame-coloured frock, open almost to the waist. Cordelia felt the tutor stiffen, saw his eyes fixed on the new arrival with an intense, half anxious, half supplicating look, which she had seen before. Her heart sank. She would be lucky now to get any more information. Desperately trying to recapture his attention, she said:

"I'm not sure that Mark did kill himself. I think it could have been murder."

He spoke inattentively, his eyes on the newcomers.

"Unlikely, surely. By whom? For what reason? He was a negligible personality. He didn't even provoke a vague dislike except possibly from his father. But Ronald Callender couldn't have done it if that's what you're hoping. He was dining in Hall at High Table on the night Mark died. It was a College Feast night. I sat next to him. His son telephoned him."

Cordelia said eagerly, almost tugging at his sleeve.

"At what time?"

"Soon after the meal started, I suppose. Benskin, he's one of

the College servants, came in and gave him the message. It must have been between eight and eight-fifteen. Callender disappeared for about ten minutes then returned and got on with his soup. The rest of us still hadn't reached the second course."

"Did he say what Mark wanted? Did he seem disturbed?"

"Neither. We hardly spoke through the meal. Sir Ronald doesn't waste his conversational gifts on non-scientists. Excuse me, will you?"

He was gone, threading his way through the throng towards his prey. Cordelia put down her glass and went in search of Hugo.

"Look," she said, "I want to talk to Benskin, a servant at your college. Would he be there tonight?"

Hugo put down the bottle he was holding.

"He may be. He's one of the few who live in college. But I doubt whether you would winkle him out of his lair on your own. If it's all that urgent, I'd better come with you."

⋙◦⋘

The college porter ascertained without curiosity that Benskin was in the college and Benskin was summoned. He arrived after a wait of five minutes during which Hugo chatted to the porter and Cordelia walked outside the Lodge to amuse herself reading the college notices. Benskin arrived, unhurrying, imperturbable. He was a silver-haired, formally dressed old man, his face creased and thick skinned as an anaemic blood orange, and would, Cordelia thought, have looked like an advertisement for the ideal butler, were it not for an expression of lugubrious and sly disdain.

Cordelia gave him sight of Sir Ronald's note of authority and plunged straight into her questions. There was nothing to be gained by subtlety and since she had enlisted Hugo's help, she had little hope of shaking him off. She said:

"Sir Ronald has asked me to enquire into the circumstances of his son's death."

"So I see, Miss."

"I am told that Mr. Mark Callender telephoned his father

639

while Sir Ronald was dining at High Table on the night his son died and that you passed the message to Sir Ronald shortly after dinner began?"

"I was under the impression at the time that it was Mr. Callender who was ringing, Miss, but I was mistaken."

"How can you be sure of that, Mr. Benskin?"

"Sir Ronald himself told me, Miss, when I saw him in college some few days after his son's death. I've known Sir Ronald since he was an undergraduate and I made bold to express my condolences. During our brief conversation I made reference to the telephone call of 26th May and Sir Ronald told me that I was mistaken, that it was not Mr. Callender who had called."

"Did he say who it was?"

"Sir Ronald informed me that it was his laboratory assistant, Mr. Chris Lunn."

"Did that surprise you—that you were wrong, I mean?"

"I confess that I was somewhat surprised, Miss, but the mistake was perhaps excusable. My subsequent reference to the incident was fortuitous and in the circumstances regrettable."

"But do you really believe that you mis-heard the name?"

The obstinate old face did not relax.

"Sir Ronald could have been in no doubt about the person who telephoned him."

"Was it usual for Mr. Callender to ring his father while he was dining in College?"

"I had never previously taken a call from him, but then answering the telephone is not part of my normal duties. It is possible that some of the other college servants may be able to help but I hardly think that an enquiry would be productive or that the news that college servants had been questioned would be gratifying to Sir Ronald."

"Any enquiry which can help ascertain the truth is likely to be gratifying to Sir Ronald," said Cordelia. Really, she thought, Benskin's prose style is becoming infectious. She added more naturally:

"Sir Ronald is very anxious to find out everything possible about his son's death. Is there anything that you can tell me, any help that you can give me, Mr. Benskin?"

This was perilously close to an appeal but it met with no response.

"Nothing, Miss. Mr. Callender was a quiet and pleasant young gentleman who seemed, as far as I was able to observe him, to be in good health and spirits up to the time he left us. His death has been very much felt in the college. Is there anything else, Miss?"

He stood patiently waiting to be dismissed and Cordelia let him go. As she and Hugo left college together and walked back into Trumpington Street she said bitterly:

"He doesn't care, does he?"

"Why should he? Benskin's an old phoney but he's been at college for seventy years and he's seen it all before. A thousand ages in his sight are but an evening gone. I've only known Benskin distressed once over the suicide of an undergraduate and that was a Duke's son. Benskin thought that there were some things that the college shouldn't permit to happen."

"But he wasn't mistaken about Mark's call. You could tell that from his whole manner, at least I could. He knows what he heard. He isn't going to admit it, of course, but he knows in his heart he wasn't mistaken."

Hugo said lightly:

"He was being the old college servant, very correct, very proper; that's Benskin all over. 'The young gentlemen aren't what they were when I first came to college.' I should bloody well hope not! They wore side whiskers then and noblemen sported fancy gowns to distinguish them from the plebs. Benskin would bring all that back if he could. He's an anachronism, pottering through the court hand in hand with a statelier past."

"But he isn't deaf. I deliberately spoke in a soft voice and he heard me perfectly. Do you really believe that he was mistaken?"

"Chris Lunn and his son are very similar sounds."

"But Lunn doesn't announce himself that way. All the time I was with Sir Ronald and Miss Leaming they just called him Lunn."

"Look, Cordelia, you can't possibly suspect Ronald Callender of having a hand in his son's death! Be logical. You accept, I suppose, that a rational murderer hopes not to be found out. You admit, no doubt, that Ronald Callender, although a dis-

641

agreeable bastard, is a rational being. Mark is dead and his body cremated. No one except you has mentioned murder. Then Sir Ronald employs you to stir things up. Why should he if he's got something to hide? He doesn't even need to divert suspicion; there has been no suspicion, there is no suspicion."

"Of course I don't suspect him of killing his son. He doesn't know how Mark died and he desperately needs to know. That's why he's taken me on. I could tell that at our interview; I couldn't be wrong about that. But I don't understand why he should have lied about the telephone call."

"If he is lying there could be half a dozen innocent explanations. If Mark did ring the college it must have been something pretty urgent, perhaps something which his father didn't particularly want to make public, something which gives a clue to his son's suicide."

"Then why employ me to find out why he killed himself?"

"True, wise Cordelia; I'll try again. Mark asked him for help, perhaps an urgent visit which Dad refused. You can imagine his reaction. 'Don't be ridiculous, Mark, I'm dining at High Table with the Master. Obviously I can't leave the cutlets and claret just because you telephone in this hysterical way and demand to see me. Pull yourself together.' That sort of thing wouldn't sound so good in open court; coroners are notoriously censorious." Hugo's voice took on a deep magisterial tone. " 'It is not for me to add to Sir Ronald's distress, but it is, perhaps, unfortunate that he chose to ignore what was obviously a cry for help. Had he left his meal immediately and gone to his son's side this brilliant young student might have been saved.' Cambridge suicides, so I've noticed, are always brilliant; I'm still waiting to read the report of an inquest where the college authorities testify that the student only just killed himself in time before they kicked him out."

"But Mark died between seven and nine p.m. That telephone call is Sir Ronald's alibi!"

"He wouldn't see it like that. He doesn't need an alibi. If you know you're not involved and the question of foul play never arises, you don't think in terms of alibis. It's only the guilty who do that."

"But how did Mark know where to find his father? In his evidence Sir Ronald said that he hadn't spoken to his son for over three weeks."

"I can see you have a point there. Ask Miss Leaming. Better still, ask Lunn if it was, in fact, he who rang the college. If you're looking for a villain Lunn should suit admirably. I find him absolutely sinister."

"I didn't know that you knew him."

"Oh, he's pretty well known in Cambridge. He drives that horrid little closed van around with ferocious dedication as if he were transporting recalcitrant students to the gas chambers. Everyone knows Lunn. Seldom he smiles and smiles in such a way as if he mocked himself and scorned his spirit that could be moved to smile at anything. I should concentrate on Lunn."

They walked on in silence through the warm scented night while the waters sang in the runnels of Trumpington Street. Lights were shining now in college doorways and in porters' lodges and the far gardens and inter-connecting courts, glimpsed as they passed, looked remote and ethereal as in a dream. Cordelia was suddenly oppressed with loneliness and melancholy. If Bernie were alive they would be discussing the case, cosily ensconced in the furthest corner of some Cambridge pub, insulated by noise and smoke and anonymity from the curiosity of their neighbours; talking low voiced in their own particular jargon. They would be speculating on the personality of a young man who slept under that gentle and intellectual painting, yet who had bought a vulgar magazine of salacious nudes. Or had he? And if not, how had it come to be in the cottage garden? They would be discussing a father who lied about his son's last telephone call; speculating in happy complicity about an uncleaned spade, a row of earth half dug, an unwashed coffee mug, a quotation from Blake meticulously typed. They would be talking about Isabelle who was terrified and Sophie who was surely honest and Hugo who certainly knew something about Mark's death and who was clever but not as clever as he needed to be. For the first time since the case began Cordelia doubted her ability to solve it alone. If only there were someone reliable in whom she could confide, someone who would reinforce her

confidence. She thought again of Sophie, but Sophie had been Mark's mistress and was Hugo's sister. They were both involved. She was on her own and that, when she came to think about it, was no different from how essentially it had always been. Ironically, the realization brought her comfort and a return of hope.

At the corner of Panton Street they paused and he said:

"You're coming back to the party?"

"No, thank you, Hugo; I've got work to do."

"Are you staying in Cambridge?"

Cordelia wondered whether the question was prompted by more than polite interest. Suddenly cautious, she said:

"Only for the next day or two. I've found a very dull but cheap bed and breakfast place near the station."

He accepted the lie without comment and they said good-night. She made her way back to Norwich Street. The little car was still outside number fifty-seven, but the house was dark and quiet as if to emphasize her exclusion and the three windows were as blank as dead rejecting eyes.

❦

She was tired by the time she got back to the cottage and had parked the Mini on the edge of the copse. The garden gate creaked at her hand. The night was dark and she felt in her bag for her torch and followed its bright pool round the side of the cottage and to the back door. By its light she fitted the key into the lock. She turned it and, dazed with tiredness, stepped into the sitting-room. The torch, still switched on, hung loosely from her hand, making erratic patterns of light on the tiled floor. Then in one involuntary movement it jerked upwards and shone full on the thing that hung from the centre hook of the ceiling. Cordelia gave a cry and clutched at the table. It was the bolster from her bed, the bolster with a cord drawn tight about one end making a grotesque and bulbous head, and the other end stuffed into a pair of Mark's trousers. The legs hung pathetically flat and empty, one lower than the other. As she stared at it in fascinated horror, her heart hammering, a slight

breeze wafted in from the open door and it swung slowly round as if twisted by a living hand.

She must have stood there rooted with fear and staring wild-eyed at the bolster for seconds only, yet it seemed minutes before she found the strength to pull out a chair from the table and take the thing down. Even in the moment of repulsion and terror she remembered to look closely at the knot. The cord was attached to the hook by a simple loop and two half-hitches. So, either her secret visitor had chosen not to repeat his former tactics, or he hadn't known how the first knot had been tied. She laid the bolster on the chair and went outside for the gun. In her tiredness she had forgotten it, but now she longed for the reassurance of the hard cold metal in her hand. She stood at the back door and listened. The garden seemed suddenly full of noises, mysterious rustlings, leaves moving in the slight breeze like human sighs, furtive scurryings in the undergrowth, the bat-like squeak of an animal disconcertingly close at hand. The night seemed to be holding its breath as she crept out towards the elder bush. She waited, listening to her own heart, before she found courage to turn her back and stretch up her hand to feel for the gun. It was still there. She sighed audibly with relief and immediately felt better. The gun wasn't loaded but that hardly seemed to matter. She hurried back to the cottage, her terror assuaged.

It was nearly an hour before she finally went to bed. She lit the lamp and, gun in hand, made a search of the whole cottage. Next she examined the window. It was obvious enough how he had got in. The window had no catch and was easy to push open from outside. Cordelia fetched a roll of Scotch tape from her scene-of-crime kit and, as Bernie had shown her, cut two very narrow strips and pasted them across the base of the pane and the wooden frame. She doubted whether the front windows could be opened but she took no chances and sealed them in the same way. It wouldn't stop an intruder but at least she would know next morning that he had gained access. Finally, having washed in the kitchen, she went upstairs to bed. There was no lock on her door but she wedged it slightly open and balanced a saucepan lid on the top of the frame. If anyone did

645

succeed in getting in, he wouldn't take her by surprise. She loaded the gun and placed it on her bedside table, remembering that she was dealing with a killer. She examined the cord. It was a four-foot length of ordinary strong string, obviously not new and frayed at one end. Her heart sank at the hopelessness of trying to identify it. But she labelled it carefully, as Bernie had taught her, and packed it in her scene-of-crime kit. She did the same with the curled strap and the typed passage of Blake, transferring them from the bottom of her shoulder bag to plastic exhibit envelopes. She was so weary that even this routine chore cost her an effort of will. Then she placed the bolster back on the bed, resisting an impulse to sling it on the floor and sleep without it. But, by then, nothing—neither fear nor discomfort—could have kept her awake. She lay for only a few minutes listening to the ticking of her watch before tiredness overcame her and bore her unresisting down the dark tide of sleep.

Chapter Four

⊰∽⊙⊂⊱

Cordelia was awakened early next morning by the discordant chattering of the birds and the strong clear light of another fine day. She lay for several minutes stretching herself within her sleeping-bag, savouring the smell of a country morning, that subtle and evocative fusion of earth, sweet wet grass and stronger farmyard smell. She washed in the kitchen as Mark had obviously done, standing in the tin bath from the shed and gasping as she poured saucepans of cold tap water over her naked body. There was something about the simple life which disposed one to these austerities. Cordelia thought it unlikely that, in any circumstances, she would willingly have bathed in cold water in London or so much relished the smell of the paraffin stove superimposed on the appetizing sizzle of frying bacon, or the flavour of her first strong mug of tea.

The cottage was filled with sunlight, a warm friendly sanctum from which she could safely venture out to whatever the day held. In the calm peace of a summer morning the little sitting-room seemed untouched by the tragedy of Mark Callender's death. The hook in the ceiling looked as innocuous as if it had never served its dreadful purpose. The horror of that moment when her torch had first picked out the dark swollen shadow of the bolster moving in the night breeze now had the unreality of a dream. Even the memory of the precautions of the night before were embarrassing viewed in the unambiguous light of day. She felt rather foolish as she unloaded the gun, secreted the ammunition among her underclothes, and hid the pistol in the elder bush, watching carefully to see that she wasn't observed. When the washing-up was done and the one teacloth washed through and hung out to dry, she picked a small posy of pansies,

cowslips and meadow-sweet from the far end of the garden and set them on the table in one of the ribbed mugs.

She had decided that her first task must be to try to trace Nanny Pilbeam. Even if the woman had nothing to tell her about Mark's death or his reason for leaving college, she would be able to speak about his childhood and boyhood; she, probably better than anyone, would know what his essential nature had been. She had cared enough about him to attend the funeral and to send an expensive wreath. She had called on him in college on his 21st birthday. He had probably kept in touch with her, might even have confided in her. He had no mother and Nanny Pilbeam could have been, in some sense, a substitute.

As she drove into Cambridge Cordelia considered tactics. The probability was that Miss Pilbeam lived somewhere in the district. It was unlikely that she actually lived in the city since Hugo Tilling had only seen her once. From his brief account of her, it sounded as if she were old and probably poor. It was unlikely, therefore, that she would travel far to attend the funeral. It was apparent that she hadn't been one of the official mourners from Garforth House, hadn't been invited by Sir Ronald. According to Hugo, none of the party had even spoken to each other. This hardly suggested that Miss Pilbeam was the elderly and valued retainer of tradition, almost one of the family. Sir Ronald's neglect of her on such an occasion intrigued Cordelia. She wondered just what Miss Pilbeam's position in the family had been.

If the old lady lived near Cambridge, she had probably ordered the wreath at one of the city florists. Villages were very unlikely to provide this kind of service. It had been an ostentatious wreath, which suggested that Miss Pilbeam had been prepared to spend lavishly and had probably gone to one of the larger florists. The likelihood was that she had ordered it personally. Elderly ladies, apart from the fact that they were seldom on the telephone, like to attend to these matters direct, having, Cordelia suspected, a well-founded suspicion that only face-to-face confrontation and the meticulous recital of one's precise requirements extracted the best service. If Miss Pilbeam had come in from her village by train or by bus, she had probably

selected a shop somewhere near the centre of the city. Cordelia decided to begin her search by enquiring of passers-by if they could recommend the name of a good florist.

She had already learned that Cambridge was not a city for the cruising motorist. She drew up and consulted the folding map at the back of her guide book and decided to leave the Mini on the car park next to Parker's Piece. Her search might take some time and would be best done on foot. She daren't risk a parking fine nor the impounding of the car. She checked her watch. It was still only a few minutes after nine o'clock. She had made a good start to the day.

The first hour was disappointing. The people of whom she enquired were anxious to be helpful but their ideas of what constituted a reliable florist somewhere near the centre of the city were peculiar. Cordelia was directed to small greengrocers selling a few bunches of cut flowers as a side line, to the supplier of gardening equipment who dealt in plants but not in wreaths, and once to a funeral director. The two florists' shops which at first sight seemed possible had never heard of Miss Pilbeam and had provided no wreaths for the Mark Callender funeral. A little weary with much walking and beginning to feel despondent, Cordelia decided that the whole quest had been unreasonably sanguine. Probably Miss Pilbeam had come in from Bury St. Edmunds or Newmarket and had bought the wreath in her own town.

But the visit to the undertakers was not wasted. In reply to her enquiry, they recommended the name of a firm which provided "a very nice class of wreath, Miss, really very nice indeed." The shop was further from the centre of the city than Cordelia had expected. Even from the pavement it smelt of weddings or funerals, as one's mood dictated, and as she pushed open the door Cordelia was welcomed by a gush of sweet warm air which caught at the throat. There were flowers everywhere. Large green buckets lined the walls holding clumps of lilies, irises and lupins; smaller containers were packed tight with wall flowers and marigolds and stocks; there were frigid bundles of tight budded roses on thornless stems, each flower identical in size and colour and looking as if it had been cultivated in a test tube. Pots of

649

indoor plants, decorated with variegated ribbon, lined the path to the counter like a floral guard of honour.

There was a room at the back of the shop where two assistants were working. Through the open door Cordelia watched them. The younger, a languid blonde with a spotted skin, was assistant executioner, laying out roses and freesias, predestined victims, graded according to type and colour. Her senior, whose status was denoted by a better fitting overall and an air of authority, was twisting off the flower heads, piercing each mutilated bloom with wire and threading them closely on to a huge bed of moss in the shape of a heart. Cordelia averted her eyes from this horror.

A buxom lady in a pink smock appeared behind the counter apparently from nowhere. She was as pungently scented as the shop, but had obviously decided that no ordinary floral perfume could compete and that she had better rely on the exotic. She smelt of curry powder and pine so strongly that the effect was practically anaesthetizing.

Cordelia said her prepared speech:

"I'm from Sir Ronald Callender of Garforth House. I wonder whether you can help us? His son was cremated on 3rd of June and their old nurse very kindly sent a wreath, a cross of red roses. Sir Ronald has lost her address and very much wants to write to thank her. The name is Pilbeam."

"Oh, I don't think we executed any orders of that type for 3rd June."

"If you would be kind enough to just look in the book——"

Suddenly the young blonde looked up from her work and called out:

"It's Goddard."

"I beg your pardon, Shirley"? said the buxom lady repressively.

"The name's Goddard. The card on the wreath said Nanny Pilbeam, but the customer was a Mrs. Goddard. Another lady came to enquire from Sir Ronald Callender and that was the name she gave. I looked it up for her. Mrs. Goddard, Lavender Cottage, Ickleton. One cross, four foot long in red roses. Six pounds. It's there in the book."

"Thank you very much," said Cordelia fervently. She smiled

her thanks impartially at the three of them and left quickly in case she got embroiled in an argument about the other enquirer from Garforth House. It must have looked odd, she knew, but the three of them would no doubt enjoy themselves discussing it after she had left. Lavender Cottage, Ickleton. She kept repeating the address to herself until she was at a safe distance from the shop and could pause to write it down.

Her tiredness seemed miraculously to have left her as she sped back to the car park. She consulted her map. Ickleton was a village near the Essex border about ten miles from Cambridge. It wasn't far from Duxford so that she would be retracing her steps. She could be there in less than half an hour.

But it took longer than she had expected to thread her way through the Cambridge traffic and it wasn't until thirty-five minutes later, that she came to Ickleton's fine flint and pebble church with its broach spire, and drove the Mini close to the church gate. It was a temptation to take a brief look inside, but she resisted it. Mrs. Goddard might even now be preparing to catch the Cambridge bus. She went in search of Lavender Cottage.

It wasn't, in fact, a cottage at all but a small semi-detached house of hideous red brick at the end of the High Street. There was only a narrow strip of grass between the front door and the road and neither smell nor sight of lavender. The iron knocker, in the form of a lion's head, fell heavily, shaking the door. The response came, not from Lavender Cottage, but from the next house. An elderly woman appeared, thin, almost toothless and swathed in an immense apron patterned with roses. She had carpet slippers on her feet, a woollen cap decorated with a bobble on her head and an air of lively interest in the world in general.

"You'll be wanting Mrs. Goddard, I daresay?"

"Yes. Could you tell me where I could find her?"

"She'll be over at the graveyard, I don't doubt. She usually is this time of a fine morning."

"I've just come from the church. I didn't see anyone."

"Bless you, Miss, she's not at the church! They haven't been burying us there for many a year now. Her old man is where

651

they'll be putting her in time, in the cemetery on Hinxton Road. You can't miss it. Just keep straight on."

"I'll have to go back to the church for my car," said Cordelia. It was obvious that she was going to be watched out of sight and it seemed necessary to explain why she was departing in the opposite direction to the one indicated. The old woman smiled and nodded and came out to lean on her gate for a better view of Cordelia's progress down the High Street, nodding her head like a marionette so that the bright bobble danced in the sun.

⋙○⋘

The cemetery was easily found. Cordelia parked the Mini on a convenient patch of grass where a signpost pointed the footpath to Duxford and walked the few yards back to the iron gates. There was a small flint chapel of rest with an apse at the east end and beside it an ancient wooden seat green with lichen and spattered with bird lime which gave a view of the whole burial ground. A wide swathe of turf ran straight down the middle and on each side were the graves, variously marked with white marble crosses, grey headstones, small rusted circles of iron heeling over towards the smooth turf and bright splashes of flowers patchworked over the newly dug earth. It was very peaceful. The burial ground was surrounded by trees, their leaves scarcely stirring in the calm, hot air. There was little sound except the chirruping of crickets in the grass and from time to time the nearby ringing of a railway level-crossing bell and the swooping horn of a diesel train.

There was only one other person in the graveyard, an elderly woman bending over one of the far graves. Cordelia sat quietly on the seat, arms folded in her lap, before making her way silently down the grass path towards her. She knew with certainty that this interview was going to be crucial yet paradoxically she was in no hurry to begin. She came up to the woman and stood, still unnoticed, at the foot of the grave.

She was a small woman dressed in black whose old-fashioned straw hat, its brim wreathed with faded net, was screwed to her hair with an immense black bobbed hat pin. She knelt with her

back to Cordelia showing the soles of a pair of mis-shapen shoes from which her thin legs stuck out like sticks. She was weeding the grave; her fingers, darting like a reptile's tongue over the grass, plucked at small, almost undetectable weeds. At her side was a punnet holding a folded newspaper and a gardening trowel. From time to time, she dropped into the punnet her little mush of weeds.

After a couple of minutes, during which Cordelia watched her in silence, she paused satisfied and began smoothing the surface of the grass as if comforting the bones beneath. Cordelia read the inscription carved deep on the headstone. "Sacred to the memory of Charles Albert Goddard beloved husband of Annie who departed this life 27th August 1962, aged 70 years. At rest." At rest; the commonest epitaph of a generation to whom rest must have seemed the ultimate luxury, the supreme benediction.

The woman rested back for a second on her heels and contemplated the grave with satisfaction. It was then that she became aware of Cordelia. She turned a bright much wrinkled face towards her and said without curiosity or resentment at her presence:

"It's a nice stone, isn't it?"

"Yes, it is. I was admiring the lettering."

"Cut deep that is. It cost a mint of money but it was worth it. That'll last, you see. Half the lettering here won't, it's that shallow. It takes the pleasure out of a cemetery. I like to read the grave stones, like to know who people were and when they died and how long the women lived after they buried their men. It sets you wondering how they managed and whether they were lonely. There's no use in a stone if you can't read the lettering. Of course, this stone looks a bit top-heavy at present. That's because I asked them to leave space for me: 'Also to Annie his wife, departed this life, . . .' and then the date: That'll even it up nicely. I've left the money to pay for it."

"What text were you thinking of having?" enquired Cordelia.

"Oh, no text! At rest will be good enough for the both of us. We shan't be asking more of the good Lord than that."

Cordelia said:

"That cross of roses you sent to Mark Callender's funeral was beautiful."

"Oh, did you see it? You weren't at the funeral were you? Yes, I was pleased with it. They made a nice job of it, I thought. Poor boy, he hadn't much else, had he?"

She looked at Cordelia with benign interest:

"So you knew Mr. Mark? Would you be his young lady perhaps?"

"No, not that, but I care about him. It's odd that he never talked about you, his old nurse."

"But I wasn't his nurse, my dear, or at least, only for a month or two. He was a baby then, it meant nothing to him. No, I was nurse to his dear mother."

"But you visited Mark on his twenty-first birthday?"

"So he told you that, did he? I was glad to see him again after all those years, but I wouldn't have pushed myself on him. It wouldn't have been right, his father feeling as he did. No, I went to give him something from his mother, to do something she had asked me to do when she was dying. Do you know, I hadn't seen Mr. Mark for over twenty years—odd, really, considering that we didn't live that far apart—but I knew him at once. He had a great look of his mother about him, poor boy."

"Could you tell me about it? It's not just curiosity; it's important for me to know."

Leaning for support on the handle of her basket, Mrs. Goddard got laboriously to her feet. She picked at a few short blades of grass adhering to her skirt, felt in her pocket for a pair of grey cotton gloves and put them on. Together they made their way slowly down the path.

"Important, is it? I don't know why it should be. It's all in the past now. She's dead, poor lady, and so is he. All that hope and promise come to nothing. I haven't spoken to anyone else about it, but then who would care to know?"

"Perhaps we could sit on this bench and talk together for a time?"

"I don't see why we shouldn't. There's nothing to hurry home for now. Do you know, my dear, I didn't marry my husband until I was fifty-three and yet I miss him as if we had been

childhood sweethearts. People said I was a fool to take on a man at that age but you see I had known his wife for thirty years, we were at school together, and I knew him. If a man's good to one woman, he'll be good to another. That's what I reckoned and I was right."

They sat side by side on the bench gazing over the green swathe towards the grave. Cordelia said:

"Tell me about Mark's mother."

"She was a Miss Bottley, Evelyn Bottley. I went to her mother as under-nursemaid before she was born. There was only little Harry then. He was killed in the war on his first raid over Germany. His Dad took it very hard; there was never anyone to match Harry, the sun shone out of his eyes. The master never really cared for Miss Evie, it was all the boy with him. Mrs. Bottley died when Evie was born and that may have made a difference. People say that it does, but I've never believed it. I've known fathers who loved a baby even more—poor innocent things, how can they be blamed? If you ask me, it was just an excuse for not taking to the child, that she killed her mother."

"Yes, I know a father who made it an excuse too. But it isn't their fault. We can't make ourselves love someone just because we want to."

"More's the pity, my dear, or the world would be an easier place. But his own child, that's not natural!"

"Did she love him?"

"How could she? You won't get love from a child if you don't give love. But she never had the trick of pleasing him, of humouring him—he was a big man, fierce, loud talking, frightening to a child. He would have done better with a pretty, pert little thing, who wouldn't have been afraid of him."

"What happened to her? How did she meet Sir Ronald Callender?"

"He wasn't Sir Ronald then, my dear. Oh, dear no! He was Ronny Callender the gardener's son. They lived at Harrogate you see. Oh, such a lovely house they had! When I first went into service there they had three gardeners. That was before the war, of course. Mr. Bottley worked in Bradford; he was in the wool trade. Well, you were asking about Ronny Callender.

I remember him well, a pugnacious, good-looking lad but one who kept his thoughts to himself. He was clever that one, oh he was clever! He got a scholarship to the grammar school and did very well."

"And Evelyn Bottley fell in love?"

"She may have done, my dear. What there was between them when they were young, who can tell. But then the war came and he went away. She was wild to do something useful and they took her on as a V.A.D., though how she passed the medical I'll never know. And then they met again in London as people did in the war and the next thing we knew they were married."

"And came to live here outside Cambridge?"

"Not until after the war. At first she kept on with her nursing and he was sent overseas. He had what the men call a good war; we'd call it a bad war I daresay, a lot of killing and fighting, imprisonment and escaping. It ought to have made Mr. Bottley proud of him and reconciled to the marriage but it didn't. I think he thought that Ronny had his eye on the money, because there was money to come, no doubt about that. He may have been right, but who's to blame the boy? My mother used to say, 'Don't marry for money, but marry where money is!' There's no harm in looking for money as long as there's kindness as well."

"And do you think there was kindness?"

"There was never unkindness that I could see, and she was mad about him. After the war he went up to Cambridge. He'd always wanted to be a scientist and he got a grant because he was ex-service. She had some money from her father and they bought the house he lives in now so that he could live at home when he was studying. It didn't look the same then, of course. He's done a lot to it since. They were quite poor then and Miss Evie managed with practically no one to help, only me. Mr. Bottley used to come and stay from time to time. She used to dread his visits, poor darling. He was looking for a grandchild, you see, and one didn't come. And then Mr. Callender finished at the university and got a job teaching. He wanted to stay on at college to be a don or something like that, but they wouldn't have him. He used to say it was because he hadn't influence, but I think he may not have been quite clever enough. In

Harrogate we thought he was the cleverest boy in the grammar school. But then, Cambridge is full of clever men."

"And then Mark was born?"

"Yes, on the 25th April 1951, nine years after they were married. He was born in Italy. Mr. Bottley was that pleased when she became pregnant that he increased the allowance and they used to spend a lot of holidays in Tuscany. My lady loved Italy, always had, and I think she wanted the child to be born there. Otherwise she wouldn't have gone on holiday in the last month of her pregnancy. I went to visit her about a month after she came home with the baby and I've never seen a woman so happy. Oh, he was a lovely little boy!"

"But why did you visit her; weren't you living and working there?"

"No, my dear. Not for some months. She wasn't well in the early days of her pregnancy. I could see that she was strained and unhappy and then one day Mr. Callender sent for me and told me that she had taken against me and that I'd have to leave. I wouldn't have believed it, but when I went to her she just put out her hand and said: 'I'm sorry, Nanny, I think it would be better if you went.'

"Pregnant women have strange fancies, I know, and the baby was so important to them both. I thought she might have asked me to come back afterwards and so she did, but not living in. I took a bedsitting room in the village with the postmistress and used to give four mornings a week to my lady and the rest to other ladies in the village. It worked very well, really, but I missed the baby when I wasn't with him. I hadn't seen her often during her pregnancy but once we met in Cambridge. She must have been near the end of her time. She was very heavy, poor dear, dragging herself along. At first she pretended that she hadn't noticed me and then she thought better of it and came across the road. 'We're off to Italy next week, Nanny,' she said. 'Isn't it lovely?' I said: 'If you're not careful, my dear, that baby will be a little Italian,' and she laughed. It seemed as though she couldn't wait to get back to the sun."

"And what happened after she came home?"

"She died after nine months, my dear. She was never strong,

as I said, and she caught influenza. I helped look after her and I'd have done more but Mr. Callender took over the nursing himself. He couldn't bear anyone else to be near her. We only had a few minutes together just before she died and it was then that she asked me to give her prayer book to Mark on his twenty-first birthday. I can hear her now: 'Give it to Mark when he's twenty-one, Nanny. Wrap it up carefully and take it to him when he comes of age. You won't forget will you?' I said: 'I'll not forget, my darling, you know that.' Then she said a strange thing. 'If you do, or if you die before then, or if he doesn't understand, it won't really matter. It will mean that God wants it that way.' "

"What do you think she meant?"

"Who's to say, my dear? She was very religious was Miss Evie, too religious for her own good, I sometimes thought. I believe we should accept our own responsibilities, solve our own problems, not leave it all to God as if He hadn't enough to be thinking about with the world in the state it is. But that's what she said not three hours before she died and that's what I promised. So when Mr. Mark was twenty-one, I found out what college he was at and went to see him."

"What happened?"

"Oh, we had a very happy time together. Do you know, his father had never spoken about his mother. That sometimes happens when a wife dies but I think a son ought to know about his mother. He was full of questions, things that I thought his father would have told him.

"He was glad to get the prayer book. It was a few days later that he came to see me. He asked the name of the doctor who had treated his mother. I told him that it was old Dr. Gladwin. Mr. Callender and she had never had any other doctor. I used to think it a pity sometimes, Miss Evie being so frail. Dr. Gladwin must have been seventy then, and although there were people who wouldn't say a word against him, I never thought much of him myself. Drink, you know, my dear; he was never really reliable. But I expect he's gone to his rest long since, poor man. Anyway, I told Mr. Mark the name and he wrote it down. Then we had tea and a little chat and he left. I never saw him again."

"And no one else knows about the prayer book?"

"No one in the world, my dear. Miss Leaming saw the florist's name on my card and asked them for my address. She came here the day after the funeral to thank me for attending but I could see it was only curiosity. If she and Sir Ronald were so pleased to see me, what was to stop them from coming over and shaking hands? She as good as suggested that I was there without an invitation. An invitation to a funeral! Who ever heard of such a thing?"

"So you told her nothing?" asked Cordelia.

"I've told no one but you, my dear, and I'm not sure why I've told you. But no, I didn't tell her. I never liked her, to tell you the truth. I'm not saying there was anything between her and Sir Ronald, not while Miss Evie was alive anyway. There was never any gossip and she lived in a flat in Cambridge and kept herself to herself, I'll give her that. Mr. Callender met her when he was teaching science at one of the village schools. She was the English mistress. It wasn't until after Miss Evie died that he set up his own laboratory."

"Do you mean that Miss Leaming has a degree in English?"

"Oh, yes, my dear! She wasn't trained as a secretary. Of course she gave up the teaching when she started working for Mr. Callender."

"So you left Garforth House after Mrs. Callender died? You didn't stay on to care for the baby?"

"I wasn't wanted. Mr. Callender employed one of those new college-trained girls and then, when Mark was still only a baby, he was sent away to school. His father made it plain that he didn't like me to see the child and after all, a father has his rights. I wouldn't have gone on seeing Mr. Mark knowing that his father didn't approve. It would have only put the boy in a false position. But now he's dead and we've all lost him. The coroner said that he killed himself, and he may have been right."

Cordelia said.

"I don't think he killed himself."

"Don't you, my dear? That's kind of you. But he's dead, isn't he, so what does it matter now? I think it's time for me

659

to go home. If you don't mind, I won't ask you to tea, my dear, I'm a little tired today. But you know where to find me, and if ever you want to see me again, you'll always be welcome."

They made their way out of the burial ground together. At the gates, they parted. Mrs. Goddard patted Cordelia on the shoulder with the clumsy affection she might have shown to an animal, then walked off slowly towards the village.

As Cordelia drove round the curve of the road, the level-crossing came into sight. A train had just passed and the barriers were being raised. Three vehicles had been caught at the crossing and the last in line was quickest away, accelerating past the first two cars as they bumped slowly over the rails. Cordelia saw that it was a small black van.

Later Cordelia remembered little of the journey back to the cottage. She drove fast, concentrating on the road ahead, trying to control her rising excitement by meticulous attention to gears and brakes. She drove the Mini hard against the front hedge, careless of whether it were seen. The cottage looked and smelt just as she had left it. She had almost expected to find it ransacked and the prayer book gone. Sighing with relief, she saw that the white spine was still there among the taller and darker covers. Cordelia opened it. She hardly knew what she expected to find; an inscription perhaps, or a message, cryptic or plain, a letter folded between the leaves. But the only inscription could have no possible relevance to the case. It was written in a shaky, old-fashioned hand; the steel nib had crawled spider-like over the page. "To Evelyn Mary on the occasion of her confirmation, with love from her Godmother, 5th August 1934."

Cordelia shook the book. No slip of paper fluttered out. She skimmed through the pages. Nothing.

She sat on the bed drooping with disappointment. Had it been unreasonable to imagine that there was something significant in the bequest of the prayer book; had she fabricated a promising edifice of conjecture and mystery on an old woman's confused recollections of a perfectly ordinary and understandable

action—a devout and dying mother leaving a prayer book to her son? And even if she hadn't been wrong, why should the message still be there? If Mark had found a note from his mother, placed between the leaves, he might well have destroyed it after reading. And if he hadn't destroyed it, someone else might have done so. The note, if it ever existed, was now probably part of the shifting heap of white ash and charred debris in the cottage grate.

She shook herself out of her despondency. There was still a line of enquiry to pursue; she would try to trace Dr. Gladwin. After a second's thought she put the prayer book in her bag. Looking at her watch, she saw that it was nearly one o'clock. She decided to have a picnic lunch of cheese and fruit in the garden and then set off again for Cambridge to visit the central library and consult a medical directory.

Less than an hour later she found the information she wanted. There was only one Dr. Gladwin still on the register who could have attended Mrs. Callender as an old man of over seventy, twenty years ago. He was Emlyn Thomas Gladwin who had qualified at St. Thomas's Hospital in 1904. She wrote down the address in her note book: 4 Pratts Way, Ixworth Road, Bury St. Edmunds. Edmunds town! The town which Isabelle had said that she and Mark had visited on their way to the sea.

So the day hadn't been wasted after all—she was following in Mark Callender's footsteps. Impatient to consult a map she went over to the atlas section of the library. It was now two-fifteen. If she took the A45 road direct through Newmarket she could be in Bury St. Edmunds in about an hour. Allow an hour for the visit to the doctor and another for the return journey. She could be home at the cottage before half past five.

She was driving through the gentle unemphatic countryside just outside Newmarket when she noticed the black van following her. It was too far away to see who was driving but she thought it was Lunn and that he was alone. She accelerated, trying to keep the distance between them, but the van drew a little nearer. There was no reason, of course, why Lunn shouldn't be driving to Newmarket on Sir Ronald Callender's business, but the sight of the squat little van perpetually in her driving

mirror was disconcerting. Cordelia decided to throw him off. There were few side turns on the road she was travelling and the country was unfamiliar to her. She decided to wait until she reached Newmarket and seize what opportunity offered.

The main through street of the town was a tangle of traffic and every turn seemed to be blocked. It was only at the second set of traffic lights that Cordelia saw her chance. The black van was caught at the intersection about fifty yards behind. As the light turned green, she accelerated quickly and swung round to the left. There was another turn to the left and she took it, then one to the right. She drove on through unfamiliar streets, then after about five minutes, stopped at an intersection and waited. The black van did not appear. It looked as if she had succeeded in shaking him off. She waited for another five minutes, then made her way slowly back to the main road and joined in the flow of eastward traffic. Half an hour later she had passed through Bury St. Edmunds and was driving very slowly down the Ixworth Road, watching for Pratts Way. Fifty yards farther on she came to it, a row of six small stucco houses standing back from a lay-by. She stopped the car outside number four remembering Isabelle, biddable and docile, who had obviously been told to drive further on and wait in the car. Was that because Mark thought the white Renault too conspicuous? Even the arrival of the Mini had provoked interest. There were faces at upper windows and a small group of children had mysteriously appeared, clustered around a neighbouring gate and watching her with wide and expressionless eyes.

Number four was a depressing house; the front garden was unweeded and the fence had gaps where the planks had rotted or had been wrenched apart. The external paint had flaked away to the bare wood and the brown front door had peeled and blistered in the sun. But Cordelia saw that the bottom windows were shining and that the white net curtains were clean. Mrs. Gladwin was probably a careful housewife, struggling to keep up her standards but too old for the heavy work and too poor to afford help. Cordelia felt benevolently towards her. But the woman who, after some minutes, finally opened to her knock —the bell was out of order—was a disconcerting antidote to her

662

sentimental pity. Compassion died before those hard distrustful eyes, that mouth tight as a trap, the thin arms clasped in a bony barrier across her chest as if to repell human contact. It was difficult to guess her age. Her hair, screwed back into a small tight bun, was still black but her face was deeply lined and the sinews and veins stood out in the thin neck like cords. She was wearing carpet slippers and a gaudy cotton overall. Cordelia said:

"My name is Cordelia Gray. I wondered if I could talk to Dr. Gladwin, if he's in. It's about an old patient."

"He's in, where else would he be? He's in the garden. You'd better go through."

The house smelt horrible, an amalgam of extreme old age, the sour taint of excreta and stale food, with an overlay of strong disinfectant. Cordelia went through to the garden, carefully avoiding looking at the hall or kitchen since curiosity might seem impertinent.

Dr. Gladwin was sitting in a high Windsor chair placed in the sun. Cordelia had never seen a man so old. He seemed to be wearing a woollen track suit, his swollen legs were encased in immense felt slippers and there was a knitted patchwork shawl across his knees. His two hands hung over the arms of the chair as if too heavy for the frail wrists, hands stained and brittle as autumn leaves which trembled with a gentle insistence. The high-domed skull, spiked with a few grey bristles, looked as small and vulnerable as a child's. The eyes were pale yokes swimming in their glutinous blue-veined whites.

Cordelia went to him and called him gently by his name. There was no response. She knelt on the grass at his feet and looked up into his face.

"Dr. Gladwin, I wanted to talk to you about a patient. It was a long time ago. Mrs. Callender. Do you remember Mrs. Callender of Garforth House?"

There was no reply. Cordelia knew that there wouldn't be. Even to ask again seemed an outrage. Mrs. Gladwin was standing beside him as if displaying him to a wondering world.

"Go on, ask him! It's all in his head you know. That's what he used to tell me. 'I'm not one for records and notes. It's all in my head.' "

663

Cordelia said:

"What happened to his medical records when he gave up practice? Did any one take them over?"

"That's what I've just told you. There never were any records. And it's no use asking me. I told the boy that too. The doctor was glad enough to marry me when he wanted a nurse, but he didn't discuss his patients. Oh, dear no! He was drinking all the practice profits away, but he could still talk about medical ethics."

The bitterness in her voice was horrible. Cordelia could not meet her eyes. Just then she thought she saw the old man's lips move. She bent down her head and caught the one word. "Cold."

"I think he's trying to say that he's cold. Is there another shawl perhaps that he could have round his shoulders?"

"Cold! In this sun! He's always cold."

"But perhaps another blanket would help. Shall I fetch it for you?"

"You let him be, Miss. If you want to look after him, then look after him. See how you enjoy keeping him clean like a baby, washing his nappies, changing the bed every morning. I'll get him another shawl, but in two minutes he'll be pushing it off. He doesn't know what he wants."

"I'm sorry," said Cordelia helplessly. She wondered whether Mrs. Gladwin was getting all the help available, whether the District Nurse called, whether she had asked her doctor to try to find a hospital bed. But these were useless questions. Even she could recognize the hopeless rejection of help, the despair which no longer had energy even to look for relief. She said:

"I'm sorry; I won't trouble either of you any further."

They walked back together through the house. But there was one question Cordelia had to ask. When they reached the front gate she said:

"You talked about a boy who visited. Was his name Mark?"

"Mark Callender. He was asking about his mother. And then about ten days later we get the other one calling."

"What other one?"

"He was a gentleman all right. Walked in as if he owned the place. He wouldn't give a name but I've seen his face somewhere.

664

He asked to see Dr. Gladwin and I showed him in. We were sitting in the back parlour that day as there was a breeze. He went up to the doctor and said 'Good afternoon, Gladwin' loudly as if talking to a servant. Then he bent down and looked at him. Eye to eye they were. Then he straightened up, wished me good day and left. Oh, we're getting popular, we are! Any more of you and I'll have to charge for the show."

They stood together at the gate. Cordelia wondered whether to hold out her hand but sensed that Mrs. Gladwin was willing her not to go. Suddenly the woman spoke in a loud and gruff voice, looking straight ahead.

"That friend of yours, the boy who came here. He left his address. He said he wouldn't mind sitting with the doctor on a Sunday if I wanted a break; he said he could get them both a bit of dinner. I have a fancy to see my sister over at Haverhill this Sunday. Tell him he can come if he wants to."

The capitulation was ungracious, the invitation grudging, but Cordelia could guess what it had cost her to give it. She said impulsively:

"I could come on Sunday instead. I've got a car, I could get here sooner."

It would be a day lost to Sir Ronald Callender, but she wouldn't charge him. And even a private eye was surely entitled to a day off on Sundays.

"He won't want a slip of a girl. There's things to do for him that need a man. He took to that boy. I could see that. Tell him he can come."

Cordelia turned to her.

"He would have come, I know he would. But he can't. He's dead."

Mrs. Gladwin did not speak. Cordelia put out a tentative hand and touched her sleeve. There was no response. She whispered:

"I'm sorry. I'll go now." She nearly added: "If there's nothing I can do for you," but stopped herself in time. There was nothing she or anyone could do.

She looked back once as the road bent towards Bury and saw the rigid figure still at the gate.

Cordelia wasn't sure what made her decide to stop at Bury and walk for ten minutes in the Abbey gardens. But she felt she couldn't face the drive back to Cambridge without calming her spirits and the glimpse of grass and flowers through the great Norman doorway was irresistible. She parked the Mini on Angel Hill, then walked through the gardens to the river bank. There she sat for five minutes in the sun. She remembered that there was money spent on petrol to be recorded in her notebook and felt for it in her bag. Her hand brought out the white prayer book. She sat quietly thinking. Suppose she had been Mrs. Callender and had wanted to leave a message, a message which Mark would find and other searchers might miss. Where would she place it? The answer now seemed childishly simple. Surely somewhere on the page with the collect, gospel and epistle for St. Mark's Day. He had been born on April 25th. He had been named after the Saint. Quickly she found the place. In the bright sunlight reflected from the water she saw what a quick rustle through the pages had missed. There against Cranmer's gentle petition for grace to withstand the blasts of false doctrine was a small pattern of hieroglyphics so faint that the mark on the paper was little more than a smudge. She saw that it was a group of letters and figures.

E M C
A   A
14.1.52

The first three letters, of course, were his mother's initials. The date must be that on which she wrote the message. Hadn't Mrs. Goddard said that Mrs. Callender had died when her son was about nine months old? But the double A? Cordelia's mind chased after motoring associations before she remembered the card in Mark's wallet. Surely these two letters under an initial could only show one thing, the blood group. Mark had been B. His mother was AA. There was only one reason why she should have wanted him to have that information. The next step was to discover Sir Ronald Callender's group.

She almost cried out with triumph as she ran through the gardens and turned the Mini again towards Cambridge. She

666

hadn't thought out the implications of this discovery, or even whether her arguments were valid. But at least she had something to do, at least she had a lead. She drove fast, desperate to get to the city before the post office closed. There, she seemed to remember, it was possible to get a copy of the Executive Council's list of local doctors. It was handed over. And now for a telephone. She knew only one house in Cambridge where there was a chance of being left in peace to telephone for up to an hour. She drove to 57, Norwich Street.

Sophie and Davie were at home playing chess in the sitting-room, fair head and dark almost touching over the board. They showed no surprise at Cordelia's plea to use the telephone for a series of calls.

"I'll pay, of course. I'll make a note of how many."

"You'll want the room to yourself, I expect?" said Sophie. "We'll finish the game in the garden, Davie."

Blessedly incurious they carried the chess board with care through the kitchen and set it up on the garden table. Cordelia drew a chair to the table and settled down with her list. It was formidably long. There was no clue about where to begin but perhaps those doctors with group practices and addresses near the centre of the city would be the best bet. She would start with them, ticking off their names after each call. She remembered another reported pearl of the Superintendent's wisdom: "Detection requires a patient persistence which amounts to obstinacy." She thought of him as she dialled the first number. What an intolerably demanding and irritating boss he must have been! But he was almost certainly old now—forty-five at least. He had probably eased up a bit by now.

But an hour's obstinacy was unfruitful. Her calls were invariably answered; one advantage of ringing a doctor's surgery was that the telephone was at least manned. But the replies, given politely, curtly or in tones of harassed haste by a variety of respondents from the doctors themselves to obliging daily women prepared to convey a message, were the same. Sir Ronald Callender was not a patient of this practice. Cordelia repeated her formula. "I'm so sorry to have troubled you. I must have misheard the name."

But after nearly seventy minutes of patient dialling she struck lucky. The doctor's wife answered.

"I'm afraid you've got the wrong practice. Dr. Venables looks after Sir Ronald Callender's household."

This was luck indeed! Dr. Venables wasn't on her preliminary list and she wouldn't have reached the V's for at least another hour. She ran her finger quickly down the names and dialled for the last time.

It was Dr. Venables' nurse who answered. Cordelia spoke her prepared piece:

"I'm ringing for Miss Leaming from Garforth House. I'm sorry to trouble you but could you please remind us of Sir Ronald Callender's blood group? He wants to know it before the Helsinki Conference next month."

"Just a minute, please." There was a brief wait; the sound of footsteps returning.

"Sir Ronald is Group A. I should make a careful note of it if I were you. His son had to ring a month or so ago with the same enquiry."

"Thank you! Thank you! I'll be careful to make a note." Cordelia decided to take a risk.

"I'm new here, assisting Miss Leaming, and she did tell me to note it down last time but stupidly I forgot. If she should happen to call, please don't tell her that I had to trouble you again."

The voice laughed, indulgent to the inefficiency of the young. After all, it wasn't likely to inconvenience her much.

"Don't worry—, I shan't tell her. I'm glad she's got herself some help at last. Everyone's well, I hope?"

"Oh, yes! Everyone's fine."

Cordelia put down the receiver. She looked out of the window and saw that Sophie and Davie were just finishing their game and were putting the pieces back in the box. She had just finished in time. She knew the answer to her query but she still had to verify it. The information was too important to leave to her own vague recollection of the Mendelian rules of inheritance gleaned from the chapter on blood and identity in Bernie's book on forensic medicine. Davie would know, of course. The quickest way would be to ask him now. But she couldn't ask Davie. It

would mean going back to the public library, and she would have to hurry if she were to be there before it closed.

But she got there just in time. The librarian, who by now had got used to seeing her, was as helpful as ever. The necessary reference book was quickly produced. Cordelia verified what she had already known. A man and wife both of whose bloods were A could not produce a B group child.

❦

Cordelia was very tired by the time she got back to the cottage. So much had happened during one day; so much had been discovered. It seemed impossible that less than twelve hours previously she had started out on her search for Nanny Pilbeam with only a vague hope that the woman, if she could be found, might provide a clue to Mark Callender's personality, might tell her something about his formative years. She was exhilarated by the success of the day, restless with excitement, but too mentally exhausted to tease out the tangle of conjecture which lay knotted at the back of her mind. At present the facts were disordered; there was no clear pattern, no theory which would at once explain the mystery of Mark's birth, Isabelle's terror, Hugo and Sophie's secret knowledge, Miss Markland's obsessive interest in the cottage, Sergeant Maskell's almost reluctant suspicions, the oddities and unexplained inconsistencies which surrounded Mark's death.

She busied herself about the cottage with the energy of mental overtiredness. She washed the kitchen floor, laid a fire on top of the heap of ash in case the next evening should be chilly, weeded the back flower patch, then made herself a mushroom omelette and ate it sitting, as he must have done, at the simple table. Last of all, she fetched the gun from its hiding place and set it on the table beside the bed. She locked the back door carefully and drew the curtains across the window, checking once more that the seals were intact. But she didn't balance a saucepan on the top of her door. Tonight that particular precaution seemed childish and unnecessary. She lit her bedside candle then went

669

to the window to choose a book. The night was balmy and windless; the flame of the candle burned steadily in the still air. Outside, darkness had not yet fallen but the garden was very quiet, the peace broken only by the distant crescendo of a car on the main road or the cry of a night bird. And then, seen dimly through the gloaming, she glimpsed a figure at the gate. It was Miss Markland. The woman hesitated, hand on the latch, as if wondering whether to enter the garden. Cordelia slipped to one side, back pressed against the wall. The shadowy figure was so still that it seemed as if she sensed a watching presence and had frozen like an animal surprised. Then, after two minutes, she moved away and was lost among the trees of the orchard. Cordelia relaxed, took a copy of *The Warden* from Mark's row of books, and wriggled into her sleeping-bag. Half an hour later, she blew out the candle and stretched her body comfortably for the slow acquiescent descent into sleep.

She stirred in the early hours and was instantly awake, eyes wide open in the half darkness. Time lay suspended; the still air was expectant as if the day had been taken by surprise. She could hear the ticking of her wrist watch on the bedside table and could see beside it the crooked, comforting outline of the pistol, the black cylinder of her torch. She lay and listened to the night. One lived so seldom in these still hours, the time most often slept or dreamt away, that one came to them tentative and unpractised like a creature newly born. She wasn't aware of fear, only of an all-embracing peace, a gentle lassitude. Her breathing filled the quiet room, and the still, uncontaminated air seemed to be breathing in unity with her.

Suddenly, she realized what had woken her. Visitors were coming to the cottage. She must subconsciously in some brief phase of uneasy sleep have recognized the sound of a car. Now there was the whine of the gate, the rustle of feet, furtive as an animal in undergrowth, a faint, broken murmur of voices. She wriggled out of her sleeping-bag and stole to the window. Mark hadn't attempted to clean the glass of the front windows; perhaps he hadn't had time, perhaps he welcomed their occluding dirt. Cordelia rubbed her fingers with desperate haste against the gritty accretion of years. But, at last, she felt the cold smooth

glass. It squeaked with the friction of her fingers, high and thin like an animal's squeal so that she thought the noise must betray her. She peered through the narrow strip of clear pane into the garden below.

The Renault was almost hidden by the high hedge but she could see the front of the bonnet gleaming by the gate and the two pools of light from the side lamps shining like twin moons on the lane. Isabelle was wearing something long and clinging; her pale figure trembled like a wave against the dark of the hedge. Hugo was only a black shadow at her side. But then he turned and Cordelia saw the flash of a white shirt-front. They were both in evening dress. They came together quietly up the path and conferred briefly at the front door, then moved towards the corner of the cottage.

Snatching up her torch, Cordelia rushed on silent, naked feet down the stairs and threw herself across the sitting-room to unlock the back door. The key turned easily and silently. Hardly daring to breath she retreated back into the shadows at the foot of the stairs. She was just in time. The door opened, letting in a shaft of paler light. She heard Hugo's voice:

"Just a minute, I'll strike a match."

The match flared, illuminating in a gentle, momentary light the two grave anticipatory faces, Isabelle's immense and terrified eyes. Then it went out. She heard Hugo's muttered curse followed by the scratch of the second match striking against the box. This time he held it high. It shone on the table, on the mute accusing hook; on the silent watcher at the foot of the stairs. Hugo gasped; his hand jerked and the match went out. Immediately, Isabelle began to scream.

Hugo's voice was sharp.

"What the hell——"

Cordelia switched on her torch and came forward.

"It's only me; Cordelia."

But Isabelle was beyond hearing. The screams rang out with such piercing intensity that Cordelia half feared that the Marklands must hear. The sound was inhuman, the shriek of animal terror. It was cut short by the swing of Hugo's arm; the sound of a slap; a gasp. It was succeeded by a second of

absolute silence, then Isabelle collapsed against Hugo sobbing quietly.

He turned harshly on Cordelia:

"What the hell did you do that for?"

"Do what?"

"You terrified her, lurking there. What are you doing here anyway?"

"I could ask you that."

"We came to collect the Antonello which Isabelle lent to Mark when she came to supper with him, and to cure her of a certain morbid obsession with this place. We've been to the Pitt Club Ball. It seemed a good idea to call here on our way home. Obviously, it was a bloody stupid idea. Is there any drink in the cottage?"

"Only beer."

"Oh God, Cordelia, there would be! She needs something stronger."

"There isn't anything stronger, but I'll make coffee. You set a light to the fire. It's laid."

She stood the torch upright on the table and lit the table lamp, turning the wick low, then helped Isabelle into one of the fireside chairs.

The girl was trembling. Cordelia fetched one of Mark's heavy sweaters and placed it round her shoulders. The kindling began to flame under Hugo's careful hands. Cordelia went into the kitchen to make coffee, laying her torch on its side at the edge of the window sill so that it shone on the oil stove. She lit the stronger of the two burners and took from the shelf a brown earthenware jug, the two blue-rimmed mugs and a cup for herself. A second and chipped cup held the sugar. It took only a couple of minutes to boil half a kettle of water and to pour it over the coffee grains. She could hear Hugo's voice from the sitting-room, low, urgent, consolatory, interposed with Isabelle's monosyllabic replies. Without waiting for the coffee to brew she placed it on the only tray, a bent tin one patterned with a chipped picture of Edinburgh castle, and carried it into the sitting room, setting it down in the hearth. The faggots spluttered and blazed, shooting out a falling shower of bright sparks which patterned

Isabelle's dress with stars. Then a stouter brand caught flame and the fire glowed with a stronger, more mellow, heart.

As she bent forward to stir the coffee Cordelia saw a small beetle scurrying in desperate haste along the ridges of one of the small logs. She picked up a twig from the kindling still in the hearth and held it out as a way of escape. But it confused the beetle still more. It turned in panic and raced back towards the flame, then doubled in its tracks and fell finally into a split in the wood. Cordelia pictured its fall into black burning darkness and wondered whether it briefly comprehended its dreadful end. Putting a match to a fire was such a trivial act to cause such agony, such terror.

She handed Isabelle and Hugo their mugs and took her own. The comforting smell of fresh coffee mingled with the resinous tang of the burning wood. The fire threw long shadows over the tiled floor and the oil lamp cast its gentle glow over their faces. Surely, thought Cordelia, no murder suspects could have been interrogated in a cosier setting. Even Isabelle had lost her fears. Whether it was the reassurance of Hugo's arm across her shoulders, the stimulus of the coffee or the homely warmth and crackle of the fire, she seemed almost at ease.

Cordelia said to Hugo:

"You said that Isabelle was morbidly obsessed by this place. Why should she be?"

"Isabelle's very sensitive; she isn't tough like you."

Cordelia privately thought that all beautiful women were tough—how else could they survive?—and that Isabelle's fibres could compare well for resilience with her own. But nothing would be gained by challenging Hugo's illusions. Beauty was fragile, transitory, vulnerable. Isabelle's sensitivities must be protected. The toughies could look after themselves. She said:

"According to you, she's only been here once before. I know that Mark Callender died in this room, but you hardly expect me to believe that she's grieving over Mark. There's something that both of you know and it would be better if you told me now. If you don't I shall have to report to Sir Ronald Callender that Isabelle, your sister and you are somehow concerned in his son's death and it will be up to him to decide whether to call in the

673

police. I can't see Isabelle standing up to even the mildest police questioning, can you?"

Even to Cordelia it sounded a stilted, sententious little speech, an unsubstantiated accusation backed up by an empty threat. She half expected Hugo to counter it with amused contempt. But he looked at her for a minute as if assessing more than the reality of the danger. Then he said quietly:

"Can't you accept my word that Mark died by his own hand and that if you do call in the police it will cause unhappiness and distress to his father, to his friends and be absolutely no help to anyone?"

"No, Hugo, I can't."

"Then if we do tell you what we know, will you promise that it won't go any further?"

"How can I, any more than I can promise to believe you?"

Suddenly Isabelle cried:

"Oh, tell her, Hugo! What does it matter?"

Cordelia said:

"I think that you must. I don't think you've any choice."

"So it seems. All right." He put his coffee mug down in the hearth and looked into the fire.

"I told you that we went—Sophie, Isabelle, Davie and I—to the Arts Theatre on the night Mark died but that, as you've probably guessed, was only three-quarters true. They had only three seats left when I booked so we allocated them to the three people mostly likely to enjoy the play. Isabelle goes to the theatre to be seen rather than to see and is bored by any show with a cast of less than fifty, so she was the one left out. Thus neglected by her current lover, she very reasonably decided to seek consolation with the next."

Isabelle said with a secret, anticipatory smile:

"Mark was not my lover, Hugo."

She spoke without rancour or resentment. It was a matter of putting the record straight.

"I know. Mark was a romantic. He never took a girl to bed—or anywhere else that I could see—until he judged that there was an adequate depth of inter-personal communication, or whatever jargon he used, between them. Actually, that's unfair.

It's my father who uses bloody awful meaningless phrases like that. But Mark agreed with the general idea. I doubt whether he could enjoy sex until he'd convinced himself that he and the girl were in love. It was a necessary preliminary—like undressing. I gather that with Isabelle the relationship hadn't reached the necessary depths, hadn't achieved the essential emotional rapport. It was only a matter of time, of course. Where Isabelle was concerned, Mark was as capable of self-deception as the rest of us."

The high, slightly hesitant voice was edged with jealousy.

Isabelle said, slowly and patiently, like a mother explaining to a wilfully obtuse child:

"Mark never made love to me, Hugo."

"That's what I'm saying. Poor Mark! He exchanged the substance for the shadow and now he has neither."

"But what happened that night?"

Cordelia spoke to Isabelle, but it was Hugo who replied.

"Isabelle drove here and arrived shortly after half past seven. The curtains were drawn across the back window, the front one is inpenetrable anyway, but the door was open. She came in. Mark was already dead. His body was hanging by the strap from that hook. But he didn't look as he did when Miss Markland found him next morning."

He turned to Isabelle:

"You tell her." She hesitated. Hugo bent forward and kissed her lightly on the lips.

"Go on, tell. There are some unpleasantnesses which all Papa's money can't entirely shield from you and this, darling, is one."

⋞⊃○⊂⋟

Isabelle turned her head and looked intently into the four corners of the room as if satisfying herself that the three of them were really alone. The irises of her remarkable eyes were purple in the firelight. She leaned towards Cordelia with something of the confiding relish of a village gossip about to relate the latest scandal. Cordelia saw that her panic had left her. Isabelle's agonies were elemental, violent but short lived, easily comforted. She would have kept her secret while Hugo instructed her to

keep it, but she was glad of his order of release. Probably her instinct told her that the story, once told, would lose the sting of terror. She said:

"I thought I would call to see Mark and, perhaps, that we would have supper together. Mademoiselle de Congé was not well and Hugo and Sophie were at the theatre and I was bored. I came to the back door because Mark had told me that the front door would not open. I thought that I might see him in the garden, but he was not there, only the garden fork in the ground and his shoes at the door. So I pushed open the door. I did not knock because I thought that I would be a surprise for Mark."

She hesitated and looked down into the mug of coffee, twisting it between her hands.

"And then?" prompted Cordelia.

"And then I saw him. He was hanging there by the belt from that hook in the ceiling and I knew he was dead. Cordelia, it was horrible! He was dressed like a woman in a black bra and black lace panties. Nothing else. And his face! He had painted his lips, all over his lips Cordelia, like a clown! It was terrible but it was funny too. I wanted to laugh and scream at the same time. He didn't look like Mark. He didn't look like a human being at all. And on the table there were three pictures. Not nice pictures Cordelia. Pictures of naked women."

Her wide eyes stared into Cordelia's, dismayed, uncomprehending. Hugo said:

"Don't look like that, Cordelia. It was horrible for Isabelle at the time and disagreeable to think about now. But it isn't so very uncommon. It does happen. It's probably one of the more innocuous of sexual deviations. He wasn't involving anyone but himself. And he didn't mean to kill himself; that was just bad luck. I imagine that the buckle of the belt slipped and he never had a chance." Cordelia said:

"I don't believe it."

"I thought you might not. But it's true, Cordelia. Why not come with us now and ring Sophie? She'll confirm it."

"I don't need confirmation of Isabelle's story. I already have that. I mean I still don't believe that Mark killed himself."

As soon as she spoke she knew that it had been a mistake. She

676

shouldn't have revealed her suspicions. But it was too late now and there were questions she had to ask. She saw Hugo's face, his quick impatient frown at her obtuseness, her obstinacy. And then she detected a subtle change of mood; was it irritation, fear, disappointment? She spoke directly to Isabelle.

"You said that the door was open. Did you notice the key?"

"It was in this side of the door. I saw it when I went out."

"What about the curtains?"

"They were like now, across the window."

"And where was the lipstick?"

"What lipstick, Cordelia?"

"The one used to paint Mark's lips. It wasn't in the pockets of his jeans or the police would have found it, so where was it? Did you see it on the table?"

"There was nothing on the table except the pictures."

"What colour was the lipstick?"

"Purple. An old lady's colour. No one would choose such a colour I think."

"And the underclothes, could you describe them?"

"Oh, yes! They were from M & S. I recognized them."

"You mean that you recognized those particular ones, that they were yours?"

"Oh, no Cordelia! They were not mine. I never wear black underclothes. I only like white next to my skin. But they were the kind I usually buy. I always get my underclothes from M & S."

Cordelia reflected that Isabelle was hardly one of the store's best customers, but that no other witness would have been as reliable when it came to details, particularly of clothes. Even in that moment of absolute terror and revulsion, Isabelle had noticed the type of underclothes. And if she said that she hadn't seen the lipstick, then it was because the lipstick hadn't been there to see.

Cordelia went on inexorably:

"Did you touch anything, Mark's body perhaps, to see if he was dead?"

Isabelle was shocked. The facts of life she could take in her stride, but not the facts of death.

"I couldn't touch Mark! I touched nothing. And I knew that he was dead."

Hugo said: "A respectable, sensible, law-abiding citizen would have found the nearest telephone and rung the police. Luckily Isabelle is none of these things. Her instinct was to come to me. She waited until the play ended, and then met us outside the theatre. When we came out she was pacing up and down the pavement on the other side of the road. Davie, Sophie and I came back here with her in the Renault. We only stopped briefly at Norwich Street to collect Davie's camera and flash."

"Why?"

"That was my idea. Obviously, we had no intention of letting the fuzz and Ronald Callender know how Mark had died. Our idea was to fake a suicide. We planned to dress him in his own clothes, clean his face and then leave him for someone else to find. We hadn't it in mind to fake a suicide note; that was a refinement somewhat outside our powers. We collected the camera so that we could photograph him as he was. We didn't know what particular law we were breaking in faking a suicide, but there must have been one. You can't do the simplest service for your friends these days without it being liable to misconstruction by the fuzz. If there were trouble we wanted some evidence of the truth. We were all fond of Mark in our different ways, but not fond enough to risk a murder charge. However, our good intentions were frustrated. Someone else had got here first."

"Tell me about it."

"There's nothing to tell. We told the two girls to wait in the car, Isabelle because she had already seen enough and Sophie because Isabelle was too frightened to be left alone. Besides, it seemed only fair to Mark to keep Sophie out of it, to prevent her from seeing him. Don't you find it odd, Cordelia, this concern one has for the susceptibilities of the dead?"

Thinking of her father and Bernie, Cordelia said:

"Perhaps it's only when people are dead that we can safely show how much we cared about them. We know that it's too late then for them to do anything about it."

"Cynical but true. Anyway, there was nothing for us to do here.

678

We found Mark's body and this room as Miss Markland described them at the inquest. The door was open, the curtains drawn across. Mark was naked except for his blue jeans. There were no magazine pictures on the table and no lipstick on his face. But there was a suicide note in the typewriter and a mound of ash in the grate. It looked as if the visitor had made a thorough job of it. We didn't linger. Someone else—perhaps someone from the house—might have turned up at any minute. Admittedly, it was very late by then but it seemed an evening for people to pop in. Mark must have had more visitors that night than during his whole time at the cottage; first Isabelle; then the unknown samaritan; then us."

Cordelia thought that there had been someone before Isabelle. Mark's murderer had been there first. She asked suddenly:

"Someone played a stupid trick on me last night. When I got back here from the party there was a bolster slung from that hook. Did you do that?"

If his surprise were not genuine, then Hugo was a better actor than Cordelia thought possible.

"Of course I didn't! I thought you were living in Cambridge not here. And why on earth should I?"

"To warn me off."

"But that would be crazy! It wouldn't warn you off, would it? It might scare some women, but not you. We wanted to convince you that there was nothing to investigate about Mark's death. That sort of trick would only convince you that there was. Someone else was trying to scare you. The most likely person is the one who came here after us."

"I know. Someone took a risk for Mark. He—or she—won't want me ferreting around. But he would have got rid of me more sensibly by telling me the truth."

"How could he know whether to trust you? What will you do now, Cordelia? Go back to town?"

He was trying to keep his voice casual but she thought she detected the underlying anxiety. She replied.

"I expect so. I'll have to see Sir Ronald first."

"What will you tell him?"

"I'll think of something. Don't worry."

Dawn was staining the eastern sky and the first chorus of birds was noisily contradicting the new day before Hugo and Isabelle left. They took the Antonello with them. Cordelia saw it taken down with a pang of regret as if something of Mark were leaving the cottage. Isabelle examined the picture closely with a grave professional eye before tucking it under her arm. Cordelia thought that she was probably generous enough with her possessions, both people and pictures, provided they were on loan only, to be returned promptly on demand and in the same condition as when she parted with them. Cordelia watched from the front gate as the Renault, with Hugo driving, moved out of the shadow of the hedge. She lifted her hand in a formal gesture of farewell like a weary hostess speeding her final guests, then turned back to the cottage.

The sitting room seemed empty and cold without them. The fire was dying and she hastily pushed in the few remaining sticks from the hearth and blew on them to kindle the flame. She moved restlessly about the little room. She was too lively to go back to bed, but her short and disturbed night had left her edgy with tiredness. But her mind was tormented by something more fundamental than lack of sleep. For the first time she knew that she was afraid. Evil existed—it hadn't needed a convent education to convince her of that reality—and it had been present in this room. Something here had been stronger than wickedness, ruthlessness, cruelty or expedience. Evil. She had no doubt that Mark had been murdered, but with what diabolical cleverness it had been done! If Isabelle told her story, who now would ever believe that he hadn't died accidentally, but by his own hand? Cordelia had no need to refer to her book on forensic medicine to know how it would appear to the police. As Hugo had said, these cases weren't so very uncommon. He, as a psychiatrist's son, would have heard or read of them. Who else would know? Probably any reasonably sophisticated person. But it couldn't have been Hugo. Hugo had an alibi. Her mind revolted at the thought that Davie or Sophie could have participated in such a horror. But how typical that they should have collected the camera. Even their compassion had been overlaid with self concern. Would Hugo and Davie have stood here, under Mark's grotesque

body, calmly discussing distance and exposure before taking the photograph which would, if necessary, exonerate them at his expense?

She went into the kitchen to make tea, glad to be free of the malignant fascination of that hook in the ceiling. Previously it had hardly worried her, now it was as obtrusive as a fetish. It seemed to have grown since the previous night, to be growing still as it drew her eyes compulsively upwards. And the sitting room itself had surely shrunk; no longer a sanctum but a claustrophobic cell, tawdry and shameful as an execution shed. Even the bright morning air was redolent with evil.

Waiting for the kettle to boil she made herself contemplate the day's activities. It was still too early to theorize; her mind was too preoccupied with horror to deal rationally with its new knowledge. Isabelle's story had complicated, not illumined the case. But there were still relevant facts to be discovered. She would go on with the programme she had already planned. Today she would go to London to examine Mark's grandfather's will.

But there were still two hours to get through before it was time to start out. She had decided to travel to London by train and to leave the car at Cambridge station since this would be both quicker and easier. It was irritating to have to spend a day in town when the heart of the mystery so obviously lay in Cambridgeshire, but for once she wasn't sorry at the prospect of leaving the cottage. Shocked and restless, she wandered aimlessly from room to room and prowled around the garden, fretting to be away. Finally in desperation she took hold of the garden fork and completed the digging of Mark's unfinished row. She wasn't sure that this was wise; Mark's interrupted work was part of the evidence for his murder. But other people, including Sergeant Maskell, had seen it and could testify if necessary, and the sight of the partly-completed job, of the fork still askew in the soil, was unbearably irritating. When the row was completed she felt calmer and she dug on without pausing for another hour before carefully cleaning the fork and placing it with the other tools in the garden shed.

At last it was time to go. The seven o'clock weather forecast

681

had prophesied thundery storms in the south-east so she put on her suit, the heaviest protection she had brought with her. She hadn't worn it since Bernie's death and she discovered that the waist band was uncomfortably loose. She had lost some weight. After a moment's thought, she took Mark's belt from the scene-of-crime kit and wound it twice round her waist. She felt no repugnance as the leather tightened against her. It was impossible to believe that anything he had ever touched or owned could frighten or distress her. The strength and heaviness of the leather so close to her skin was even obscurely comforting and reassuring, as if the belt were a talisman.

Chapter Five

❦

The storm broke just as Cordelia alighted from the number 11 bus outside Somerset House. There was a jagged flash of lightning and, almost instantaneously, the thunder crashed like a barrage round her ears and she raced across the inner courtyard between the ranks of parked cars through a wall of water while the rain spouted around her ankles as if the paving stones were being raked with bullets. She pushed open the door and stood draining pools of water on the mat and laughing aloud with relief. One or two of the people present glanced up from their perusal of wills and smiled at her, while a motherly looking woman behind the counter tut-tutted her concern. Cordelia shook her jacket over the mat then hung it on the back of one of the chairs and tried ineffectually to dry her hair with her handkerchief before approaching the counter.

The motherly woman was helpful. Consulted by Cordelia on the correct procedure, she indicated the shelves of heavy, bound volumes in the middle of the hall and explained that the wills were indexed under the surname of the testator and the year in which the document was lodged with Somerset House. It was for Cordelia to trace the catalogue number and bring the volume to the desk. The original will would then be sent for and she could consult it for a fee of 20 pence.

Not knowing when George Bottley had died, Cordelia was in some perplexity where to begin her search. But she deduced that the will must have been made after the birth, or at least the conception, of Mark, since he had been left a fortune by his grandfather. But Mr. Bottley had also left money to his daughter and this part of his fortune had come on her death to her husband. The strong probability was that he had died before her, since otherwise he would surely have made a new will. Cordelia decided to begin her search with the year of Mark's birth, 1951.

Her deductions proved correct. George Albert Bottley of Stonegate Lodge, Harrogate, had died on 26th July 1951, exactly three months and one day after the birth of his grandson and only three weeks after making his will. Cordelia wondered whether his death had been sudden and unexpected or whether this was the will of a dying man. She saw that he had left an estate of nearly three quarters of a million pounds. How had he made this, she wondered? Surely not all from wool. She heaved the heavy book across to the counter, the clerk wrote the details on a white form and pointed out the way to the cashier's office. Within a surprisingly few minutes of paying what seemed to her a modest fee, Cordelia was seated under the light at one of the desks near the window with the will in her hands.

She hadn't liked what she had heard about George Bottley from Nanny Pilbeam and she didn't like him any better after reading his will. She had feared that the document might be long, complicated and difficult to understand; it was surprisingly short, simple and intelligible. Mr. Bottley directed that all his possessions should be sold, "since I wish to prevent the usual unseemly wrangling over bric-à-brac". He left modest sums to servants in his employ at the time of death but there was no mention, Cordelia noticed, of his gardener. He bequeathed half of the residue of his fortune to his daughter, absolutely, "now that she has demonstrated that she has at least one of the normal attributes of a woman." The remaining half he left to his beloved grandson Mark Callender on attaining his twenty-fifth birthday, "by which date, if he hasn't learned the value of money, he will at least be of an age to avoid exploitation." The income from the capital was left to six Bottley relations, some of them, apparently, only distant kinsmen. The will created a residual trust; as each beneficiary died his share would be distributed among the survivors. The testator was confident that this arrangement would promote in the beneficiaries a lively interest in each others' health and survival while encouraging them to achieve the distinction of longevity, no other distinction being within their reach. If Mark died before his twenty-fifth birthday the family trust would continue until all the beneficiaries were dead and the capital would then be distributed among a formidable list of

charities chosen, as far as Cordelia could see, because they were well known and successful rather than because they represented any personal concern or sympathy on the part of the testator. It was as if he had asked his lawyers for a list of the more reliable charities, having no real interest in what happened to his fortune if his own issue were not alive to inherit it.

It was a strange will. Mr. Bottley had left nothing to his son-in-law yet had apparently been unworried by the possibility that his daughter, whom he knew not to be strong, might die and leave her fortune to her husband. In some respects it was a gambler's will and Cordelia wondered again how George Bottley had made his fortune. But, despite the cynical unkindness of its comments, the will was neither unfair nor ungenerous. Unlike some very rich men he hadn't attempted to control his great fortune from beyond the grave, obsessively determined that not one penny should ever get into unfavoured hands. His daughter and his grandson had both been left their fortunes absolutely. It was impossible to like Mr. Bottley but difficult not to respect him. And the implications of his will were very clear. No one stood to gain by Mark's death except a long list of highly respectable charities.

Cordelia made a note of the main clauses of the will, more because of Bernie's insistence on meticulous documentation than from any fear of forgetting them; slipped the receipt for 20p into the expenses page of her notebook; added the cost of her cheap day return ticket from Cambridge and her bus fare, and returned the will to the counter. The storm had been as short as it was violent. The hot sun was already drying the windows and the puddles lay bright on the rain-washed courtyard. Cordelia decided that she ought to charge Sir Ronald for half a day only and spend the rest of her time in London at the office. There might be post to collect. There might even be another case awaiting her.

But the decision was a mistake. The office seemed even more sordid than when she had left it and the air smelt sour in contrast to the rain-washed streets outside. There was a thick film of dust over the furniture and the bloodstain on the rug had deepened into a brick-brown which looked even more sinister

than the original bright red. There was nothing in the letterbox but a final demand from the electricity board and a bill from the stationer. Bernie had paid dearly—or rather, had not paid—for the despised writing paper.

Cordelia wrote a cheque for the electricity bill, dusted the furniture, made one last and unsuccessful attempt to clean the rug. Then she locked the office and set off to walk to Trafalgar Square. She would seek consolation in the National Gallery.

❖⟞○⟝❖

She caught the eighteen-sixteen train from Liverpool Street and it was nearly eight o'clock before she arrived back at the cottage. She parked the Mini in its usual place in the shelter of the copse and made her way round the side of the cottage. She hesitated for a moment wondering whether to collect the gun from its hiding place, but decided that this could wait until later. She was hungry and the first priority was to get a meal. She had carefully locked the back door and had stuck a thin strip of Scotch tape across the window sill before leaving that morning. If there were any more secret visitors she wanted to be warned. But the tape was still intact. She felt in her shoulder bag for the key and, bending down, fitted it into the lock. She wasn't expecting trouble outside the cottage and the attack took her completely by surprise. There was the half-second of pre-knowledge before the blanket fell but that was too late. There was a cord around her neck pulling the mask of hot stifling wool taut against her mouth and nostrils. She gasped for breath and tasted the dry strong-smelling fibres on her tongue. Then a sharp pain exploded in her chest and she remembered nothing.

The movement of liberation was a miracle and a horror. The blanket was whipped off. She never saw her assailant. There was a second of sweet reviving air, a glimpse, so brief that it was barely comprehended, of blinding sky seen through greenness and then she felt herself falling, falling in helpless astonishment into cold darkness. The fall was a confusion of old nightmares, unbelievable seconds of childhood terrors recalled. Then her body hit the water. Ice-cold hands dragged her into a vortex of

horror. Instinctively, she had closed her mouth at the moment of impact and she struggled to the surface through what seemed an eternity of cold encompassing blackness. She shook her head and, through her stinging eyes, she looked up. The black tunnel that stretched above her ended in a moon of blue light. Even as she looked, the well lid was dragged slowly back like the shutter of a camera. The moon became a half moon; then a crescent. At last there was nothing but eight thin slits of light.

Desperately she trod water, reaching tentatively for the bottom. There was no bottom. Frantically moving hands and feet, willing herself not to panic, she felt around the walls of the well for a possible foothold. There was none. The funnel of bricks, smooth, sweating with moisture, stretched around and above her like a circular tomb. As she gazed upwards they writhed, expanded, swayed and reeled like the belly of a monstrous snake.

And then she felt a saving anger. She wouldn't let herself drown, wouldn't die in this horrible place, alone and terrified. The well was deep but small, the diameter barely three feet. If she kept her head and took time, she could brace her legs and shoulders against the bricks and work her way upwards.

She hadn't bruised or stunned herself against the walls as she fell. Miraculously she was uninjured. The fall had been clean. She was alive and capable of thought. She had always been a survivor. She would survive.

She floated on her back, bracing her shoulders against the cold walls, spreading her arms and digging her elbows into the interstices of the bricks to get a better grip. Shuffling off her shoes, she planted both feet against the opposite wall. Just beneath the surface of the water, she could feel that one of the bricks was slightly unaligned. She curved her toes around it. It gave her a precarious but welcome foothold for the start of the climb. By means of it, she could lift her body out of the water and could relieve for a moment the strain on the muscles of her back and thighs.

Then slowly she began to climb, first shifting her feet, one after the other in tiny sliding steps, then humping up her body inch by painful inch. She kept her eyes fixed on the opposite curve of the wall, willing herself not to look down, nor up,

counting progress by the width of each brick. Time passed. She couldn't see Bernie's watch, although its ticking seemed unnaturally loud, a regular obtrusive metronome to the thumping of her heart and the fierce gasping of her breath. The pain in her legs was intense and her shirt was sticking to her back with a warm, almost comforting effusion, which she knew must be blood. She willed herself not to think of the water beneath her or of the thin, but widening clefts of light above. If she were to survive, all her energy must be harnessed for the next painful inch.

Once, her legs slipped and she slithered back several yards before her feet, scrabbling ineffectually against the slimy walls, at last found a purchase. The fall had grazed her injured back and left her whimpering with self-pity and disappointment. She scourged her mind into courage and began climbing again. Once she was gripped by cramp and lay stretched as if on a rack until the agony passed and her fixed muscles could move. From time to time her feet found another small foothold and she was able to stretch her legs and rest. The temptation to stay in comparative safety and ease was almost irresistible and she had to will herself to start again on the slow torturous climb.

It seemed that she had been climbing for hours, moving in a parody of a difficult labour towards some desperate birth. Darkness was falling. The light from the well top was wider now but less strong. She told herself that the climb wasn't really difficult. It was only the darkness and loneliness which made it seem so. If this were a fabricated obstacle race, an exercise in the school gymnasium, surely she could have done it easily enough. She filled her mind with the comforting images of rib stools and vaulting horses, of the fifth form shouting their encouragement. Sister Perpetua was there. But why wasn't she looking at Cordelia? Why had she turned away? Cordelia called her and the figure turned slowly and smiled at her. But it wasn't Sister after all. It was Miss Leaming, the lean pale face sardonic under the white veil.

And now when she knew that, unaided, she could get no further, Cordelia saw salvation. A few feet above her was the bottom rung of a short wooden ladder fixed to the last few feet of

the well. At first she thought that it was an illusion, a phantasm born of exhaustion and despair. She shut her eyes for a few minutes; her lips moved. Then she opened her eyes again. The ladder was still there, seen dimly but comfortingly solid in the fading light. She lifted impotent hands towards it knowing, even as she did so, that it was out of reach. It could save her life and she knew that she hadn't the strength to reach it.

It was then, without conscious thought or scheming, that she remembered the belt. Her hand dropped to her waist feeling for the heavy brass buckle. She undid it and drew the long snake of leather from her body. Carefully she threw the buckled end towards the bottom rung of the ladder. The first three times the metal struck the wood with a sharp crack but didn't fall over the rung; the fourth time it did. She pushed the other end of the belt gently upwards and the buckle dropped towards her until she could stretch out her hand and grasp it. She fastened it to the other end to form a strong loop. Then she pulled, at first very gently and then harder until most of her weight was on the strap. The relief was indescribable. She braced herself against the brickwork, gathering strength for the final triumphant effort. Then it happened. The rung, rotted at its joints, broke loose with a harsh tearing sound and spun past her into darkness, just missing her head. It seemed minutes rather than seconds before the distant splash reverberated round the wall.

She unbuckled the belt and tried again. The next rung was a foot higher and the throw more difficult. Even this small effort was exhausting in her present state and she made herself take time. Every unsuccessful throw made the next more difficult. She didn't count the number of attempts, but at last the buckle fell over the rung and dropped towards her. When it snaked within reach she found that she could only just buckle the strap. The next rung would be too high. If this one broke, it would be the end.

But the rung held. She had no clear memory of the last half hour of the climb but at last she reached the ladder and strapped herself firmly to the uprights. For the first time she was physically safe. As long as the ladder held she needn't fear falling. She let herself relax into brief unconsciousness. But then the wheels of

the mind which had been spinning blissfully free, took hold again and she began to think. She knew that she had no hope of moving the heavy wooden cover unaided. She stretched out both hands and pushed against it but it didn't shift, and the high concave dome made it impossible for her to brace her shoulders against the wood. She would have to rely on outside help and that wouldn't come till daylight. It might not come even then, but she pushed the thought away. Sooner or later Miss Markland would come to the cottage. Sooner or later someone would come. She could hope to hold on, thus strapped, for several days. Even if she lost consciousness there was a chance that she would be rescued alive. Miss Markland knew that she was at the cottage; her things were still there. Miss Markland would come.

She gave thought to how she could attract attention. There was room to push something between the boards of wood if only she had something sufficiently stiff to push. The edge of the buckle was possible provided she strapped herself more tightly. But that must wait until the morning. There was nothing she could do now. She would relax and sleep and await rescue.

And then the final horror burst upon her. There would be no rescue. Someone would be coming to the well, coming on quiet and stealthy feet under the cover of darkness. But it would be her murderer. He had to return; it was part of his plan. The attack, which at the time had seemed so astonishingly, so brutally stupid, hadn't been stupid at all. It was intended to look like an accident. He would come back that night and remove the well cover again. Then, some time next day or within the next few days, Miss Markland would blunder through the garden and discover what had happened. No one would ever be able to prove that Cordelia's death wasn't an accident. She recalled the words of Sergeant Maskell: "It isn't what you suspect; it's what you can prove." But this time would there even be suspicion? Here was a young, impulsive, over-curious young woman living at the cottage without the owner's authority. She had obviously decided to explore the well. She had smashed the padlock, drawn back the lid with the coil of rope which the killer would leave ready to be found, and tempted by the ladder, had let herself down those few

steps until the final rung broke beneath her. Her prints and no one else's would be found on the ladder, if they took the trouble to look. The cottage was utterly deserted; the chance that her murderer would be seen returning was remote. There was nothing she could do but wait until she heard his footsteps, his heavy breathing, and the lid was drawn slowly back to reveal his face.

After the first intensity of terror, Cordelia waited for death without hope and without further struggle. There was even a kind of peace in resignation. Strapped like a victim to the uprights of the ladder she drifted mercifully into brief oblivion and prayed that it might be so when her killer returned, that she might not be conscious at the moment of the final blow. She had no longer any interest in seeing her murderer's face. She wouldn't humiliate herself by pleading for her life, wouldn't beg for mercy from a man who had strung up Mark. She knew that there would be no mercy.

But she was conscious when the well lid began slowly to move. The light came in above her bowed head. The gap widened. And then she heard a voice, a woman's voice, low, urgent and sharp with terror.

"Cordelia!"

She looked up.

Kneeling at the rim of the well, her pale face immense and seeming to float disembodied in space like the phantasm of a nightmare, was Miss Markland. And the eyes which stared into Cordelia's face were as wild with terror as her own.

Ten minutes later Cordelia was lying slumped in the fireside chair. Her whole body ached and she was powerless to control her violent shivering. Her thin shirt was stuck to her wounded back and every shift of movement was pain. Miss Markland had put a light to the kindling and was now making coffee. Cordelia could hear her moving to and fro in the little kitchen and could smell the stove as it was turned high and, soon, the evocative aroma of coffee. These familiar sights and sounds would normally have been reassuring and comforting, but now she was desperate to be alone. The killer would still return. He had to return, and when he did, she wanted to be there to meet him. Miss Markland brought in the two mugs and pressed one into Cordelia's shivering

691

hands. She stumped upstairs and came down with one of Mark's jumpers which she wound round the girl's neck. Her terror had left her, but she was as agitated as a young girl sharing her first half-shameful adventure. Her eyes were wild, her whole body trembled with excitement. She sat down directly in front of Cordelia and fixed her with her sharp inquisitive eyes.

"How did it happen? You must tell me."

Cordelia had not forgotten how to think.

"I don't know. I can't remember anything that happened before I hit the water. I must have decided to explore the well and lost my balance."

"But the well lid! The lid was in place!"

"I know. Someone must have replaced it."

"But why? Who would have come this way?"

"I don't know. But someone must have seen it. Someone must have dragged it back."

She said more gently:

"You saved my life. How did you notice what had happened?"

"I came to the cottage to see if you were still here. I came earlier today but there was no sign of you. There was a coil of rope—the one that you used, I expect—left in the path and I stumbled over it. Then I noticed that the well lid wasn't quite in place and that the padlock had been smashed."

"You saved my life," said Cordelia again, "but please go now. Please go. I'm all right, really I am."

"But you aren't fit to be left alone! And that man—the one who replaced the lid—he might return. I don't like to think of strangers snooping around the cottage and you here alone."

"I'm perfectly safe. Besides, I have a gun. I only want to be left in peace to rest. Please don't worry about me!"

Cordelia could detect the note of desperation, almost of hysteria, in her own voice.

But Miss Markland seemed not to hear. Suddenly she was on her knees in front of Cordelia and pouring out a spate of high, excited chatter. Without thought and without compassion, she was confiding to the girl her terrible story, a story of her son, the four-year-old child of herself and her lover, who had broken his way through the cottage hedge and fallen into the well to

his death. Cordelia tried to shake herself free from the wild eyes. It was surely all a fantasy. The woman must be mad. And if it were true, it was horrible and unthinkable and she could not bear to hear it. Sometime later she would remember it, remember every word, and think of the child, of his last terror, his desperate cry for his mother, the cold suffocating water dragging him to his death. She would live his agony in nightmares as she would re-live her own. But not now. Through the spate of words, the self-accusations, the terror recalled, Cordelia recognized the note of liberation. What to her had been horror, to Miss Markland had been release. A life for a life. Suddenly Cordelia could bear it no longer. She said violently:

"I'm sorry! I'm sorry! You've saved my life and I'm grateful. But I can't bear to listen. I don't want you here. For God's sake go!"

All her life she would remember the woman's hurt face, her silent withdrawal. Cordelia didn't hear her go, didn't remember the soft closing of the door. All she knew was that she was alone. The shaking was over now although she still felt very cold. She went upstairs and pulled on her slacks then unwound Mark's jumper from her neck and put it on. It would cover the blood stains on her shirt and the warmth was immediately comforting. She was moving very quickly. She felt for the ammunition, took her torch and let herself out of the back door of the cottage. The gun was where she had left it, in the fold of the tree. She loaded it and felt its familiar shape and heaviness in her hand. Then she stood back among the bushes and waited.

It was too dark to see the dial of her wrist watch but Cordelia reckoned that she must have waited there immobile in the shadows for nearly half an hour before her ears caught the sound for which she was waiting. A car was approaching down the lane. Cordelia held her breath. The sound of the engine reached a brief crescendo and then faded away. The car had driven on without stopping. It was unusual for a car to pass down the lane after dark and she wondered who it could be.

Again she waited, moving deeper into the shelter of the elder bush so that she could rest her back against the bark. She had been clutching the gun so tightly that her right wrist ached and she moved the pistol to her other hand and rotated the wrist slowly, stretching the cramped fingers.

Again she waited. The slow minutes passed. The silence was broken only by the furtive scuffling of some small night prowler in the grass and the sudden wild hoot of an owl. And then once more she heard the sound of an engine. This time the noise was faint and it came no closer. Someone had stopped a car further up the road.

She took the gun in her right hand, cradling the muzzle with her left. Her heart was pounding so loudly that she felt its wild hammering must betray her. She imagined rather than heard the thin whine of the front gate but the sound of feet moving round the cottage was unmistakable and clear. And now he was in sight, a stocky, broad-shouldered figure, black against the light. He moved towards her and she could see her shoulder bag hanging from his left shoulder. The discovery disconcerted her. She had completely forgotten the bag. But now she had realized why he had seized it. He had wanted to search it for evidence, but it was important that, finally, it should be discovered with her body in the well.

He came forward gently on tip-toe, his long simian arms held stiffly away from his body like a caricature of a film cowboy ready for the draw. When he got to the rim of the well he waited and the moon struck the white of his eyes as he gazed slowly round. Then he bent down and felt in the grass for the coil of rope. Cordelia had lain it where Miss Markland had found it, but something about it, some slight difference perhaps in the way it was coiled, seemed to strike him. He rose uncertainly and stood for a moment with the rope dangling from his hand. Cordelia tried to control her breathing. It seemed impossible that he should not hear, smell or see her, that he should be so like a predator yet without the beast's instinct for the enemy in the dark. He moved forward. Now he was at the well. He bent and threaded one end of the rope through the iron hoop.

Cordelia moved with one step out of the darkness. She held

the gun firmly and straight as Bernie had shown her. This time the target was very close. She knew that she wouldn't fire but, in that moment, she knew too what it was that could make a man kill. She said loudly:

"Good evening, Mr. Lunn."

She never knew whether he saw the gun. But for one unforgettable second, as the clouded moon sailed into the open sky, she saw his face clearly; saw the hate, the despair, the agony and the rictus of terror. He gave one hoarse cry, threw down the shoulder bag and the rope and rushed through the garden in a blind panic. She gave chase, hardly knowing why, or what she hoped to achieve, determined only that he shouldn't get back to Garforth House before her. And still she didn't fire the gun.

But he had an advantage. As she threw herself through the gate she saw that he had parked the van some fifty yards up the road and left the engine running. She chased after him but could see that it was hopeless. Her only hope of catching up with him was to get the Mini. She tore down the lane feeling in her shoulder bag as she ran. The prayer book and her note book were both gone but her fingers found the car keys. She unlocked the Mini, threw herself in and reversed it violently onto the road. The rear lights of the van were about a hundred yards ahead of her. She didn't know what speed it could do, but doubted whether it could out-pace the Mini. She trod on the accelerator and gave pursuit. She turned left out of the lane on to the subsidiary road and now she could see the van still ahead. He was driving fast and was holding the distance. Now the road turned and for a few seconds he was out of sight. He must be getting very close now to the junction with the Cambridge road.

She heard the crash just before she herself reached the junction, an instantaneous explosion of sound which shook the hedges and made the little car tremble. Cordelia's hands tightened momentarily on the wheel and the Mini jerked to a stop. She ran forward round the corner and saw before her the gleaming, headlamp lit surface of the main Cambridge road. It was peopled with running shapes. The transporter, still upright, was an immense oblong mass blocking the sky line, a barricade slewed

across the road. The van had crumpled under its front wheels like a child's toy. There was a smell of petrol, a woman's harsh scream, the squeal of braking tyres. Cordelia walked slowly up to the transporter. The driver was still in his seat, gazing rigidly ahead, his face a mask of dedicated concentration. People were shouting at him, stretching out their arms. He didn't move. Someone—a man in a heavy leather coat and goggles—said:

"It's shock. We'd better drag him clear."

Three figures moved between Cordelia and the driver. Shoulders heaved in unison. There was a grunt of effort. The driver was lifted out, rigid as a manikin, his knees bent, his clenched hands held out as if still grasping the immense wheel. The shoulders bent over him in secret conclave.

There were other figures standing round the crushed van. Cordelia joined the ring of anonymous faces. Cigarette ends glowed and faded like signals, casting a momentary glow on the shaking hands, the wide, horrified eyes. She asked:

"Is he dead?" The man in goggles replied laconically:

"What do you think?"

There was a girl's voice, tentative, breathless.

"Has anyone called the ambulance?"

"Yeah. Yeah. That chap in the Cortina's gone off to 'phone."

The group stood irresolute. The girl and the young man to whom she was clinging began to back away. Another car stopped. A tall figure was pushing his way through the crowd. Cordelia heard a high, authoritative voice.

"I'm a doctor. Has anyone called the ambulance?"

"Yes, sir."

The reply was deferential. They stood aside to let the expert through. He turned to Cordelia, perhaps because she was nearest.

"If you didn't witness the accident, young woman, you'd better get on your way. And stand back, the rest of you. There's nothing that you can do. And put out those cigarettes!"

Cordelia walked slowly back to the Mini, placing each foot carefully before the other like a convalescent trying her first painful steps. She drove carefully round the accident, bumping the Mini on the grass verge. There was the wail of approaching sirens. As she turned off the main road, her driving mirror

glowed suddenly red and she heard a whoosh of sound followed by a low, concerted groan which was broken by a woman's high, single scream. There was a wall of flame across the road. The doctor's warning had been too late. The van was on fire. There was no hope now for Lunn; but then, there never had been.

Cordelia knew that she was driving erratically. Passing cars hooted at her and flashed their lights and one motorist slowed down and shouted angrily. She saw a gate and drew in off the road and switched off the engine. The silence was absolute. Her hands were moist and shaking. She wiped them on her handkerchief and laid them in her lap feeling that they were separate from the rest of her body. She was hardly aware of a car passing and then slowing to a halt. A face appeared at the window. The voice was slurred and nervous but horribly ingratiating. She could smell the drink on his breath.

"Anything wrong, Miss?"

"Nothing. I've just stopped for a rest."

"No point in resting alone—a pretty girl like you."

His hand was on the door handle. Cordelia felt in her shoulder bag and drew out the gun. She pushed it into his face.

"It's loaded. Go away at once or I'll shoot."

The menace in her voice struck cold even to her own ears. The pale, moist face disintegrated with surprise, the jaw fell. He backed away.

"Sorry, Miss, I'm sure. My mistake. No offence."

Cordelia waited until his car was out of sight. Then she turned on the engine. But she knew that she couldn't go on. She turned off the engine again. Waves of tiredness flowed over her, an irresistible tide, gentle as a blessing, which neither her exhausted mind nor body had the will to resist. Her head fell forward and Cordelia slept.

Chapter Six

Cordelia slept soundly but briefly. She didn't know what woke her, whether the blinding light of a passing car sweeping across her closed eyes or her own subconscious knowledge that rest must be rationed to a brief half hour, the minimum necessary to enable her to do what had to be done before she could give herself over to sleep. She eased her body upright, feeling the stab of pain in her strained muscles and the half-pleasurable itch of dried blood on her back. The night air was heavy and odorous with the heat and scents of the day; even the road winding ahead looked tacky in the glare of her headlights. But Cordelia's chilled and aching body was still grateful for the warmth of Mark's jersey. For the first time since she had pulled it over her head she saw that it was dark green. How odd that she hadn't noticed its colour before!

She drove the rest of the journey like a novice, sitting bolt upright, eyes rigidly ahead, hands and feet tense on the controls. And here at last were the gates of Garforth House. They loomed in her headlights far taller and more ornamental than she remembered them, and they were closed. She ran from the Mini praying that they wouldn't be locked. But the iron latch, although heavy, rose to her desperate hands. The gates swung soundlessly back.

There were no other cars in the drive and she parked the Mini some little way from the house. The windows were dark and the only light, gentle and inviting, shone through the open front door. Cordelia took the pistol in her hand and, without ringing, stepped into the hall. She was more exhausted in body than when she had first come to Garforth House, but tonight she saw it with a new intensity, her nerves sensitive to every detail. The hall was empty, the air expectant. It seemed as if the house had waited for her. The same smell met her of roses

and lavender, but tonight she saw that the lavender came from a huge Chinese bowl set on a side table. She recalled the insistent ticking of a clock, but now she noticed for the first time the delicate carving of the clock case, the intricate scrolls and whirls on the face. She stood in the middle of the hall, swaying slightly, the pistol held lightly in her drooping right hand, and looked down. The carpet was a formal geometrical design in rich olive greens, pale blues and crimson, each pattern shaped like the shadow of a kneeling man. It seemed to draw her to her knees. Was it perhaps an eastern prayer mat?

She was aware of Miss Leaming coming quietly down the stairs towards her, her long red dressing-gown sweeping round her ankles. The pistol was taken suddenly but firmly from Cordelia's unresisting hand. She knew that it had gone because her hand felt suddenly lighter. It made no difference. She could never defend herself with it, never kill a man. She had learnt that about herself when Lunn had run from her in terror. Miss Leaming said:

"There is no one here you need defend yourself against, Miss Gray."

Cordelia said:

"I've come to report to Sir Ronald. Where is he?"

"Where he was the last time you came here, in his study."

As before, he was sitting at his desk. He had been dictating and the machine was at his right hand. When he saw Cordelia, he switched it off, then walked to the wall and pulled the plug from the socket. He walked back to the desk and they sat down opposite each other. He folded his hands in the pool of light from the desk lamp and looked up at Cordelia. She almost cried out with shock. His face reminded her of faces seen grotesquely reflected in grubby train windows at night—cavernous, the bones stripped of flesh, eyes set in fathomless sockets—faces resurrected from the dead.

When he spoke his voice was low, reminiscent.

"Half an hour ago I learned that Chris Lunn was dead. He was the best lab assistant I ever had. I took him out of an orphanage fifteen years ago. He never knew his parents. He was an ugly, difficult boy, already on probation. School had done

699

nothing for him. But Lunn was one of the best natural scientists I've ever known. If he'd had the education, he'd have been as good as I am."

"Then why didn't you give him his chance, why didn't you educate him?"

"Because he was more useful to me as a lab assistant. I said that he could have been as good as I am. That isn't quite good enough. I can find plenty of scientists as good. I couldn't have found another lab assistant to equal Lunn. He had a marvellous hand with instruments."

He looked up at Cordelia, but without curiosity, apparently without interest.

"You've come to report, of course. It's very late, Miss Gray, and, as you see, I'm tired. Can't it wait until tomorrow?"

Cordelia thought that this was as close to an appeal as he could ever bring himself. She said:

"No, I'm tired too. But I want to finish the case tonight, now." He picked up an ebony paper-knife from the desk and, without looking at Cordelia, balanced it on his forefinger.

"Then tell me, why did my son kill himself? I take it that you do have news for me? You would hardly have burst in here at this hour without something to report."

"Your son didn't kill himself. He was murdered. He was murdered by someone he knew well, someone he didn't hesitate to let into the cottage, someone who came prepared. He was strangled or suffocated, then slung up on that hook by his own belt. Last of all, his murderer painted his lips, dressed him in a woman's underclothes and spread out pictures of nudes on the table in front of him. It was meant to look like accidental death during sexual experiment; such cases aren't so very uncommon."

There was half a minute of silence. Then he said with perfect calmness:

"And who was responsible, Miss Gray?"

"You were. You killed your son."

"For what reason?" He might have been an examiner, putting his inexorable questions.

"Because he discovered that your wife wasn't his mother, that the money left to her and to him by his grandfather had come by

fraud. Because he had no intention of benefiting by it a moment longer, nor of accepting his legacy in four years' time. You were afraid that he might make this knowledge public. And what about the Wolvington Trust? If the truth came out, that would be the end of their promised grant. The future of your laboratory was at stake. You couldn't take the risk."

"And who undressed him again, typed out that suicide note, washed the lipstick from his face?"

"I think I know, but I shan't tell you. That's really what you employed me to discover, isn't it? That's what you couldn't bear not to know. But you killed Mark. You even prepared an alibi just in case it was needed. You got Lunn to ring you at college and announce himself as your son. He was the one person you could rely on absolutely. I don't suppose you told him the truth. He was only your lab assistant. He didn't require explanations, he did what you told him. And even if he did guess the truth, he was safe, wasn't he? You prepared an alibi which you dared not use, because you didn't know when Mark's body was first discovered. If someone had found him and faked that suicide before you had claimed to have spoken to him on the telephone, your alibi would have been broken, and a broken alibi is damning. So you made a chance to talk to Benskin and put matters right. You told him the truth; that it was Lunn who had rung you. You could rely on Lunn to back up your story. But it wouldn't really matter, would it, even if he did talk? No one would believe him."

"No, any more than they will believe you. You've been determined to earn your fee, Miss Gray. Your explanation is ingenious; there is even a certain plausibility about some of the details. But you know, and I know, that no police officer in the world would take it seriously. It's unfortunate for you that you couldn't question Lunn. But Lunn, as I said, is dead. He burnt to death in a road accident."

"I know, I saw. He tried to kill me tonight. Did you know that? And earlier, he tried to scare me into dropping the case. Was that because he had begun to suspect the truth?"

"If he did try to kill you, he exceeded his instructions. I merely asked him to keep an eye on you. I had contracted for

your sole and whole-time services, if you remember; I wanted to be sure I was getting value. I am getting value of a kind. But you mustn't indulge your imagination outside this room. Neither the police nor the courts are sympathetic to slander nor to hysterical nonsense. And what proof have you? None. My wife was cremated. There is nothing alive or dead on this earth to prove that Mark was not her son."

Cordelia said:

"You visited Dr. Gladwin to satisfy yourself that he was too senile to give evidence against you. You needn't have worried. He never did suspect, did he? You chose him as your wife's doctor because he was old and incompetent. But I did have one small piece of evidence. Lunn was bringing it to you."

"Then you should have looked after it better. Nothing of Lunn except his bones has survived that crash."

"There are still the female clothes, the black pants and the bra. Someone might remember who bought them, particularly if that person was a man."

"Men do buy underclothes for their women. But if I were planning such a murder, I don't think buying the accessories would worry me. Would any harassed shop girl at the cash desk of a popular multiple store remember a particular purchase, a purchase paid for with cash, one of a number of innocuous items, all presented together at the busiest time of the day? The man might even have worn a simple disguise. I doubt whether she would even notice his face. Would you really expect her to remember, weeks afterwards, to identify one of thousands of customers and identify him with sufficient certainty to satisfy a jury? And if she did, what would it prove unless you have the clothes in question? Be sure of one thing, Miss Gray, if I needed to kill I should do it efficiently. I should not be found out. If the police ever learn how my son was found, as they well may do since, apparently, someone other than yourself knows it, they will only believe with greater certainty that he killed himself. Mark's death was necessary and, unlike most deaths, it served a purpose. Human beings have an irresistible urge towards self-sacrifice. They die for any reason or none at all, for meaningless abstractions like patriotism, justice, peace; for other men's ideals,

for other men's power, for a few feet of earth. You, no doubt, would give your life to save a child or if you were convinced that the sacrifice would find a cure for cancer."

"I might. I like to think that I would. But I should want the decision to be mine, not yours."

"Of course. That would provide you with the necessary emotional satisfaction. But it wouldn't alter the fact of your dying nor the result of your death. And don't say that what I'm doing here isn't worth one single human life. Spare me that hypocrisy. You don't know and you're incapable of understanding the value of what I'm doing here. What difference will Mark's death make to you? You'd never heard of him until you came to Garforth House."

Cordelia said:

"It will make a difference to Gary Webber."

"Am I expected to lose everything I've worked for here because Gary Webber wants someone to play squash or discuss history with?"

Suddenly he looked Cordelia full in the face. He said sharply:

"What is the matter? Are you ill?"

"No I'm not ill. I knew that I must be right. I knew that what I had reasoned was true. But I can't believe it. I can't believe that a human being could be so evil."

"If you are capable of imagining it, then I'm capable of doing it. Haven't you yet discovered that about human beings, Miss Gray? It's the key to what you would call the wickedness of man."

Suddenly Cordelia could no longer bear this cynical antiphony. She cried out in passionate protest.

"But what is the use of making the world more beautiful if the people who live in it can't love one another?"

She had stung him at last into anger.

"Love! The most overused word in the language. Has it any meaning except the particular sentimental connotation which you choose to give it? What do you mean by love? That human beings must learn to live together with a decent concern for each other's welfare? The law enforces that. The greatest good of the greatest number. Beside that fundamental declaration of common

703

sense all other philosophies are metaphysical abstractions. Or do you define love in the Christian sense, caritas? Read history, Miss Gray. See to what horrors, to what violence, hatred and repression the religion of love has led mankind. But perhaps you prefer a more feminine, more individual definition; love as a passionate commitment to another's personality. Intense personal commitment always ends in jealousy and enslavement. Love is more destructive than hate. If you must dedicate your life to something, dedicate it to an idea."

"I meant love, as a parent loves a child."

"The worse for them both, perhaps. But if he doesn't love, there is no power on earth which can stimulate or compel him to. And where there is no love, there can be none of the obligations of love."

"You could have let him live! The money wasn't important to him. He would have understood your needs and kept silent."

"Would he? How could he—or I—have explained his rejection of a great fortune in four years' time? People at the mercy of what they call their conscience are never safe. My son was a self-righteous prig. How could I put myself and my work in his hands?"

"You are in mine, Sir Ronald."

"You are mistaken. I am in no one's hands. Unfortunately for you that tape recorder is not working. We have no witnesses. You will repeat nothing that has been said in this room to anyone outside. If you do I shall have to ruin you. I shall make you unemployable, Miss Gray. And first of all I shall bankrupt that pathetic business of yours. From what Miss Leaming told me it shouldn't be difficult. Slander can be a highly expensive indulgence. Remember that if you are ever tempted to talk. Remember this too. You will harm yourself; you will harm Mark's memory; you will not harm me."

❧◦❧

Cordelia never knew how long the tall figure in the red dressing-gown had been watching and listening in the shadow of the door. She never knew how much Miss Leaming had heard or at

what moment she had stolen quietly away. But now she was aware of the red shadow moving soundlessly over the carpet, eyes on the figure behind the desk, the gun held closely against her breast. Cordelia watched in fascinated horror, not breathing. She knew exactly what was going to happen. It must have taken less than three seconds but they passed as slowly as minutes. Surely there had been time to cry out, time to warn, time to leap forward and wrench the gun from that steady hand? Surely there had been time for him to cry out? But he made no sound. He half rose, incredulous, and gazed at the muzzle in blind disbelief. Then he turned his head towards Cordelia as if in supplication. She would never forget that last look. It was beyond terror, beyond hope. It held nothing but the blank acceptance of defeat.

It was an execution, neat, unhurried, ritually precise. The bullet went in behind the right ear. The body leapt into the air, shoulders humped, softened before Cordelia's eyes as if the bones were melting into wax, and lay discarded at last over the desk. A thing; like Bernie; like her father.

Miss Leaming said:

"He killed my son."

"Your son?"

"Of course. Mark was my son. His son and mine. I thought you might have guessed."

She stood with the gun in her hand gazing with expressionless eyes through the open window to the lawn. There was no sound. Nothing moved. Miss Leaming said:

"He was right when he said that no one could touch him. There was no proof."

Cordelia cried out appalled:

"Then how could you kill him? How could you be so sure?"

Without releasing her hold on the pistol, Miss Leaming put her hand into the pocket of her dressing-gown. The hand moved over the desk top. A small gilt cylinder rolled over the polished wood towards Cordelia, then rocked into stillness. Miss Leaming said:

"The lipstick was mine. I found it a minute ago in the pocket of his dress suit. He hadn't worn that suit since he last dined in Hall

on Feast night. He was always a magpie. He put small objects instinctively into his pocket."

Cordelia had never doubted Sir Ronald's guilt but now every nerve was desperate for reassurance.

"But it could have been planted there! Lunn could have put it there to incriminate him."

"Lunn didn't kill Mark. He was in bed with me at the time Mark died. He only left my side for five minutes and that was to make a telephone call shortly after eight o'clock."

"You were in love with Lunn!"

"Don't look at me like that! I only loved one man in my life and he's the one I've just killed. Talk about things you understand. Love had nothing to with what Lunn and I needed from each other."

There was a moment's silence. Then Cordelia said:

"Is there anyone in the house?"

"No. The servants are in London. No one is working late at the lab tonight."

And Lunn was dead. Miss Leaming said with weary resignation:

"Hadn't you better phone the police?"

"Do you want me to?"

"What does it matter?"

"Prison matters. Losing your freedom matters. And do you really want the truth to come out in open court? Do you want everyone to know how your son died and who killed him? Is that what Mark himself would want?"

"No. Mark never believed in punishment. Tell me what I have to do."

"We've got to work quickly and plan carefully. We have to trust each other and we have to be intelligent."

"We are intelligent. What must we do?"

Cordelia took out her handkerchief and dropping it over the gun, took the weapon from Miss Leaming and placed it on the desk. She grasped the woman's thin wrist and pushed her protesting hand against Sir Ronald's palm, pulling against the instinctive recoil, forcing the stiff but living fingers against the soft unresisting hand of the dead.

706

"There may be firing residue. I don't really know much about that, but the police may test for it. Now wash your hands and get me a pair of thin gloves. Quickly."

She went without a word. Left alone, Cordelia looked down at the dead scientist. He had fallen with his chin against the desk top and his arms swinging loosely at his sides, an awkward, uncomfortable-looking pose which gave him the appearance of peering malevolently over his desk. Cordelia could not look at his eyes, but she was conscious of feeling nothing, not hatred, or anger, or pity. Between her eyes and the sprawled figure swung an elongated shape, head hideously crooked, toes pathetically pointed. She walked over to the open window and looked out over the garden with the casual curiosity of a guest kept waiting in a strange room. The air was warm and very still. The scent of roses came in waves through the open window, alternately sickening sweet and then as elusive as a half-caught memory.

This curious hiatus of peace and timelessness must have lasted less than half a minute. Then Cordelia began to plan. She thought about the Clandon case. Memory pictured herself and Bernie, sitting astride a fallen log in Epping Forest and eating their picnic lunch. It brought back the yeasty smell of fresh rolls, butter and tangy cheese, the heavy fungoid smell of summer woods. He had rested the pistol on the bark between them and had mumbled at her through the bread and cheese. "How would you shoot yourself behind the right ear? Go on, Cordelia—show."

Cordelia had taken the pistol in her right hand, index finger lightly resting on the trigger, and with some difficulty had strained back her arm to place the muzzle of the gun against the base of the skull. "Like that?" "You wouldn't, you know. Not if you were used to a gun. That's the little mistake Mrs. Clandon made and it nearly hanged her. She shot her husband behind the right ear with his service revolver and then tried to fake a suicide. But she pressed the wrong finger on the trigger. If he'd really shot himself behind the right ear he'd have pressed the trigger with his thumb and held the revolver with his palm round the back of the butt. I remember that case well. It was

707

the first murder I worked on with the Super—Inspector Dalgliesh, as he was then. Mrs. Clandon confessed in the end." "What happened to her, Bernie?" "Life. She'd probably have got away with manslaughter if she hadn't tried to fake a suicide. The jury didn't much like what they heard about Major Clandon's little habits."

But Miss Leaming couldn't get away with manslaughter; not unless she told the whole story of Mark's death.

She was back in the room now. She handed Cordelia a pair of thin cotton gloves. Cordelia said:

"I think you'd better wait outside. What you don't see you won't have the trouble of forgetting. What were you doing when you met me in the hall?"

"I was getting myself a nightcap, a whisky."

"Then you would have met me again coming out of the study as you took it up to your room. Get it now and leave the glass on the side table in the hall. That's the kind of detail the police are trained to notice."

Alone again, Cordelia took up the gun. It was astonishing how repulsive she found this inert weight of metal now. How odd that she should ever have seen it as a harmless toy! She rubbed it thoroughly with her handkerchief erasing Miss Leaming's prints. Then she handled it. It was her gun. They would expect to find some of her prints on the butt together with those of the dead man. She placed it again on the desk top and drew on the gloves. This was the more difficult part. She handled the pistol gingerly and took it over to the inert right hand. She pressed his thumb firmly against the trigger, then wound the cold, unresisting hand round the back of the butt. Then she released his fingers and let the gun fall. It struck the carpet with a dull thud. She peeled off the gloves and went out to Miss Leaming in the hall, closing the study door quietly behind her.

"Here, you'd better put these back where you found them. We mustn't leave them lying around for the police to find."

She was gone only a few seconds. When she returned, Cordelia said:

"Now we must act the rest just as it would have happened. You meet me as I come out of the room. I have been with Sir

Ronald about two minutes. You put down your glass of whisky on the hall table and walk with me to the front door. You say—what would you say?"

"Has he paid you?"

"No, I'm to come in the morning for my money. I'm sorry it wasn't a success. I've told Sir Ronald that I don't want to go on with the case."

"That's your concern, Miss Gray. It was a foolish business in the first place."

They were walking out of the front door now. Suddenly Miss Leaming turned to Cordelia and said urgently and in her normal voice:

"There's one thing you had better know. It was I who found Mark first and faked the suicide. He'd rung me earlier in the day and asked me to call. I couldn't get away until after nine because of Lunn. I didn't want him to be suspicious."

"But didn't it occur to you when you found Mark that there might be something odd about the death? The door was unlocked although the curtains were drawn. The lipstick was missing."

"I suspected nothing until tonight when I stood there in the shadows and heard you talking. We're all sexually sophisticated these days. I believed what I saw. It was all horror but I knew what I had to do. I worked quickly, terrified that someone would come. I cleaned his face with my hankerchief dampened with water from the kitchen sink. It seemed that the lipstick would never come off. I undressed him and pulled on his jeans which had been thrown over the back of a chair. I didn't wait to put on his shoes, that didn't seem important. Typing the note was the worst part. I knew that he would have his Blake with him somewhere in the cottage and that the passage I chose might be more convincing than an ordinary suicide note. The clattering of the typewriter keys sounded unnaturally loud in the quietness; I was terrified that someone would hear. He had been keeping a kind of journal. There wasn't time to read it but I burnt the typescript in the sitting-room grate. Last of all, I bundled up the clothes and the pictures and brought them back here to be burnt in the lab incinerator."

"You dropped one of the pictures in the garden. And you didn't quite succeed in cleaning the lipstick from his face."

"So that's how you guessed?"

Cordelia didn't reply immediately. Whatever happened she must keep Isabelle de Lasterie out of the case.

"I wasn't sure if it was you who had been there first but I thought it must have been. There were four things. You didn't want me to investigate Mark's death; you read English at Cambridge and could have known where to find that Blake quotation; you are an experienced typist and I didn't think that the note had been typed by an amateur despite the late attempt to make it look like Mark's work; when I was first at Garforth House and asked about the suicide note you spoke the whole of the Blake quotation; the typed version was ten words short. I first noticed that when I visited the police station and was shown the note. It pointed direct to you. That was the strongest evidence I had."

They had reached the car now and paused together. Cordelia said:

"We mustn't waste any more time before ringing the police. Someone may have heard the shot."

"It's not likely. We're some distance from the village. Do we hear it now?"

"Yes. We hear it now." There was a second's pause then Cordelia said:

"What was that? It sounded like a shot."

"It couldn't have been. It was probably a car back-firing."

Miss Leaming spoke like a bad actress, the words were stilted, unconvincing. But she spoke them; she would remember them.

"But there isn't a car passing. And it came from the house."

They glanced at each other, then ran back together through the open door into the hall. Miss Leaming paused for a moment and looked Cordelia in the face before she opened the study door. Cordelia came in behind her. Miss Leaming said:

"He's been shot! I'd better phone the police."

Cordelia said:

"You wouldn't say that! Don't ever think like that! You'd go up to the body first and then you'd say:

710

" 'He's shot himself. I'd better phone the police.' "

Miss Leaming looked unemotionally at her lover's body, then glanced round the room. Forgetting her role, she asked:

"What have you done in here? What about finger prints?"

"Never mind. I've looked after that. All you have to remember is that you didn't know I had a gun when I first came to Garforth House; you didn't know Sir Ronald took it from me. You haven't seen that gun until this moment. When I arrived tonight you showed me into the study and met me again when I came out two minutes later. We walked together to the car and spoke as we have just spoken. We heard the shot. We did what we have just done. Forget everything else that has happened. When they question you, don't embroider, don't invent, don't be afraid to say you can't remember. And now—ring the Cambridge police."

⋙∘⋘

Three minutes later they were standing together at the open door waiting for the police to arrive. Miss Leaming said:

"We mustn't talk together once they're here. And, afterwards, we mustn't meet or show any particular interest in each other. They'll know that this can't be murder unless we two are in it together. And why should we conspire together when we've only met once before, when we don't even like each other?"

She was right, thought Cordelia. They didn't even like each other. She didn't really care if Elizabeth Leaming went to prison; she did care if Mark's mother went to prison. She cared, too, that the truth of his death should never be known. The strength of that determination struck her as irrational. It could make no difference to him now and he wasn't a boy who had cared over much what people thought of him. But Ronald Callender had desecrated his body after death; had planned to make him an object, at worse of contempt, at best of pity. She had set her face against Ronald Callender. She hadn't wanted him to die; wouldn't have been capable herself of pressing the trigger. But he was dead and she couldn't feel regret, nor could she be an instrument of retribution for his murderer. It was expedient, no more than that, that Miss Leaming shouldn't be

punished. Gazing out into the summer night and waiting for the sound of the police cars, Cordelia accepted once and for all the enormity and the justification of what she had done and was still planning to do. She was never afterwards to feel the least tinge of regret or of remorse.

Miss Leaming said:

"There are things you probably want to ask me, things I suppose you've a right to know. We can meet in King's College Chapel after Evensong on the first Sunday after the inquest. I'll go through the screen into the chancel, you stay in the nave. It will seem natural enough for us to meet by chance there, that is if we are both still free."

Cordelia was interested to see that Miss Leaming was taking charge again. She said:

"We shall be. If we keep our heads this can't go wrong."

There was a moment's silence. Miss Leaming said:

"They're taking their time. Surely they should be here by now?"

"They won't be much longer."

Miss Leaming suddenly laughed and said with revealing bitterness:

"What is there to be frightened of? We shall be dealing only with men."

So they waited quietly together. They heard the approaching cars before the headlamps swept over the drive, illuminating every pebble, picking out the small plants at the edge of the beds, bathing the blue haze of the wisteria with light, dazzling the watchers' eyes. Then the lights were dimmed as the cars rocked gently to a stop in front of the house. Dark shapes emerged and came unhurriedly but resolutely forward. The hall was suddenly filled with large, calm men, some in plain clothes. Cordelia effaced herself against the wall and it was Miss Leaming who stepped forward, spoke to them in a low voice and led them into the study.

Two uniformed men were left in the hall. They stood talking together, taking no notice of Cordelia. Their colleagues were taking their time. They must have used the telephone in the study because more cars and men began to arrive. First the police

surgeon, identified by his bag even if he hadn't been greeted with:
"Good evening Doc. In here please."

How often he must have heard that phrase! He glanced with brief curiosity at Cordelia as he trotted through the hall, a fat, dishevelled little man, his face crumpled and petulant as a child when forcibly woken from sleep. Next came a civilian photographer carrying his camera, tripod and box of equipment; a fingerprint expert; two other civilians whom Cordelia, instructed in procedure by Bernie, guessed were scenes-of-crime officers. So they were treating this as a suspicious death. And why not? It was suspicious.

The head of the household lay dead, but the house itself seemed to have come alive. The police talked, not in whispers, but in confident normal voices unsubdued by death. They were professionals doing their job, working easily to the prescribed routine. They had been initiated into the mysteries of violent death; its victims held no awe for them. They had seen too many bodies: bodies scraped off motorways; loaded piecemeal into ambulances; dragged by hook and net from the depths of rivers; dug putrefying from the clogging earth. Like doctors, they were kind and condescendingly gentle to the uninstructed, keeping inviolate their awful knowledge. This body, while it breathed, had been more important than others. It wasn't important now, but it could still make trouble for them. They would be that much more meticulous, that much more tactful. But it was still only a case.

Cordelia sat alone and waited. She was suddenly overcome with tiredness. She longed for nothing but to put down her head on the hall table and sleep. She was hardly aware of Miss Leaming passing through the hall on her way to the drawing room, of the tall officer talking to her as they passed. Neither took any notice of the small figure in its immense woollen jersey, sitting against the wall. Cordelia willed herself to stay awake. She knew what she had to say; it was all clear enough in her mind. If only they would come to question her and let her sleep.

It wasn't until the photographer and the print man had finished their work that one of the senior officers came out to her. She was never afterwards able to recall his face but she remembered his voice, a careful, unemphatic voice from which every

713

tinge of emotion had been excluded. He held out the gun towards her. It was resting on his open palm, protected by a handkerchief from the contamination of his hand.

"Do you recognize this weapon, Miss Gray?"

Cordelia thought it odd that he should use the word weapon. Why not just say gun?

"I think so. I think it must be mine."

"You aren't sure?"

"It must be mine, unless Sir Ronald owned one of the same make. He took it from me when I first came here four days ago. He promised to let me have it back when I called tomorrow morning for my pay."

"So this is only the second time you've been in this house?"

"Yes."

"Have you ever met Sir Ronald Callender or Miss Leaming before?"

"No. Not until Sir Ronald sent for me to undertake this case."

He went away. Cordelia rested her head back against the wall and took short snatches of sleep. Another officer came. This time he had a uniformed man with him, taking notes. There were more questions. Cordelia told her prepared story. They wrote it down without comment and went away.

She must have dozed. She awoke to find a tall, uniformed officer standing over her. He said:

"Miss Leaming is making tea in the kitchen, Miss. Perhaps you would like to give her a hand. It's something to do, isn't it?"

Cordelia thought; they're going to take away the body. She said:

"I don't know where the kitchen is."

She saw his eyes flicker.

"Oh, don't you, Miss? You're a stranger here, are you? Well, it's this way."

The kitchen was at the back of the house. It smelt of spice, oil and tomato sauce, bringing back memories of meals in Italy with her father. Miss Leaming was taking down cups from a vast dresser. An electric kettle was already hissing steam. The police officer stayed. So they weren't to be left alone. Cordelia said:

"Can I help?" Miss Leaming did not look at her.

"There are some biscuits in that tin. You can put them out on a tray. The milk is in the fridge."

Cordelia moved like an automaton. The milk bottle was an icy column in her hands, the biscuit tin lid resisted her tired fingers and she broke a nail prising it off. She noticed the details of the kitchen—a wall calendar of St. Theresa of Avila, the saint's face unnaturally elongated and pale so that she looked like a hallowed Miss Leaming; a china donkey with two panniers of artificial flowers, its melancholy head crowned with a miniature straw hat; an immense blue bowl of brown eggs.

There were two trays. The police constable took the larger from Miss Leaming and led the way into the hall. Cordelia followed with the second tray, holding it high against her chest like a child, permitted as a privilege to help mother. Police officers gathered round. She took a cup herself and returned to her usual chair.

And now there was the sound of yet another car. A middle-aged woman came in with a uniformed chauffeur at her shoulder. Through the fog of her tiredness, Cordelia heard a high, didactic voice.

"My dear Eliza, this is appalling! You must come back to the Lodge tonight. No, I insist. Is the Chief Constable here?"

"No, Marjorie, but these officers have been very kind."

"Leave them the key. They'll lock up the house when they've finished. You can't possibly stay here alone tonight."

There were introductions, hurried consultations with the detectives in which the newcomer's voice was dominant. Miss Leaming went upstairs with her visitor and reappeared five minutes later with a small case, her coat over her arm. They went off together, escorted to the car by the chauffeur and one of the detectives. None of the little party glanced at Cordelia.

Five minutes later the Inspector came up to Cordelia, key in hand.

"We shall lock up the house tonight, Miss Gray. It's time you were getting home. Are you thinking of staying at the cottage?"

"Just for the next few days, if Major Markland will let me."

"You look very tired. One of my men will drive you in your own car. I should like a written statement from you tomorrow.

Can you come to the station as soon as possible after breakfast?
You know where it is?"

"Yes, I know."

One of the police panda cars drove off first and the Mini
followed. The police driver drove fast, lurching the little car
around the corners. Cordelia's head lolled against the back of
the seat and, from time to time, was thrown against the driver's
arm. He was wearing shirt sleeves and she was vaguely conscious
of the comfort of the warm flesh through the cotton. The car
window was open and she was aware of hot night air rushing
against her face, of the scudding clouds, of the first unbelievable
colours of day staining the eastern sky. The route seemed strange
to her and time itself disjointed; she wondered why the car had
suddenly stopped and it took a minute for her to recognize the
tall hedge bending over the lane like a menacing shadow, the
ramshackle gate. She was home. The driver said:

"Is this the place, Miss?"

"Yes, this is it. But I usually leave the Mini further down
the lane on the right. There's a copse there where you can drive
it off the road."

"Right, Miss."

He got out of the car to consult the other driver. They moved
on slowly for the last few yards of the journey. And now, at
last, the police car had driven away and she was alone at the
gate. It was an effort to push it open against the weight of the
weeds and she lurched round the cottage to the back door like
a drunken creature. It took some little time to fit the key into
the lock, but that was the last problem. There was no longer a
gun to hide; there was no longer need to check the tape sealing
the windows. Lunn was dead and she was alive. Every night
that she had slept at the cottage Cordelia had come home tired,
but never before had she been as tired as this. She made her
way upstairs as if sleepwalking and, too exhausted even to zip
herself into her sleeping-bag, crept underneath it and knew
nothing more.

And at last—it seemed to Cordelia after months, not days, of waiting—there was another inquest. It was as unhurried, as unostentatiously formal, as Bernie's had been, but there was a difference. Here, instead of a handful of pathetic casuals who had sneaked into the warmth of the back benches to hear Bernie's obsequies, were grave-faced colleagues and friends, muted voices, the whispered preliminaries of lawyers and police, an indefinable sense of occasion. Cordelia guessed that the grey-haired man escorting Miss Leaming must be her lawyer. She watched him at work, affable but not deferential to the senior police, quietly solicitous for his client, exuding a confidence that they were all engaged in a necessary if tedious formality, a ritual as unworrying as Sunday Matins.

Miss Leaming looked very pale. She was wearing the grey suit she had worn when Cordelia first met her but with a small black hat, black gloves and a black chiffon scarf knotted at her throat. The two women did not look at each other. Cordelia found a seat at the end of a bench and sat there, unrepresented and alone. One or two of the younger policemen smiled at her with a reassuring but pitying kindness.

Miss Leaming gave her evidence first in a low, composed voice. She affirmed instead of taking the oath, a decision which caused a brief spasm of distress to pass over her lawyer's face. But she gave him no further cause for concern. She testified that Sir Ronald had been depressed at his son's death and, she thought, had blamed himself for not knowing that something was worrying Mark. He had told her that he intended to call in a pr vate detective, and it had been she who had originally interviewed Miss Gray and had brought her back to Garforth House. Miss Leaming said that she had opposed the suggestion; she had seen no useful purpose in it, and thought that this futile and fruitless enquiry would only remind Sir Ronald of the tragedy. She had not known that Miss Gray possessed a gun nor that Sir Ronald had taken it from her. She had not been present during the whole of their preliminary interview. Sir Ronald had escorted Miss Gray to view his son's room while she, Miss Leaming, had gone in search of a photograph of Mr. Callender for which Miss Gray had asked.

The coroner asked her gently about the night of Sir Ronald's death.

Miss Leaming said that Miss Gray had arrived to give her first report shortly after half past ten. She herself had been passing through the front hall when the girl appeared. Miss Leaming had pointed out that it was late, but Miss Gray had said that she had wanted to abandon the case and get back to town. She had showed Miss Gray into the study where Sir Ronald was working. They had been together, she thought, for less than two minutes. Miss Gray had then come out of the study and she had walked with her to her car; they had only talked briefly. Miss Gray said that Sir Ronald had asked her to call back in the morning for her pay. She had made no mention of a gun.

Sir Ronald had, only half an hour before that, received a telephone call from the police to say that his laboratory assistant, Christopher Lunn, had been killed in a road accident. She had not told Miss Gray the news about Lunn before her interview with Sir Ronald; it hadn't occurred to her to do so. The girl had gone almost immediately into the study to see Sir Ronald. Miss Leaming said that they were standing together at the car talking when they heard the shot. At first she had thought it was a car backfiring but then she had realized that it had come from the house. They had both rushed into the study and found Sir Ronald lying slumped over his desk. The gun had dropped from his hand to the floor.

No, Sir Ronald had never given her any idea that he contemplated suicide. She thought that he was very distressed about the death of Mr. Lunn but it was difficult to tell. Sir Ronald was not a man to show emotion. He had been working very hard recently and had not seemed himself since the death of his son. But Miss Leaming had never for a moment thought that Sir Ronald was a man who would put an end to his life.

She was followed by the police witnesses, deferential, professional, but managing to give an impression that none of this was new to them; they had seen it all before and would see it again.

They were followed by the doctors, including the pathologist,

who testified in what the court obviously thought was unnecessary detail to the effect of firing a jacketed hollow-cavity bullet of ninety grains into the human brain. The coroner asked:

"You have heard the police evidence that there was the print of Sir Ronald Callender's thumb on the trigger of the gun and a palm mark smudged around the butt. What would you deduce from that?"

The pathologist looked slightly surprised at being asked to deduce anything but said that it was apparent that Sir Ronald had held the gun with his thumb on the trigger when pointing it against his head. The pathologist thought that it was probably the most comfortable way in which to hold the weapon, indeed the only comfortable way, having regard to the position of the wound of entry.

Lastly, Cordelia was called to the witness box and took the oath. She had given some thought to the propriety of this and had wondered whether to follow Miss Leaming's example. There were moments, usually on a sunny Easter morning, when she wished that she could with sincerity call herself a Christian; but for the rest of the year she knew herself to be what she was—incurably agnostic but prone to unpredictable relapses into faith. This seemed to her, however, a moment when religious scrupulosity was an indulgence which she couldn't afford. The lies she was about to tell would not be the more heinous because they were tinged with blasphemy.

The coroner let her tell her story without interruption. She sensed that the court was puzzled by her but not unsympathetic. For once, the carefully modulated middle-class accent, which in her six years at the convent she had unconsciously acquired, and which in other people often irritated her as much as her own voice had irritated her father, was proving an advantage. She wore her suit and had bought a black chiffon scarf to cover her head. She remembered that she must call the coroner "sir".

After she had briefly confirmed Miss Leaming's story of how she had been called to the case, the coroner said:

"And now, Miss Gray, will you explain to the court what happened on the night Sir Ronald Callender died?"

"I had decided, sir, that I didn't want to go on with the case.

I hadn't discovered anything useful and I didn't think there was anything to discover. I had been living in the cottage where Mark Callender had spent the last weeks of his life and I had come to think that what I was doing was wrong, that I was taking money for prying into his private life. I decided on impulse to tell Sir Ronald that I wanted to finish the case. I drove to Garforth House. I go there at about ten-thirty. I knew it was late but I was anxious to go back to London the next morning. I saw Miss Leaming as she was crossing the hall and she showed me straight into the study."

"Will you please describe to the court how you found Sir Ronald."

"He seemed to be tired and distracted. I tried to explain why I wanted to give up the case but I'm not sure that he heard me. He said I was to come back next morning for my money and I said that I only proposed to charge expenses, but that I would like to have my gun. He just waved a hand in dismissal and said, 'tomorrow morning, Miss Gray. Tomorrow morning.' "

"And then you left him?"

"Yes, sir. Miss Leaming accompanied me back to the car and I was just about to drive away when we heard the shot."

"You didn't see the gun in Sir Ronald's possession while you were in the study with him?"

"No, sir."

"He didn't talk to you about Mr. Lunn's death or give you any idea that he was contemplating suicide?"

"No, sir."

The coroner doodled on the pad before him. Without looking at Cordelia, he said:

"And now, Miss Gray, will you please explain to the court how Sir Ronald came to have your gun."

This was the difficult part, but Cordelia had rehearsed it. The Cambridge police had been very thorough. They had asked the same questions over and over again. She knew exactly how Sir Ronald had come to have the gun. She remembered a piece of Dalgliesh dogma, reported by Bernie, which had seemed to her at the time more appropriate advice for a criminal than a detective. "Never tell an unnecessary lie; the truth has great

authority. The cleverest murderers have been caught, not because they told the one essential lie, but because they continued to lie about unimportant detail when the truth could have done them no harm."

She said:

"My partner, Mr. Pryde, owned the gun and was very proud of it. When he killed himself I knew that he meant me to have it. That was why he cut his wrists instead of shooting himself, which would have been quicker and easier."

The coroner looked up sharply.

"And were you there when he killed himself?"

"No, sir. But I found the body."

There was a murmur of sympathy from the court; she could feel their concern.

"Did you know that the gun wasn't licensed?"

"No, sir, but I think I suspected that it might not have been. I brought it with me on this case because I didn't want to leave it in the office and because I found it a comfort. I meant to check up on the licence as soon as I got back. I didn't expect ever to use the gun. I didn't really think of it as a lethal weapon. It's just that this was my first case and Bernie had left it to me and I felt happier having it with me."

"I see," said the coroner.

Cordelia thought that he probably did see and so did the court. They were having no difficulty in believing her because she was telling the somewhat improbable truth. Now that she was about to lie, they would go on believing her.

"And now will you please tell the court how Sir Ronald came to take the gun from you?"

"It was on my first visit to Garforth House when Sir Ronald was showing me his son's bedroom. He knew that I was the sole owner of the Agency, and he asked me if it wasn't a difficult and rather frightening job for a woman. I said that I wasn't frightened but that I had Bernie's gun. When he found that I had it with me in my bag he made me hand it over to him. He said that he didn't propose to engage someone who might be a danger to other people or herself. He said that he wouldn't take the responsibility. He took the gun and the ammunition."

"And what did he do with the gun?"

Cordelia had thought this one out carefully. Obviously he hadn't carried it downstairs in his hand or Miss Leaming would have seen it. She would have liked to have said that he put it into a drawer in Mark's room but she couldn't remember whether the bedside table had had any drawers. She said:

"He took it out of the room with him; he didn't tell me where. He was only away for a moment and then we went downstairs together."

"And you didn't set eyes on the gun again until you saw it on the floor close to Sir Ronald's hand when you and Miss Leaming found his body?"

"No, sir."

Cordelia was the last witness. The verdict was quickly given, one that the court obviously felt would have been agreeable to Sir Ronald's scrupulously exact and scientific brain. It was that the deceased had taken his own life but that there was no evidence as to the state of his mind. The coroner delivered at length the obligatory warning about the danger of guns. Guns, the court were informed, could kill people. He managed to convey that unlicensed guns were particularly prone to this danger. He pronounced no strictures on Cordelia personally although it was apparent that this restraint cost him an effort. He rose and the court rose with him.

After the coroner had left the bench the court broke up into little whispering groups. Miss Leaming was quickly surrounded. Cordelia saw her shaking hands, receiving condolences, listening with grave assenting face to the first tentative proposals for a memorial service. Cordelia wondered how she could ever have feared that Miss Leaming would be suspected. She herself stood a little apart, delinquent. She knew that the police would charge her with illegal possession of the gun. They could do no less. True, she would be lightly punished, if punished at all. But for the rest of her life she would be the girl whose carelessness and naïveté had lost England one of her foremost scientists.

As Hugo had said, all Cambridge suicides were brilliant. But about this one there could be little doubt. Sir Ronald's death would probably raise him to the status of genius.

Almost unnoticed, she came alone out of the courtroom on to Market Hill. Hugo must have been waiting; now he fell into step with her.

"How did it go? I must say death seems to follow you around, doesn't it?"

"It went all right. I seem to follow death."

"I suppose he did shoot himself?"

"Yes. He shot himself."

"And with your gun?"

"As you will know if you were in court. I didn't see you."

"I wasn't there, I had a tutorial, but the news did get around. I shouldn't let it worry you. Ronald Callender wasn't as important as some people in Cambridge may choose to believe."

"You know nothing about him. He was a human being and he's dead. That fact is always important."

"It isn't, you know, Cordelia. Death is the least important thing about us. Comfort yourself with Joseph Hall. 'Death borders upon our birth and our cradle stands in the grave.' And he did choose his own weapon, his own time. He'd had enough of himself. Plenty of people had had enough of him."

They walked together down St. Edward's Passage towards King's Parade. Cordelia wasn't sure where they were making for. Her need at present was just to walk, but she didn't find her companion disagreeable.

She asked:

"Where's Isabelle?"

"Isabelle is home in Lyons. Papa turned up unexpectedly yesterday and found that mademoiselle wasn't exactly earning her wages. Papa decided that dear Isabelle was getting less—or it may have been more—out of her Cambridge education than he had expected. I don't think you need worry about her. Isabelle is safe enough now. Even if the police decide that it's worthwhile going to France to question her—and why on earth should they?—it won't help them. Papa will surround her with a barrage of lawyers. He's not in a mood to stand any nonsense from Englishmen at present."

"And what about you? If anyone asks you how Mark died, you'll never tell them the truth?"

"What do you think? Sophie, Davie and I are safe enough. I'm reliable when it comes to essentials."

For a moment Cordelia wished that he were reliable in less essential matters. She asked:

"Are you sorry about Isabelle leaving?"

"I am rather. Beauty is intellectually confusing; it sabotages common sense. I could never quite accept that Isabelle was what she is: a generous, indolent, over-affectionate and stupid young woman. I thought that any woman as beautiful as she must have an instinct about life, access to some secret wisdom which is beyond cleverness. Every time she opened that delicious mouth I was expecting her to illumine life. I think I could have spent all my life just looking at her and waiting for the oracle. And all she could talk about was clothes."

"Poor Hugo."

"Never poor Hugo. I'm not unhappy. The secret of contentment is never to allow yourself to want anything which reason tells you you haven't a chance of getting."

Cordelia thought that he was young, well-off, clever, even if not clever enough, handsome; there wasn't much that he would have to forgo on that or any other criteria.

She heard him speaking:

"Why not stay in Cambridge for a week or so and let me show you the city? Sophie would let you have her spare room."

"No thank you, Hugo. I have to get back to town."

There was nothing in town for her, but with Hugo there would be nothing in Cambridge for her either. There was only one reason for staying in this city. She would remain at the cottage until Sunday and her meeting with Miss Leaming. After that, as far as she was concerned, the case of Mark Callender would be finished for good.

❧❍❧

Sunday afternoon Evensong was over and the congregation, who had listened in respectful silence to the singing of responses, psalms and anthem by one of the finest choirs in the world, rose and joined with joyous abandon in the final hymn. Cordelia

rose and sang with them. She had seated herself at the end of the row close to the richly carved screen. From here she could see into the chancel. The robes of the choristers gleamed scarlet and white; the candles flickered in patterned rows and high circles of golden light; two tall and slender candles stood each side of the softly illuminated Reubens above the high altar, seen dimly as a distant smudge of crimson, blue and gold. The blessing was pronounced, the final amen impeccably sung and the choir began to file decorously out of the chancel. The south door was opened and sunlight flooded into the chapel. The members of the college who had attended divine service strolled out after the Provost and Fellows in casual disarray, their regulation surplices dingy and limp over a cheerful incongruity of corduroy and tweed. The great organ snuffled and groaned like an animal gathering breath, before giving forth its magnificent voice in a Bach fugue. Cordelia sat quietly in her chair, listening and waiting. Now the congregation was moving down the main aisle—small groups in bright summer cottons whispering discreetly, serious young men in sober Sunday black, tourists clutching their illustrated guides and half-embarrassed by their obtrusive cameras, a group of nuns with calm and cheerful faces.

Miss Leaming was one of the last, a tall figure in a grey linen dress and white gloves, her head bare, a white cardigan slung carelessly around her shoulders against the chill of the chapel. She was obviously alone and unwatched and her careful pretence of surprise at recognizing Cordelia was probably an unnecessary precaution. They passed out of the chapel together.

The gravel path outside the doorway was thronged with people. A little party of Japanese, festooned with cameras and accessories, added their high staccato jabber to the muted Sunday afternoon chat. From here the silver stream of the Cam was invisible but the truncated bodies of punters glided against the far bank like puppets in a show, raising their arms above the pole and turning to thrust it backwards as if participating in some ritual dance. The great lawn lay unshadowed in the sun, a quintessence of greenness staining the scented air. A frail and elderly Don in gown and mortarboard was limping across the grass; the sleeves of his gown caught a stray breeze and billowed

out so that he looked like a winged and monstrous crow struggling to rise. Miss Leaming said, as if Cordelia had asked for an explanation:

"He's a Fellow. The sacred turf is, therefore, uncontaminated by his feet."

They walked in silence by Gibbs Building. Cordelia wondered when Miss Leaming would speak. When she did, her first question was unexpected.

"Do you think you'll make a success of it?"

Sensing Cordelia's surprise, she added impatiently:

"The Detective Agency. Do you think you'll be able to cope?"

"I shall have to try. It's the only job I know."

She had no intention of justifying to Miss Leaming her affection and loyalty to Bernie; she would have had some difficulty in explaining it to herself.

"Your overheads are too high."

It was a pronouncement made with all the authority of a verdict.

"Do you mean the office and the Mini?" asked Cordelia.

"Yes. In your job I don't see how one person in the field can bring in sufficient income to cover expenses. You can't be sitting in the office taking orders and typing letters and be out solving cases at the same time. On the other hand, I don't suppose you can afford help."

"Not yet. I've been thinking that I might rent a telephone answering service. That will take care of the orders although, of course, clients much prefer to come to the office and discuss their case. If I can only make enough in expenses just to live, then any fees can cover the overheads."

"If there are any fees."

There seemed nothing to say to this and they walked on in silence for a few seconds. Then Miss Leaming said:

"There'll be the expenses from this case anyway. That at least should help towards your fine for illegal possession of the gun. I've put the matter in the hands of my solicitors. You should be getting a cheque fairly soon."

"I don't want to take any money for this case."

"I can understand that. As you pointed out to Ronald, it

falls under your fair deal clause. Strictly speaking you aren't entitled to any. All the same, I think it would look less suspicious if you took your expenses. Would thirty pounds strike you as reasonable?"

"Perfectly, thank you."

They had reached the corner of the lawn and had turned to walk towards King's Bridge. Miss Leaming said:

"I shall have to be grateful to you for the rest of my life. That for me is an unaccustomed humility and I'm not sure that I like it."

"Then don't feel it. I was thinking of Mark, not of you."

"I thought you might have acted in the service of justice or some such abstraction."

"I wasn't thinking about any abstraction. I was thinking about a person."

They had reached the bridge now and leaned over it side by side to look down into the bright water. The paths leading up to the bridge were, for a few minutes, empty of people. Miss Leaming said:

"Pregnancy isn't difficult to fake, you know. It only needs a loose corset and judicious stuffing. It's humiliating for the woman, of course, almost indecent if she happens to be barren. But it isn't difficult, particularly if she isn't closely watched. Evelyn wasn't. She had always been a shy, self-contained woman. People expected her to be excessively modest about her pregnancy. Garforth House wasn't filled with friends and relations swopping horror stories about the ante-natal clinic and patting her stomach. We had to get rid of that tedious fool Nanny Pilbeam, of course. Ronald regarded her departure as one of the subsidiary benefits of the pseudo pregnancy. He was tired of being spoken to as if he were still Ronnie Callender, the bright grammar school boy from Harrogate."

Cordelia said:

"Mrs. Goddard told me that Mark had a great look of his mother."

"She would. She was sentimental as well as stupid."

Cordelia did not speak. After a few moments silence Miss Leaming went on:

"I discovered that I was carrying Ronald's child at about the same time as a London specialist confirmed what the three of us already guessed, that Evelyn was most unlikely to conceive. I wanted to have the baby; Ronald desperately wanted a son; Evelyn's father was obsessional about his need for a grandson and was willing to part with half a million to prove it. It was all so easy. I resigned from my teaching job and went off to the safe anonymity of London and Evelyn told her father she was pregnant at last. Neither Ronald nor I had any conscience about defrauding George Bottley. He was an arrogant, brutal, self-satisfied fool who couldn't imagine how the world would continue without his issue to supervise it. He even subsidized his own deceit. The cheques for Evelyn began to arrive, each with a note imploring her to look after her health, to consult the best London doctors, to rest, to take a holiday in the sun. She had always loved Italy, and Italy became part of the plan. The three of us would meet in London every two months and fly together to Pisa. Ronald would rent a small villa outside Florence and, once there, I became Mrs. Callender and Evelyn became me. We had only daily servants and there was no need for them to look at our passports. They got used to our visits and so did the local doctor who was called in to supervise my health. The locals thought it flattering that the English lady should be so fond of Italy that she came back month after month, so close to her confinement."

Cordelia asked:

"But how could she do it, how could she bear to be there with you in the house, watching you with her husband, knowing that you were going to have his child?"

"She did it because she loved Ronald and couldn't bear to lose him. She hadn't been much success as a woman. If she lost her husband, what else was there for her? She couldn't have gone back to her father. Besides, we had a bribe for her. She was to have the child. If she refused, then Ronald would leave her and seek a divorce to marry me."

"I would rather have left him and gone off to scrub doorsteps."

"Not everyone has a talent for scrubbing doorsteps and not everyone has your capacity for moral indignation. Evelyn was

728

religious. She was, therefore, practised in self-deception. She convinced herself that what we were doing was best for the child."

"And her father? Didn't he ever suspect?"

"He despised her for her piety. He always had. Psychologically he could hardly indulge that dislike and at the same time think her capable of deceit. Besides, he desperately needed that grandchild. It wouldn't have entered his mind that the child might not be hers. And he had a doctor's report. After our third visit to Italy we told Doctor Sartori that Mrs. Callender's father was concerned about her care. At our request he wrote a reassuring medical report on the progress of the pregnancy. We went to Florence together a fortnight before the baby was due and stayed there until Mark arrived. Luckily he was a day or two before time. We'd had the foresight to put back the expected date of delivery so that it genuinely looked as if Evelyn had been caught unexpectedly by a premature birth. Dr. Sartori did what was necessary with perfect competence and the three of us came home with the baby and a birth certificate in the right name."

Cordelia said:

"And nine months later Mrs. Callender was dead."

"He didn't kill her, if that's what you're thinking. He wasn't really the monster that you imagine, at least, not then. But in a sense we did both destroy her. She should have had a specialist, certainly a better doctor than that incompetent fool Gladwin. But the three of us were desperately afraid that an efficient doctor would know that she hadn't borne a child. She was as worried as we were. She insisted that no other doctor be consulted. She had grown to love the baby, you see. So she died and was cremated and we thought we were safe for ever."

"She left Mark a note before she died, nothing but a scribbled hieroglyphic in her prayer book. She left him her blood group."

"We knew that the blood groups were a danger. Ronald took blood from the three of us and made the necessary tests. But after she was dead even that worry ended."

There was a long silence. Cordelia could see a little group of tourists moving down the path towards the bridge. Miss Leaming said:

"The irony of it is that Ronald never really loved him. Mark's grandfather adored him; there was no difficulty there. He left half his fortune to Evelyn and it came automatically to her husband. Mark was to get the other half on his twenty-fifth birthday. But Ronald never cared for his son. He found that he couldn't love him, and I wasn't allowed to. I watched him grow up and go to school. But I wasn't allowed to love him. I used to knit him endless jerseys. It was almost an obsession. The patterns got more intricate and the wool thicker as he grew older. Poor Mark, he must have thought that I was mad, this strange, discontented women whom his father couldn't do without but wouldn't marry."

"There are one or two of the jerseys at the cottage. What would you like me to do with his things?"

"Take them away and give them to anyone who needs them. Unless you think I ought to unpick the wool and knit it up into something new? Would that be a suitable gesture, do you think, symbolic of wasted effort, pathos, futility?"

"I'll find a use for them. And his books?"

"Get rid of them too. I can't go again to the cottage. Get rid of everything if you will."

The little group of tourists was very close now but they seemed engrossed in their own chatter. Miss Leaming took an envelope out of her pocket and handed it to Cordelia.

"I've written out a brief confession. There's nothing in it about Mark, nothing about how he died or what you discovered. It's just a brief statement that I shot Ronald Callender immediately after you had left Garforth House and coerced you into supporting my story. You'd better put it somewhere safe. One day you may need it."

Cordelia saw that the envelope was addressed to herself. She didn't open it. She said:

"It's too late now. If you regret what we did, you should have spoken earlier. The case is closed now."

"I've no regrets. I'm glad that we acted as we did. But the case may not be over yet."

"But it is over! The inquest has given its verdict."

"Ronald had a number of very powerful friends. They have

730

influence and, periodically, they like to exercise it if only to prove that they still have it."

"But they can't get this case reopened! It practically takes an act of parliament to change a coroner's verdict."

"I don't say that they'll try to do that. But they may ask questions. They may have what they describe as a quiet word in the right ear. And the right ears are usually available. That's how they work. That's the sort of people they are."

Cordelia said suddenly:

"Have you a light?"

Without question or protest Miss Leaming opened her handbag and handed over an elegant silver tube. Cordelia didn't smoke and was unused to lighters. It took three clicks before the wick burst into flame. Then she leaned over the parapet of the bridge and set fire to the corner of the envelope.

The incandescent flame was invisible in the stronger light of the sun. All Cordelia could see was a narrow band of wavering purple light as the flame bit into the paper and the charred edges widened and grew. The pungent smell of burning was wafted away on the breeze. As soon as the flame tinged her fingers, Cordelia dropped the envelope, still burning, and watched it twist and turn as it floated down small and frail as a snowflake to be lost at last in the Cam. She said:

"Your lover shot himself. That is all that either of us need to remember now or ever."

They didn't speak again about Ronald Callender's death, but walked silently along the elm-lined path towards the Backs. At one point Miss Leaming glanced at Cordelia and said in a tone of angry petulance:

"You look surprisingly well!"

Cordelia supposed that this brief outburst was the resentment of the middle-aged at the resilience of the young which could so quickly recover from physical disaster. It had only taken one night of long and deep sleep to return her to the state which Bernie, with irritating coyness, used to describe as bright eyed

and bushy tailed. Even without the benison of a hot bath the broken skin on her shoulders and back had healed cleanly. Physically, the events of the last fortnight had left her unscathed. She wasn't so sure about Miss Leaming. The sleek platinum hair was still swathed and shaped immaculately to the bones of the head; she still carried her clothes with cool distinction as if it were important to appear the competent and unharassed helpmate of a famous man. But the pale skin was now tinged with grey; her eyes were deeply shadowed, and the incipient lines at the side of the mouth and across the forehead had deepened so that the face, for the first time, looked old and strained.

They passed through King's Gate and turned to the right. Cordelia had found a place and had parked the Mini within a few yards of the gate; Miss Leaming's Rover was further down Queen's Road. She shook hands firmly but briefly with Cordelia and said goodbye as unemotionally as if they were Cambridge acquaintances, parting with unusual formality after an unexpected meeting at Evensong. She didn't smile. Cordelia watched the tall, angular figure striding down the path under the trees towards John's Gate. She didn't look back. Cordelia wondered when, if ever, they would see each other again. It was difficult to believe that they had met only on four occasions. They had nothing in common except their sex, although Cordelia had realized during the days following Ronald Callender's murder the strength of that female allegiance. As Miss Leaming herself had said, they didn't even like each other. Yet each held the other's safety in her hands. There were moments when their secret almost horrified Cordelia by its immensity. But these were few and would get fewer. Time would inevitably diminish its importance. Life would go on. Neither of them would ever forget completely while the brain cells still lived, but she could believe that a day might come when they would glimpse each other across a theatre or restaurant or be borne unprotestingly past on an underground escalator and would wonder whether what they both recalled in the shock of recognition had really once happened. Already, only four days after the inquest, Ronald Callender's murder was beginning to take its place in the landscape of the past.

There was no longer anything to keep her at the cottage. She spent an hour obsessionally cleaning and tidying rooms which no one would enter, probably for weeks. She watered the mug of cowslips on the sitting-room table. In another three days they would be dead and no one would notice, but she couldn't bear to throw out the still living flowers. She went out to the shed and contemplated the bottle of sour milk and the beef stew. Her first impulse was to take both and empty them down the lavatory. But they were part of the evidence. She wouldn't need that evidence again, but ought it to be completely destroyed? She recalled Bernie's reiterated admonition: "Never destroy the evidence." The Super had been full of cautionary tales to emphasize the importance of that maxim. In the end she decided to photograph the exhibits, setting them up on the kitchen table and paying great attention to exposure and light. It seemed a fruitless, somewhat ridiculous, exercise and she was glad when the job was done and the unsavoury contents of bottle and pan could be disposed of. Afterwards she carefully washed them both and left them in the kitchen.

Last of all she packed her bag and stowed her gear in the Mini together with Mark's jerseys and books. Folding the thick wool, she thought of Dr. Gladwin sitting in his back garden, his shrunken veins indifferent to the sun. He would find the jerseys useful, but she couldn't take them to him. That kind of gesture might have been accepted from Mark, but not from her.

She locked the door and left the key under a stone. She couldn't face Miss Markland again and had no wish to hand it back to any other member of the family. She would wait until she got to London, then send a brief note to Miss Markland thanking her for her kindness and explaining where the key could be found. She walked for the last time round the garden. She wasn't sure what impulse led her to the well but she came up to it with a shock of surprise. The soil around the rim had been cleared and dug and had been planted with a circle of pansies, daisies and small clumps of alyssum and lobelia, each plant looking well established in its hollow ring of watered earth. It was a bright oasis of colour among the encroaching weeds. The effect was pretty but ridiculous and disquietingly odd. Thus

strangely celebrated, the well itself looked obscene, a wooden breast topped by a monstrous nipple. How could she have seen the well cover as a harmless and slightly elegant folly?

Cordelia was torn between pity and revulsion. This must be the work of Miss Markland. The well, which for years had been to her an object of horror, remorse and reluctant fascination, was now to be tended as a shrine. It was ludicrous and pitiable and Cordelia wished that she hadn't seen it. She was suddenly terrified of meeting Miss Markland, of seeing the incipient madness in her eyes. She almost ran out of the garden, pulled the gate shut against the weight of the weeds and drove finally away from the cottage without a backward glance. The case of Mark Callender was finished.

Chapter Seven

Next morning she went to the Kingly Street office promptly at nine o'clock. The unnaturally hot weather had broken at last and, when she opened the window, a keen breeze shifted the layers of dust on desk and filing cabinet. There was only one letter. This was in a long stiff envelope and was headed with the name and address of Ronald Callender's solicitors. It was very brief.

"Dear Madam, I enclose a cheque for £30.00 being expenses due to you in respect of the investigation which you carried out at the request of the late Sir Ronald Callender into the death of his son Mark Callender. If you agree this sum, I would be grateful if you would sign and return the attached receipt."

Well, as Miss Leaming had said, it would at least pay part of her fine. She had sufficient money to keep the Agency going for another month. If there were no further case by that time, there was always Miss Feakins and another temporary job. Cordelia thought of the Feakins Secretarial Agency without enthusiasm. Miss Feakins operated, and that was the appropriate word, from a small office as squalid as Cordelia's own, but which had had a desperate gaiety imposed upon it in the form of multi-coloured walls, paper flowers in a variety of urn-like containers, china ornaments and a poster. The poster had always fascinated Cordelia. A curvaceous blonde, clad in brief hot pants and laughing hysterically, was leap-frogging over her typewriter, a feat she managed to perform with a maximum of exposure while clutching a fistful of five pound notes in each hand. The caption read:
"Be a Girl Friday and join the fun people. All the best Crusoes are on our books."

Beneath this poster Miss Feakins, emaciated, indefatigably cheerful and tinsled like a christmas tree, interviewed a dispirited trail of the old, the ugly and the virtually unemployable. Her

milch cows seldom escaped into permanent employment. Miss Feakins would warn against the unspecified dangers of accepting a permanent job much as Victorian mothers warned against sex. But Cordelia liked her. Miss Feakins would welcome her back, her defection to Bernie forgiven, and there would be another of those furtive telephone conversations with the fortunate Crusoe made with one bright eye on Cordelia, a brothel madam recommending her latest recruit to one of her fussier customers. "Most superior girl—well educated—you'll like her—and a worker!" The emphasis of amazed wonder on the last word was justified. Few of Miss Feakins' temporaries, beguiled by advertisements, seriously expected to have to work. There were other and more efficient agencies but only one Miss Feakins. Bound by pity and an eccentric loyalty, Cordelia had little hope of escaping that glittering eye. A series of temporary jobs with Miss Feakins' Crusoes might, indeed, be all that was left to her. Didn't a conviction for illegal possession of a weapon under Section I of the Firearms Act 1968 count as a criminal record, barring one for life from socially responsible and safe jobs in the civil service and local government?

She settled down at the typewriter, with the yellow telephone directory to hand, to finish sending out the circular letter to the last twenty solicitors on the list. The letter itself embarrassed and depressed her. It had been concocted by Bernie after a dozen preliminary drafts and, at the time, it hadn't seemed too unreasonable. But his death and the Callender case had altered everything. The pompous phrases about a comprehensive professional service, immediate attendance in any part of the country, discreet and experienced operators and moderate fees, struck her as ridiculously, even dangerously, pretentious. Wasn't there something about false representation in the Trades Description Act? But the promise of moderate fees and absolute discretion was valid enough. It was a pity, she thought drily, that she couldn't get a reference from Miss Leaming. Alibis arranged; inquests attended; murders efficiently concealed; perjury at our own special rates.

The raucous burr of the telephone startled her. The office was so quiet and still that she had taken it for granted that no

736

one would call. She stared at the instrument for several seconds, wide-eyed and suddenly afraid, before stretching out her hand.

The voice was calm and assured, polite but in no way deferential. It uttered no threat, yet to Cordelia, every word was explicit with menace.

"Miss Cordelia Gray? This is New Scotland Yard. We wondered whether you would be back at your office yet. Could you please make it convenient to call here sometime later today? Chief Superintendent Dalgliesh would like to see you."

It was ten days later that Cordelia was called for the third time to New Scotland Yard. The bastion of concrete and glass off Victoria Street was, by now, fairly familiar to her although she still entered it with a sense of temporarily discarding part of her identity, like leaving shoes outside a mosque.

Superintendent Dalgliesh had imposed little of his own personality on his room. The books in the regulation bookcase were obviously textbooks on law, copies of regulations and Acts of Parliament, dictionaries and books of reference. The only picture was a large water colour of the old Norman Shaw building on the Embankment painted from the river, an agreeable study in greys and soft ochres lit by the bright golden wings of the R.A.F. Memorial. On this visit, as on previous occasions, there was a bowl of roses on his desk, garden roses with sturdy stems and thorns curved like strong beaks, not the etiolated scentless blooms of a West End florist.

Bernie had never described him; had only fathered on him his own obsessive, unheroic, rough-hewn philosophy. Cordelia, bored by his very name, had asked no questions. But the Superintendent she had pictured was very different from the tall, austere figure who had risen to shake her hand when she first came into this room and the dichotomy between her private imaginings and the reality had been disconcerting. Irrationally, she had felt a twinge of irritation against Bernie for so putting her at a disadvantage. He was old of course, over forty at least,

but not as old as she had expected. He was dark, very tall and loose-limbed where she had expected him to be fair, thick set and stocky. He was serious and spoke to her as if she were a responsible adult, not avuncular and condescending. His face was sensitive without being weak and she liked his hands and his voice and the way she could see the structure of his bones under the skin. He sounded gentle and kind, which was cunning since she knew that he was dangerous and cruel, and she had to keep reminding herself of how he had treated Bernie. At some moments during the interrogation she had actually wondered whether he could be Adam Dalgliesh the poet.

They had never been alone together. On each of her visits a policewoman, introduced as Sergeant Mannering, had been present, seated at the side of the desk with her notebook. Cordelia felt that she knew Sergeant Mannering well having met her at school in the person of the head girl, Teresa Campion-Hook. The two girls could have been sisters. No acne had ever marked their shiningly clean skins; their fair hair curled at precisely the regulation length above their uniformed collars; their voices were calm, authoritarian, determinedly cheerful but never strident; they exuded an ineffable confidence in the justice and logic of the universe and the rightness of their own place in it. Sergeant Mannering had smiled briefly at Cordelia as she came in. The look was open, not overtly friendly since too generous a smile might prejudice the case, but not censorious either. It was a look which disposed Cordelia to imprudence; she disliked looking a fool before that competent gaze.

She had at least had time before her first visit to decide on tactics. There was little advantage and much danger in concealing facts which an intelligent man could easily discover for himself. She would disclose, if asked, that she had discussed Mark Callender with the Tillings and his tutor; that she had traced and interviewed Mrs. Goddard; that she had visited Dr. Gladwin. She decided to say nothing about the attempt on her life or about her visit to Somerset House. She knew which facts it would be vital to conceal: Ronald Callender's murder; the clue in the prayer book; the actual way in which Mark had died. She told herself firmly that she mustn't be drawn into discussing

the case, mustn't talk about herself, her life, her present job, her ambitions. She remembered what Bernie had told her. "In this country, if people won't talk, there's nothing you can do to make them, more's the pity. Luckily for the police most people just can't keep their mouths shut. The intelligent ones are the worst. They just have to show how clever they are, and once you've got them discussing the case, even discussing it generally, then you've got them." Cordelia reminded herself of the advice she had given to Elizabeth Leaming: "Don't embroider, don't invent, don't be afraid to say you can't remember."

Dalgliesh was speaking:

"Have you thought of consulting a solicitor, Miss Gray?"

"I haven't got a solicitor."

"The Law Society can give you the names of some very reliable and helpful ones. I should think about it seriously if I were you."

"But I should have to pay him, shouldn't I? Why should I need a solicitor when I'm telling the truth?"

"It's when people start telling the truth that they most often feel the need of a solicitor."

"But I've always told the truth. Why should I lie?" The rhetorical question was a mistake. He answered it seriously as if she had really wanted to know.

"Well, it could be to protect yourself—which I don't think likely—or to protect someone else. The motive for that could be love, fear, or a sense of justice. I don't think you've known any of the people in this case long enough to care for them deeply so that rules out love, and I don't think you would be very easy to frighten. So we're left with justice. A very dangerous concept, Miss Gray."

She had been closely questioned before. The Cambridge police had been very thorough. But this was the first time she had been questioned by someone who knew; knew that she was lying; knew that Mark Callender hadn't killed himself; knew, she felt desperately, all there was to know. She had to force herself to an acceptance of reality. He couldn't possibly be sure. He hadn't any legal proof and he never would have. There was no one alive to tell him the truth except Elizabeth Leaming and herself. And she wasn't going to tell. Dalgliesh could beat against her

will with his implacable logic, his curious kindness, his courtesy, his patience. But she wouldn't talk, and in England there was no way in which he could make her.

When she didn't reply, he said cheerfully:

"Well, let's see how far we've got. As a result of your enquiries you suspected that Mark Callender might have been murdered. You haven't admitted that to me but you made your suspicions plain when you visited Sergeant Maskell of the Cambridge police. You subsequently traced his mother's old nurse and learned from her something of his early life, of the Callender marriage, of Mrs. Callender's death. Following that visit you went to see Dr. Gladwin, the general practitioner who had looked after Mrs. Callender before she died. By a simple ruse you ascertained the blood group of Ronald Callender. There would only be point in that if you suspected that Mark wasn't the child of his parents' marriage. You then did what I would have done in your place, visited Somerset House to examine Mr. George Bottley's will. That was sensible. If you suspect murder, always consider who stands to gain by it."

So he had found out about Somerset House and the call to Dr. Venables. Well, it was to be expected. He had credited her with his own brand of intelligence. She had behaved as he would have behaved.

She still didn't speak. He said:

"You didn't tell me about your fall down the well. Miss Markland did."

"That was an accident. I don't remember anything about it, but I must have decided to explore the well and overbalanced. I was always rather intrigued by it."

"I don't think it was an accident, Miss Gray. You couldn't have pulled the lid free without a rope. Miss Markland tripped over a rope, but it was coiled neatly and half-hidden in the undergrowth. Would you have even troubled to detach it from the hook if you'd only been exploring?"

"I don't know. I can't remember anything that happened before I fell. My first memory is hitting the water. And I don't see what this has to do with Sir Ronald Callender's death."

"It might have a great deal to do with it. If someone tried to

kill you, and I think that they did, that person could have come from Garforth House."

"Why?"

"Because the attempt on your life was probably connected with your investigation into Mark Callender's death. You had become a danger to someone. Killing is a serious business. The professionals don't like it unless it's absolutely essential and even the amateurs are less happy-go-lucky about murder than you might expect. You must have become a very dangerous woman to someone. Someone replaced that well lid, Miss Gray; you didn't fall through solid wood."

Cordelia still said nothing. There was a silence, then he spoke again:

"Miss Markland told me that after your rescue from the well she was reluctant to leave you alone. But you insisted that she should go. You told her that you weren't afraid to be alone in the cottage because you had a gun."

Cordelia was surprised how much this small betrayal hurt. Yet, how could she blame Miss Markland? The Superintendent would have known just how to handle her, probably persuaded her that frankness was in Cordelia's own interest. Well, she could at least betray in her turn. And this explanation, at least, would have the authority of truth.

"I wanted to get rid of her. She told me some dreadful story about her illegitimate child falling down the well to his death. I'd only just been rescued myself. I didn't want to hear it, I couldn't bear it just then. I told her a lie about the gun just to make her go. I didn't ask her to confide in me, it wasn't fair. It was only a way of asking for help and I hadn't any to give."

"And didn't you want to get rid of her for another reason? Didn't you know that your assailant would have to return that night; that the well cover would have to be dragged clear again if your death were to look like an accident?"

"If I'd really thought that I was in any danger I should have begged her to take me with her to Summertrees House. I wouldn't have waited alone in the cottage without my gun."

"No, Miss Gray, I believe that. You wouldn't have waited there alone in the cottage that night without your gun."

For the first time Cordelia was desperately afraid. This wasn't a game. It never had been, although at Cambridge the police interrogation had held some of the unreality of a formal contest in which the result was both foreseeable and unworrying since one of the opponents didn't even know he was playing. It was real enough now. If she were tricked, persuaded, coerced into telling him the truth, she would go to prison. She was an accessory after the fact. How many years did one get for helping to conceal murder? She had read somewhere that Holloway smelt. They would take away her clothes. She would be shut up in a claustrophobic cell. There was remission for good conduct but how could one be good in prison? Perhaps they would send her to an open prison. Open. It was a contradiction in terms. And how would she live afterwards? How would she get a job? What real personal freedom could there ever be for those whom society labelled delinquent?

She was terrified for Miss Leaming. Where was she now? She had never dared ask Dalgliesh, and Miss Leaming's name had hardly been mentioned. Was she even now in some other room of New Scotland Yard being similarly questioned? How reliable would she be under pressure? Were they planning to confront the two conspirators with each other? Would the door suddenly open and Miss Leaming be brought in, apologetic, remorseful, truculent? Wasn't that the usual ploy, to interview conspirators separately until the weaker broke down? And who would prove the weaker?

She heard the Superintendent's voice. She thought he sounded rather sorry for her.

"We have some confirmation that the pistol was in your possession that night. A motorist tells us that he saw a parked car on the road about three miles from Garforth House and when he stopped to enquire if he could help he was threatened by a young woman with a gun."

Cordelia remembered that moment, the sweetness and silence of the summer night suddenly overlaid by his hot, alcoholic breath.

"He must have been drinking. I suppose the police stopped him for a breath test later that night and now he's decided to come up with this story. I don't know what he expects to gain

by it but it isn't true. I wasn't carrying a gun. Sir Ronald took the pistol from me on my first night at Garforth House."

"The Metropolitan Police stopped him just over the force border. I think he may persist in his story. He was very definite. Of course, he hasn't identified you yet but he was able to describe the car. His story is that he thought you were having trouble with it and stopped to help. You misunderstood his motives and threatened him with a gun."

"I understood his motives perfectly. But I didn't threaten him with a gun."

"What did you say, Miss Gray?"

"Leave me alone or I'll kill you."

"Without the gun, surely that was an empty threat?"

"It would always have been an empty threat. But it made him go."

"What exactly did happen?"

"I had a spanner in the front pocket of the car and when he shoved his face in at the window I grasped that and threatened him with it. But no one in his right senses could have mistaken a spanner for a gun!"

But he hadn't been in his right senses. The only person who had seen the gun in her possession that night was a motorist who hadn't been sober. This, she knew, was a small victory. She had resisted the momentary temptation to change her story. Bernie had been right. She recalled his advice; the Superintendent's advice; this time she could almost hear it spoken in his deep, slightly husky voice: "If you're tempted to crime, stick to your original statement. There's nothing that impresses the jury more than consistency. I've seen the most unlikely defence succeed simply because the accused stuck to his story. After all, it's only someone else's word against yours; with a competent counsel that's half-way to a reasonable doubt."

The Superintendent was speaking again. Cordelia wished that she could concentrate more clearly on what he was saying. She hadn't been sleeping very soundly for the past ten days—perhaps that had something to do with this perpetual tiredness.

"I think that Chris Lunn paid you a visit on the night he died. There's no other reason that I could discover why he

743

should have been on that road. One of the witnesses to the accident said that he came out in the little van from that side road as if all the devils in hell were following him. Someone was following him—you, Miss Gray."

"We've had this conversation before. I was on my way to see Sir Ronald."

"At that hour? And in such a hurry?"

"I wanted to see him urgently to tell him that I'd decided to drop the case. I couldn't wait."

"But you did wait, didn't you? You went to sleep in the car on the side of the road. That's why it was nearly an hour after you'd been seen at the accident before you arrived at Garforth House."

"I had to stop. I was tired and I knew it wasn't safe to drive on."

"But you knew too, that it was safe to sleep. You knew that the person you had most to fear from was dead."

Cordelia didn't reply. A silence fell on the room but it seemed to her a companionable not an accusing silence. She wished that she wasn't so tired. Most of all, she wished that she had someone to talk to about Ronald Callender's murder. Bernie wouldn't have been any help here. To him the moral dilemma at the heart of the crime would have held no interest, no validity, would have seemed a wilful confusion of straightforward facts. She could imagine his coarse and facile comment on Eliza Leaming's relations with Lunn. But the Superintendent might have understood. She could imagine herself talking to him. She recalled Ronald Callender's words that love was as destructive as hate. Would Dalgliesh assent to that bleak philosophy? She wished that she could ask him. This, she recognized, was her real danger—not the temptation to confess but the longing to confide. Did he know how she felt? Was this too, part of his technique?

There was a knock at the door. A uniformed constable came in and handed a note to Dalgliesh. The room was very quiet while he read it. Cordelia made herself look at his face. It was grave and expressionless and he continued looking at the paper long after he must have assimilated its brief message.

She thought that he was making up his mind to something. After a minute he said:

"This concerns someone you know, Miss Gray. Elizabeth Leaming is dead. She was killed two days ago when the car she was driving went off the coast road south of Amalfi. This note is confirmation of identity."

Cordelia was swept with relief so immense that she felt physically sick. She clenched her fist and felt the sweat start on her brow. She began to shiver with cold. It never occurred to her that he might be lying. She knew him to be ruthless and clever but she had always taken it for granted that he wouldn't lie to her. She said in a whisper:

"May I go home now?"

"Yes. I don't think there's much point in your staying, do you?"

"She didn't kill Sir Ronald. He took the gun from me. He took the gun——"

Something seemed to have happened to her throat. The words wouldn't come out.

"That's what you've been telling me. I don't think you need trouble to say it again."

"When do I have to come back?"

"I don't think you need come back unless you decide that there's something you want to tell me. In that well-known phrase, you were asked to help the police. You have helped the police. Thank you."

She had won. She was free. She was safe, and with Miss Leaming dead, that safety depended only on herself. She needn't come back again to this horrible place. The relief, so unexpected and so unbelievable, was too great to be borne. Cordelia burst into dramatic and uncontrollable crying. She was aware of Sergeant Mannering's low exclamation of concern and of a folded white handkerchief handed to her by the Superintendent. She buried her face in the clean, laundry-smelling linen and blurted out her pent-up misery and anger. Strangely enough—and the oddness of it struck her even in the middle of her anguish—her misery was centred on Bernie. Lifting a face disfigured with tears and no longer caring what he thought of her, she blurted out a final, irrational protest:

"And after you'd sacked him, you never enquired how he got on. You didn't even come to the funeral!"

He had brought a chair over and had seated himself beside her. He handed her a glass of water. The glass was very cold but comforting and she was surprised to find how thirsty she was. She sipped the cold water and sat there hiccuping gently. The hiccups made her want to laugh hysterically but she controlled herself. After a few minutes he said gently:

"I'm sorry about your friend. I didn't realize that your partner was the Bernie Pryde who once worked with me. It's rather worse than that, actually. I'd forgotten all about him. If it's any consolation to you, this case might have ended rather differently if I hadn't."

"You sacked him. All he ever wanted was to be a detective and you wouldn't give him a chance."

"The Metropolitan Police hiring and firing regulations aren't quite as simple as that. But it's true that he might still have been a policeman if it hadn't been for me. But he wouldn't have been a detective."

"He wasn't that bad."

"Well, he was, you know. But I'm beginning to wonder if I didn't underrate him."

Cordelia turned to hand him back the glass and met his eyes. They smiled at each other. She wished that Bernie could have heard him.

⬡⬡

Half an hour later Dalgliesh was seated opposite the Assistant Commissioner in the latter's office. The two men disliked each other but only one of them knew this and he was the one to whom it didn't matter. Dalgliesh made his report, concisely, logically, without referring to his notes. This was his invariable habit. The A.C. had always thought it unorthodox and conceited and he did so now. Dalgliesh ended:

"As you can imagine, sir, I'm not proposing to commit all that to paper. There's no real evidence and as Bernie Pryde used to tell us, hunch is a good servant but a poor master. God, how

that man could churn out his horrible platitudes! He wasn't unintelligent, not totally without judgment, but everything, including ideas, came apart in his hands. He had a mind like a police notebook. Do you remember the Clandon case, homicide by shooting? It was in 1954 I think."

"Ought I to?"

"No. But it would have been helpful if I had."

"I don't really know what you're talking about, Adam. But if I understand you aright, you suspect that Ronald Callender killed his son. Ronald Callender is dead. You suspect that Chris Lunn tried to murder Cordelia Gray. Lunn is dead. You suggest that Elizabeth Leaming killed Ronald Callender. Elizabeth Leaming is dead."

"Yes, it's all conveniently tidy."

"I suggest we leave it that way. The Commissioner incidentally has had a telephone call from Dr. Hugh Tilling, the psychiatrist. He's outraged because his son and daughter have been questioned about Mark Callender's death. I'm prepared to explain his civil duties to Dr. Tilling, he's already well aware of his rights, if you really feel it necessary. But will anything be gained by seeing the two Tillings again?"

"I don't think so."

"Or by bothering the Sureté about that French girl who Miss Markland claims visited him at the cottage?"

"I think we can spare ourselves that embarrassment. There's only one person now alive who knows the truth of these crimes and she's proof against any interrogation we can use. I can comfort myself with the reason. With most suspects we have an invaluable ally lurking at the back of their minds to betray them. But whatever lies she's been telling, she's absolutely without guilt."

"Do you think that she's deluded herself that it's all true?"

"I don't think that young woman deludes herself about anything. I took to her, but I'm glad I shan't be encountering her again. I dislike being made to feel during a perfectly ordinary interrogation that I'm corrupting the young."

"So we can tell the Minister that his chum died by his own hand?"

"You can tell him that we are satisfied that no living finger pressed that trigger. But perhaps not. Even he might be capable of reasoning that one out. Tell him that he can safely accept the verdict of the inquest."

"It would have saved a great deal of public time if he'd accepted it in the first place."

The two men were silent for a moment. Then Dalgliesh said:

"Cordelia Gray was right. I ought to have enquired what happened to Bernie Pryde."

"You couldn't be expected to. That wasn't part of your duties."

"Of course not. But then one's more serious neglects seldom are part of one's duty. And I find it ironic and oddly satisfying that Pryde took his revenge. Whatever mischief that child was up to in Cambridge, she was working under his direction."

"You're becoming more philosophical, Adam."

"Only less obsessive, or perhaps merely older. It's good to be able to feel occasionally that there are some cases which are better left unsolved."

⟫∘⟪

The Kingly Street building looked the same, smelt the same. It always would. But there was one difference. Outside the office a man was waiting, a middle-aged man in a tight blue suit, pig eyes sharp as flint among the fleshy folds of the face.

"Miss Gray? I'd nearly given you up. My name's Fielding, I saw your plate and just came up by chance, don't you know."

His eyes were avaricious, prurient.

"Well now, you're not quite what I expected, not the usual kind of Private Eye."

"Is there anything I can do for you, Mr. Fielding?"

He gazed furtively round the landing, seeming to find its sordidness reassuring.

"It's my lady friend. I've reason to suspect that she's getting a bit on the side. Well—a man likes to know where he stands. You get me?"

Cordelia fitted the key into the lock.

"I understand, Mr. Fielding. Won't you come in?"